A BETTER PLACE

To Berry & Sandy,
Good friends. Go PAT ♥!

A BETTER PLACE

Steven M. Forman

Steven M. Forman

MANDEVILLA
PRESS

A BETTER PLACE

Copyright 2019 by Steven M. Forman
All rights reserved
Published by: Mandevilla Press
                Lakewood Ranch, Florida 34211

MANDEVILLA
PRESS

First Edition - Published by Mandevilla Press

Printed in the United States of America

Digital ISBN - 978-1-62704-050-1

Print ISBN - 978-1-62704-049-5

To Barbara and our family

PRAISE FOR A BETTER PLACE

"From the trenches of World War I to the post-Vietnam era in North Platte, Nebraska, A Better Place is a wonderfully written, dramatic, multi-generational saga of soldiers and lovers, goodness and evil. Diverse, complex, and unforgettable characters. Well done!"

— **Deborah Shlian**- Award-winning author of Rabbit in the Moon, Silent Survivor, and more.

ACKNOWLEDGMENTS

*T*o Peter Bochner and John Paine for their editing and creative suggestions. To Jamie Snell for her precise copy editing. Without her, I was lost. To my agent, Bob Diforio, who helps me navigate the ever-changing book publishing industry. I couldn't do it without him. To Debbie Shlian for all her support.

FROM A BETTER PLACE

"Would the world be a better place if we could forget our bad memories and prejudices at the end of each day?"

"You mean, begin each day with a clean slate?"

"Yeah. What do you think?"

TABLE OF CONTENTS

PROLOGUE

July 15, 1918
THE GHOST

He had already killed twice, and the night was young. He had slashed a throat with his M17 trench knife and broken a neck with his bare hands. He was a big man; still, his victims never saw him coming. He was a phantom, appearing and disappearing like an apparition in No Man's Land, that 250 yards of ravished ground between Allied and enemy lines. He was called the Ghost, *le Fantome, das Gespenst.* But there had been a time, long ago and far away, when he had been the Golden Boy.

He had killed over a hundred men in less than a year on the Western Front—a 400-mile stretch of trenches zigzagging through France, Belgium, and the Swiss border. His country had given him a Silver Star for killing, but he took no pride in it. In a war of attrition, he killed only to end the killing.

It had been raining for two days, and No Man's Land was a foul-smelling quagmire. Slithering through slime, the Ghost came face to face with a rat the size of a house cat. Battlefield rats ate the dead, infected the living, and killed more soldiers than combat. The Ghost raised his M17 trench knife, and before the rat lunged, plunged the razor-sharp blade through the rodent's humped back and out its bloated belly. *Die, you son of a bitch*; he snarled through clenched teeth. He scraped the rat guts off his blade into the muck, feeling good. Killing rats saved lives.

He heard sounds from a bomb crater ahead. Snaking forward, his M17 in hand, he peeked over the rim of the five feet deep crater and saw the enemy—an alert, grizzled veteran—and the enemy saw him. The element of surprise was gone, but the Ghost still had the advantage of being a superior force. As the German reached for his rifle, the Ghost swooped like an attacking crowned eagle—his talons a trench knife and a clenched fist. Illuminated from behind by a bright flare in the night sky, splattered with mud and blood, his eyes glowing red like the devil's own—the Ghost was terrifying. The German frantically struggled to aim his rifle, but the knife plunged twice into his heart, killing him instantly—his eyes still open.

The Ghost propped the corpse against the mud wall and searched his uniform for documents. That was one of a trench raider's jobs. Primarily his role was to infiltrate No Man's Land *after* a battle, capture enemy survivors, and bring them behind Allied lines for interrogation. But the Ghost took no prisoners. He took lives and documents. Trench raiders had a one-week life expectancy in No Man's Land. The Ghost had survived forty weeks and saw no reason to change his methods.

He read the dead soldier's papers: Sergeant Helmut Jory. Age: 30. Town: Marzahn.

A whisper from above startled him. "Sergeant Jory, it's Private Adenauer. Are you okay?"

The Ghost hid against the wet wall. "My God," Adenauer gasped, seeing his blood-soaked sergeant.

Impulsively, the Ghost reached up, grabbed the front of Adenauer's coat, and yanked him into the hole. The German landed on his head and flopped forward onto his back. The Ghost pounced and stabbed. The soldier gurgled and died.

The Ghost propped Adenauer's body next to Jory's. Their lifeless eyes stared at him. The Ghost searched Adenauer's uniform. He found only ID papers. *Joseph Adenauer, 18, Marzahn.* The Ghost grimaced. *Damnit. Another kid.* The Ghost could no longer kill without caring—especially a kid. At least the sergeant was a professional soldier with a fighting chance. But, killing a teenager took part of the Ghost's soul. Both soldiers had died for long-forgotten leaders, for long-forgotten reasons—dead before they had a chance to live—their lives pledged before they were born. *It's not fair,* the Ghost thought as he reached across the trench and closed their eyes.

Flares overhead cast an eerie glow on No Man's Land. The Ghost saw a light flicker in a forward crater. *Fool.* He crept to the rim and spied a young German soldier, on his back, shining his flashlight on an object in his hand. The boy wept. The Ghost swooped again, landing next to the startled soldier, his knife at his throat.

"The Ghost," the boy gasped.

The Ghost had never hesitated before, but this time he did. Holding his knife to the soldier's throat, he snatched the object from his hand. It was a family photograph. "My parents, my sister, and me," the terrified soldier said. The Ghost said nothing. His papers identified the boy as Klaus Schmidt, nineteen years old, from Munich. On impulse, the Ghost decided Klaus Schmidt would be his first prisoner. He took the boy's rifle and tossed it out of the hole. "Stay," he commanded. Schmidt nodded.

The Ghost scrambled from the crater and crawled east. He checked for land mines by tapping the ground ahead with his knife. Satisfied that the next few yards were safe, he was turning back for his prisoner when he heard the whistling of a falling bomb. It sounded close. *Shit!* He buried his face in the mud and covered his helmet with his arms.

The explosion, only yards behind, heaved up the ground under him like a punch in the gut. A German helmet, a broken rifle, and chunks of earth rained down around him. When the smoke cleared, he rose to his elbows, gasping for breath. The small crater where he'd left Klaus Schmidt was smoking. A direct hit. A boot lay nearby with a foot and part of a leg still inside. A severed hand held remnants of a shredded photo that fluttered between lifeless fingers until a puff of wind carried it away. The family of Klaus Schmidt would never see him again.

More bombs fell. The Ghost cursed and crawled toward Allied lines, approximately a hundred yards west. It was slow going, feeling for mines, pausing for whistling bombs. The sun would rise soon, and he would lose the cover of darkness. But he couldn't hurry. *Slow and steady*, he chided himself. Finally, he saw the front line of the Allied trenches. *The front*—the most dangerous of all trenches…represented safety for the Ghost.

"Who goes there?" a shaky voice called from the forward trench.

"The Ghost," he said in a harsh whisper.

"Who?" the sentry asked again.

"The Ghost, asshole," he growled. "Want the whole German Army to know?"

"Sorry. Proceed."

Before the war, he had never cursed. His mother detested profanity, and the Ghost revered his mother, a devout Lutheran. *But trenches are godless, motherless hellholes,* he rationalized. *So, fuck it.*

He slid on his stomach, head first, down the mud wall of the six-foot-deep trench and somersaulted forward to the far wall, three feet away. His face was covered with battlefield sludge. He was drenched in gore, his bloody knife in his belt—the bogeyman from every child's nightmare. Around him, twenty men huddled against the mud walls. Some sections of the wall had been revetted with wood to stop them from collapsing in on them.

"You the Ghost?" a doughboy asked.

The huge man nodded.

"How do you survive out there?"

The Ghost shrugged and slid his helmet over his eyes. He stretched out his six-foot, six-inch frame, crossed his long arms over his broad chest, and tried for sleep. A few hundred yards away, thousands of Germans wanted to kill him. *Sleep? Sure. No problem.*

"That's the Ghost," the doughboy said to his comrades.

"Heard he killed three hundred Germans with that knife," another said.

The Ghost smiled. He had been credited with an impossible number of kills, improbable acts of bravery, and inhuman feats of strength. He denied nothing. If exaggerated claims gave hope to the hopeless, he saw no harm in that. He closed his eyes, remembering who he was before he was the Ghost.

PART 1

CHAPTER 1

1896–1913
JONAS & DUKE

Before he was the Ghost, before he killed nearly two hundred men in battle, he was Jonas Hensen, a gentle giant known as the "Golden Boy" in his home town of North Platte, Nebraska. He was born in 1896, a big baby who got bigger fast. He was six feet two by the age of thirteen but never used his inordinate size to make his friends feel small.

"Are you trying your hardest?" his littlest friend, Mickey Caroline, asked one day when they were rough-housing.

"Hard enough," Jonas said.

"Why don't you try harder?" Mickey asked.

"If you were my size, I would," Jonas said, and that said it all. He wanted life to be fair.

There was another thirteen-year-old in North Platte of comparable size and strength to Jonas but his direct opposite in temperament. Duke Hannigan, son of cattle baron Liam Hannigan, was a mean-spirited bully like his father. Jonas and Duke had sized each other up from a distance … but didn't meet until their freshman year in high school. Duke had gone to a private Catholic school until then and transferred to North Platte High so he could play football. His arrival was eagerly anticipated.

The school only had enough boys for a varsity football team. Freshmen could participate, but rarely played in games. Jonas and Duke were expected to be exceptions because of their size and athleticism. Curious fans turned out for the first practice of the 1909 season. The consensus was that Duke's nasty disposition was better suited for football than Jonas's gentle nature.

It was also the first season North Platte football players would use protective equipment. Until then, the game had been played without helmets, padding, or spiked shoes. But, twenty-three football-related deaths nationally, made playing the sport unprotected, unacceptable to North Platte Coach, Emmitt Parsons.

The fans at the practice field behind the school heard the *clack, clack, clack,* of football spikes on cement as the players walked from the locker room to the field. The initial sight of twenty-three young men in padded jerseys, football pants, and hard-leather helmets was impressive—the helmets and cleats making each player three inches taller. Duke Hannigan and Jonas Hensen looked enormous, even bigger than the older players on the team. Duke and Jonas walked far apart from one another as if separated by a natural antipathy. Actually, Jonas had approached Duke in the locker room before practice to introduce himself and was rebuffed. "Stay away from me Hensen, or you're going to get hurt." Duke had said. Jonas said nothing, but he fumed inside. He didn't like being threatened. Today he would try his hardest.

Duke was as expected: big, strong, and fast. Jonas was the surprise, jostling for a position next to Duke for each drill, he showed he was bigger, stronger, and faster. The much-anticipated contest between the two was no contest at all. Duke Hannigan simply couldn't keep pace with Jonas Hensen. Standing on the sidelines, Liam Hannigan seethed. His son was disappointing him.

During a break, Liam approached Coach Parsons and had an animated conversation with him. When practice resumed, the coach announced they would have a tackling drill. "Normally, I don't have contact for the first few days of practice, but I want to accommodate Mr. Hannigan, who generously donated the football equipment to the school. He wants to see how it holds up to hard hitting. Let's try it out with our two big freshmen. Hensen, Hannigan, face each other, ten yards apart. The rest of you form a circle around them. Hensen, you run straight at Duke, and Duke, you try to bring him down. Second time around, we'll switch roles."

On Coach Parsons' signal, Duke set himself in a tackling crouch and growled. Jonas charged, knees high, pumping like pistons, arms working in unison. An instant before impact, Jonas lowered his head and purposely hit Duke flush in the face with the top of his hard leather helmet. Stunned, Duke toppled flat on his back.

Jonas kept running. His left spiked shoe landed on Duke's thigh; then his right stomped Duke's chest and the left narrowly missed his face. Literally run over, Duke lay motionless on the ground, blood on his face, tears in his eyes.

"Hannigan, you okay?" Coach Parsons asked. "It's your turn to run."

Duke waved him off.

"Okay," Coach Parsons said. "Join us when you're ready."

The team trotted off. Liam Hannigan walked over to his son's supine figure. "I told Parsons to run that drill so you could show everyone how tough you are," he said. "You humiliated me." He kicked his son's hip. "Get up and get your sorry ass back in that practice."

Duke Hannigan dragged himself to his feet, humiliated and vengeful.

Jonas arrived home from practice anxious to share his experience with his parents, Alf and Bea Hensen. They had emigrated from Denmark two years before he was born. Bea, a devout Lutheran, named her son Jonas after Justus Jonas, a sixteenth-century Lutheran theologian. She hoped he would follow the church's teachings as religiously as she had. Her husband, Alf, was ambivalent about religion, giving as much credence to his Viking heritage as he did to Martin Luther's vision.

"You are not to talk about that game in this house," she said. "It's barbaric and will only bring out the worst in you."

"We agreed he could try it," Alf said.

"No. I was overruled. But I won't have you talk about that game in front of me."

Jonas was a foot taller than his mother and had to bend down to kiss her on the forehead. "Mom, I'm sorry. But I feel I was meant to play this game like you were meant to be religious."

"Don't you dare compare football to religion, Jonas Hensen. I'm doing God's work. You're playing the devil's game."

"I was only comparing the dedication."

She gave him a withering look and walked away.

❀   ❀   ❀

The first game of that first season set the tone for the future of Duke Hannigan and Jonas Hensen. Jonas was brilliant, graceful, powerful, and dynamic on the field. A sportsman, he would knock his opponent down then help them up. The fans loved him.

"That Hensen kid is terrific," a man in the stands said.

"Best on the field," said another. "How old is he?"

Alf Henson turned around. "Thirteen."

"Thirteen? That's all? Are you sure?"

"He's my son," Alf said.

"Good Lord. What's he gonna be when he's a senior?"

"Bigger and better, I imagine," Alf said, with a small smile.

Duke plodded through the game, his competence overshadowed by his petulance.

"That Hannigan kid's good, but he plays dirty," a fan observed.

"He's hurt two of their players already," another said.

"That's *after* the referees warned him."

Eventually, Duke was ejected from the game for repeated unnecessary roughness penalties. He sat on the bench alone. No one approached or consoled him. No one cared.

"Waste of talent," a man said.

North Platte won 21–0, and when it was over, Alf joined other parents on the field with their sons. He hugged Jonas and said, "Good game. I've never seen you so aggressive before."

"I never played strangers before. I was afraid to lose. I played as hard as I could."

"You should always play hard," Alf said. "But don't be afraid to lose. It happens."

"Not to me. People expect me to win."

"Don't let people put pressure on you," Alf said.

"I put pressure on myself. I don't want to disappoint anyone," Jonas admitted.

"You didn't disappoint me," his friend Mickey Caroline said, walking toward them. "I finally got to see you do your best. If you played like that with your friends, you'd have killed me."

"I enjoy playing for fun with my friends," Jonas said.

"You sure weren't playing for fun today," Mickey said.

"They weren't my friends."

Chapter 2

1913
SHIRLEY

"I can't believe it's been four years," Jonas remarked to Emmitt Parsons in the coach's small office at North Platte High. "It seems like yesterday."

The coach nodded. "The older you get, the faster time passes. Imagine how I feel." He pointed to the memorabilia on display in his office; autographed leather footballs, the first helmets used in a Nebraska high school football game, playbooks dating back to 1900, and a framed picture of Walter Camp, pioneer of American football. "All these people," the coach sighed picking up a leather ball off a shelf, spinning it. "All the innovations. The practices. The games. Amazing, and it's just the beginning."

"It seems like a dream," Jonas said.

"It *was* a dream for you. You graduated with honors, made the All-State football team twice, and you're headed to the University of Nebraska on a football scholarship. I'd say you were pretty damn close to perfect. The Golden Boy."

"Thanks, Coach," Jonas said, aware that his six feet six inch, two hundred and twenty-five-pound facade kept his imperfections hidden. Only he knew the Golden Boy was not *pretty damn close to perfect*. There were times he feared his girlfriend of four years, Shirley Kelley, knew he was not perfect, but she never said anything. She was the prettiest girl in school from the wealthiest family, and she wanted to be his golden girl forever. But that's not what he wanted, and she knew it.

One night, after they had made love on a blanket in a secluded spot near the North Platte River, she asked, "Why aren't I enough for you, Jonas?" They had parked her Model T Ford Roadster outside city limits, facing north, the Great Plains sprawled in front of them, all the way to Canada. "Aren't I pretty enough?"

"You're the prettiest girl in town."

"But you're always looking at other girls."

"I like to look."

"And next year you'll have all those co-eds in college to look at."

She was right, and he said nothing.

"We could have such a wonderful life together," she continued, her voice wistful. "You could work on my father's ranch; we'd have plenty of money, we could have lots of babies..."

"I could never work for your father," Jonas said. "He's Liam Hannigan's partner. I don't like the Hannigans, especially Duke."

"My father doesn't like the Hannigans either. They're only partners because their grandfathers were partners. You could change that if we got married."

"Why are you in such a hurry to get married?"

"I need to be wanted, and I want to be needed," she said. "Marriage affirms that. What do you want, Jonas? What do you need? You can tell me your secrets."

"No, I can't," Jonas told her with certainty and thought...

Without my secrets, there's no Golden Boy. If I told you I'm a sexually obsessed atheist, that I picture every girl in school naked— their mothers too; even the lunchroom lady. That I get hard just looking at the bumps under girls' sweaters or that I masturbate all the time, would you still think I'm the Golden Boy? I don't think so. And, how can I tell anyone in this small, deeply religious town that I don't believe in God; that I laugh at Bible stories? What if my mother, my friends knew? It would be... bye, bye, Golden Boy.

His prolonged silence told Shirley all she needed to know. "That's what I thought," she said. "You don't need me. You don't need anyone. I love you, Jonas, but it hurts too much knowing you're leaving me soon. I have to stop seeing you now, so I can start getting over you."

"I'm sorry you feel that way," he said though secretly he was relieved.

Amanda Bersten was ten years old and blonde, with a cute freckled face that promised to be beautiful someday. She was tall and a bit of a *tomboy*; the fastest runner in her class—including the boys.

When her father, Hugo, asked her to go with him to a North Platte High football game on Saturday, she was thrilled. She remembered how he had taken her older brother, Michael, to games. But Michael had died of muscular dystrophy when he was nine, and she was five. She knew her father missed Michael, and she wanted to be both daughter and son to him.

As her first game began, she looked around the playing field behind the school. Portable stands on either sideline were filled with students and fans from both high schools. She was excited by the crowd and the action. After a short while, she asked, "Daddy, who is number eleven?"

"That's Jonas Hensen," her father said. "He's our best player."

Amanda became fascinated with him. He was graceful for someone so big, and he seemed to always be in the middle of the action. Each time he collided with another player, she cringed, and each time he got up, she breathed a sigh of relief. At one point, he came out of the game and took off his helmet. His face was covered with blood. Her eyes filled with tears. *Why am I crying? I don't even know him.* Jonas Hensen was her first crush—the Golden Boy.

She carried that crush for two more years, attending every game, watching him. Her crush turned to puppy love and she felt she had to tell him how she feels.

In the spring of 1912, she followed him and three of his friends to Mel's Diner, a sports-themed hangout for North Platte High athletes and their friends. There were pictures of local and professional teams on the wood walls and above the wood tables. The 1900 Omahogs, a professional baseball team from Omaha, had their picture on the wall along with the Omaha Indians of 1902, the Packers of 1904, and the Omaha Rourks of 1906. The pictures all looked the same because it was basically the same players with the new owner's jerseys each year.

Jonas usually shared a table with his inner circle of friends, mostly from the football team: Tommy Hennessey, the left halfback; Donny Hootstein, the quarterback; and Joe Davis, the fullback. Jonas, the right halfback. Occasionally, team manager, Mickey Caroline would join them, but not today. They were laughing and joking, talking about graduation when Amanda approached. She could hear her heart pounding. "Jonas Hensen, I love you," she said in a shaky voice.

His friends laughed. He didn't. "Thanks," he said, smiling. "Who are you?"

"Amanda Bersten. And I'm going to marry you someday."

More laughter ... but not from Jonas. "How old are you?"

"Twelve."

"That's too young to think about marriage."

"I know. Will you wait for me?"

"I'll have to think about that."

"Okay. While you're thinking, can I have a kiss?"

"No way. You're just a kid."

"I'm talking about a kid's kiss. On the cheek?"

"Okay," he said and pointed to his cheek. She kissed the spot.

"You are so nice," she said and ran away to grow up.

"Looks like Shirley Kelley has competition," Tommy said.

"Shirley and I broke up," Jonas told them. "She knows I'm not marrying her or anyone else right now. I'm going to college with all those beautiful college girls to meet. It's a big world out there, and I don't want to be tied down to anyone."

❧ ❧ ❧

The news of their breakup made the girls in North Platte High happy. Jonas Hensen was now available. The boys were happy because Shirley Kelley was unattached, even though she told everyone she still loved Jonas.

To Duke Hannigan, it meant another confrontation with his father. "Now's your chance," Liam said when Duke told him about the breakup of the Golden couple. "I've been pushing you to date her for two years, but you always used Hensen as an excuse."

"I also told you I don't like her. You seem to have forgotten that."

"I don't care if you like her or not."

"Oh yeah, I forgot. It's a good business opportunity," Duke said.

"That's right," Liam snapped. "If you marry her someday, it will help me get rid of her father as a business partner. Michael Kelley's too goddamn honest. I could do much better without him."

"So, buy him out and leave me alone."

"I already explained that. If you marry his daughter, he'll trust me more, and it will be easier to take advantage of him."

"You want me to marry the daughter, so you can screw the father."

"Exactly. Business is business," his father said.

Duke then pointed out what everyone at school knew. "She still loves Hensen."

"So, change her mind."

"How?"

Liam thought for a moment. "Listen. Everyone thinks Hensen is this unbeatable Golden Boy. So, if you beat the shit out of him in front of the whole school, you'll look like a hero to her."

"What makes you think I can beat the shit out of him? He's bigger and stronger."

"You're a Hannigan, and Hannigans are winners, no matter what it takes. Let me show you something." Liam opened the middle drawer of his desk and removed a small black box. He handed it to his son. "Open it."

Duke opened the box and removed a black, palm-sized piece of metal. "This is heavier than it looks," Duke said, hefting it.

"It's lead. I call it the *Equalizer*. Hold it in the palm of your hand and make a fist."

The lead disappeared in Duke's big hand. He pounded his fist into his other palm. "Wow. This thing could kill someone," he said.

"It has. I used it fighting my way up in the cattle business. Just get in the first punch and you win."

"What if I don't get in the first punch?"

"Then you're a bigger loser than I thought," Liam said. "Just pick your spot and sucker-punch him. No one will remember *how* you won. They'll just remember who won. The man who beats the legend becomes the legend."

Duke liked the sound of that. "I have to pick the exact right moment," he said.

"I got one for you. Do it right after the graduation ceremony when all the kids gather behind the school. Start a fight. Hit first. He'll go down, and you'll go up in Shirley Kelley's eyes."

Duke was more excited about getting revenge than winning Shirley Kelley.

Duke carried the weight of his father's Equalizer in his pocket and the burden of his grudges on his shoulders. Liam Hannigan had always been ashamed of his Irish past: the poverty, drunkenness, and discrimination. He had to fight for everything he had and expected his son to do the same. No excuses.

It was a North Platte High tradition that after the graduation ceremony the seniors would gather behind the school to exchange congratulations, sign yearbooks, and say goodbye. No parents or teachers allowed. His father had suggested this moment, and Duke agreed it was perfect. He approached Jonas face to face—the Equalizer clenched tightly in his right hand and growled, "I think it's time we settled things, Hensen."

Jonas took a step back. "We have nothing to settle. You don't like me. I don't like you. Let's leave it at that."

"No. I'm challenging you to a fight to prove I'm a better man."

"You've had four years to do that. Why now?"

"Because I want Shirley Kelley," Duke said, loud enough to draw attention. "But she still thinks you're so special; I say you're not."

Curious students formed a circle around them. Hearing her name, Shirley pushed to the front. The sight of her emboldened Duke. "So, *Golden Boy*, you gonna fight me or not?"

"No, thanks," Jonas said. "Go fight yourself."

Some laughed. Duke grimaced.

"I'm leaving," Jonas said and waved. "Congratulations, everyone," he turned away.

Now! While his back is turned. Duke hurried after Jonas, his fist cocked. Jonas heard footsteps. He turned and saw the punch coming, but too late. Duke's fist exploded on the left side of Jonas's face, breaking his jaw. Felled like a tree, Jonas landed hard on his left shoulder. Duke was after him, kicking him in the ribs with steel-toed boots he wore for the occasion. Two ribs broke.

"Duke! Stop!" Shirley screamed. But Duke was out of control. He continued kicking Jonas—to the back, face, and chest. Kick after kick until Jonas tucked himself into a fetal position and rolled away from the assault. Duke's head was pounding. He was gasping for air—hyperventilating. The excitement of certain victory was intoxicating. He paused to catch his breath and enjoyed the moment. He surveyed the crowd. Shirley looked shocked. *Everyone* looked shocked. Duke Hannigan was beating the Golden Boy. Exuberantly, Duke raised his arms over his head and slowly turned in a full circle. *Look at me. I'm number one.*

All eyes were on Duke while Jonas struggled to one knee, then to his feet. There was a collective gasp from the crowd when he was upright. Alerted, Duke turned. *How did he get up?* He wondered. *But, so what? Look at him. He's finished.*

Jonas was swaying, his eyes glassy. Blood was drooling from his open mouth—his broken jaw unable to close. *This is even better,* Duke thought. *One more solid punch and he'll never get up.* He moved forward, cocking his right arm confidently—forgetting that a wounded animal is the most dangerous.

"Duke, no!" Shirley shouted. "You've proved your point to me."

This isn't about you, Shirley, this is about me, Duke thought.

Duke watched Jonas turn sideways to make himself a smaller target. Then he watched Jonas stagger, almost losing his balance. Duke smirked and stopped. "Not so tough anymore, are you, Golden Boy?" he taunted, loving the moment.

"Duke, please stop," Shirley pleaded again.

Duke turned to her "Who's the Golden Boy now?" he shouted.

Shirley's eyes were looking beyond him now as surprise registered on her face. Duke was confused. *What?*

He wondered as he turned back toward Jonas. The punch hit him flush in the face, a ferocious straight right, thrown with evil intent. The blow broke Duke's nose, loosened his front teeth, busted his lips and broke his jaw. Duke's feet left the ground, and when he landed, his head cracked on the cement. The last thing Duke remembered was the Equalizer flying out of his hand.

Jonas stood, staring down at Duke's inert body. He wanted to say *fuck you*, but his broken jaw wouldn't let him.

Impulsively, Shirley burst from the crowd and rushed by Jonas, toward Duke. Jonas grabbed her arm. She stopped abruptly and whispered an explanation. "He needs me," she said softly. "You don't." Jonas let her go.

She knelt by Duke and lifted his bloody head and ruined face onto her lap. Her dress became covered with his blood.

Bad choice, Jonas thought before dizziness forced him to one knee.

Two ambulances arrived. Both injured fighters were rushed to the hospital. The area cleared. Those who were there said they would never forget the scene; *the Golden Boy battered, facing defeat, rising from the abyss—hitting Duke so hard he rearranged his face and knocked him unconscious.* One student described the sound of the back of Duke's head hitting the cement as being like *a baseball bat smashing a pumpkin.* That description made that moment legendary.

A week later, Alf drove Jonas to the scene of the fight. Using flashlights, they searched the bushes. "Here it is," Jonas mumbled through his wired jaw, handing the piece of lead to his father. "I knew I saw something."

"Jesus," Alf said hefting the *Equalizer*. "He could have killed you with this. We have to tell the police."

"I don't want to tell anyone," Jonas said. "Duke knows he's a loser and a cheat and I learned a lesson. That's enough."

"What did you learn?"

"Never to turn my back on a loser and a cheat," Jonas said.

The next day they called the University of Nebraska and told them he would be unable to join the team in the fall. He would take a year to heal and return better than ever.

CHAPTER 3

1914–1917
WAR I

A year later, in the fall of 1914, a bigger, stronger, faster Golden Boy entered the University of Nebraska. He quickly realized that college teams were comprised primarily of Golden Boys like him—star athletes from their hometowns. He was just one of many, and he loved the new experience—the challenge. His fear of losing was replaced by the thrill of winning. Victories were appreciated, instead of expected. He was outplayed at times, and that just made him try harder. He wasn't expected to be perfect. He was expected to do his best, and that was usually enough.

On campus, no one cared if he was religious, and he could talk openly about sex with his friends. He felt like he had escaped a *prison of perfect*, and it was liberating. College life suited him. He was popular, a good student, and a star athlete. Girls loved him, and he loved girls. Lots of girls. No exclusive relationships for him. Monogamy could wait.

He remained in contact with his former teammates from high school; Tommy Hennessey, Donny Hootstein, and Joe Davis. By Jonas's senior year, Hennessey was at Nebraska Law School, Hootstein was at Harvard Law, and Joe Davis worked for the North Platte Park Department. While they enjoyed their youth, Europe's youth was at war.

The Central Powers of Austria-Hungary, Germany, the Ottoman Empire, and Bulgaria were at war with the Allies of Britain, France, Russia, and Italy. The United States had remained neutral, but after years of provocation, President Wilson was forced to declare war on Germany in April of 1917. Jonas was home for spring break with his friends at Mel's when the declaration of war was announced to the public.

"What are the odds we'll be called?" Hennessey asked.

"A hundred percent," Jonas said. "The Army needs over four million men—fast."

"We could apply to be officers," Hootstein suggested.

"Not me," Hennessey chimed in. "I don't want to lead men into war," Jonas and Joe Davis nodded.

When their draft notices came, Jonas had just graduated, Hootstein and Hennessey were home for the summer, and Davis was always home. After one drunken night together, the four best friends said goodbye and went to war.

Before reporting for basic training at Camp Sherman in Chillicothe, Ohio, Jonas researched the war, gathering disturbing information. In three years, from 1914 to 1917, before America entered the war, there had been twenty million war-related deaths or casualties. *The Civil War was only fifty years ago,* Jonas knew, *and lasted four years. Less than a million men died in that war. The Inquisition and the Hundred Years War combined didn't have 20 million casualties. What's going on in Europe?*

After more research, Jonas understood. Weapons had changed, tactics hadn't. Machine guns were now firing thousands of bullets per minute into hordes of men charging in frontal assaults. *Madness*, Jonas concluded. After a week of basic training, he approached his drill sergeant, Dillard Grundy of Dillard, Texas. Grundy was a homely man with a pockmarked face, a thick neck, and a protruding, caveman brow. "Can we talk, Sergeant?"

"About what, college boy?" Grundy asked.

"About these frontal assaults you're teaching us."

"Great, ain't they?" Grundy grunted. "Scared the shit out of the Huns."

"Actually, I don't think they're great, and they scare the shit out of me."

"You a coward boy?" Grundy growled. "I went up San Juan Hill on a frontal assault. No problem."

"You went up Kettle Hill, Sarge," Jonas said.

"Don't matter. A frontal assault got us to the top."

"Gatling guns firing eight hundred bullets a minute got you to the top," Jonas said. "You had them. The enemy didn't."

"Still a frontal assault."

"Yeah, but not against machine guns, Sarge. The Germans have machine guns now that fire over a thousand bullets a minute."

"You learn that in college?"

"I read it in a book."

"Don't read much, myself."

What a surprise, Jonas thought.

"Anything else on your mind?"

"As a matter of fact, yes. What about Big Bertha?"

"A girl?"

"No. A German cannon. Fires an eighteen hundred pound shell nine miles."

"What's your point?"

"My point is that frontal assaults are suicidal now," he said.

"I'm willing to die for my country."

"I'd rather live for my country," Jonas said.

"You afraid, college boy?"

"Sure, I'm afraid. I'm not an idiot. I'll refuse to go on a frontal assault."

"You'll be shot for disobeying orders."

"And I'll be shot for obeying them," he explained. "It's idiotic."

"You calling me an idiot?"

"No," Jonas lied. "I'm saying frontal assaults are idiotic."

"I'll tell General Pershing."

"Great. In the meantime, is there anything I can do for my country besides dying in a frontal assault? Anything that gives me a fighting chance?"

"Sure. You can be a fuckin' trench raider," Grundy said and laughed.

"What's a fuckin' trench raider?" Jonas asked.

"A trench raider goes into No Man's Land *after* a battle and looks for wounded enemy soldiers to bring back for interrogation. Trench raiders have to survive machine guns, falling bombs, land mines, enemy soldiers, rats—everything."

"Do trench raiders get to make their own decisions?" Jonas asked.

"Sure, they're on their own out there."

"I'll take the job."

"Don't be stupid," Grundy said. "Trench raiders last a week at most."

"I'll take my chances. Make me a trench raider."

"Nobody volunteers. It's a punishment."

"Punish me."

In the winter of 1917, on his first night on the Western Front, Jonas met PFC Walter Jackson from Congo Bottom, Tennessee. The terrified teenager asked Jonas why he had volunteered to be a trench raider.

"I'll explain it to you after your first frontal assault."

Jackson never got his explanation. During his first frontal assault, he was in a shell hole when a Big Bertha shell landed in his lap. He was blown to smithereens, and weightless flakes of Walter fluttered onto No Man's Land like dirty snow.

Later that night, Jonas watched Sergeant Grundy prepare to lead his men on their first frontal assault. Grundy checked his rifle, gas mask, and bayonet then put his foot on the bottom rung of the trench ladder. *There's no fear in that man*, Jonas marveled, as Grundy looked back and commanded, "Follow me, men," just as he had done on Kettle Hill. But this wasn't Kettle Hill. This time both sides had machine guns. Just as Sergeant Grundy's head cleared the rim of the trench, four machine gun bullets stitched a path across his forehead. His lifeless body fell back into the trench and landed at Jonas's feet.

Jonas looked down. It was the first violent death he'd ever seen. Suddenly, there was another body falling—landing next to Grundy. He'd been shot in the neck and was nearly decapitated. An instant later, another body fell, landing face up and faceless. It was raining mutilated, dead bodies. The men trying to mount a frontal assault were being blown back into the trench by walls of bullets. Twenty million deaths suddenly made sense. Fifty million made sense. World War I was a slaughterhouse.

He huddled against the trench wall furthest from the exit ladders to avoid being buried under falling bodies. He watched in horror as American boys fell dead having never fired a shot, their deaths in vain—their lives wasted. Jonas covered his helmet with his arms, drew his legs up into a fetal position, and hoped he would not be killed by a stray bullet.

Chapter 4

1918
DRINA

The Great War ended in 1918 after a do-or-die German offensive died. Kaiser Wilhelm requested an Armistice rather than a German surrender. The war-weary Allies agreed. Though the Armistice was between France, Great Britain, and Germany, Jonas was selected to be part of a U.S. honor guard to accompany the Allied contingent to Compiegne, France. A captain and two enlisted men were sent. Jonas noticed that each man was over six feet tall. *To impress the enemy,* he figured. They were even issued clean uniforms.

The formal Armistice took place on the eleventh day of the eleventh month, at the eleventh hour at Commander Ferdinand Foch's railroad car in a forest clearing near Compiegne. Although the Armistice became official at 5:00 a.m., November 11, the formal signing did not take place until 11:00 a.m. In those six hours, thousands of soldiers were killed in combat.

Two hours before the signing, Jonas stood outside Foch's railroad car with the French and British honor guards, also consisting of two enlisted men and one captain. The

German contingent, of four enlisted men and two captains, kept their distance.

The French wore their traditional uniforms consisting of a blue jacket and red pants with a blue cap known as a kepi. *Not very military*, Jonas thought. The British uniform, like the American, was drab olive green. The enlisted men wore their steel Brodie helmets with Sam Browne belts around their waists and over their right shoulders. The captains wore peaked caps.

The Germans were in gray, wearing long coats, secured at the waist by cartridge belts. The officers wore peaked caps, and their men were in helmets.

Jonas eyed the German captains. One looked dangerous. One looked civilized and wore a medal Jonas recognized. He approached and nodded his greeting. The civilized one returned his nod; the dangerous one glared. Jonas read their name tags. The civil one was Franz Goldschmidt, who appeared to be in his early thirties. The nasty one, Captain Emil Koenig, looked closer to Jonas's age.

"The Blue Max, Captain Goldschmidt?" Jonas asked, pointing.

"Yes," Goldschmidt said.

"Don't fraternize with the enemy, Goldschmidt," Koenig growled.

"The war is over, Koenig," Goldschmidt snapped. "Let it go."

Ignoring Koenig, Jonas asked, "What did you do to earn the Blue Max?"

"I was a pilot with over twenty kills—not a pleasant subject, I realize."

"War," Jonas shrugged as if that said it all.

Goldschmidt pointed. "Your Silver Star, Hensen. For what?"

Jonas had forgotten he was wearing a medal. It was contrary to policy, but an officer had pinned it on him shortly before departing for the ceremony. Jonas guessed it was to impress the enemy—like his height.

"I was a trench raider," he answered, "With over a hundred kills."

Goldschmidt raised his eyebrows. "You are the Ghost?"

Jonas nodded.

"You are famous."

Koenig said, "If we met in the trenches, I would have killed you."

"You would have tried," Jonas said, staring at Koenig until the man walked away.

Goldschmidt held out his hand.

"To peace, Hensen," he said.

"To peace, Goldschmidt," Jonas said and shook the German's hand.

It rained on Armistice Day. At night a bright full moon lighted Compiegne. People danced in the streets. Soldiers celebrated surviving, and the chance to grow old. A voice boomed over a loudspeaker. *The Krug Brother's Circus Is Now Open—Servicemen Free! Come One, Come All!* Jonas followed the raucous crowd and calliope music to a field near a rail siding where a circus tent stood. There was a large sign over the entrance:

The Krug Circus—The Greatest Show in Europe

A man on stilts, dressed like Uncle Sam, was smiling, waving, and saying, "I want you…under the Big Top." He was an avuncular Uncle Sam compared to the stern-faced one on recruiting posters.

An adolescent girl handed Jonas cotton candy on a stick and kissed his cheek. He was reminded of the young girl in North Platte who had kissed him the same way. *What was her name?*

A throng jostled Jonas into the Big Top. A dazzling array of sights and sounds assaulted his senses. Clowns danced, ponies pranced, tightrope walkers teetered, jugglers juggled, rope dancers dangled. A raucous calliope created a cacophony. Jonas became disoriented. For twelve months, he had heard only war sounds—sounds of dying. *Now, this crazy celebration of life jarred his senses.*

He found a seat in the stands. Three men in dirty clothes followed and sat next to him. They smelled of alcohol, sweat, and foul breath. Their eyes were glazed, and they spoke the nonsensical gibberish of the intoxicated. He turned away, not letting them spoil the moment.

The tent lights went low, and the entertainers disappeared. A spotlight illuminated the ringmaster, standing alone in the ring, wearing a black top hat and splendid red jacket. He introduced himself as Fredrik Krug, the owner of the circus. He looked to be in his forties. He expressed his gratitude to the servicemen in the tent, and everyone applauded. A few patted Jonas on the shoulder. Krug then introduced the *Hungarian Gypsy Rope Dancers.*

A young woman, looking to be in her teens appeared. She was dressed in a form-fitting red sequined costume and was followed by two men in equally tight blue outfits. The three of them were small and dark-skinned, though the woman had a lighter complexion and her features were more delicate. Three ropes hung from a beam high above the ring. Each performer climbed a rope. The girl kept pace with the men. *She's amazing,* Jonas thought.

When she reached the top, she began twisting and turning. Upside down, right side up, long black hair flowing, bright eyes flashing, delicate hands painting exotic images in the air. He was mesmerized. *I survived to meet her,* he convinced himself.

The three drunks were sneaking drinks from brown paper bags. The more they drank, the more annoying they became. When the act ended, they staggered from their seats and departed, braying like donkeys.

The rope dancers descended and took their bows. The woman exited promptly while the two males remained, helping prepare the ring for the next act. Jonas went outside and wandered the midway, looking for the rope dancer. After a few minutes, he saw a colorful clown weaving toward him like a drunk. As he got closer, Jonas saw the clown was wearing a name tag that read, Bongo, and he was bleeding from a gash on his forehead.

"They took Drina," Bongo said, desperation in his voice.

"Who are you talking about?"

"Drina. The rope dancer. Three men dragged her into the woods near the tracks, right over there." He pointed. "I tried to stop them, but they knocked me down."

"I'll go after her," Jonas said. "You get help."

Bongo stumbled away. The moon provided enough light to see a trail of broken underbrush. Jonas charged through and over the bushes. He heard them before he saw them, their drunken laughter, her desperate screams. Then he saw two men pushing and pulling Drina, with the third lagging behind the three drunks from the circus. Drina's shirt was torn, and she was bleeding from a cut above one eye. She was fighting but losing.

Infuriated, Jonas charged through the underbrush, channeling the Ghost he thought he had left behind in the trenches. He grabbed the startled straggler by the throat with one hand, raised him off the ground, and smashed the back of his head against a tree trunk. He dropped the limp body to the ground. Instinctively, he sensed someone attacking from his left. He thrust his left arm above his head just as a broken tree limb, wielded like an axe, smashed into his forearm and his head. The Ghost went down, dazed, and rolled away from his attacker. He staggered to his feet, disoriented. Blood ran into his eyes from the top of his head. His vision was blurred, but he could see his attacker approaching, poised to strike again.

The Ghost knew his left arm was useless, hanging at his side. The man charged, brandishing the limb above his head again. When he chopped down, the Ghost leaned right, avoiding the descending blow. The limb crashed into the ground. The Ghost slammed his right fist down into the man's jaw and felt bones shatter and skin shift on the man's skull. The assailant went down, face first, and didn't move.

The Ghost turned toward Drina who was struggling with the third drunk. Her hair covered half her face. The Ghost weaved toward them. The drunk shoved Drina aside and held up a knife. Losing his balance, the Ghost dropped to one knee. The drunk leered and lunged. *I can't believe this is how I'm going to die,* Jonas thought as his world went dark.

CHAPTER 5

1918
JONAS & DRINA

Jonas awoke disoriented and in pain. A gas lamp with a Tiffany shade cast a soft light on what appeared to be a large, long bedroom. *Where am I?* He wondered, touching the bandage on his head. He was propped on his right side, naked under a blanket. He smelled of disinfectant. His left arm was in a cast. He didn't know if hours or days had passed.

He vaguely remembered being carried on a stretcher, put on a bed, undressed, and washed. He recalled liquor being poured down his throat, and a series of pinpricks in his head. He could still feel the wrenching pain in his left arm. But mostly he remembered Drina, the beautiful rope dancer he had tried to rescue. *Was she alright? Did I save her?*

Drina sat in the dark near her Pullman railcar, with Krug Brothers Circus emblazoned in red on the side. She had bathed, cleaned her wounds, and dressed in a long robe with sandals. She was thinking of the man in her bed, who had likely saved her life. She knew he was the white knight she had been waiting for since childhood—the man in her dreams who would change her world.

Uncle Fredrik approached. "How is he?" he asked.

"He'll live," Drina answered. "Stitches in his head and a cast on his arm. It would have been worse if Bongo hadn't got there and hit that drunk on the back of the head with a juggling club—just about killed him. I think our guy killed the other two. Never saw a man fight like that."

"He's a warrior, alright," Uncle Fredrik told her. "He has a Silver Star for bravery pinned to his uniform. He's a combat hero. His ID papers say his name is Jonas Hensen. He has blonde hair and green eyes. Best of all, for you, he's very white, like the man in your dreams."

"He's the one," Drina said. "I'm sure of it."

"Will you tell him your dream and your plan?"

"No. He would never understand or agree."

"Then, you'll be taking advantage of him."

Drina smiled and lowered her eyes. "In the nicest possible way...and only if he is a good man. He can't be just anyone."

"You know I don't approve of what you're doing."

"I know. But you'll help me, anyway."

"When have I ever said no to you?"

Drina kissed her uncle on the cheek and went inside.

Jonas was surprised when she appeared by the bed. "How do you feel?" she asked.

"Better," he said and saw a bruise on her face. "How are you?"

"I'm fine, thanks to you. You're a hero."

"No. I'm just a man."

"Obviously a very special man," she said. "Who are you?"

"It's a long story."

"We have time," she said, sitting on the bed next to him.

⚜ ⚜ ⚜

Talking about the past was cathartic for Jonas, reminding him of who had been before the war. When he finished, Drina said, "A Golden Boy and a Ghost, I knew you were special when I first saw you."

"What did you see when you first saw me?"

"A beautiful, talented woman."

"Did the color of my skin bother you?"

"Not at all. I've never been that way. People are people."

"Excellent answer," she said.

"Are you testing me?"

"In a way. I want to know if you are as good on the inside as you are on the outside."

"I don't know," Jonas said. "I just try to do the right thing."

"Like saving me?"

"Saving you was definitely the right thing."

"And I want to thank you for that," she said, unbuttoning her robe and letting it fall.

Jonas held up his arm as if to shield her nakedness. "You don't have to thank me that way," he said, his voice shaky.

"I want to," she sighed, sliding under the covers.

He loved her smell, her silky skin, lush hair, and full lips. He grew hard, and she found him under the covers. He gasped. She fondled him then mounted him carefully. "Let me do everything. You just enjoy."

He closed his eyes and tried to make it last. But it was too intense for him and ended quickly. "I'm sorry," he said. "It's been so long."

She leaned down and kissed him. "It was perfect," she said. "Now rest."

He fell asleep. Hours later, his desire proved stronger than his fatigue, and he reached for her again. The second time was longer and better.

They slept for hours and awoke facing each other. He kissed her lips and asked, "And who are you, besides a beautiful angel?"

"I'm no angel," she said. "I'm a Romani from Spain. A Gypsy. Drina Santiago."

"The ringmaster introduced you as Hungarian."

"My partners are Hungarian. My Uncle Fredrik, the ringmaster, keeps the introductions simple. He says white Europeans think all mud people look the same."

"Mud people?"

"Not brown, black, or white. The color of mud."

"What a terrible expression."

"Is your word, *nigger*, any better?" Drina said.

"No. Hate is ugly no matter what word you use."

"The men who attacked me think all mud women are whores."

"Those men were monsters."

A pained look crossed her face. "Did I say something wrong?" Jonas said.

"My parents died because of a monster like them."

"What happened?"

"I was only three, so Uncle Fredrik told me the story. My parents were trapeze artists. A white newspaper reporter wrote that Romani trapeze performers lacked the courage and skill to perform without a net. My parents were offended and took down the net for one performance. They fell and died trying to prove themselves to an ignorant racist, who later wrote ... *I told you so.* He was a monster, and his hateful words killed my parents."

"Things will change someday."

"White monsters will never change. It's their world. Coloreds have to change."

"How? What can they do?"

"There are ways," Drina said. "I have plans."

"Can I help?" Jonas asked.

"You already have," she said and reached for him again.

CHAPTER 6

1918
UNCLE FREDRIK

Three days of making love made Jonas feel human again. On his last night before rejoining his unit, Fredrik Krug invited him to dinner in his lavish club car with Drina. Jonas was impressed by the sumptuous interior. A chandelier in the center gave the space a warm glow, and Tiffany lampshades added color. Silk shades covered the windows, and rich dark walnut paneling adorned the walls. The lounge chairs were upholstered with a rich maroon fabric, and the sofa was the same. A bed at the opposite end of the car had a low partition separating the space.

"It's hard to believe this is a railcar," Jonas said.

Fredrik Krug chuckled. "George Pullman would be insulted. This is called a Pullman Luxury Sleeping Car, custom-made for me. Seventy-five feet long—over eight feet wide. Extravagant, but it's my home. So, where have you two been for the past three days?"

Drina blushed. "Uncle! You embarrass me."

"I'm sorry. I think it's a blessing you two found each other."

"I agree," Jonas said. Drina lowered her eyes and said nothing.

They talked of many things, including the death of Drina's parents. "Pride killed them," Fredrik said. "I should never have let them perform without a net."

Drina touched Fredrik's hand. "It was not your fault, Uncle."

He smiled at her. "My late wife couldn't have children, so Drina became our daughter after she was orphaned. She means everything to me."

"I can understand why," Jonas said.

After dinner, Drina encouraged the two men to go for a walk while she cleaned up. They strolled along the disassembled midway, Krug greeting all the workers by name. Jonas saw trapeze swings on the ground, prepared for packing. The first time he saw them, they were high overhead. "You must love circus life," he said, glancing at Krug.

"I do. My great-grandfather started with a magic show, and now we're the largest traveling circus in Europe. We have a three-ring version at our home base in Zurich, but it's too difficult to move this time of year."

"I'm sure. How did you manage to get to Compiegne the night of the Armistice?"

"We were given a month's notice."

"But the Armistice was only announced a week ago," Jonas responded, puzzled.

"Obviously, the date was known before the announcement."

"You mean the date was known a month ago?" Jonas stammered. "And we continued fighting? Thousands died needlessly during that time."

"Actually, millions died needlessly the entire time," Fredrik said. "But what's done is done. What matters now is the future. Do you have plans?"

"Only that I rejoin my company tomorrow," Jonas told him, still seething over the Armistice debacle.

"Then what?"

"I assume I'll be shipped home in the spring."

"What about Drina?" Fredrik asked.

"I was thinking of coming back for her, but we haven't talked about it."

"Do you love her?"

"I don't know," Jonas admitted. "I think I do."

"If you loved her, you'd know for sure," Fredrik opined. "Do you think she loves you?"

"I'm not sure. Everything happened so fast. It doesn't seem real."

"Because it's not real," Fredrik said. "It's an illusion. You survived hell, met an angel, and think you're in heaven. But you're not. You're in a place you don't belong."

"You're confusing me. What do you think I should do?"

"My advice? Go home. See your family and friends. Give your old life a chance. You can always return."

"What if Drina doesn't wait for me?" Jonas asked.

"Then it wasn't meant to be."

"Do you know what Drina wants?"

"Yes. She wants to change the world, one person at a time."

That night in bed, Drina rested her head on his shoulder. "Thank you again for saving my life," she said.

"Thank you for saving mine," he responded and fell asleep.

When Drina awoke in the morning, Jonas was gone. She hoped he had left part of him with her, but only time would tell.

Jonas remained in France with his company through the New Year. They helped clean up some of the mess left from the Great War while he struggled with the knowledge that the Army had withheld information about the Armistice and allowed thousands of men to die for nothing.

Drina learned she was pregnant in January, and before her pregnancy showed, she announced she was leaving the circus, and returning to her family in Spain. She told everyone her departure was prompted by the attack she suffered. In actuality, it was part of the long-term plan she made with her Uncle Fredrik years ago to save the world—one person at a time.

Jonas was shipped home in May onboard a makeshift troop ship named the *Philippines*. Upon arrival in New York harbor, the ship was immediately quarantined for influenza. After a prolonged period, the soldiers were finally released, and Jonas booked a train ticket home. He telegrammed his schedule to his parents.

The *Eastern Limited* arrived at the North Platte outdoor train station, the morning of the 23rd of May. Jonas wasn't surprised to see the platform filled with people carrying signs welcoming him home. He assumed his parents had announced his arrival.

He saw his mother and father standing apart from the crowd; his father dressed incongruously in a suit and tie. His mother wore a dark blue dress, the kind she wore to church on Sundays. They looked different, smaller than he remembered them. They were only in their forties, and he hadn't been gone long enough for them to have changed so noticeably. *Am I seeing things differently?* He wondered. *Was the war so big everything else seems small?*

A cheer erupted when he stepped off the train. His parents rushed to greet him, and they hugged. A man he didn't recognize shook Jonas's hand, introduced himself as the mayor and ushered the Hensens to a black Packard convertible. Jonas sat in the back with his parents as they were driven slowly down Main Street behind a small marching band. The street was lined with people cheering and waving American flags. It was a grand homecoming for a war hero. By chance, Jonas saw Shirley Kelley in the crowd. She looked good. She waved. Jonas waved back. He wondered if she was happy with Duke. He had no regrets.

They arrived in front of City Hall, where a temporary wooden platform had been erected. Three folding chairs had been placed behind a portable podium where the mayor stood while the Hensens sat. *"Today we welcome home a local hero,"* the mayor began, reading from a notecard. *"From the playing fields of Nebraska to the battlefields of Europe, Jonas Hensen made us all proud."* Applause. *"With Tom Hennessey, Don Hootstein, and Joe Davis, Jonas was part of the greatest backfield in North Platte High football history."* More applause. *"Sadly, as we all know, Jonas is the sole survivor of that illustrious group. Hennessey, Hootstein, and Davis along with team manager, Mickey Caroline, were all killed in the Argonne Forest shortly before the Armistice."*

Jonas bolted from his seat. "What? They're all dead?" he shouted.

"I thought you knew," the mayor said, turning around—embarrassed.

"We wrote you, son," his father said, reaching up to touch his arm.

"I didn't get a letter," Jonas shouted. "I didn't know."

"I'm so sorry," the mayor said.

"They didn't have to die," Jonas shouted, thinking of the delayed Armistice announcement. "Our army lied."

The crowd didn't understand his words but felt his pain. They watched with sympathy as Jonas ran off the stage and down the street.

"Jonas," his father called after him, but he didn't stop. He couldn't stop.

He ran through the streets of North Platte, tears streaming down his face—directionless. In an empty field outside of town, he fell to his knees and vomited until there was nothing left in him. He cursed the men who started the war and those who prolonged it. It had all been for nothing. He got up and started running again and didn't stop for a long time.

CHAPTER 7

1919
JONAS

Jonas's Silver Star was displayed at City Hall and his All-American plaques at the North Platte Museum of History. He showed no interest in them or anything else. Nightmares had begun attacking him like snapping dogs. He couldn't sleep. Men he killed in the war came back to haunt him in nightmares that woke him—screaming.

One night, Sergeant Grundy appeared in his dream with four holes in his head. *"I tried to warn you about those guns,"* Jonas recalled.

"I couldn't change," Grundy said and faded in the mist.

Another night, the young German soldier with the family photo, appeared. He was being sent home one piece at a time, and his family was putting him back together like a jigsaw puzzle.

Jonas felt weak and vulnerable for the first time in his life. He avoided people, leaving the house in the early morning and staying out till dark. When he returned home, he barely spoke to his parents. He had nothing to say. The family doctor told Bea and Alf that Jonas had survivor's guilt. "Some come out of it," he said. "Some don't."

Bea prayed for him. Alf hoped.

Early one humid, cloudless Sunday morning in August, Jonas walked three miles to downtown North Platte, drifted west on Front Street for another mile and came to Bailey Yard. He hadn't been there in years and wondered if it had changed as much as he had.

He stood on a slope overlooking the yard that held millions of memories for thousands of people. Jonas remembered childhood visits to the yard with his father. *"Bailey is the biggest railroad transferring yard in the world,"* his father had told him. *"Three thousand acres. Eight miles long, two miles wide. A hundred and fifty trains and a thousand railcars go through Bailey Yard every day. Over two thousand people, like me, work here."*

Bailey Yard was always busy, even on a Sunday morning. Jonas watched railroad cars coupling, uncoupling, and switching tracks. He tried to imagine living his father's life for the next forty years and knew he couldn't. Compared to war, everything else seemed meaningless.

He returned to the center of town and sat on a wooden bench in front of City Hall. The church bell clanged eight times. It's only eight o'clock. What will I do for the rest of my day? The rest of my life? He tilted his head back and looked at the morning sun. Football season was a few weeks away. When he was young, there was a season for everything. But once school days ended, one day melted into the next ... and time passed faster.

He closed his eyes and wondered where to walk next. Yesterday he had gone to the North Platte River and visited the spot where he had made love to Shirley Kelley. Before that, he had walked to Scout's Rest Ranch, Bill Cody's four thousand-acre spread west of downtown. It had been closed for several years, but at one time, it was the home base for Buffalo Bill's Wild West Show and the highlight of North Platte.

When Jonas was nine, he had met Buffalo Bill while trespassing on his land. The showman was about to run him off when Jonas asked him how he got his nickname. Bill explained that he had already killed over four thousand buffalo when a man named Medicine Bill Comstock claimed he had killed more. They decided to have a *buffalo killing* contest for the legal right to use the Buffalo designation. Bill Cody won.

"What if you had killed all the buffalo?" Jonas had asked the official Buffalo Bill.

"That couldn't happen," Bill has assured him. "There were millions of them."

Jonas had enjoyed knowing Buffalo Bill, but now his ranch was nothing but memories. The house was still standing, but the characters who had brought the ranch to life were gone. Bill was dead for three years. Johnny "Cowboy Kid" Becker, Frank Butler, Annie Oakley, and Calamity Jane had moved away or died. He didn't realize how special those times and people were…until they were gone.

The bell atop City Hall clanged nine times and woke him. Jonas stood, stretched, and heard someone call his name. He immediately recognized the voice. "Coach," he said, smiling at Emmitt Parsons, his former high school coach and teacher. They hugged and clapped each other on the back.

"How long has it been?" Coach Parsons asked.

"Since before the war, I think."

"Got time for a cup of coffee with your old coach?"

They went to the North Platte Diner, took a booth, and ordered coffee from a young waitress who recognized them.

"We're all proud of you, Jonas," she said, and he thanked her. "How's the team look this year, Coach?" He assured her they looked good.

"I'm proud of you too, Jonas," Parsons said after the waitress went for their coffee. "Only two of my former players ever made All-American. You and Vic O'Connor."

"Vic was the best," Jonas said. "I played with him for two years in high school and college. I know he went to war. Did he make it back?"

"He did. Came back to North Platte and opened a law practice. The two of you are local success stories."

"Vic's a success. Not me."

"I heard you're having a hard time. What's up?"

"I don't know. Everything seemed so much easier in high school," Jonas rationalized.

"You were passionate about everything back then."

"The war took my passion, Coach. I feel like nothing I do matters anymore. Did you ever feel that way?"

"Never. I always thought what I did mattered," Coach Parsons said. "I like to think that I had a positive influence on my students and players."

"You did a lot for me," Jonas told him. "I wanted to be like you when I grew up."

"That means a lot coming from you," the coach thanked him. "Duke Hannigan doesn't think as highly of me as you do. I saw him last year, and he claimed he never learned a thing from me."

"Duke's a fool," Jonas snapped. "He never learned anything from anyone because he never listened. I hope you didn't pay attention to him."

"I didn't. I'm proud of what I've done. And I'm going to miss it."

"What do you mean? Where are you going?"

"Haven't you read the papers? I'm retiring. One more year."

"No. I hadn't heard. Why retire?"

"I'm sixty-five, Jonas. It's time."

Jonas had noticed the gray hair at the temples and the wrinkles around his coach's eyes, but he hadn't thought much about it. "You still have a lot of good years left in you," he said.

"I hope so, and I'd like to spend them relaxing. Trouble is, my assistant coach is my age, and he's retiring too. I start interviewing applicants for my job tomorrow. Whoever I choose will be my assistant this year, and then take over as head coach next year. He'll need to be able to teach history, too. Not easy to find."

I could do that, Jonas thought and felt his heartbeat quicken. *I'd love to do that. Teach kids. Coach kids.* "What about me?" he asked impulsively.

"What about you?"

"I could coach and teach," Jonas said. "I love kids, and I'm qualified."

"You're overqualified."

"So, can I apply for your job?"

"Of course, you can. In fact, if you're serious, don't bother applying. You're hired."

"What about the other applicants?"

"You're the only North Platte, All-American football player and Silver Star recipient I expect to apply," the coach told him and laughed. "The job is yours if you want it."

"I want it. I think it's what I've been looking for. A chance to do something important. I can't thank you enough, Coach."

"For what? Offering you a low-paying job?"

"For offering me hope."

The Golden Boy felt like he had finally come home.

On July 29, 1919, Drina Santiago gave birth to a son. He was several weeks premature but weighed a reasonable five pounds. When Fredrik Krug received word of the early birth, he left the circus for Annecy. Before leaving, he lied to his assistants. He told them his distant cousin and her husband had been killed in a car accident, leaving their newborn son an orphan. "I'm going to see what I can do to help."

No one questioned him. Hadn't he taken Drina in as his own after her parents died? Certainly, he'll do no less for his own flesh and blood.

Things are going as planned, Fredrik thought on his way to Annecy. *I'll return with the baby claiming he's a Krug. Later, Drina will return to the circus, explaining she missed circus life. Then, I'll ask her to be the baby's nanny. That way, she can raise her own child, and he can enjoy the advantages of the white world as a Krug.* That's what she wanted. That was her plan to improve the world, one person at a time. Give one child a fair chance.

Fredrik sat at Drina's bedside at the Annecy Hospital, holding her baby boy in his arms. "You look tired," he said, understating her sickly appearance. There were dark circles under her eyes, and her skin looked pasty and translucent.

"I'm fine," she said, sounding weak. "Isn't my son beautiful?"

"He looks like his father. He can easily pass for white."

"My dream came true," Drina said.

"Will you tell Jonas now?"

"No. He'd feel obligated. I planned this child. He didn't."

"You know I've never approved of all this. I only agreed because I love you."

"I know," she said and touched his arm. Her hand felt clammy.

"Have you thought of a name?"

She smiled wanly. "I like the name Niko," she said then flinched.

"Are you alright?"

"No." Her voice cracked. She looked under the sheets. "Oh God, I'm gushing blood."

"Get a doctor!" Uncle Fredrik shouted at the attending nurse.

Drina's head fell back on the pillow. "I can't breathe," she gasped.

"Help!" Uncle Fredrik shouted, grasping Drina's hand.

The baby began to cry. Drina continued gasping, her eyes wild. She squeezed his hand and drew him closer. "Promise me you'll raise him white," she whispered.

"Don't talk like that. You'll raise him yourself."

"Promise," she said, gritting her teeth.

"I promise."

A doctor came running, but he was too late. Drina's uterus had ruptured, and she bled out in minutes. The stillness of death replaced her spark of life. Drina died before she could close her eyes. She was only eighteen.

Her newborn son cried, and the nurse reached for him. "I'll take him to the nursery," she said. "Does he have a name?"

"Niko Santiago Krug," Fredrik Krug said.

"Religion?"

"Catholic."

"Race?"

"Caucasian."

"But his mother was Gitano," the nurse said.

"Caucasian," he repeated. "Write it down. The boy is Caucasian."

Fredrik had Drina's body cremated in Annecy. When he returned to Zurich, he scattered her ashes on the circus grounds, with her parents, among friends.

The circus people never doubted the boy was a Krug. Some even said he looked like Fredrik. No one thought about the big, blond doughboy who had saved Drina one night and stayed with her for a few days. If anyone remembered Jonas Hensen, they would have known that Niko Krug looked exactly like him.

CHAPTER 8

1915–1920
AMANDA

In 1915, Amanda Bersten was a fifteen-year-old sophomore at North Platte High. Long-legged and thin, she showed great potential as a long-distance runner on the girl's track team until the day it all ended during a race. She had passed another runner, the third in the last half mile, and realized there was no one in front of her. She was winning with only a half mile to go! She had finished third once—never first. *Today's my day*, she thought, feeling like she was flying.

Suddenly, her right leg cramped and weakened. She tried to continue, but it grew worse. She began limping and soon she was walking. The pain persisted, and her leg grew weaker. She stopped, covered her face with her hands, and started crying. One of the girls she'd passed caught up to her. "Are you okay?"

No, I'm not okay, Amanda thought, remembering her brother's cramps and weakening muscles. He had died from Duchenne muscular dystrophy. It was a man's disease, but her parents had always feared she might develop another form. *And, here it is,* she thought as she slumped to the ground. At first, she sat, but the pain forced her down on her side. She did not try to get up. She knew her running days were over. Maybe even her life.

The headline of the August 29, 1919, *North Platte Ledger* read:

THE GOLDEN BOY RETURNS
Jonas Hensen, All-American football player and decorated war hero, is returning to North Platte High as coach and teacher.

The reporter went on to extol Emmitt Parsons for his long coaching career and his wisdom in selecting Jonas to replace him.

The Golden Boy's first practice, days later, drew nearly a hundred spectators. Enrollment for football the previous day had set a school record. Coach Parsons was popular, but Jonas Hensen was a legend. Jonas was all positive energy that first afternoon. Coach Parsons directed him, and he performed. The players loved the mix of an old pro's experience and a young lion's enthusiasm.

After practice, some of the spectators formed a line to talk to Jonas. They were mostly fans who remembered his playing days. At the end of the line, Jonas noticed a tall, young woman who looked vaguely familiar. She had long blonde hair, blue eyes, and a sprinkling of freckles on her cheeks. She wore a colorful blouse and a long skirt, ending at her ankles. She had a narrow waist and a full figure. Finally, she was next in line. "Hi Jonas," she said. "Remember me?"

"You look familiar," he said. "But I can't place you."

"A long time ago I told you I was going to marry you."

"That was you? I remember—but not your name. Was it…?"

"Amanda Bersten," she said.

"Sure. You were a scrawny kid back then."

"I grew up," she said.

"You certainly did. You're beautiful," he told her, thinking she was a different kind of beauty than the one he had left behind in Europe, less delicate—more robust.

She smiled and blushed. "Thank you. I had such a crush on you."

"That was a long time ago."

"Nearly eight years. I was ten."

"I've been to college and war since then."

"I know. I read all about you. The whole state was proud of you." She smiled again, charming him.

"Amanda Bersten," Coach Parsons called, walking toward them, breaking the spell.

"Hi, Coach," she smiled and hugged him.

"How've you been?"

"Holding my own."

"That's good, right?"

"Yes."

What does she mean…'holding my own?' Jonas thought.

"Do you two know each other?" Coach Parsons asked.

"We met a long time ago," Amanda said.

"A reunion. Great. Jonas, I need to talk to you when you're done."

"Okay, Coach," Jonas said. Turning to Amanda, he asked, "Would you like to get together sometime? Get reacquainted?"

"I'd love that."

"I'll call you."

"Great. Now don't keep the coach waiting."

After he talked football with Coach Parsons, he asked about Amanda.

"Wonderful girl," Coach Parsons said. "Unfortunate situation."

"What's unfortunate?"

"I'm sorry. I thought you knew. She has muscular dystrophy. Her older brother had it too. He died a while back."

"I didn't know," Jonas said, stunned and suddenly depressed.

"She seems to be doing fine, though," Parsons added quickly.

Jonas nodded. He felt numb. "I gotta go," was all he could say.

That night Jonas had a new nightmare. It began with Amanda's enchanting face—her cute freckles, her radiant smile, and her bright blue eyes. In his dream, those bright eyes dimmed, her limbs shriveled, and she was in a wheelchair. Then he was lowering her limp body into a grave when he lost his balance and fell in with her. He screamed, opened his eyes, and found himself on his bedroom floor.

Jonas struggled to his feet; pulled on a pair of jeans, and went outside, shirtless and barefoot. He sat on the top step of the front porch and looked up at a cloudless sky. *I've seen too many young people die. I can't watch this girl die too.*

After two weeks she called him. "Hi, Jonas. I'd expected to hear from you. Are you okay?"

"I'm busy right now," he told her. "I'll call you back."

Jonas felt guilty but couldn't bring himself to call. *I can't get involved in her life,* he told himself. *Enough death. Enough loss.*

One day after practice, Coach Parsons said, "What's wrong, Jonas? You seem distracted lately."

"Sorry. I didn't know it showed. It's a personal problem."

"Does it have anything to do with Amanda Bersten?"

"How did you know?"

"I could tell you were very upset when I told you she had MD."

"I was attracted to her, but when you told me she was dying…"

"Hold on," Coach Parsons interrupted. "I never said she was dying."

"You said her brother died from MD."

"He did. But he had Duchenne's. Almost always fatal. Amanda has myotonic dystrophy. It's more manageable. She could live a normal life."

"I thought she would just wither away and die."

"She might. And she might outlive us all."

Jonas nodded but wasn't convinced.

"Jonas, a few weeks ago, you were wondering why you survived the war. Right?"

"Yes. But, not anymore. This job gave me a new purpose."

"Is it possible you survived the war to find Amanda … and not this job?"

"Not really. I barely know the girl."

"You seem to like her a lot. I'm just asking if it's possible."

The more Jonas thought about Amanda Bersten, the more he thought Coach Parsons might be right. He was attracted to her. She seemed attracted to him. *Maybe.*

CHAPTER 9

1919
AMANDA & JONAS

Jonas got the Berstens' address, borrowed his father's truck, and drove to Amanda's neighborhood. Amanda lived in a modest two-level white house with a picket fence framing a small lot, near downtown North Platte. There was a veranda in front with two rocking chairs and a swing-style loveseat. Jonas got out of the truck and cleared the two steps to the veranda in one stride. He pressed the button and heard the bell ring inside. He heard a woman's voice say, "I'm coming." The door opened, and Jonas saw what Amanda might look like in twenty-five years.

"Can I help you?" Amanda's mother asked, then recognized him. "You're the Hensen boy. The war hero."

"Jonas Hensen. Bea and Alf's son."

"Of course, your father works at the Bailey Yard with my husband, Hugo. I'm Amanda's mother, Hannah. What can I do for you, Jonas?"

"I came to see Amanda."

"I didn't know you two knew each other. Is she expecting you?"

"No. I just dropped by to say hello."

"I'm afraid Amanda's not feeling well. You do know she's been ill."

"I heard. But I saw her a few weeks ago, and she looked great."

Mrs. Bersten nodded, and her eyes welled up. "She's had a setback," she said and bit her lower lip. "I'm sorry. I'm just not myself when she's not well. This is not our first time."

"I understand," Jonas said, his voice soft and respectful.

She looked at him and cleared her throat. "Anyway, I'll go upstairs and tell her you're here. Don't be insulted if she doesn't want to see you. I brought her lunch about a half hour ago, but she didn't even look at it. She was just sitting by the window, looking out. It breaks my heart."

"Can I just go up? That way, she can't refuse to see me."

"You might upset her."

"I might cheer her up."

"That would be nice. She is all dressed and looks so pretty." Mrs. Bersten sniffled. "Try. What harm could it do? First door on the left at the top of the stairs. Be sure to knock. Don't be upset if she tells you to go away."

"No problem," Jonas nodded, loped up the stairs, and knocked.

"Mom, I'm not hungry," Amanda said. "You can take the tray away if you want."

He opened the door. Amanda was sitting in a wooden armchair, staring out the window, her back to him. She was wearing a blue dress with white and black saddle shoes. He walked slowly to her side and pulled a straight-back wooden chair next to her. She continued staring out the window.

"Mom, I don't want company," she said, without turning.

Jonas picked up the bowl of soup from the portable table and held the spoon to her mouth.

"Mom don't feed me," Amanda said. "I'm not a baby." She turned her head, saw him, and gasped. He touched her lower lip gently with the spoon.

"Eat something," he said.

She just stared.

"The soup is cold, but the vegetables will be good for you."

Without taking her eyes off him, she opened her mouth. He fed her. Her face was bright red, and Jonas thought she was beautiful. He felt his own face getting warm.

"That's a good start," he said, spooning out more.

"What are you doing here?" she asked, her voice soft, shaky, and a little angry.

"I wanted to see you," he said. "But never mind me. Just eat. Take your time. I'm not going anywhere."

She opened her mouth again, still staring at him. She finished the soup and a few bites of a toasted cheese sandwich.

"Okay, I've eaten," she said. "Why are you here?"

"I came to apologize for not calling."

Her eyes welled up, just like her mother's had. "You made me cry," she said, looking like she might cry now.

"I'm sorry," he apologized, feeling a strong desire to hold and comfort her.

"You must know about my MD," she said, searching his eyes for a reaction.

"I do. Coach Parsons told me."

"Did he tell you my older brother died from MD?"

"Yes. But he said yours is different. More manageable."

"I have a chance to live a normal life," she said. "But that's wishful thinking. A dream, really. I like my dreams better than my reality."

"Why?"

"In my dreams, I'm not sick, and you love me like I love you," she explained.

He didn't know what to say. She broke the moment's silence with a wave of her hand.

"Don't worry. It's just my fantasy, not yours. I won't bother you again. Promise."

"Can we talk about that?"

"About silly dreams and childhood fantasies? Why bother?"

Not knowing what to say, Jonas impulsively leaned forward and kissed her lips lightly.

"Why did you do that?" she asked, her fingers going to her lips.

"I've been thinking about doing that for two weeks."

Her eyes glistened, "Are you teasing me?"

"I wouldn't do that."

"I don't want you feeling sorry for me."

"I'm not. I actually can't get you out of my mind."

"Don't lie to me, Jonas Hensen. I couldn't stand that."

"I'm not. Look, when I learned you were sick, I got depressed. I saw so many horrible things during the war; I couldn't bear seeing something bad happen to you. That's why I didn't call. I was afraid."

"I thought you just didn't like me."

"I *really* like you," he said and kissed her again. This time she kissed him back.

"That was nice," she said, her eyes still closed, her lips touching his.

He broke away first. "We should go downstairs. Your mother might be worried."

Hannah Bersten was waiting at the bottom of the stairs and was relieved to see a smile on her daughter's face. "You're feeling better, I see."

"I am," Amanda said, her smile expanding. "Jonas got me to eat. We're going to sit on the porch and talk, now. Okay?"

"Wonderful," her mother said, pleased.

Jonas and Amanda sat on rocking chairs, facing one another. Jonas took her hands and she smiled. *I like making her smile*, he thought.

"Things are happening so fast," Amanda said.

"It's timing," Jonas said. "You're not twelve anymore, and I'm not at war. We can get to know each other now."

"I'd like that."

After that day, they were together every night. Their relationship became a whirlwind courtship. Amanda had been in love with Jonas since she was ten, and her puppy love had matured with her. His perspective was entirely different. Their first meeting was only a vague memory for him. He remembered how cute and determined she had been, but little else. Now there was something about her that enchanted him. He delighted in making her happy, and she seemed happy just to be with him. Jonas had known many women, but he had never felt before what he was feeling for Amanda. He became obsessively possessive and protective of her. He held her hand when they were walking because he knew she liked the closeness. He loved the way she rested her head on his shoulder when they sat side by side.

After a month, they began exploring each other's bodies with their hands. One night in his car, she asked, "Do you want to make love to me?"

"I don't want to rush you," he said. "I can wait."

"Wait for what?"

"More time together. You're still a kid to me."

"I'm nearly nineteen," she pouted.

"I'm twenty-three. Sex is important to me, but I want it to be special with you."

She loved feeling special.

After dinner with her parents, they were sitting on her front porch on a nippy November evening, wearing jackets, huddled on the loveseat. "They adore you," she told him. "My father loves that I'm dating the local hero. My mother loves you for making me so happy."

"How about making me happy by starting that exercise program we talked about. We need to strengthen and stretch your muscles every day and make sure you eat the right foods and get plenty of sleep. I'll do it with you."

"Including the sleeping part?"

"I've thought about that too," he said.

"Oh, really? What did you think?"

"Remember when you said you were going to marry me someday?"

"Of course, I remember."

"Well, how about it?"

"How about what?"

"How about marrying me?"

She bolted upright. "Did you just propose to me?"

"I did."

Instead of being elated, Amanda became conflicted and said nothing.

Uncomfortable, Jonas asked, "Did I say something wrong? I know we haven't talked about marriage. Was it a shock?"

"Yes. I'm speechless."

"Okay. Then just nod your head for yes or shake it for no."

"First, I need to tell you something that might change your mind," she said. "Doctors think, with my condition, it could be dangerous for me to have children."

Jonas said nothing but couldn't help thinking about how much he loved children. Looking intently at Amanda, he made his choice. "I still want to marry you."

"But you want children," she said. "I know you do."

"I want you more. Are you going to marry me or not?"

Despite her anxieties, she jumped on his lap and kissed his face over and over. "Yes," she said with each kiss. "I've loved you all my life."

"And I love you now."

They were married December 29, 1919, in the Lutheran church where Jonas had pretended to believe in God. The bride and groom had no close friends anymore and came from small families. But the church was filled with towns-people who had come to witness the marriage of the Golden Boy to a local girl. The entire high school football team was there. Coach Parsons was the best man.

When her father walked her down the aisle, Amanda whispered, "So many people are here. We only expected family."

"You're marrying a local hero," her father said.

"I know," Amanda said and hoped she could make a hero happy.

CHAPTER 10

1919
WHY ME?

The old farmhouse was big enough to accommodate the newlyweds. With no time or money for a honeymoon, their first night in bed together was in Jonas's old room, filled with memorabilia from his past... as they began their future.

There was some awkwardness at the outset, but soon their love-making came naturally and was enjoyable for both of them. Jonas was delighted with her, and Amanda seemed happy with married life. No one could tell there was a storm brewing inside her.

"Will you regret not having children?" she asked one night after they made love.

"No. You gave me a choice, and I chose you."

"I know," she said. *But why?* She wondered. *Why would this incredible man choose me... when so many healthy, beautiful women would love to have him and his child? It doesn't make sense.*

For years, her dream of marrying Jonas had been a comforting fantasy, but the reality of actually having him terrified her. She knew Jonas had no idea she felt that way. He was focused on teaching, coaching, and caring for her. He was determined to make her stronger and healthier through exercise and diet. He massaged her muscles and joints every night, keeping them stretched and flexible. He walked miles with her to build her stamina. They did strength training together. They cooked healthy foods together. It seemed ideal. Still, she was troubled, until one night, her emotions boiled over.

It began at a North Platte High faculty party in the school gym shortly after the new year. Teachers, city officials, town leaders, and their families were invited. Duke Hannigan, the town's biggest taxpayer and benefactor, came with his wife, Shirley. The best plastic surgeon in Nebraska couldn't make Duke's face look the same after Jonas had punched him years ago. He resembled a losing prizefighter. But, by losing the fight, Duke had won Shirley Kelley and made his father happy. Business is business.

As usual, Jonas was the center of attention. He didn't do anything to attract attention. People simply gravitated to him. He was polite to everyone while being solicitous of Amanda. He held her hand constantly and included her in every conversation. Still, she felt insecure. Everyone vied for his attention. *He doesn't need me*, she thought, just as he squeezed her hand reassuringly. *All these people want him. The mayor wants a picture with him. The chief of police. That buxom councilwoman who keeps pressing against him. Shirley Hannigan can't take her eyes off him. Probably wondering what he sees in me.*

The drafty gym was chilly, but Amanda was sweating, her face flushed. She excused herself, went to the ladies' room, and splashed cold water on her face. In the mirror, she saw several women enter, see her, and whisper to one another. *Vultures. You can't have him. He's mine.*

She hurried out and bumped into a big man standing outside the door. Duke Hannigan! *Has he been waiting for me?*

He looked down at her. "Aren't you Jonas Hensen's wife?"

You know very well who I am, she thought, saying nothing.

"You look beautiful tonight, Mrs. Hensen," he said, looking her up and down like a prize heifer. "Jonas always had an eye for pretty girls. But I'm surprised he married you, knowing your family health issues."

"You're disgusting!" Amanda attempted to slap his face.

He grabbed her wrist. "What do you think you're doing?" he asked, grinning.

"Trying to be the second Hensen to break your nose," she said.

His grin became a grimace. "Bitch," he said softly. "After you're gone, every woman in town will line up to fuck your husband."

"I'm sure your wife will be first in line," she said and hurried away. Her lips were trembling, her face pale. She felt faint. She returned to the gym and pushed through the crowd surrounding her husband. "I don't feel well," she whispered. "I have to leave."

"Of course," he said, excusing himself.

When they were in the car, he asked, "What's wrong?"

"Nothing."

They rode home in silence. When they arrived, she rushed into their bedroom, slamming the door behind her. He found her lying on the bed in a fetal position, facing the wall—crying. He sat and put his hand on her shoulder. She pulled away.

"Do you need a doctor?" he asked.

"No."

"Do you have a fever?"

"No."

"You have to tell me what's wrong, so I can help."

She sat up and glared at him. "You're what's wrong."

Stunned, Jonas said. "Me? What did I do wrong?"

"You married me."

"What in the world are you talking about?"

"There were so many healthy girls you could have chosen."

"Probably. But I chose you. What upset you tonight?"

"Nothing."

"Nonsense. Something brought this on."

"Duke Hannigan cornered me and said, after I die, girls will line up for you."

Jonas gritted his teeth. His face turned red. "That son of a bitch."

"He's right, though. I will die young, and you will find someone else."

"Amanda, how long have you felt this way?"

"Since you proposed. I never understood why you wanted me."

"Why didn't you ask me then?"

"I didn't want to know. I just wanted you. Now I need to know."

"Okay, I'll tell you. Can I lay next to you?" She nodded, sniffling. She put her head on his shoulder when he was next to her. "I have to tell you about the war first."

He told her everything he could remember; the killing, the Ghost, the trenches, the rats, walls of bullets, dead horses, headless horsemen, insides outside, the screams, the stench, the dead floating among the living in flooded trenches. "I can't stop seeing the faces of all the men I killed," he said. "I hated myself for being so good at it. But it was them or me until the war ended."

He described the Armistice ceremony in the Argonne and the German pilot named Goldschmidt, a good man in a bad time. He spoke of the Krug circus—how he saved a Gypsy girl named Drina—their passionate affair.

"Did you love her?"

"At that time, in that place, I think I did. But not like I love you."

"You still haven't explained that."

"I will. When I returned to North Platte, I was confused. I was being honored for killing people. When I learned my friends were dead, I wanted to die. I had horrible nightmares; the worst was of men with their legs blown off, still trying to walk on the stumps. It got so bad; I considered suicide."

"Oh my God, Jonas. I had no idea. What stopped you?"

"You."

"Me? What did I do?"

"You replaced my nightmares. I started dreaming of you instead of war. Coach Parsons said I survived the war for a reason, and that reason could be you. I think he's right. You're my reason. You're my redemption. Saving you saves me."

Tears came to her eyes, "Oh, Jonas. You can't save me. I'm too sick."

"Amanda, do you love me?"

"With all my heart."

"Then let me save you. I need you."

"You *need* me?" she said, tears streaming down her cheeks.

"Yes. I thought I'd never need anyone. I was wrong. I need you."

They held each other for several minutes. Finally, he leaned back. "I think we should make love," he said.

"Right now?" she asked.

"Why not? We missed your massage today," he said. "We can do both."

He sat up and began undressing her slowly. She watched him intently, excited by his touch. When she was naked, he lifted her from the bed like a bride and put her, face up, on the massage table in their bedroom. He didn't cover her and began taking off his clothes. She watched—unable to take her eyes off this magnificent man who needed her. Now it all made sense.

He began massaging her lovingly, from her scalp to her toes. He stretched every muscle without hurting her. "Your disease shortens muscles," he said. "We won't let that happen."

His powerful fingers prodded, pulled, and stretched her with such loving intensity that her body tingled. "You're tearing me apart." she gasped.

"No," he said. "I'm keeping you together."

When he was done massaging her, he bent over the table and kissed her lips. She wrapped her arms around his neck. "Don't let go," he said. Slowly he straightened his back, while her arms held fast to his neck. He lifted her off the table. "Put your legs around my waist," he told her. She did. They met in the middle and coupled perfectly. His hands cupped her buttocks and held her there. She buried her face in his shoulder. He lifted her, held her in place, then slowly lowered her onto him. She gasped.

"This feels perfect," she said.

"It is perfect. We were made for each other. Now, look at me."

She leaned back. They were eye to eye.

"Tell me why I chose you?" he said, lifting her.

She sighed. "Because ... because you *need* me."

"And I love you," he added. "What else?" he lowered her.

"Oh," she moaned. "You need to save me ... to save yourself."

He lifted her up again and whispered, "Now say ... if I die, you'll die."

"If I die ... you'll die," she said and gasped as he let her down again.

He carried her to the bed. Still inside her, he lowered her on her back without losing their connection. Then he was on top of her. She wrapped her legs around him. They continued making love to a shuddering climax. He eased off her, and lay on his side, next to her. He kissed her softly. "Any more questions?"

"None," she said.

CHAPTER 11

1925
ODINA

In June 1925, blonde-haired, blue-eyed, fair-skinned Hilda Knudson was in the Omaha General Hospital giving birth to her third child. With two blond, blue-eyed boys, ages six and four, she hoped for a girl, though any healthy child was welcome. Her blond-haired, blue-eyed husband, Bo, felt the same.

In the delivery room, Hilda's doctor encouraged her. "You're almost there," he said. "One more push. That's it. And here comes your baby … and—Oh my!"

"What?" Hilda asked, frightened. "Is something wrong? The infant squalled.

"No, not really," the doctor said. "The baby is fine."

"Thank heavens. Girl or boy?"

"Girl," the doctor said.

"A girl! Wonderful!" She held out her arms.

The doctor carefully handed Hilda the little bundle. Her smile faded when she saw the brown-skinned, brown-eyed, black-haired baby. "Oh, my!"

Bo Knudson rushed into the hospital room to meet his new daughter. No doctors or nurses were present. "They wanted us to be alone," Hilda said.

Bo held out his arms. "Let me see our new daughter."

She handed him the baby. "Bo, I've never been with another man."

Bo said nothing. He just stared. Finally, he said, "I'll be damned."

"Bo, I swear I don't know what happened."

Bo laughed. "I do. It's amazing."

"Why are you laughing? This isn't funny. I'm a good wife. You know that."

"I know," he said, sitting on the bed next to her and putting the brown baby between them. "Say hello to my great-grandmother, Winona Wild Wolf, of the Oglala Sioux nation. She's come back."

Winona Wild Wolf was born in 1840, just prior to the start of the Great Indian Wars of the American frontier. In 1860, her warrior father, Iron Fist, was killed in battle. It was rumored that Iron Fist had killed Custer, but that was never confirmed. Winona and her mother, White Buffalo, were relocated to the Sioux Reservation in the panhandle of northern Nebraska. White Buffalo had been a *Wayazan anwanyanka* in her tribe—one who cares for the injured and sick—a healer who could not heal herself. She had tuberculosis and, fearing her death was imminent, taught Winona her *Wayazan anwanyanka* secrets. The young girl learned quickly. When White Buffalo died, Winona became the new *Wayazan* of her tribe. Filled with compassion, she healed both Indians and white men alike. She did not see color. She saw people. It was not long before all the sick and wounded—regardless of color, sought her care. They came from miles around to be healed by *Wayazan* Winona Wild Wolf.

The Knudson family emigrated from Denmark in 1859 and traveled to Nebraska as homesteaders, arriving in 1860. Able Knudson, the twenty-year-old, blond, blue-eyed, fair-skinned oldest Knudson son, fell ill shortly after arriving. The family was advised to see *Wayazan* on the Sioux reservation.

Fortunately for Able, he only had pneumonia—not deadly smallpox that was decimating settlers and Indians alike. Winona knew how to treat pneumonia, and she knew how to treat a handsome man like Able Knudson. He recovered, they fell in love and married, despite protestations and pessimism from their tribes. Their marriage lasted forty years, ending when Able died in 1900. Winona lived three more years, surrounded by her two children, six grandchildren, and nine great-grandchildren. All of Winona's descendants married Caucasians, and with each passing generation, traces of her Sioux heritage faded—until Bo and Hilda's dark-skinned baby girl arrived.

They gave their brown daughter a Scandinavian name. They called her Odina, leaving no doubt as to her origins. Still, while growing up, she would stand out like a currant raisin in a batch of golden sultanas. "She'll have a tough time growing up," Hilda said. "Being different isn't easy."

"If it doesn't break her, it will make her special," Bo said.

Chapter 12

1926
NIKO

Niko Santiago Krug grew up a child of the circus. He lived with his Uncle Fredrik, but his primary caregivers were the circus women. Performers, workers, wives, and mothers. Gypsy mothers, primarily Hungarians, and Spanish adored him. By four, he'd been exposed to multiple languages and cultures.

At six years old, he began asking questions. "Uncle Fredrik, why don't I have parents like other kids?"

His uncle told a half-truth to keep his word to Drina. "They died."

"Tell me about them."

Should I tell the same lie I tell everyone—that his mother was my cousin who died in a car accident with his father? How many lies can I tell before I start tripping over my own words? Will he hate me when he learns the truth? He decided to take a chance. "Niko, can you keep an important secret?"

Niko nodded. "I won't tell anyone, Uncle. Promise."

"Okay, no one in the circus knows this secret. Everyone thinks your mother and father died in a car crash and I adopted you. That's not true. I lied."

"Why?"

Fredrik took a deep breath and prepared to tell another half-truth. "Your mother was a very beautiful Spanish Romani Gypsy. She died right after you were born."

"So, I'm a Gypsy?" Niko said, seemingly unaffected by the disclosure.

"Half. Your father was white. An America soldier," Fredrik said, telling the truth before adding another lie. "They fell in love and planned to marry, but he was killed in the war. He never knew about you. Your mother loved you and asked me to care for you before she died. And here we are."

"So, I'm half-Gypsy and half-white?"

"Yes. But that's the secret you must keep. Your mother made me promise to raise you as white."

"Why?"

"With a white father and a Gypsy mother, you're considered colored by white people."

"So, what? I like my color."

"I know," Uncle Fredrik said, wondering how to explain prejudice to an unsullied six-year-old. "Your mother believed that powerful white people don't give colored people, especially children, a fair chance in life."

"You're white, and you give me everything."

Fredrik searched for the right words. "Some white people are good—some are bad. The bad ones don't like colored people."

"Was my father a good white man?"

"The best," he said, relieved to tell the truth. "That's why your mother chose him."

"Is this why I'm darker than white kids and whiter than colored kids?"

"Yes. But your mother wanted everyone to believe you're all white so you could go to the best schools and have the same opportunities as the all-white kids. Understand?"

"I think so—but I don't like it."

"Nor do I. So, can you keep this secret?"

"For how long?"

Smart kid. "How about until after college? Then you can be whoever you want."

Niko smiled, mischief on his mind. "If I do this, will I be fooling the bad white people?"

"Yes. You'll be fooling all of them," Uncle Fredrik said, returning the smile.

"Okay. It'll be fun."

Niko was big for his age. When he was seven, he looked ten. "It's in your genes," Uncle Fredrik told him, remembering the size of Jonas Hensen. "You're big like your father."

Without a mother to coddle him, Niko became independent at an early age. The circus educated him in its own way. Stashu, the strongman, taught him how to build muscle. Styzmon, the wrestler, taught him leverage and grappling. Boxer Bob taught him how to use his fists. Abdul Haddad, the knife thrower, taught Niko his art. But his favorite teacher was Greta, the Horseback Princess. When he was small, they rode double in the saddle, with the back of his head pressed between her breasts. He loved riding lessons.

He would tease the Gypsy daughters and play tricks on their mothers, and they adored him. To them, he was Fredrik Krug's nephew, a white boy who acted like a Gypsy. They let his dark black hair, grow to his shoulders—a complementary contrast with his bright green eyes. When he was eight, his faux-uncle allowed him to feed the animals. He loved doing that. On hot summer days, he would wander shirtless and shoeless between the cages wearing ragged shorts, carrying heavy pails of food. A Gypsy woman pointed at him one day and called, "Hey, Jungle Boy!" The nickname stuck. "Jungle Boy, come here…" "Jungle boy, do this…" He didn't mind. He liked being the Jungle Boy.

His favorite animal was King, the African lion. King's trainer, South African Pieter Vandenhoff, had raised King from a cub. "King is exceptional," Pieter told Niko. "He never lived in the wild, so he's comfortable with people. But you must never forget that he is the king of beasts—five hundred pounds of muscle, fangs, claws, and attitude. You must respect what he is and treat him with care. Talk to him. He likes that."

So, Niko talked to King every day. "How are you today, King?"

Blink—Blink—Yawn.

"Did you have enough to eat?"

Blink—Blink. King would lick around his mouth with his huge tongue and look inscrutably at the Jungle Boy.

After a while, when Niko brought King his food, the lion would meet him at the bars and stare at him. *What are you thinking, King? Do you know I'm your friend?* One night, Niko dared pat King's big paw that rested near the bars. King watched, then licked his hand. After that, Niko slept outside King's cage most nights and talked to him until they fell asleep.

When Niko was nine, the circus performed in Zagreb, Yugoslavia. He was mucking out a stall when he heard King roar. The lion only roared when he was hungry or angry. Niko had just fed him, so he knew something was wrong. He ran to King's cage and found three local teenagers tormenting his lion. They jabbed King with long sticks and threw rocks at him. King showed his fangs and roared. The kids laughed and poked from a safe distance.

"Stop," Niko said, moving in front of the cage. "Leave him alone."

The teenagers were bigger, but the Jungle Boy was fearless.

"Get out of the way, kid," the biggest teenager said and pushed him down to the ground. King roared.

"No, leave him alone," Niko said again, standing up and standing his ground.

The boy rushed Niko to shove him aside. Using what Styzmon the wrestler had taught him; the Jungle Boy side-stepped and pushed the boy against the cage. The boy held out his arm to stop his momentum, but it passed through the bars into the cage. King roared again and swiped with his massive paw. The boy screamed and yanked his arm away. Blood spurted, and the boy collapsed. King roared again and paced in his cage.

The noise attracted two security guards. One used his belt to tie a tourniquet around the boy's arm. The other called for an ambulance that arrived quickly. The injured boy was put on a stretcher and whisked away. As a crowd gathered, Fredrik Krug appeared.

"What happened?" he demanded.

"King mauled a boy's arm," one of the security men told him.

"King's never attacked anyone before," Krug said. "He's accustomed to people. Did you boys provoke him?"

"No, sir," one of the teenagers lied. "He attacked for no reason." The other boy nodded.

"They're lying!" Niko shouted. "They were teasing him with sticks."

A Zagreb constable arrived with a deputy carrying a rifle. Krug held up his hand to stop them. "What's the rifle for?"

"To shoot the lion, of course," the constable said as if he were talking to a child. "He attacked a human and has to be destroyed."

"No. He was protecting me," Niko said, standing in the deputy's path.

"Lions don't protect people, they eat them," the constable said. "Get out of my deputy's way so he can get this over with."

"I believe my nephew," Uncle Fredrik said, raising a hand to stop the deputy.

The constable looked impatient. "Those two boys say the lion wasn't provoked. That's good enough for me."

Krug stepped in front of the shooter, the gun inches from his chest. "I said, I believe my nephew."

"Herr Krug, get out of the way, or I'm going to have to arrest you."

"I won't let you shoot our lion," Krug insisted.

No one noticed that Niko had slipped away until a woman screamed and pointed at the lion's cage. Nine-year-old Niko was in the cage, face to face with the African lion.

"How the hell did that kid get in there?" the constable asked.

"He feeds the animals. He has the key," Krug explained.

"Tell him to get out before that lion bites his head off."

"Niko," Krug called, but the boy was totally focused on the lion.

"Hello, King," Niko said, in the soothing voice he always used with him. A low rumble came from the beast. "I can tell you're upset, but you have to show these people what a good boy you are."

The crowd watched as King approached Niko until they were almost nose to nose.

"Oleg, shoot that damn lion before it's too late."

The deputy raised the rifle and aimed.

As King began to lick Niko's face, a gunshot shattered the air.

The lion flinched and skittered away. Fredrik Krug had pushed the rifle barrel upward, just in time to redirect the bullet skyward. King opened his cavernous mouth and roared. Niko stood his ground and let the lion pace around him. "It's okay, boy," he said, his voice still calm. He patted his thigh, encouraging the beast to come closer. The big cat inched forward, sniffed, and licked the boy's face again. Niko stroked the lion's mane. The crowd was mesmerized.

"Okay, Niko," Fredrik called. "You proved your point. Please come out of there."

"Not until the deputy puts his rifle away," Niko said.

"Yeah, put it down," someone shouted. The deputy lowered his rifle.

"Now make those boys tell the truth," Niko said.

All eyes went to the teenagers who blurted out confessions.

"Okay, son. You saved your lion," the constable said. "Now, come out."

Niko put his face close to King. He could smell the raw meat he had recently fed him. "Good boy," he said, patting the lion's mane again before he left the cage.

His uncle hugged him. "How could you take such a risk?"

"I was protecting my friend," Niko said.

His uncle nodded and hugged him again.

Later, Tian, the diminutive Chinese cook, approached Niko and spoke to him in broken English. "You very brave boy," he said. "Protect lion."

"He's my friend," Niko explained again.

"To protect friends, must be unbeatable fighter. Tian can teach."

Niko smiled. "I already had Styzmon, Stashu, and Boxer Bob teach me to fight."

"Tian can defeat all of them," the cook told him.

Niko laughed. "No, you can't," he said. "You're too small."

"Not too small. Tian very good fighter. Try to hit me."

"I don't want to hit you."

"No hit Tian. Just try."

Niko shrugged and swung a half-hearted punch at Tian. The little man avoided Niko's reach, grabbed his wrist, and flipped him over his shoulder, to the ground.

Niko scrambled to his feet, unhurt, but looking surprised.

Tian laughed. "Try again."

This time Niko charged forward. Tian sidestepped and flipped Niko over his hip.

Niko got up laughing and excited. "How did you do that?"

"Ancient Chinese art."

"Can you teach me?"

"Tian can teach but must promise, only fight for good. Like protecting friends."

"I promise. Can I be as good as you?"

Tian nodded and added, "Niko will grow very big and strong someday. Tian teach you to use that strength—make you unbeatable—must listen—work hard."

"I will," Niko said. "Make me unbeatable."

And he did.

CHAPTER 13

1926–1936
NAZIS

Niko's first school was the circus, and Uncle Fredrik was his teacher. He learned geography from traveling with the circus and studying maps. He learned math by adding ticket sales and multiplying by the price to get the total. He used a similar technique for division and subtraction. He learned history from stories his uncle told him and books he read.

Eventually, Fredrik decided Niko needed a more formal education and enrolled him in a small, exclusive private school in Zurich: *Ecole Nouvelle de la Suisse.* "Thank you for your generous donation, Herr Krug," the school principal said.

"Thank you for accepting my nephew," Krug said.

"He's bright and belongs here, despite ambiguities in his application."

The scions of wealthy families accepted Niko because he was a Krug and the Krug Brothers Circus was famous throughout Europe. Niko was deferential to this clique of heirs but avoided becoming close with any of them. They unknowingly offended him with their smug remarks and supercilious attitudes—making him feel vindicated deceiving them.

When he was fourteen, during summer vacation in Vienna, Niko lost his virginity to an eighteen-year-old Viennese girl who thought he was older. When he told Greta, the Horseback Princess, she was disappointed. "I wanted to be your first," she said pouting. "I was waiting for you to grow up."

"If you hurry, you can be my second," Niko told her.

By the time he turned fifteen Niko was six feet, two inches tall and growing fast. His boyish features had matured and bore a remarkable resemblance to his father—with only a difference in their coloring. By sixteen he had grown another four more inches—the exact height of the father he'd never met.

In June of 1936, Uncle Fredrik handed Niko two tickets and a letter. "Tickets to the Berlin Olympics and a letter from Heinrich Himmler."

Niko picked up the letter:

To Whom It May Concern,
The bearer of this letter, Mr. Fredrik Krug, is my dear friend. Extend him every courtesy while he is visiting Berlin to attend the Olympics and search for suitable locations for his world-famous circus tour.

The letter was on official Nazi stationery and signed by Himmler.

"Himmler is a maniac," Niko said. "How can you be his friend?"

"I am not his friend. It's a long story."

"I don't want to hear it. And I will not go to Hitler's Olympics."

"You can see Jesse Owens. He could win three gold medals."

"The Nazis are racist thugs," Niko objected. "They already barred Johan Tillman, Germany's middleweight boxing champion because he's Romani. Jews are also barred. Hitler's a monster. I'd love to see Owens perform, but I refuse to go to Hitler's Germany."

Hours later, Fredrik gave Niko a second thought. "Let's go to Berlin and do our own investigation of Hitler's Germany. If things are as bad as you think, we can spread the word when we return. And while we're there, we can watch Owens."

"Under those terms, I'll go," Niko agreed. "You're very clever Uncle Fredrik."

Berlin looked idyllic. No anti-Semitic or anti-Romani signs anywhere; but Nazi flags, banners, and signs were ubiquitous. The streets were spotless. The Nazis were unfailingly civil and solicitous. Niko was frustrated by the deception but said little, patiently waiting for the monster to rear its ugly head.

In three days, Jesse Owens won three gold medals; the hundred-meter dash, the two hundred-meter, and the long jump. Krug nudged his nephew after the jump event. "Spectacular, eh?"

"Incredible. Hitler can't be happy with a black man winning so many medals."

"Be careful what you say," Fredrik whispered, looking around nervously.

He noticed female spectators nearby stealing glances at Niko. *Understandable,* Uncle Fredrik thought. *He's tall, well-built, and handsome. Classic Roman profile; straight nose, high cheekbones, full lips, indeterminate origins. Drina's dream.*

The crowd roared, startling Fredrik from his reverie. "There's Luz Long," Niko said, pointing at the German long jumper on the field—his arm around Jesse Owens's shoulder. "A real sportsman. He helped Owens with advice on his last jump."

"So, not all Germans are monsters?" Uncle Fredrik said.

"No," Niko replied. "All Nazis are monsters—not all Germans are Nazis."

They departed the stadium and located Krug's Rolls Royce in the parking lot. Fredrik's chauffeur, Joseph Schultz, an amicable Austrian, had been with the Krug Brothers Circus for thirty years. He was a stocky man, filling every inch of his driver's uniform. He sported a neat mustache under his nose.

"Was Owens triumphant?" Schultz asked.

"Yes. Today he won the long jump," Krug said.

"Three gold medals. You should have seen him," Niko said.

"Unfortunately, my job is to protect this car from panhandlers and Gypsies like you," Schultz said and grinned. He was the only person in the circus Fredrik had trusted with Niko's true identity. "But there are no Romani around here. Very unusual. Something's wrong."

A local policeman was passing by. "Excuse me, Officer," Schultz said. "I was just asking why there are no Romani peddlers here, like always, at public events."

"All Gypsies were relocated," the policeman told them with a broad smile.

"All?" Schultz said. "There must have been a thousand in the city."

"More like seven hundred...but *poof*...now there are none," the policeman said, moving his hands like a magician who had just made a rabbit disappear. "Why all this interest in undesirables?"

Fredrik interceded. "We're circus people from Switzerland. Perhaps this will explain." He handed the policeman Himmler's letter. He read and nodded respectfully. "Welcome to Berlin, Herr Krug." He returned the letter with a flourish. "I've been to your circus. It's wonderful."

"Thank you, Officer Hess," Fredrik said, reading the man's name tag. "Since you've been to our circus, you know we have several Gypsies in the show. And I'm always looking for good Romani workers."

"You will not find them here anymore. New laws, you know."

"I know your new laws," Niko said, obviously bothered. "They take away people's rights."

Before Hess could respond, Niko turned and walked away.

"Your young friend should be more respectful, Herr Krug," Hess cautioned. "Nazi officials are not as tolerant as a Berlin policeman, like me."

"My nephew is just sixteen," Fredrik said.

"He is very big for his age," Hess said.

"Very big, yes, but very young. You know how it is with teenagers, I'll speak to him."

"For his own safety, you understand."

"Yes, but, tell me, where did you move so many Gypsies?"

"Marzahn, I think."

"I know that place. It's about twenty miles northeast of here."

"Yes," Hess answered. "Well, I must be going." He touched the bill of his cap courteously, looked suspiciously at Niko, and walked away.

"Take us to the Aldon," Fredrik said to Schultz.

On the way to Berlin's most luxurious hotel, they passed the famous Brandenburg Gate, topped by the Quadriga, a chariot of four horses, driven by the goddess of war.

"Impressive," Schultz said.

"German monuments are fixated on war," Niko added then said, "Okay, Uncle, tell me about your friend Himmler. I'm ready to listen."

"I already told you … Himmler is not my friend," Uncle Fredrik, insisted. "I met him about fifteen years ago before the Nazis came to power. He approached me after a circus performance in Munich—told me he was a chicken farmer, and all his chickens were dying."

"What did he want from you?" Niko asked.

"He thought I could help him because I kept so many animals healthy in the circus. I felt bad for him and looked at his stock the next day. Unfortunately, his chickens were infected with herpes viruses and had to be destroyed. He was devastated. I wanted to help him, so I offered him a loan. I told him to pay me back whenever he could. He was extremely grateful. I didn't hear from him again until a year ago when he sent me a letter with a check for the entire amount of the loan. In his letter, he wrote about the rebirth of German pride and his new position in the Nazi party. He said he had never forgotten my kindness and offered his assistance in the future. When Germany was awarded the Olympics, I wrote and asked if he could assist me with Olympic tickets and locating sites for the circus, should we tour Germany again. He responded with the letter I showed you and two Olympic tickets. He also invited me to call him when I was in Berlin."

"Do you intend to call him?"

"Of course not."

"So, what do you think of his new Germany?" Niko asked.

"I'll know more after we see Marzahn," Uncle Fredrik said.

It was late in the afternoon when they entered Marzahn. They drove through a bucolic area of small farms and passed an old working windmill on a hillside.

"I feel like we've gone back in time," Schultz said.

"Don't let the windmill fool you," Krug said, pointing to a sign that read: *Zigenunerrastplatz, Gypsy Open Air Camp.* "The Third Reich is here."

The camp was situated on an open field between an old municipal cemetery and a sewage dump. Schultz parked the limo on the side of the road, and they looked out the windows. There appeared to be several hundred Gypsies as Hess had indicated—excised from Berlin by Hitler's iron scalpel. These poor souls had been forced to ride in their decrepit wagons to Marzahn and had been dumped like trash on this fetid field. Niko looked at the prisoners and wondered if he could somehow be related to any of them. "This place isn't fit for pigs," he observed.

"No temper tantrums," Uncle Fredrik said. "Control yourself."

"I'll try."

They got out of the car and walked toward the field. A palpable stink stopped them like a stone wall. Schultz bent at the waist, put his hands on his knees and vomited. "Sorry," he sputtered, wiping his mouth on his sleeve.

Niko counted three water spigots and two outhouses for hundreds of people. Diseased horses grazed on infected brown grass, their toxic droppings baking in the sun. Four armed guards walked the perimeter while workmen completed erecting a wire-fence enclosure. Gypsy caravans with flat tires were clustered on the festering field. Wagons painted festive colors created an even more macabre scene. An old Gitano guitarist played flamenco music with gnarly fingers. He wore a yellow scarf around his neck, fastened at his throat by an ornate ring. In his youth, he might have given the scarf and ring to a sweetheart as a sign of his love, but now it served only as a reminder of better times. A middle-aged Romani couple danced to his music on top of this cesspool, dressed stylishly, their clothes ragged from hardship. A few children tried to play, but most sat silently in the dirt with flies circling their heads. Hitler had stolen their childhood.

Madness, Niko thought, his head throbbing. He held his hands to his temples and rubbed them. "Not feeling well," he said and walked toward the woods.

Fredrik and Schultz were approached by a German officer, who asked, "Is your friend alright?"

"He feels a little sick, Captain," Krug explained.

"I understand. This place is sickening," the German agreed. "Why are you here?"

Fredrik showed him Himmler's letter.

"Captain Fritz Berger, at your service, Herr Krug," the Nazi officer said—clicking his heels, creating a puff of dust. "But I'm afraid this is not a place for your circus."

"I can see that now," Krug acknowledged. "Tell me, why only four guards for so many prisoners?"

"We're guarding sheep," he told them. "Gypsies are docile, like Jews. There's no threat here."

Fredrik nodded as Niko approached, wiping his mouth.

"You should get your friend to a doctor," Berger suggested.

"I'll give him a few minutes to recover, and then we'll leave."

"Give my regards to Himmler," Berger said and walked away.

A ragged woman approached from the area where the fence was incomplete. She was carrying a bundled blanket. She showed it to Niko. It was a dead baby boy, his face bluish gray. The woman's face was marred by excrescences, and she seemed close to death herself. "Please take my son and bury him in clean earth," she asked Niko, who reached for the bundle.

"You! Get away," Captain Berger shouted, running toward them. He drew his pistol and pointed at the woman. She shielded her dead baby with her body. Berger grabbed the grieving woman's arm, threw her to the ground, and kicked her. She yelped and crawled inside the designated prisoner's area. Niko's face clouded with anger.

"What did she want?" Berger asked, pointing his pistol at Niko.

Niko's left hand moved with the lightning quickness Tian had instilled in him. He grabbed the pistol barrel, expertly twisting it from the German's hand and tossed it in the dirt. The rattled German officer shouted, "Guard!"

A soldier came running, aiming his rifle at Niko. Krug stepped in front of his nephew.

"Captain Berger," he said. "Your guard has a gun pointed at my nephew. I don't think this is the hospitality Herr Himmler had in mind."

"Your nephew attacked me," Berger said, flustered by the Himmler reference.

"No, Captain. He disarmed you."

Berger said nothing, not wanting to fight with Himmler's friend.

"A misunderstanding then," Krug tried to compromise.

"Agreed," Berger gladly accepted the truce offer. "No need to mention this to Himmler?"

"None," Krug nodded, shaking Berger's hand. He turned away and led his two companions to the limo.

"We could have been arrested or worse," Uncle Fredrik whispered to his nephew.

They rode in silence, as dusk replaced daylight. After a few miles, Niko said, "Stop."

Schultz steered to the side of the road. Niko got out and stuck his head through the open front window. "I have to go back and free those people. Otherwise, they'll die."

Fredrik grasped Niko's arm. "What do you think you can do for them?" he asked.

"They have machine guns. You're unarmed," Schultz added.

"They're overconfident. You heard Berger. He thinks they're guarding sheep."

"Maybe you're the one who's overconfident. You could get yourself killed."

"Maybe. But I have to do something," Niko said and ran off into the night.

CHAPTER 14

1936
NIKO

Niko ran the two miles to the camp, his mind and body burning with rage. *Who the hell are these Nazis bastards, to put people in a cage?*

He smelled the camp before he saw it and ducked into the woods. Three spotlights swept the enclosure. The fence was completed, and there was a lock on the front gate. He took a deep breath, trying to ignore the mephitic smell. Watery sludge oozed from a waste pipe and plopped into the sewage pond. One spotlight illuminated the gravestones, and another lit the sea of shit. The third circled the perimeter. There was little activity among the Gypsies now. Some huddled in small circles, talking in hushed tones. Some appeared to be sleeping or dead. The old man was still holding his guitar but wasn't playing.

Niko's eyes scanned the area. He saw a dim light shining from the window of a small shack he hadn't noticed in the afternoon. It was located less than fifty yards outside the fence. Set among the trees, it was easy to miss. Niko guessed it was temporary quarters for the Nazis. Three guards manned the three spotlights, meaning the fourth was inside.

Niko moved silently to the shack and peeked over a window sill. He saw three beds, a stove, and a table with chairs. Captain Berger sat at the table writing in a journal, his back to the only door. Niko sidled to the door and carefully turned the knob. It creaked. Berger turned. The look of annoyance on his face quickly turned to terror when he saw Niko charging. He started to rise, but Niko was on him, his arms wrapping around the Nazi's head, covering his mouth. He pushed and pulled in opposite directions and heard a snap when the lower vertebrae in Berger's neck broke. The Nazi was dead.

Niko opened the door a sliver and peered outside. The light continued to sweep the area. He hefted Berger's corpse on his shoulder and carried it outside to the edge of the sewage dump. Lowering the body to the ground, he emptied the Nazi's pockets: a knife, papers, keys, and the pistol from his holster. He emptied his own pockets, not wanting the contents to get lost or soiled. Next, he gathered rocks and stuffed them into the Nazi's uniform.

Taking a deep breath, Niko lifted the weighted corpse on his shoulder again and carried it into the sewage pond. When the muck reached his waist, he lowered the corpse into the sludge and watched it sink, disappearing in the muck. He stood on Berger's chest, grinding him deeper into the soft bottom. He slogged back to land and collapsed on his back. His hands were shaking, and his heart was pounding. He was revolted by the stink, but excited by the kill.

He heard footsteps and held his breath. There was a knock on the door of the shack. "Captain Berger?" a guard called. "Are you in there?" the guard opened the door and entered.

Niko grabbed Berger's knife and scrambled beside the open door. He stood flat against the wall. "Where the hell is he…" the guard muttered, exiting the shack.

STEVEN M. FORMAN

Niko let him pass and attacked from behind. He wrapped his arm around the guard's forehead, pulled his head back, and slashed his throat so fast not a sound was made. He lowered the gurgling guard to the ground and let him bleed out. He saw the SS Party pin on the dead man's collar and felt good. *Another Nazi.* He gathered more rocks for ballast and repeated Berger's burial.

Back on dry land, he put the knife in his belt and checked the pistol. It was loaded. He headed to the nearest search-light. The guard was leaning against a fence post, napping. Niko swapped the gun for the knife and approached from the front. Covering the guard's mouth with one hand, he thrust Berger's knife just below the third rib and up into his heart. The guard's eyes opened wide and remained that way after he died. He was buried in shit with the others.

The fourth guard heard Niko coming. He was reaching for his rifle when Niko shot him between the eyes. Once again, he noted the Nazi insignia on the collar. He had killed four Nazis and was exhilarated. After burying the fourth, he rested.

Finally, he trudged back to the barracks and tried unsuccessfully to clean himself. He still smelled and looked like shit.

He went to the front gate and tried several of Berger's keys on the lock. Eventually, he found the right one. Several Romani prisoners had gathered on the opposite side of the fence. He swung the doors open. "Go," he said.

"Where?" one man asked, holding out his hands, palms up.

"I don't know. But you'll die if you stay here."

"No," another man said. "The police told us we'd be peacefully relocated."

"They lied," Niko said, raising his voice.

"What are they going to do, kill us all?" another man asked.

"Yes," Niko said. "That's exactly what they'll do."

"Impossible," the man said.

"Where are the guards?" another man asked, worried.

"Gone," Niko said.

"Did you kill them?" a woman cried. "Oh, God. The Nazis will blame us."

"What's the matter with you people?" Niko asked. Their blank faces told Niko they had no idea the horrors that awaited them.

The woman with the dead baby pushed her way through the crowd and held her bundle out to Niko. "Thank you for coming back."

Niko took the bundle from her. "Leave this place," he said to her.

"I can't," she whispered. "The others would suffer because of me."

"Don't you understand?" he said. "There's no hope here."

A few prisoners decided to heed his advice and ran off into the night. Most remained. Niko departed with the dead baby in his arms. When he reached the tree line, he looked back. The front gate was locked again. The prisoners had become their own jailers.

Niko buried the unknown child in a shallow grave beneath a tree on a small hill. "Rest in peace, little one," he said before trotting down the hill onto the road that led to Berlin. He ran west until he saw the silhouette of his uncle's limo. He was surprised they waited. He tapped the rear fender. The driver's window and a rear window opened simultaneously.

"God, you smell like shit," Schultz said.

Niko got in the back, looking like he had bathed in a cesspool.

"Good God, Niko," Krug said, gasping. "What happened?"

He told them.

"You killed four men?" Krug said.

"I killed four Nazis."

"And put us all in danger," his uncle said, unhappy.

"Why? the prisoners only saw me tonight," Niko said.

"Yes. But they saw us all together this afternoon," Uncle Fredrik said. "If the Nazis question the prisoners about the missing guards, we'll all be implicated."

"Should we leave for Switzerland immediately?" Schultz asked.

"That will do more harm than good," Krug said. "They know who I am. If we run, we'll look guilty. The Nazis will demand the Swiss government return us. It will create tension between Switzerland and Germany."

"I never thought of that," Niko said.

"You never think of consequences, Niko," Krug said. "You're too hot-headed. Schultz, drive to Berlin. I need time to think of a way out of this."

They drove an hour before Fredrik said, "I have an idea."

"Good," Schultz said. "I've come up with nothing."

"I think this will work," Uncle Fredrik said. "When we get to Berlin, I'll arrange with a contact of mine to hide Niko."

"You have contacts in Berlin besides Himmler?" Niko asked.

"I'm an international businessman, Niko. I have contacts everywhere."

Niko knew his uncle was wealthy but never looked below the surface.

"Once you're safe, Schultz and I will go to police headquarters and file a missing person report. We'll show Himmler's letter to give us credibility."

"With that letter, they'll probably believe anything you say," Schultz said.

"I'm counting on it. I'll say the three of us went to Marzahn to scout out possible circus locations. If the Nazis check my story, the prisoners will confirm that the three of us were there in the afternoon. They'll say they saw Niko and Berger's confrontation and my intervention ending in a handshake. No one needs to lie. That's what happened. We'll tell the Berlin police Niko disappeared at a rest stop after we left the camp, and never returned. This way, it will look as if Niko acted on his own that night."

"It sounds plausible," Schultz said.

"After we file the report, we'll sneak Niko out of Berlin."

"To where?" Niko asked. "I can't go back to Switzerland like you said."

"If the Nazis start looking for you, nowhere is safe in Europe. I'll arrange passage for you to America."

"I don't know anyone in America," Niko said.

"I do," Fredrik said."

"Who do you know in America?"

"I'll tell you later after I make the arrangements."

"I'm sorry I caused us so much trouble," Niko said.

"You have a good heart, Niko." Uncle Fredrik told him. "But you need to use your head sometimes."

CHAPTER 15

1936
EICHMANN

Adolf Eichmann sat at his desk in his Berlin office. Sitting across from him was Franz Goldschmidt, and his daughter, Ida. Goldschmidt was the president of the family-owned Federal Bank and the winner of the Blue Max during the Great War. Eichmann knew Goldschmidt was nervous and admired his composure under the circumstances.

This is a brave man, Eichmann thought. *A war hero.*

Goldschmidt thought Eichmann resembled a vulture; narrow head, emotionless eyes, beaked nose, and predatory mouth. The banker glanced at his eighteen-year-old daughter, Ida, sitting next to him. He wished she hadn't come, but she insisted. Her penchant for insolence worried him. He had warned her about Nazi intolerance, but she was insouciant and arrogant. Goldschmidt felt responsible for his daughter's attitude. His wife Ilse, Ida's mother, had died when the girl was eight and he was at war. Ida was cared for by an elderly grandmother who never disciplined her. When he returned from the war, he found a spoiled, haughty child.

She had dressed expensively for the meeting. Her father had suggested more conservative attire, but she said, "Eichmann should know that he's not dealing with Jewish peasants."

Eichmann looked up from his reading, nodded at the former captain, and glanced contemptuously at Ida. Ida sighed, feigning boredom. Eichmann ignored her. "This is your service record," he said to Goldschmidt, pushing the folder toward the captain. "You were awarded the Blue Max. Very impressive."

"He is a hero," Ida said.

Eichmann glared at her. "I was talking to your father," he said, in a voice as cold as a Russian winter. He turned to the captain. "I asked you to come because of your outstanding service to the Fatherland."

"I was ordered to come," Goldschmidt said. "Is something wrong?"

"Yes. Something is very wrong, Captain. You are a Jew in a country that no longer wants its Jews. I have been assigned to expedite the emigration of special Jews."

"What makes me special?"

"Your war record and your ability to pay for passage to another country. When Jews leave, they must relinquish all their property and money to the Third Reich."

"That's preposterous," Ida said, raising her voice. "We're not leaving. We own property here. We own banks. We're wealthy. How dare you treat a war hero this way."

Eichmann took a deep breath, showing more restraint than Goldschmidt had expected. "It is *because* your father is a war hero that I can make this offer. Soon there will be no offers."

"Hitler will be voted out in the next election," Ida said.

Eichmann laughed. "There will be no more elections in Germany."

"If we refuse to go?" Ida said.

"That would be unwise," Eichmann said. "Here are the documents for your signature, Captain. I advise you to sign them."

"Don't sign, Father," Ida said. "They can't do this to us."

"Perhaps we should talk alone, Herr Goldschmidt," Eichmann said.

"You will do no such thing," Ida said.

Eichmann lost his patience. His face turned red, and he slammed his open palms on the desk. He stood and leaned across the desk toward Ida. "Shut up!" he screamed, inches from her startled face.

Ida recoiled. "You have no right…" she stammered.

"I have every right!" Eichmann shouted. "It is you Jews who no longer have rights. Now, wait outside for your father." He pointed to the door.

Terrified, she hurried from Eichmann's office.

Eichmann sat down again, cleared his throat, and straightened his uniform. "Excuse my outburst. Your daughter's insolence was intolerable. She simply doesn't understand, but I believe you do, Captain. I urge you to accept my offer. Leave Germany while you can. The Fuhrer could change the policy at any moment."

"What more could Hitler do to us? He's taken away all our rights."

"He could close the borders and not let Jews leave."

After an extended pause, the Nazi said, "I have nothing against Jews," he began. "I'm the government's liaison with Germany's Jews because I understand you people. I speak Hebrew and Yiddish. I know Jewish customs and traditions. But I also know Adolf Hitler. He blames the Jews for all of Germany's problems."

"You know that's not the truth," Goldschmidt said.

"It's Hitler's truth, and that is the only truth that matters in Germany now. The *Queen Mary* leaves for America in a few days. I urge you to be on that ship."

Goldschmidt asked, "What will Hitler do with the Jews who can't or won't leave? There are millions of us. Does he plan to kill us all?"

"Please don't wait to find out," Eichmann implored, finding no pleasure pressuring this war hero—this brave man—this incredibly skilled pilot. He knew that Hitler could use men like Franz Goldschmidt in his war machine. If only the Fuhrer's mindless hatred of the Jews was not so all-consuming—so self-destructive. How can he convince this man that leaving Germany now, right now, was his last chance? He would have no problem sending Goldschmidt's daughter to the camps—but not this good man. What could he say to him that would make him understand? Finally, he found the words.

"Mr. Goldschmidt," Eichmann said with all the compassion he could muster. "Believe it or not, I am trying to save your life." Then the Nazi reverted to form and added, "You are dismissed."

CHAPTER 16

1936
AMERICA

When Fredrik Krug, Schultz, and Niko arrived in Berlin, they went to the east side of the city where they were met by a small, raggedy, fidgety man who took them to a fourth-floor apartment. Krug had a brief conversation with the man, gave him money, and let him out.

"Who was that man?" Niko asked.

"An associate," Krug said. "I called him when we stopped for gas."

"I didn't know you had friends in Berlin," Niko said.

"He's not a friend. You can trust a friend. An associate's trust costs money."

"What if someone offers him more money?"

"A good businessman makes sure that doesn't happen. We'll come for you in a day or two. You have enough food and drink. Don't leave this apartment for anything. Don't open the door for anyone but us."

They returned in a day. "You are now officially a missing person," Schultz said. "The police are looking for a tall man with long hair." He held up a pair of scissors. Schultz cut Niko's hair and gave him a cap. "Wear this low on your head and slouch."

They drove from Berlin to Hamburg where Niko was to board a cruise ship to Southampton. From there, the *Queen Mary* would take him to New York City. Fredrik handed Niko a packet. "These are all your tickets."

He shuffled through the tickets. "Why am I going to Nebraska?" he asked.

"To meet your father."

"What?" Niko gasped—shocked. "You said my father died in the war."

"I lied. Another promise I made to your mother."

"You made too many promises with my life," Niko said.

"Sorry. It's what she wanted. Now, I'll tell you the truth about your father and mother."

After hearing the story, Niko was angrier. "It sounds like I'm the result of a breeding experiment."

"Your mother would disagree. She'd say you're a dream come true. Now, repeat what I told you."

Niko took a deep breath. "My father's name is Jonas Hensen. He's forty years old. A local legend in North Platte, Nebraska. A football and war hero. He won the Silver Star for bravery. Now he's a high school history teacher and a football coach. He has no children. His wife has an illness."

"Excellent," Uncle Fredrik said. "You have a good memory."

"How do you know all this about him?"

"I told you," Uncle Fredrik said, smiling. "I have connections everywhere."

"Okay. So, *why* do you know all this about him?"

"I thought you two might need each other someday."

"What if he doesn't want a long-lost son?" Niko expressed his concern.

"I think he will. Give him a chance. What have you got to lose?"

The ship's horn blasted. It was time to end one life and start another. "Uncle Fredrik, how can I ever thank you for all you've done?"

"Forgive all the lies and enjoy your life."

"I'll do my best. Take care of my lion."

"I will."

Niko shook Schultz's hand, hugged his uncle, and walked to the ship, thinking he was leaving Europe forever.

Two days later, Niko stood at the stern of the *Queen Mary*, watching Southampton fade from view. He had checked into his first-class cabin and gone to the main deck. He wore the blue suit and white shirt his uncle had bought him in Berlin. *Dress and act like you belong in first class,* his uncle had said. *You'll fit right in.*

Niko walked the thousand feet of the main deck, from stem to stern and back again. He soon lost count of the round trips, preoccupied with thoughts of the future. He walked until the sun went down, and the warm breeze became a brisk wind. He glanced at his watch. It was nearly eight. He was hungry.

He entered the first-class dining room; two decks high, wide as the ship, and opulently furnished. The maître d' escorted Niko to a table. Several women noticed him, but that was nothing new. He attracted female attention like a magnet. He enjoyed it.

He was seated, reading the menu when he sensed someone hovering. An attractive dark-haired woman wearing a black dress with a plunging neckline looked down at him. He stood, and she looked up at him. "My, you're a big one," she remarked. "May I join you?" she was holding a drink.

"With your husband?" Niko gestured to her wedding band.

"No. He's in New York, working. He's always working."

"What does he do?"

"Works for Meyer Lansky," she said as if that should explain everything. It didn't.

"Is that the name of a company or a man?"

"You never heard of Meyer Lansky—the most famous Jewish gangster in America."

"I'm Swiss—not American," Niko explained. "What does your husband do for Meyer Lansky?"

"His nickname is Digger—as in undertaker. What do you think?"

"Really? What's your husband's real name?"

"Bruce Leonard. But never call him Bruce." She wagged her index finger at him.

"I won't," Niko said. "Would you care to join me for dinner, Mrs. Leonard?"

"Call me Renee," she said, and they sat. She drained her drink, put the glass on the table, and cupped her hands under her chin. She gazed at him, her eyes half-closed. "You're very handsome, you know."

"Thank you. How many drinks have you had?"

"Three," she smiled. "Martinis. You can buy me my fourth."

"If that's what you want. Tell me, Renee, are you Jewish too?"

"Why do you ask?" she said, slurring a word.

105

"Just curious," he said, hoping she wouldn't get sick or pass out.

"Curioushh to shee a Jewish woman naked?" she slurred her words and giggled.

"Definitely—but not you, I'm afraid."

"Is that an insult?" she said, managing a pout.

"Not at all. You're very pretty," he said. "But you're married."

"Don't let that bother you."

"I'm afraid it does," Niko said. "So, tell me, Renee, why were you in Europe?"

"Meyer sent me to help get Jews out of Germany, to the States or Israel. He pulled a lot of strings to get me in and get them out."

"Why you? Why not your husband or someone else?"

"I have no criminal record. I can get a passport. Plus, he trusts me."

"Did you have any luck with the Jews?"

"It wasn't luck. We paid for what we got. The Nazis are greedy."

"They're also killers."

"So's my husband. To hell with all killers. Let's talk 'bout us."

"I'm ordering a steak first. Are you hungry?"

"No. But, I'll have another drink."

"Maybe you shouldn't."

"I'm old enough to be your babysitter," she said, laughing.

He ate steak, and she consumed two more martinis. They made small talk until her eyes became slits, and her conversation gibberish.

He stood and helped her up. "Let's get you to your cabin," he said.

"I thought you'd never ask," she whispered, slumping against him and stumbling as they walked. He found her cabin key in her pocketbook and opened the door. He picked her up and carried her across the threshold like a bride. "How romantic," she managed before her eyes closed and she passed out.

He put her on the bed, undressed her to her slip, and tucked her under the covers. She began to snore lightly. He wrote a note and left it on the pillow next to her head; *"You're going to hate the way you feel in the morning, but you won't hate yourself."*

Returning to the main deck, Niko walked toward the bow again, enjoying the smell of the ocean, the feel of the chilly ocean air, and the sight of a sky filled with stars. He noticed an incongruous couple walking toward the stern. The man looked dignified, wearing a long black raincoat with a white silk scarf at his throat. His hands were deep in his coat pockets. His hair was gray and combed straight back. He had perfect posture—eyes front—military style. *Impressive*, Niko thought.

Conversely, the woman was repugnant with the unfriendly face of a Doberman Pinscher. *Must be his daughter*, Niko thought. *No mistress could look like that.*

The two men nodded as they passed each other.

"That young man looked familiar," Franz Goldschmidt remarked to his daughter.

"We don't know anyone on this ship," she growled like a Doberman.

"Not from this ship," he clarified. "Another place. I know that face from somewhere."

"He's a third your age."

"Maybe he just reminds me of someone."

"Forget it. You don't know him or anyone else where we're going."

"We have distant cousins in Boston, I told you. They'll help us."

"I'd never help a stranger."

"I know, Ida," Franz Goldschmidt said with regret. They walked on.

When Niko woke the next morning, there was a note under his door; *Niko, You're a gentleman. If you ever need a friend in New York City, this is my number. Renee.*

He put the note in his wallet. Now he had a friend in America he'd just met and a father he'd never met.

Chapter 17

1936
NIKO

On the afternoon of September 3, 1936, Niko stepped off a train in North Platte, Nebraska. He entered the station and rented a locker for his suitcase. At the ticket counter, he asked a clerk how to get to the high school.

The agent looked up, his jaw dropped, and so did his pen.

"Are you alright?" Niko asked.

The man blinked rapidly and cleared his throat. "I'm fine," he replied, obviously unnerved. He gave Niko directions, staring at him the whole time. *Strange,* Niko thought, leaving the office.

The strangeness persisted as Niko walked through downtown North Platte. People seemed startled when they first saw him, and then they stared. *Why?* He wondered. Niko was accustomed to second looks because of his size. But these reactions felt as different to him as North Platte looked. There were no grand buildings like the twin-spired *Grossmunster* or the impressive *Fraumunster* in Zurich. If ornate churches with Chagall windows represented old-world elegance, North Platte was wild west simplicity—short and squat. But none of that mattered. Europe was his past. America was his future.

Niko arrived at North Platte High and found the football field behind the school. From the shadows, he watched the players stretching and exercising under the supervision of a tall man in a black sweat suit. The man's back was to Niko, but the way he moved looked familiar. Niko watched the practice from there. He didn't understand the game, but he could appreciate the coach's enthusiasm and the respect he commanded from his players.

The practice lasted nearly two hours, and when it was over, the players ran off the field as a unit. The coach walked behind, jotting notes on a clipboard. When the field was empty except for the coach, Niko stepped out of the shadows. They were about thirty yards apart when the coach looked up. *My God*, Niko thought, stunned, and suddenly understanding why he had shocked so many townspeople. He looked exactly like his father.

Jonas dropped his clipboard when he saw the dark-skinned, younger replica of himself approaching. His mind flashed back to Compiegne and Drina—the beautiful Gypsy rope dancer. This boy had her skin color and big brown eyes— with his face and body. *I have a son*, Jonas thought and knew in an instant his life would never be the same.

When they were only a few feet apart, they stopped, both speechless. Jonas found his voice first. "I didn't know," he said.

"I didn't either … until recently," Niko said.

"How old are you?"

"Seventeen."

He nodded. The math made sense. "What's your name?"

"Niko Santiago Krug."

Jonas nodded again. "I can't believe I didn't know you existed."

"My mother didn't want you to feel obligated," Niko said.

"Is that what she told you?"

"No," Niko sighed. "She died giving birth to me."

Jonas grimaced. "How awful," he said. "She was so beautiful. I can still see her, up high, dancing like an angel. You know she was an acrobat?"

"A rope dancer."

"Yes, that's right," Jonas said, "She was so young."

"Eighteen when she died," Niko said. "Uncle Fredrik told me the whole story just recently. He promised my mother to keep you a secret."

"Fredrik Krug was a good man. How did he know where to find me?"

"He told me he has a lot of international connections," Niko explained. "To locate you, he used a contact in Zurich…who knew a man in New York…who knew a man in Omaha…"

Jonas nodded. "I understand. But, why bother, after all these years?"

"He thought we might need each other now."

"Do we?" Jonas asked.

"That's up to you, I guess. He thought you needed to meet your only male descendant."

Jonas thought about that and said, "He's right. My wife and I have no children. I have no siblings. You're the last of my bloodline."

"Fredrik said he wouldn't have sent me here if you had children. He said that would have been unfair to your family."

Jonas thought of how he had chosen Amanda over having children. If he had made a different choice, married another woman, and had children, Niko Santiago Krug would not be standing there. He never regretted choosing Amanda. Now he was certain he made the right choice— that it was fate. *Maybe my son is another reason I survived the Great War*, Jonas thought. He nodded at Niko and said, "Okay. I understand why Fredrik thought I might need to meet you. Do you need me?"

It was Niko's turn to nod. "I have nowhere else to go," Niko said. "I got in trouble in Europe and had to leave in a hurry. Uncle Fredrik sent me here. But I understand I'm a stranger to you. You owe me nothing. I'll leave if you want."

"No. I don't want you to leave. We just found each other. I want you to meet my wife. Let's see where this goes."

Niko sighed with relief and said, "Thank you."

They retrieved Niko's suitcase from the train station and headed for the Hensen farmhouse in Jonas's truck. "Two generations of Hensens have lived in our house," Jonas told his long-lost son. "I'm the first Hensen born in America. My parents immigrated from Denmark in 1894. They were homesteaders, meaning the government gave them the land to farm. After a year, they decided they didn't want to be farmers. They expanded and improved the house instead, hoping that would satisfy the government. No one from the government ever came to check. My father, your grandfather, was a good mechanic and got a job with the railroad."

"Are your parents still alive?" Niko asked.

"No. My father was killed in an accident at Bailey railroad yard six years ago. Got caught between two coupling railcars. My mother had a heart attack not long after. They were both around sixty-five, we think. Records from the old country aren't that dependable."

"What about your wife? Will I be a shock to her?"

"Maybe. Maybe not," Jonas said. "I told her everything about my past. She knows I had a love affair after the war. I think she'll be okay… after the initial shock."

He parked in front of the farmhouse. Amanda was sitting at the kitchen table cutting vegetables. Her face showed her pain. Her fingers ached, and her shoulders were stiff. Everything was an effort today. It was not a good day for her MD. Some days were worse than others, but Jonas never knew. She kept it from him. When she heard the door knob turn, her pained expression changed to a big smile. "You're home early," she said, looking up. "And who's that big guy trying to hide behind you?"

Jonas stepped aside, held out his arm, and announced, "Amanda, this is my son, Niko."

"Oh, my goodness," Amanda gasped, staring. She got up and walked to him, her bright blue eyes filled with life. "You look so much like Jonas," she said. Her fingers touched his cheek, but she withdrew them immediately. "I'm sorry. Do you mind?"

"Not at all," Niko said.

She traced his cheek again with her fingertips. "A miracle," she said, smiling.

"I must be a shock to you."

"Not entirely," she told him. "Jonas told me about your mother. Where have you been all this time? Here, sit at the table and tell us everything."

Niko gave them a brief history, including Marzahn and his escape from Europe.

"You killed four men. How did you feel about that?" Jonas wanted to know.

"Honestly, I felt like I made the world a better place."

"A better place for who?" Jonas asked. "Certainly not those four men."

"The Nazis are a curse," Niko insisted. "The world is better off without them."

"From what I hear, the Nazis think the world would be a better place without Jews, Gypsies, and anyone who disagrees with them. That doesn't make them right—or you."

"You asked how I felt about killing them—not if I felt I was right."

"I don't think the world can be a better place for everyone," Amanda added. "People want different things."

"I agree," Niko said.

"Who am I to disagree?" Jonas said. "I killed over a hundred Germans myself."

"Yes, but you were at war. You had no choice," Amanda touched his hand.

Jonas smiled at her. "There's always a choice, sweetheart," he told them.

"This was my bedroom as a child," Jonas told Niko. "Unpack and rest a while."

Niko was too excited to rest. He looked at framed memorabilia on the wall; his father with various football teams, his All-American Certificates, his high school and college diplomas. He felt a sense of pride for a father he didn't know. *This man is part of me*, he thought. *And he accepts me.* The realization comforted him. He took a deep breath and continued perusing the room. He was wondering about the drawing of a Viking longboat and why there was no memorabilia about the Great War when Amanda called him for dinner.

At the table, Amanda said, "You mentioned you were entering your twelfth year of school."

Niko nodded. "Yes, ma'am."

"That would make you a senior in our school system," Jonas said.

"You should finish school," Amanda said.

"I have other things to worry about. You do, too—like how to explain me."

"Let's sleep on those worries," Amanda said. "And talk in the morning."

They left the uncertainties unanswered and finished eating.

After dinner, Jonas showed Niko sepia photographs from Denmark and the Hensens' early days in America. He told Niko about their Viking ancestry and his father's theory. "I was so aggressive playing football, my mother said I was possessed by the devil," Jonas said. "My father thought it was just as likely I inherited Viking warrior genes from the old country. He said great warriors like Erik the Red and Ragnar Lodbrok could be in our bloodline."

"That would be amazing," Niko said.

"Whenever I would do crazy things, I blamed it on the Vikings," Jonas said and laughed.

"I do a lot of crazy things, myself," Niko said, smiling. "I'll use that excuse, too."

Jonas checked his watch. "Amanda needs her sleep. We'll talk more tomorrow."

Niko said, "Can I ask one more question, Mrs. Hensen?"

"Call me, Amanda."

"Amanda. My Uncle Fredrik said you were ill. But you don't look sick. You look great."

"Thank you. Your uncle is right. I have muscular dystrophy," she explained. "Your father and I are fighting it together. He won't let me be sick."

As they were leaving the kitchen, Niko asked Jonas, "What should I call you?"

"For now, use my name," Jonas said. "We'll see what happens."

That night Niko lay in bed surrounded by memories, none of them his own. He felt comfortable with the Hensens but disconcerted with the circumstances. He slept fitfully and woke before dawn.

"You're up early," Jonas said to Niko, finding him sitting at the kitchen table the next morning. Amanda followed him into the room.

"I couldn't sleep. I have a lot on my mind," Niko told them.

"Us too," Jonas admitted. "We were talking about you last night."

"I hope it wasn't anything bad."

"Not at all," Amanda answered. "We were wondering if you'd like to finish high school here in North Platte," Amanda said.

"Funny," Niko replied. "I was wondering if I should leave. I'm not easy for you to explain."

"You're Jonas's son," Amanda said. "What else is there to explain?"

"A lot," Niko told them. "Jonas is a highly respected teacher and coach in this town. A war hero. People trust him with their kids. How would they feel if they learn their hero had an affair with a Gypsy circus performer seventeen years ago and had a half-breed, bastard son?"

"It sounds sordid when you put it that way," Amanda observed.

"But it's the truth, and I didn't even include the four Nazis I killed."

"Some things are better left unsaid," Jonas said.

"Exactly," Niko said. "I have to be explained in a way that doesn't offend or alarm the people of North Platte and ruin your reputation."

"Any ideas?" Amanda asked.

Niko nodded. "I've been passing for white my whole life by telling half-truths—combining fact with fiction. We could do that to explain me."

"What would we say?" Jonas asked.

"We could say my mother was the daughter of a wealthy Spanish family instead of a Gypsy rope dancer...and Jonas met her at a fancy Armistice celebration in Compiegne...instead of the circus."

"That does sound better," Amanda said.

"And it's half true," Niko said. "Then we say they fell in love, but her parents forbid the relationship. So, they had a secret affair."

"How romantic," Amanda said.

"It's a fairy tale," Jonas said and laughed.

"I know. But it's still romantic. What happens next, Niko?"

"Jonas ships out for America not knowing she's pregnant. He writes her, but her parents intercept the letters, and she never sees them. So, when Jonas receives no replies, he thinks he's lost her and goes on with his life. When she dies in childbirth, her parents raise the boy for the next seventeen years. When they pass away, Niko is sent to live with an uncle. While settling the estate, the uncle finds Jonas's letters and decides to reunite father and son in America. And here I am."

"What a beautiful, heartwarming story," Amanda said." I don't care that it's not true. I love it, Niko."

"I've had a lot of practice telling stories," Niko said.

"It has several loose ends if someone investigates closely," Jonas said.

Niko spread his arms wide to indicate the whole community. "People love you here," he said. "They'll want to believe you. No one will investigate."

"He's right," Amanda agreed. "No one will question you."

Niko nodded. "In Europe, everyone believed I was white because Fredrik Krug said I was white. Even though my skin was dark, no one doubted him. No one will doubt you, either. But it's your choice. The whole truth would hurt you, and I'd leave town before I'd let that happen."

"No. We want you to stay," Amanda said. "We'll tell everyone your fairy tale."

As predicted, Niko and his half-truths were accepted without question. When he was tested to determine if he was qualified to be a high school senior in America, it was determined he was overqualified. Jonas proudly enrolled him at North Platte High as his son.

One morning, before school started, while Jonas and Amanda were taking their daily walk, they saw Niko standing in a clearing in the woods. He was gracefully raising his arms above his head, slowly moving his legs apart, until he descended into a perfect split.

"What's he doing?" she asked.

"Exercising, I think," Jonas said.

"It hurts just looking at that split," Amanda said.

Niko remained stretched for minutes before leaning to his right and touching his toes with both hands. He repeated the motion to the left.

"He's got great flexibility," Jonas observed.

They watched as Niko got up and went through a series of strenuous kicks and punches, springing up, rolling over, flipping like an acrobat.

"A natural athlete," Jonas said. "I asked him if he wanted to try football."

"What did he say?"

"Said he never played but would try so he could spend more time with me."

"What a nice thing to say."

"He's a nice person. Very sensitive. Fredrik Krug did a good job bringing him up."

Niko was doing chin-ups from a tree limb when he saw Amanda and Jonas. He dropped from the limb and trotted to them.

"Good morning," he said, his face shiny with sweat.

"You certainly do some unconventional exercises," Amanda said.

"The Chinese cook with the circus taught me martial arts exercises," Niko explained. "Now you'll teach me to play football."

"It won't be easy," Jonas said. "Lots of rules."

"I'll do my best," Niko said. "See you at home." He ran off.

"I'm worried," Amanda said, watching his long powerful strides.

"Don't be," Jonas said. "Niko can handle himself."

"I know," she said. "I'm worried for the other boys."

CHAPTER 18

1936
BETH

When Niko walked through the front door of North Platte High School his first day, he was immediately the center of attention.

He's huge.

He's handsome.

He's gorgeous, Beth Hannigan thought, standing next to her locker. The seventeen-year-old daughter of cattle baron Duke Hannigan was beautiful, spoiled, wild, and promiscuous. All the boys wanted her. She wanted a select few. Right now, she wanted Niko Hensen.

She caught his eye as he passed and used her best smile to stop him. He noticed her but didn't stop. *What's with him?* She thought. *No boy ignores me.*

Later that day, she tried again by bumping into him in the corridor, breasts first. "Sorry," she said, leaning against him.

"My fault," he said, aware of her body language.

"I'm Beth Hannigan," she said, looking up.

"Niko Hensen," he said. "Coach Hensen's son."

"You look like him," Beth said. "Going to the senior assembly?"

"On my way."

"Good." She grabbed his arm. "We can go together."

They entered the auditorium and sat in the last row together. Several girls rolled their eyes, intimating, *that figures.*

On stage, Principal Vanhooten, a short, bald man in a blue suit and red bow tie, stood behind the lectern. He welcomed the students and droned on about the challenges they faced as seniors and the opportunities the high school offered. The students looked bored. "Lastly, I want to introduce a new student from Europe. His name is Niko Hensen, and he is Coach Hensen's son. Niko, please stand up."

Niko slowly unfolded his six-and-a-half-foot frame. Beth's body tingled. She crossed her legs reflexively. She noticed other girls do the same and smiled. *Not a chance, girls*, she thought, *He's mine.*

"Niko, would you like to tell us anything about yourself?"

He smiled, thinking, *imagine if I told them the truth.* "Hello, everyone," he said. "Nothing much to tell. I grew up in Europe, and I'm just glad to be here." He sat down again.

"A man of few words," Vanhooten said. "That's it then. Have a great year, seniors."

As they walked out, Beth asked Niko, "Can you ride a horse?"

"Yes," he said.

"Want to go riding with me? I have horses on my father's ranch."

"That sounds great. When?"

"After school, today?" she said, anxious to get him alone.

"I can't today. I'm trying out for the football team."

"Do you like football?" she made a face showing she didn't.

"Never played. My father told me a little about it."

"It's very rough."

"I don't mind."

Me neither, she thought.

"I'll come watch," she said, kissed his cheek, and walked away.

A handful of fans normally attended pre-season practice. But more than fifty came to watch the big new kid—the coach's son. If he had any of this father's ability, he would be great. Students were curious and older fans hopeful.

It was a clear, summer's end afternoon, the temperature in the low seventies. The smell of fresh-cut grass and churned up dirt was strong. The familiar thumps, bumps, and grunts of football announced the start of a new season. The players all looked alike in drab practice uniforms... except for Niko who stood out like a lighthouse on a promontory point. He was the biggest and fastest on the field like his father a generation ago. No one could elude him. No one could catch him.

I'll catch you, Beth thought, watching his every move.

Beth was not the only Hannigan watching. On a hill, a few hundred yards from the field, Beth's father, Duke, was peering through powerful binoculars, gnashing his teeth. He had heard about Jonas Hensen's long-lost son and needed to see for himself. It was easy to recognize the physical resemblance: the height, the impressive physique, the fast, smooth, effortless movements... like a big cat. "Son of a bitch," Duke muttered.

Duke had only one possession he knew Jonas Hensen coveted: children. Duke had three: Beth and his twin boys Elvis and Eli. The boys were big, like him, but lazy and unmotivated. Duke had let them play football for Hensen when they were in high school, hoping their presence would annoy the coach—maybe cause him to do something unprofessional and get fired. But Jonas had handled them well for four years and got the most out of them. Their size and his coaching skills enabled the twins to have decent high school football careers. Duke wasn't satisfied with their achievements. He was never satisfied with anything they did.

The practice ended, and fans joined the players on the field. Duke continued to focus his binoculars on Hensen. When Niko took off his helmet, Duke was stunned by the strong facial resemblance to Jonas. Except for the son's darker complexion and black hair, they were lookalikes. Duke was even more surprised to see his daughter's face appear in his lenses next to Hensen. *What's she doing here? She hates football.*

When he saw Beth kiss Hensen's cheek and push herself against him, he lost his temper. *Bastard*, he thought, *another fuckin' Hensen to worry about.* He threw the expensive binoculars to the ground and stomped to his red Lincoln Zephyr convertible. His tires churned up dirt and gravel behind him as he sped away. When he was frustrated like this, he usually took his anger out on his defenseless, dependent mistress, Randi Renart.

She had been Duke's mistress for eight years, bound to him by golden handcuffs. She had a daughter from a teenage pregnancy and an abandoned mother to support, and Duke filled that need. For his part, Duke enjoyed the power he had over her as much as the sex. To him, they were the same thing. Although they were careful never to be seen together, it was the worst kept secret in North Platte.

That afternoon at Randi's house, Duke was rougher with her than usual. When they were done, she asked, "Have you been drinking?"

"I had a few before I got here."

"You're a mean drunk," she said. "You really hurt me."

"I've hurt you before."

"That doesn't make it right."

"Our relationship is about money, not right or wrong."

"If it's business, why don't you hire a whore? It would be cheaper."

"Owning you is more fun."

He knew Randi hated herself for being someone's victim all her life. Her father had been a harmless alcoholic who disappeared when she was seven. Her mother was an uneducated cleaning lady who worked the night shift at the Bailey Yard's executive offices. She earned just enough to live dirt poor. With little in the way of parental guidance, Randi learned life by trial and error. She had above-average intelligence, a pretty face, and a voluptuous body that made her popular with the boys at North Platte High. She had been queen of the senior prom, but her king knocked her up that night and skipped town. An unwed mother at nineteen, she had enough clerical skills to get a day job in the same Bailey Yard office her mother cleaned by night.

Duke saw Randi working there and made a callous offer to buy her sexual services. Surprisingly, she agreed if he agreed to pay her enough to support her family. He paid, and she performed, fulfilling his sexual fantasies and soothing his ego.

She sat on the bed, watching Duke dress. He still was an imposing man. Six-foot-four, two hundred and forty pounds of muscle, with just a hint of middle-aged thickness around his waist. She rubbed her left shoulder where he had hit her. "You really hit me hard," she said. "You haven't been this abusive since your wife threatened to divorce you for cheating her parents."

His face turned red, and he slapped her face. She yelped and fell back on her bed.

"Jesus..." she whimpered.

"Don't ever talk about that again," he said.

"Those are...those are...your own goddamn words," she stammered. "You said you screwed them. You said they never had a chance."

"That's for me to say, not you," he growled. "The Kelleys got what they deserved. They were weak. I made us the biggest cattlemen in Nebraska—not the fuckin' Kelleys."

He finished dressing and withdrew a wad of cash from his pocket. He threw it on the bed. "Next month's allowance," he said and exited her house.

Duke loved driving up to his twenty-room mansion. He deliberately had his house built slightly larger than Buffalo Bill's Scout's Rest Ranch, five miles away. He copied Bill's Victorian style, complete with mansard roofs, small towers, and twin chimneys. His red barn, used only for storage, was bigger than Bill's, too.

He arrived home too late for dinner and went to the den. His wife was at the bar, mixing Seagram's 7 with 7 Up. His ponderous twenty-one-year-old twin sons lolled across a large sectional sofa designed for six. Beth was squeezed into the small space they didn't use.

"You two take up the whole damn sofa," Duke said, entering the room. To Beth, he added, "What were you doing at football practice today?"

"What were you doing there?" Beth asked, typically defiant.

"I like football," he said. "You hate it."

"I met a new boy at school today and went to watch him play."

"Do you always kiss boys you just meet?"

"I can't believe you were spying on me," Beth exclaimed, angry.

"I wasn't spying. Everyone saw you."

"It just so happens I like him, and he likes me. His name is Niko Hensen. He's Coach Hensen's son."

"I know who he is, but we don't know anything about him."

"I know he's gorgeous and all the girls want him."

"I don't care if all the boys want him too," Duke said, "Stay away."

"Why?"

"Because his father and your father fought over me," Shirley interrupted.

Beth rolled her eyes. "Yes, Mother. I know. A hundred years ago. No one cares anymore."

"Your father does," Shirley said, her eyes drooping.

"You're drunk," Duke said. "How many drinks have you had today?"

"Counting breakfast…seven," she told him. "And it's not enough."

"You're disgusting," Duke said and turned to Beth again. "I don't want you seeing that boy because we don't know anything about him. His father probably had sex with a hundred women in Europe during the war and obviously impregnated at least one of them. So, seventeen years later, one of his bastards shows up. Well, who is he? Where's he been? Who's his mother? Did you notice he's dark enough to be a half-breed? Would you like that?"

"He's not a half-breed," Beth said.

"How do you know? They say his mother was a wealthy Spaniard. Was she a Catholic? A Jew? There are Spanish Jews, you know. Would you like that? Or an Eye-talian? You know how I feel about them."

"Yes, you hate anyone who isn't a white Irish Catholic," Shirley slurred. "Mexicans, Chinamen, Indians, Negroes, and Jews. Did I leave anyone out?"

"Drunks," he said.

"I'll drink to that," Shirley said. She turned to Beth. "Tell me, dear, does he look like his father?"

"Yes. Younger and darker."

"He must be gorgeous."

"He is," Beth said.

"Go for it."

"Like your mother did," Duke said.

"I don't regret it for a minute."

"Enough!" Beth said. "All you two do is fight. I'm sick of it." She left the room.

"You missed dinner," Shirley said to Duke. "I guess you were with your whore."

Before Duke could answer, Beth returned shouting, "And I'll date whoever I want."

"I better not see you with him again," Duke shouted back.

"You won't see me," Beth said. "I promise you that."

"What are you going to do ... sneak around?"

"That's what you do," Beth said.

Shirley laughed. "Like father, like daughter," she said.

"This family is crazy," Beth said and left the room again.

"Damn it," Duke shouted and kicked over an end table. He went to the bar and poured two shots of scotch into a glass. He gulped it down and slammed the glass down. "Fuck it," he said and stormed out of the room.

Shirley passed out on her lounge.

Beth drove to the Hensen house in her new red MG convertible. Amanda answered the front door. "Beth, what a pleasant surprise."

"Hi, Mrs. Hensen. Is Niko home?"

"He is, dear," she said and called out his name. Niko appeared, saw Beth, and smiled.

"Hi, Niko, want to go for a ride?" Beth asked.

"Sure. Is it okay with you, Amanda?"

She nodded.

Beth drove Niko to the secluded spot near the North Platte River, where *her* mother had made love to *his* father as teenagers. She brought a blanket, and they spread it on the grass. There was no preliminaries or awkwardness. They both had experience. They both had the desire. They lunged for each other. Beth was accustomed to control. Niko changed all that.

CHAPTER 19

1936
NIKO

In the fall of 1936, North Platte had a second Golden Boy named Hensen, and the timing was perfect. In the depths of the Great Depression, the town needed a hero. He led the high school football team to a perfect season and gave the townspeople hope. If their sons could become undefeated champions, anything was possible.

The town was fascinated by Niko, and he was fascinated by his father. The man he had long thought dead was larger than life: a war hero, a local legend, an inspiration, and a teacher. Niko was proud to be his son, and Amanda had become the mother he never had. He adored her.

Niko had never known the love of parents until now, though he was no stranger to love. He had loved his uncle, a lion, several Gypsy surrogate mothers, and friends like Tian. He had made love without love involved and learned that love and lust were the closest emotions to hate. He was experiencing that love-hate relationship with Beth Hannigan now, and he didn't like it. The passion he had felt for her had cooled to the point where he no longer liked her. She was a contradiction, fawning over him while deliberately being mean to others. He hated her meanness.

She said she loved him, but he believed it was their image she loved. The best-looking couple. The football hero and his girl. She loved possessing what the other girls wanted. But he was no one's possession.

Most of all, he despised when she talked about her father. *My father hates your father. My father doesn't want me to see you. My father thinks you're a half-breed. My father's a bigot. My father… my father… my father…*

Fuck your father, Niko thought, disliking everything Duke Hannigan represented.

Niko began receiving football scholarship offers through the mail shortly before the New Year. They piled up on the kitchen table. An offer from the University of Nebraska sat on top. One night they sifted through the pile. "Niko, have you thought about where you want to go?" Amanda asked.

"Actually, I'd like to stay here with you," Niko said.

"But these are great opportunities," she replied, surprised.

"I thought you wanted to go to college," Jonas added.

"I do. I just don't want to go now."

"Most kids your age, *want* their independence," Jonas said.

"Most kids my age had parents all their lives. I didn't. Now that I have a mother and a father, I want to spend more time with them."

Jonas was touched. "I'm glad you feel that way," he said. "I just thought you'd go to Nebraska like I did."

"I'd love to follow in your footsteps," Niko assured him. "Just not now."

"Maybe next year?" Jonas asked.

"Maybe," Niko said. "And, something else. Would it be okay if I called you Mom and Dad?"

Amanda bit her lower lip. "I'd love that," she said.

"If that's how you feel, that would be fine," Jonas said.

"That's how I feel," Niko said. "And I'm glad you understand about college. It's been bothering me for a while."

"I should call my friend, Larry Babbitt, the athletic director at Nebraska, and tell him you won't be coming," Jonas said. "He's called me a couple of times about you."

"I hope this isn't a problem for you."

"No. He'll understand."

Two hours later, Jonas asked for a family meeting. "I spoke to Larry, and he understood," Jonas said. "But the new head coach, Biff Jones, didn't."

"I thought it was decided, I'm staying here with you," Niko said.

"Hear me out," Jonas persisted. "This is Coach Jones's first year. He really wants you. He's hiring staff now and offered me an assistant coaching job if you come with me."

"That very nice. But you love coaching here at the high school." Niko said.

"I'd love to coach at Nebraska," Jonas said. "It's sort of my dream job. Coach Jones can arrange a leave of absence for me here … until you finish your four years there."

"Really? How can he promise that?" Amanda asked.

"Football is serious business in Nebraska," Jonas said. "He has influence."

"Well, I love Lincoln," Amanda said. "If that matters."

"Of course, it matters," Niko said. "I'm not going without you."

❧ ❧ ❧

Later that night, Niko told Jonas his feelings about Beth Hannigan.

"I don't know how I got so involved with a girl like her."

"I do," Jonas said. "Your world was upside down when you got here, and the prettiest girl in town seduced you before you got right-side up."

"The seduction was mutual," Niko said.

Jonas laughed. "I understand," he said. "I've seen the chemistry between you two at school. Lust is a powerful emotion."

"But when lust turns to dislike. What then?"

"End it before it turns to hate and fighting. Hannigans fight dirty."

"Did they get rich fighting dirty?"

"Not originally."

"Tell me about them."

"The original Hannigans and Kelleys who immigrated here from Ireland during the '45 Potato Famine were dirt poor. But worked hard and had foresight. They went to work for the transcontinental railroad laying tracks, east to west. When they reached Nebraska, they saw herds of cattle coming here from Texas for a rail shipment east. They saw the value of raising cattle closer to the railroads and went into business doing just that. That one idea led to their cattle dynasty today. The dirty fighting started later."

"I heard that you fought Duke Hannigan for Shirley Kelley. Is that true?"

Jonas shrugged. "Not exactly," he smiled. "But we did have a fight."

"Did he fight dirty?"

"He did," Jonas said, remembering the piece of lead he'd found.

"So, you lost?"

"No. I won."

"But he got the girl," Niko said, confused.

"I didn't want her," Jonas explained. "She wanted to get married. I didn't."

"And Duke did."

"I think he was pushed into it by his father for business reasons."

"Not very romantic," Niko said, shaking his head.

"The Hannigans aren't very romantic," Jonas said. "Or honorable. When the U.S. became involved in the Great War, Duke's father, Liam, used bribes to keep Duke out of the army."

"Duke wasn't drafted?" Niko asked, surprised.

"No. He was deferred-stayed home. He took charge of the business under Liam's supervision. The Kelleys weren't paying attention. They figured, since Duke was family, they could trust him. They were wrong. Duke made sure his illegal maneuverings implicated the Kelleys, too. By the time they were made fully aware of their legal exposure, they wanted no part of the business. Liam was able to buy them out at a greatly reduced price."

"How do you know all this?"

"Rumors, gossip, and common knowledge," Jonas said. "The business was too big to be a secret. The Kelleys left North Platte, wealthy and bitter. Shirley never forgave Duke and only remained with him for the children."

"Duke Hannigan is worse than I imagined," Niko said. "The children would have been better off without him," he said. "Shirley should have left him."

"She never should have married him," Jonas opined. "She was at a vulnerable stage in her life, and she made a terrible mistake. She became an alcoholic just to cope with him."

"Do you still have feelings for her?"

"Yes. I feel sorry for her. I like her. She deserved better."

"And Beth?"

"The Kelleys were good people, and she's half-Kelley. So, maybe she's not all bad. But I wouldn't want even half a Hannigan in my life."

Niko stood up.

"Where are you going?"

"To get rid of my Hannigan."

"Be careful."

CHAPTER 20

1936
DUKE

Niko drove to the Hannigan Ranch. The huge house had always impressed him when Beth took him there to go horseback riding in Duke's absence. A hundred yards behind the house, Niko saw the fenced-in bullpen for *The One and Only Romeo*, Duke's prized stud bull. Duke loved that bull more than most people.

The horse barn and the ranch house for workers were several hundred yards away in the opposite direction. As far as the eye could see was Hannigan land. Niko was nervous but determined when he knocked on the front door. Beth answered. "Niko, what are you doing here?" she whispered.

"We need to talk."

"Not now," she whispered again. "My father's here."

They heard footsteps in the hall. Duke called, "Beth, come back in here. Father Coughlin's radio show is starting. He's introducing William Pelley. I want you to hear them." He entered the foyer and saw Niko, stopped abruptly, and stared. Niko could feel the hate.

"Daddy, this is Niko Hensen," Beth told him, nervous.

"I know who he is," Duke snapped.

"I was just leaving," Niko reached for the doorknob.

Duke held up his hand. "Since you're here, Hensen, we might as well have a little talk."

"We have nothing to talk about," Niko replied.

"I think we do. Come in."

Concerned but unafraid, Niko followed them to a large wood-paneled den. A set of Texas longhorns seven feet across were affixed to large stones above a cavernous fireplace. The walls were decorated with awards and photos memorializing the history of the K&H Ranch. In one corner, a stuffed brown bear reared on its hind legs, fangs and claws bared, a bullet hole between its marble eyes.

Elvis and Eli sprawled on the sofa. Duke sat down in his big armchair. Beth stood by, looking apprehensive. Shirley Hannigan, reclining on her lounge, drink in hand, looked up at Niko and said, "Oh, my God."

Niko smiled down at her. "Mrs. Hannigan," he said. "I'm Jonas Hensen's son, Niko."

The likeness was remarkable. "Of course, you are," she said gawking.

"My father told me nice things about you, Mrs. Hannigan."

"He did?" she smiled, flattered.

"Bet he didn't say nice things about me," Duke laughed.

"No, sir, he didn't," Niko said. "So, what do you want to talk about?"

"I'd like to know what you think of Father Coughlin and William Pelley."

"Why do you care what I think?"

"I want to know what kind of American you are."

Niko took a deep breath. Duke Hannigan irritated him. *Pompous asshole*, he thought. "Okay, I'll tell you what I think,"

Niko began. "I think Coughlin's a disgrace to the Catholic religion, and Pelley's a fraud. They're both anti-Semites, bigots, racists, and Nazis."

Beth cringed. Shirley laughed. Elvis and Eli looked confused.

"I agree. They are anti-Semites and bigots. And I support them. Jews, niggers, and half-breeds are ruining America. We need strong leaders like Pelley and Coughlin to keep America a white Christian Nation."

Niko's mind returned to the Gypsy prison camp in Marzahn. "Pelley and Coughlin are Nazi sympathizers."

"Damn right they are," Duke said. "Nothing wrong with the Nazi philosophy."

"Nazis sterilize and euthanize people they don't like. Do you approve of that?"

"No, he doesn't," Beth said, not wanting her father to answer.

"I'm in favor of anything that gets rid of inferior races."

"I can't believe you said that," Shirley said. "You *are* a Nazi."

"I know what I am," Duke said, pointing at Niko. "The question is, what is he? We don't know anything about him. He's dark enough to be part-nigger. Who was your mother, boy?"

Niko could feel the rage building inside him. He glared at Duke and wanted to hurt him. He wanted to shove his self-righteous superiority down his throat. He lost control. "I'll tell you exactly who I am," Niko said, advancing into the room, making it seem smaller. "I'm the son of Jonas Hensen and Drina Santiago. My mother was a Gypsy circus performer. She died giving birth to me."

"No!" Beth screamed. "Don't tell him that. He'll tell everyone. He'll ruin you."

"I knew it!" Duke crowed. "A half-breed. A Gypsy."

"And I killed four Nazis in Germany. That's why I had to flee to America."

"A half-breed murderer," Duke said. "Beautiful. What else you got, son?"

"I'm your daughter's lover."

A punch to the face couldn't have done Duke more damage. A look of pain crossed his face like he'd been kicked in the balls. He stood up. "You son of a bitch!" He growled and looked over at his sons. "Boys, throw this half-breed bastard out of here!"

"No, don't," Shirley said, holding up a hand to stop them. "Don't go near him."

"You can't protect him," Duke shouted.

"You idiot, I'm trying to protect my sons!" Shirley screamed.

"Don't worry, Mrs. Hannigan," Niko said. "I'll leave on my own."

"The hell you will," Duke growled.

Niko turned his back on the Hannigans the way his father had years ago. Duke took an iron poker from the hearth. "Get him!" he ordered his sons.

"No!" Shirley shouted. She tried to rise but swooned to the floor.

Beth went to her while her brothers lumbered after Niko. Duke followed, brandishing the poker. Elvis reached Niko first and slapped his huge hand on Niko's shoulder. In a seamless motion, Niko grabbed the hand and flipped the three-hundred-pound Elvis over his shoulder, dropping him to the hardwood floor. Wine glasses jumped from a shelf behind the bar and shattered on the floor. Elvis lay on the floor, gasping, making no effort to rise.

Eli engulfed Niko in a bear hug from behind and lifted him in the air. Niko dropped his head forward until his chin touched his chest, then snapped his head backward like a slingshot. The back of his head bashed Eli's face, flattening his nose and splitting his lips. Eli collapsed on the floor, unconscious.

Niko took two steps toward Duke, who waved the iron poker. "C'mon, half-breed, I'll split your fuckin' head open!"

Niko turned sideways and before Duke could react, thrust the heel of his boot into Duke's chest. The blow knocked Duke back onto his armchair. His momentum flipped the chair over and dumped him on the floor. He lost his grip on the poker.

"Are we done yet?" Niko asked, unfazed.

"Get out of my house!" Duke screamed, struggling to his feet.

Niko backed away. "Beth, tell your mother I'm sorry." He glanced sideways to make sure Duke was not going after the poker again.

"Don't worry about my wife," Duke said. "I'm going to ruin you."

"Threatening me is a very bad idea."

"I got plenty of guys on my payroll tougher than you."

"No, you don't," Niko said, and closed the door on the Hannigans.

"I'm sorry," Niko said after he told Jonas and Amanda what happened. "I just wanted to hurt that man. I lost control. I do that a lot. It's my biggest weakness."

"How bad did you hurt his boys?"

"Not nearly as bad as I could have. I was careful. But can Duke really ruin us?"

"He'll try," Jonas confirmed, thinking that Duke's influence could cause his family a lot of trouble. "He buys influence. He'll use his contacts on the school board to get me fired, and you expelled. Then he'll pressure the university to withdraw your scholarship."

"This is all my fault," Niko said. "I don't care about my scholarship, but I can't let anything happen to you. I'll apologize and leave town."

"No, you won't," Jonas said. "It was self-defense."

"Yes. But I provoked him."

"Why did you do that?" Amanda asked.

"He reminded me of those Nazi guards at the Gypsy camp. Pure evil."

"He is a nasty man," she said.

"Well, now we've got a fight on our hands," Jonas said.

"I don't want him to ruin things for you," Niko said.

"We'll deny everything he says," Amanda said. "People know Duke is a liar."

"But he's telling the truth this time," Niko said.

"Won't matter. His reputation will precede him," Jonas said.

"What about his influence?"

"Let him do his worst," Jonas decided. "Then I'll do mine."

CHAPTER 21

1936
ROMEO

The next morning when Niko and Jonas went to the high school, a local policeman stopped them at the main entrance. "Sorry, Jonas," he said. "I can't let Niko in, and you're to report to Mr. Vanhooten's office."

"Damn it," Niko said.

"Relax," Jonas said. "He got in the first punch the last time we fought, too. He lost then, and he'll lose now."

When Jonas entered Vanhooten's office, the Principal looked embarrassed. "How are you, Jonas?" he asked, uncomfortable.

"You know how I am. Why the suspensions?"

"Hannigan claims Niko attacked him and his sons last night."

"It was self-defense."

"That's not what he says. Anyway, I can't let him in the school."

"What about innocent till proven guilty?"

Vanhooten grimaced. "You know what I'm up against, Jonas."

"I know Duke's got powerful connections in this town."

"He's got powerful connections in this state," Vanhooten said. "I'm sure he plans to contact the university, too. He made some pretty serious allegations against you and Niko."

"All lies," Jonas said, gritting his teeth. "But I'll handle it. One way or another."

Niko and Jonas gave Amanda the bad news when they returned home.

"What now?" she asked.

"I was the Ghost once. I can be the Ghost again," Jonas told them.

That night, Duke bragged to Shirley about what he had done.

"You didn't," she said.

"I did. This is war."

"And he's a warrior. You're not."

Always jealous of her admiration for Jonas, Duke blustered. "I have enough money and connections to destroy your hero."

"He won't let you hurt his family. He'll kill you first."

"I'm not afraid of him," Duke said.

"Because you're a goddamned fool. He almost killed you once before."

"Things are different now," Duke said.

"They certainly are," she agreed. "He's killed over a hundred men since then."

"I'm not worried," Duke insisted and stomped out of the room. In the foyer, he phoned his head of security. "Put ten extra men on duty guarding the house tonight, and every night until I tell you differently."

"Expecting trouble, boss?"

"Nothing we can't handle."

As forecasted, torrential rain had been falling since midnight. By three a.m. the ground was mud. Dressed for the storm, Jonas crawled atop a low rolling hill overlooking the Hannigan mansion. Heavy raindrops hammered his black, waterproofed Stetson Bozeman. His black pommel slicker and backpack were rain-repellent and provided excellent camouflage. He had charcoaled his face, making him invisible from ten yards. He was alone, having insisted that Niko stay home and watch Amanda.

The rain slashed the ground like razors. Rivulets ran down the slope toward the house. He saw several armed guards patrolling the periphery of the main house and smiled. He had not come for the Hannigans. He had come for Romeo, Hannigan's 1,700-pound Polled Hereford, the best stud bull in Nebraska. He was referred to as *The One and Only Romeo* because he was one of a kind. Romeo was Duke's most prized possession. He valued the animal more than his family.

Duke had built a customized bullpen for Romeo a few hundred yards behind the house. It was a large space determined by observing Romeo's roaming habits. Whatever space he used, he got. The land was enclosed by a pole fence and had a one-bull barn built in the middle. Duke had installed four automatic overhead, retractable doors at each side of the square. In the winter, the doors were closed when necessary, and two wood-burning stoves provided heat. When it was hot, all doors were opened for maximum ventilation. Duke had alfalfa planted for grazing and other tasty plants for Romeo's snacks. The troughs were always filled with the proper amounts of feed for the day.

Tonight, all four doors were open. Duke's orders: *Romeo likes rain. Leave the doors open if the temperature is above forty.*

Jonas crawled through the wet grass toward Romeo's pen. He shimmied under the fence and crab-crawled to the barn. The bull stood stoically, illuminated by the glow of a single gas lamp. When Jonas stepped into the light, the bull snorted.

"Easy, big guy," Jonas said, putting his hand gently on the animal's wide forehead. Romeo was used to humans and had a mild disposition. He relaxed immediately.

Jonas took off his bulky backpack and set it on the ground. He squatted, unbuttoned the top of the pack, and carefully withdrew a six-inch, needle-thin package tightly wrapped in a clean white cloth. He put it in his slicker pocket. Next, he removed two hollow three-foot aluminum poles and snapped them together. It had one pointed end and a J-hook at the other end. He reached into the pack and removed a transparent bag the size and shape of a small pillow, containing a clear liquid. Two more pillow-packs followed, containing darker liquids. Jonas put on two rubber surgical gloves, stood, petted Romeo on the head, and walked to the edge of the shelter.

He needed time to collect his thoughts. He leaned against a support pole and watched the rain. He was reluctant to take the next step, but it was the best way to deal with the situation. He knew Duke wouldn't understand. He was counting on Shirley to explain his actions.

The rain slowed, and a flash fog formed, inches above the cold ground. Thickening and expanding, the fog obscured visibility until the landscape was indistinguishable. He took a deep breath and turned to face Romeo. "You did nothing to deserve this, lover boy."

He removed the wrapped object from his pocket, unwound the cloth carefully, and took out a long syringe. "Sorry," Jonas said and, using both hands, drove the needle deep into the bull's neck, near the muscles above his shoulders. Romeo bellowed in protest and stomped his front hooves. The needle remained embedded in his shoulder, draining its contents. "Relax, big fella," Jonas said. "Just let it happen."

Several minutes passed before Romeo's two front legs buckled. Slowly, his hindquarters followed. The animal's eyes closed as he toppled helplessly on his side. Twice he tried to rise but failed. Finally, the bull snorted and went still.

Now for the worst part. Jonas lifted the javelin with both hands and held it over his head. "You won't feel a thing," Jonas said and stabbed down hard. Romeo quivered. The pole was deeply embedded. "That should do it." Jonas went to his backpack. He removed several items, placing them near Romeo's priceless testicles.

An hour later, the grisly deed was done. Jonas and Romeo were covered with blood. Jonas snapped off the rubber gloves. He took one last look at the bloody bull, then made his way out of the pen into the high grass.

At five o'clock the next morning, the ground fog still blanketed the Circle H when Carson Bodine parked his pickup truck in the gravel lot near Romeo's pen. The sixty-five-year-old ranch hand felt like eighty. He'd been a cowboy since fifteen, and it showed in his weathered face and bow-legged limp. Carson had worked for the Hannigans and Kelleys for thirty years, and now his only job was to take care of Romeo. The life expectancy for a pampered Hereford was about twenty-two years, and Carson expected this to be his last job, which suited him fine.

"Damn fog," Carson said. "Can't see shit."

When he reached Romeo's pen, he whistled between his teeth, waiting to hear the bull's familiar trot. On a clear day, Romeo would quick-step to the fence to get the two apples Carson always had for him in his denim jacket. Carson whistled again. Nothing.

He found the gate with his hands, opened it, and walked tentatively toward Romeo's shelter. Squinting, he finally saw a large mound of... something. The closer he got, the more the mound took shape.

"Oh, my God!" Carson said. Romeo was lying on his right side, his left side covered with blood. His left eye appeared gouged out, raw, bloody goo in its place. There was blood at his throat and a puddle of blood near his backside with hanging entrails where his testicles should have been. "Help!" he screamed, then turned away and stumbled blindly in the direction of the main house.

An armed guard, rifle at the ready, appeared out of the fog. "Carson," he said. "What's the problem?"

"Some sick bastard castrated Romeo and killed him!"

"Oh Jesus," the guard said. "Hannigan will castrate us."

"You were paid to watch the fuckin' bull," Carson said.

"Last night we were all ordered to guard the house, not the bull."

"This is bad," Carson said.

The sun eased up, and the fog slowly lifted. Duke Hannigan came out on his front porch pulling on his boots. His jeans were unzipped, his hair mussed, and his shirt unbuttoned.

"What's all the fuckin' noise?" he asked.

Carson, shaking, told his boss about his prized bull. Duke's ruddy complexion turned pale. Without a word, he led the gathering group to Romeo's pen. They stood at the fence looking at the bull's bloody body on the ground, some thirty yards away. It was a gruesome sight—blood and guts everywhere.

Tears ran from Duke's eyes. His hands were clenched into fists.

"Who would butcher such a magnificent animal?" Carson asked.

"Jonas Hensen," Duke snarled. "That dirty son of a bitch."

"Why would a nice guy like him do a thing like this?" one of the guards asked.

"Because Duke declared war on him and his family yesterday," Shirley said, coming up behind them. She wore a long sheepskin coat over her nightgown. Her arms were wrapped around her midsection to ward off the morning chill. She wore bedroom slippers and looked hungover.

Duke was seething. "Come see what your war hero did."

She looked at the bloody heap in the pen before saying, "Jonas Hensen would never do that."

"Why? He butchered over a hundred Germans, didn't he? You said so yourself."

"That was war."

"This is war, too!" Duke screamed. "And I'm gonna kill him. Did everyone hear me? I'm gonna kill Jonas Hensen for this."

"Don't be killing no one just yet," Carson said. "Romeo's rising."

Everyone turned toward the pen. Romeo was standing now on wobbly legs, shaking his head from side to side. Snorting, confused.

"What the fuck?" Duke shouted.

Carson held up a hand like a traffic cop. "Let me go to him first," he ordered. "He knows me."

Carson rushed to Romeo's side and patted his forehead. "My poor baby," he said, and squatted down to check for testicles. Carefully, he removed clumps of sticky entrails from the area until he uncovered the bull's balls. Caron stood up. "His jewels are fine!" he announced. A cheer erupted. "Everything's fine. None of the blood is his. It's all been faked."

"The cows will be thrilled," one guard said, getting a laugh.

"What's so funny?" Duke snapped. "Who would fake slaughter a prized bull?"

"Jonas Hensen," Shirley said. "This he would do. To warn you."

Duke dismissed the other workers. He and Shirley walked toward the bull and stopped a few feet away. "Okay, how did he do this and why?" he asked.

"How?" Shirley repeated and looked around. "Seems like he left you a blueprint. First, he gave Romeo a sedative by injection. The needle is still in his shoulder, for chrissakes."

Duke looked at Romeo's shoulder and nodded. "I missed that," he admitted. "How did he keep him asleep all night?"

"He hung a slow-drip sedative from that pole," Shirley pointed.

"I didn't notice the pole or the bag," Duke confessed, embarrassed.

"You didn't see a goddamn thing."

"I was too upset. But I don't understand. Why didn't he just kill Romeo?"

"Jonas wouldn't kill for spite," Shirley told him. "He staged all this to warn you—give you a chance to back down."

"I won't back down," Duke promised. "He caught me by surprise. Won't happen again."

"Of course, it will," Shirley said. "You declared war on a warrior and went to sleep. He went to war. What did you expect?"

"Okay, so I'll hire a warrior to kill him."

"You damn fool," Shirley cursed her husband. "You just told twenty witnesses you were going to kill Jonas Hensen. If something happens to him now, you'll be blamed and lose everything—your fancy houses, your bull, and your whores."

Duke finally realized Hensen had *him* by balls, not Romeo. "What does he expect me to do? Apologize?"

"No. Just call off your dogs. Leave his family alone."

"I can't. It's a matter of pride."

"No, it's a matter of time ... before he kills you."

"He hasn't got a chance. I have every advantage."

Just then, Carson approached carrying a small pouch. "Sorry, boss, I just found this near Romeo. It has your name on it."

Duke snatched the pouch and opened it. A startled look crossed his face.

"What is it?" Shirley asked.

"Nothing," he said, knowing it was everything.

"Bullshit," she said. "He left it here for a reason."

"Forget it," Duke said, putting the *Equalizer* in his jacket pocket. He had lost it years ago—never expecting to see it again. It was a reminder to Duke that he was no match for Jonas Hensen—even with every advantage.

The next day Duke dropped all charges against the Hensens.

Niko approached Jonas.

"Why didn't you just kill the bull?"

"There was no need."

"That man deserved it."

"Maybe. But the bull didn't."

"You would have taught Hannigan a lesson."

"I taught him two lessons. One—where there's life there's hope—two, death is final and ends all negotiations."

CHAPTER 22

1936–1939
MEYER LANSKY

Beth was despondent when she went to Boston to attend Simmons College in September. The abrupt and violent end to her relationship with Niko had traumatized her, and her parents hoped a change in environment would help her recover. Her acceptance to Simmons had been bought and paid for, but she had no real desire to go. Her father forced the issue by flying to Boston with her and moving her into the ornate Lenox Hotel two weeks before school opened. He told her, "See the city. Enjoy yourself. Forget that half-breed bastard."

She learned her way around Boston by taking long, solitary walks. As usual, men were attracted to her, but she wasn't interested. She missed Niko terribly—half-breed or not.

Walking through the Public Gardens one Sunday, she made eye contact with a handsome young man who reminded her of Niko. He approached her. He was tall, not as tall as Niko. He was handsome, not as handsome as Niko. But he would do.

He introduced himself. "Hi, I'm Lucho Romero."

She noticed he had an accent. "I'm Beth Hannigan. Where are you from?"

"Peru. I'm a senior at Harvard."

"You must be very smart."

He shook his head. "My father is very rich and influential."

"Like my father," she said.

They spent the afternoon together, and by the end of that time, Beth felt a spark. Beguiled by his resemblance to Niko, she went with him to his apartment in Cambridge that night and tried to fall in love again. It didn't happen. Lucho was a good lover, but after the sex, she began to cry.

"Was I that bad?" he joked.

"No," she said and told him about Niko. "I used you, and I'm sorry."

"It was my pleasure," he told her—grinning.

"No. I'm serious," she said. "I'm very unhappy."

"I can make you happy," he said

"Not with sex," she said. "This was a mistake."

"I have something better than sex."

"What?"

"I'll show you," he said and went to the bathroom, returning with a cloth pouch. She watched him shake a small amount of white powder from the pouch onto the back of his hand between his thumb and index finger. Then he sniffed the powder up to his nose. Gradually, his smile broadened, and his eyes grew glassy. He leaned back on his pillow and closed his eyes. "Beautiful," he sighed.

"What is it?" she asked, fascinated.

"Cocaine, a plant my family grows and processes in Peru," he told her.

"What does it do?"

"It takes away all the sadness."

"Can I have some?"

Duke Hannigan had been a Nazi sympathizer since Adolf Hitler became chancellor of Germany in 1933. When American Nazi, William Pelley, campaigned for President of the United States in 1936, Duke enthusiastically supported him. He sent a $2,500.00 donation to Pelley's campaign headquarters in Nashville, North Carolina along with an application for membership in Pelley's Silver Shirt Legion. The Legion was an American version of Hitler's Brown Shirts in Germany. A few weeks later Duke received a letter from Pelley, thanking him for his generous donation, welcoming him to the Silver Shirts, and asking if he would consider starting a Chapter in Nebraska. Duke jumped at the offer and began asking associates in Lincoln County to join him. He was encouraged by the number of potential members he found and reported his results to Pelley. A campaign worker responded, asking for his patience while they focused on the Presidential election.

When Pelley received less than 1,600 votes, he abandoned his presidential aspirations but increased his political activism. Duke remained an ardent supporter, corresponding and regularly donating to Pelley's organization. In the summer of '39, his persistence was rewarded. He received a phone call from Pelley himself, telling him that a Nebraska Chapter of the Silver Shirts Legion had finally become a priority.

✤ ✤ ✤

September 3, 1939, was a clear, warm Saturday in Lincoln, Nebraska. The University of Nebraska's football season was to open September 30, against Indiana at Memorial Stadium in Bloomington. Jonas and Niko were anxious for the games to begin. The previous season had been a disappointment for Nebraska. Several key players were injured, leaving a young and inexperienced team to stumble to a 3-5-1 record. Niko had never been part of a losing team and hated the feeling. He hoped the '39 season would be better.

That afternoon, Niko sat with his parents in the house they were renting, reading newspapers. Niko was looking at a two-day-old *Lincoln Union Star* with the headline:

EUROPE AT WAR— GERMAN PLANES BOMB POLISH CITIES

"Germany attacked Poland," he told Jonas. "War is coming."

"War is here," Jonas replied. "Look at this." He handed Niko the *North Platte Ledger.*

CATTLE BARON FORMS SILVER SHIRTS
Meeting September 10—Legion Hall—2:00 pm
William Dudley Pelley, National Founder of the pro-Nazi Silver Shirts, has announced that Duke Hannigan of North Platte has been appointed President of the Silver Legion's Nebraska Chapter. Mr. Hannigan, a well-known businessman and civic leader, said over two hundred people have joined his chapter.

Mr. Hannigan purchased the defunct Farmer's Union Hall building in North Platte and has converted it to the Silver Legion Building.

It will be used for meetings and education. "I expect hundreds of concerned citizens to attend the Grand Opening of our new facility on September 15," Mr. Hannigan said. "I urge all who support a white Christian America to join us. In New York City and Minneapolis, Silver Shirt Chapters have been attacked by Jewish gangsters and closed. We will not tolerate Jewish gangsters in Nebraska."

"Why did Jewish gangsters attack Silver Shirts in those cities?" Amanda asked.

"There are a lot of Jews in New York and Minneapolis," Jonas said. "Meyer Lansky in New York and Davie 'The Jew' Berman in Minnesota are very dangerous men."

"Meyer Lansky," Niko said. "I've heard that name before."

"He's infamous. Maybe you saw his name in the newspapers."

Niko shook his head. "No, I remember someone telling me something about him."

"Whatever it was, it wasn't good," Jonas said.

"Nazis in North Platte isn't good either," Amanda said.

Jonas nodded. "Maybe we should contact Meyer Lansky for his help," he joked.

Amanda laughed. "You have his number, don't you, dear?"

Jonas laughed. Niko didn't. He removed his wallet from his back pocket, thumbed through the contents, removed a worn piece of paper, and handed it to Jonas.

"Three years ago, this phone number led to Meyer Lansky."

"You're joking," Jonas said, looking dubiously at the number. "Why would you have Meyer Lansky's phone number?"

"It's not *his number*," Niko explained. "It belongs to a friend of his." He told them about Renee Leonard on the *Queen Mary.*

"Interesting story," Jonas said. "But we're not calling Meyer Lansky."

"Why not?" Niko said. "There must be a reason I kept this note for three years."

"Maybe you were interested in that Leonard woman," Jonas guessed.

"No, that's not it," Niko denied the implication. "I forgot all about her until now."

"Maybe it's fate," Amanda said.

"Maybe it is," Niko said. "I think I should call the number. If no one answers or it's been disconnected, we'll drop it. If she's there, maybe it is fate."

"Go ahead," Jonas said. "What have we got to lose?"

Niko placed the call through an operator. A woman answered.

"Renee Leonard?" the operator asked.

"Who's wants to know?"

"You have a long-distance call from North Platte, Nebraska."

"Is this a joke?" Niko heard her say.

"Renee, it's Niko," he shouted over the operator. "We met on the *Queen Mary*. Don't hang up."

"Niko? Tall, dark, and handsome Niko who wouldn't let me seduce him?"

"Madam, are you Renee Leonard?" the operator interrupted.

"I am. Niko, baby. Having second thoughts about me?"

Niko laughed. "Of course. I'm twenty-one now."

"Legal and gorgeous. What can I do for you, sweetheart?"

He told her, concluding with, "I heard what Lansky did to the Silver Shirts in New York. I was hoping Digger could convince him to help us here."

157

"Sweetheart, Digger's a hindrance, not a help."

"Wasn't he at the Silver Shirt riot in New York with Lansky?"

"Yeah. He threw a guy out a window," she said. "He hates Nazis. But that doesn't mean he's going to travel to half-assed, Nebraska, to fight them."

Niko heard a gruff voice ask, "Who ya talkin' to?"

She covered the mouthpiece to explain. Niko heard a gruff voice say, "Give me the fuckin' phone. Hey kid, you think I care about Nazis in Bum Fuck, Nebraska?"

"It's North Platte, Nebraska," Niko said. "Not Bum Fuck or half-assed."

"What makes you think I give a shit?" Leonard growled.

"You're a Jew. You've already fought the Silver Shirts in New York City. If they succeed this time in Nebraska, they'll be back in New York, stronger than ever."

"Maybe," the gangster said, slightly mollified. "Why do you care? You Jewish?"

"No, but I'm half-Gypsy. We're on Hitler's shit list too."

"Lucky us, huh," Digger said. "But why call me?"

"You've done this kind of thing before."

"Yeah, and it ain't easy," Digger said. "People get hurt. People get killed. I don't suppose a nice guy like you ever killed a man?"

"I killed four—Nazis guarding a concentration camp," Niko said.

"No shit. You saw a concentration camp?" Digger sounded impressed.

"Yes. It was awful. Men, women, and children rotting away and dying."

"Nazi cocksuckers," Leonard said. "Let me think about this. I'll get back to you."

Renee was back on the line. "Charming, ain't he? Give me your phone number."

He did. "Renee, this meeting is on September 15. Will he get back to me in time?"

"I'll make sure he does. One way or another."

A week of worrying passed slowly. Finally, Renee called.

"Hey, handsome. Digger says not to worry."

"What does that mean?"

"Don't worry."

CHAPTER 23

1939
DUKE

Saturday, September 15, 1939, was a perfect day for a parade. At noon the air was crisp, the sky was clear, and the mood festive. The mile-and-a-half parade route would weave through the center of the city, and the rally would be held in front of the new *Silver Legion Center.*

William Pelley could not attend but sent the Legion's Silver Trumpets Marching Band. Crowds lined the sidewalks. Niko and Jonas waited outside the new Center, uninterested in the festivities, caring only about the message.

"Big crowd," Niko said.

"Parades are free. People are curious," Jonas answered.

The sound of a bass drum in the distance announced that the show was beginning. It took twenty-five minutes for the parade to turn the corner onto Rodeo Road where Jonas and Niko waited. The band looked ceremonial, wearing black campaign hats, silver shirts tucked into black Jodhpur pants, tucked into high black boots. There was a scarlet "L" on the left front of the shirts. As soon as the band came into view, the trumpets began blaring "*When the Saints Come Marching In.*" The crowd cheered.

"Are they cheering the music or the Silver Shirts?" Niko asked.

"We'll see," Jonas said.

Following the brass band came a band of bigots; stern-faced Silver Shirt soldiers, wearing the same uniforms. Jonas estimated there were a hundred of them.

Duke Hannigan, chest puffed, a whistle in his mouth led the silent soldiers. "Looks like a goddamn peacock," a farmer said.

"They all look silly if you ask me," his wife said, giggling.

One soldier carrying a Christian Patriots banner received a smattering of applause, but the man carrying the Silver Legion L flag next to the American flag was jeered. "That flag don't belong next to ours," a man shouted.

God bless Nebraskans, Jonas thought.

The march stopped at the new Center with a snare drum flourish and sparse applause.

Niko surveyed the crowd. "See any Jewish gangsters?"

"What do they look like?"

"Skull caps and machine guns."

Jonas laughed. "Did you really expect them to come?"

"I thought Lansky might do something after hearing from Leonard."

"*If* he heard from Leonard. You can't trust gangsters."

An elevated wooden stage had been erected in front of the Center. Jonas thought of the one erected in front of city hall twenty years ago, to welcome him home from the war. *Two sad occasions*, he thought.

The Silver Trumpets marched off to the side of the stage while the Silver Shirt soldiers formed a protective perimeter around it. They stood at attention, faces impassive, watching the crowd.

Duke marched up three wooden steps and stood behind a lectern. He tested the microphone and smiled. Before he could speak, angry voices came out of the crowd.

"Hannigan, take down those Nazi flags!"

"Go live in Germany if you like it so much!"

"Hey, Duke, where's Adolf?"

Hannigan leaned closer to the microphone. "Sergeant Simms, our flags are upsetting some people. Lower them, please. We're here to make friends."

The crowd cheered as the flags were lowered.

Duke waved in response to the cheers. "Welcome to the opening of the Silver Legion Center," he said. "We hope this building will become a symbol of a new world order."

His words were greeted with conservative murmuring.

"Most of you here have known me since I was a kid..."

"We didn't like you then either," a man shouted, getting a laugh.

Hannigan nodded and smiled deferentially. "I know I wasn't very popular in those days, but I always loved my country—"

"Why didn't you fight in the war like I did?" shouted a one-armed man.

More cheers.

"Nebraskans can smell bullshit a mile away," Jonas whispered to Niko.

Undaunted, Hannigan tried again. "The Army classified me as a key man in a vital industry. My family worked around the clock to feed the troops... at no profit."

There was a smattering of applause from the uninformed.

"He's lying," Jonas whispered. "His family made a fortune overcharging the military."

"Hey, Hannigan! If you're such a patriot, why represent Germany?" a man shouted.

"We don't," Duke answered. "We represent American Christian patriots."

"Your organization endorses Nazis and Fascists!" another yelled.

Before Duke could respond, a light flashed from a second-floor window of the Center behind him, followed by a muffled percussive *boom*.

"What was that?" a man asked—startled.

"Part of the show, I guess," another said.

"Sounded like a bass drum," a woman commented.

Another flash—another muffled boom—then another and another—ten in all—in rapid succession. Five from the right and five from the left, meeting in the middle. *Wow! What a show!* Fascinated, the crowd held its breath, waiting for a finale. They didn't wait long. Slowly, the left side of the Silver Legion Center sagged. Then the right. Then the middle. With a *whoosh*, a rumble, and a cloud of dust, the entire building collapsed inward until a heap of debris was all that remained. A reddish dust wafted over the stunned observers, making them all resemble faded bronze statues. No one screamed. No one was hurt. Everyone was stunned.

"What do you think?" Jonas asked Niko. "Poor construction or Bruce Leonard?"

"My money's on Bruce Leonard," Niko guessed and smiled.

His smile vanished when they learned that an elderly security guard was stationed inside the Silver Legion Center. Zebalon "Buster" Brown, was nowhere to be found. Thinking he could be buried in the rubble, Niko and Jonas worried they were indirectly responsible.

"What should we do?" Niko asked.

"Let's wait till they search the rubble, and we know more," Jonas suggested.

The search began and much to everyone's relief, Buster straggled into town later that afternoon while the search for him was still in progress. Buster told the three cops on the scene that he'd been kidnapped at gunpoint by two bulky, masked men in trench coats and fedoras. "They blindfolded me, put me in a car, and drove out of town. Told me if I cooperated, I wouldn't get hurt."

"What did you do?" the top-ranking cop, a Captain, asked.

"I ain't hurt."

"How did you get away?"

"They let me go."

"Just like that?" the Captain asked.

"No. They drove me about two miles short of Sutherland. Let me out on the side road and gave me a couple of sandwiches and water. Told me, if I was smart, I'd stay out of North Platte till late afternoon. So here I am, late afternoon. I ain't stupid. I hitched a ride to town."

"You think they were Jewish gangsters Duke was talking about?" one of the cops asked.

"I wouldn't know a Jewish gangster from a Hindu one," Buster said.

"When could the building have been wired to explode?" the third cop asked.

"Workers were coming and going all the time," Buster said.

"Why bother to kidnap Buster?" the first cop asked. "I don't get it."

Jonas did. "They didn't want anyone to get hurt," he volunteered.

"Gangsters don't care if people get hurt," the cop disagreed. "That explosion could have killed a bunch of us."

"You're wrong," Jonas argued. "That wasn't an explosion. It was an *implosion*...no flying objects or collateral damage. Right, Captain?"

"That's right," the captain agreed, taking advantage of Jonas's tactful hint.

"And that's why they took Buster out of danger," Jonas added. "No injuries."

"Why would gangsters care?" a cop persisted.

"They were here to kill an idea—not people. They were sending the Nazis a message."

"What message?"

"Get out of our town," Jonas suggested. "You're not welcome here."

"Speaking of Nazis," Niko interjected. "Has anyone seen Duke since the implosion?"

No one answered.

Searchers combed the wreckage, and no bodies were found. Duke Hannigan was missing. Police began an investigation.

Niko and Jonas returned to Lincoln. A month later, Randi Renart moved out of North Platte with her mother and daughter. She left no forwarding address. Eli Hannigan told Elvis he was leaving town to start a new life. He wanted to separate himself from the family and the business. He didn't know where he was going. "I'll contact you with a bank to wire my trust money," he said. "I'm not coming back."

"What if Dad comes back?"

Eli didn't answer.

Chapter 24

1941
SHIRLEY

On New Year's Day, 1941, Nebraska lost the Rose Bowl 21 to 14 to an undefeated Stanford team. Niko was frustrated. "We should have won," he told Jonas. "We were better."

"We got outcoached," Jonas took the blame. "We weren't fully prepared for the T."

"The T formation is just trickery," Niko disagreed. "It's not football."

"It is now," Jonas countered. "The sport changed, and we didn't."

"Don't blame yourself, Dad. You're a great coach."

"Not today," Jonas insisted. "None of us were. No excuses. We got outcoached. It won't happen to me again. I hope you learn a lesson from this loss, so I won't feel so bad."

"What lesson?"

"Don't be afraid of change—embrace it," Jonas advised his son. "Try new things—find a better way. Can you do that?"

"Sure, but…"

"No buts about it, Niko, and no excuses," Jonas insisted. "Promise me you'll learn from my mistakes and not repeat them. If you do that, you can change this loss into a win."

"Okay, Dad, I promise."

Niko made All-American and was accepted to Nebraska Law School. As promised, Jonas got his coaching job back at North Platte High, and the Hensen family returned to North Platte. Jonas spent the summer learning the T formation and planned to implement it at the high school for the coming season. Niko found work at Bailey Yard and did the suggested reading for his first year of law school. He found contracts and wills boring and thought maybe law wasn't for him.

On a Sunday afternoon in late August, the doorbell rang. Amanda answered. Jonas was in the kitchen with Niko when he heard Shirley Hannigan's voice. He hurried to the front door, joining Amanda. "Hello, Shirley," he said. "This is a surprise." He hadn't seen her in years. She was still pretty but looked worn. Standing next to Shirley was her son, Elvis, who looked like he'd been in a fight and lost. His eyes and lips were swollen, and he had several stitches on his cheek. "I'm sorry to intrude, Jonas," Shirley said, her lower lip quivering. "I didn't know where else to turn."

"Come in," Jonas said. "Amanda, this is Shirley Hannigan."

"I've heard so many nice things about you," Amanda said, smiling.

Shirley returned her smile, wanly.

"I know you've met Niko," Jonas said.

"Under difficult circumstances," Shirley said, embarrassed.

Niko nodded but said nothing.

"What brings you here?" Jonas asked. "Is this about Duke?"

"No. Duke is still missing. This is about Beth," she said, on the verge of tears.

Amanda led them to the kitchen, where they sat at the kitchen table. Niko remained standing. Shirley leaned against her son's shoulder. "This is hard for me," she said. "I don't know where to begin."

"Is Beth okay?" Jonas asked.

"No, she's not," Shirley said, but couldn't continue. She began to cry.

Elvis took over. "Beth's in Boston in serious trouble," he said. "She's a drug addict."

"Oh, my," Amanda said. "How did this happen?"

"It's been going on for years," Elvis said. "I knew she was using drugs, but she made it sound like a casual thing. I was so busy with my mother's health, my father's disappearance, and the ranch, I didn't pay enough attention to Beth."

"I've been such a burden for him," Shirley said. "I drink too much, and Elvis has to take care of me. I feel terrible."

Amanda rubbed Shirley's shoulder in sympathy.

"Start at the beginning," Niko said, wondering where this was going.

Elvis began. "During Beth's first year at Simmons, she met a Peruvian guy going to Harvard, Lucho Romero. He introduced her to cocaine. His father grows the stuff in Peru. Apparently, they're big-time."

"Did she tell you this originally?" Niko asked.

"She mentioned him. Not the drugs."

"When did the trouble start?" Niko asked.

"It was gradual," Elvis said. "She stopped coming home for holidays, claiming she had too much schoolwork or social stuff. I sensed something was wrong but ignored it."

"I was drinking too much to notice," Shirley confessed, lowering her eyes.

"It came to a head a few weeks ago," Elvis went on. "She called—sounding desperate. Told me she was totally addicted and was trading sex for drugs with Lucho and his friends. She said they had started abusing her and wouldn't let her go. She asked me to come get her. She gave me the address."

"Why didn't she call the police?" Niko asked.

"Lucho terrified her, warned her not to go to the police, threatened to kill her if she did. She thought maybe I could buy her way out. I went there to do that. Figured they'd be happy to get rid of her. I never expected what happened."

"What *did* happen?" Jonas asked.

"I knocked on the door and was met by this Lucho guy," Elvis began. "He insisted Beth wasn't there. I offered him money for her, and he refused, said he didn't need my money. When I tried to push by him to search the house, two muscular guys with shaved heads rushed into the room, and the rough stuff started. It was three against one. I'm lucky they didn't kill me."

"Who slashed your face?" Niko asked. "It looks like a knife wound."

"It is," Elvis nodded. "There was this fourth guy. Little shit. Dressed all in black. He came into the room last. I was already beaten up and barely conscious. He made a big show of his knife. Cut my cheek for no reason and said the next time it would be my throat. They threw me down the front stairs. Lucho said I was a dead man if I came back."

"Dear God," Amanda said, touching Shirley's shoulder. Shirley cried softly.

"Why do they even want her?" Jonas wondered.

"It's a power thing, Dad," Niko answered. "Drug dealers are like Nazis, you can't reason with them."

"Why did you come to us?" Niko asked.

"It was Elvis's idea," Shirley said.

"I saw you fight once," Elvis explained. "I think I need your kind of help."

"I know we have no right to ask this of you," Shirley said.

Jonas intervened. "Shirley, you can always ask me for help," he told her. "We go back a long way. But I can't speak for Niko. Do you want to get involved, son?"

"Not really," Niko said. "I don't like the Hannigan's politics."

Elvis understood. "Niko, the only Nazi in our family is my father," he insisted. "I swear."

"It's true," Shirley agreed. "We all hated what he was doing ... even Beth."

Niko glanced at his father. "You can believe Shirley," Jonas told him.

Amanda spoke up. "I want to help, but it's Niko's decision."

Niko nodded. "Okay, Mom, I'll help— but on one condition."

All eyes were on him when Niko turned to Shirley. "Mrs. Hannigan, you have to stop drinking," he told her and the rest of the people in the room. "I won't bring home one addict to live with another addict. They'll enable each other, and it won't work."

Now all eyes turned to Shirley.

"I don't know if I can stop," Shirley admitted, her voice shaking.

"You can get professional help if you need it," Niko suggested. "But, if you want me to take the risk of rescuing Beth, those are my terms."

Shirley gritted her teeth. "Okay. I'll do it," she committed herself.

"Then we have a deal," Niko confirmed.

"Good. When do we go to Boston?" Jonas asked.

"*We* don't, Dad," Niko said. "*I do.* You're staying here with Mom like I did the night you visited Romeo. Elvis, I'll want you to come. When can you leave?"

"Any time you want."

"Okay. Check the flight schedules. Omaha to Chicago to Boston, I guess. Let me know."

"I'll get right on it," Elvis promised.

When the Hannigans departed, Jonas asked Niko, "Won't you need help?"

"No. The drug dealers will need help," Niko said.

Niko planned to arrive in Boston late in the day and use the cover of darkness to escape. They booked flights accordingly and used the travel time to talk. After they had boarded the first plane, Elvis asked Niko, "Do you have a plan?"

"I want to get as many of these guys in one room at one time," Niko explained. "It's easier to take out multiple opponents in a small space."

"Maybe not," Elvis said. "Those muscle guys were really strong."

"I know how to use their strength against them. Don't worry."

"How can you be so sure of yourself?"

"I was trained for this—since I was a kid."

"Can I ask you a question?"

"Sure," Niko told him.

"When you flipped me over your shoulder, years ago, did you take it easy on me?"

Niko nodded. "I didn't slam you to the ground as hard as I could have."

"That's what I thought. You could have killed me; I'll bet."

"Yes," Niko said. "But I didn't want to. I hated your father, not you."

"What about these guys holding my sister. What will you do to them?"

"Whatever it takes."

"Would you kill them?"

"If that's what it takes," Niko said. "Can we talk about something else?"

"Sure," Elvis said, and they were silent for a moment. Niko glanced out the airplane window. Middle America's farmland looked like a multi-colored quilt from this height. Elvis broke the silence. "How did you kill the four Nazis in Germany?"

"I thought we were finished talking about killing."

"Last question," Elvis promised.

"I broke one guy's neck, stabbed one, cut a throat, and shot another."

"Amazing," Elvis said, folded his arms across his chest, and closed his eyes.

They transferred planes in Chicago and arrived in Boston at dusk.

CHAPTER 25

1941
BETH

They took a cab from Logan Airport through Sumner Tunnel to the North End and headed west. "Their house is in Brookline about a half hour away," Elvis said, obviously nervous and wondering how Niko could be so relaxed.

Finally, after a prolonged silence, Niko said, "Tell me about these guys again."

"Okay. Lucho is tall and well built." Elvis began.

"How tall?" Niko interrupted.

"Not as tall as you and not as big either."

"Is he quick?"

"Hard to tell. I was overwhelmed by the two muscular guys."

"Describe them."

"Short and stocky. Strong and slow."

"The little guy with the knife?"

"Just a mean little prick. He didn't need to cut me. He wanted to."

"What kind of knife?"

"I don't know. Long and thin."

"Was it a switchblade?"

"No. He pulled it out of a sheath. Why?"

"A sheathed knife can be thrown with accuracy. That's an important detail."

"I'm positive it was in a sheath," Elvis said, then held up his hand. "Wait. Stop here."

The driver pulled to the curb on Beacon Street. A streetcar came out of a tunnel at the same time and passed them on the left. Beacon Street was divided by the tracks, and traffic ran east and west on either side. Elvis paid the driver and led Niko to a side street on the corner. Old apartment buildings on Beacon Street reminded Niko of row houses in London. They turned onto a quiet street lined with modest two-story houses. They walked about two hundred yards before Elvis stopped. "There it is," he said, pointing a few feet ahead, at a nondescript, two-story white house with five steps leading to a front porch. "There's a large window behind that big oak tree," Elvis explained. "It's the living room window. You can see inside from the street."

Niko nodded, calmly assessing the situation.

"What's the plan?" Elvis asked

"I always plan on speed and surprise. But a lot depends on what's going on inside the house. Can we get a closer look?"

"Once we pass the tree, we can see better."

They moved slowly past the tree, dusk providing some cover. The light was on in the living room. "Can't see much," Niko said and tiptoed up the stairs with Elvis close behind. Suddenly, he put his hand back to stop Elvis. Through the window, they saw Beth stumble into the living room, followed closely by a tall young man. "Lucho," Elvis whispered. Beth looked frightened. Lucho grabbed a fistful of her hair from behind, pulled her toward him, and slapped her hard across the face. Niko flinched and clenched his fists. Lucho pointed a finger at her and shouted in her face. Niko couldn't hear him, but he'd seen enough.

"That son of a bitch," Niko said. "I'm going in."

"What about the other three guys?"

"I'm expecting them," Niko said, then looked at Elvis. "You don't have to follow me."

"I'll be right behind you."

Niko moved to the solid front door, bent his knee, raised it to his chest, and rammed the heel of his boot into the center of the wood door. The impact broke the lock, and the door flew open with a loud bang. Niko dashed inside and saw Lucho approaching, a look of confusion on his face. Instinctively, Niko took two quick steps forward and launched himself into the air. The look on Lucho's face turned to terror as he saw a six foot six, two-hundred and twenty-five-pound human projectile hurtling toward his face. Before Niko drove his boot into the startled Peruvian's face, he had decided against lethal force. Lucho had damaged Beth, but he hadn't killed her. Fair is fair. He drove the sole of his boot into Lucho's face with enough force to crush, maim, and render useless, but not kill. Consequently, Lucho's nose flattened, his four front teeth were torn out at the roots, and he tumbled backward, unconscious, but not dead. Niko landed lightly, already looking at the two muscle heads rumbling down the staircase from the second floor. Elvis came to Niko's side, and one of the muscle heads snarled, "You came back—you dumb bastard." He charged. *Untrained street fighters*, Niko calculated. *No problem.* Before he could help Elvis, the second bullet head rushed him—head down—snorting like a bull. Niko sidestepped him like a matador grabbing the back of the man's shirt collar and the back of his belt at the waistband. Using the man's momentum, Niko swung him underhand into the wall behind him. The top of his shaved head cracked on contact with the wall and blood spurted. He dropped to the floor, alive but unconscious.

Niko turned to see Elvis grappling with the other bald muscleman. They were on the floor, trading punches. Elvis was on the bottom, getting the worst of it. The stitches on his cheek had re-opened. Niko went to them, clutched a pressure point in the bald man's shoulder, and squeezed. Tian had called this maneuver the *Dokko*. With the right amount of pressure on the right nerve, it rendered a man unconscious instantly. *Lights out.* The muscle head went limp, and Niko yanked him off Elvis. He held him up just enough to reshape his face with a thunderous right fist to the mouth. More blood. More teeth. "He'll stay unconscious longer," Niko explained the last punch. They were face to face when Elvis looked over Niko's shoulder and shouted, "Niko, look out!"

Niko whirled in time to see a small man, dressed in black, finishing a throwing motion. *Shit*, Niko thought, knowing he was about to be impaled by a knife. He felt Elvis grab him from behind and yank him downward. The knife entered high and deep in his left shoulder—six inches above his heart. Elvis had saved his life.

Niko wrestled free from Elvis's grip. Without hesitation, he yanked the knife from his left shoulder with his right hand and, in one continuous motion, he flung the knife backhand at the little man in black. It struck him directly in the heart—killing him instantly. He died with a look of disbelief on his face.

Niko slumped on a chair, his shoulder burning. "Shit, I'm slowing down," he said.

Elvis examined the wound. "It missed your vitals."

"Thanks to you."

"It's the least I could do," Elvis said, focused on the wound. "We have to stop the bleeding." He hurried from the room and returned with towels. "Found them in the kitchen," he explained as he staunched the bleeding.

"We need to get out of here," Niko said, standing. He took one of the towels and went to the dead man in black. He wiped his fingerprints from the knife handle protruding from the man's chest. Then he went to Beth, who was sitting in a catatonic state on the sofa. She stared blankly ahead, only partially aware of what was happening. Niko sat next to her, holding a towel against his wound. Her eyes tried to focus on him. Her pupils were dilated, and her nostrils were white with powder. "Beth?" he said.

She recognized his voice through the fog. "Niko. You're here."

"I'm here too, Beth," her brother said.

"Elvis, you came back." She smiled. "How nice." Her eyes closed.

In a bathroom upstairs, Elvis found boxes of bandages. "They must have been expecting bloodshed," he said, shaking his head. He dressed Niko's wound and helped him into a clean shirt from a closet. "Lucho's," he guessed. "It almost fits." Niko bandaged Elvis's cheek after washing it. "We're a mess, huh," Elvis said.

"And we're the winners," Niko joked. They both laughed, more in relief than victory.

It was dark outside by the time they were ready to leave. Niko rechecked the condition of the four drug dealers.

Three were still unconscious and badly wounded; the man in black was dead. Niko emptied a glass of water on Lucho's bloody face. His puffy eyes opened slightly. Niko knelt beside him. "Listen to me, asshole," he said. "You didn't kill Beth, so I didn't kill you. But one chance is all you get. If you and your two friends aren't out of this country by tomorrow, I'll kill you both. Understand?"

Lucho nodded. "But I have three friends," he mumbled.

"You *had* three friends. Now you have two. You also had front teeth. Now you don't."

Lucho closed his eyes and hoped this crazy man would be gone when he opened them again.

They put Beth between them, with each of her arms slung over one of their shoulders. They dragged her out of the house and down the steps. "They won't let us on a plane like this," Niko said.

"Maybe we should let her rest overnight," Elvis suggested. "I stayed at a hotel last time I was here. It's a short subway ride from here."

The trolley driver eyed them suspiciously when they boarded but said nothing.

They got off at the next stop, Kenmore Square, and Elvis led them to the Braemore Hotel. They took adjoining rooms, and the clerk asked no questions. Beth shared one room with her brother, and Niko took the other. They dropped Beth onto one of the twin beds, and she was asleep in minutes.

"She's still a beautiful woman," Niko said.

"Yes, on the outside," Elvis said. "Inside she's a mess."

They washed Niko's wound again and re-bandaged it. "You didn't lose much blood, and the wound is clean," Elvis said. "You'll be all right till we get to Nebraska."

"I need some sleep," Niko said. "I'll leave the adjoining door open if you need me."

"Thanks, Niko," Elvis said. "You were amazing tonight."

"You too," Niko said and crawled into bed.

Beth awoke in the middle of the night, disoriented. She knew Niko was near. She had heard him say he would be in the adjoining room and that she was still beautiful. She slid out of bed and staggered to the adjoining room. She saw him in bed. *He's still beautiful too.*

She undressed and got into bed next to him. He grew hard in her hand, and she mounted him, carefully manipulating him inside. He moaned, between asleep and awake. She moved slowly at first then faster until his eyes snapped open. "Oh, Jesus," he said, exploding in her. He gasped for breath. "What have you done?" he asked, shoving her off him.

"I wanted you," she said, her mind muddled and jumbled.

He was disgusted. "It's always about what you want. What if you get pregnant?"

"I won't. I promise."

From the adjoining room, Niko heard Elvis call, "Is my sister with you?"

"Yes," Niko answered. "She was just leaving."

Not soon enough.

CHAPTER 26

1941–1942
WAR II

On December 7, 1941, the Japanese attacked Pearl Harbor. The following day, President Roosevelt declared war on Japan. December 11, Hitler declared war on the United States. The world was at war for the second time in the twentieth century.

Niko phoned Jonas after the attack and again after the war declaration. "Dad, I know you're anti-war, but I'm dropping out of law school and enlisting in the army."

"I always said survival was the only good reason to go to war," Jonas reminded him. "You've got that reason now."

"Thanks for understanding. I'm enlisting in Lincoln right after we hang up."

"Okay, but listen to me carefully," Jonas urged. "You have to insist on being stationed in Europe, not the far east."

"Okay. But will they listen to me?"

"Make them listen. If necessary, ask for the highest-ranking officer on duty. This is very important. I survived my war and did the most good because I put myself in the right position. You have to do the same."

❧   ❧   ❧

Niko stood in a long line outside the Army Recruitment Center on D Street in Lincoln. Everyone in line was waiting to enlist. But he was not like everyone. He already possessed fighting skills far beyond army standards. He didn't need basic training. He needed special training.

The enlistment hall was designed for mass processing, not individual requests. It wouldn't be easy to get someone's attention. There were long, rectangular tables in the room, manned by sergeants. Every volunteer signed without question until it was Niko's turn. "I only want to fight in Europe," he said to a Sergeant named Posey.

"This ain't a restaurant, kid," Posey said. "You don't get to choose. Sign the paper."

"I'd like to speak to the officer in charge."

"I'm in charge."

"No, you're not. You're a sergeant. I want an officer."

Posey stood. "If you're not going to sign, get out of line."

"I want to enlist, but I want to speak to the officer in charge."

Hearing the exchange, a tall, slim man in uniform, walked behind Posey and stopped. "I'm Captain Unger. I'm in charge. As you can see, we're a little busy right here signing up men like you."

"With all due respect, Captain, there aren't any other men like me here."

"Oh, really? And what makes you special?"

"I grew up in Europe and speak German," Niko said. "I want to serve there."

"The army decides where you serve," Posey interfered.

181

The Captain held up his hand to silence Posey. "How well do you speak German?"

"Fluently."

"Really?" the Captain said, sounding skeptical. "Anything else make you special?"

"I'm an expert marksman and a master of martial arts. I already killed four Nazis."

"That's bullshit!" Posey shouted. "America just entered the war."

Niko told them about Marzahn. "And my father won a Silver Star on the Western Front."

"I was on the Western Front," Captain Unger said.

"Ever hear of the Ghost when you were there?"

"Of course," Unger said. "I think his name was John ..."

"Jonas Hensen," Niko interrupted.

"Yeah, that sounds right. What about him?"

"He's my father."

Captain Unger raised his eyebrows in surprise then said, "Come with me, young man."

On January 20, 1942, Adolf Eichmann arrived at the Wannsee Villa, northwest of Berlin, for a meeting with fifteen military and civilian officials. It was very cold and overcast. Eichmann gave his overcoat and gloves to an SS man at the door, blew into his hands, and rubbed them together. He nodded to fellow officers and strode purposely toward General Reinhard Heydrich. Eichmann looked prosaic—Heydrich impressive.

The General was six feet six inches tall, blond, with an autocratic deportment. Known as The Hangman, he was one of Hitler's favorites. His ice-blue eyes were as cold as the frigid weather. Standing in front of the large, blazing fireplace, dressed in his black SS uniform, Heydrich looked like an Aryan executioner. Eichmann looked like an accountant. He was thirty-four and balding, with aquiline features, more Semitic than Aryan. He was of unimpressive height and weight. Only his SS uniform and rank indicated his importance.

Eichmann and Heydrich were completely different, bonded only by one maniacal order from their maniacal Fuhrer: plan and expedite the extermination of millions of non-Aryan sub-humans like the Jews, Gypsies, Slavs, homosexuals, sickly, insane, and all enemies of the Third Reich.

Eichmann gave the Nazi salute. "Heil Hitler."

Heydrich returned the greeting. "Eichmann. How is your family?"

"Fine, sir. Klaus is six, Horst is two, and Vera is expecting again."

"Excellent. Have you chosen a name?" Heydrich asked, his smile disingenuous.

"For a boy, Dieter. For a girl, Gertrude."

"Strong Aryan names. Very good."

Eichmann nodded respectfully. "Thank you, sir."

The large fire, tended by an SS sergeant, crackled and glowed but did not generate enough heat to warm the chilly room.

Heydrich directed Eichmann to an unoccupied area near a rear window. Outside, thin, ice-encrusted tree limbs, buffeted by icy winds, tapped the rear windows like skeletal fingers. On Great Wannsee Lake, whitecaps raced across the black water.

"Your latest statistics were impressive," Heydrich said.

"Thank you, sir."

"Hitler's plan for extermination is working well, then?"

"Yes, sir," Eichmann said. "Auschwitz can kill twelve thousand people a day, Treblinka and Dachau about seventy percent of that. Belzec half, Sobibor, Chelmno and Majdanek, perhaps twenty-five percent."

"Excellent," Heydrich said. "How can I help?"

"We can only fit a hundred and twenty people per railcar."

"So, you need bigger railcars?"

Eichmann nodded.

"Done," Heydrich said, looking at his watch. "I will start the meeting soon. As recording secretary, you are not to write the word *extermination* at all. Not once. We'll talk about it but nothing in writing. Substitute innocuous words for incriminating ones. Understood?"

"Understood," Eichmann said.

Heydrich called the meeting to order. "We are here to discuss the Fuhrer's new extermination policy issued in October."

Eichmann wrote: *Meeting Purpose—Discuss immigration policy.*

For ninety minutes, the group discussed extermination methods. Eichmann took notes creatively. *Gas became chemicals; concentration camps—detention centers; ghettos—ethnic neighborhoods; killing efficiency—productivity.* At the end of the meeting, Heydrich spoke in confidence. Eichmann stopped writing.

"Lieutenant Colonel Eichmann was chosen to supervise this effort because of his efficiency and his knowledge of Jews. Those fools trust him. We estimate there are eight million

Jews and more than eleven million other *Untermenschen* to exterminate. He needs your cooperation. Any questions?"

There were none.

Eichmann felt important. Heydrich felt like God.

While the Nazis were planning the death of millions of unwanted European Jews, one unwanted Jew was born in Boston on January 20, 1942. "It's a boy," the doctor said, knowing the mother would not be happy.

"I wanted a girl," Ida Zorn whined. "I don't want a boy."

The doctor held the baby upside down and slapped his backside. The infant cried.

"You should slap his father's ass, too," the dour woman said. "This was his idea."

Dr. Harold Reitman pitied Harry Zorn and his newborn son. They would never be able to satisfy this irascible woman. "Be thankful," he told her.

"For what? In Germany, we owned banks. We lived in a mansion. We were envied by others. Now I have nothing."

"You have your family."

"My family," she snapped. "My husband's a failure, and now I have a fat little boy who'll grow up to be a fat little man—a loser like his father."

"Be thankful you're alive. Many Jews in Germany have lost their lives."

"I lost my life too. We were rich. Now we're poor. My brilliant father can't find a decent job in this country because his English is not good enough. My husband can't pass the CPA exam because he's stupid."

❧ ❧ ❧

Harry Zorn had always been fat. Growing up in Boston, the other kids called him *fatso, tubby, fat boy, lard ass*. He learned to live with it. He met Ida while attending Northeastern University in Boston where he majored in accounting. She was working in a coffee shop nearby.

It was never about love with Harry and Ida. It was about settling. She didn't like his appearance, but when she learned a CPA could make a decent living, he looked better. They married in 1940. By 1941, he had flunked the CPA exam twice. Harry accepted his failures, but Ida felt victimized. *He tricked me*, she thought and never forgave him.

The baby squalled again. "He's hungry," the assisting nurse said.

"Don't look at me," Ida said, crossing her arms over her flat chest. The cries grew louder. "Make him stop," Ida wailed.

"I'll get him fed at the nursery," the nurse said and scurried away.

"Don't feed him too much. He's fat enough already," Ida shouted.

"It's baby fat," Dr. Reitman said. "He'll grow out of it."

"His father never did."

The doctor changed the subject. "Have you chosen a name?"

"Harry wants Isadore in memory of his father, Israel. I hate that name."

"Which one? Isadore, Israel, or Harry?"

"All of them."

"Mrs. Zorn, why did you have a baby?"

"My husband talked me into it. He said we might have a baby girl. My mother died when I was young. He knew I wanted a baby girl, so I could give her what I missed as a child. Instead, I get a fat baby boy to remind me of his fat father."

With the world at war and people mourning death, Ida Zorn mourned life.

CHAPTER 27

1942
NIKO & BETH

The U.S. Army spent twelve weeks testing and ranking two hundred candidates for special assignments. Niko ranked high. "Hensen doesn't know fear," an army psychologist said in his report. "The prospect of killing for a cause doesn't bother him at all." His martial arts instructor reported, "He should be teaching me. He's the best I've ever seen."

Because of his special skills, Niko was sent to Camp X in March of 1942. Located on the northern shore of Lake Ontario and operated by the British Special Operations Executive (SOE), Camp X was originally intended to teach top rated British soldiers the art of sabotage. But the day after it opened, the Japanese attacked Pearl Harbor, dragging the United States into the war and sending America's special warriors to Camp X.

It was two below zero outside when Niko and a hundred other candidates attended their first meeting at Camp X. A British captain addressed them. "Welcome to Camp X," he began. "You're here because you've displayed an outstanding aptitude for what we teach. At Camp X, you'll learn advanced sabotage, subversion, deception, military intelligence, and a wide range of silent killing techniques for assassinations and furtive attacks. We call this place the School of Mayhem and Murder. If you succeed here, you'll be sent to Scotland for more training. If you pass muster there, you Americans will become U.S. Rangers and you Brits will be designated Commandos. Work hard. We need you."

Months earlier, after being rescued by Niko and Elvis in Boston, Beth Hannigan had been able to convince her brother she was in no condition to return to North Platte. "It will break our mother's heart to see me like this," she said. "I need some time to get myself together." Despite Niko's protests, Elvis left her at a detox facility at the Boston City Hospital.

"You're making a mistake," Niko warned, on their trip home. "She can't be trusted."

"I know," Elvis said. "But my mother would fall apart if she saw Beth like this."

Niko said nothing. It wasn't his problem.

After two days in the detox center, Beth checked herself out and disappeared. Weeks later, she contacted Elvis, saying she was living clean in a one-bedroom apartment on Beacon Street and needed money. He assumed she was lying but wired her money anyway. He didn't want her home. What he didn't know was that she was also pregnant and uncertain of the father. She had had recent sex with the four Peruvians in the drug house and several others. Any one of them could be the father, including Niko. There was no way of knowing. What she did know was she did not want anyone's baby.

Her new drug supplier had turned her onto heroin, and she hoped the dangerous substance would kill the fetus. When the drug didn't work, she tried to abort the baby herself with a wire hanger. This only resulted in a raging infection. She took herself to the Boston Hospital for Women, where she was treated with streptomycin and released—still pregnant.

Just die, she begged the life inside her. *It sucks out here.*

She returned to Nebraska when it became apparent she was going to give birth. She contacted Elvis from Omaha and told him her condition and asked for his help.

"When this baby is born, get rid of it. I don't care how," she said.

"You make me sick."

"I make myself sick. Will you help me or not?"

"I'll help," he said, disgusted with her. "You're still my sister."

"Don't tell mother about this."

"I won't. She's still on the wagon. Something like this would ruin everything."

She gave birth in May to a premature baby girl at the Omaha General Hospital emergency room. It was a breech delivery, and the baby girl's right leg was damaged by forceps in the hands of a flustered intern. The nurse tried to show her the baby, but Beth turned her head away. "I never want to see her," she said. When Elvis arrived, Beth said, "Just get rid of her."

"No one will adopt the poor thing," Elvis told her. "The doctor told me she's sickly, drug-addicted, and has a deformed leg. There's a possibility she's deaf and brain-damaged."

"I tried to kill the little bastard, but she wouldn't die."

Elvis recoiled. "We should have left you in that drug house," he said. "I'll take care of the baby, but I'm done with you."

"I don't blame you," Beth said.

Elvis's inquiries led him to the Midwest Institute for Disabled Children, twenty miles northwest of Omaha. The gloomy facility was originally built back in 1840 as a hospital. When it closed in 1901, the state of Nebraska bought it for use as a home for mentally disabled children. Elvis brought the infant to the institute.

"Think of this facility like a nursing home for children—brought here by people who can't or won't take care of them," Richard Gibbs, the Institute director, told Elvis. Gibbs was a pleasant looking man in his fifties, dressed in the white coat of a doctor. "We take care of the basic needs of children with serious mental and physical disabilities. We don't treat their problems—we're not qualified to treat their problems. If your niece is retarded or deaf, as you fear, we can't help her. We're strictly maintenance. We simply maintain them for however long they live. Sounds cruel, I know—but they're far better off with us than if they were wards of the state."

"I understand," Elvis said, hating his sister more. "I'm afraid I have no choice."

"If the mother or father shows up someday and wants the baby..."

"That's not going to happen," Elvis interrupted.

"Alright, then. There are some papers you'll have to sign."

Elvis signed the forms and left Jane Doe in storage, classified as an abandoned baby without identification. He told Director Gibbs that a fund would pay the expenses and gave him his contact number in the event of emergencies. Otherwise, Elvis instructed Gibbs that he expected no contact.

Elvis returned home and never told his mother she was a grandmother.

On the night of May 22, 1942, Niko stood at the open door of a Handley Page Halifax four-engine bomber waiting for the red jump light to flash. He stared into the blackness at fifteen hundred feet. The coordinates were set for him to land in an open field, forty miles northeast of Pilsen, ten miles south of Prague. He was to rendezvous with four Czech members of the Operation Anthropoid team. It was his first assignment as a U.S. Ranger—an assassination of a Nazi general.

The target—Reinhard Heydrich, Hitler's favorite general—Reich Protector of Moravia and Bohemia—part of the Czech Republic under German rule. Photographs of Heydrich showed the perfect Nazi: tall, blonde, imperious looking with a long, austere face. He was cruel and heartless and targeted for death.

Niko felt the plane descending. The red light flashed, and he jumped without thinking. The cold air at a thousand feet slapped his face. He dropped away from the plane, spread-eagled. When he was comfortable, he did an exuberant tuck and roll, head over heels. Then he pulled the ripcord and watched his chute stream up, billow out, and ease him slowly into the belly of the beast.

Niko landed in an empty field, fifteen miles east of Prague. When he'd finished burying his chute, the Operation Anthropoid team came out of the darkness to join him. They introduced themselves: Adolf Opalka, Josef Valcik, Jan Kubis and Josef Gabcik. Using bicycles left for them at a partisan farm adjacent to the field, they began their eight-mile ride on mostly unpaved roads to a safe house in Prague. They arrived without incident and gathered around a table. It was three-thirty in the morning, but they were wide awake, fueled by adrenaline.

"Kubis, tell Hensen the plan," Opalka said.

"You know Heydrich must be assassinated by a Czech," Kubis began.

Niko nodded. "But if all of you are killed first, I am to finish the job."

"Correct," Opalka said. "Go on, Kubis."

"Heydrich lives in Pamanske Brezany, about a twenty-minute drive from his office at Prague Castle. Each day he is driven by SS Sergeant Johannes Klein, a loyal and fierce bodyguard. Heydrich rides in the back of a Mercedes 320 B convertible. The top is always down, and he has no armed escort. He is daring us to kill him."

"And we will," Gabcik said.

"Klein must negotiate a hairpin turn near the Bulovka Hospital," Kubis said. "We've been watching him every day, and Klein slows to almost a full stop to make that turn."

"We will strike there," Gabcik interrupted. "There is a tram station where Kubis and I will be waiting. Valcik will be about a hundred meters north and will signal when the car is near. I will have a Sten under my coat, and when Klein slows, I'll step in front of the car and open fire. Kubis will attack from behind. He'll remove anti-tank grenades from a briefcase he'll be carrying and throw them into the back-seat. They are very powerful grenades. Heydrich will not survive."

"Then we run in different directions," Kubis said. "That's where you come in. You cover our escape. If you survive, you go to a safe house. We will show you the location and fastest route in advance. Any questions?"

"Where will you be?" Niko asked Opalka.

"At the safe house waiting for you. I will handle your escape from the country."

"Okay," Niko said. "Can I see the area before the attack?"

"The location is nearby. We'll go there early. Get some sleep."

"I'll stand guard," Niko volunteered.

"No. I'll go first," Gabcik offered. "I'm too anxious to sleep."

"Okay," Niko told them and was asleep in minutes.

"He's not even nervous," Gabcik gestured toward Niko. "It's not normal."

"If he was normal, he wouldn't be here," Opalka pointed out.

The morning of May 27, 1942, was sunny with good visibility. Niko watched from a doorway across the street from the tram station. He was dressed in workman's clothes and a cap with a brim to shield his face. Gabcik and Kubis were at their positions near the hairpin turn, dressed in old suits.

At 10:30 a.m., Valcik gave the signal. The Hangman was near.

The Mercedes rounded the bend. The top was down, as usual. When the car slowed before the sharp curve, Gabcik stepped off the curb, aimed his Sten gun at Heydrich and pulled the trigger. *Nothing.* The gun had jammed. Gabcik threw it aside and went for his pistol.

"Stop the car," Heydrich shouted in German. He stood up in the back seat, drew his Lugar from a hip holster and aimed at Gabcik. Niko flinched when he saw the barrel flash, but Gabcik did not go down. Heydrich had missed.

Gabcik was aiming his pistol now. Another barrel—flash. Another miss.

Niko saw Kubis approach from behind and throw a large, anti-tank grenade toward the back seat. The grenade fell short, hit the right rear fender above the right wheel, and exploded. The loud blast tore the bumper apart, spewing shrapnel. Heydrich was hit in the lower back and Kubis, the right leg. Bleeding, Kubis limped away.

By now, Gabcik's pistol had also jammed, and he ran.

Niko watched Heydrich stagger from the smoldering car, the back of his uniform soaked with blood. He saw him order Klein to pursue Gabcik before slumping on the car hood.

Now, Niko thought, stepping from the doorway and walking calmly toward the car. Removing his pistol from his coat, Niko aimed at the Nazi's head and fired. Heydrich's head snapped back, and his hat went flying. He went down.

Niko kept walking. *Is he dead?* He wondered. He saw a crowd gathering near the car and four German soldiers, rifles at the ready, running toward the wreckage. Another clear shot was no longer available.

Niko's mind raced. *Heydrich is supposed to be killed by a Czech. If I press the attack now, that possibility is lost. Maybe the blast or the head shot killed him.* He decided it was better for him to live to fight another day and ran off in the direction Klein and Gabcik had gone. Two blocks later he saw Klein on the ground, bleeding profusely from a leg wound. He ignored the Nazi, more concerned about Gabcik's survival. He found Gabcik, a block later, hiding in a doorway. "I shot Klein," he gasped.

"In the leg," Niko said. "He's still alive."

"Damn. Is Heydrich dead?"

"I shot him, but I don't know," Niko said. "We have to go."

They ran off in different directions. Niko found Opalka at the safe house and briefed him.

"So many mistakes," Opalka said, shaking his head.

"Killing someone is never easy."

Two nights later, a small plane landed in an open field near a Czech farm in Pilsen. Niko shook hands with Opalka, wished him luck, and boarded the plane.

Ten days after the assassination attempt, Heydrich died from his injuries. Shrapnel and horse hairs from the car's upholstery had entered his body through his back, and the detritus caused a virulent infection that killed him. A non-fatal bullet gouge was found across the top of his skull, missing his brain by millimeters. Doctors confirmed the blood infection was the cause of death. Heydrich had been killed by a Czech. Mission accomplished.

Operation Anthropoid resulted in the death of one Nazi and approximately 5,000 Czechs. Reprisals were widespread. Based on the false belief that the assassins were from Lidice, Hitler ordered the town razed and all males fifteen and older, killed. The order was carried out on June 10. A hundred and seventy-three men were killed. Eighty-eight women and over fifty children were sent to concentration camps. The town of Lezaky met a similar fate.

The assassins were betrayed by a misguided countryman who disclosed their hiding place in the Cyril and Methodius Cathedral in Prague. Opalka, Valcik, Kubis, and Gabcik were martyred in a fourteen-hour firefight.

So many lives for one. Operation Anthropoid was considered a success.

CHAPTER 28

May 1945
NIKO & KING

On an evening in May 1945, Jonas and Amanda sat reading in their living room. Jonas had a book on the Civil War, and Amanda was browsing through the latest edition of *Life* magazine. The cover featured General Eisenhower and the liberation of concentration camps throughout Europe. The black-and-white photographs sickened Amanda: piles of stick-thin dead bodies stacked like firewood—staring, living skeletons standing near electrified fences, brick chimneys belching smoke fueled by incinerated corpses, ovens still filled with human ash and bones. She turned another page and saw a photograph of General Eisenhower at Buchenwald. "Ike" was surrounded by American soldiers and German civilians who had been ordered to witness the Nazi horror. Amanda scanned the photo and gasped when she saw her stepson standing near Eisenhower. Niko's fists were clenched, his face dark with rage. She handed the magazine to Jonas, who stared at the picture.

"He'll never be the same," Jonas predicted, remembering his own war. "This will change him." A letter from Niko arrived two weeks later, confirming Jonas's suspicions.

April 12, 1945

Dear Mom and Dad, I hope you are well. As for me, I survived the war unhurt physically but damaged emotionally. I witnessed atrocities I had not previously dreamed possible, and I've changed. I no longer believe people are born innocent or that evil is acquired or learned. I believe people like Hitler and his Nazis are born evil and predisposed to do evil things. No amount of teaching or experiences can change that predisposition. Consequently, I now believe it is necessary to destroy evil, at first sight, before it grows into a world-wide menace like Hitler and his Nazis.

To this end, I joined a secret service organization, a new organization created to find and fight evil on behalf of our country. My commitment starts now so I will not be home soon, as planned. I hope you understand.

I am writing from a train to Switzerland, where I will visit Uncle Fredrik.

You and I owe him so much. I will give him your regards.

Love,

Your son, Niko.

Niko had wired Uncle Fredrik from Germany telling him he wanted to visit him in Switzerland. They had not communicated during the war, so Niko was thrilled when he received a cable response: *Can't wait to see you.*

Niko made his way to the winter home of the circus. Uncle Fredrik was outside, talking to workmen when he saw Niko approaching. He raised his arms and shouted, "Welcome home." Niko ran to greet him, and they came together in a ferocious hug. Uncle Fredrik held him for several minutes. Finally, he let go. "Look at you," he said. "All grown up. You look just like your father."

"Much darker, though," Niko said.

"Of course, like your beautiful mother. And how do I look?"

"The white hair becomes you."

"The war gave me white hair. Come to my office; we can sit and talk."

They sat across from one another in comfortable chairs. Uncle Fredrik poured them each a glass of brandy and leaned back. "How long has it been?" he said, then snapped his fingers. "Of course, Hitler's Olympics, 1936. That animal. You were sixteen or seventeen."

"I'm twenty-six now. So, tell me what happened. How did the circus survive?"

"I kept it together with my own money. We were forced to do an occasional show for the Nazis, and then the Allies used us to entertain their men. We survived."

"Did you lose many people?"

"Some. The allied bombings weren't supposed to hit Switzerland, but they did. We had to rebuild and replace. Greta and her horse vanished one night. Tian was killed in a bombing raid."

Niko's eyes burned as he remembered his *Shifu* (skilled master) and the countless hours they spent together. "It took a bomb to stop him," Niko said.

Fredrik nodded. "The same raid killed Stashu the Strong Man and Pieter the Lion Tamer."

Niko was saddened by the bad news. "What about King?" he asked, fearing the answer.

"Still alive—barely. He survived the bombs but not the passage of time."

"Where is he?"

"His cage is in the same place. Do you remember?"

"Of course. Can I have the key?"

Uncle Fredrik didn't hesitate. "He's not a threat anymore."

"He was never a threat to me."

Niko found King lying on his side in his cage. His breathing was shallow, and his exposed flank was moving in and out like a heartbeat. His once regal mane was mangy, and his body was thin and bony. *Look what life does when it lasts too long.*

"King, it's Niko," he said, in the soothing voice he always used with his friend.

The old lion opened his eyes and tried to rise but only got to his haunches.

"I'll come to you," Niko said, opening the gate. He walked to the old lion, sat next to him, and stroked his mane. "Hello, old friend," he whispered. "It's been a long time."

Blink, Blink. King licked Niko's face.

"Did you wait to say goodbye to me?"

Blink, Blink. King purred as Niko scratched his bony frame.

"Remember when you were five hundred pounds of muscle, fangs, and claws. The King of Beasts?"

Blink, Blink.

"Now it's time to let the young lions roar," Niko said and eased King's great head down, so he rested on his side again. He lay next to him, nose to nose and passed his hand gently over King's eyes. There was no resistance, only a deep sigh. They rubbed noses until they fell asleep.

An hour later, Niko awoke. King did not.

Chapter 29

1945
ODINA

Wayazan Winona Wild Wolf's descendant, Odina Knudson, grew up to be breathtakingly beautiful. She was tall and slender with shoulder-length black hair and bright green eyes that glowed like emeralds against her golden-brown skin. Her smile was both innocent and beguiling. She was twenty years old in June 1945 when she reported for a summer nursing job at the Midwest Institute for Disabled Children in Omaha. She had just completed her second year at Creighton School of Nursing.

She met with Director Richard Gibbs in his office. "I'm delighted you're here," he said. "Top-ranked Creighton students typically choose more modern facilities."

"I want to work with disabled children," Odina said.

"You understand, we don't treat patients here. We merely maintain them."

"I still want the experience."

There was a knock on the door. "Your tour guide is here," Gibbs said. A short blonde woman entered. "Nurse Goodman, Nurse Knudson."

The two women shook hands. Physically they were opposites. Odina was nearly six feet tall, long, and loose-limbed. RN Elyse Goodman, barely over five feet, was a tightly wrapped bundle of energy. "We're the long and short of it," Goodman said, smiling. Gibbs was quick to start them on their tour.

"Call me Elyse when we're alone," Goodman said, as they left his office.

"I'm Odina."

"With a name like Knudson, I expected another Nebraska blue-eyed blonde."

"My parents did too," Odina said.

"I hope your mother had a good explanation."

"She did," Odina said. "A Knudson ancestor had married a Sioux Indian girl named Winona Wild Wolf. After four generations of blonde, blue-eyed babies—I arrived."

"Winona had some strong genes, I guess."

"I'm told she was a strong woman," Odina said.

"Did you inherit her strength?"

Odina smiled. "My father said growing up a brown raisin among all the golden sultanas in Nebraska made me strong, like Winona. I also heard she was very compassionate. She was a Wayazan—the healer in her tribe."

"Like a doctor?" Elyse asked.

"More like a nurse. She nursed Indians and whites, alike."

"Did you inherit her compassion?"

"I like to think so. I want to help people."

"We don't help the helpless here," Elyse said. "We're a home for the hopeless."

"If I can help one child, I'll be happy," Odina said.

They walked the shadowed corridors, Elyse talking, Odina listening. The patients are tranquil.

"Are they all sedated?" Odina asked.

"Just the violent ones," she said, pointing. "Like that one. She throws fits and bites."

Odina looked at the girl strapped in a wheelchair. The girl looked back. Odina guessed she was three or four. "What's wrong with her?" she asked.

"What isn't?" Elyse said. "Born drug-addicted. Cried for weeks in withdrawal. Deaf. Retarded. One leg disfigured during a breech delivery. Very sad."

Her eyes seem alert, Odina thought. "Has she ever been tested?"

"I told you, we don't do that here. But her condition is fairly obvious."

"What's her name?"

"No name. We call her Jane Doe."

Jane Doe's eyes followed Odina. *She's trying to tell me something,* Odina thought.

Elyse took Odina's arm. "We have to continue. There's a lot more to show you."

As they walked away, Jane Doe began shaking her wheelchair and grunting.

"She doesn't want us to go," Odina said.

"She doesn't know what she wants."

"I'm not so sure about that," Odina said. "There's something about her."

"There's something about every one of them. C'mon, Pocahontas."

The tour took over two hours. "It's a big place," Goodman said. "We'll review everything tomorrow. I'm going home. You can go too. Where are you staying?"

"The nurse's dorm next door."

They said goodnight in the front lobby. Odina decided to tour the facility again. It was nearly seven when she returned to the second floor where she had seen Jane Doe. She wanted to see her again. The night nurse gave her the room number with an admonition. "Careful. She bites."

Odina entered the dimly lit room. She saw the girl's arms and legs were strapped down to the bed. She switched on the table lamp, and Jane Doe opened her eyes. She struggled against the straps. Odina bent over and looked in the child's eyes. *"I'm in here,"* they seemed to shout at her. Odina recoiled, unnerved. Jane Doe grunted and pulled harder at her restraints. She shook her head from side to side. *"Look at me,"* the child's eyes screamed.

Odina saw a light behind Jane Doe's eyes—a glimmer of intelligence. "I see you," she said aloud, surprising herself. Impulsively, she unstrapped the girl's restraints. Released, Jane Doe lunged. Her arms went around Odina's neck, and her fingers locked like a vice.

Bent over the bed, Odina struggled to free herself, but the girl clung to her like grim death. Fearing she had made a terrible mistake, Odina tried prying the girl's fingers loose but couldn't. She was growing panicky until she felt Jane Doe frantically rub her cheek against her own. It was then she realized the girl wasn't attacking. She was hugging, expressing herself the only way she could. Odina stopped resisting and put her arms around the child, hugged her back and stroked her hair gently. The little girl whimpered and stroked Odina's hair, babbling incoherently. "I hear you, sweetheart," Odina said, straightening her back, lifting Jane Doe with her. "I know you're in there."

❧ ❧ ❧

Odina told the night nurse to contact Director Gibbs at home and tell him to return to the Institute for an emergency. Gibbs arrived within an hour and was amazed to see Odina sitting in an armchair with Jane Doe nestled contentedly in her arms.

"She never let anyone hold her before," he said. "What happened?"

"We made a connection," Odina said. "Watch."

Odina put Jane Doe in her wheelchair, facing her. Odina raised her hand in the air. Jane Doe raised her hand in the air. Odina raised two hands. Jane Doe did the same.

"She understands," Gibbs said, surprised.

"I don't think she has brain damage," Odina said.

The director nodded. "You could be right," he said. "I have to make a call."

Gibbs went to his office, located Jane Doe's file, and phoned Elvis Hannigan. "Jane Doe may not be brain-damaged, after all," he said. "Come see for yourself."

Elvis arrived the next morning. Gibbs took him to view Jane Doe. When Elvis saw the child through a glass window, he gasped.

"Is something wrong?" Gibbs said.

"She looks just like her father," he mumbled—astounded.

"I thought you didn't know who the father was."

"I didn't, back then. But she's changed a lot in four years. There's no doubt."

"Do you think the father knows about her?"

"Definitely not."

"Difficult situation," Gibbs said and rapped on the window gently.

The nurse looked up. *What a beautiful woman,* Elvis thought. Gibbs signaled her. The nurse nodded and performed her mimicking exercises with the child.

"Remarkable," Elvis said. "Who is the nurse?"

"Odina Knudson," Gibbs said. "A student nurse. She has a gift."

"Obviously," Elvis said, fascinated by her. "Where can I make a phone call?"

Elvis used the phone in Gibbs' office to contact Jonas and tell him he needed to come to Omaha with Amanda as soon as possible. "I can't tell you why on the phone. But trust me and come."

"It's a long ride for Amanda," Jonas said.

"Take a plane. I'll pay for the flight. It's important."

"If you say so," Jonas said. "We'll see you tomorrow."

❧ ❧ ❧

Jonas and Amanda arrived at six the next evening. Elvis met them at the airport.

"Elvis, you look different," Amanda said. "I guess I haven't seen you in a while."

"I lost sixty pounds," Elvis said.

"You look great," Jonas said. "Now tell us what's so important? We're worried."

"I'm sorry. Elvis said. "I didn't want to say anything on the phone to influence your reaction. I appreciate you coming based on my word."

He drove directly to the Institute where Director Gibbs accompanied them to the second floor. He pointed through a glass window where Jane Doe and Odina sat facing each other. Amanda's mouth dropped open. "Oh my," she said. "She looks just like Niko."

"I'm glad you see it, too," Elvis said, relieved. "I was afraid you wouldn't."

"It's obvious," Jonas said. "But I'm confused. Who is the mother?"

"My sister," Elvis said. He reminded them of Beth's Boston rescue four years ago.

"Obviously, Niko did more than just rescue her," Jonas said.

"He's not to blame," Elvis said. "This is all my sister's fault."

"Does Niko know?" Amanda asked.

"No," Elvis said. "She wasn't even sure he was the father."

"It was a difficult time for her," Amanda rationalized.

"My sister doesn't deserve your sympathy, Mrs. Hensen," Elvis said. "She contacted me after she gave birth and asked me to get rid of the baby. There was no family resemblance yet. I thought of adoption, but the poor baby was a mess: drug-addicted, infected, deaf, retarded, and a mangled leg from the delivery. No one would have adopted her. I was lucky to find this place. I've been paying for her care for four years, not knowing Niko was the father. All I knew was she was my niece."

"And our granddaughter," Amanda said.

Jonas nodded. "Where is Beth?" he asked.

"Who knows? I wire money to her at various banks. It changes. Where's Niko?"

"Still working for the government. He was in Berlin last week."

"Should we let him know he has a daughter?" Elvis asked.

"He has to be told," Amanda answered.

"I can send a telegram to D.C., and they'll forward it to him," Jonas said.

"He shouldn't hear this news by telegram," Amanda said.

"He should come here like we did, and see for himself," Jonas said. He sent Niko a telegram to the Central Intelligence Group in Washington:

NEEDED IN OMAHA/STOP/
FAMILY OK/STOP/ DAD/END

They provided the Institute's address and phone number. Two hours later, they received Niko's response.

COMING TOMORROW/STOP/NIKO/END

CHAPTER 30

1945
DOROTHY

When he received the telegram from his father, Niko was in Washington, D.C., pending reassignment. He knew his father wouldn't ask him to come to Omaha unless it was important.

The next morning, he hitched a ride on a military plane departing from Bolling Field, arriving in Offutt Air Base in Bellevue, Nebraska at three o'clock. He phoned the Institute when he arrived, told them he was on his way, checked out a government car, and drove ten miles to the Institute.

When he arrived, his parents and Elvis greeted him in the lobby. Amanda was the first to hug him. She held him tight. "I've missed you."

"I missed you too, Mom. You look wonderful."

"Your father won't let me be sick," she said, smiling.

Niko turned to his father and hugged him. "Dad, it's been a while."

"Four years and then some."

"How are you?"

"Pretty good for an old man."

"Elvis, you look great," Niko said, turning to his friend.

"I lost some weight," Elvis said.

"It shows. So, tell me why I'm here."

"Come see for yourself."

Director Gibbs arrived. Elvis introduced him, and they went to the second floor.

Standing behind the glass, looking at the nurse's back and the little girl's face, Niko was furious. "She's about four years old, right?" he said, his face red with anger.

Elvis nodded. "She didn't look like you at birth. I had no idea until two days ago."

"Your sister promised me there would be no baby," Niko said, clenching his teeth.

Elvis told Niko about the failed abortion attempts, the condition of the child at birth, choosing the institution, and the recent breakthrough. "When I saw her for the first time in four years, I knew she was yours. I called your parents for verification."

"Does Shirley know?" Niko asked.

Elvis shook his head. "She's sober but very fragile. I don't want to upset her."

"What about your father?"

"Still missing," Elvis told him. "We're the only ones who know."

Niko glanced at the baby just as Odina turned her head toward the window. *She's beautiful,* Niko couldn't help thinking. "Who's the nurse?" he asked.

"Odina Knudson, a student nurse," Gibbs said. "Very talented. Would you like her to bring you your daughter?"

Niko turned away from the window. "No. I want nothing to do with her."

"Niko, she's yours," Amanda said, visibly upset with him.

"Biologically, yes. Emotionally, no," Niko said.

"Let's move to the conference room," Gibbs said, uncomfortable with this development. "I'll tell Nurse Knudson to take Jane Doe to her room."

The Hensens and Elvis were seated at the conference table when Odina and Gibbs entered. Odina's bright green eyes flashed with anger as she looked around the room. *Very beautiful*, Niko thought—reacting viscerally to her. He stood and said, "I'm Niko Hensen. You must be upset with me."

Odina was awed by his inordinate size, imposing physique, and handsome face. The resemblance between father and daughter was remarkable. *Extraordinary*, she thought, clearing her throat and mind, determined not to be intimidated. "Upset and confused," she said, managing to keep her voice steady. "I'm told you want nothing to do with your daughter."

"That's right," Niko answered, his face impassive.

"How can you be so insensitive?" she asked, her anger flashing.

"You shouldn't judge people you don't know," Niko said.

"I know you're turning your back on your own flesh and blood," Odina said. "What else do I need to know?"

"The whole story," Niko said and sighed. "Let me ask you a question, Nurse Knudson. In fact, let me ask all of you a question. If I was a woman who had been raped, impregnated, and forced to give birth...would you understand if I didn't want anything to do with the baby?"

"Are you saying Beth Hannigan raped you?" Odina asked, incredulous.

"That's exactly what I'm saying. I was asleep when she crept into my bed—half asleep when she had sex with me and not truly awake until it was too late. When I realized what she had done, I made her promise not to have a child if she got pregnant. She promised. She lied. Jane Doe is the result of that lie."

"This innocent child shouldn't pay for her mother's sins."

"Nor should I," Niko said. "I'll send money for her support, but that's all."

"We don't need your money," Elvis said. "I'll handle that. She's my niece."

"You're a better man than I am," Niko said. "I hope you understand how I feel."

"And I hope you understand how I feel," Amanda said, standing. "She's our granddaughter and our responsibility now. She needs us."

"She needs a lot of things," Odina said. "She needs examinations to determine her capabilities and limitations. She needs a name."

"I'm prepared to start right now," Amanda said.

"I'm not. I'm leaving," Niko said. "I took a room at the Omaha City Hotel and have an early military flight in the morning."

"Do you want to meet later?" Jonas asked.

"No. I won't talk about this again," Niko said. "Not now. I'm too upset."

"Then we'll say goodbye, now," his father said. They hugged.

Amanda had tears in her eyes when they embraced. It was an awkward time.

"I'm sorry to disappoint you," Niko said.

"You could never disappoint me," she said. "I understand how you feel. But I don't agree with you. This child is yours … ours really. I can't turn my back on her."

"Do what you have to do," he said, kissed her forehead, and closed the door behind him.

There was a prolonged silence until Odina said, "What just happened?"

"My son is obviously not ready to be a father," Jonas told her.

"He's selfish," Odina said.

"No, he's not," Elvis interjected. "I understand how he feels. My sister lied to him."

"He should still help his daughter," Odina replied.

"He'll help when he's ready," Jonas said. "Right now, we need to focus on the child."

"First, we need to establish a status for Jane Doe," Gibbs suggested.

They agreed to change her legal classification from Orphan Jane Doe to the daughter of Niko Hensen and Beth Hannigan, abandoned at birth by the mother and father. They would petition the state to grant custody to the paternal grandparents.

"The child will need a name," Gibbs added.

Amanda suggested Dorothy. "In Danish—meaning Gift from God."

"I like it," Jonas said. "Dorothy Hensen."

Niko sat alone at a table in the small lobby bar of the modest Omaha City Hotel. He sipped his second scotch on the rocks.

He was still angry. Beth disgusted him; the child offended him; the nurse intrigued him. Odina Knudson—beautiful, compassionate, fiery, and obviously talented. She had looked him in the eye and challenged him. That took courage. She was intriguing, but under the circumstances—impossible.

He closed his eyes and tried to relax but remained restive. He had disappointed his parents and left them in anger. He had never done that before. *I'll write and apologize,* he thought before sensing someone hovering over him. He looked up and there she was. Odina Knudson. Magnificent—breathtaking. He couldn't help smiling. "Nurse Knudson. What brings you here?"

"You."

"Why? Are you going to lecture me on fatherhood again?"

"No. I'm here to tell you what we're doing with your daughter," she told him a half-truth. The whole truth was she had experienced an uncontrollable urge to see him again.

"I thought I made myself clear," he said, his voice calm. "I have no interest in her."

"Will you at least listen?"

He shrugged and with a hand gesture, invited her to sit down. She sat beside him.

"I'm listening."

"We named your daughter Dorothy ... Dorothy Hensen."

"My parents were okay using their last name?"

"It was your mother's idea. They intend to raise her as their grandchild."

"Amanda shouldn't take care of anyone but herself."

"I know about her MD and agreed to stay on as Dorothy's nanny and your mother's helper."

"Big commitment," he said, not hiding his surprise. "And what else?"

"We're arranging medical and mental tests for Dorothy. We're having an ear, nose, and throat specialist determine if her deafness is reversible."

"Is that even possible?"

"In some cases—depending on the cause. See, you *are* interested."

"Don't mistake curiosity for interest."

"Don't you feel anything for her? She is your daughter."

"Yes. I feel pity and anger."

"Nothing more than that?"

Niko stared at her without responding. Looking at her was making his heart race.

"Do you think you'll ever accept her?" Odina finally broke the silence.

Niko sighed. "I can't even accept myself since the war. I've got a lot of issues to deal with … including you."

"Me?" Odina said, feeling butterflies in her stomach. "What did I do?"

"You didn't do anything. To be honest, I find you incredibly attractive."

"Really?" she said, surprised, flustered and flattered— feeling her face get warm.

"Really," he replied, staring directly into her eyes. "I think you're spectacular."

Her heart was pounding now. She said the first thing that came to mind. "I don't know if I like you very much, but I'm definitely attracted to you, too."

They gazed at each other for a moment. Niko blinked first and abruptly stood up.

"Well, our timing is terrible," he told her—sounding contrite. "I'm leaving for Europe soon, and I may not make it back. It's just the wrong time to start a relationship." He removed his room key from his jacket pocket. She noticed the number, 320.

"Good luck with Dorothy," he said, holding out his hand. She took it.

"Please don't go," she said, surprising herself.

He studied her for a moment, then said, "Staying would lead nowhere. I have too many problems to resolve and battles to fight. Sorry about everything."

He turned and walked away. She watched him go. It didn't feel right. Frustrated, she got up and walked slowly toward the exit. As she was about to leave the hotel, she stopped. "To hell with it," she said aloud, turned, and headed for the elevators. She didn't stop again until she was standing in front of room 320. *This is a mistake*, she thought. *I don't even like him.*

She knocked.

"Wait a minute," she heard Niko's voice. When he opened the door, he had a towel wrapped around his waist, and his hair was wet. His body overwhelmed her. He was all sharp angles and ripped muscles. Without clothes, he looked even bigger. Odina thought he was the most beautiful man she had ever seen.

"Sorry. I needed a cold shower," he said. "Did you forget to tell me something?"

"Yes. I'm a virgin," she blurted out.

"You won't be if you come in this room."

Without hesitation, she entered and closed the door behind her.

They embraced and kissed. His towel slid to the floor, and her clothes followed. Making love with Niko Hensen was perfect for her maiden voyage. He was gentle and thoughtful, making her first time a pure pleasure—her second time even better.

Odina was showering when Niko pulled back the curtain and joined her. They dried each other and made love again. This time it was more intense. They knew each other better. She loved every caress, every touch, every kiss—every minute. She gasped and bit his neck at the end.

After, they lay together, her head on his chest.

"We both have such dark skin," she said, holding her arm against his stomach.

"My mother was a Spanish Gypsy," he told her.

"But, Amanda…"

"My step-mother."

She nodded. "We have something in common," she said. "One of my ancestors was a Sioux Indian."

"Two half-breeds," Niko said.

They were silent for a moment.

"Why are you going to Europe?" she asked.

"Can't talk about that—secret stuff," he told her, rolling his eyes. "Let's talk about you."

She told him about Winona Wild Wolf and her own awkward childhood. "I was tall, dark, and clumsy. A brunette among blondes; A scarecrow; Teased a lot. Through it all, I always liked people and always wanted to help. I think I got more from Winona than just her color."

"You have her gift. You gave Dorothy a second chance at life. I wish I had more time to get to know you."

"Don't go away. Hitler, Mussolini, and Tojo are dead. There's no one left to fight."

"There's Stalin, Mao, and the communists. Someone has to stop them."

"Why you?"

"Because I can."

"Please stay."

"I can't."

"I hate you."

"I understand."

In the morning, she had regrets. Mostly she regretted he wasn't there.

PART 2

CHAPTER 31

February 1953
ZIGGY

Eleven-year-old Ziggy Zorn looked like a loser, felt like a
loser, and acted like a loser. Fat, slovenly, and lazy, he
was the bullseye on every bully's target. Even his nickname,
Ziggy, was the work of bullies. His given name, Isadore,
morphed into Icky somehow, then Iggy, and finally, Ziggy.
He didn't like the name, but it was better than Fatso.

Trudging home on a cold February afternoon, one of
those Massachusetts winter days when the sky was the color
of slate and hung low like a ceiling, he was the last one out
of Temple Beth Am Hebrew School. He was a born straggler. The fat kid in school, always last.

It hadn't snowed in a week, but Ziggy was wearing bulky
rubber boots. His mother didn't care that the other kids
teased him about wearing galoshes on snowless streets. She
only cared about having to replace shoes ruined by sidewalk
salt. Ziggy wore a cap with earflaps pulled tightly over his
head, tied securely under his second chin. His tight brown
coat was zipped up to his neck. The zipper pinched the soft
skin of his flabby neck. Under the parka, his shirttails hung
out of his waistband, and his pants were baggy from being

stretched out of shape. His overall appearance could be likened to a bag of dirty laundry. Still, he was Sarah Zorn's favorite person in the whole world, and her devoted big brother loved her like crazy—even though she wasn't his real sister.

Sarah had been adopted by the Zorn's during the Baby Scoop Era, after World War II. A rash of premarital pregnancies had prompted the federal government to encourage the adoption of babies born to unwed mothers. Ida thought she wanted a baby girl and badgered Harry to adopt one for her and insisted it would make her happy. Harry relented, as always, but it was a mistake. He should have known. Nothing could make Ida happy.

Ziggy was three when Harry brought his baby sister home. Ida named her Sarah. "I'm finally happy," Ida announced, with her new blue-eyed blonde baby on her lap. "She's perfect."

Sarah was perfect—perfectly normal. But Ida wanted fantasy-world perfect and with each soiled diaper, cry in the night, and childhood fever, Ida became more disenchanted, until she wanted nothing to do with Sarah at all.

Ziggy filled the void in Sarah's life left by a delusional mother. For five years, Ziggy and Sarah were inseparable. She was his best friend—his only friend, really, and when she fell seriously ill a week before her eighth birthday, Ziggy was devastated. He would never forget that awful morning Sarah awoke screaming. "Ziggy, I can't move." Then the doctor's nightmarish pronouncement; "Sarah has polio," followed by his mother's accusation, "You picked a sick one, Harry. It's your fault."

Harry said nothing. It was pointless.

Sarah was put in an iron lung, with only her head and face visible. The rest of her little body was in a seven-foot-long, eight-hundred-pound cylinder. Pumps underneath the apparatus went up and down, hissed and breathed for her.

"Ziggy…" she paused while the machine hissed. "Why can't (pause—hiss) I move?"

"You have an infection, Sarah," he told her. "The doctors will make you better."

But they didn't. Sarah got worse. She could only speak when the machine exhaled, fifteen times a minute. Ziggy visited her every day and brought little gifts. He entertained her with finger puppets. Sometimes she would laugh. It was a forty-minute walk to the hospital, but Ziggy didn't care. He never missed a day. On weekends Harry would drive him and Papa Franz. Ida never visited. Ziggy loved that little girl so much. And she loved him.

Daydreaming about his sister, Ziggy carelessly dropped his Hebrew book on the ground. *Shit. Am I supposed to kiss the book?* He wondered. *I forget the book-kissing rule. So many unexplained religious rules. Like standing and sitting during services. The congregation will please rise.* Why? *Be seated.* When? A few pages later, *Rise-Sit-Rise-Sit-Rise-Sit.* He felt like a Jewish-Jack-in-the-Box. *Who made up these rules?* He picked up the book and kissed it, got dirt on his lips, and spit it out. *Fuck.* Ziggy cursed silently. He never cursed out loud, but it gave him a sense of power when he did it silently. Subliminally, he was a blasphemous pirate.

He hated Hebrew school and the idea of a bar mitzvah. There was too much to learn. He wasn't stupid. He was lazy and unmotivated. *No matter what I do,* he rationalized, *I'll still be me. So, why bother?*

He lived on Westbourne Terrace, off Washington Street and when he turned onto the street, he hoped the one-eyed cat he fed yesterday would be near the playground again today. The scrawny animal had hissed at Ziggy when he first approached, but Ziggy won him over by sitting at the curb and sharing his Baby Ruth candy bar. Today, he had little scraps of meat and cheese he had taken from the school cafeteria, wrapped in a napkin he had hidden his pocket. He sat on the curb, took out the package, and waited.

The cat appeared within minutes from under cardboard boxes. He rubbed against Ziggy's jacket and purred. Ziggy fed him with one hand and petted him with the other. When the food was gone, the cat snuggled against the boy for warmth. Ziggy thought about bringing him home, but knowing his mother would never allow an animal in the house, he abandoned the idea. He struggled to his feet, and the cat skittered away. "Stay warm," he said and started trudging home again.

He lived in a three-bedroom apartment with his father, mother, Sarah, and his maternal grandfather, Franz Goldschmidt. Across the street from their apartment was the paved playground of the Driscoll School. Two of Ziggy's classmates, Anthony Martignetti and Daniel Ross, were playing basketball at a solitary basket with no net. *Someone should put up a net,* Ziggy thought. *Not me, of course. But, someone.* He watched the two boys play. Ross was the better athlete. Things came easy for him—he was blessed. A good student, a good athlete, and handsome. He wondered how Ross would do if things ever got hard for him.

Despite the cold, the boys wore short sleeve jerseys. Ziggy envied their slim, athletic physiques. His body was made of jelly, and he had bigger boobs than the girls at school. The boys teased him, and he would laugh…but inside, he cried and raged. *You think I wanted this body, you, assholes?* Ross and Martignetti never teased him. They were indifferent. In his world of negatives, indifference was a positive.

When he turned to leave, he saw three boys approaching he didn't recognize. He knew most everyone in this insular Jewish neighborhood, so these three had to be invaders. *Let's see,* Ziggy thought. *Florid faces, little noses, light hair, thin lips, and mean expressions. They were the worst—Irish invaders.*

Brookline was ethnically divided. The Irish ghetto was Brookline Village and Whiskey Point. *What kind of a name is Whiskey Point?* The lower-middle-class Jews occupied the area from Coolidge Corner to Cleveland Circle. Jews with money lived in South Brookline. If Jewish kids wandered into Whiskey Point, they were lost, looking for an escape route. If Irish kids wandered into a Jewish neighborhood, they were usually looking for fat Jewish boys to pummel.

A pugnacious Irish kid put his red face into Ziggy's space. *Gargoyle ugly,* Ziggy thought—but said nothing.

"You a kike, fat boy?" the Irish kid asked.

"A what?" Ziggy asked, wondering why the kid had no upper lip. Or did it just look that way.

"A Jew," the Irish kid snarled.

Should I answer or pretend to be deaf?

"Hit him, Sean," another marauder said.

The third kid knocked the Hebrew book out of Ziggy's hand, onto the ground.

Okay, now you have to kiss it, Ziggy thought. The boy stomped on the book.

Okay. Forget the kiss.

Kevin tried again. "Hit him, Brian."

What's with this kid?

"Anybody ever tell you you're a fat shit, Jew boy?" Brian said.

No, asshole. You're the first to notice.

Brian pushed him, and Ziggy fell. *They won't kick a man when he's down.*

Brian kicked him. *Shit. Try crying.* He began crying, but Brain kicked him again. *Try the unconscious routine.*

Before he could feign unconsciousness, he heard Daniel Ross say, "Leave him alone."

Saved, Ziggy thought.

"Looks like another Jew, huh, Sean?" Brian said, agitated.

"Definitely," Sean concurred. "You looking for trouble, Jew boy?"

Without a word, Ross punched Sean in the mouth, and Sean went down.

He's dead, Ziggy thought.

CHAPTER 32

1953
GOLDSCHMIDT

Sean wasn't dead. He had plenty of life left in him. He got up and charged Ross, trying to tackle him. They wrestled to the sidewalk and grappled to a draw. In the meantime, Brian and Kevin had attacked Martignetti. While Brian held Martignetti from behind, Kevin tried to line up a clear punch, but Martignetti struggled mightily, twisting and turning.

"Hold him still, Brian," Kevin said.

"I'm trying."

Two against one, Ziggy thought. *Someone should do something. Not me, of course, but someone.* Ziggy saw a smaller boy appear out of nowhere, running toward them. *Run the other way*, Ziggy thought. But the kid kept coming. He had short, sandy hair, a compact, thin body and a cut on the bridge of his nose. Without hesitating, the little kid jumped on Kevin's back, wrapped his left arm around the bigger boy's neck, and began punching him in the face with his right fist. *Unbelievable.*

"What the fuck?" Kevin said, trying to free himself.

But the little kid hung on, like a bronco rider, punching Kevin's face like a woodpecker; *Bap, bap, bap.* The right side of Kevin's face turned red and lumpy. He began to bleed from a cut above his right eye. Choking, Kevin dropped to his knees. The woodpecker tightened his grip. "I can't breathe," Kevin gasped.

"You give up?" the kid asked.

"Fuck you."

Bap, bap, bap.

"Okay, I give up … you little shit."

The kid released Kevin's neck and slid down his back to the ground. Kevin fell face first in the dirt, gasping for air, bleeding from his nose and above his eye. The little kid stood behind him. Calm. He was shorter than all of them. *How did he do that?* Ziggy wondered. *That was amazing.*

Ross and Sean had disengaged by now and were on their feet, glaring at each other. Martignetti had Brian in a headlock on the ground, content with his advantage. When Kevin collapsed, Martignetti released Brian and stood up. "Pick up your friend and get out of here," he ordered.

They picked up Kevin. "We'll be back," Sean said, without conviction.

"Can't wait," the little kid said.

The Irishmen withdrew, undoubtedly to fight another day—but not here.

"Thanks," Martignetti patted the little guy's shoulder. "What's your name?"

"Eddie Perlmutter."

"How old are you, Eddie?"

"Almost nine."

Nine? No way. Ziggy thought.

"You just beat the shit out of a twelve-year-old," Martignetti told him.

"No big deal."

"Yes, it is," Martignetti enthused. "You could be a prize-fighter someday."

"Nah. I'm gonna be a cop."

"Then the robbers are in trouble," Martignetti predicted.

He helped Ziggy to his feet. "You okay?" Martignetti asked. Ziggy nodded, wiping tears from his eyes. Ross said nothing. He was upset. The fight hadn't gone the way he thought it would. Things hadn't come easy this time. Ziggy could tell Ross was flustered. He walked away,... rattled. Martignetti followed.

"Stop crying, for chrissakes," Eddie said to Ziggy. "Next time, fight back."

Ziggy hung his head, and his body language said, *There's no fight in me.*

Eddie got the message. "Hey, it's your life," he said and departed.

Ziggy dragged himself up three floors. The moment he entered the apartment, his mother screamed. "You split your pants! You think it's easy finding pants for a fatty like you?"

He knew she hated him for being a fat little boy instead of the pretty little girl she thought she wanted. *Why don't you ask what happened?* He wondered. *Why don't you ask if I'm okay?*

"What happened to you, Isadore? Are you okay?" Papa Franz asked.

His mother's father was as kind as she was cruel; a hero in the Great War—for the wrong side. A wealthy bank owner in Germany, he had been banished from his homeland, forced to leave his fortune behind. On the ocean crossing to America, he had thrown his war medal into the Atlantic and never looked back, unlike his daughter.

Papa Franz sat at the kitchen table with Ziggy's father. Harry Zorn resembled a forlorn Humpty Dumpty. A good man in a bad life and a cheap suit. An underpaid bookkeeper, he had failed the CPA exam five times. Ziggy told them about the fight, explaining how Eddie Perlmutter had intervened.

"He's only nine years old and half your size," Ida interrupted. "You're pathetic. Like your father."

"Stop it, Ida," Papa Franz ordered. He was the only person who could silence her. Muttering, she put dinner on the table, slamming down each plate. The only sound after that was clinking silverware and chewing. No conversation. Ziggy and Harry hunched over their food devouring mountains of mashed potatoes and piles of pot roast in gravy. Papa Franz sat with perfect posture and ate with discipline. He had lived a disciplined life, fought a wasted war with distinction, worked hard for success, and had been a devoted husband to his late wife, Ilsa. He regretted not being a better father to his only child, Ida. He looked at her across the table, and his heart ached. Ilsa had been a beautiful, compassionate woman. Ida was a mean-spirited, homely caricature of her mother. He watched her peck at her food with quick, vulturine movements and turned his attention to Ziggy. "How do you feel, Isadore?"

"I'm okay, Papa," Ziggy said, smiling vapidly. "Eddie Perlmutter's really brave. He's not afraid of anything."

"What are you afraid of, Isadore?" Papa Franz asked.

"Everything, I guess."

"Why? You're a big boy," his father said.

"I'm not big, Dad. I'm fat."

"You can lose weight and learn to defend yourself," Papa Franz said.

"I'd rather avoid trouble. It's easier."

"Sometimes you can't avoid trouble. Like today."

"I'll be more careful from now on," Ziggy said, thinking about Eddie Perlmutter's heroics again. "Who's the bravest person you ever knew, Papa Franz?"

His grandfather thought a moment. "An American soldier known as, the Ghost."

"Why the Ghost?"

"He was invisible to his enemies until it was too late," Papa Franz said.

I wish I was invisible sometimes, Ziggy thought. "What was his real name?"

"Jonas Hensen. He killed over a hundred soldiers, most with his bare hands."

"Wow! Did you ever fight him?"

"No. We met after the war."

"If you did fight him, you would have won. Right?"

"In the air, maybe. The ground, no. He was unbeatable. He was also a good man."

The phone rang. They got very few calls. *Sarah*, Ziggy thought, worried.

The phone continued ringing until Harry picked it up. He listened, said, "Okay," then hung up. "Dr. Schimmel says we should go to the hospital right now. Sarah's failing."

"I bought her a present," Ziggy said. "It will make her feel better." He ran to his room and returned with a light brown teddy bear.

"You idiot," his mother said. "She's dying. She doesn't need this." Ida wrestled the bear from Ziggy and threw it in the trash.

Ziggy said nothing and wondered if other kids hated their mothers.

CHAPTER 33

North Platte 1953
DOROTHY

The air was redolent with the smell of cabbage, cauliflower, and kohlrabi from nearby farms. Odina sat on a rocking chair on the front porch of the Hensen house, watching eleven-year-old Dorothy approach. She was returning from school, and there was no mistaking her awkward gait. Her left leg was bowed, rail thin, and an inch shorter than her right. A custom shoe, with a one-inch lift compensated for the difference, but she would never have a normal stride. Still, she was a miracle. Seven years ago, she was thought to be mentally and physically impaired, unable to walk, talk, or hear. Now she did all those things, and she did them well.

Dorothy reached the front porch and crawled onto Odina's lap, rested her head on her nanny's shoulder, and sighed.

"Hard day at school, love?" Odina asked, stroking Dorothy's long brown hair.

"Sixth grade's hard, Nanny O," Dorothy sighed, using her special name for Odina.

"It's not easy being number one. Don't forget where you started."

Dorothy would never forget her silent, empty world before Nanny O saw the light in her eyes. She could still recall the doctor in Omaha removing gobs of wax from her ears before repairing her perforated eardrums and treating her infected inner ears with penicillin. She would always remember Odina's voice as the first sound she ever heard and that voice teaching her everything she'd missed in her isolation. They were like a mother and child, with Dorothy's birth coming the moment Odina saw the light. They were inseparable and talked about everything. No subject was off limits. Still, everyone was surprised one night at dinner when Dorothy asked, "Nanny O, are you a lesbian?"

"Dorothy," Amanda raised her voice, which she seldom did. "Where did you hear that word?"

"At school in Current Events," Dorothy said. "It was in our *Weekly Readers.*"

"That's what they're teaching in school, nowadays?" Amanda couldn't believe it.

"Only once," Dorothy said. "There was an article in the *Reader* about the people President Eisenhower said were not allowed to work for the federal government."

"And that word was on the list?" Amanda asked.

"Not just the word lesbian," Dorothy explained. "The list included criminals, immoral people, drunks, drug addicts, and sexual perverts. Mrs. Thompson, our teacher, explained sexual perverts to us, including homosexuals and lesbians."

"It's wrong to teach that at school," Amanda said. "I'm going to complain."

"Better she learns it from a teacher in school than from kids in the schoolyard," Jonas suggested.

"At her age, she shouldn't be hearing these things at all," Amanda disagreed. "And why would you think your Nanny O is one of those … you know."

"Lesbians?" Dorothy said, without embarrassment. "I'm not even sure what a lesbian is. I think it's a woman who doesn't have a man, like Nanny O."

"It's true I don't have a man," Nanny O agreed, "But I'm not a lesbian."

"You don't have to talk about this, Odina," Amanda interrupted.

"I don't mind. I want Dorothy to have it explained the right way."

Odina then carefully explained women with women to Dorothy. She stressed love, not sex, as the primary reason. "I don't think it's a choice someone makes," Odina concluded. "It's just who they are. But, it's not who I am."

"Okay, so did you have boyfriends when you were my age?" Dorothy asked.

"No. I was skinny, awkward, and homely. The boys teased me a lot."

"I get teased, too. When does it stop?"

"When you change, or they change," Odina told her.

"So, you never had a boyfriend?"

"No. I was too angry at boys."

"Were you ever in love with a man when you grew up?" Dorothy asked.

"No," Odina said. "I was very attracted to a man once, the most handsome man I ever saw."

"Really? What did he look like?" Dorothy was excited to know.

"He was big and beautiful, like an oak tree," Odina said. "I never met another man like him—before or since."

"What happened?"

"Nothing. He was beautiful on the outside but troubled on the inside."

"Uncle Elvis is beautiful inside and out," Dorothy said. "Could you love him?"

"I do love him," Odina said. "Like a brother. There are all kinds of love."

"Love is very confusing," Dorothy said.

"Yes, it is," Odina agreed. "Let's talk about something else."

"Let's eat," Amanda suggested, relieved.

After dinner, they moved to the living room and listened to the Philco radio. The voice of Perry Como serenaded them with "Don't Let the Stars Get in Your Eyes." "How about putting on the news with John Cameron Swayze?" Jonas asked.

"I don't want to hear about President Eisenhower's golf game," Amanda made a face.

They laughed and continued to listen to Perry Como, followed by Frank Sinatra and Tony Bennett. After Odina put Dorothy to bed, she rejoined the Hensens.

"I never heard you mention a special man before," Amanda said.

"It wasn't worth mentioning," Odina said.

"I couldn't help thinking you were describing Niko," Amanda said.

"Why would you think that?" Odina asked, nonplussed—totally unprepared.

"Yeah, why?" Jonas asked, equally surprised.

"Her description," Amanda explained. "*Big and beautiful like an oak tree. The most handsome man she ever saw.* Who else fits that description besides Niko?"

"No one I know," Jonas admitted. "But, maybe Odina's got someone else in mind."

"I don't think so," Amanda teased a little. "I remember the way you looked at him the first time you saw him."

"That was years ago," Odina pointed out. "And I was nasty to him."

"That you were. But I could tell you were a little awed by him," Amanda recalled. "He has such an imposing presence."

"Maybe, so," Odina said. "But it's irrelevant. We had nothing in common."

"How do you know?" Amanda asked. "You were only focused on Dorothy."

"She was the only one who mattered, at that time," Odina defended herself.

"Odina's right," Jonas interrupted. "It is irrelevant. Niko's been gone for years."

"He might come back," Amanda rationalized.

Jonas shook his head. "Not likely," he said. "He's still at war with evil."

Amanda noticed that Odina's face had turned red when Niko's name was mentioned, and she knew he was the man she was talking about. *Why do we always want what we can't have?* She wondered, remembering how long she had dreamed of a man so long ago. *Sometimes dreams do come true.*

CHAPTER 34

1953
NIKO

Niko stood by the second-floor window of the American Embassy in Tehran. Outside, a CIA-instigated riot raged. Code name, Operation Ajax. "Look at the fuckin' mess we've made," Niko said. "I'm ashamed of myself."

"You're taking this too personally," fellow CIA agent Richard Price said.

"Remember this date, August 15, 1953. America will pay for this riot someday."

"You make it sound like we're the bad guys here, Niko."

"We are. We're sponsoring the overthrow of a legally elected prime minister. Muhammed Mosaddegh is a good man, and we're replacing him with a corrupt shah?"

"I understand," Price said. "Mosaddegh wants Iranian oil to benefit Iranians and the CIA thinks that's un-American."

"That's not funny."

"You're right. It's ludicrous. The shah will allow America to maintain control of forty percent of Iran's oil at the expense of the Iranian people, to the benefit of big oil. *That's* the American way. We're just doing our job."

"Our job sucks."

"Yes, but we're good at it," Price joked. A Harvard graduate, Price was one of many CIA agents from the Ivy League. Of average height, weight, and appearance, Price preferred cerebral solutions to violence—but killed when necessary. He was Niko's best friend in the agency, a fellow cynic with a sense of humor. "Besides," Price continued, "the agency's done much worse than this. How about my job in Germany after the war—smuggling Nazis out of Europe? Me. A Brooklyn Jew. Did that make any sense?"

"None," Niko agreed. "And you weren't very good at it either. Three out of four of your prisoners died in their cells."

Price shrugged. "Nobody's perfect," he countered. "And fuck those Nazis, anyway."

"Nazis are yesterday's news," Niko said. "Now we have communists."

"Right. The CIA says Mosaddegh's a communist."

"The CIA is full of shit. Mosaddegh's no communist. He's just tired of the U.S. screwing Iran. He wants Iranian oil controlled by Iranians."

"As I said, that's un-American," Price joked.

"Still not funny," Niko replied, turning from the window and walking to the door.

"Where are you going?"

"To join our men in the streets."

"Kermit wants us to stay inside," Price reminded him.

"Fuck Kermit Roosevelt, our illustrious Far East director," Niko cursed Teddy's grandson.

"Like it or not, the President's grandchild has ordered us to stay indoors today."

"I didn't hear him say that. Kermit has to speak up." Niko disregarded the warning and went outside.

The protesters were marching toward Prime Minister Mosaddegh's house, and Niko stayed on the fringe of the crowd. A U.S. built tank, driven by an Iranian, fired its cannon at random government buildings. Facades crumbled. Niko watched a man stumble from a recently hit building. He was bleeding from the head and holding his hands to his ears as if he had gone deaf from the explosion. It was a living nightmare, conceived by the CIA.

Niko recognized several mercenaries he had recruited, marching side by side with gangsters he knew. He heard talk that six hundred people had already been killed. *Could that be true,* Niko wondered, feeling sick.

The crowd reached the Prime Minister's house, and a gun battle erupted. A tank shell exploded, knocking down the front wall of the house. Inside, in what looked like a foyer, a chandelier lay smashed on the floor along with marble statues. A sofa was on fire. Paintings on the walls were shredded. Chunks of rock and glass were scattered throughout the grounds. Niko was upset to see Mosaddegh being hauled from the house, bloody and bewildered. The man only wanted what was best for Iran. The CIA only wanted what was best for America. Disgusted, Niko headed back to the Embassy. He'd seen enough.

As he passed an alley strewn with rubble, he heard a woman scream. He ran into the alley, picking his way through the debris. In a clearing, he saw three men attacking an Iranian woman and a young girl. One man was sitting on the girl's chest, slapping her face repeatedly. Her dress was torn and lifted to her waist. The other two men had the older woman exposed, and one was mounting her.

Niko went berserk and rushed to the child. He grabbed her assailant by the back of his shirt collar, pulled him to his feet, and spun him around. The thug's eyes were glazed with lust, and Niko recognized that he had recruited him. His name was Amin.

"Hensen," Amin said. "Let me go. You can have her next."

He thinks I'm like him, Niko thought, aghast. He grabbed Amin by the throat with one hand. The Iranian's eyes bulged with panic. "Okay, go first," he rasped.

Niko tightened his powerful grip, crushing Amin's windpipe. The Iranian's body went limp, and Niko tossed him aside like a ragdoll.

The two rapists across the alley had heard the commotion and were coming to Amin's aid. They saw Niko discard their friend's body and turn toward them. They froze. He recognized them: Farhad and Hassan, two CIA recruits.

"Hensen, what have you done?" Farhad said, staring at his friend on the ground.

Niko charged them. When he was within striking distance, he slammed the palm of his hand upward, into Farhad's nose, driving his nasal bone into his brain. Niko watched him topple backward onto the rubble, dead.

Hassan tried to run, but Niko caught him from behind and pushed him into the wall, face first. He grabbed the man's head in both hands, twisted it violently, and broke his neck. He let Hassan's lifeless body drop to the dirt.

He went to the older woman, who had crawled across the alley and was cradling the young girl's bloody head in her arms. She looked up at Niko, took his hand, and kissed it. "Thank you for saving us."

"Don't thank me," Niko said, pulling his hand away. "This is my fault."

❧   ❧   ❧

On August 19, 1953, the Shah returned to power, regally. Mosaddegh went to prison, quietly. Hensen and Price departed Iran, inconspicuously.

"I can't do this anymore," Niko said. "I want to resign."

"I feel the same. But we're under contract."

"I think mine expired while we were in Iran."

Price looked perplexed. "They didn't send a renewal?"

Niko shook his head.

"We joined about the same time," Price said. "I think I'll quit with you."

When they got to CIA headquarters in D.C., they learned that both their contracts had expired. An oversight. "What a system," Price said. "We've been free for more than two months."

They reported to their supervisor, as ordered. Howard Woolf was an ex-marine and commando—like Niko. They respected him but no longer shared his enthusiasm for the agency.

"Welcome home," Woolf enthused, motioning them to sit. "You guys did great."

"That depends on how you look at it," Niko said.

"Only one way to look at it," Woolf said. "America won."

"By putting a democratically elected prime minister in jail," Niko said.

"Mosaddegh is a communist," Woolf said.

"Horseshit," Niko cursed. "He's an Iranian patriot."

Woolf made a face like something smelled bad. "Are you going soft on me?"

"Howard, a thousand people were killed during Operation Ajax," Price cited.

"That's bad, even by our standards," Niko told him. "We were wrong."

"We're not the Boy Scouts," Woolf rationalized. "We can't question U.S. policy."

"I understand. Which is why I quit," Niko decided.

"The same goes for me," Price added.

"Very funny, guys. Both of you have contracts with the agency."

"Wrong," Price corrected him. "Our contracts expired while we were in Iran."

Woolf pressed a button. "Miss Tully, bring me Price and Hensen's contracts."

Woolf's secretary, pretty and petite, entered and placed two folders on his desk. Woolf checked both. "Shit. You guys are right. Miss Tully, bring me two extension forms."

"Don't bother," Niko declined. "We're not extending."

"Be serious, guys," Woolf pleaded.

Their silence confirmed their seriousness.

"But we have a good versus evil situation waiting for you in Guatemala," Woolf pleaded.

"Which one are we?" Price asked. "Lately we're not even the lesser of two evils."

"I don't believe you're talking like this."

"Iran did me in, Howard," Niko admitted. He told him about the rapists.

"I know that sounds bad," Woolf agreed. "But look at the bright side. You killed three bad men. That's a good thing."

"Except I hired them in the first place," Niko pointed out. "We do evil in the name of what we think is good. I'm not doing that anymore."

"We're the CIA, boys. We don't have to let you just walk away."

"Do you really want us as enemies?" Niko asked.

"Of course not," Woolf agreed. "You're two of our best agents."

"Then treat us like that," Niko demanded. "We've earned it."

After two days of debriefing and sworn statements, the CIA cut them loose.

Standing outside Woolf's office, Price said, "What now?"

"I'm going home," Niko told him.

CHAPTER 35

August 1953
CHICAGO

The next morning at seven, Niko sat alone in the last row of the half-empty bus leaving Washington for Chicago. It would take approximately eleven hours to Chicago, another eight to Omaha, and four more to North Platte. He had spent the previous night with Richard Price, drinking and reminiscing before they both went to sleep on the bus station's benches. Price had only one bus to take to New York City later that morning and was still sleeping when Niko departed.

He found a *Chicago Tribune* dated August 19, 1953, on the empty seat next to him. *Yesterday's news*, he thought, figuring the edition had been left behind by a Chicago to D.C. passenger the night before. He put the newspaper on his lap, closed his eyes, and slept for hours.

When he awoke, the bus was west of Cleveland, and his hangover had been replaced by anxiety. *What now?* He wondered. Since, December 7, 1941, he had been fighting evil at the Army's direction and the CIA's discretion. When he was ordered to do evil in the name of good, he had decided to quit. Now, with no one giving him orders, he felt directionless.

He was also apprehensive about what he would find at home. *Would Jonas and Amanda look the same? Had the past seven years been kind to them? Is Odina still there caring for the daughter he didn't want?* He had thought of them often during the past seven years, with a vague sense of regret. When he first went away, his mother had written about Dorothy's amazing progress and Odina's dedication. But, when he didn't respond to her prompts, she stopped mentioning them. *How will I feel if they're both still there?* He wondered. *How will I feel if they're both gone?*

Odina was not at the forefront of his mind, but neither was she in the recesses. She was always there, a gentle memory—soft and warm. There had been other women over the seven years; two in Iran, one in Germany, others elsewhere. But they paled in comparison to the one he had left behind. He sighed, picked up the *Tribune*, and read the headline.

TRUMBULL PARK RACE RIOTS RAGE
South Deering Reeling Over Segregated Apartments

Betty Howard, a light-skinned Negro woman, appeared alone at the rental office of the legally segregated Trumbull Park Apartments. The rental agent assumed she was white. Mrs. Howard filled out an application and rented an apartment. Weeks later, her husband, Mr. Donald Howard, obviously a Negro, moved in with her. Realizing their mistake, the rental agent asked the Howards to leave. They refused. Trumbull Park residents reacted violently. Riots erupted and grew worse each day.

A photo showed rioting whites fighting with Chicago police. Niko noticed swastika armbands on the sleeves of three rioters. The caption: *Rioters and police clash at Trumbull Park. The White Christian Socialist Party, a neo-Nazi group, joins riots.*

Niko closed the paper, no longer worried about being directionless. He didn't need the Army or the CIA to find evil. It was everywhere. He would start his personal crusade in Chicago.

The bus reached the Greyhound station in Chicago at six p.m. Niko walked one block to the weathered Sherman Hotel, where an old man at the front desk checked him in. He took the elevator to the tenth floor. The furniture in his room was tired-looking, but the room itself was spacious and clean. He tossed his suitcase on the bed and walked to the large window overlooking the Chicago skyline. "*Hog butcher for the world,*" Niko recited the first line from Carl Sandburg's famous poem, *Chicago*. He took a shower, got dressed, and returned to the lobby. The old man was still at the front desk.

"Can I help you?" the old man asked.

"You can, Mr....."

"No mister," the old man held up a hand to stop him. "I'm Al...Al Shapiro, the night manager."

"Okay, Al. How do I get to Trumbull Park?"

"You don't. There's a riot there."

"I know."

"You like riots?"

"Depends. Tell me about the White Christian Socialist Party."

"Nazi bastards," Shapiro told him.

"You know them?"

"Sure. Bastards had a recruiting meeting here once, in one of our conference rooms. Small crowd. They distribute *anti-everything* propaganda all over the city. They rent a storefront on the South Side, in the white section. They have a goon squad for intimidation. I think they're the bastards attacking old Jews in Lawndale."

"Anyone try to stop them?"

"The cops patrol but haven't arrested anyone."

"How about the Jewish community?"

"They write letters to the editor."

"A waste of time. Nazis only understand force," Niko said.

"Are you volunteering?"

"Maybe. Where's the store front?"

"Don't go there," Shapiro advised. "Those people are dangerous. You're big but they've got someone even bigger. I saw him at their meeting. Must be seven feet tall, over three hundred pounds. They call him *Crusher*. He's a bull."

"Ever seen a bullfight?"

"No."

"The bull usually loses."

Shapiro smiled, went to a desk drawer, and rummaged. "Okay, Mr. Matador," he hummed. "Let's see what we have here. They left a few business cards here. Ah, here's one. Their office is on 63rd Ave. on the east corner of Cottage Grove. Can you remember that?"

"Sure," Niko said.

"That's too bad. You seem like a nice kid. I hope you don't get hurt."

The cab stopped at 63rd and Cottage Grove in front of *The White Christian Socialist Party* storefront. Niko paid the driver and read the paper signs taped on the front window.

GONE TO RIOT! KEEP TRUMBULL PARK WHITE
THE HOLOCAUST NEVER HAPPENED

Remembering Buchenwald, Niko was incensed. He peeked into the office. It was filled with desks, chairs, and printing equipment. He wondered why no effort had been made to conceal the contents. No drapes. No blinds. Lights on—daring someone to vandalize the place. It reminded Niko of *Reinhard Heydrich*, riding in an open-air car, daring the Czechs to attack. The Czechs dared. Heydrich died. Now it was time for the White Christian Democrats to meet a similar fate.

Niko looked around. Garbage cans and trash bags littered the sidewalks awaiting pickup. By the curb was an old rusty file cabinet, six drawers high. There was a badly damaged Remington typewriter on top. Useless as a typewriter, the Remington could still be useful as a projectile. Niko carried the bulky machine to the storefront. A dim light illuminated a large U.S. flag pinned to the back wall next to a Nazi flag. Niko gritted his teeth, recalling Duke Hannigan's flags during his Silver Shirts parade in North Platte. *Idiots*, he thought.

He lifted the Remington above his head, bent his elbows, and lowered the typewriter behind his neck. He took two quick steps forward for momentum, lowered his head and heaved the Remington forward, into the *HOLOCAUST* sign. The window shattered as the typewriter flew through, landed on a desktop, bounced in the air, and crashed to the floor. The noise was cause for alarm … but no alarm sounded. *Overconfidence*, Niko thought. He stepped over the empty window frame into the office. He lifted a heavy photocopier from the first desk and threw it against the nearest wall. It would never copy Nazi propaganda again.

A door at the back of the room flew open and slammed against the wall behind it. A mountain of a man emerged. He wasn't quite seven feet tall, but close. He had to lower his head to fit under the door frame. Brandishing a baseball bat, the giant glared at Niko and bellowed, "I'm going to kill you!"

Niko didn't flinch and calmly appraised Crusher. *Massive and slow. No problem.*

Crusher paused. Usually, just the sight of him was enough to create terror and prompt flight. Not this time. He sensed no fear from this man, and it confused him. He gripped the bat with both hands, growled, and took a threatening step forward. The trespasser growled back and stepped forward, too. Bewildered, and with no alternative strategy, Crusher swung the bat at the man's head.

Niko ducked deftly and delivered a short, hard blow to the giant's solar plexus. Crusher heard himself grunt as the air gushed from his lungs... and felt the bat fly from his hands, crashing into the wall across the room. Gasping, the man-mountain felt a searing pain in his back as a fist pummeled his left kidney. Crusher reared back, stiff-legged, and Niko drove his right boot into the outside of Crusher's left knee. Cartilage tore, and ligaments ruptured. Crusher screamed, dropped to his knees, and toppled face first on the tiled floor. He writhed in excruciating pain. The slaughter was over in seconds. Niko dragged the gasping giant to a support beam and sat him against it. He pulled an unattached telephone wire from the wall and used it to tie Crusher's hands behind his back around the pole. He squatted next to the moaning monster and whispered, "Tell your Nazi friends to get out of Chicago, or I'll be back to kill all of you. Understand?"

Crusher nodded, gritting his teeth and groaning, certain he was dealing with a crazy man.

Niko crunched his way over the broken glass, stepped carefully through the shattered front window, and disappeared into the night—his anxiety gone.

Next stop—North Platte, Nebraska.

Chapter 36

1953
DOROTHY

On a hot, humid Sunday afternoon, Jonas and Amanda went shopping after church while Odina and Dorothy remained at home. Dorothy was sitting on the front porch, rocking the rocking chair, reading a book her Uncle Elvis had given her. Entitled, *A Valley Grows Up*, the book portrayed the history of a valley, from prehistoric times to the 20th century. It was one of the many gifts Uncle Elvis had given her over the years, and she loved him dearly. She wished Nanny O had loved him enough to say "Yes" when he proposed to her a year ago. But she had declined, saying she wasn't ready for marriage. Elvis had been understanding, but eleven-year-old Dorothy had not. *What is she waiting for?* she wondered. *She'll never find anyone nicer than Uncle Elvis.*

Despite the August heat, Dorothy wore long pants to hide her deformed leg. She couldn't hide her limp, but she could cover the cause. It was a constant reminder of how different she was from the other kids, and it bothered her.

Restless and uncomfortable, she went inside.

Odina heard the screen door slam. "Hot out there?" she called from the kitchen.

"Like an oven," Dorothy said.

"Come here, darling. I'll cool you off."

They stood at the sink, and Nanny O rubbed Dorothy's neck and face with a wet, cold towel. "That feels good," Dorothy said.

"Roll up those long pants, and I'll do your legs."

Dorothy didn't care if Nanny O saw her bad leg, so she sat on a chair and pulled up her jeans. Nanny O washed Dorothy's legs, lingering on the damaged one. "You know what this leg is, don't you?" she asked.

"Yes. It's ugly."

"That depends on how you look at it," Odina said. "I think it's a miracle." She put aside the cloth. "Now help me with the dishes; I'll wash, you dry."

They worked for a few minutes before they heard a knock on the front door. Dorothy looked through the window above the sink. "There's no car outside. Someone walked here."

"In this heat? Crazy. Go see who it is," Odina said. "I'll use the bathroom."

Still drying a dish, Dorothy limped to the front door. She looked through the screen door, gasped, and dropped the porcelain plate on the hardwood floor. It shattered. She looked up at a towering stranger. She recognized him immediately though they had never met. She knew his face from photos, but pictures had not prepared her for him in real life. He was larger than life; startling, intimidating, and awesome. His white T-shirt was soaked in sweat, clinging to him like a second skin. His body reminded her of a statue of a Greek god. Instinctively, she knew he was the man Odina had spoken about. *Big and beautiful like an Oak tree,* she remembered Nanny O's words. *This is the man she was talking about—and I hate him.*

The unwanted daughter glared at the unforgiving father. Not knowing what to say, they were silent until Niko asked, "Do you know who I am?"

"Yes. Do you know who *I* am?"

"You're Dorothy," he said emotionless.

"That's right. Your daughter."

"I know, we have the same face."

"It looks better on you. What do you want?" she asked, impolite and angry.

"This is my home."

"You left it a long time ago."

"Yes, and now I'm back."

"Why?"

"To see my parents."

"And Nanny O."

"Who?"

"Odina. I call her Nanny O."

"Oh, Odina, the nurse," he said, feigning indifference, "we only met once."

"Well, she remembers you," Dorothy said, her voice challenging.

"She was very pretty, as I recall."

"She's beautiful...inside and out," Dorothy replied, then added. "She thinks you're beautiful too, but only on the outside."

"Really?" Niko said with a small smile.

"Yes. She told me you were troubled inside."

"She's right," Niko agreed.

"She said she could never love a man like you," Dorothy lied.

"I understand."

Odina had returned to the kitchen and picked up a dish when she heard Dorothy ask, "Did you ever think of us?"

Who is she talking to? She wondered.

"Of course, I thought of you," she recognized Niko's voice immediately. Her heartbeat quickened. It had been so long.

"Really? What did you think?" Dorothy persisted.

"I wondered how you were and hoped you were well."

"If you cared, why did you leave us? Why didn't you write?" Dorothy asked. Odina cringed.

"I had problems after the war," Niko answered, uncomfortable with her and her questions.

"The war has been over for years."

"Not for me," he said—getting testy. "Now if you don't mind, I'd like to come in and see my parents."

"They're not here," Dorothy said. "Come back later." she slammed the door shut.

"Dorothy," Odina said, rushing around the corner and opening the door. She saw him through the screen and dropped the dish she was holding. It shattered, the remnants comingling with the dish Dorothy had just dropped. Niko laughed and quipped, "You break a lot of dishes around here, don't you?" he said.

Odina was embarrassed. "Not usually. I apologize for Dorothy's rudeness," she said, thinking, *Amanda was right, he is awesome.* She thought of them making love years ago and blushed. She knew her face was bright red.

"No need to apologize," Niko said. "I understand how she feels."

Odina opened the screen door and stepped aside so he could enter. He picked up his suitcase and sidled past her through the front door. They were only inches apart. The mutual attraction was palpable. Their bodies seemed to remember meeting before. He fought the urge to kiss her. She had the same impulse.

Odina cleared her throat nervously and glanced at Dorothy. *She's jealous*, Odina thought, feeling guilty. Niko set his suitcase on the floor. "Let me help clean up these dishes then I'd like to clean up myself if that's okay," he said.

"Of course," Odina said. "I'll get you a towel."

In the bathroom, he peeled off his T-shirt and dropped it on the floor. He was splashing water on his face when Odina came to the open door with a towel. He turned to her and smiled. "Thank you," he said, reaching for the towel. She couldn't help staring. Flustered, she turned away, bit her lower lip, and walked away, her face burning.

This wouldn't be easy.

CHAPTER 37

1953
NIKO

Niko had dried his face and combed his hair when he heard a car pull into the yard. He took a fresh shirt from his suitcase and went out to welcome Amanda and Jonas.

"Niko," Amanda exclaimed—rushing to him. They hugged and kissed while Jonas waited his turn. Then they all went inside, gathered around the kitchen table, and reconnected after so many years. Niko declined to talk much about his experiences except to say he had become disenchanted with the CIA and resigned. Sensing his reticence, no one pressed him for details.

"So, what's been going on here in North Platte?" Niko asked.

"Not much has changed," Jonas replied. "They renamed Bulldog Field to Parsons Memorial Field, in memory of my old coach, Emmitt Parsons. You know you're getting old when things are named in memory of people you knew."

"If not for Coach Parsons, we might never have gotten together," Amanda said. "God bless that man."

"Amen," Jonas said.

"Mom, I can't get over how good you look," Niko said. "You haven't aged a bit."

"Thank you," Amanda said. "Doctor says I'm stronger than I was ten years ago."

"You're amazing," Niko said, reaching across the table and taking her hand in both of his. Odina watched him, transfixed, and tingling.

I haven't felt like this since he went away, she thought—realizing how much she missed the feeling.

"How's Shirley Hannigan?" he asked.

"Still sober," Amanda said. "She's become a good friend."

"And, Duke?"

"Not a word," Amanda said. "It's like he vanished off the face of the earth. Some think he's dead. Most think he ran away with his mistress, Randi Renart."

"Jeez. Did everyone in town know Duke had a mistress?" Niko asked.

"There was never any proof. But it was common knowledge," Jonas shrugged.

"Without proof, it's just a rumor—not common knowledge," Niko said

Jonas nodded. "I suppose. But why do you care?"

"I don't really. I just feel bad for Shirley."

"She doesn't talk about Duke anymore," Amanda told him. "I think she'd rather forget him."

"I can't blame her," Niko agreed. "How's Elvis?"

"He's an angel," Amanda answered. "A great friend to us and uncle to Dorothy."

"I love him," Dorothy exclaimed, staring at Niko. "He asked Nanny O to marry him, you know."

Her words startled Niko. "No, I didn't know," he said, trying not to show his surprise. His head began pounding.

"Dorothy, that's personal," Odina scolded, embarrassed.

"Well, he did propose," Dorothy persisted.

"Are congratulations in order?" Niko asked, forcing a smile.

"Not at all," Odina said. "I told him I'd think about it and I'm still thinking."

Dorothy stood up and stomped her foot. "You should have said, *yes*," she shouted. "I wish I had a father like him." she turned and stomped from the room.

"Forgive her," Amanda said. "She adores Elvis. He's been so good to her."

"Elvis is a good man," Niko agreed, remembering how Elvis had saved his life in Boston. He rubbed his eyes and massaged his temples.

"Niko, are you alright?" Amanda asked.

"To tell you the truth, I'm a little beat."

"Why not lie down in your old room and get some rest?" Amanda suggested.

"I think I will," Niko said. "Just for a while."

He lay on his back on his old bed and covered his eyes with one arm. He was surprised by his extreme reaction to Elvis's proposal. *Why am I so upset?* He wondered. *A lot of men must want her, and I've been gone for years.*

During his time away, Odina had been a pleasant, gauzy, memory, a romantic reminiscence of what had happened between them and what might have been—had things been different. But when he saw her today, things *were* different, and she was no longer a gossamer figment of his imagination. She was real and more extraordinary then he remembered. He had been excited to have a second chance with her until he learned she might already be lost to a man he could not challenge for her affection—a man who had saved his life. His excitement had turned to depression in an instant, and his system had short-circuited. He felt physically ill. Exhausted, he fell into a deep, dreamless sleep.

Later in the afternoon, Amanda looked in on him then went to the front porch where Jonas, Dorothy, and Odina had congregated. "He's still asleep," she told them. "I'm afraid we'll wake him if we go inside. Why don't we leave him a note and go to town for dinner?"

"Not me," Odina said. "I'm a little tired myself. You three go."

"I'll stay with you, Nanny O," Dorothy said.

"No. Come with us, Dorothy," Amanda urged. "We'll buy you those new records you've been asking for. What were they, again?"

"*Your Cheating Heart* by Hank Williams, *Gee* by the Crows, and *Crazy Man Crazy* by Bill Haley and His Comets."

"They sound perfectly awful," Amanda commented. "But, if that's what you want, we'll get them for you."

"Is it alright with you if I go, Nanny O?"

"Sure. Take advantage of their offer."

"Will you be okay alone with him?" she asked, rolling her eyes.

Odina laughed. "Don't be silly," she said. "He's not an ogre. He'll probably sleep through the night, anyway. He looked exhausted. Go get your records, and we'll listen to them together when you get back."

Amanda glanced at Odina and nodded. *She knows*, Odina realized and smiled back.

❧ ❧ ❧

After they had gone, Odina sat alone on the front porch, ruminating. Seeing Niko for the first time in seven years had awakened her repressed desire for him. It had laid dormant but had not waned. If anything—it had intensified. No man before him or since had this effect on her. She had the barely undeniable urge to touch him, to make love to him again. She wanted him passionately ... and this time he would not be gone in the morning.

She heard the screen door open behind her. "Hello, there," she greeted him. "Feel better?"

"Yes, a little," he answered, stretching his arms out wide and yawning. "I heard the truck leave and thought everyone was gone."

"They went to town for dinner," Odina said. "I was too tired."

"I'm glad," he said, sitting next to her. "Gives us a chance to talk."

Apprehensive, she asked, "What do you want to talk about?"

"Our relationship."

"What relationship?" she quickly responded. "I haven't seen you in seven years."

"Did you miss me?" he asked, smiling as if he was joking.

"Did *you* miss *me*?" she asked, not returning his smile— not joking.

"To be honest," he said, leaning toward her, "I didn't realize how much I missed you until I saw you again today."

"I felt the same," she said and reached out and touched his hand. It was spontaneous combustion, and they both felt the heat. It couldn't be ignored.

"What about Elvis?" he said. "Do you love him?"

"Like a brother," she said. "I could never marry him."

That was all the encouragement Niko needed. He stood and pulled her up with him. Their bodies came together naturally. They kissed, tentatively at first, then passionately. No words were necessary to lead them to his bedroom. They undressed each other in haste. Her naked body felt at home next to his, and both were reminded of the first time as if no time had passed. They knew they belonged together.

Lying in bed, luxuriating in the afterglow, Odina lifted her head off Niko's shoulder and looked in his eyes. "Are you staying or going this time?" she asked.

"I plan to stay. But what will you tell Elvis?"

"I'll tell him I won't marry him," she said.

"Will you tell him about us?"

"I'll have to," she said. "I think he'll understand. I know Dorothy won't."

"What won't she understand? Why you won't marry him or that you're involved with me?"

"Both," Odina said. "She loves him and hates you. How do you feel about her, now?"

"I'm impressed," he admitted. "She's come a long way. It's remarkable. But I can't look at her without thinking of her mother, and that spoils everything."

"Do you think you'll ever be able to accept her as your daughter?"

"No. I feel nothing for her but regret."

"No guilt?"

"None."

"Can you live with her under the same roof?"

"For your sake and my parents, I will," Niko said.

"Good. But you have to understand; if you make me choose between Dorothy and you, I'll choose her," Odina said.

"I understand," Niko said. "I'll try to never make you choose."

CHAPTER 38

1953
ELVIS

The next night Elvis and Shirley came for dinner at the Hensen house. Shirley was happy just being with the Hensens. Amanda had become her dear friend, and her love for Jonas had evolved into an undying affection. She was glad Duke was gone, though she still feared his return. She no longer asked about Beth.

When Elvis saw Odina and Niko interact, he understood the situation immediately. The chemistry between them was apparent in their furtive glances, suggestive smiles, and smoldering eye contact. He realized Odina would never look at him that way. He wasn't heartbroken. He knew Odina's feelings for him were platonic, almost sisterly, but he had hoped they would change with time. Now he knew that would never happen. He just hoped that someday a woman would look at him the way Odina was looking at Niko now.

After dinner, Niko invited Elvis to take a walk with him. The hundred and sixty acres of the Hensens' homestead had never been farmed and consisted mostly of uncultivated, tall grass and planted trees. The original house, built by the first homesteaders, sat in the middle of the acreage.

Niko's grandfather, Alf, had added a second floor to the house and planted the many trees on the land. After fifty years of growth, there was a small patch of woodland on the property, not common to the area.

The two big men walked slowly on the unpaved path that bisected the main road leading the three miles to North Platte.

"There's something I want to talk to you about," Elvis said, stopping. They faced one another. "I can see there's something between you and Odina."

Niko said nothing.

"I just want you to know that I proposed to her," Elvis said.

Niko nodded. "Dorothy told me."

"Odina told me she would think about it, but the truth is, she's doesn't love me, and she never will."

"She does love you, Elvis," Niko told him.

"I know—like a brother," Elvis repeated Odina's words. "That's not what I had in mind. I guess you're the better man."

"That's not true," Niko said. "You're as good a man as anyone, Elvis. You take care of your mother and brother. You risked your life for your sister, and you took care of my daughter when I wouldn't. And you saved my life."

"When you put it that way, I do sound pretty good," Elvis decided.

"You're great," Niko said. "Odina may not love you with the passion you want, but passion isn't a choice. It's a natural reaction. It's either there, or it isn't. Someday a woman will love you with that passion, and if you love her the same way, that's the one you want... not the one you need to convince."

"You make it sound so logical."

"Nothing about love is logical."

"You're right," Elvis said. "Now if only I can find the right woman."

"Who knows? Maybe she'll find you."

"Should I tell Odina she can stop thinking about my proposal," Elvis asked.

"That's up to you."

"You tell her. It will be less embarrassing that way."

"You're a good man, Elvis," Niko said. They shook hands and started walking again. "Now, let's talk about your father. Why hasn't your mother declared him legally dead after all these years? It's ridiculous."

"There's no proof he's dead. She's afraid he might come back someday."

"After fourteen years? Either someone killed him, or he killed himself."

"Not likely he killed himself. He's too selfish," Elvis said.

"Let's think about it then," Niko said. "Duke had been publicly humiliated the day he disappeared. A bully would need to rebuild his ego by picking on someone weaker— someone who wouldn't fight back. Any ideas?"

"My entire family," Elvis said and laughed.

"Okay. Did he go after anyone in the family that day?"

"I was joking. But, no, none of us saw him after the parade."

"Anyone else he'd pick on ... who wouldn't fight back?"

"Employees?" Elvis guessed. "His mistress, maybe."

"Who is she? What's she like?"

"Randi Renart. Single mom. Very pretty," Elvis remembered. "Financially dependent on him, I think. That's what

I heard, anyway. She left town right after my father went missing. I figured they had run off together."

"If not, she's a perfect murder suspect."

"Not likely," Elvis said. "Duke was big and strong. She wasn't. She would have needed a weapon to kill him. Plus, even if she shot him, she'd have to move his two hundred and forty pounds somewhere, somehow. She couldn't have done it alone."

"What if she had a big, strong accomplice, like you or your brother?"

"Oh, so now we're suspects," Elvis shook his head.

"Why not? You hated your father. Did you know Randi Renart?"

"No. Never met her," Elvis said, shaking his head. "Only saw her a couple of times. Eli said he met her once…said she was nice."

"That could mean something," Niko said. "Didn't Eli leave town after your father disappeared?"

Elvis nodded.

"Maybe she ran off with your brother, not your father."

"Never," Elvis disagreed without hesitation, but then paused—put his hands on his hips and looked at the ground. He seemed to be thinking. "I suppose it's possible," he conceded. "Randi's mother and thirteen-year-old daughter lived with her and disappeared with her. Duke would never have taken them along. He was too selfish. But Eli has a good heart. He would have taken them. Jesus. I never thought of that. A lover's triangle."

"A fight between two big men over a woman. An accidental death."

"Hold on. If it was an accident, why wouldn't Eli just tell the police?"

"Good question. Let's ask him. Where is he?"

"I don't know. I wire him money monthly from his trust fund. That's all."

"Where do you wire the money?"

"The Bank of Steinauer," Elvis said. "His choice."

"So, he must live near there."

"I asked him once. He told me he doesn't live near Steinauer. Just uses the bank."

"And you believed him?"

"Eli was never a liar," Elvis said. "Then again, he changed a lot after Dad disappeared. When he came to North Platte a while ago, I hardly recognized him. He'd lost over a hundred pounds, had a bushy beard and long, straggly hair. Dressed like a farmer, in overalls and a floppy old hat."

"Sounds like he was hiding."

"From what?"

"Let's find him and ask."

"Where do we start?"

"We follow the money," Niko suggested.

"I won't feel right, hunting my brother," Elvis admitted.

"We're not hunting him. We're trying to find him."

"But if Eli is involved in our father's disappearance … and we tell the police …"

"Who said anything about the police? We're just looking for the truth."

"In that case, let's start in Steinauer," Elvis said.

Steinauer, Nebraska; population seventy-five, one square mile, a four-hour drive from North Platte on Route 80. Elvis and Niko left early the next day and arrived near noon.

A hot wind tossed dust around Steinauer's deserted Main Street, reminiscent of a ghost town.

"I can't imagine Eli living here," Elvis commented, looking around.

"Can you imagine him hiding here?" Niko asked.

It was easy to find the bank, a two-story wood building in the center of town. The bank itself occupied the ground floor. There was no one inside, except for a pretty, blonde woman at the teller's window. She appeared to be in her late twenties. As Elvis approached, he couldn't help but notice her size. She was big. Not fat, big, as in tall, at least six feet with broad shoulders, and a buxom, full figure. When she asked, "Can I help you?" her smile was wide, showing big white teeth topped by big blue eyes. "I'm Zoe Gredisson, the assistant manager."

"Miss Gredisson, I'm Elvis Hannigan. This is my associate, Niko Hensen. I wire money to this bank regularly for my twin brother Eli Hannigan."

She studied him. "I can see the resemblance."

"So, Eli comes here," Niko confirmed.

"Yes, from time to time."

"We're here to see my brother, but we only have his account number. We need his address or phone number."

"I'm sorry. I can't give out client information without their prior consent."

"This is obviously his twin brother," Niko persisted. "You said so yourself."

"I-I understand," she stammered. "But…"

"Miss Gredisson," Niko interrupted. "We've just driven four hours. Please give us the address, and we'll be on our way."

A pained expression crossed her face.

"Excuse my associate," Elvis interceded, "it's just that we've come a long way, and it's important we find my brother."

"I'd like to help," she said. "But I can't. I'd lose my job."

"Can we speak to the manager?" Niko asked.

"That would be Mr. Steinauer, the owner," she said.

"The bank owner has the same name as the town?" Niko asked.

"His family founded the town," she explained. "The town has his name."

"Okay, can we see Mr. Steinauer?"

"He's not here till tomorrow. Can you come back?"

Niko rolled his eyes, exasperated, and headed for the door without a word.

"I understand your situation, Miss Gredisson," Elvis said, reluctant to leave. "We'll find my brother some other way."

He offered his hand across the counter. She took it in hers. "Goodbye," Elvis said, enjoying the warm feel of her big hand and long fingers. She continued holding on for an awkward moment and finally, released him.

"Goodbye, Mr. Hannigan," she said, looking sad.

Niko was already outside. Elvis had reached the bank's front door when she called after him. "Mr. Hannigan, I think your brother lives nearby."

Elvis turned. "Why do you say that?"

"I saw him leave the bank once when I was outside. He drove to the northwest corner and turned onto Junction Street, which dead-ends at Junction Crossing. Nothing there but a defunct auto body shop and a few houses. He might live in one of them."

"Thank you, Miss Gredisson," Elvis waved. "You're very nice."

271

"So are you, Mr. Hannigan. Come back soon."

Outside, Niko was in the truck. "What do you think?" Elvis asked, getting in.

"Waste of time," he said.

"No. What did you think of the girl?"

Niko rolled his eyes. "Who cares?" he said. "She wouldn't help us."

"I care," Elvis said. "And she did help us."

"How?"

"First, tell me if you think she's pretty."

"Yes. I think she's pretty. A little buxom for my taste."

"I like that," Elvis said. "Do you think I should ask her out?"

"It didn't take you very long to get over Odina."

"You said the right one could be right around the corner."

"Steinauer isn't around the corner from anywhere. Besides, maybe she's married."

"No ring, I checked."

"Really? You plan to commute four hours for a date?" Niko said.

"Maybe. I thought she was really nice." After a few seconds, Elvis opened the truck door again. "I'm going to ask her out."

"Your business. How did she help us? You never said ... aw dammit."

Elvis had already entered the bank.

CHAPTER 39

1953
ELI

Niko waited patiently for Elvis, glad he was interested in the bank teller. He deserved a good woman. Twenty minutes later, Elvis returned.

"She said, yes!"

"That took twenty minutes?"

"No. We got to know each other a little."

"What's a nice girl like Zoe doing in a small town like this?"

"She's originally from Steinauer but had been living in Omaha for four years, working at a bank there. Her mother died a year ago, and she came home to help her ailing father. She's a really good person."

"So are you. Good luck. Now, what did she tell you about your brother?"

They reached the T at the end of Junction Street. It was as Zoe described. To the left were three typical Nebraska five-room homes—two on one side of the road, one farther down the road on the other side—isolated. They saw a man working in a vegetable garden behind the house.

"Is that Eli?" Niko asked.

Elvis looked. "If it is, he's even thinner and shaved off his beard."

As they got closer, Elvis recognized him. "Yeah, that's him," he confirmed. They stopped the truck and got out.

When Eli saw who it was, his shoulders slumped.

"Hello, Eli," Elvis said.

Eli offered neither a handshake nor a hug. He simply said, "Elvis."

"You told me you didn't live in Steinauer," Elvis said.

"I lied. How did you find me?"

"Niko was with the CIA. He can find anyone," Elvis said, covering for Zoe.

"The last time I saw you—you broke my nose," Eli recalled.

"That was a long time ago. Before your father disappeared."

"If you're here to talk about my father, I have nothing to say."

The rear door of the house opened, and Randi Renart emerged.

"I'll be goddamned," Elvis whispered. "You were right."

Randi approached. "Couldn't you just let us be, Elvis?"

"It was my idea, not his," Niko said.

"It was a bad idea," Eli told them. "My family is none of your business."

"Your mother is like family to me," Niko said. "I made it my business."

Eli's face softened. "Is my mother okay?" he asked.

"Yes, except she thinks your father is still alive and won't move on with her life," Niko explained.

"What's that got to do with me?" Eli asked, sounding defensive.

"Thought you might know something about your father's disappearance."

Eli stared at Niko. "I don't have to talk to you," he said.

"Eli, if you know anything, our mother deserves the truth," Elvis said.

"We're not here looking to hurt you," Niko added.

Eli gritted his teeth. "Just leave us alone."

Randi put her hand on Eli's shoulder. "Calm down. Let's all go inside and talk."

"This is a bad idea," Eli told her.

Randi shook her head. "It's time we stopped living like this," she said.

They went inside and sat in the small living room. Randi and Eli shared the sofa, Elvis and Niko used wooden chairs.

"Are your mother and daughter living here?" Elvis asked.

"My mother died of cancer years ago. Taylor ran away a year later, at eighteen."

"We don't need to know about Taylor," Niko said. "We're here about Duke."

"It's all connected."

"Randi, stop," Eli said, agitated.

Randi put her hand on his arm. "Maybe they can help us," she said.

At first, Randi's words trickled out before a flood of dammed-up emotions burst out. She related her early history, an alcoholic father, a teenage pregnancy, and eventually, Duke's proposition. "He saw me working as a secretary at Bailey Yard," she told them. "He wanted me. I had a mother and daughter to support, so I became his mistress. I suppose that makes me a whore to you."

"No. It makes you a victim," Niko said. "You sacrificed yourself for your family."

"To survive, I made a deal with the devil."

"You're not the first person to do that," Niko said. "What about you and Eli?"

"Met by chance in town," she explained. "I knew who he was, but he didn't know about his father and me. He started calling me for dates. I told him, no, and I told him to stop calling. He wouldn't. Finally, I told him the truth."

"How did he take it?"

"Not good. He hung up. But later he came to my house. Said he wanted me anyway. I refused, but he persisted. I was confused. I didn't love him, but he was so nice, not at all like his father, and he was so damned persistent. We started seeing each other secretly. This went on for two years. My feelings for him changed."

"One day she told me she loved me," Eli said, smiling for the first time.

"You grew on me," she said and touched his hand.

"We started praying for a miracle," Eli said.

"And you got one when Duke disappeared," Niko said. "What happened that day?"

Another flood of words followed; *Silver Shirts parade— stayed home—Taylor napping—mother away—Duke showed up drunk—covered in dust—raving—'fuckin' Jews—Gypsy bastards—crazy stuff—pushes me—hits me. I'm terrified—saw kitchen knife—grab it—Duke discards it—knocks me down, straddles me—rips at my clothes— threatens to rape me.* At this point, Randi began hyperventilating.

"Calm down, Randi," Eli comforted her. "Take a deep breath."

She breathed slowly before continuing. "I struggled with him but didn't scream. I didn't want to wake Taylor. Duke was hitting me. I was dizzy. Suddenly, I saw Taylor standing behind him, her eyes crazy, like a wild animal. I see she's holding the discarded kitchen knife. Duke didn't know she was there. Taylor raised the knife over her head and screamed, *you son of a bitch, you'll never touch us again.* Then she stabbed Duke low in the neck, near his shoulder. He screamed and reared back. She stabbed him again, and again, and again. Higher on his neck, his face, his right eye. She didn't stop stabbing till he fell off me. I knew he was dead. She kept screaming; *you'll never touch us again.* I'll never forget those words."

"So, Duke was molesting her too?" Niko asked.

"Yes. She told us later," Eli revealed. "That sick bastard."

"It was my fault," Randi sobbed. "I left her with him."

"How old was Taylor?" Niko asked.

"Twelve," Randi said, still crying. "My poor baby."

"I can't believe my father molested a twelve-year-old." Elvis stammered.

"I couldn't believe it either, Elvis," Eli admitted. "But it's true."

"Why not call the police?" Niko asked Randi. "It was justifiable homicide."

"She called me instead," Eli answered. "I went to their house. They told me what my father had done..."

"Why didn't *you* call the police?" Niko interrupted.

"I wanted to," Eli said. "But Taylor went crazy. Said she didn't want anyone to know she had killed someone or that she had been sexually molested. She threatened to kill herself. Randi was frantic. She was sure no one would believe anything she said."

"Think about it," Randi said. "I was having an affair with a father and his son, and the father was molesting my daughter."

"I might have been in shock—I don't know," Eli said. "But when they pleaded with me to make it go away, I did."

"How?" Elvis asked.

"They cleaned up the house, and I got rid of the body," Eli confessed.

"Where?"

"In the Calhoun Ravine, north of Omaha."

"The Haunted Ravine?" Elvis asked. "Where that murder took place?"

"Yes, in 1919," Eli said. "It's abandoned—like a haunted house."

"That's a four-hour drive from here," Elvis said. "Why there?"

"I tried to imagine what Duke would have done after the parade if he hadn't gone to Randi's house," Eli explained. "I imagined him speeding along Route 80 in his little sports car, drinking whiskey to drown his sorrows."

"Sounds like something he would do," Elvis agreed.

"He would have passed through Omaha around 1:00 a.m., and reached Calhoun fifteen minutes later," Eli said. "A narrow dirt road leads to the ravine. The car could have easily gone over the edge, tumbled down the ravine, hit a tree and exploded. If it went into some trees, it could remain unseen for years."

"A lot could have gone wrong with a plan like that," Niko commented.

"But it didn't," Eli responded. "I wrapped Duke's body in blankets and put him in the trunk. Randi kept whiskey in the house for him, and I took the bottle with me. I drove Duke's car to the ravine, put him behind the wheel, doused him with the booze, set his shirt on fire, and pushed him over the edge. The car bounced into some trees going fast, hit something hard, and exploded. I watched it burn for a while, then walked back to Route 80, where Randi picked me up in my car as planned. Years later, here we are."

A fitting end for Duke Hannigan, Niko thought. *Burning in hell.*

"No accident was ever reported at Calhoun Ravine," Randi added.

"We never thought it would go unnoticed this long," Eli said.

"You got lucky," Elvis said.

"You call living like this lucky?" Eli said, looking around at their shabby surroundings. "It's been a nightmare."

"After that, my daughter fell apart, talking to herself, fighting with friends until she had none. Her eyes had this crazy look in them all the time, like when she stabbed Duke. She worried us, and when she ran away, we were actually relieved."

"We were afraid she'd kill us or someone else," Eli admitted.

"I don't think so," Niko disagreed. "Duke was probably an isolated incident. He had been abusing her and her mother when she struck back—unplanned. She killed an evil man, and the world is a better place without him. I'm leaving it at that. I'm not telling anyone what you told me."

"Me neither," Elvis said.

"Thank you," Eli said. "Now what?"

"Come out of hiding," Niko said. "Go home and see your mother."

"Shirley would never accept Duke's mistress, and I'm not leaving her."

"I thought of that," Niko said. "Can anyone prove Randi was Duke's mistress?"

"Did anyone ever catch them in the act, you mean? No," Elvis said.

"Did Duke ever admit to an affair with Randi?" Niko asked.

"Never," Eli said. "He always denied it. But everyone knew."

"Everyone *assumed*," Niko said, thinking of how the CIA taught him to lie with conviction. "I was told that Duke asked her to be his mistress and she refused."

"That's not true. Who told you that?" Elvis asked.

"I forget. But the same guy told me Randi was in love with Eli all these years."

"You just made that up," Eli accused.

"Show me one bit of evidence it's not true," Niko said.

"I can't. But no one will believe you," Eli retaliated.

"Odina, Amanda, and Jonas will believe me," Niko insisted. "Your mother will believe it too. Especially if Eli comes home with Randi."

"I'm not so sure about that," Elvis disagreed.

"She'll want to believe it," Niko said. "That's half the battle."

"What have we got to lose?" Randi asked.

"Nothing," Eli nodded. "Let's go home."

CHAPTER 40

1953–1958
CHANGES

Elvis visited Zoe every weekend after that for two months. On his eighth visit, he proposed. She accepted. He brought her home to North Platte to meet his family.

"She's perfect for you," Odina told him. "I'm so happy you found each other."

"In Steinauer of all places," Elvis said. "I went looking for Eli and found Zoe."

Eli and Randi eventually returned to North Platte and told their lies. They were greeted with skepticism by some, support from others, and indifference by many. It was old news, and Niko was right. People believe what they want to believe.

"Do you think Eli and Randi are telling the truth?" Jonas asked Niko.

"I do. Why?"

"Their story leaves a big unanswered question. Where's Duke?"

"They don't know. And I don't care. Do you?"

"I care about the truth."

"The truth? The truth is, everyone's happy Duke's gone, and no one wants him back," Niko told his father. "Shirley's happy that Eli's home. She's accepted Randi. What more truth do you need?"

Duke never cared about the truth, Jonas thought. *He almost killed me with a lead pipe and tried to ruin my family. He was a racist and a Nazi.*

"You're right," Jonas concluded. "To hell with Duke."

With that issue resolved, Jonas changed the subject. "I realize you haven't been home long, but have you given any thought to your future? Do you plan on staying here a while?"

"I plan on staying. Why do you ask?"

"Shirley mentioned to Amanda that Elvis intends to offer you a job."

"Really? I don't know the ranching business," Niko told him. "Why would they want me?"

"They trust you," Jonas said, and that said it all.

As predicted, Elvis offered Niko a job the next day.

"What would I do?"

"Be our general manager," Elvis said. "We can teach you all you need to know."

"Who's my boss?"

"Shirley. She's the largest stockholder besides my father."

"Your father's dead," Niko said. "And I won't work for his ghost. Sooner or later you have to convince Shirley to declare Duke legally dead."

"That might take some time," Elvis said. "But I promise to work on it."

"When do I start?"

Franz Goldschmidt's short-term memory was failing. He could remember the distant past but not the previous day.

He could easily describe the Fokker triplane he flew during the Great War: "It was black and gold, incredibly fast diving or climbing, but difficult to maneuver."

He could remember April 21, 1919, the day his group leader, Manfred von Richthofen, the *Red Baron*, was killed: "He flew too low and was shot from the sky by a rifle on the ground." He could even recall the Red Baron's last words, "*Ich bin Kaput.*" (I am utterly finished). All this he could remember ... but not his way home.

On a clear September afternoon, during one of his daily walks, he became disoriented and wandered behind a strip of stores. Trucks were loading and unloading in the area, and one of them was backing up. The driver didn't see Franz until the last second. He slammed on his brakes. The tires squealed, and Papa Franz turned toward the noise.

"I barely touched him," the driver told the policeman later. "See, there's no blood."

The patrolman squatted next to Goldschmidt. "The sharp edge of your loading deck hit him on the temple. See the indentation? It killed him instantly. Not your fault."

"Poor old guy," the driver said because that's all he saw on the ground. He didn't see the highly decorated war pilot who flew with reckless abandon and received his country's highest military honor. He couldn't know the old man had once been a war hero, beloved husband, wealthy bank president, and a German Jew, *saved* by Adolf Eichmann. What the driver saw was a mirage—a dead old man without a story.

In 1954, Elvis married Zoe, and Eli married Randi in a twin ceremony at the Hannigan mansion. It was a small gathering attended by family and a few friends. Elvis and Zoe moved into the Hannigan mansion with Shirley, who loved having them there. Eli and Randi moved into a small house they had built on the land formerly used as Romeo's private playpen. The area became known as the Hannigan Compound.

Niko moved into the expanded Hensen house with Odina, Dorothy, and his mother and father. It was a house filled with love, except for the continued distant relationship between Niko and Dorothy. She couldn't forgive him for leaving or returning. He couldn't look at her without thinking of Beth's deceit. Under the circumstances, Niko and Odina didn't discuss marriage. The only time Niko brought it up, Odina said, "Don't make me choose," and that was that.

Niko was working as the general manager of the Hannigan's ranch.

"Do you like working for the Hannigans?" Jonas asked one evening as they sat on the front porch after dinner.

"I do," Niko said. "The cattle business is fascinating, and they treat me well."

"What if Duke comes back?"

"I'd leave. I couldn't work for him."

"Do you think he'll ever come back?" Jonas asked.

"No, I don't," Niko answered—knowing the truth. "I think he's gone forever."

"Dead?"

"Probably."

"So why doesn't Shirley declare him legally dead?"

"I don't know," Niko said, shrugging. "I've asked her a dozen times. I've also asked her to get rid of the Chamanskis."

"The accountants?"

Niko nodded. "They make my skin crawl," he said. "They don't give me a straight answer when I ask a question. I just don't trust them."

"What does Shirley say about them?"

"She defends them by saying they were hired by Liam and kept by Duke, so they're obviously important."

"You don't agree?"

"No. They're obviously crooked, for the same reasons," Niko countered.

"What will you do?"

"Four years ago, I promised her I'd stay two years at most. Those two years flew by, so I gave her two more. Nothing changed at the ranch or at home. Something has to give."

CHAPTER 41

1958
DOROTHY

Dorothy turned sixteen in the fall of 1958. She was at the top of her class scholastically and the bottom socially. Her shyness was mistaken for aloofness. She wasn't pretty, and she wasn't homely. She was tall and slim with a well-developed figure, but her awkward gait made her feel unattractive. Lonely and vulnerable, she was easy prey.

Her predator arrived on a Harley in front of North Platte High. She saw him talking to several tittering girls gathered around his motorcycle. Dorothy admired his dark good looks. When her Spanish teacher passed by, she asked, "Mr. Rios, who is that boy?"

"Hola, Dorothy," he said and looked where she was pointing. "Steve Diamond from Omaha. I hear he's trouble. You best stay away from him."

Walking to the bus stop, Dorothy was surprised to hear the soft growl of a motorcycle engine alongside her. She turned and saw Steve Diamond. "Hey, good looking," he said. "Need a ride?"

She was flattered by his compliment. "No, thank you," she said.

"Why not? It looks like you hurt your leg."

"I have a bad leg."

"Well, there ain't nothing wrong with the rest of you. You're sexy."

No one had ever called her sexy. "Is that your idea of a compliment?"

"Sure."

"What are you doing here? I heard you're from Omaha."

"I go where I want," he said. "Now, how about that ride. I won't bite."

Impulsively, she accepted, forgetting all predators bite. She got on the back of his Harley, putting her schoolbooks between them, and wrapping her arms around his waist. The speed, the cool September air whipping her hair, the vibration of the motor between her legs, and the driver's good looks all excited her. She enjoyed having her arms around his narrow waist and hard, flat stomach. *He thinks I'm sexy*, she thought.

Her fascination ended when Diamond unclasped her fingers and moved her hand to his crotch. She could feel his hardness through his jeans. She panicked and yanked her hand away, causing the cycle to shimmy.

"Easy, girl, you'll get us killed."

"I want to get off," she said, her voice shaking.

He pulled the bike into a wooded area. They both got off. Dorothy grabbed her books and limped away. Diamond grabbed her shoulders and turned her around.

"What's your fuckin' problem?" he scowled.

Frightened, she said, "This was a mistake. I'm not that kind of girl."

"I thought a gimp like you would be grateful for my attention," he said.

She slapped his face—he pushed her—she fell to the ground—dropping her books. Diamond leaned over her prone body and jammed his hand inside her blouse. Buttons popped, and her shirt opened. He felt her well-developed breasts while she screamed, "Stop!" He ignored her and pulled at her pants. She kicked, but he wouldn't stop. When he got her pants down to her ankles, he said, "Holy shit, that is one ugly leg. I'll have to close my eyes to fuck you." He pulled her pant leg over her custom shoe.

She looked up through her tears and saw he had lowered his jeans to his thighs and was holding his erect penis in his hand—like a weapon. Bending her freed leg toward her chest, she thrust it up forcefully. The hard heel of her shoe hit him squarely in the scrotum.

Diamond howled and staggered back, bent over, holding his crotch. Dorothy sat up and reached for her pants. Before she could get them on, Diamond pushed her on her back again, straddled her, and punched her face twice. She could barely see out of her puffy eyes, and her nose and mouth were bleeding, but still, she tried to fight him off. Finally, he gave up, pulled up his pants, and got back on his Harley. "You tell anyone about this; I'll kill you," he said and roared away, leaving her in the dirt.

Dorothy pulled up her pants and struggled to her feet. She staggered to the highway, crying, and flagged down an elderly man in a pickup truck who rushed her to the North Platte Hospital. The emergency room nurses removed her dirty, torn clothes, and dressed her in a hospital gown. They were cleaning her superficial wounds when three survivors of a car crash were rushed in and became the priority.

Dorothy was left alone behind a curtain, lying on a gurney. She saw a surgical knife on a tray nearby. A nurse pulled back the curtain just in time to see Dorothy stab the knife into the side of her twisted leg, below the knee, and drag it down toward her ankle. As blood gushed onto the floor, Dorothy passed out.

Outside Dorothy's hospital room, Dr. McKenzie told Niko, "Your daughter is very brave."

Niko rarely thought of Dorothy as his daughter. After five years of living under the same roof, they were basically strangers, hardly talking or interacting. They only co-existed because they both loved Odina, and Odina loved them.

"We reset her broken nose and put ice on her face," Dr. McKenzie continued. "She needed nineteen stitches in her leg. Do you know why she cut herself?"

"I have no idea," Niko told him. "Have the police been to see her?"

"Yes. A Captain Frank Cassidy came early this morning."

"Why a captain?"

"The Diamond and Hannigan families are prominent. The incident could get a lot of attention."

"I've never heard of the Diamonds," Niko admitted.

"They're well-known in Omaha," the Captain related. "Steve Diamond is an eighteen-year-old senior at Omaha Central High. He's a star football player, heavily recruited. He's nearly as big as you. He's wild and tough like his father, an ex-marine and federal marshal. Well-connected in Omaha."

"Connected to what?"

"Politicians, lawyers, judges... organized crime."

"The Mafia?" Niko asked. The Mafia had been in Omaha since Prohibition.

The doctor said, "Captain Cassidy can tell you more."

Niko thanked him and opened the door to Dorothy's room. The Hensen and Hannigan families were gathered around her bed. "There are too many visitors in here already," a harried nurse said before taking a look at Niko and hurrying out.

Everyone turned to Niko. Dorothy's head was propped on pillows. She looked him in the eye, and Niko recalled Odina telling him, *"The first time Dorothy talked to me was with her eyes."* Now those eyes were talking to him, saying, *"I can handle this myself."* He saw no self-pity in her, although he sensed a vulnerability that indicated she wouldn't mind a hug from her father but could live without one. Inexplicably, that defiant look and vulnerable eyes moved him. *She's just like me,* he realized, making him think they had more in common than facial similarities. For the first time, Niko was able to see his daughter for who she was and who she wasn't. She was *not* a symbol of his weakness or her mother's deceit. She was her own person, strong enough to survive and thrive the misfortunes of her birth. She was not like her mother; she was like him. She looked like him, was tough like him, stubborn like him. *Two fools,* he thought, and decided, *Enough.* He took a deep breath and walked to her bedside.

No one knew what to expect. Father and daughter had established no relationship over the years. They simply coexisted. Now, they stared at each other for several moments, saying nothing.

What's he thinking? Dorothy wondered.

What's she thinking? Niko wondered.

What are they thinking? Everyone else in the room wondered.

Finally, Niko leaned over and kissed his daughter on the forehead. Everyone was stunned, especially Dorothy. He had never kissed her before. When he whispered in her ear, he used the same words Odina told him she had used the night she connected with Jane Doe. "I see you," he said, so only she could hear. Dorothy threw her arms around her father's neck as she had done with Odina twelve years ago. She bit her lower lip, trying not to cry.

"Just rest," he whispered. "I'll come back tomorrow when you're alone, and we can talk. Okay?"

Dorothy nodded.

"Don't worry," he said. "I'm with you now. I'll take care of everything."

Niko left the room, and Odina followed. "What just happened?" she asked.

"I finally saw my daughter."

"It's about time, don't you think?"

"I'm a little slow," he smiled. "For instance, I think it's time we got married."

"I'm happy just being together. I don't need a document."

"My daughter needs a mother, not a nanny. So, will you marry me?"

"If your daughter approves."

The next morning, Niko returned to Dorothy's hospital room. She was alone and waiting. He kissed her for the second time in five years.

Dorothy said, "How could I hate you for so long, and love you in an instant?"

"I feel the same," Niko said. "We're very much alike."

"Is that good or bad?"

"Both."

A uniformed policeman entered the room. "Hello again, Dorothy," he said and turned to Niko. "Captain Frank Cassidy. You must be Dorothy's father."

"Niko Hensen. What's up, Captain?"

"Steve Diamond was at my office first thing this morning."

"Contradicted everything in Dorothy's statement, I'm guessing," Niko said.

"He did." Cassidy proceeded to relate Diamond's version.

"He's lying about everything," Dorothy said. "I didn't ask him for a ride. I didn't grope him. I wasn't sexually aggressive. He assaulted me."

"He admits he hit you, but claims it was self-defense. After you kicked him in the groin."

"That's not how it happened," Dorothy said.

"It's his word against yours," Cassidy said. "If you pursue this case, be prepared for some very embarrassing questions from Diamond's side."

"Like what?"

"Like, are you a virgin? How many times have you had sex?"

"They can ask me that?"

Cassidy nodded. "I'm afraid so. Diamond's father is a powerful man. He'll stop at nothing to defend his son. He's very well-connected."

"This is North Platte, not Omaha," Niko said.

"He has a long reach," Cassidy said. "He's also intimidating. Ex-Marine Corps, heavyweight boxing champ during the war, martial arts instructor now. Never lost a fight. That man scares the hell out of most people."

"I'm not most people," Niko said. "I'll go to Omaha and have a talk with him."

"I advise against that," Cassidy said. "Joe Diamond is an associate of Anthony Biase, the Omaha Mafia boss. You may have to deal with him if you go after Diamond."

"I don't want you involved with the Mafia," Dorothy said, alarmed.

"Don't worry. I'll talk to Biase before Diamond."

"What makes you think Biase will listen to you?" Cassidy asked.

"I have a way with people. Where can I find him?"

"I hear he operates out of the Owl Cigar Shop in Omaha," Cassidy said. "But I think you're making a big mistake. These are very dangerous men."

"I'm a dangerous man myself, Captain."

"I believe you," the captain said. "You look like you can handle yourself. But don't say I didn't warn you."

"Maybe you should warn them," Niko said. Cassidy shrugged.

"Suit yourself, Mr. Hensen," he said and left the room.

"I know you're a war hero," Dorothy said. "But are you still a dangerous man?"

Niko nodded. "The Diamonds have more to worry about than I do," he told her.

"I guess I don't know anything about you. We've hardly talked all these years."

"We'll make up for lost time later," Niko said. "But let's talk about you now."

"My life is not very interesting," she said.

"That's not what I heard," Niko said. "But I'd like to hear it from you."

Dorothy spoke of her years of fighting limitations and exceeding expectations. "What you've accomplished is amazing," he told her.

"I owe it all to Nanny O," Dorothy said. "I was living on the dark side of a one-way mirror, where no one could see me … until she did."

"I owe her a lot too," Niko said. "In fact, yesterday, I asked her to marry me."

Dorothy looked conflicted until Niko quickly added, "She turned me down."

Dorothy's expression turned to shock. "But why? I know she loves you."

"Apparently, she loves you more," Niko said. "She said she wouldn't marry me unless you approve. She said if she had to choose between us, she'd choose you."

"She really said that?"

Niko nodded.

Dorothy smiled. "Well, she doesn't have to choose," she said. "I approve. She can have us both."

"She'll have to hear that from you."

"I'll tell her right away," Dorothy said. "And I want you to forget about the Diamonds. I finally have a father, and I don't want to lose you."

"Sorry," Niko said. "But no one hurts my daughter and gets away with it."

CHAPTER 42

1958
DIAMONDS

The next morning, Niko left North Platte at five a.m. and arrived at the Owl Cigar Shop at nine-thirty. The shop didn't open till ten, so he went to the Owl Coffee Shop next door. Two waitresses, one blonde, one brunette, scrambled to serve the tall, handsome stranger first. The blonde won. "Hi, I'm Pearl," she said, pad and pencil in hand. Niko thought she was pretty in a brassy sort of way.

"Just coffee, Pearl," he said and smiled.

She poured him a cup of coffee. "You're not from around here, are you?"

"No. North Platte."

"Bailey Yard, right?"

Niko nodded.

"What brings you all the way to Nebraska's biggest city?"

"I'm looking for Anthony Biase. Know him?"

"Of course. You a cop?"

"No. Why?"

"Nowadays, mostly cops and lawyers are looking for Mr. Biase."

"Not me. I'm here to ask him for a favor."

"Why would Mr. Biase do a favor for a stranger?"

"It's in his best interest."

"Will it stop his indictments?"

"What indictments?"

"He's about to be indicted for dealing drugs and a bunch of other stuff. It was in all the papers. Everybody knows."

"Not me," Niko replied.

Just then, a young man passed. "Morning, Pearl," he greeted her—kept walking while adding, "You're looking fine today."

"Thank you, Mr. Buffett. You always say the right thing. Any tips for me?"

Buffet looked back over his shoulder. "Yes. Work hard and save your money."

"He's a financial genius, that Warren Buffet," Pearl declared, watching him exit the front door. "Hey, see that guy next to him, outside the front window?"

Niko looked. "No, missed him. Who was it?"

"Frankie Florio—Mr. Biase's top man; opens the cigar store every morning. Easy to spot. No shape. No neck. No waist. The bulge in his jacket is a gun."

Niko paid for the coffee and left a nice tip. "Thanks, Pearl."

Outside, Niko saw the back of a shapeless man in a long, wrinkled raincoat opening the door of the cigar store. Niko approached from behind. "Frankie Florio?" he said. The man's right hand reached inside the right pocket of his raincoat. *Shit*, Niko thought. Florio turned, holding a .38 caliber Colt in his right hand.

Niko swept his left arm up fast into Florio's right wrist, causing the gun to point at the sky. Then he expertly wrested the Colt away and pointed it at Florio.

"Whoa, that was fast," the gangster exclaimed, raising his hands. "Don't shoot."

"Don't move."

"I won't. What the fuck do you want?"

"I want to talk to Anthony Biase," Niko said.

"Why?"

"I have a problem with one of Mr. Biase's friends."

"Which one?"

"Joe Diamond—and I don't want to have a problem with Mr. Biase, too. Understand?"

"Understood," the rumpled, droopy-eyed gangster said. "Where you from?"

"North Platte."

"I've been there. The land of cows, trains, and the fuckin' Chamanskis."

"You know the fuckin' Chamanskis?"

"Sure. Those scumbags have been doin' Mr. Biase's books since Prohibition, no secret there. Jerzy Chamanski's a fuckin' thief. His ugly fuckin' sons, too. You do business with them?"

"My boss does," Niko said.

"Is your boss a drug dealer?"

"No. She's legitimate. The Chamanskis do her books."

"Then your boss is getting screwed."

I was right about them, Niko thought. "Why do you say that?"

"The Chamanskis keep two sets of books for everyone, and they're big-time drug dealers, too. A legitimate operator shouldn't have anything to do with them."

"You're sure about this?" Niko asked.

"Positive. Mostly they sell designer drugs to housewives. *Mother's Little Helpers*, they call them. Very addictive."

A bell went off in Niko's head, prompted by two words—
Addictive and Housewife. He knew someone who fit that
description.

"Besides, pal, you got old information. Joe Diamond
ain't Mr. Biase's friend no more. Mr. Biase's got problems
with the government, and Joe Diamond knows too much
about Mr. Biase's business. If someone got rid of him, they'd
be doin' Mr. Biase a favor."

"That's good to know. Where can I find Joe Diamond?"

"How the fuck should I know?" Florio snapped.

"You should be more helpful to a man pointing a gun
at your balls."

"Good point. Try Boys Town."

Niko cocked the hammer. "Hey, I'm serious," Florio
said, holding his hands in front of his jewels. "Diamond
teaches a self-defense class at Boys Town. He recruits tough
kids for his street gangs there. Fucker has no soul. I hate the
son of a bitch."

"Why? He's just a criminal, like you."

"No way. I don't hurt kids," Florio said. "That's an *infa-
mia*. Pure fuckin' evil."

Florio's attitude was like the CIA, where the definition
of evil was malleable. "How did a bad guy like Diamond get
a job at a clean place like Boys Town?"

"Father Flanagan died in the late thirties with no num-
ber-two guy. The place got fucked up. Diamond slipped
through the cracks with the help of dirty politicians."

"That was twenty years ago. Why is Diamond still
there?"

"People owe him or fear him. He's tough and connected."

"I'm going to disconnect him."

"Be my fuckin' guest."

Boys Town is nine miles west of downtown Omaha, on West Dodge Road. Niko turned at a thirty-foot-high pylon sign that displayed BOYS TOWN vertically. He drove past the unmanned gatehouse and noticed a white limestone statue of one boy carrying a smaller boy on his back. The inscription read: *"He ain't heavy, he's my brother."*

Saplings and hedges bordered pathways and round-abouts; he parked in front of the administration building. In the lobby, he saw framed pictures and plaques, highlighting the forty-one-year history of Boys Town. Photographs of Spencer Tracy and Mickey Rooney, from the 1938 movie were displayed. Niko read that Boys Town was originally founded as an orphanage in 1917 by Father Edward Flanagan, a Jesuit priest who welcomed all races and religions. *The world could use more Father Flanagans*, he thought.

Niko saw a man leaving the athletic director's office. He looked to be in his thirties, at least a foot shorter than Niko, but with a gymnast's solid physique. "Can I help you?" the man asked with a smile. "I'm Jim Bemis, Athletic Director."

"Niko Hensen. I'm looking for Joe Diamond."

Bemis's smile faded. "Are you a friend of his?"

"No. I was told I might find him here."

"Who told you?"

"Frankie Florio."

The man made a face like something smelled bad. "Are you a friend of *his?*"

Niko laughed and explained himself.

"So, you're here to ask Joe Diamond for a favor?"

"I'm here to ask him to do the right thing."

"Joe Diamond doesn't do the right thing. He's a bad man with dangerous friends."

"You're referring to Anthony Biase, I assume."

"For one," Bemis nodded.

"Mr. Diamond and Mr. Biase are no longer friends."

"That's news to me. Even so, Joe Diamond is not to be taken lightly."

"Neither am I. Where can I find him?"

"Follow me."

As they walked together, Niko said, "Tell me about Joe Diamond."

"He's a mean bastard," Bemis said. "He intimidates people with his size and temper. Be careful what you say. You don't want to upset him."

Niko laughed. "I think it's funny how a man's reputation precedes him. I'm six-six, two hundred and twenty-five pounds, and you're worried I might upset Joe Diamond?"

"Diamond's big, too. And on top of that, he's never lost a fight."

"And how many have I lost?"

"I have no idea," Bemis shrugged.

"I'm undefeated too. So, maybe you should be warning Diamond."

"This I gotta see," Bemis said, opening the door to the gymnasium.

The gym was small, with an undersized basketball court and old gymnastic gear. Ropes for climbing hung from the ceiling, and there was a heavy punching bag in the corner. Niko spotted Joe Diamond immediately, strutting and lecturing a group of boys seated on exercise mats looking up at him. He wore a gray T-shirt and shorts that accentuated his muscular physique. His hair was cut flat-top style, enhancing his tough-guy image. Niko studied him. *Thick neck, twenty inches around, he estimated. He can take a head punch.*

Heavy legs. Bulging biceps. Strong and ponderous. Probably over-confident. Speed and surprise will take him out fast.

"What do you want, Bemis?" Diamond shouted. "I'm trying to teach these kids, and you're distracting me."

"Sorry about that, but I've got someone here who wants to meet you."

Diamond looked at Niko. "I'm a little busy right now," he said.

"That's okay, I'll wait," Niko said. "I'd like to watch your technique."

"Who the hell are you?" Diamond said.

"Niko Hensen."

"Never heard of you."

"Your son tried to rape my daughter. Did you hear that?"

Diamond's face turned red—his anger rising. Niko liked that.

Diamond smirked. "The way I heard it, some horny bitch got physical with my boy, and he had to straighten her out."

"You heard wrong," Niko said, with boys snickering in the background. "I just don't want you using your influence to fix the trial."

Diamond laughed. "What are you—a fuckin' comedian?"

"No, I'm dead serious."

Diamond puffed up his chest and flexed his pectoral muscles, so they moved under his shirt. "Listen, asshole; my son is going to Nebraska next fall on a football scholarship. No bitch is going to spoil that with some phony assault charge. I'll do whatever it takes to make sure that doesn't happen. Understand? Now get lost."

A few boys guffawed until Niko said, "I'm not going anywhere," and began walking across the gym, pointing at Joe Diamond but looking at the kids. "You think this guy is funny?" he asked. "His son tried to rape my daughter. When she resisted, he beat her up—left her bleeding by the side of the road." He singled out one of the boys. "What if she was your sister? Would that be funny, too?"

The boy squirmed but didn't answer. The gym was silent.

"Get lost," Diamond broke the silence. "Or I'll leave you by the side of the road."

"Give it your best shot," Niko said, standing still, his arms at his sides.

Diamond stepped forward. Niko did the same. They were inches apart. Diamond was accustomed to looking down—not eye to eye. He felt awkward. Niko knew that.

A boy said, "Mister, back off. Mr. Diamond's the toughest man in Nebraska."

Niko shook his head. "Son, he's not even the toughest guy in this gym."

An undefeated fighter expects to win. An unbeatable fighter knows he'll win. So, when Diamond threw his right hook, he expected to break Niko's jaw and knock him out. It had happened countless times before. But, when Niko saw the roundhouse right coming, he knew he'd already won. *The man is sucker-punching himself,* Niko thought, thanking Tian for teaching him so well.

CHAPTER 43

1958
DIAMOND CUTTERS

Niko ducked deftly; his fists raised to either side of his chin. Diamond's punch whiffed harmlessly over his head. Niko unleashed Tian's favorite weapon—the left hook *shovel punch* up into Diamond's liver—causing immediate damage—excruciating pain.

Stepping farther left, he quickly delivered a left hook to Diamond's unprotected right kidney. This time, Diamond reared back, his mouth open, trying to scream—no sound coming out. His body had shut down. He was frozen in place, like a statue.

The overhand right Niko launched next, to the center of Diamond's face, was superfluous. The man was already out on his feet. *That's for insulting my daughter,* Niko thought as it landed.

Diamond toppled back, his face shattered. A canvas mat broke his fall. The gym was deathly quiet. The only evidence that Diamond was still alive was the rise and fall of his chest.

The fight had lasted half a minute, three punches—two of Tian's favorites.

"Enough," Bemis said, stepping in front of the unconscious Diamond.

"Actually, it was one more than enough," Niko said.

"How badly is he hurt?" Bemis asked.

"He'll live," Niko said, glancing down with disgust at Diamond. "But his fighting days are over. Call an ambulance."

One student said, "I can't believe you did that to him. He was our hero."

"Heroes care about people," Niko told them. "Like Mr. Bemis here. He's a hero."

"Thanks for the plug," Bemis whispered.

An ambulance and a police car arrived. Diamond was whisked away while Niko was approached by the two remaining cops. "These guys could be on Diamond's payroll," Bemis warned Niko out of the corner of his mouth. "Careful what you say."

Niko eyed the cops. "You guys on Diamond's payroll?" he asked. Bemis groaned.

The boys who witnessed the fight gave their testimony at the scene, but Niko was asked to go to police headquarters to sign a statement. The cops were treating Niko circumspectly. Not only had he defeated the "toughest guy in Omaha" in less than a minute, but he had asked two officers an incriminating question. What would he do next? Bemis volunteered to go to the station with Niko as a precaution.

After giving his statement, Niko told Bemis he wanted to return to Boys Town and snoop around. "If Diamond recruits kids into street gangs, we should put an end to his pipeline—clean things up."

"There are plenty of good men in Boys Town and the Omaha police department who can do that," Bemis said. "Not everyone's crooked."

"I'm sure," Niko said. "But let's give them a hand. I'd like to talk to some of the kids under Diamond's supervision, see if they can point us in the right direction."

Niko spent the rest of the day with Bemis. They reassembled Diamond's class and talked to them. One boy asked if Niko would teach their martial arts class. "Sorry, I have a job," Niko said. "But I'm sure Mr. Bemis will find a good replacement."

"Can you just teach us that first punch you threw?" the boy asked.

"The shovel punch," Niko nodded. "That was taught to me by a great man ... who made me promise only to use it to fight for good. You'll have to do good before I teach you."

"How will you know if we're good?" the boy asked. "You won't be here."

"Mr. Bemis will tell me."

After Bemis gave Niko a tour of Boys Town, they had dinner and said goodbye, each knowing they had made a new friend. Niko called Odina at ten o'clock from his room at the Omaha City Hotel and told her he would return to North Platte in the morning.

The phone in his hotel room rang at one in the morning, waking him. It was Captain Cassidy calling from North Platte. "Sorry if I woke you, Mr. Hensen. Your wife told me to call you in Omaha to prove you couldn't be involved in an incident here in North Platte tonight."

"She's right, I'm four hours away, and I've been here since nine-thirty this morning." He checked the clock in the room. "Yesterday morning, actually. Plenty of witnesses. What is it I'm no longer suspected of doing?"

"Steve Diamond was assaulted. He's in the North Platte Hospital."

"What a coincidence, I put his father in an Omaha hospital last night."

"What happened?"

"We had an altercation," Niko told him.

"You started a fight with Joe Diamond?"

"Actually, he started it. I finished it."

"I underestimated you, Mr. Hensen."

"So did Joe Diamond. What happened to his son?"

"He was in North Platte to see his lawyer," Cassidy explained. "After their meeting, they went to dinner. The lawyer says he left Diamond around nine. Two hours later, Diamond was found unconscious in the alley behind the old Fox Theater. He had a wound to the back of his head, and he had two shattered kneecaps. Looks like someone with a lot of experience and power, like you, did a job on him with a baseball bat. I think his football career is over."

"Any suspects besides me?"

"Your whole family," Cassidy suggested. "But everyone has an alibi."

Niko returned to North Platte in the morning and told Dorothy about his trip to Omaha. She listened, in wide-eyed awe. "That's amazing," she said. "And while you were taking care of Joe Diamond, someone attacked his son."

"Captain Cassidy told me," Niko said. "Any ideas?"

"No," Dorothy said. "Cassidy questioned all of us." She shook her head. "Ridiculous. Who in our family, aside from you, would attack anyone?"

"Well, he had to ask," Niko said. "We all have a motive."

"We all had alibis too," Dorothy said. "The four of us were home, together. Grandma and Grandpa went to bed early. Odina and I turned in around eleven."

"Good," Niko said. "The truth is the best alibi."

"Should we still press charges against Steve Diamond?"

"I think justice has been served. Don't you?"

"Yes. It's fair now."

Two days later, Niko requested a meeting with Elvis and Eli at the North Platte Diner. Seeing them sitting side by side, Niko remembered how different they looked from when they first met. The big, bulky boys were now lean, handsome men. The only negative Niko saw was their growing resemblance to their father. Fortunately, the likeness ended there. They were good men, and Niko liked working for them.

"Thanks for meeting me here," Niko began.

"Why a business meeting outside the office without my mother?" Elvis asked.

"Because I don't want your mother to know about it."

"No business secrets in our family," Eli reminded him. "You know that."

"I do. But your mother seems to have forgotten."

"What are you talking about?" Eli asked, irritated by the implication.

Niko took a deep breath. "You two know how unhappy I've been with your father's unresolved status and the Chamanskis involvement at Circle H."

"Yes. You tell us twice a year and quit twice a year," Elvis said, glancing at Eli.

Niko leaned forward across the table. "And each time I bring it up, your mother says she has good reasons for not making changes."

"Correct. She's afraid Duke is still alive, and she insists she needs the Chamanskis."

Niko nodded. "Right. And we all know Duke's not coming back."

"But we can't tell her," Eli whispered. "And we agreed not to pressure her about the Chamanskis."

"Well, now I think we have to pressure her," Niko said, producing a folder from the seat next to him. "I learned some things in Omaha two days ago that prompted me to visit North Platte City Hall when I got back and go over our records."

"About the Chamanskis again?" Elvis asked, raising his voice. "Enough already, Niko. My mother insists we need them."

"Your *mother* needs them," Niko retorted. "*Not* the business."

"What the hell does that mean?" Elvis shouted, drawing attention.

Niko held up his hand to quiet Elvis. "Just listen," he asked. Referring to papers in the folder now, he said, "In the corporate records your father is still listed as president, stockholder, and board member. Shirley and you two are the same."

"We know all that," Elvis said, rolling his eyes at Eli.

Niko saw the disrespectful gesture but did not react. Instead, he spoke calmly. "Do you also know that Jerzy Chamanski is a de facto board member—with power of attorney for your mother and father?"

Both brothers were dumbfounded. After a prolonged silence, Elvis asked, "How is that possible?"

"Your mother added him over a year ago," Niko told them.

"Why in the world would she do that?" Elvis asked.

"It's a long, very sad story," Niko said. "When I was in Omaha, I learned that the Chamanskis also do the books for Anthony Biase."

"The Mafia, boss?" Elvis asked, obviously surprised.

"That's right," Niko confirmed, looking around the restaurant to make sure no one was listening. "A Biase associate told me the Chamanskis are in the drug business with Biase's organization."

"Jesus," Eli said. "Does this affect us?"

"Indirectly, yes."

"How?"

Niko beckoned the twins to move closer. "As we all know," he whispered, "your mother has an addictive personality. It took her years to get off alcohol."

Both boys nodded. "It was very difficult for her," Elvis confirmed.

"I don't like where this is going," Eli noted.

"I'm sorry, I don't like it either," Niko concurred. "But I believe the Chamanskis have hooked Shirley on drugs and are manipulating her. Nothing else could explain her irrational business decision."

"I don't believe this," Elvis said.

"Believe it," Niko insisted. "And if I'm right, the Chamanskis can take control of the Circle H anytime they want with their power of attorney for both parents."

"Then why haven't they?"

"I think they're just biding their time and stealing you blind," Niko theorized. "No one is watching them. They do what they want."

Elvis rubbed his eyes. "Jesus. What do we do now?"

"We intervene and get rid of the Chamanskis."

"You could be wrong about the drugs," Eli said.

"That would be worse," Niko said. "It would mean your mother lost her mind."

"Okay," Elvis said downcast. "How do we fix this?"

"Leave that to me."

The intervention came first and included Amanda and Jonas. It was emotionally draining, and brief. Within fifteen minutes, Shirley denied, confessed, and decried her drug use. "They made it sound so innocent. An anti-anxiety pill. Then a stronger pill. I thought they were my friends."

"The Chamanskis are nobody's friend," Niko said. "They're bloodsuckers."

"We'll get through this together," Amanda told Shirley, touching her shoulder.

Niko was more pragmatic. "No. This time you need professional help, Shirley. There's a detox clinic in Grand Island. You're going there and staying there until you're well."

Shirley didn't argue.

Elvis, Eli, and Niko took Shirley to the clinic. They insisted Amanda not come. "We all love Shirley," Niko said. "But she needs tough love now."

The two-and-a half hour ride was solemn but optimistic. "Forget about everything except getting better, Mom," Elvis said. "We'll take care of business."

"Can you fix the mess I made?"

"It will be my pleasure," Niko said.

Chapter 44

1958
CHAMANSKIS

The Chamanski Group owned a single-tenant office building on Route 5 not far from Buffalo Bill's abandoned ranch. It was a foreboding fortress built of brick and stone. *All it needs is a moat*, Niko thought, parking in front. The lobby furniture was old and heavy; the receptionist too.

Niko gave his name. "You can go right in," she said. "They're ready for you."

No one's ever ready for me, Niko thought.

Jerzy Chamanski was a little old man sitting behind a large, old desk. He wore a blue suit, formally buttoned, with a white shirt and blue tie. He was flanked by two younger men, with fire hydrant bodies. They wore ill-fitting, expensive suits. *Three homely bastards*, Niko thought.

"Have a seat," the old man said, smiling disingenuously.

"I'll stand."

The fake smile vanished.

He has a nose like a knackwurst, Niko noticed. There was no hair on top of his head, but plenty on the sides covering his ears, giving him a Ben Franklin look. Niko guessed he was in his mid-seventies.

311

He glanced at the sons and concluded, *Knackwurst noses run in the family*. They appeared to be in their mid-forties and sported the same hairstyle as their father, though they still had some thinning hair clinging to the top.

The old man said, "These are my sons, Bezyli and Alexji."

Niko did not extend a hand. The sons glared malevolently. Niko glared back. They looked away first.

"You asked for this meeting," Jerzy said. "What can we do for you?"

"You can relinquish your power of attorney for Circle H, return all stolen money and land, resign as our accountant, and leave town."

The old man laughed. "Be serious, Mr. Hensen."

"I'm as serious as death," Niko said, his voice menacing.

The elder Chamanski cleared his throat. "Does Shirley know about this?"

"Shirley's in a clinic, being detoxed off the drugs you've been giving her."

The Chamanskis blinked rapidly like they'd just come out from under a rock and were blinded by the light. "I don't know what you're talking about," Jerzy tried.

Niko slammed his fist down on the desk. The phone's handpiece flew off the cradle. A desk calendar hit the floor. The Chamanskis flinched and turned pale. Veins bulged in Niko's neck. "It must have been easy for you to hook an alcoholic," he growled. "First, Milltown, mother's little helpers, to ease anxiety. Then stronger doses until she was addicted. I'm sure it was simple to manipulate her after that, get power of attorney, and anything else you wanted."

"We have signed documents to support our legal position in court," Bezyli said.

"I have no intention of going to court," Niko said.

"If you're threatening us you should know we have very powerful connections and protection," the old man said, feigning confidence he didn't feel.

"Who? Anthony Biase?" Niko said, watching their nervous reaction. "He's got problems of his own right now. And I was told by a reliable source, that you're one of his problems. You may need protection from your protection."

Bezyli turned ashen. "Who told you that?"

"Does the name Frankie Florio ring a bell?"

"Jesus," Jerzy said.

"We have other connections," Bezyli tried.

"Joe Diamond won't help you either," Niko informed them. "I met him in Omaha the other day. We had a disagreement. He's in the hospital."

The old man wiped his brow with a handkerchief. "What do you want, Mr. Hensen?"

"I told you. A return of all stolen Circle H assets and your resignations."

"Don't be ridiculous. You can't prove we stole anything," Alexji said.

"An IRS forensic audit can," Niko said and watched the three of them squirm.

"We need time to think this over," the old man said, pale and perspiring.

"While you're thinking," Niko advised, "I suggest you call the Omaha General Hospital and check on the condition of Joe Diamond since our disagreement. You know—as a reference. I'll be at the North Platte Diner tomorrow morning at eight. Be there, or I'll assume we have a serious disagreement too and will act accordingly."

❦ ❦ ❦

They met at the diner promptly at eight and huddled in a corner.

"How's Joe?" Niko asked.

"His condition is critical," Jerzy said. "They wouldn't give me any details."

"You want details?" Niko said. "The fight lasted thirty seconds. He's got a ruptured liver and kidney. His jaw and nose are broken. He's probably missing a few teeth. Now, what about my offer?"

"This is extortion," the old man said, his voice weak.

"Thanks for your legal analysis," Niko sneered. "Now, what's your answer?"

The Chamanskis exchanged glances. "If we agree, do you guarantee no publicity, no contacting the IRS, and no acts of vengeance in the future?"

"Guaranteed. But I still want an audit to determine how much you stole."

"No audit," the old man said.

"No deal," Niko replied.

Jerzy hesitated then said, "Okay, it's a deal," and held out a hand. Niko ignored it. "Do we have a deal or not, Mr. Hensen?"

"We have a deal. I just don't want to shake your hand."

The independent audit of Circle H confirmed a net worth of twenty million, sixteen million more than listed on the last Chamanski statement. Undeclared land, undervalued inventory, phony invoices, and hidden cash accounted for the missing value. The Chamanskis settled the debt with land transfers, vendor credits, missing inventory, and a certified check. They resigned their power of attorney and prepared to leave Nebraska.

"Where did they get all that cash to pay us?" Elvis asked.

"It's an accumulation. They've been stealing from you and other ranchers for years," Niko said. "We're just one of many."

"Should we tell other ranchers?"

"I promised no further recriminations against the Chamanskis. I keep my word."

"Doesn't seem fair," Eli said.

"It's fair for us."

A week later the Chamanski office building burned to the ground.

Jerzy called Niko. "I thought we had a deal," he shouted into the phone.

"We do," Niko insisted.

"My office building was destroyed by a fire last night."

"I swear I had nothing to do with it," Niko said.

"I don't believe you."

"I don't care."

"If you didn't do it, who did?"

"Anthony Biase, maybe? Looking to burn you and your two sets of books."

There was a pause before Chamanski said, "You're not done with us yet."

"Even you are not stupid enough to mess with me again," Niko said.

"It's not what we'll do. It's what's already been done," Jerzy said, and the line went dead.

Shirley came home from Grand Island rejuvenated and eager to get back to work. At the first meeting of the board of directors, she asked, "What do we do with the money we didn't know we had?"

They discussed options: sell the ranch, maintain the status quo, expand, invest in other businesses. Niko proposed an entirely new direction based on changes that had taken place in the beef industry recently. "As we all know, grain-fed beef has become extremely popular over the past few years," he digressed. "People prefer the flavor and texture. I believe the demand will only increase in the future. Agreed?"

"Agreed," Elvis said, and the others nodded. "So, what's your idea?"

"Grain feeding, instead of grazing, will result in a consolidation of processing locations. Cattle growers like us would be smart to build large feedlots near progressive processors and grow with them."

"Sounds logical," Shirley said. "Which processors are most likely to grow?"

"I'm recommending one in particular," Niko said. "Have you heard of A.D. Anderson or Currier Holman?"

"I read about them in a trade magazine a couple of years ago," Elvis said. "They had some crazy idea of doing all beef processing under one roof. No more shipping of swinging sides of beef east. Sounded unrealistic to me."

"It's totally realistic," Niko said. "Anderson and Currier formed a new company called Iowa Beef Processors. They plan to streamline the processing and packaging of beef and pork under one roof. Every meat cut is to be sealed in airtight packages, in a box. They call it *box beef*. I believe it's the wave of the future. They have solid financing and are building a plant in Denison, Iowa, right now. I think Circle H should get behind them."

"How?" Eli asked.

"Buy acres of land near the factory, invest heavily in feed mills, storage tanks, and holding pens to grain feed thousands of animals for sale to IBP."

Eli whistled. "You're talking about a major investment to support one customer."

"Eli's right," Elvis said. "What happens if you're wrong? What if IBP fails?"

"IBP won't fail. Their idea is revolutionary but sound. If I am wrong, Circle H will just own more land and equipment than we need. We're flush with cash now, so we can handle it. But if I'm right, Circle H can become one of the largest cattle growers in the world."

"Sounds exciting," Elvis said.

Eli said, "If you're right, a lot of small ranches will go out of business."

"Probably," Niko nodded. "Change always hurts someone. My Nebraska football team lost to Stanford in the 1941 Rose Bowl because they changed, and we didn't."

"That's right. Wasn't that the introduction of the T formation?" Eli recalled.

"Exactly," Niko answered. "A major change."

"I vote in favor of Niko's idea," Elvis said, and Eli agreed.

Shirley said, "You have my vote too, Niko, and my gratitude for all you've done for our family, and for me, personally. That's why I'm gifting you some of my Circle H stock. I want you to share in the future with us."

"I'm honored," Niko said.

"But, in return, I expect you to stay with the company. No more talk of leaving. Agreed?"

"Agreed," Niko said, committing himself to the Hannigans, marveling at the irony.

PART 3

CHAPTER 45

1962–1970
THE SIXTIES

In May of 1962, *Life* magazine ran a cover story entitled, *The New Cattle Barons.* The article included photos of the Hannigan and Hensen families and the IBP founders. The cover depicted the face of a Hereford bull, and the inside subtitle was, *From Prairie to Plate.*

"In retrospect, I wish we hadn't agreed to do that article," Niko said.

"Why?" Odina said. "It's very flattering."

"I'm just not comfortable with strangers knowing our business," Niko said.

"What could happen?"

"I'll know when it happens."

She injected the needle into her arm, watched the syringe empty, and waited for the numbness to relieve her pain. She was in a motel room in Las Vegas, where she had been living for a year. Monthly checks from her brother paid her expenses though most of the money was spent on drugs.

Outside, the sun blazed, but her room faced north and got no direct sunlight. The window shades were kept down, and the drapes were drawn tight. The air conditioner pumped in arctic air, so the room was always frigid. Still, she felt hot and sweaty. The only light came from the red neon VACANCY sign outside her window that made the room glow like St. Elmo's Fire.

Las Vegas was not her home. She had no home anymore. This place was just another stop on her road to nowhere. She wept as she reached for the issue of *Life*, she had taken from the motel lobby. The picture of a Hereford bull and the words *Cattle Barons* on the cover had caught her attention. Standing in the lobby, she had flipped through the pages. The pictures inside made her feel faint. She choked on a sob, clutched the magazine to her chest, and stumbled from the lobby to her room. Groggy from the drug, she opened the magazine again.

Niko Hensen smiled at her from the glossy page. *He's still gorgeous.* She vaguely remembered horseback riding with him and making love. The words under his picture described him as an All-American football player and war hero. Another picture showed Niko sitting next to a beautiful dark-skinned woman with a young boy on her lap. The caption read, *Niko Hensen, his wife Odina, and their son Erik, 2.* She wept.

Her brothers, Elvis and Eli, were so thin she hardly recognized them. They both had attractive wives, and Elvis had a cute two-year-old daughter.

Her mother Shirley looked healthy and happy. The article quoted her; *"I've been blessed. I have wonderful family and friends. I only wish my daughter was here with us. But she chose a different life."* More tears, more pain.

The final picture in the article was of a dark-haired girl staring at her. *Who are you?* She wiped tears from her cheeks. *You look just like Niko.* She read the name under the picture: DOROTHY HENSEN. She was identified as Niko's daughter from a previous relationship. Beth's heart raced. *My daughter! I tried to kill that girl.* She didn't want to read more but couldn't stop. *Overcoming severe handicaps caused by prenatal problems, Dorothy is now a high honors student at the University of Nebraska and plans to join her father working for Circle H.*

An anguished cry escaped her lips. She staggered from the bed to the bathroom. She needed more relief from the pain.

Beth Hannigan was found dead on the floor of her motel room the next morning. The copy of *Life* lay next to her, opened to a picture of Dorothy Hensen. Her family claimed her body, took her home to North Platte and buried her in the Hannigan section of the North Platte Cemetery. "I told you that article wouldn't do us any good," Niko said at Beth's graveside.

Jonas Hensen hated war. He had fought one and lived through four; the terrible waste of World War I, the fight for survival of World War II, the political conflict in Korea, and the national nightmare of Vietnam. *"The only war worth fighting is a war of survival,"* he told his students at North Platte High. *"The United States didn't belong in Korea, and we don't belong in Vietnam. It's their civil war. But you could be sent there unless you protest."*

By October of 1964, at sixty-nine years old, his politics cost Jonas his job.

"We'd like you to retire at the end of this school year," Clayton Morgan, chairman of the school committee, told Jonas. "You're nearly seventy years old. It's time."

"This is about my political views, isn't it, Clayton?" Jonas had replied.

"To be honest, Jonas, yes. People don't like what you're teaching our kids. They think it's unpatriotic. To be honest, I agree."

"But times have changed, Clayton."

"Not in Nebraska."

Jonas retired—no longer the Golden Boy.

"People should be ashamed of themselves, after all you've done," Amanda had objected to his forced retirement. Jonas was more understanding.

"It's the war," he excused the townspeople. "The whole country is divided, not just North Platte."

"What will you do now?"

"Teach without a classroom," he told her, and that's what he did.

By the late sixties, millions of students across the nation were protesting. It became a decade of change and turmoil in America. The nation's youth took to the streets chanting slogans like…"Hell no, we won't go."— "One, two, three, four, we don't want your fucking war."— "Make love, not war."— "Flower power."

As a new decade dawned, four student protestors at Kent State University were shot and killed by members of the Ohio National Guard. Young Americans killing young Americans. Jonas was devastated.

A national demonstration protesting these killings and the Vietnam War, in general, was scheduled for May 9, 1970. Over 100,000 people were expected in D.C. and another 100,000 in San Francisco. Jonas asked Amanda to go with him to Washington.

"Do we have to go?" she asked. "I don't think I'm physically up to it."

"You don't have to go—but I do," he told her. "The antiwar movement is important to me."

"I understand. You go. I'll stay here, supporting you."

He departed a day prior to the demonstration.

At 3:30 in the morning, the day of the rally, Jonas lay wide awake in his bed at the Lombardy Hotel. He couldn't sleep. The frustrated faces of the young protestors he had seen walking the streets in D.C. kept him awake. He was reminded of the lifeless faces of the two young German soldiers he had killed fifty years ago. They had died for nothing as had his best friends, Hennessey, Hootstein, Davis, and Caroline. Now history was repeating itself with another senseless war. But this time, American kids were refusing to fight. They were rioting in the streets, and Jonas was right there with them—along with other educators and radical leaders.

✤ ✤ ✤

Wide awake, Jonas got out of bed. *How can anyone sleep at a time like this?* He wondered, getting dressed. He exited the Lombardy and walked to the Lincoln Memorial, less than a mile away. As he approached, he saw protesters milling near Lincoln's statue. It was 4:00 a.m. *I guess a lot of people couldn't sleep tonight*, he thought.

He saw a black limousine parked at the curb in front of the monument and wondered why it was there. He climbed the fifty-seven steps to the base of Lincoln's statue and got his answer. About forty young people were standing there, quietly listening to a middle-aged man dressed in a suit and tie. "Probably most of you think I'm an SOB," President Nixon was saying. "But I want you to know that I understand just how you feel." *Even the President of the United States couldn't sleep tonight,* Jonas thought.

Nixon rambled on about Neville Chamberlain and Winston Churchill, making several esoteric remarks that no one understood. Soon he was ready to leave. He shook a few hands and was departing when a student said, "I hope you realize we're prepared to die for what we believe," to which Nixon replied, "It wasn't that long ago my generation felt the same." As Jonas watched Nixon's limo drive away, he realized he had just witnessed history only because he couldn't sleep.

Finally, feeling like he needed a nap, the 74-year-old Golden Boy made his way back to his hotel and slept until mid-afternoon. He awoke with a headache. He showered, dressed, and walked to the rear of the White House, where a scheduled peace rally was happening. Wooden barricades kept thousands of protesters at a safe distance from the South Lawn. Police patrolled the perimeter, watching for trouble.

It started peacefully enough with protesters singing, tossing Frisbees, and interacting amicably with the cops. But as the afternoon gave way to dusk, the atmosphere changed. Hard hat workers and blue-collar agitators gradually found their way to the location, creating a potentially explosive situation. The mix of alcohol and marijuana in the air smelled like trouble.

The cops sensed the growing tension and urged the crowd to disperse. But their tactics backfired. Volatile drunks in the crowd grew restive, the protesters agitated. A beefy, red-faced hard hat threw a punch at a long-haired protester. When a policeman stepped in to separate them, the hard hat punched the cop, who retaliated by rapping the man's forehead with his nightstick. Blood streamed. More punches flew. The cop went down, and the crowd became a mob and attacked him—reason was abandoned.

Jonas instinctively wanted to help the cop and pushed towards him. Some rioters pushed back, and one threw a punch at Jonas—then another—his long grey hair confusing some into thinking he was an easy target—a dangerous assumption. In a flurry of motion, a Ghost from the past awakened and hell broke loose. First, a right fist to the nose of the man in front of the Ghost—eliminated one obstacle. A knee to the balls cleared away another. An elbow to a throat scythed another. A boot to an instep—another to a knee—gradually cleared a path to the cop who was curled into a fetal position on the ground. He looked badly hurt.

"Give me your hand!" Jonas shouted, extending his arm. The cop, bruised and bleeding, grabbed ahold. Jonas yanked him to his feet. The crowd closed in again. Jonas reacted by shouting, "Run! The cop pulled his gun!"

Chaos. Running. Screaming. Dispersing. Jonas hustled the cop out of harm's way and sat him on a bench. More police arrived and formed a protective circle around them. "Thanks, man," the injured cop said to Jonas. "You saved my life. Hey, are you okay?"

Jonas was gasping for air. "Out of breath," he managed.

"You don't look so good," the cop said.

"Can't catch my breath," Jonas said, his hand on his chest.

"He may be having a heart attack," another cop said. "I'll call an ambulance."

Jonas winced. "No, I'll be fine," he said. "Just need to breathe—rest." He slumped. The cop caught him under the arms and eased him to the ground. Someone put his head on a folded coat. Jonas closed his eyes. Images and memories whirled through his mind until Amanda's face was all he could see. She was smiling, her face hallowed by a soft light. *If you die… I'll die*, he thought. A sharp pain in his chest. A siren wailing. And then nothing at all.

CHAPTER 46

1970
JONAS

When Jonas collapsed in Washington, Amanda was standing at the kitchen sink in North Platte pouring herself a cup of coffee. Without warning, she dropped the coffee pot and slid to the floor in a sitting position.

Dorothy heard the noise and came running. "Grandma, what happened?"

Amanda reached for her granddaughter. "Help me up," she mumbled.

Dorothy managed to get Amanda up and in bed. Amanda's eyes fluttered, and she managed two unintelligible words. Dorothy put her ear next to Amanda's lips. "What did you say, Grandma? I can't hear you."

"Jonas... gone," Amanda whispered.

"Yes. He's in Washington," Dorothy reminded her.

Amanda shook her head, "No. Jonas... *gone*," she insisted, then went still.

Dorothy called the doctor and the two families to the mansion.

After Dr. McKenzie examined Amanda, he spoke to everyone gathered in the bedroom. "I don't know what to say. Two weeks ago, she was in excellent health. But right now, she has all the symptoms of advanced muscular dystrophy. I can't explain it."

"Maybe I can," Niko interrupted, entering the room, his voice shaky, his face pale, his eyes red-rimmed and teary. "I just received a phone call from a police detective in Washington. Two hours ago, my father suffered a fatal heart attack at the demonstration; he's gone."

Amanda tugged on Dorothy's sleeve. They looked at each other.

"There must be a mistake," Shirley suggested, distraught, her voice breaking.

"No mistake," Niko was emphatic. "The man I spoke with was at the scene. He got our number from Jonas's identification card."

"Jesus…" Elvis exclaimed. "What happened?"

"A rioting crowd attacked a cop," Niko explained. "Jonas fought them off and saved the cop. Then his heart gave out. The captain called him a hero."

"He was always a hero," Shirley said, tears streaming down her face.

"Dorothy, when did Grandma collapse?" Niko asked.

"A couple of hours ago."

"And Jonas died a couple of hours ago," Niko confirmed.

"Are you suggesting a connection?" Dr. McKenzie asked incredulously.

"It's a hell of a coincidence, don't you think?" Niko said, not liking the doctor's tone of voice.

"Coincidence, yes. Connection? No. Impossible."

"Impossible?" Niko said. "For years, Amanda's condition has been impossible. It never worsened. You yourself couldn't explain that."

"I still can't. MD is a progressive disease. Hers never progressed until today."

"And now you can't explain how Jonas's death and Amanda's collapse coincide."

"Medically, no, I can't."

"Maybe it's not medical," Dorothy interjected. "Grandma once told me she and Jonas made a vow when they were first married. Five words. *If you die, I'll die.* He died. And now she's dying."

"Nonsense," the doctor said. "Amanda collapsed before we knew Jonas had died."

"No. Amanda told me Jonas was gone before Niko told us about the phone call," Dorothy insisted. "I swear she did."

"That makes no sense," the doctor said.

"Maybe not to you," Dorothy said. "But it makes sense to me. I believe Amanda was living all these years for Jonas. Fighting off her disease for him. When he died, she stopped fighting."

"Well, she's not dead yet," the doctor said. "I'm calling an ambulance."

Amanda moaned and tugged at Dorothy's sleeve again. Dorothy put her ear next to her grandmother's mouth and listened intently. Tears were in her eyes when she looked up. "Grandma says she wants to wait here for Grandpa to come home."

"Then that's what we'll do," Niko said. "We'll get him for her."

Amanda closed her eyes, satisfied.

"She needs a hospital," Dr. McKenzie insisted.

"She needs her man more," Dorothy disagreed.

The family left the doctor with Amanda and met in the living room. "I'll take the Gulfstream," Niko said, referring to the new million-dollar company plane.

"Of course," Shirley said. "I'll call ahead and make arrangements for you."

Niko, Elvis, and Eli departed on the Gulfstream II Jet at five the next morning. They flew from Lee Bird Field in North Platte and arrived in D.C. slightly after 11 a.m. Shirley had contacted the Circle H lawyer in D.C. with instructions. She ordered an oversized coffin to accommodate Jonas's large body and the extra quantity of dry ice necessary to preserve him without embalming. She wanted Jonas's body to look as life-like as possible for Amanda. "Don't worry about the cost," Shirley said.

Everything was ready for the Gulfstream when it landed in D.C. They put Jonas in the coffin, loaded it, and departed for North Platte in just over an hour.

They brought Jonas's body to the house where he was born. The coffin was placed in the living room on a table low enough for Amanda to view him from a chair. She was asleep when they arrived, and they did their best not to wake her. Niko asked to be alone while he viewed his father's body. He didn't want Amanda to see any signs of deterioration and hoped the dry ice and quick trip had worked. He opened the coffin lid.

The Golden Boy looked perfect—larger than life, even in death. Niko removed the packaging from the mostly-evaporated dry ice, disposed of it, and returned to the open coffin. He bent down and kissed his father's forehead. Death and dry ice had turned Jonas as cold as a winter grave, but Niko let his lips linger before straightening up again.

I thought Superman wasn't supposed to die; he spoke silently to his father, tears in his eyes. *I was seventeen before I knew you existed. I remember the first time I saw you. You were coaching young men who obviously adored you. Then you coached me, and I adored you too. You were amazing. I'm told you died the way you lived—fighting for what you believed was right. I'm not surprised. That's who you were.*

Sorry I never found the answer to what would make the world a better place for everyone, but I promise to keep looking.

The love of your life is waiting for you. I'll bring her to you. Rest in peace, Dad.

Niko and Dorothy helped Amanda into the room, holding her under each arm. Odina walked behind them. The Hannigans remained in the other room. Amanda shuffled along as best she could. There were no tears, even the hint of a smile on her face. When she saw Jonas, her smile broadened.

Dorothy bit her lower lip, trying not to cry. She wondered if she would ever love someone the way her grandmother loved her grandfather. Amanda whispered in her ear. Dorothy smiled and said, "Yes, Grandma, he is very handsome."

Amanda then whispered something to Niko. "I know Dad loved me, Mom," he said. "But he loved you more than anyone in the world. You *were* his world."

Amanda smiled again and nodded. She gestured, indicating she wanted to be alone with Jonas. Dorothy held her while Niko got a chair. She sat where she could still see his face.

"We'll be outside, Grandma," Dorothy said and closed the door.

Amanda's hands rested on the edge of the large casket. She noticed the space around his body, unaware of the care used to preserve his appearance. Soon her mind wandered to other things—*the first time she saw him—when she told him they would marry— the night he proposed—the night he explained why he needed her—and the life they had shared.*

She remembered the night she had lied for him to the police. *He had gone after Steve Diamond, that night saying, "Niko will take care of the father. I'll take care of the son." How he returned home later that night, satisfied. "I was like the Ghost again," he told her. "He never saw me coming." She was afraid he had killed that boy, but he assured her he hadn't. "He'll live,"* Jonas had told her, *but he'll never play football or attack another woman again."* He was sixty-two years old that night, the same age he was when he burned down the Chamanski's office building.

He was seventy-four the day he died and still her hero. Nothing had changed between them. She bent over the casket and kissed his lips, mindless of how cold they were. *If you die, I'll die…* was the last thing she said.

After a half-hour passed, Niko said, "I think we should check on her."

"Let her be," Dorothy said. "She's saying goodbye."

They waited another fifteen minutes. "That's long enough," Niko said and opened the door. The room was empty except for the coffin.

"Where is she?" Niko said.

"I don't know," Dorothy said. "She can't walk without help."

"The coffin lid is down," Niko said. "It was open when we left her."

At Circle H, time seemed to stand still … before it moved on … as always.

CHAPTER 47

1971
ZIGGY

Ziggy Zorn had been feeling better about himself since graduating high school. Numbers had started talking to him in college, during his third cycle through Northeastern's six-month work-study program. After eighteen months, numbers had become his best friends. Debits and credits made perfect sense to him. Fellow students asked him questions. His teachers complimented him, and employers praised him. His appearance hadn't changed much, but he felt different now that he was good at something.

He had been working for The Discount Store for seven years and was very good at what he did. Professionally, his self-confidence had grown, and personally, he had his first girlfriend. Her name was Hope Wolfson, a plump and proper Jewish girl working under his supervision in the accounting department. She admired his skills, and he admired her boobs, which she let him touch from time to time. The couple had reached the hugging, kissing, and touching stage, and Ziggy was hopeful she would be the one to take his virginity.

He felt it would have happened already if he had been living in his own apartment instead of with his mother. He had been in the process of looking for a place a year ago when his father was diagnosed with cancer and committed suicide rather than suffer through the treatments. Harry went peacefully with pills and alcohol, leaving his burdens behind with Ziggy; unpaid rent, unpaid bills, and a wife even her son couldn't love. His own apartment would have to wait.

Still, the future looked promising, and it would not be interrupted by the draft board. In 1966 the Army had rejected him as physically unfit. He was accustomed to rejection, but this was the first time rejection had saved his life. Over 16,000 American boys were healthy enough to die in Vietnam that year, and Ziggy would have been one of them had he not been classified as ... *too fat to fight.* It was the first time Ziggy did not resent his body.

On Valentine's Day, Ziggy picked up Hope in his 1965 Buick Roadmaster for a night out. They were engaged now, but neither was excited about it. Their relationship was based on a lack of options. Ziggy was a good man with a good job, but women couldn't get past his Humpty Dumpty appearance and meek demeanor. Hope was plump, plain, and painfully needy. She had few second dates. Ziggy and Hope weren't meant for each other ... but they weren't meant for anyone else either.

Ziggy drove from Brookline to East Boston in the Roadmaster, which wallowed like a boat on the road. Lombardo's Restaurant was totally sold out for the "One Night Only" appearance of popular singer Sergio Franchi. Ziggy dropped Hope off in front and found a parking space four blocks away. It was a frigid twenty degrees in Boston, but despite the cold, Ziggy was sweating when he met her by the coatroom.

Steven M. Forman

"How did Lombardo's get such a big star?" Hope asked.

"Mr. Gershman said something about family connections."

"It was nice of him to give you his tickets."

"He also gave me four twenty-dollar bills to tip his friends," Ziggy said. "Frankie, Little Vinnie, Big Ralph, and Tilly Rags."

"I'm Frankie," a big man in a black suit suddenly appeared and led them to a prime table close to the elevated stage. Ziggy inconspicuously slipped a twenty-dollar bill into Frankie's large paw. Pocketing the bill discreetly, Frankie said, "Mr. Gershman is a classy guy."

"He asked me to say hello to some of his friends."

"I'll send them over," Frankie said.

"I'm impressed by the way you handled the tip," Hope said.

"I know a few things," Ziggy said, not mentioning that Mr. Gershman had coached him. A waiter took their drink order, and a man even bigger than Frankie, approached their table. *This must be Big Ralph*, Ziggy thought.

"Good evening, folks," the man said. "I'm Little Vinnie."

"Nice to meet you," Ziggy said, making another smooth hand-off.

Big Ralph was next, a mountain. Tilly Rags, a weasel, got the last twenty. Ziggy thought they all looked like gangsters in their black suits, fancy white shirts, dark ties, and slicked-back dark hair.

Mr. Gershman had recommended they order the house specialty, dry gin martinis. They did. Sipping from an elegant, long-stemmed martini glass, Hope's eyes glistened. She reached for Ziggy's hand. "I'm having a wonderful time," she said. She had never said that before. *Was this the*

338

night? The tiny diamond on her engagement ring twinkled. Ziggy sipped his drink and coughed. The gin burned his throat, but it made Hope look pretty, stuffed in her pink dress. Ziggy's blue suit was a size too small, but he didn't care. There was magic in the air—and gin.

They each ordered another martini and Lombardo's chicken dinner. Stimulated by the gin and the glamorous atmosphere, Hope began rubbing Ziggy's thigh under the table. With each sip, her hand traveled higher. She winked, ordered a third martini, and her fingers found ground zero. Ziggy's eyes opened wide, and his hips involuntarily thrust forward. *Holy shit,* he thought, losing control. Hope withdrew her hand to applaud Sergio Franchi's entrance, and Ziggy ejaculated in his underwear. The ovation drowned out his yelp. While Sergio sang his opening number, Ziggy squirmed uncomfortably, feeling his semen glue his sensitive skin to his *Fruit of the Looms. What a disaster,* he thought, drained, flustered, and frustrated.

Twenty minutes into the show, Hope said, "That woman is disgusting."

"What woman?" Ziggy asked, fidgeting in his seat.

"Two tables to your right."

He looked and saw a table of four raucous fifty-something brunettes in heavy makeup. One of them pointed at Sergio, then at his crotch, and mouthed the words, *Eat me.* The singer looked away and kept singing. The *eat me* woman continued heckling. Ziggy was surprised no one else was complaining.

"Someone should do something," Hope whined.

Not me, Ziggy thought.

"Why don't you?" Hope said.

"Me? No way," Ziggy said. "Just ignore them."

"I can't. They're too distracting."

"Maybe Frankie will say something," Ziggy said.

"He's not even looking. Besides, I want you to do it...for me." Her hand was on him again, fondling. *Jeez.*

Emboldened and horny, Ziggy stood. His sticky underwear tore free from his skin. "Shit," he said and sat down quickly, rocking back and forth.

"What's the matter?" Hope asked.

"Cramp," he said, still rocking.

The obnoxious heckler was standing now, dancing and making lewd gestures at Sergio, who continued to ignore her.

"Ziggy, do something," Hope said. "I'm losing that loving feeling."

Don't do that. He got up again, slower this time, and walked to the gyrating woman. When she saw him, she stopped dancing and glared malevolently. Out of the corner of his eye, Ziggy saw Frankie and Tilly Rags, watching—horrified. *I think I'm making a terrible mistake.*

"Excuse me," he said respectfully. "You're a great dancer, but you're distracting my fiancée. Would you mind stopping?"

The woman didn't say a word. She just glared at Ziggy, her eyes bulging. To his surprise, she sat down. "Thank you so much," he said and humbly backed away. He sat down at his table, sweating.

"See, that wasn't so hard, was it?" Hope said.

I almost shit my pants. Ziggy thought. "Is she still staring at me?"

"Yes, and I'll stare right back."

"No. Don't," Ziggy whispered.

Sergio was singing, the woman was glaring, and Ziggy was shaking. Tilly Rags appeared. "I think you should leave," he said, handing them their coats.

"Why?" Hope said. "That woman caused all the trouble."

Tilly Rags leaned over and whispered. "That woman is Gerry Angel's wife."

The Mafia boss?

"We don't want trouble," Tilly said. "Just go." He urged them up from their seats.

"I have to pay the bill," Ziggy said.

"Fuck the bill," Tilly Rags said, pushing Ziggy toward the door.

They were on the street a minute later. "This isn't fair," Hope pouted.

"Forget fair," Ziggy said, his voice cracking, his body shaking. "We have to get out of here." He pulled her arm, but she pulled away.

"Stop that," she said. "Are you crying? For God's sake. I don't believe it."

"I've got a bad feeling about this," he said. "Please, let's go."

"How far away is the car?"

"Four blocks."

"I'm not walking four blocks in these shoes in this cold. I'll wait inside."

"Please come with me," he said, glancing at the front door.

"Stop acting like a baby. Go get the car."

The door to Lombardi's burst open and two huge men emerged, followed by Mrs. Angel. Hope passed by them on her way back inside, without noticing.

"Oh, shit," Ziggy whimpered and walked away as fast as he could. He heard footsteps following him. Tears were freezing to his cheeks. He had managed to go two blocks when he was grabbed from behind, lifted off the ground, and pushed into an alley. He hung limply between two enormous men and peed his pants.

Theresa Angel stood in front of them. "Do you know who I am, fat boy?" she sneered. He nodded. "You can't come into my neighborhood and embarrass me."

"I didn't mean to embarrass you. I made a mistake. I'm sorry."

"Too late," she said. "Anthony, just break his nose and make it fast. I'm freezing my ass off out here."

Just break his nose? Is that supposed to be a favor?

One of the men grabbed his arms from behind.

"I'm on probation," Anthony said. "A two-time loser. I shouldn't be involved."

Right, Ziggy thought. *He shouldn't be involved.*

"I'll be sure to tell my husband," Mrs. Angel said, glaring.

Fuck, Ziggy thought, knowing he was doomed.

He saw the punch coming but couldn't move. The pain and the sound of breaking bones sickened him. He tasted his own blood and heard someone scream. It was him. His head was spinning. They let him fall on the icy sidewalk.

He heard the sound of running shoes on the pavement and a new voice shouting, "Hey, what's going on here?"

"Shit, it's a cop," Anthony said. "I can't get caught."

BANG!

Was that a gunshot? Ziggy pretended to be unconscious, and then he was.

CHAPTER 48

1971
DOROTHY

While Ziggy Zorn's world was falling apart, Dorothy Hensen's was coming together. She had graduated from the University of Nebraska, summa cum laude, then finished graduate school in June of '64, earning her master's degree in business. As anticipated, she joined Niko at the Circle H Ranch and seemed to have her father's talent for business.

Just as he had predicted the rise of IBP in the early sixties, his daughter predicted their decline in the seventies. Just as he had advocated the purchase of land and feedlot equipment to support IBP's spectacular growth, Dorothy had urged the divestiture of these assets ten years later. Both their ideas were sound and their timing exquisite. But it hadn't been easy.

In the sixties, Niko had to convince the Hannigans that IBP was a sound investment. That began with a trip to Dennison, Iowa, in March 1960 where entrepreneurs Currier Holman and A.D. Anderson had opened the first IBP slaughterhouse.

On the train back to North Platte, Niko and the Hannigans discussed what they had seen. *"I think IBP is going to be a great investment for us,"* Niko had said. *"They've already realized substantial cost-cutting. No shipping live cattle. No stock-yards. No middlemen. State-of-the-art factories on one floor instead of those old Swift and Armor three-story buildings. The strategic location of our land and feedlots will be worth a fortune by 1970."*

"We should go wherever IBP goes," Elvis had said.

And they did, becoming the number one supplier of grain-fed beef to IBP's growing empire. Then came growing pains and Dorothy's plan for the seventies.

After visiting all eight IBP plants in 1970, Dorothy submitted a report to her father. *"It's highly speculative,"* he said after reading it. *"Nothing you presented represents common knowledge or current opinion."*

"Dad, I spent two weeks visiting eight IBP factories getting inside information," Dorothy said. *"If you wanted common knowledge, you could have read the newspaper, and I could have stayed home. I presented you with new, firsthand information. Isn't that why you sent me?"*

"Yes. But you're making risky recommendations."

"If you didn't think I was qualified, you should have gone yourself."

"Don't be so sensitive. Disagreements are healthy in business."

"Okay. Where do we disagree?"

"Why are you so sure IBP's purchase of Blue Ribbon Beef will be disallowed?"

"It violates anti-trust laws. Any B-school graduate can see that," she said.

"We're making a large investment to support the Blue Ribbon purchase."

"I know, and I think it's a mistake. I recommend you cancel the deal."

"If you're wrong, we'll lose a big opportunity."

"If I'm right, you'll save millions. It's a reasonable risk."

Niko nodded and thumbed through the report. "You predict IBP's Dakota City workers will go on strike. No one here thinks they will."

"No one here had dinner with the president of the union last week. I did. He guaranteed his union would strike."

"A strike will hurt IBP's production capacity by about thirty percent," Niko said.

"Maybe more," she said.

Niko dropped her report on the table. "I think your prediction that Currier Holman will be criminally indicted for racketeering is nonsense. He's the president and founder of IBP, for God's sake."

"He's also guilty. To get his product into the New York City market, he made deals with organized crime."

"Dorothy, if he goes to jail, IBP could go out of business."

"Not a chance. IBP's long-term prospects are excellent. But the company grew too fast and made some big mistakes that will cost them in the short term. They'll get bad publicity, and they'll suffer large losses. Their stock will plummet in the short term. In the long-term, though, IBP is a solid company with a great product. They'll come back stronger than ever. Our assets are at a peak right now. I think we should sell our IBP support system before all this negative information becomes common knowledge. We'll make millions fast."

"It's a very bold plan," Niko said. "I'm not as sure of it as you are."

"Nothing in business is without risk. But I'm confident."

"If you're wrong?"

"We'll make less money," she said. "But we can't lose... selling assets."

"Let's present it to the Hannigans and see what they think."

Dorothy presented her long-term plan to the board of directors.

"We'll be out of the ranching business if we follow your plan," Shirley noted.

"Yes. But, if I'm right, we'll make so much, we can be in any business we want."

"If you're wrong?"

"We'll just make less money. I don't see any downside risk."

Her confidence won the day. The vote in favor of her plan was unanimous.

Months later, as Dorothy predicted, thousands of union members in IBP's Nebraska and Iowa plants, went on strike against unfair wages and conditions. Production, profits, cash flow, and stock prices plummeted. At the same time, IBP lost civil anti-trust battles and criminal suits brought by the government. Their stock value plummeted further.

Circle H, cash-rich from selling its feedlots, cattle, and land inventories at peak prices, used this cash to buy IBP stock at reduced prices. As IBP settled the strikes, paid its fines, reorganized its operations, and returned to profitability, Circle H gradually sold its stock at rapidly escalating prices. Rumors circulated that Circle H earned in the $500 million range from Dorothy's strategy.

Jane Doe had come a long way.

CHAPTER 49

1971
ZIGGY

Ziggy was at Boston City Hospital, semi-conscious, for two days. When he awoke, it took him several moments to get acclimated. He was in a hospital room with one bed and a window to his left. It was overcast outside, but he saw enough light to determine it was daytime. His head hurt, his throat was sore, and he was depressed.

A man who looked vaguely familiar entered the room.

"Mr. Zorn, how are you feeling?"

"Groggy," Ziggy responded. "Who are you?"

"Detective Eddie Perlmutter. Boston Police."

"I know you from somewhere."

"We grew up in the same neighborhood."

Ziggy immediately remembered the fight with the Irish kids and hoped Perlmutter had forgotten. "Right. I still live there."

"Some things don't change. The last time we talked, you had just been beaten up."

Damn, he does remember. "The story of my life," he moaned.

"Sorry to hear that," Perlmutter replied. "But, this time it's serious."

347

"Getting beaten up is always serious."

"I was referring to the policeman who was killed."

Ziggy recoiled. *Policeman? Killed?* He vaguely recalled a gunshot. "I don't know anything about that," he insisted, not wanting to get involved. "What happened?"

"A policeman was shot and killed that night. His body was found next to you in the alley. Did you hear or see anything?"

"No. I must have been unconscious," Ziggy lied, feeling guilty.

"Could you identify the man who hit you?"

Oh shit. "I don't think so," Ziggy kept lying, his voice shaky.

"Was Mrs. Angel at the scene?"

"I don't remember."

"I think you're lying, Mr. Zorn."

Damn. How does he know that? "Why would I lie?"

"To avoid getting involved," Perlmutter guessed.

How does he know that, too?

"We heard all about your confrontation with Mrs. Angel."

"Who told you?"

"Plenty of witnesses. Everyone was cooperative except your fiancée," Perlmutter disclosed, referring to his notepad. "Miss Hope Wolfson. She said she saw you approach Mrs. Angel in the restaurant. Claims she doesn't know why you approached her or what you said."

She's lying, he thought. *Why?* Then he knew. *She doesn't want to get involved.*

"Insists she wasn't with you during the attack."

Ziggy said nothing.

"We know you were asked to leave Lombardi's, and Mrs. Angel, Anthony Anastasia, and Ralphie Santucci followed you. I figure you said something to Mrs. Angel that upset her, and she had her bodyguards assault you in retaliation. The officer was just in the wrong place at the wrong time."

"If you know all this, why are you asking me?"

"When we arrived, only you and the policeman's body were in the alley. We don't know who hit you or who shot the officer. We need someone who can put Mrs. Angel and her two bodyguards in that alley with you."

Ziggy's heartbeat quickened. He felt the familiar wave of cowardice drain him. It was like air seeping from a balloon, leaving him totally deflated and flaccid. "I don't know anything," he said, hating himself for his impotence.

"Are you sure?" Perlmutter persisted, leaning forward.

Ziggy didn't respond. Perlmutter had his answer.

"Dammit, Zorn," Perlmutter fumed, omitting the respectful *Mister* this time. "You've been letting people walk all over you your whole life. I don't know how you live with yourself."

It isn't easy.

Perlmutter dropped a card on the bed. "If you grow a pair of balls, call me."

Confused and despondent, Ziggy called Hope. She didn't sound happy to hear from him. "Why did you lie to the police?" he asked.

"Those gangsters got to me first," she told him. "I was terrified."

"How did they get your number?"

"Probably from Mr. Gershman."

That made sense. "What did they ask?"

"They wanted to know what I said to the police. I told them I said nothing. They warned me to keep it that way, and I intend to do just that. I hope you said nothing, too."

349

"I said I didn't remember anything, but I don't think he believed me."

"Who cares?" Hope was dismissive. "Stick to your story. Those hoodlums mean business."

"I know. This is terrible. Why did you make me approach that horrible woman?"

"Oh, so now you're blaming me. You're the one who insulted her."

"I did not insult her," he protested.

"She said you did."

"And you'd believe a gangster's wife before your fiancé?"

"That's another thing," she said, her voice cold. "You're not my fiancé anymore."

"What? Why not?"

"You cried like a baby," she said. "I was mortified. "I can't marry you." *CLICK!*

Can things get any worse? He wondered. Then his mother called.

Hysterically, she told him the police had contacted and informed her he was in the hospital. He thought she might ask what happened. She didn't. Instead…"What about me?" she asked. "Who will send money?"

Ziggy told her not to worry and hung up.

The next phone call was also about money. "You're fired, you, asshole," Ziggy's boss, Robert Gershman, shouted into the phone causing him to hold the phone away from his ear. "I told you not to embarrass me. So, what do you do? You get into a fight with Gerry Angel's wife. Jesus, Zorn."

"It wasn't a fight," Ziggy tried to explain. "I just asked—"

"I don't give a shit what happened. Angel's furious with me."

350

"I'm sorry," Ziggy apologized. "This is all a big misunderstanding."

"Misunderstanding, my ass. You're fired."

"You can't be serious. I do a great job for you."

"You do," Gershman agreed. "But you can be replaced."

"You have no one qualified to replace me."

"Is that so?" Gershman retorted. "Your ex-fiancé said she could do your job."

Ziggy recalled how curt Hope had been on the phone. "When did she say that?"

"Today, when I told her I was firing you," Gershman revealed.

"I don't believe this," Ziggy whined. "She stabbed me in the back."

"She did," Gershman concurred. "You're lucky she dumped you. She's sneaky."

"But you're giving her my job?"

"I'll have to keep an eye on her, I guess."

"This doesn't make any sense."

"When you're dealing with Gerry Angel, nothing makes sense," Gershman explained. "But don't worry. You'll find another job. You're good at what you do. In fact, you're great. I hate to lose you."

"You're not losing me. You're firing me."

"Whatever."

"This is not fair."

"That's life, Zorn," Gershman said and hung up.

With tears in his eyes, Ziggy got out of bed and shuffled to the bathroom. He looked in the mirror above the sink. His eyes were black and blue, and his nose was packed with cotton. He had a three-day beard. He looked and felt like shit. His fiancé and his job were gone, and no one cared.

The phone rang. It was his best friend, Robert Reiss. "Ziggy, how are you feeling?"

Finally, someone cares. "Terrible," he complained. "I have a broken nose and two black eyes. I just lost my job, and my fiancé broke up with me."

"That's why I'm calling," Robert explained. "Hope told me *you* dumped *her.* So, I asked her out. She said yes."

"Wait a minute; *she* broke up with *me,*" Ziggy wailed, blinking back tears.

"Whatever," Robert said, uninterested in the details. "We're going out tomorrow night. Is that okay with you?"

Ziggy held the phone away from his ear again. He couldn't believe what he was hearing. It was absurd. No one cared about him. No one respected him. *I'm a good man, but people treat me like shit anyway,* he thought.

He felt like crying but, inexplicably, he laughed instead. He dropped the phone on the floor, walked to the sink, and looked in the mirror again. "Asshole," he called his image and smashed his forehead into the glass—once, twice, three times.

Chapter 50

HOPELESS

Finally, the glass shattered, and he collapsed on the floor, next to the phone. The last thing he heard was Robert Reiss calling his name through the phone.

A nurse found him, unconscious, face down on the floor, in a pool of blood and glass.

Ziggy regained consciousness in his hospital bed. He touched the bandage on his forehead and groaned. He tried getting out of bed, felt dizzy, and fell back. He rested before trying again. Finally, he was able to stagger to his feet and weave to the bathroom. His head throbbed.

Using both hands, he leaned on the sink and looked at the broken mirror. Only a small sliver remained to reflect his image. The self-inflicted wounds had been bandaged. His nose was still packed, and his eyes were blacker and bluer. His thin hair was sticking up at crazy angles. *What a fuckin' mess*, he thought, then laughed at himself. He had reached rock bottom. He had never been on top, but this was a new low. He had nothing left to lose.

His nurse entered, looking concerned. "Mr. Zorn, are you alright?"

"Just great," he told her and laughed again, shaking his head slowly, unsure if he was losing his mind or finding it.

"You gave yourself quite a blow to the head. It's no laughing matter."

"Yes, it is," Ziggy disagreed. "It's hilarious."

"You should get back in bed. You're not yourself, right now."

"Good," Ziggy sounded delighted. "I don't want to be myself ever again."

The nurse didn't know how to respond, so she shrugged and left the room.

I do feel different, Ziggy thought. *I'm not worried about anything because I have nothing left to lose. I've lost everything. Everyone I ever loved is gone—my grandfather, my father, my sister, my best friend, my fiancé, my job… all gone. My mother hates me. I hate my mother. No one cares if I live or die.* Realistically he shouldn't be laughing, but he was anyway. *I'm so pathetic, it's funny.*

His stomach growled, startling him. *What's that?* He wondered. *With my luck, it's probably some rare gastric disease.* It took a moment to register. He was hungry. He couldn't remember the last time he was hungry. He always ate before hunger happened. He remembered he hadn't eaten since he'd been punched in the nose. He'd been living on intravenous nourishment and fruit juice for days. It felt strange to be hungry, but it didn't hurt. *Fuck it. I'm not going to eat so much anymore,* he decided. *I'm sick of being fat. I'm sick of being treated like shit. No more.*

Impulsively Ziggy reached for the phone and dialed a private number he knew by heart. "Hello, Mr. Gershman, Ziggy Zorn."

"If you're calling to ask for your job back, forget it," Gershman snapped.

"Fuck you," Ziggy shouted.

"Did you just say *fuck you* to me?"

"I did. What are you gonna do? Fire me? Now, shut up and listen."

"Did you just tell me to shut up?"

"Yes. Are you deaf?" Ziggy demanded, raising his voice. "I'm calling to tell you I want a year's severance pay."

"First you tell me to go fuck myself," Gershman said, raising *his* voice. "Then you tell me to shut up, and then you demand a year's severance pay. Are you out of your fuckin' mind?"

"As a matter of fact, I'm perfectly sane—finally," Ziggy declared. "I deserve severance."

"If I say no?"

Good question, Ziggy thought, then came up with a good answer. "I've overlooked your illegal tax deductions for years and saved you thousands of dollars."

"That was your job."

"No, that was breaking the law. You ordered me to certify your income tax evasion," Ziggy explained. "I could have lost my CPA license because of you. Maybe gone to jail."

"You got paid for that, you dumb shit."

"I'll contact the IRS and see who they think is a dumb shit. Tax evasion is a sleep away crime. Then I'll call the FBI and tell them about your buddy-buddy relationship with Gerry Angel."

"You wouldn't dare."

"Yesterday I wouldn't dare," Ziggy told him. "Today, I dare."

"That hit to the head must have knocked you senseless."

"Actually, it knocked some sense *into me*. I'm sick and tired of taking shit from everyone. I want one year's severance, and I don't want Hope to get my job."

"Why not?"

"First, because she stabbed me in the back, and second, she's not qualified. In fact, she can't handle her own job without my help. If I were you, I'd fire her, not promote her."

"Can I quote you on that?"

"Sure. And one more thing. I'm going to put all this in writing, just in case you or your East Boston friends should decide to drop a piano on my head. If something happens to me, this information will happen to you. You should pray for my good health." He hung up. He felt great. He felt like a new man.

The new Ziggy called Eddie Perlmutter and told him about that night. "Mrs. Angel was in the alley," he confessed. "I saw the man who hit me. I did not see anyone shoot that policeman, but I did hear a gunshot before I passed out."

"Will you testify in court?"

"You're goddamn right I will."

"What happened to you?"

"I decided I couldn't live with myself anymore."

"Do you want police protection?"

"No. I'll protect myself."

CHAPTER 51

1971
JANICE & JAMES

Ziggy lived with his mother for the next two months while he recovered. It felt like forever. Without his father to buffer his mother's constant complaining, he became the brunt of her venom. By the end of April, she had become insufferable, and he needed to get away from her—the farther, the better.

He was looking and feeling better. The swelling in his nose and eyes had healed, and the black and blue marks had faded. He had lost a lot of weight. He planned to lose more. But his mother weighed him down, and he planned to lose her, too.

He received a check for one year's severance from Gershman and deposited it in full at the Shawmut Bank where the manager smiled at him for the first time in five years. In anticipation of his planned escape from New England, he went to the Discount Store and bought new pants and shirts that fit his new body. His waist was down six inches and his shirts, two sizes. He wore and carried his new clothes leaving the store. At the door, he saw Hope Wolfson, changing prices in the men's department. "Hello, Hope," he said.

She looked at him blankly before recognizing him. "Ziggy? You look different."

"I lost weight. What are you doing in this department?"

"I was demoted. Right after you left."

"I thought you were getting my job."

"I thought so too. Someone told Mr. Gershman I wasn't qualified."

"I did."

"You? Why?"

"Because you're not qualified," he said. "Besides, you stabbed me in the back with my boss and my best friend."

She lowered her eyes. "I don't know why I did that."

"I do. You don't respect me," he told her. "Truth is, I never earned your respect. But it doesn't matter anymore. I hope your date with Robert Reiss was worth it."

"We only went out once. He was horrible. He only wanted sex."

Ziggy smiled. "Not your favorite thing, as I remember."

Hope was embarrassed. "You were always such a gentleman about that. Maybe we should try again."

"No, thanks. Quite honestly, Hope, I deserve better than you."

He turned and walked away thinking, *boy, did that feel good!*

Ziggy stood at the front door of his mother's apartment, saying goodbye. His car was packed, and he was eager to leave his old life behind. "How can you abandon me?" Ida Zorn screamed. "I'm too old to take care of myself." She wore her old housecoat over frayed pajamas.

"You're fifty-four," Ziggy said. "President Nixon is only four years older."

"But I'm losing my memory. I need help."

"I offered to move you to a nursing home."

"I'm too young for a nursing home," she said frowning. "You're a terrible son."

"And you're a terrible mother. We're even."

"Don't forget to send money," she spit, ignoring his comment.

"*Money*, you can remember. Goodbye, mother."

"Good riddance," she shouted and slammed the door in his face.

Ziggy laughed. He was done with guilt. He was done with fear. He was done with self-pity. Best of all, he was done with her.

The cavernous trunk of his Roadmaster easily held a suitcase full of new wash-and-wear clothing and toiletries. On the seat next to him were roadmaps and directions he had marked in red. He planned to drive west, with a vague destination of California but would stop whenever and wherever he wanted. He was excited by the possibilities. His life had always been regimented by the plans others made for him. No more. He made a mental note of the date: Friday, April 23, 1971. *Free at last!*

He took I-90 to the New York Thruway. The weather was clear, the big Buick was comfortable, and the traffic was sparse. He was surprised by how long it took to drive nearly 400 miles across New York state. As he approached Erie, Pennsylvania, his eyelids began to droop. He saw a sign for a rest stop with a restaurant and gas station, one mile off the highway. He took the exit and found a White Castle restaurant. *Never heard of it*, he thought, looking at a small white

Enterprise

building with the tacky castle façade and a sign announcing, "29 cent hamburgers."

He got out of the car, stretched, and checked his watch. It was 4:45 p.m. He estimated he'd been driving for more than eight hours. He ordered a burger and a Coke and sat at a table. He was studying the roadmap when he heard a girl's voice say, "Excuse me, sir."

He looked up. A girl he guessed was in her late teens was standing next to his table. She was blonde and blue-eyed, with a pleasant smile. "Hi. I'm Janice Cooper, and I'm hitchhiking home from college with a friend. We're looking for a ride west. Any chance?"

"I've never picked up hitchhikers," Ziggy said, always suspicious of hitchhikers. "Where's home?"

"Omaha, Nebraska."

"That's a long way. Where's college?"

"Berklee School of Music in Boston," she said.

"I know Berklee, I'm from Brookline," Ziggy enthused, relaxing a little. "What instrument do you play?"

"I play strings; guitar, banjo, stuff like that. I also play the piano. My friend plays wind instruments; trumpet, sax, flute. You name it. He is so talented. Oh, here he comes. James, I just asked this nice man from Boston for a ride."

Ziggy turned to see James. *Oh jeez! A Negro!* Ziggy thought. He had nothing against Negroes. He just didn't know any. This one was well-dressed and pleasant-looking, but Ziggy was uncomfortable.

James held out his hand, "James Jackson," he said. When Ziggy hesitated, James smiled. "The black doesn't rub off."

"I know," Ziggy said, embarrassed, taking the offered hand. "I was just surprised. I don't know any Negroes."

"Most white people don't," James said. "Think of this as a new experience."

Ziggy nodded. "Why are you two hitchhiking to Nebraska? Why not take a bus?"

"Our parents think we did," Janice said. "We wanted an adventure instead."

"A dangerous adventure, if you ask me," Ziggy told them.

"You mean, a colored boy hitchhiking with a white girl," James said.

"Hitchhiking is dangerous without the race thing," Ziggy said. "You have no idea what kind of crazy person might give you a ride."

"That's why I asked you," Janice said. "You don't look crazy."

"I'm not. But I could be. You're taking a risk. How old are you?"

"We're both eighteen," Janice said. "We've been friends for years."

Ziggy was conflicted. *Do I want two strangers in my car? A Negro? I've never even talked to a Negro before. The girl looks nice and says he's her friend. Both musicians.* He thought about the timing that had brought the three of them to the same place at the same time. *Maybe it's fate. Maybe I'm meant to give these kids a ride and keep them safe.* "Okay, I'll give you a ride," the new Ziggy decided, excited.

"Thank you," Janice exclaimed, hugging him. "I knew you were a nice man."

"I'll pass on the hug," James said. "But thanks, man."

"How far west are you going?" Janice said.

"To make sure no crazies pick you up, I'll take you to Omaha."

Janice clapped her hands. "See James; we're having an adventure already with our new friend." She kissed Ziggy on the cheek, exuberantly.

"What's our new friend's name?" James asked. Ziggy told him.

"What kind of a name is Ziggy?" Janice asked.

"A nickname," Ziggy told her. "It's a long story."

"We have about a thousand miles to go," James mentioned. "Is that enough time?"

Janice was traveling with her guitar, James his harmonica and flute. They both had small backpacks that fit easily into the car's trunk. James sat in the back, and Janice joined Ziggy in front. After the Roadmaster was cruising at sixty, Ziggy told them the story behind his nickname. He felt comfortable talking to them, and the nickname story segued into the reasons behind his trip west. When he was finished, Janice said. "People were so mean to you."

"I've been mistreated because of the way I look," Ziggy said.

"Me too," James added.

"You mean because you're a Negro and I'm fat?"

"You're not fat anymore, Ziggy," Janice pointed out.

"I lost forty pounds, but I'll always think of myself as fat."

"But you could change," James said. "I can't. I'll always be someone's nigger."

"I never use that word," Ziggy told them.

"I got news for you," James announced. "Even negro is a bad word nowadays."

"Really? Since when?"

"Since Malcolm X said so. He says Negro is a white man's word. He thinks since white men call themselves white, black men should call themselves black, or African-American."

"It'll take some getting used to," Ziggy predicted.

"Change takes time," James said.

"I'm tired," Janice announced, curling up.

Soon, they were both asleep.

Ziggy drove on, pleased at how easily two strangers had become friends.

CHAPTER 52

1971
LEGENDS

Ziggy stopped for the night at the Holiday Inn east of Cleveland. He had driven eleven hours and was weary. Janice and James had napped fitfully and were still tired. Ziggy got a room and offered them the floor, but they chose to sleep in the car. They met in the motel's coffee shop late the next morning.

"I looked at the map," Ziggy told them. "Davenport, Iowa, should be our next overnight. It's about ten hours if we drive straight through. From Davenport, it's only four hours to Omaha. If we keep to this schedule, you should be home at a reasonable time, Sunday."

They got in the car, and Ziggy pulled back onto I-90. "Is Omaha a nice place to live?" he asked, after a few miles.

"It was," James told him. "But now there's a lot of racial tension."

"I met James our freshmen year at Omaha Central High in the Advanced Placement Music Program," Janice said. "We became best friends, like brother and sister. But if not for that program, we probably never would have met. The races just don't mix anymore."

"Boston has racial problems, too," Ziggy said.

"I know," James agreed. "But I think Omaha's different."

"In what way?"

James thought a moment. "It's more polarized, I think," he speculated. "After World War I, thousands of black people in the south moved to Omaha for jobs in the railroad and meat industries. The workers already living there were mostly white immigrants from Eastern Europe and Ireland. They had congregated in North Omaha. When the blacks started moving into their neighborhood, the whites moved out—to West Omaha."

"So, the north became a black ghetto," Ziggy said. "Like Roxbury in Boston."

"Right," James agreed. "But then Omaha's stockyards closed, and the railroads consolidated. Thousands of jobs were lost all at once. Omaha became a disaster area."

Ziggy shook his head, looking contrite and noted, "I always associated Omaha with Boys Town, from the Mickey Rooney movie."

Both kids laughed, and James replied, "Technically, Boys Town isn't even in Omaha. It's an independent city."

"Did it survive?"

"It did. Some rich people helped," James explained. "Janice, tell Ziggy the story about Niko Hensen and Joe Diamond."

"You want to hear an Omaha legend?" Janice asked.

"Sure," Ziggy enthused. "I love legends."

When Janice was done telling the story about the Diamonds, Niko Hensen, and his daughter Dorothy, Ziggy asked, "When did this happen?"

"About twelve years ago," Janice said.

"Reminds me of a Clint Eastwood movie," Ziggy noted. "A stranger comes to town and runs the bad guys out."

"Except this story is true," Janice said. "And the stranger was Niko Hensen from North Platte, Nebraska—instead of Clint Eastwood from Hollywood, California,"

"What happened to the bad guys?"

"Never heard from the Diamonds again. I think they moved away."

"And the Hensens?"

"Still a prominent family in Nebraska along with the Hannigans," Janice said. "Made a fortune in cattle and the stock market. Niko Hensen became a major benefactor of Boys Town."

"They're a very generous family," James said. "The money Janice and I got for Berklee came from a scholarship fund established by Dorothy Hensen in Omaha."

"That's the girl Steve Diamond attacked, right?"

"Right," James confirmed. "She turned out to be a brilliant businesswoman."

"She was born with serious physical and mental problems," Janice said. "And overcame them all. So, every year, she gives a scholarship to a student who was able to overcome challenges and succeed."

"But you both got a scholarship the same year," Ziggy said.

"It was an unusual situation," James said. "Miss Hensen couldn't decide which one of us deserved the scholarship more—so, she gave one to each of us. She's very generous."

"You must both be exceptional musicians."

"We try," James answered, being modest. He removed his flute from its case and played a haunting melody that filled the confines of the Roadmaster.

"That was beautiful," Ziggy said. "What's the name?"

"El Condor Pasa," James said. "Written in 1913—and still popular today. It's on one of Simon and Garfunkel's albums."

"There must be lyrics if Paul Simon's involved," Ziggy suggested.

"Of course," Janice confirmed. "I'll sing them for you."

James played—Janice sang.

When they finished, Ziggy was complimentary. "I'd applaud if I wasn't driving,"

he told them. "I loved the words— 'I'd rather be a hammer than a nail.' I've been a nail my whole life."

⚜   ⚜   ⚜

When they stopped for gas, Janice got her guitar from the trunk. James got his harmonica. With the music and singing accompanying his driving, the hours flew by like the landscape, and Ziggy didn't want the ride to end.

It was dark when they saw a sign that read "Davenport, 40 miles." A few miles down the road was another sign, "Local Exit—Rest Area—1 mile."

"I need a ladies' room," Janice announced.

Ziggy pulled off the highway onto a poorly lit side road. He drove a few hundred yards and saw a neon Budweiser sign in the window of a one-level wood building that had clearly seen better days. "Skip's Bar and Grill," Ziggy read aloud as he pulled into the gravel parking lot.

His headlights illuminated three metal garbage cans, a beat-up pick-up truck, and a baseball bat leaning against the wall, next to a flat tire. "Awful-looking place," Ziggy observed.

"Who cares? I gotta go," Janice insisted. She got out of the car and dashed for the door. James and Ziggy followed, walking. The door had a CLOSED sign on it. Through the drawn window shades, they could hear Neil Diamond singing "Cracklin' Rosie" on the jukebox. Janice pounded on the door.

"Janice, the place is closed," Ziggy said. "Let's go."

"I'm gonna go in my pants!" she whined, pounding on the door again.

The door opened a crack. A boozy voice growled, "Can't you fuckin' read?"

"Please, I need a ladies' room bad," Janice said.

The sound of a woman's voice was a door opener. Ziggy looked at the wiry, disheveled drunk standing in the doorway. *Shit.* He had seen men like this before—bleary-eyed bastards with nasty dispositions. The swastika tattoo on his neck said it all.

"Hello, little lady," he slurred with a jackal's smile. "Ladies room shhtraight ahead." He stepped aside with an exaggerated sweep of his hand, and she dashed ahead. Ziggy saw two larger men standing at a pool table, ogling her as she passed. Each one had a swastika tattoo. *This is a mistake*, Ziggy thought as he started to enter the bar.

The neo-Nazi drunk put his hand on Ziggy's chest. "Sorry, it's Ladies' Night at Skip's," he said. "No niggers or Jews allowed. You look like a Jew to me, and I can plainly see Sambo there is a nigger."

James scowled but said nothing.

"Are you Skip?" Ziggy asked, trying to make a personal connection.

"Skip Junior," he said. "Senior died and left me this dump. It's closed permanently. I just come by to drink the booze till it's gone. Only good thing my old man ever done for me."

"He did visit you in the joint a couple of times," one of his friends interjected.

"That he did, Bubba," Skip Junior said, taking another swig of beer.

"Skip, let me in to wait for my friend," Ziggy said and tried again to push by.

Skip continued to stand in his way. "No trespassing."

"I just want to get my friend and leave."

Janice emerged from the ladies' room and was heading for the exit when one of the men blocked her way. "How about a dance, little girl?" he said, grabbing her hands.

"Please let me go," Janice said.

The other man moved behind her. "Let's all dance," he said, pressing against her.

James pushed by Skip and moved toward Janice. "Let her go," he shouted.

As James passed, Skip turned. He was holding a billiard ball in his free hand and smashed it into the back of James's head. James went down to his hands and knees. Skip danced in front of him and kicked him in the jaw. James flipped over on his back, unconscious.

"You all seen that? Nigger was trespassing," Skip shouted, laughing. "Breaking and entering. Place is closed. Nigger broke in. Jew boy too."

Skip sucker punched Ziggy in the mouth. Janice screamed, still sandwiched between Skip's friends. Ziggy stumbled back but didn't fall. The punch wasn't powerful—not like the one that had broken his nose in East Boston—but it hurt. Skip moved toward Ziggy, who hesitated a moment, then turned and ran.

CHAPTER 53

1971
KISSIMMEE STICK

He barged through the front door, tripped in the gravel parking lot, and went flying. He fell on his knees and palms, and his momentum propelled him forward so that his face hit the jagged stones. They tore into his skin like little razors. He scrambled up and ran again—Skip in pursuit—laughing. "Where are you going, Jew boy? Running out on your friends?"

Ziggy gritted his teeth in pain as he ran toward his car. Rounding a corner, he saw what he was looking for—the baseball bat he'd noticed pulling into the parking lot. He picked it up. It was labeled *Kissimmee* Stick, and it was heavy. *Good.* Ziggy thought just as he heard Skip approaching, giggling. "Where's my little Jew boy?" Ziggy drew the Kissimmee Stick back in his best imitation of a baseball batter.

When Skip turned the corner, Ziggy swung. Not being athletic, Ziggy probably would have missed a baseball—but Skip's head was more the size of a slow-moving basketball. The thirty-six-ounce Kissimmee Stick made solid contact with Skip's mouth, snapping his head back and sending his legs flying out from under him. Skip went airborne before crashing to the gravel—out cold—his face a bloody mess. *Fuck you, Skip*; Ziggy thought as he ran to the front door and kicked it open. James was still on the floor, unconscious but stirring; Janice was fighting off Skip's two pals who pawed at her from either side. They were trying to lay her out on the pool table. Her blouse was torn at the buttons, and her jeans were pulled down to her ankles. She was bleeding from the nose, and her face looked swollen. *Animals*, Ziggy thought, filled with rage and disgust as he moved toward them, bat cocked.

One of the two assailants saw him coming. "Hey, Bubba. Look who's back with your bat."

Bubba turned to see Ziggy approaching. "Hey, that's mine," the lummox said.

"Here, take it," Ziggy growled, before hitting the moose below his nose, across his upper lip with a mouthful of Northern White Ash. Bubba screamed and stumbled back, blood gushing from his mouth and nose. Three teeth fell on the floor.

When Bubba moved his hands to protect his face, Ziggy swung at his kneecaps. The big man screamed again, fell flat on his back, and blubbered, "Jackson, help me."

But Jackson was running for the door.

Ziggy caught him from behind and swung the bat like an axe, chopping down on Jackson's right shoulder. Jackson went to his knees, screaming. Ziggy walked in front of him and jammed the fat, round top of the bat into his mouth, splitting his lips and knocking him over.

"Move, and I'll kill you," Ziggy said. Seeing the crazed look in Ziggy's eyes, Jackson lay very still.

❧ ❧ ❧

Ziggy helped James to his feet. He was woozy and bloody, with a lump on the back of his head … but still able to walk. Janice had pulled up her pants and was shaking with fear. "Let's get out of here," she implored, grabbing Ziggy's arm for balance. He got them to his car, put Janice in the front and James in the back. James slumped over, groaning. Janice was quiet but shaking.

Ziggy sped back to the highway and pushed the Roadmaster to eighty. His head whirled with violent images: Skip's bloody face, Bubba's broken teeth, Jackson's crushed shoulder, Janice's battered face. His mind raced like the Buick, and they got to Davenport in under half an hour. Ziggy saw a blue H sign indicating a hospital, and he took that exit. He followed the H signs all the way to the Genesis Medical Center and screeched to a halt at the Emergency Room door.

When he tried to get out of the car, Janice grabbed his arm. "Where are we?" she asked weakly.

"A hospital in Davenport."

"Ziggy, my parents can't know about this."

"Don't worry about that now," Ziggy said and got out of the car.

He saw an ER attendant at the entrance. "I have two emergencies," he shouted.

The attendant nodded and ran inside, returning with another attendant. They were both pushing gurneys. After James and Janice were secured, Janice grabbed Ziggy's arm again. "You can't tell anyone about this," she pleaded. "If our parents learn we lied and were traveling together, they'll never let us go back to school. You have to promise."

"Janice, I'm worried about you two, not your parents," Ziggy told her.

"Please keep this a secret," she implored him. "We're friends. I'd do it for you."

I know you would, Ziggy thought. "Okay, I promise."

"Thank you." She squeezed his hand. Her swollen eyes were closing as the attendants rushed her away. Her bruises looked worse in the hospital lights.

As he walked toward his car, it started to rain.

Ziggy sat in the car, watching the rain collect on the windshield. The Roadmaster felt empty without his new friends. He wanted to stay with them but realized he'd be asked a lot of questions he had just promised not to answer. *Better leave*, he decided, starting the car and heading for the highway. While driving, he noticed his hands were trembling on the steering wheel. The horror at Skip's was finally impacting him. He had never acted so recklessly before in his life. He hadn't cared about himself or what he did to those three drunks. His only concern was to save his friends, and he had succeeded. *I can't believe I did that!* He thought.

Without a specific destination, Ziggy was drawn to Omaha. He just felt he belonged there. He noticed the bloodstains on the car seats and the bloody *Kissimmee Stick. Damn!* He thought, frantically throwing the bloodied bat into the back seat without looking. He drove on like a mad man.

He saw a sign— "Omaha 300 miles." It was past midnight, and it would take him over four hours. He was too hyper to rest, so he pushed on. The Roadmaster roared along the highway as the rain grew harder, then stopped abruptly, leaving him in a dense fog. The last sign Ziggy saw clearly was for Council Bluffs. The visibility was deteriorating quickly. The car was moving too fast for the weather conditions. Nervous, he took a sharp turn at the next exit sign he saw. The visibility dropped to zero on the side road, and Ziggy stepped hard on the brakes. The Roadmaster skidded off the soft shoulder on the side road and slammed into a sign pole. Ziggy flew forward. His forehead hit the steering wheel. The horn blared, and he saw black instead of fog.

CHAPTER 54

1971
ZIGGY

The fog lifted early the next morning. Police found Ziggy's Roadmaster crushed against an ENTERING OMAHA sign pole. Ziggy was still in the driver's seat, his forehead against the steering wheel.

"Sir—are you okay?" a policeman asked through the driver's side window. Ziggy stirred, lifted his head, and opened his eyes. He squinted in pain, unaware of the dried blood on his face from the new gouge in his forehead. He touched the wound tentatively, confused and disoriented.

"Where am I?" Ziggy asked, groggy. "Who are you?"

"Officer Smith, Omaha police," the policeman said. "Officer McNulty at the other window. What happened to you?"

Ziggy looked at Smith, then McNulty. "Lost in the fog," he told them, disoriented and shaky. "Skidded. Hit something."

"This pole," Smith pointed at the Entering Nebraska sign. "It appears you smacked your head on the steering wheel."

Ziggy looked at the sign pole. "Thought I was in Iowa," he mumbled.

"No, sir. You're at the Nebraska state line."

Ziggy removed his hand from his aching forehead and looked at his fingers.

"The blood dried," Smith said. "We should get you to a hospital."

"Blood stains on the passenger seat and door," McNulty told his partner.

Janice, Ziggy thought, nervous.

"Sir, was there someone with you last night?" Smith asked.

Ziggy remembered his promise to Janice. "No," he lied.

"Can you explain the blood on the passenger seat?" McNulty questioned him.

"No."

"Your license and registration, sir," Smith ordered.

Oh jeez, Ziggy thought reaching for the glove compartment, producing the papers.

"Isadore Zorn," Smith read. "You're a long way from home, Mr. Zorn."

Ziggy nodded—apprehensive.

"More blood in back," McNulty announced. "And a black harmonica case."

"Yours?" Smith asked.

"No," Ziggy said.

"Whose is it, then?"

Ziggy said nothing, realizing his silence was making him look suspicious. He didn't care. *I gave my friend my word,* he thought.

"Smitty," McNulty called out. "There's a baseball bat covered with blood back here, too."

Smith drew his gun from his hip holster, stepped back, and pointed it at Ziggy. "Mr. Zorn, please give me your car keys and step out of the car, hands raised."

Ziggy complied. "You don't need a gun," he told Smith.

"I'll be the judge of that," Smith retorted. "Check the trunk, Mac."

Smith tossed McNulty the keys and kept his gun aimed at Ziggy. McNulty returned with a guitar and two backpacks. "Check 'em out," Smith said.

McNulty searched the backpacks. He found two student ID cards.

"Who are Janice Cooper and James Jackson?" McNulty asked.

Ziggy shrugged.

"Mac, call headquarters. Get the lab folks out here. Have them treat this car as a possible crime scene. Mr. Zorn, we're taking you to the police station for questioning."

Ziggy nodded, keeping his hands in the air. He looked at his car, the front fender and hood were wrapped around the pole. Smith noticed. "Don't worry about your car," he said. "Worry about yourself." He cuffed Ziggy, his hands behind his back, and helped him into the rear seat of the police car.

Ziggy listened as McNulty reported their findings to headquarters on the cruiser's radio. The words *crime scene, blood-stained baseball bat,* and *missing Omaha kids* ricocheted around the station. Local police and beat reporters heard bits and pieces and passed on their versions to their respective newsrooms.

When McNulty, Smith, and Ziggy arrived at the Central Omaha Police Station, a half dozen reporters were already at the scene along with television and newspaper photographers. Ziggy got out from the back seat of the police car and inadvertently looked directly at the television camera and photographers. The flashbulbs blinded him, and reporters bombarded him with questions. *What did you do with those kids, Zorn? Why do you have a bloody baseball bat in your car? Did you kill those kids? Where are their bodies?*

Ziggy stared straight ahead—a deer in the headlights. *I'm innocent,* he conveyed with his eyes. *I don't hurt people. People hurt me.*

Inside the station, he was marched to an interrogation room where he was seated at a rectangular table. His handcuffs were removed. A doctor was called to treat his new wounds and look at his old ones. He whispered his conclusions to the arresting officers and departed.

A middle-aged man entered the room and sat across from Ziggy. He introduced himself as Chief Detective Ed Davidson. He wore a shirt and tie, his shirt opened at the collar, and his sleeves rolled up to his elbows. "Mr. Zorn, I've been briefed by Officers Smith and McNulty. I'd like to ask you a few questions."

Ziggy shrugged.

"Do you want a lawyer?"

"Am I being arrested?"

"You're a suspect, as of now."

"When I'm arrested, I'll want a lawyer," Ziggy said.

"Okay. Can you tell me about Janice Cooper and James Jackson?"

"No, I can't," Ziggy said.

"Then let me tell you what we already know," Davidson said. "We called the Cooper and Jackson homes and talked to their mothers. Both told us the same thing. Each kid was supposed to be coming home on a bus from Boston, where they go to college. Mrs. Jackson said her son, James, and Janice Cooper are not friends. Janice Cooper's mother said the same things about her daughter and James Jackson. Can you explain that?"

Yes, their parents are racist, Ziggy thought but shook his head.

"Can you tell me why their backpacks are in your car?"

"No, I can't," Ziggy said.

"You can't, or you won't?"

"Both."

"Mr. Zorn, did you do something bad to those kids?"

"No," he said.

"Can you tell us where they are?"

"No."

"These evasive answers aren't doing you any good, Mr. Zorn."

"They're the only answers I can give you."

"Why?"

"Can't tell you that either."

The door to the room opened. A uniformed policeman entered and said gruffly, "Has the suspect said anything pertinent?"

"Nothing."

"Mr. Zorn," the man in uniform said. "I'm Chief Larry Davidson. If you're not going to tell us anything, we have probable cause to arrest you."

"I told him that," Detective Davidson said. "He won't talk."

"Suit yourself," the chief snapped. "Read him his rights and put him in a holding cell. He'll see a judge tomorrow. Now, come outside for a minute."

They met outside the door. "Eddie, I have to go to Boys Town for a building dedication. Keep working on this guy. We could have a horror show on our hands. I'll be back late afternoon."

Detective Ed Davidson returned to the room. "Are you related to the Chief?" Ziggy asked. "You have the same last name, and you look alike."

"He's my older brother," Detective Ed Davidson said.

"That must be awkward—answering to your brother."

"That's none of your business," the detective ended the conversation.

"Sounds like I hit a nerve."

"You have the right to remain silent…"

CHAPTER 55

1971
BOYS TOWN

Dorothy and Odina sat in an audience of two hundred people listening to Niko dedicate the new athletic building at Boys Town. It had been paid for by The Hensen Family Charitable Trust. When Niko had come to Boys Town twelve years ago for Joe Diamond, he also found a new cause to support. He befriended Jim Bemis and took a special interest in the Boys Town athletic department.

"Great speech, Dad," Dorothy said, looking business-like in a black bell-bottom pantsuit. She always wore pantsuits to hide her damaged leg.

"It's a beautiful facility, Niko," Odina said.

The procession of well-wishers included Police Chief Larry Davidson in full dress uniform. "Boys Town is lucky to have you as a benefactor, Mr. Hensen," he said to Niko.

"Thanks, Chief. Will you stay for lunch and a tour of the building?"

"I can't. I've got an urgent case—two missing teenagers."

"Omaha High School students?" Dorothy asked.

"Former students actually," the chief told her. "They attended college in Boston this year. They were traveling home when they went missing—James Jackson and Janice Cooper."

"Those names ring a bell," Dorothy said.

"They're music students at Berklee College in Boston," the chief said.

"Is he black and she's white?"

"Yes. Do you know them?"

"I think I do," Dorothy replied. "I believe I gave them scholarships just last year. What's happened to them?"

"Right now, they're just missing. But it doesn't look good," the chief told them. "We have a suspect—a blood-stained car—a bloody bat."

"Oh, dear," Odina said.

Dorothy said, "Do you think the suspect harmed them?"

Davidson shrugged. "He looks like a harmless accountant. But you never know. You'll probably see it all on the news tonight."

After the luncheon, the Hensens drove back to Omaha. In the early evening, they went to Cinema Center, a new two-screen movie theater, where they chose *The Last Picture Show* over, *Dirty Harry*. They had a late dinner at Delmonico's, one of Niko's favorite Omaha restaurants. After dinner, they returned to the historic Magnolia Hotel, where the family had adjoining rooms. While they prepared for bed, Odina put on the television. "Maybe we can hear about those missing kids," she said.

"Call me if something comes on," Dorothy said from her room.

They half-listened to the national news for Sunday, April 25, 1971. "A U.S. Army lieutenant named William Calley was found guilty of murdering twenty-two Vietnamese civilians in a place called My Lai…

"And now, in a local story..."

"Dorothy," Odina called. "This could be it."

Dorothy went to her parents' room. The television screen showed previously recorded film while a newscaster spoke over it. "Today, a man from Boston, Massachusetts, —a still photo of Ziggy filled the screen— identified as Isadore Zorn, was taken into police custody and questioned about the disappearance of two Omaha teenagers."

He looks harmless, Dorothy thought, looking at Ziggy's sad brown eyes, and wondering why she felt empathy for a stranger suspected of a heinous act.

Ziggy's photo was replaced by two photos of the missing boy and girl. "Janice Cooper and James Jackson..."

"That's them," Dorothy said.

Niko held up a hand to shush her. The announcer continued.

"...Advanced Placement graduates of Omaha Central High last year have been reported missing and foul play is suspected. According to their parents, the two gifted music students were supposed to be on a Greyhound bus from Boston, where they attend the prestigious Berklee School of Music. Their parents say their children are not friends and have no idea why they would be traveling together."

The reporter went on to describe the bloody bat and car and promised more information when available. "The FBI is involved because the suspect crossed state lines. They'll question Zorn tomorrow. Boston police revealed Zorn is involved in an investigation concerning the Angel crime family." The picture of Ziggy appeared again.

Nonsense, Dorothy thought, looking intently at the photo. *That man is not in organized crime. I just know it.*

Niko switched off the TV. "You were saying . . . you know those kids?"

"Yes. I gave them both scholarships last June at the Omaha Central graduation. Great kids. Amazing musicians. We couldn't select one over the other, so we awarded two scholarships. First time we ever did that. I can't believe they're missing."

"Something in that report doesn't make sense," Niko said. "Two kids from Omaha Central High, in the Advanced Placement Music Program, in Boston at the same time, at the same school, on Dorothy Hensen scholarships. How can they not be friends? It doesn't seem possible."

"Maybe it's a black and white thing," Dorothy said. "Last year, there were race riots in Omaha over Vivian Strong, that fourteen-year-old black girl who was shot by a white cop at the Logan Fontenelle Project."

"I remember," Odina said. "You almost canceled your visit to the high school."

"I'm glad I didn't, but it was ugly," Dorothy said. "The audience was racially divided, physically and emotionally. Cheering for graduates was strictly along racial lines. No interracial mingling after the ceremony. I think some of the kids were intimidated by their parents."

"Maybe the kids are friends but don't want their parents to know," Niko said.

"Possible?" Odina said. "I just hope that man didn't hurt them."

"He didn't," Dorothy said.

"How do you know?" Niko asked.

"He looked totally harmless," Dorothy said. "I saw it in his eyes."

"You could hardly see his eyes in that photo," Odina said.

"I could see them clearly. He was looking directly at the camera," Dorothy said.

"He looked like a normal guy with normal eyes, to me," Odina said.

"Didn't you look in my eyes once … and see what no one else saw?"

"She's got you there," Niko said. "I'm sure we'll know more tomorrow."

In the morning, Dorothy asked Niko if he could arrange for her to meet Zorn at the police station. "I want to help, and I have a good feeling about that man."

Niko rarely refused his daughter. Odina said he indulged her to make up for lost years. "Maybe," Niko conceded. "But, really, she's never asked for anything I didn't think she deserved."

He called Chief Davidson. The Hensens were major donors to the Nebraska Police, and influential in the whole state. It was difficult to say no to them. "It's a highly unusual request," Chief Davidson said. "But for you, and because of Dorothy's connection to the missing kids, I'll make an exception. You know my younger brother, Eddie. He's in charge of this case. I'll contact him and make arrangements. But make it early. The FBI will be there this afternoon."

The Hensens went directly to the station. Detective Ed Davidson whisked Dorothy into an interrogation room with Ziggy, who was handcuffed to the conference table. He looked disheveled after a night in jail.

"I'd like to be alone with him," Dorothy said.

"I think I should stay," Detective Davidson said.

"Detective," Dorothy said. "The man is handcuffed to a table. It's okay."

"You never know."

"I accept full responsibility," she said.

"Yes, ma'am," Davidson said. "I'll station someone outside the door just in case."

When he left the room, Dorothy sat across from Ziggy. Their eyes met. *I know he didn't hurt those kids*, she thought. *So, what's he hiding?*

"Hello, Mr. Zorn, I'm Dorothy Hensen."

He recognized the name "As in...Dorothy Hensen Scholarships?"

"How do you know that?"

"Someone told me."

"The missing kids?"

"I can't say," Ziggy replied, angry with himself for saying too much.

"What *can* you say about those kids?"

"Nothing."

"Why not?"

"I can't even tell you that," Ziggy said, looking sheepish.

"Mr. Zorn..."

"You can call me Ziggy."

"What kind of a name is that?"

"A nickname. I got it from a bully a long time ago."

"Were you bullied as a child?"

"All the time."

"So was I," she said. "But I fought back."

"I didn't. I was afraid," he said, embarrassed.

"Of what?"

"Everything."

The poor man, Dorothy thought. "Well, since you won't tell me anything," she said. "Can I tell you what I think?"

Ziggy shrugged. "Sure."

"I think you picked up those kids hitchhiking. Along the way, something bad happened, which would explain the blood in your car and your injuries. I think the kids are okay and you're protecting them from something. How am I doing?"

"I can't answer you," he said, but she could tell by his expression that she was on the right track. "But why do you think I didn't hurt those kids? Everyone else thinks I did."

"I got a good feeling about you when I saw you on television," she said.

"And now that you've met me ..."

"I'm positive you didn't hurt those kids. But what are you hiding?"

"I can't tell you, but thanks for believing in me."

Detective Davidson burst into the room, startling them. "Come with me," he said, waving his arm like a traffic cop. "Hurry."

"I'm handcuffed to the table," Ziggy said, holding up his arm.

Davidson released him, and they rushed through the squad room to the station's spacious foyer. Odina and Niko saw them and followed. A circle of photographers and reporters were there, jabbering like a murder of crows. The human circle moved toward the Chief's office; the reporters were shouting questions.

Davidson stood on a chair to see. "I'll be damned," he said.

"Who is it?" Dorothy asked.

"Janice Cooper and James Jackson."

CHAPTER 56

1971
DOROTHY & ZIGGY

The two teenagers were rushed into Chief Larry Davidson's office. The door slammed behind them. A cacophony of voices filled the foyer until the Chief's door opened. "Where the hell is Ziggy Zorn?" he shouted.

"With me," his brother Eddie shouted back.

"Well, bring him here. He's a goddamn hero."

The room buzzed with excitement as Detective Davidson brought a bewildered Ziggy through the horde.

Dorothy smiled at Odina.

"Don't say I told you so," Odina whispered, poking her with her elbow. "I hate that."

Janice and James emerged from the Chief's office and ran to Ziggy. Janice threw her arms around his neck and hugged him. James joined them in a circle, arms over shoulders, their foreheads touching. "I'm so glad you're okay," Ziggy said.

"Nothing serious," James said. "A few stitches and a concussion. We left the hospital as soon as we saw you on television."

"We called the police station here from a pay phone," Janice said. "But they treated us like crank callers."

"Who the hell did that?" Chief Davidson bellowed. No one answered.

"We took a bus to Omaha and got here as soon as we could," Janice said. "I can't believe you got arrested for keeping your promise. You're a real friend."

"Thank you," Ziggy said, glowing inside. *I have real friends!*

Janice turned to the crowd. "Ziggy Zorn saved me from being raped and probably saved my life, too."

"Mine, too," James said.

An instantaneous uproar followed. A reporter shouted over the din. "Ziggy. Why didn't you just tell the police what happened?"

Janice answered, "I made him promise not to."

"Why?"

"That's personal," she said.

Chief Larry Davidson interrupted the questioning. "That's enough for now. These folks have to give their statements."

He led Janice and James back to his office, but Ziggy hesitated, looking for Dorothy. Seeing her, he said to the chief, "I need a minute," and approached her.

"Miss Hensen, thank you for believing in me."

"I knew you were a good person," she said. "I didn't know you were a hero."

Ziggy blushed. "I'm no hero. We ran into some bad characters. I couldn't let them hurt these kids."

"You fought them off with that bloody baseball bat, didn't you?"

Ziggy nodded. "I needed the bat. There were three of them, and I'm basically a wimp."

"Nonsense," she said. "You're very brave."

Chief Davidson poked his head out of his office. "Mr. Zorn, please."

"I have to go," Ziggy said.

"What will you do after you give your statement?" Dorothy asked.

"I don't know. Get my car repaired and hit the road again, I guess."

"Where are you going?"

"California... I think."

"What's in California?"

"Nothing. I'm just running away from home. Thanks again."

❧ ❧ ❧

An hour later, Ziggy, Janice, and James emerged from Chief Davidson's office. The area had been cleared of civilians, except for Dorothy Hensen and two others. Ziggy guessed the man standing next to her was her father. There was a strong resemblance. The dark-skinned woman standing with them did not look like Dorothy's mother. Ziggy wondered why they were still at the station.

"Miss Hensen," Janice called out to Dorothy. "Remember us?"

"Of course," Dorothy said. "My scholarship winners."

They exchanged hugs.

"Are you here because of us?" James asked.

"We were in Omaha on business and came here to see if we could help."

"That was so nice of you. Have you met our friend Ziggy Zorn?" Janice beckoned for Ziggy to join them.

"I have. Before you showed up, I was trying to get him to talk to me about you, but he wouldn't."

"I made him promise not to say a word."

"Why all the secrecy?" Dorothy asked.

Janice took a deep breath. "We disobeyed our parents. They told us to take a bus, but we hitchhiked instead. We didn't want them to know. They don't want us to be friends, but we are. We didn't want them to know that either."

"I understand your parents not wanting you to hitch-hike," Dorothy said. "But why not be friends?"

"It's a color thing," James said. "Her parents hate blacks. My parents hate whites."

"I remember a lot of racial tension last year at gradua-tion," Dorothy said.

"There would have been more if you hadn't given two scholarships," Janice said.

James nodded and said, "My father was convinced Janice was going to win because she's white. He thinks all white people are racists. I don't. Not all of them, anyway."

A middle-aged black couple entered the station. James looked like the man who was obviously his father. They both approached. The heavy-set black woman looked frazzled as she hugged her son. The man scowled and asked a police-man, "Is my son free to go?" The policeman nodded.

Without acknowledging anyone else, the father grabbed his son's arm roughly and dragged him toward the door. James wrestled his arm away and stopped. The father poked his finger into his son's chest and shouted in his face. Ziggy couldn't hear the words, but he could feel the anger. He was surprised when James stood his ground and talked back. They turned to look in his direction. James pointed at him, and the man nodded.

They approached Ziggy. "My son says you saved his life," the man said. "Thank you."

"Yes, thank you," the black woman said, touching Ziggy's shoulder, tentatively.

"You're welcome," Ziggy replied. "Your son was very brave, himself. He got hurt trying to help Janice. We helped each other."

"They never should have been there in the first place," Mr. Jackson huffed, angry.

"You're right," Ziggy agreed. "Sometimes, people make mistakes and are in the wrong place at the wrong time. But your son is safe now, and that's all that really matters."

Mr. Jackson looked hard at Ziggy. "He was lucky," he said, still fuming.

"Lucky he was with friends," Ziggy added.

Jackson shrugged. "Thank you again," he muttered and turned to go.

"See you in September, James," Janice called after them. James waved, smiling. On their way out, the Jacksons passed a middle-aged white couple coming in.

"My parents," Janice said. "They know the Jacksons but won't say hello."

Ziggy watched as the Jacksons and the Coopers passed like strangers.

"Wish me luck," Janice said and went to greet her parents.

"That's going to be a hard fight for both kids," Dorothy said.

"Change is worth fighting for," Niko said.

Dorothy looked at Ziggy then gestured to Niko. "Ziggy, this is my father, Niko Hensen and my stepmother, Odina."

They shook hands. "Why are you still here, Miss Hensen?" Ziggy asked.

"Call me Dorothy," she offered. "And I waited for you."

"You did?" Ziggy responded, surprised.

"Yes, I wanted to talk to you. You mentioned you had to get your car fixed before you move on. I thought we could help."

"You don't have to do that," he said, surprised by their kindness.

"We'd like to," she said. "You could come with us to North Platte and stay a day or two at our house. We can have your car towed and fixed there. My parents said it was alright with them."

"That's so nice of you. But you don't even know me."

"We know all we need to know from what you did for those kids," Dorothy enthused. "We'd like to get to know you better."

"Why would important people like you want to know a nobody like me?"

"We don't think you're a nobody," Odina interjected. "We admire what you did."

Just then, two FBI agents from Omaha arrived.

Chapter 57

1971
ZIGGY

The agents were brought up to date by the Omaha police, and the senior FBI agent told them, "After we received your report, we immediately dispatched agents from our Davenport office to Skip's Bar. Our people there know about Skip Junior. He's an ex-con with a long record. We're expecting a report soon. When we know more, where can we reach you?"

Before Ziggy could answer, Dorothy said, "He'll be staying with us," and gave the agent her phone number. *What does she want with me?* He wondered. He'd never experienced such positive attention from a woman before. *She must think I'm someone I'm not.*

Ziggy was invited to sit in the front seat of Niko's new Jensen FF coupe. The women sat in the back.

"This is a beautiful car," Ziggy noticed. "Very unusual."

"It's from England," Niko told him. "My friend Alan Jensen custom-made this one for me. It's bigger than the standard Grand Tourer."

"What's the FF mean?"

"Ferguson Formula," Niko said. "Signifying it's a four-wheel drive."

"He's like a kid with a new toy," Odina said from the back.

Ziggy was impressed by the Jensen and the Hensens. *I don't belong with these extraordinary people,* he thought. *They'll realize that soon enough.* But the miles passed pleasantly, and he felt welcome.

When Niko asked Ziggy why he had decided to head west, Ziggy told them about his *Valentine's Day massacre* in Boston. Niko said, "It's none of my business, but your boss, your fiancé, your best friend, and your mother sound like terrible people."

"Not terrible—just selfish," Ziggy explained his personal circle. "They took advantage of me because I let them. It's the story of my life."

"Why?" Niko asked.

"Well, look at me," Ziggy said as if his appearance would explain everything.

"Okay, I'm looking, and I see a very nice man," Dorothy told him.

Ziggy glanced back at her, looking for a hint of sarcasm. He saw none. It was a compliment—plain and simple. He blushed. "Thank you," he said.

When they stopped for gas, everyone got out of the car. Dorothy made a phone call. When they resumed driving, Odina moved to the front, and Ziggy sat in back with Dorothy. He was delighted by the new arrangement, though apprehensive.

"Why was Robert Reiss your best friend?" Dorothy asked. "He sounds awful."

"He was the only best friend I could get," Ziggy explained.

"And your fiancé?"

"Same reason."

"Your mother?"

"A bitter woman. She only cared about what she'd lost, not what she had."

"I never met my real mother," Dorothy remarked.

"You can have mine," Ziggy joked.

Dorothy laughed. "My mother tried to kill me before I was born."

"My mother tried to kill me *after* I was born."

Laughter and light-hearted banter continued throughout the long drive.

They arrived in North Platte in the early evening and went directly to the Hannigan mansion. "What a house!" Ziggy said, intimidated. *What am I doing here?*

"It's not ours," Dorothy said. "My grandmother, Shirley Hannigan, lives here with one of her twin sons, Elvis, his wife Zoe, and their twelve-year-old daughter, Althea."

"Is there a Grandfather Hannigan?"

"He's dead," she said quickly.

"Who lives in that smaller house?"

"The other twin, Eli, and his wife Randi," Dorothy said.

The family greeted them in the big foyer. Nearly everyone towered over Ziggy, even Niko's twelve-year-old son, Erik. The only one at Ziggy's level was twelve-year-old Althea. The enthusiastic greeting made Ziggy feel welcome but uncomfortable. *I'm not special like all of you*, he thought. *I'm just an unemployed accountant from Boston.*

When they were seated in the large dining room, Ziggy asked Dorothy, "Do you have gatherings like this often?"

"We get together a lot, but this is a special occasion. I called ahead to let everyone know you were coming. They all wanted to meet you. Your story is news here too."

"I keep telling you … I'm no one special."

"Tonight, you are," she told him.

Dinner was delicious and delightful.

When it was time to go, the Hensens drove to their smaller house a few miles away. Odina and Niko were in front, and their son Erik sat between Ziggy and Dorothy in back. *This is nice*, Ziggy thought.

Dorothy showed Ziggy a guest bedroom and acclimated him. "Sleep well," she said. "I'll see you in the morning." She closed the door. He hated to see her go. She had made him feel so welcome and wanted. He liked the feeling.

He was in bed, under the covers, thinking of her, when there was a knock on the door. "Ziggy, it's Dorothy. Can I come in?"

He wondered what she could want now. "Sure. I'm under the covers."

She entered wearing a long bathrobe. "I just wanted to make sure you're comfortable. We added this room a year ago, and you're the first guest."

"I'm honored. It's really nice."

"My home office is down the hall. Niko's too. We work from the house sometimes. Our business office is downtown." She sat on the foot of the bed. His heart raced. *What's happening?*

"My family likes you," she said.

"I like them, too," Ziggy said, clearing his throat nervously. "Your father and stepmother seem like a perfect couple."

"They were made for each other," Dorothy said. "Funny, when they first met, they didn't get along. They fought over me."

"Why?"

"It's a long story," she said. "But, seven years after they met, they fell in love. Five years after that, they got married."

"Twelve years?"

"Amazing, right?"

Ziggy nodded. "Quite a love story."

"It's nothing compared to my grandparent's love story," Dorothy told him.

"I'd like to hear it."

"Tomorrow when I take you sightseeing, if that's okay with you."

"I'd like that," he told her, keenly aware of her being so close.

Impulsively, Dorothy leaned over and kissed his cheek. "I'm glad you're here," she said, went to the door, and closed it behind her.

It took Ziggy an hour to fall asleep.

The next morning, Dorothy took Ziggy to the North Platte Cemetery and the gravesite of her grandparents, Jonas and Amanda Hensen. "Notice anything unusual?" she asked, pointing to the headstone. Ziggy studied it for a few moments.

"There are two names on one stone," he said. "And it says they died the same day. Is that right?"

"Very observant," she complimented him. "Emotionally, they died the same moment—physically, they died only hours apart. It's part of the love story I want to tell you." She took a deep breath and began the story. She finished it by telling him how Amanda had climbed into the coffin, lay next to the love of her life, and died. "And that's how they were laid to rest. Together forever."

"It's like she willed herself to die with him," Ziggy commented, still gazing at the stone.

"Just like she willed herself to live for him, all those years."

"I can't imagine a love like that," Ziggy said, glancing at Dorothy for her reaction and was surprised to see her looking at him.

CHAPTER 58

1971
ZIGGY & NIKO

The next morning, Ziggy rose at sunrise and stood in front of the Hensen house, wondering what he was doing in Nebraska. The vagaries of the open road had carried him from Boston to North Platte like the tornado whisked the movie character Dorothy from Kansas to Oz. He felt out of place, surrounded by super men and women who had accepted him as an equal when he wasn't. It didn't make sense.

"You're up early," Niko said, quietly closing the screen door behind him.

"Couldn't sleep," Ziggy said. "I have a lot on my mind."

"Want to talk about it? Sometimes that helps."

Ziggy liked Niko's directness. "Okay," he accepted the offer and took a deep, nervous breath. "I feel out of place here with people like you."

"What kind of people do you think we are?"

"Super people. War heroes, great athletes, multimillionaires, and philanthropists. I'm just an unemployed East Coast Jew who did the right thing one time in his life ... and you're all judging me by that."

Niko held up his hand. "Stop right there, Ziggy," he told him. "First of all, our family doesn't care about your religion or where you're from, and we don't judge people. We take to people based on their actions. What you did with those kids proved to me you're a good man. You not only saved them, but you also kept your word to them at your own risk. That says a lot to me about who you are."

"Are you speaking for your whole family?"

Niko smiled. "C'mon, Ziggy, you're not asking about my whole family," he said. "You're asking about Dorothy, right?"

"Well, yeah," Ziggy said and blushed. "She's been really nice to me, and I'm not accustomed to such positive attention from an attractive woman. I'm more accustomed to rejection."

"Dorothy's a genuinely nice person."

"So, she's probably nice to everyone."

"She is, but you're the first man she ever invited home," Niko said.

"Really? Do you think that means something?" Ziggy asked.

"I'd say it means she's comfortable with you. But you'll have to ask her."

"What if she tells me to hit the road?"

Niko laughed. "At least you'll know where you stand."

"You're right. Any advice?"

"Just be yourself, Ziggy. That's what got you here."

That afternoon Odina and Dorothy had lunch alone in the Hensen house. Niko and Ziggy had gone to watch Erik play baseball. Dorothy was quieter than usual, saying little, thinking a lot. She couldn't get Isadore "Ziggy" Zorn out of her mind. There was something about him that had enthralled her from the moment she saw him on the television screen. His eyes had attracted her first. She saw a vulnerable kindness in them that convinced her he hadn't harmed those missing students. When she met him in person at the police station, she was certain he was innocent… and special. He wasn't handsome or attractive. He was comfortable. She was not usually comfortable with men outside of her family. Her violent experience with Steve Diamond had scarred her physically and emotionally, and she had never fully recovered. She could not forget the image of Steve Diamond, brandishing his manhood at her, like a weapon. She had normal sexual urges but equated sex with Diamond's obscene behavior, and her few relationships with men had all ended badly. Ziggy seemed different, kind, and gentle, and she wanted to get to know him better—if she got the chance.

"Ziggy's car is almost ready," Odina told Dorothy as if reading her mind. "He'll be leaving soon. How do you feel about that?"

"I'll miss him," Dorothy confessed, saddened by the prospect.

"Why not ask him to stay?"

"He's heading to California to start a new life."

"He could start a new life here," Odina said.

"What's in North Platte for him?"

"You," Odina said.

Dorothy blushed. "We've only known each other a week."

"It's obvious you like him, and I think he *really* likes you," she said, raising her eyebrows suggestively.

"Romantically, you mean? Don't be ridiculous," Dorothy said, dismissing the notion but liking the idea.

"I've seen the way he looks at you. He follows you around like a little puppy."

Dorothy giggled. "He's never even tried to kiss me."

"He's probably afraid of you," Odina said. "You're a rich and powerful woman. You intimidate men."

"Are you kidding? Men intimidate me."

"One man intimidated you … a long time ago. Ziggy's not Steve Diamond."

"I know," Dorothy said. "But I need another reason to ask him to stay, besides me. What if he doesn't really like me? It would be awkward."

"How about offering him a job?"

"What job?"

"You know Niko is considering buying an interest in a public company, right?"

Dorothy nodded. "He's trying to emulate that guy in Omaha, Warren Buffett. He says the man's a genius."

Odina laughed and said, "He heard that from a waitress in an Omaha coffee shop. Anyway, when you buy a public company, you come under a lot of scrutiny. You have to be squeaky clean."

"What does that have to do with Ziggy?"

"Niko wants to do an internal audit to see if Liam or Duke left any skeletons in the Circle H closet. He doesn't want outside auditors to have access to this confidential information. So, he's at an impasse. Ziggy's a CPA. Maybe Niko would use him for the audit."

"Ziggy's an outsider, too," Dorothy pointed out.

"Yes, but Niko likes him."

"No harm in asking, I suppose," she agreed.

When Niko came back from the baseball game, Dorothy approached him about Ziggy. His answer was predictable. "You know I don't trust outsiders."

"You trust Ziggy to sleep in the same house with your family," she said.

"Good point," he said. "Is this personal for you?"

"A little. But I think he's the right man for the job, too."

"I trust your judgment. I'll talk to him."

Ziggy was excited about the new opportunity and took the job immediately. He began with the original incorporation papers and moved forward. The numbers in the Circle H books told him a story of railroad rascals, range wars, cross-breeding cattle, double-crossing people, courage, cleverness, and criminality. Ziggy spent days at City Hall, poring through old records, deeds, land purchases, and sales, reconstructing the cattle empire that led to Circle H Holdings.

The downtown offices of Circle H were housed in a non-descript commercial building on Main Street. Headquarters consisted of one big room for five clerical workers, framed by five private offices for the Hensens and Hannigans. There was a conference room for meetings. The second floor consisted of rooms used for storage and files. The current Circle H business consisted of diversified real estate holdings, international commodities, stock trading, and large investments. Ranching was history. Circle H now had affiliates in several U.S. cities run by diversified joint venture partners.

Occasionally, Dorothy shared some of the company's current deals with Ziggy while he searched the company's past deals. "We recently made a big investment in a company named *Systems and Services*. They do business as Sysco. Our partner in Houston says Sysco is the future of the food-service industry in America. We're betting big on them. Niko also made a huge investment on Berkshire Hathaway stock—Warren Buffett's company. He's really impressed by that man."

"You're betting on your future, and I'm auditing your past," Ziggy said.

"Have you found anything we should know about?" she asked.

"Maybe. But I can't tell the boss's daughter before I tell the boss."

She laughed. "Do you really think of me as the boss's daughter?"

"Sometimes. Mostly I just think of you as a very nice person."

"Thank you," she blushed, averting her eyes. "Are you enjoying the work?"

"I love it, and I love being here."

"We love having you here."

What about just you—do you love having me here? He thought but didn't ask.

They had few chances to socialize once Ziggy began his audit. The time was lost to long hours of research and analysis. Ziggy spent his time between City Hall and the downtown office. He would often return to the house after dinner and some nights after the Hensens had gone to bed. Niko trusted Ziggy enough to give him a house key for those late nights. After a month of twelve-hour days, Ziggy had learned to read between the lines of the Circle H story and saw a pattern emerging he didn't like. When his suspicions

were confirmed, he decided it wasn't enough for him to just identify the problem. He had to find a solution.

In June, five weeks after he started working for Circle H, Ziggy asked for a meeting of the board to report his findings. They met in the Circle H conference room. Ziggy stood at the head of the table. Dorothy thought he looked thinner than when they'd first met. His belt was pulled tight, and his pants looked a size too big. His thinning hair was neatly combed. He looked trim and professional. They exchanged nervous glances. She wanted him to do well. Ziggy cleared his throat. "I was asked to find anything in your company's past that could negatively impact your future ... and I'm sorry to tell you that I found something."

"I'm afraid to ask," Shirley interrupted. "It must be something my husband did."

"Not just him," Ziggy told them. "Duke did plenty—black market activities during both world wars, price fixing, illegal government payoffs, falsified financial statements; you name it Liam and Duke did it."

"You learned all this just by reading our books?" Elvis asked.

"I read numbers like most people read words," Ziggy explained. "I also learned that your auditors, the Chamanskis were thieves."

"They were. But how could you know?" Shirley asked.

"It was easy. Huge amounts of money and inventory went missing. Cash disappeared. The entries didn't make sense. The year you terminated them, you had a multimillion-dollar cash infusion. Unless I'm wrong, that was settlement money from them."

Nods around the table confirmed he was correct and gave him the confidence to continue.

Listening carefully, Dorothy was impressed. Ziggy was a savant with numbers. When he talked numbers, he even looked different, stood taller, made eye contact, spoke without deference. A man in his element. Yet when she said, "Ziggy, you're amazing," he blushed. She found that endearing about him.

"You think all those crimes will come back to haunt us?" Niko asked.

"Not all of them," Ziggy said. "Every big company has its scandals and scoundrels. Cornelius Vanderbilt liked prostitutes. John D. Rockefeller liked illegal trusts. Joseph Kennedy was a bootlegger. Yet his son was still elected president because people tend to forgive the sins of the fathers. What I'm concerned about is a time bomb that was planted in your books that could explode in your faces, unless you defuse it first."

Shirley grimaced. "What did they do?"

"They stole land," Ziggy said. "Circle H holds titles to thousands of acres of stolen land."

CHAPTER 59

1971
ZIGGY

"What? How do you steal land?" Eli asked.

"By exploiting loopholes in the system," Ziggy answered.

"What loopholes?" Shirley asked.

"What system?" Eli said.

"In the old days of the wild frontier, the only way to protect privately-owned land was to fence it in. Building fences was difficult, expensive, and time-consuming. But the invention of barbed wire in 1867 made building fences fast and easy."

"You learned this from our books?" Elvis asked.

"I did some additional research at City Hall, but yes, I found large purchases of barbed wire back then," Ziggy said. "Liam took advantage of this new fencing and the lack of government supervision by erecting barbed-wire fences around both his private land and thousands of acres of public land. No one was watching."

"I'm not surprised," Niko said.

"I didn't know the man," Ziggy said. "But he seems like a plundering pirate."

"Sound like you did know him," Eli confirmed.

Ziggy continued. "Liam also took advantage of the Homestead Act, which granted as much as six hundred and forty acres of free land per family for farming. Liam bought this land cheap from homesteaders, who preferred a quick profit to slow and risky farming. He fenced in that land too. By illegally fencing in all this land, Liam was able to deprive his cattle-raising competitors of valuable grazing land and water rights. When the federal government sent inspectors to check complaints, nothing happened. Liam either paid them off or got rid of them."

"What do you mean … got rid of them?" Shirley asked.

"One federal agent got in a fist fight with Liam at a local bar and died from a punch to the head," Ziggy said. "The report is at City Hall. A shouting match turned into a shoving match before punches were thrown. It was ruled self-defense."

Niko nodded, remembering the lead in Duke's fist that nearly killed Jonas. He finally knew where it came from.

"How did you uncover all this?" Dorothy asked.

"It's all in the records. Missing bills of sale and bad forgeries," Ziggy said.

"Wait a minute," Eli interrupted. "You said people tend to forgive the sins of the fathers. We can claim we didn't know anything about stolen land."

"That might work but only if we make that claim before anyone else releases this information," Ziggy said. "Otherwise, it will look like you were hiding something for years. If that happens, people won't believe a word you say. You have a reputation to protect. Shirley has done so much to undo the resentment built up against the Hannigans over the years, and it would be a shame if that was wasted.

The Hensens are revered as heroes around here. People love and admire you. This could destroy all that goodwill."

"Damn," Niko said. "Jerzy Chamanski said I hadn't heard the last of him. This must be what he was talking about. We've got land fraud in our records, and he's probably waiting for an opportune time to blackmail us."

"A time like now," Dorothy observed. "With you trying to buy a public company."

"Or any other major move we might want to make," Shirley concluded.

"It's not just the Chamanskis," Ziggy said. "You have to deal with this problem before *anyone* finds out and makes it known. Otherwise, you'll be on the defensive."

"Do you have any ideas?" Dorothy asked, hoping Ziggy had an answer. He did.

"If I was a local hero, like you people, I'd try to turn a negative into a positive."

"How?" Eli asked.

"I would go to the BLM…"

"What's the BLM?" Shirley interrupted him.

"Bureau of Land Management," Ziggy elaborated. "You should tell them everything."

"Tell the feds we stole their land?" Eli said. "That's crazy. Who does that?"

"Heroes do," Ziggy said. "And, it's not what you say, it's how you say it. I suggest you send someone to the BLM—tell them that a recent audit revealed the *possibility* of irregularities, and that you need their cooperation to confirm your suspicions."

"Don't you think we might antagonize the agency if we make them look bad?" Niko asked.

"That's right," Elvis said. "Civil servants don't like to look bad."

"I thought of that, and I did some related research," Ziggy said.

You did? Dorothy thought, impressed.

"The BLM wasn't even formed until 1946," Ziggy explained. "Liam and Duke had already stolen their land. Before 1946 there were two agencies. One was the General Land Office, formed in the 1800s to give away land the government stole from the Indians."

"Jesus, everyone was stealing land in those days," Elvis said.

"Apparently," Ziggy nodded. "The other land agency was Grazing Services, formed in 1934 to manage grazing rights." Ziggy paused, took a deep breath, and continued. "So, two understaffed agencies, formed over a hundred years apart, were responsible for managing 264 million acres of government land. Of course, they couldn't. For better control, the government consolidated these two agencies into one—the BLM—in 1946. There is no evidence, to this day, that control of this land improved under the BLM. The agency looks like a bad idea whose days could be numbered. Now, imagine if someone from the BLM miraculously recovers thousands of acres of missing land."

"He'd be a goddamn hero," Elvis said.

"And Circle H..." Ziggy prompted.

"We'd all be goddamn heroes," Eli exclaimed.

"Which you already are," Ziggy noted. "But you'd be bigger goddamn heroes."

"And everyone wins," Niko summarized.

"Which is always the best outcome," Ziggy emphasized.

"I'll go to Washington," Niko volunteered.

Everyone agreed, and Dorothy added, "Dad, I think you should take Ziggy."

"I wasn't planning on going without him."

After one day in D.C., Niko returned and called another meeting of the board. Before he could say a word, Dorothy asked, "Where's Ziggy?"

"Still in Washington."

"Why aren't you with him?"

"He doesn't need me."

"Why not?" Dorothy asked apprehensively.

"Because Ziggy is a goddamn genius and I was just in his way."

Dorothy breathed a sigh of relief.

"What did he do?" Shirley asked.

"He started our meeting with BLM agent Les Rich by telling him he *thinks* he's found several thousand acres of government land wrongly registered as private land by Circle H. Then he insisted he couldn't verify his findings without the cooperation of a competent BLM agent. Rich got so excited, I thought he'd fall off his chair. He realized he was being handed an opportunity to do something special in an agency that had done nothing special in thirty years."

"So where is Ziggy now?"

"He's still in Washington working with Rich, leading him by the nose, to all the fenced-in government land that Liam and Duke stole. When they're done, I believe Les Rich and Circle H are going to be declared heroes in Washington. I can't wait to see how this is handled."

He didn't have to wait long. Two days later, the *Associated Press* released the story under the headline THIS LAND IS YOUR LAND! The article praised Circle H Holding Company of North Platte, Nebraska, and its independent auditor, Isadore "Ziggy" Zorn, for helping the Bureau of Land Management recover thousands of acres of public land wrongly recorded as private. Les Rich of the BLM was quoted: *"The discrepancies in title were found by Mr. Isadore Zorn, an independent auditor, while conducting an internal audit on behalf of Circle H. Unable to verify his findings, Mr. Zorn was sent by Circle H General Manager, Niko Hensen, to the BLM for verification. Mr. Zorn and I worked together for several days to untangle confusion that occurred over a hundred years ago. The results were well worth the effort. The cooperation between Circle H and the BLM yielded an extremely positive result for the public domain. Many thanks to Mr. Zorn and Circle H."*

Ziggy was quoted as saying: *"Circle H is thrilled with the results of our joint venture with the BLM. The invention of barbed wire and its use by overzealous cattle ranchers resulted in a multitude of errors in land ownership on our wild frontier. Circle H is proud to be part of the solution and to return this land to the public."*

"Ziggy turned a negative into a positive, just like he said," Niko told the board.

"He didn't even have to lie," Eli remarked.

"Do you think we could get him to stay as our full-time CFO?" Shirley asked.

"We can ask," Niko concurred, glancing at Dorothy, who avoided his eyes.

"Send the private jet back to D.C. to pick him up," Shirley said. "He's earned it."

Ziggy sat alone, watching the District of Columbia grow smaller through the port window of the ascending Circle H Gulfstream II. The pilot and co-pilot had met him at the bottom of the air-stairs used for boarding. "Good afternoon, Mr. Zorn. Let me take your suitcase. Just pick a seat on board, make yourself comfortable, and we'll depart when you're ready."

It was a clear day, perfect for flying. The take-off was smooth.

"Mr. Zorn," the pilot's voice came over a speaker, "we're going to level off at 30,000 feet and cruise at a speed of 425 miles per hour. With a slight tailwind, we should have you on the ground in North Platte in approximately three hours. There are cold drinks and snacks in the compartment to your left. The restroom is in the rear. Lean back, relax, and leave the flying to us."

Ziggy was soon deep in thought. He was a different man than the one who escaped from Boston two months ago. He had lost another twenty pounds. His weight had gone from two hundred and fifteen pounds to a healthy one hundred and sixty. At five-foot-six inches, he was trim. He had only one chin now, his former pumpkin face lean. He felt good about himself. *All I ever needed was motivation.*

He was motivated to belong with the Hensens and Hannigans. He was motivated by his new job offer at Circle H. Most of all, he was motivated by Dorothy Hensen. He wanted her to like him ... maybe even love him someday.

And why not? *If I can convince the U.S. government that thousands of acres of stolen land were an oversight ... and that Liam and Duke Hannigan were just a couple of rascals ... I can do anything.*

CHAPTER 60

1971
ZIGGY & DOROTHY

Ziggy returned to a hero's welcome. Townspeople visited Circle H's downtown office to thank the Hensens and Hannigans for what they'd done. Everyone wanted to meet the genius, Ziggy Zorn. "Fine thing you did, young man," one rancher told Ziggy. "Always knew Liam and Duke were up to no good," said another. "Thank you for doing the right thing."

Ziggy was busy handling the land exchange and still had little time to spend with Dorothy. Finally, she suggested a Sunday picnic.

"Great!" Ziggy said. "I have something I want to talk to you about."

Dorothy got a queasy feeling. *What does he want to talk about? Is he going to tell me he's leaving?*

On Sunday, they took Ziggy's repaired Buick to a secluded spot near the North Platte River where her paternal grandfather Jonas, and maternal grandmother Shirley, had gone as teenage sweethearts. They never married each other, but they became her grandparents anyway. Dorothy spread a blanket and laid out cheese, fruit, bread, and a bottle of wine. "So, what do you want to talk to me about?" she asked. When he hesitated, she said, "If you're going to tell me you're leaving, I'll understand. You don't have to worry about hurting my feelings."

"What? Why would you say that?"

"To make it easy for you. I thought you might be tired of North Platte and me."

"Not at all. I was afraid you were tired of me. I even told your father."

"You told my father what?" Dorothy said, surprised.

"I told him how much I liked you but was afraid I wasn't good enough for you."

"What did he say?"

"He told me to tell you how I feel ... so I am."

Her eyes got misty. "I really like you too," she said. "I was thinking you're too good for me."

"That's ridiculous," Ziggy protested. "No one is too good for you. You're smart, generous, beautiful—"

"I am *not* beautiful," Dorothy interrupted.

"I think you are," Ziggy said. Impulsively, he leaned over and kissed her quickly on the lips.

"Oh. I wasn't expecting that," she said, touching her lips with her fingertips.

"Neither was I. It just happened."

"You can do it again if you want."

Their lips met again, and the kiss was softer and longer this time. Soon, they were kissing passionately, lying on the blanket in an embrace. Ziggy got aroused. When Dorothy felt his hardness against her thigh, she recoiled. An evanescent image of Steve Diamond, exposed and erect, flashed through her subconscious, destroying the moment for her.

She pushed Ziggy away, scrambled to her feet, and backed up. "Don't touch me," she said, unable to get over one man's cruelty.

"What's wrong?" Ziggy asked, confused.

"I want to go home," she said, gathering her belongings and hobbling to the car.

Ziggy followed. "Dorothy, what did I do?"

She didn't answer, and they rode back to the house in silence. When they arrived, Dorothy left him in the car and limped into the house, slamming her bedroom door behind her.

Ziggy trudged to his room, bewildered. He flopped on his bed, covered his eyes with his arm, and wondered, *what went wrong? Everything seemed so perfect*, he reflected, then thought, *I knew it was too good to be true.*

His newfound self-confidence drained away until he was empty, reduced to hoping that Dorothy would come to him and explain what had gone wrong. But, by dusk, he accepted that his time with Dorothy in Oz was over. *I should leave soon*, he thought, *Avoid confrontations and explanations. Leave a note for Niko thanking him for everything.* He packed his suitcase and lay down to rest before beginning a long drive to nowhere. He fell asleep. An hour later, he was awakened by a noise in the dark room.

"Who's there?" he said, bolting up.

"Dorothy," she said. "Where are you going?"

"How do you know I'm going anywhere?"

"I just tripped over your suitcase."

"Sorry, I wasn't expecting you. I'm leaving for California tonight."

"I don't want you to go," she said, sitting on the bed next to him.

"I'm confused. This afternoon you hated me."

"I know. It's my fault." She said and sat on the bed and told him about Steve Diamond; how he wielded his penis at her like a weapon.

Ziggy laughed.

"It's not funny," she said, angry. "I never got over it."

"I'm not laughing at you," Ziggy said. "I'm laughing at me."

"I don't understand."

"No part of my body will ever be confused with a weapon," he said. "Well, a Derringer, maybe."

Unexpectedly, Dorothy laughed. "That was funny," she said, the specter of Steve Diamond losing its clarity.

"And if I did have a weapon, I'd use it to protect you— not hurt you."

Her eyes welled with tears. "That's so nice," she said and snuggled next to him. "Why do you have all your clothes on?"

"I had planned on a quick getaway. Hey, why are you unzipping my fly?"

"I want to see if you scare me." She pulled down his zipper, reached in his underwear, and found him. Ziggy's heart pounded. She removed his erect penis and felt it up and down. "I'm not afraid of this."

"You really know how to hurt a guy," he told her.

She kissed him. "It's perfect," she said.

It became a night for firsts. The first, two virgins lost their status. Secondly, two former virgins said *I love you* to someone outside their immediate family.

But, the next morning, when Dorothy awoke, Ziggy was gone. She got out of bed, limped to the window, and saw that his Roadmaster was not there. She looked around the room. His suitcase was not there, either. *It can't be*, she thought. *He said he loved me. Why would he lie? I hate him! I hate men.*

She flopped on her back on the bed, covered her face with a pillow, and tried to smother herself. She couldn't, so she kicked her legs up and down in a tantrum. *"Bastard, liar, son of a bitch,"* she said. From under the pillow, she heard his voice.

"You called?"

He's here? He heard me? She thought, lifting the pillow. "Oh … hi," she said as if nothing had happened.

"Have you been crying?"

"Me? Crying? No. Why would I be crying?"

"You thought I left you, didn't you?"

She was embarrassed. "Well, you weren't here. Your car and suitcase were gone. I thought…"

"You thought I left you. Well, too bad. I'm never leaving you."

She sniffled. "Good. Where were you? Where was your car and suitcase?"

"I needed something in my suitcase and didn't want to wake you. I took it to the kitchen and opened it, got what I wanted, then I drove to town to buy wrapping paper for a gift I have for you."

She finally noticed he had been standing with his hands behind his back the whole time. "Is that what you're hiding?"

He nodded and presented an irregular-shaped wrapped package. "Open it. It comes with a story."

She tore off the wrapping paper. "A used teddy bear?" she said, confused.

"Technically, it's not used. It's just stained on the right ear. That's part of the story. A long time ago, I loved a girl more than anyone in the world."

"More than you love me?"

"Different. She was my adopted sister, Sarah." Ziggy told her how Sarah died from polio and what happened the night she died.

"I can't believe your mother threw the bear in the trash. That was so mean."

"That's my mother. Later, I took the bear from the trash and hid it in my closet. I promised myself I'd save it for someone who I loved as much as I loved Sarah. That's how much I love you, Dorothy."

She hugged the stuffed animal. "Now I'll show you how much I love you."

Dorothy pulled her nightgown up so Ziggy could see her damaged leg.

"I knew you were hiding it from me last night," he said.

"I never let anyone see my leg. It's so ugly. But I'm trusting you with all of me."

"It's not ugly. It's part of what makes you so special," he said, touching the leg with his fingertips. "How did you get the scar?"

She told him. Before she could stop him, Ziggy lowered his face and kissed the scar. "Don't ever hurt yourself again. Promise?"

She nodded. "I had to promise my father the same thing."

They lay side by side, holding each other. "I'm not letting go," he said.

"You better not."

Later that night, they joined Odina and Niko in the living room. "We're in love," Dorothy announced with a big smile.

"Wonderful," Odina said. "You two are a perfect match." Niko agreed.

The phone rang, and Niko answered it. A quizzical look crossed his face.

"How did you get this number?" he asked. "Hold on." He put his hand over the mouthpiece. "Ziggy, Eddie Perlmutter in Boston wants to talk to you. He says Chief Davidson gave him this number."

Ziggy nodded and took the phone. "Hi, Detective. What's up?"

"Your real estate story made the *Boston Globe*," Eddie Perlmutter said.

"Shit."

"Right. You may be a hero to some, but you're a target to others. I'm afraid Anthony Anastasia might want to visit you in Nebraska."

"Why? I thought you said my testimony wouldn't hold up in court."

"Not for murder. Assault. Anastasia's a two-time loser already. A third felony conviction could put him away for a long time. I want you in witness protection right away."

Ziggy thought about leaving Dorothy. "I'll call you back, okay?"

"Make it soon, Zorn. This is no joke."

"I'm not laughing."

Ziggy reminded the Hensens of the trouble he had in Boston. "According to Detective Perlmutter, Boston hitmen might come here to kill me. He wants me in witness protection right away."

"You're not going anywhere without me," Dorothy said. "I just found you."

"No one is going anywhere," Niko said. "I'll take care of this."

"Niko, this is my problem, not yours," Ziggy said.

"My daughter loves you," he said, "that makes your problem my problem."

"These are professional killers, Niko. No one will be safe around here."

"They won't ever get here."

"Don't underestimate these guys," Ziggy said.

"Don't underestimate me. You take care of Dorothy. I'll take care of everything else."

"Odina, tell Elvis to get the Gulfstream ready. I'm leaving for Boston tomorrow morning. Tell Eli I'll want certain things on board. I'll give you a list. I also want him to research Gerry Angel. Everything. Use our Boston lawyers and connections for the information. Let's get moving. We have a lot to do."

CHAPTER 61

1971
THE ANGELS

Two days later, the black maid looked for Angel, the white Shih Tzu, in the black-and-white kitchen of the red brick mansion in Lynnfield, Massachusetts. It was nine-fifteen on a Wednesday morning, and Angel would normally be looking for her breakfast by now. The sharply dressed man of the house would have already scratched her tummy and departed in his black chauffeur-driven limo. *Where's that damn dog?* the maid wondered. Sometimes, at twilight, Angel would exit via the doggy door that led to the fenced-in backyard and chase shadows for a while. If she tired herself out, she would occasionally sleep in the carpeted dog house in the yard.

The maid opened the back door and called, "Angel!" When the furball didn't come running, she stepped outside and called again. No Angel. Concerned, she went farther out into the yard until she saw a white mound lying on the lush grass by the dog house. She approached the mound for a closer look.

When she realized what it was, she screamed. Angel lay motionless in the grass, her long white hair matted and red with blood.

The young nurse began her morning rounds of the luxury suites at the Meadows Nursing Home in West Roxbury, Massachusetts. The luxury suites had larger rooms, better accommodations, and more nurses than the rest of the home. Currently, the only patient in the suites was a ninety-three-year-old matriarch of an undisclosed, wealthy Boston family. Unlike other patients, the woman's name was not known by the nurses, and they were instructed not to talk to her. The old woman always wore a surgical mask, so the nurses didn't know what she looked like. There was an armed guard at her door at all times.

The nurse wondered why this apparently wealthy woman was not being cared for in her own home. *Maybe it's a security issue,* she thought—but why would a ninety-three-year-old woman need security? *Strange.*

When the nurse arrived at the woman's room at 9:15—the same time the Shi Tzu was late for breakfast in Lynnfield—she was surprised to see no guard on duty. *Strange.* She knocked. No answer. Had the old woman died during the night? The nurse opened the door a crack. The patient was there, in her bed, facing the window. She was either still sleeping or dead.

Walking toward the bed, the nurse noticed a streak of red on the back of the woman's white hair. Alarmed, she rushed to the window side of the bed. The old woman's eyes were closed, and she wasn't wearing her surgical mask. Her face was unremarkable for a woman her age, but there was a black dot between her eyes, surrounded by red. The nurse screamed.

❧ ❧ ❧

Gerry Angel did not arrive at his Prince Street office in Boston's North End until nearly noon. He had spent the morning with his current mistress, a woman less than half his fifty-nine years. She made him feel young again, and that was worth all the aggravation that came with an affair.

He got out of the back of the limo, straightened his tie, and buttoned the middle button of his bespoke Zegna suit. Gerry Angel looked the part of a Mafia Don; neat, sharp and dangerous. He was not a handsome man. His large Roman nose overpowered his face and eliminated any chance of being considered good-looking. He was too short and stocky to look suave, but he did the best with what he had. His full head of white hair was always perfectly coiffed, and his fingernails manicured and polished. His hands showed no trace of the blood that was certainly on them. He looked like a gentleman, but when he spoke, he revealed his hardscrabble origins.

A flunky ran to him. "Boss, where you been? I've been trying to find you all morning."

Angel slapped the back of the man's head and growled, "I told you, never ask me where I been. Now, what's the fuckin' emergency?"

The flunky rubbed the back of his head. "Your moulin-yan maid called and said your dog had to be rushed to a fuckin' dog doctor."

Angel slapped the back of the man's head again. "A veterinarian, stunad, not a dog doctor. So, what's with my Angel?"

The man shrugged, rubbing his head again. "The mou-linyan said the dog was all bloody but breathing. She woke

Mrs. Angel and Mrs. Angel took the dog to the dog doc— to the vet-rah-whatevah."

"What the fuck?" Angel said, sighed, and walked to the front door of his building. He'd been born in this neighborhood and emotionally never left. Despite his fancy clothes, cars, and homes, he was still a North End wise guy.

"Oh, I almost forgot, boss. Your mother's nursing home called. Said it was an emergency."

Angel turned. "You tell me about my fuckin' dog before you tell me about my mother?"

"Sorry. My memory's bad. Maybe I get hit on the head too much."

"Moron," Angel said and opened the door. The first floor was arranged like a clubhouse. There were folding tables and chairs, a pool table, and a jukebox. In the back was a full kitchen, with a refrigerator and freezer in a separate room. It was a hangout for Angel's inner circle. His large office was the only room on the second floor. The third and fourth floors were unoccupied and used for storage.

The phone was ringing. Another flunky answered it. "Ravens Club," he said and listened. "Who's dis?" he listened again. "Boss, you want to talk to some fuckin' nursing home?"

Angel grabbed the phone. "What's with my mother?" he asked and listened. "You're kidding me, right? But she's okay? Good. Where was her fuckin' bodyguard? In the closet, tied up? He's got a fuckin' gun, for chrissakes. What do you mean, he still had his gun, but it was empty?"

Angel listened some more. "Enough. I'll be there this afternoon." He hung up.

"Boss, you got another call on line two," another flunky said. "Your wife."

"Theresa, what's up with the dog?" He listened, and his eyes opened wide. "I don't fuckin' believe it. No, we're not at war with anyone. We're even okay with those Irish motherfuckers on Winter Hill. I got no idea. I'll call you later." He hung up. "Where the fuck is Anthony Anastasia?"

"Probably shacked up, boss," another thug said. "He gets very horny every spring."

"Find his fuckin' shack and get him here," Angel said, walking up the stairs. He opened the door to his office and gaped. "What the fuck?"

Blood everywhere—on his desk, floors, walls, file cabinets, ledgers, coffee machine. A 1959 Celtics World Championship autographed team photo was slopped in blood. He couldn't see Bill Russell's face through the stains. The glass covering the framed photo of him posing with Mayor Kevin was shattered. There was an ice-pick protruded from Angel's forehead in the picture. *A message.*

He had seen a lot of bloody scenes in his day, but this was different. This wasn't spatter. This was specific and superfluous. Deliberate and excessive—a sloppy paint job. Aghast and confused, Gerry Angel backed out of the room, locked the door and went downstairs. "I'm going to the European," he shouted in the general direction of his guys. "Find Anastasia and send him there. Fast." He left without saying a word about his office. It defied description.

An hour later, Anastasia slid into the secluded booth across from his boss. "What's the fuckin' emergency?" he asked.

Angel told him.

"Let me get this straight," Anastasia said. "Some stronzos drugged your mother and your dog last night, covered them in blood, but didn't hurt them?"

Gerry Angel nodded.

"Who was guarding your mother?"

"Jumbo Lafontana."

"*Marone.* Jumbo's a monster. Nobody gets by him."

"This guy did."

"Unbelievable. How?"

"I just talked to Jumbo. He says the guy was bigger than him. Disarmed him with some judo shit."

"*Minchia*—I don't believe it," Anastasia said.

"Jumbo don't lie. He said the guy grabbed his shoulder, squeezed, and it was lights out. The next thing he knows he's in the closet, tied up, and gagged."

"Who the fuck is this guy?"

"Don't sound like anyone we know."

A waiter approached, carrying a phone. "Mrs. Angel on the phone, Mr. Angel," he said, plugging the phone into a wall jack. "Says it's important."

"Theresa. What's up?" he asked, then listened. "Holy shit. You could be right. Makes sense. Good thinking." He hung up. "Theresa's got an idea who this guy might be."

"Who? I'll kill the bastard before dinner."

"I don't think so," Gerry Angel said. "Theresa reminded me that the article in the Globe said Zorn is living in Nebraska with a huge, former World War II U.S. Ranger and CIA agent named Hensen. Sounds like a guy who could put Jumbo to sleep with a squeeze."

"World War II?" Anastasia said. "An old man, from Bum Fuck, Nebraska. No problem. I'll go there and kill the bastard."

"Not so fast," Angel said. "The article also said the guy's a zillionaire, owns his own plane. Means he can fly anywhere, anytime."

"Are you saying this mamaluke flew to Boston from Nebraska, just to throw blood on your fuckin' dog…your mother…and your office?"

"That's right," Angel said. "Theresa thinks he's sending us a message."

"What message?"

"Maybe he wants us to know he can kill us, our mothers, or our fuckin' dogs anytime he wants. Maybe he's warning us to leave Zorn alone, and he'll leave us alone."

"He's warning us? Fahgetaboutit! I'll shoot the bastard in the head. Fuck him."

"No, Anthony. Fuck you," Angel said. "I'm not going to war with a crazy U.S. Ranger if I don't have to. He could be in the next booth for all we know. Look, relax. Zorn didn't see you shoot anyone. He even told the cops that. Their whole case is circumstantial. Leave Zorn and his CIA friend alone and let the case die."

"He knows I punched him in the nose. That's assault. I'm a two-time loser."

"Your word against his. No problem."

"Easy for you to say. Besides, your wife got me in this trouble. It's her fault. You owe me, Gerry."

"I don't owe you a war with a trained Ranger who can hire his own army. I'm telling you to wait. See what happens. *Capiche?*"

"I'll think about it," Anastasia said. He got up, angry.

"I'm giving you an order, Anthony."

Anastasia glared, said nothing, and walked away.

Crazy bastard, Angel thought, working himself into a rage. *No respect.*

That night, Anthony Anastasia sat at the bar in Polcari's Restaurant on Atlantic Ave. He was furious, and he was drunk. He felt Gerry Angel was taking a risk with his freedom, and his wife was to blame. Sure, Zorn hadn't seen him shoot the cop. But Zorn did remember who broke his nose Valentine's Day. Anastasia was a two-time loser. *Why risk another conviction?* He thought. *I can pop that little Jew and his CIA buddy, no problem. What the fuck is Angel worried about? I kill people all the time.*

Ralphie Santucci, the man who had been with him in the alley on Valentine's Day, arrived at Polcari's and sat on the stool next to his friend. They'd grown up together on the North End streets and were like brothers. "You're late, asshole," Anastasia said, joking.

"I was with the boss," Ralphie said. "He wanted to talk to me."

"About what?"

"About you."

"What about me?"

"He told me to make sure you were cool about Zorn and didn't do nothing crazy." The bartender put a scotch in front of Ralphie. "Thanks, Rocco," Ralphie said. "Gerry don't want a war with no ex-CIA spook. He don't want the trouble."

"Gerry's a pussy," Anastasia said, bleary-eyed. "He's losing his nerve."

Ralphie looked around nervously, concerned someone was listening. "Don't talk like that, Anthony," Ralphie advised. "Gerry's the boss. Don't forget that."

"Maybe he shouldn't be," Anthony said. Ralphie flinched and looked away.

"Quiet down, Anthony."

"Fuck it," Anthony talked louder. "Zorn can put me in the slammer for years."

"Gerry's betting he won't," Ralphie whispered.

"Gerry's betting with my life," Anastasia insisted, gulping down his new drink. "Fuck Gerry Angel. Zorn's gonna die."

Rocco, the bartender, looked at Ralphie and they exchanged eye rolls and grimaces.

Ralphie got up. "C'mon, buddy," he said to Anastasia. "I'll drive you home."

It took a lot of prodding, but Ralphie finally convinced Anastasia it was time to go. They walked toward the parking garage on Atlantic, two blocks south of Polcari's. Anastasia had his arm around his best friend's shoulder for support. "Fuckin' Gerry don't give a shit about nobody but himself," Anastasia slurred. "Maybe it's time for a new boss. Maybe me. What do ya think, Ralphie?"

"I'm a loyal soldier, Anthony," Ralphie reminded him, as they passed an abandoned building.

"I gotta take a piss," Anastasia said, turning into the boarded doorway and unzipping his fly. "I think I'll fly out to Nebraska tomorrow and do the job. Never been there. Maybe you'll come with me, Ralphie."

Ralphie sighed. "I'm not going anywhere, Anthony, and neither are you." He pulled his .38 from his suit—a silencer was attached. He cocked the hammer.

Anthony turned, sensing what was coming. "Oh fuck," were his last two words.

"Sorry," Ralphie apologized. "Bosses orders." The silencer muffled the noise.

Later that night, Niko Hensen's private jet took off—his job in Boston done.

With Anastasia dead, there was no need for a trial. Ziggy didn't want to press charges against Mrs. Angel or Santucci, explaining to Eddie Perlmutter, "I want to forget my past. My life is good now."

"I understand," Perlmutter said. "I'm proud of you for standing up for yourself."

"I'm proud of me, too," Ziggy said.

CHAPTER 62

1972
A BETTER PLACE

After a ten-month engagement, spent getting to know each other better and loving each other more, Ziggy Zorn and Dorothy Hensen were married on a Sunday afternoon in June of 1972. The nonsectarian ceremony was conducted by a district judge at the Hannigan mansion. Ziggy, a secular Jew, and Dorothy, a lapsed Lutheran, declared religion irrelevant. Janice Cooper and James Jackson were the only outsiders invited but could not attend. They phoned from Boston the morning of the ceremony.

"Sorry we can't be there, Ziggy," Janice apologized.

"We understand. Playing with the symphony orchestra sounds exciting."

"It's amazing. Let me put James on."

"Hello, Ziggy," James came on the line. "Congratulations!"

"Thanks. How are things with your parents?"

"Okay," James said. "At least they've accepted my friendship with Janice."

"One step at a time," Ziggy advised, before asking a lot of questions about the orchestra. When they said goodbye, they exchanged promises to meet again in the future.

Maybe they would. Maybe they wouldn't. But because they had met in the past, their lives had been changed forever.

After the wedding ceremony, a professional photographer took a family photo on the front steps of the mansion. For his portrait shot, he used the flagship of wedding cameras, the OM-1 from Olympus. For less-formal pictures, he took multiple shots with the new Polaroid SX-70, that wasn't even available to the public yet. When he was done, everyone gathered in the house for a cocktail hour before dinner. There were toasts and jokes and the comfortable conversations that take place between people who loved each other. Ziggy felt the warm glow of a loving family; certain he had never been happier in his life. He had an amazing woman he loved. Even more amazing, she loved him. He found it hard to believe. Every night when they went to bed, he would hold onto her, as if afraid to let her go.

"I'm here, Ziggy," she would whisper.

"Promise you'll be here when I wake up."

"I promise."

Only then could he sleep.

Before the cocktail hour ended, Dorothy surprised everyone with a copy of the photographs taken by the new Polaroid camera.

"How did you get these photos so fast?" Shirley asked. "They're beautiful."

"New technology," Dorothy explained. "Circle H just invested big in Polaroid and got an advance sample."

"Another good investment," Shirley said. "Except I look old in the picture."

"Sorry, Grandma," Dorothy said. "Enjoy your photos, everyone. Dinner in five."

Eli and Randi sat on the sofa. "We look old, too," she said, staring at their picture.

"We are old," Eli said. "I'm fifty-six, and you're—"

"Older," she cut him off. She was sixty-four.

Eli leaned closer to her "Do you ever think about my father?"

"Only bad thoughts," she said. "Do you ever think about your sister?"

"Only sad thoughts."

"Sometimes it's hard to believe what happened to us," Randi said.

"It seems like a dream sometimes," Eli said.

"At other times, it seems like a nightmare."

Elvis, Zoe, and Althea stood nearby, looking at their photo. "We're so lucky," Zoe said.

Elvis nodded. "If I hadn't gone to Steinauer looking for Eli twelve years ago, we wouldn't have our beautiful daughter today."

They both hugged Althea simultaneously.

"You two are so embarrassing," the twelve-year-old said, loving the attention.

Shirley reclined on her lounge with the photo. She smiled at those in the picture and mourned those missing. *If only I could change some things*, she thought. *My husband and my daughter.*

The years I lost to alcohol and drugs. Then she brightened, thinking of her blessings: *Eli's home again, lying to me about Randi and Duke's relationship—a good lie, and I love them for it. Elvis, Zoe, and Althea. Niko, Odina, and Erik. Dorothy, my miracle, and my only link to Beth. And Ziggy. I feel so good about him.*

Shirley sighed. She was seventy-two now and hoped that someday one of her grandchildren would point at this picture and say, *"That's Grandma Shirley. You would have really liked her. She was so nice."*

Dorothy and Ziggy sat on the loveseat, looking at the picture. "I had to go halfway across America to find you," he said.

"It took you long enough."

"If my boss didn't give me tickets to Sergio Franchi, we never would have met."

"Or if your girlfriend and your best friend hadn't betrayed you."

"Or if I hadn't picked up Janice and James going to Omaha."

"Or if your mother hadn't been so awful."

"Which reminds me. Her doctor at the nursing home called this morning and told me her Alzheimer's has gotten worse. She's lost almost all of her long-term memory."

"That's terrible."

"Not really. She's forgotten Germany and the Nazis. He said she's not so angry anymore. She's being nicer to people. She doesn't know who they are, but she's nicer."

"Would the world be a better place if we all forgot our bad memories and prejudices at the end of the day?"

"You mean, begin each new day with a clean slate?" Ziggy asked.

"Yeah. What do you think?"

"I think I'd fall in love with you all over again."

"Ziggy, we should have a baby. We have so much love to give."

"Can we start trying now?"

"I think we should wait until the party's over."

Niko, Odina, and Erik were in the kitchen. Odina pointed at the picture. "Look how tall you are, Erik. Tall, dark, and handsome, just like your father."

"Do you think I'll be as tall as Dad?"

"Probably. You two are so much alike."

"It will be hard to be as good as you, Dad," Erik said.

"As good at what?" Niko asked.

"Everything. A football player, a soldier, a businessman."

"You'll be better," Niko said. "You'll learn from what I did right and wrong. But I don't want you to be a soldier."

"What about Vietnam?" Erik asked.

"I hope that war will be over by the time you're eighteen," Odina said.

"If there is a war, I want to be a Navy Seal," Erik said. "Special forces, like Dad."

Niko couldn't help but think how much his son was like him and how much he had been like his father—each generation adding something to the preceding one. Erik would be big and athletic. *He's bigger than I was at his age. Faster too*, Niko thought. *He's learning martial arts from me quicker than I learned from Tian. He's compassionate, like his mother and Winona Wild Wolf before her. There's no limit to what he can be.*

"Your Grandpa Jonas would tell you the only war to fight is for survival," he said.

"Vietnam is not for survival," Erik said. "Why are we fighting there?"

"Good question," Odina said.

Niko put his hand on Erik's shoulder. "Don't worry about being like me and stop thinking about war," he said, "Just enjoy being twelve for now. Okay?"

Dorothy announced dinner was ready. Niko excused himself, saying he wanted to be alone for a bit. He went outside with the photo and looked up at a full moon. Only three years ago a man had been there, and already it was history. In twenty-four hours, this moment would be history. He had so many yesterdays to remember and fewer tomorrows to live.

Dorothy walked out on the veranda. "Odina told me you were here. We're serving dinner. Why are you out here all alone?"

"Just thinking about the past, present, and future," he said, holding up the photo.

"It's a nice picture, isn't it?"

"Happy families make nice pictures. I was thinking mostly about the past."

"Your parents? Well, you never knew your birth mother."

"I picture her sometimes. I see my father in the mirror every morning."

"You were so much alike," Dorothy said.

"And so different. We disagreed on what would make the world a better place for everyone. I believed in destroying evil. He believed in teaching people to reject it."

"Did you ever reach an understanding?"

"We agreed that a better place is purely subjective."

"Did either of you change your thinking?"

"Not really. I narrowed my focus from the whole world to just my personal space."

"When did that change happen?"

"In 1962," Niko remembered. "A friend from my CIA days, Richard Price, called me—said he'd become a federal marshal and wanted me to join him helping integrate southern universities. Said he was starting with the University of Mississippi and a black student named James Meredith."

"Civil rights were always important to you," Dorothy said.

"They still are. But I turned Richard down—told him about my narrower focus—my commitment to family."

"Did he argue with you?"

"Not at all. Told me he understood. I remember watching TV and seeing him with a group of other marshals, marching Meredith into a school building."

"Did you have regrets?"

"Some. But, like I told Richard, I'd changed my focus."

"You were what, forty-two then? Maybe a little too old for a fight."

"Young enough," Niko said. "I'll let you know when I need help, Mrs. Zorn."

"Can you believe it? I'm married."

"Yes, to a good man."

"I'm glad you like him, Dad. He's so good to me."

"You deserve it."

"That's what he says."

"I'm very happy for you."

"Thank you," she said, tears glistening in her eyes. "Now come inside."

His family had gathered for dinner. The bride and groom sat at the head of the table. Dorothy, radiant, holding the hand of her new husband, Ziggy Zorn, seemingly from out of nowhere. He gazed at Odina—beaming at the newlyweds, probably remembering the abandoned little girl in a wheelchair. Odina glanced up at Niko. *The love of my life*—they both thought.

Shirley sat between her grandchildren, Erik and Althea, engaged in an animated conversation about Elton John versus Frank Sinatra. She was free of her demons and at peace with her legacy. She watched Elvis and Zoe talking, touching, still amazed they had found each other and had Althea. Eli and Randi sat silently, solemn soulmates sharing an unspeakable memory that made their bond unbreakable.

Niko was happy, living in a world created by a circus of circumstances with unforgettable performers. It wasn't a perfect world, but at this moment, in this room, with these people,... he couldn't imagine a better place.

THE END

ABOUT THE AUTHOR

Steven M. Forman was born and raised in the Boston area. After graduating from the University of Massachusetts in Amherst, he founded a one-man business and built it into a multi-million-dollar worldwide enterprise.

Boca Knights was Forman's first novel published in 2009 by Forge Books. It was followed by Boca Mournings and Boca Daze—introducing an inimitable new detective hero, Eddie Perlmutter. Readers have fallen in love with Eddie.

His more recent novels include historical fiction (A Better Place–2019) and a prequel to the Boca trilogy (Eddie the Kid–2019). Books written by Steven M. Forman can be found wherever fine books are sold—in stores or online.

COMING SOON—A NEW NOVEL
BY
STEVEN M. FORMAN

Before Boca Knights, Boca Mournings,
and Boca Daze there was…

EDDIE THE KID & THE SHOTGUN MAN

Before he was the *Boca Knight*, Eddie Perlmutter was known as *Eddie the Kid*—Boston's most promoted, demoted, unparalleled super cop.

In 1974 a mystery man appeared through a puff of smoke on the streets of Boston's North End, brandishing a *one of a kind* four-barreled *Lupara* shotgun. With four thunderous blasts, he murders one of Boston's more popular Mafia figures and his two bodyguards—then vanishes. Boston newspapers sensationalize the assassin, naming him, *The Shotgun Man*. Twenty-nine-year-old Police Detective, Eddie Perlmutter is assigned the case.

Eddie the Kid & The Shotgun Man takes you back in time to the hills of Sicily, home of the Mafia, the Black Hand, old-world vendettas, and the Shotgun Man; to the factories of England's famous gunmakers, to Chicago street corners in Little Hell, and finally to the streets of Boston.

Set in the seventies against a background of forced public school integration through court-ordered busing, and the demise of honor among thieves, *Eddie the Kid & The Shotgun Man* pits a mystery man on a murderous mission against a fearless, irrepressible lawman who never backs down.

EXCERPT FROM EDDIE THE KID AND THE SHOTGUN MAN

PROLOGUE

Boston – September 11, 1974

Jimmy Lopresti was a hoodlum with a heart. He never killed anyone
who didn't have it coming. He was movie star handsome—tall and slim, with thick black hair he combed straight back off his forehead. His nose was aquiline, his lips full and sensual, his profile like the head on a Roman statue. His eyes were big and brown—bedroom eyes—the girls called them. Jimmy grew up in the North End of Boston where they called him Jimmy G—the G for gorgeous.

"Hey Jimmy G. How ya doin'?"

"Hey, Jimmy G. Looking good."

At twenty-nine years old he was on top of the world. His mother called him "Mia splendore Jimmy," and lit a candle for him every day. Kids looked up to him.

"Hey Jimmy G. When I grow up, I'm gonna be like you."

Jimmy G would answer, pointing his index finger like a gun—his thumb the hammer, "Yo, Carmine. Finish school—then we'll talk."

"Okay Jimmy G. Dig your double-breasted suit, man."

Bosses loved him. "Jimmy G got respect," they said. Bosses were big on respect.

Jimmy had been a *made-man* since '69 when he *hit* Danny "Dummy" Doyle—an Irish mobster from Winter Hill. Jimmy did such a first-class job; even the Irish gang didn't hold it against him.

"Dummy had it comin'," Doyle's best friend, Art Murphy, said. "I heard Jimmy G took him out for dinner before he popped him. That Jimmy G's got class."

Jimmy didn't enjoy killing. It was just part of *the life*, and Jimmy loved *the life*—the fast cars, the fast women, the easy money, the respect.

He was standing in front of the European Restaurant in the North End, waiting to have lunch with his boss—dangerous, deceitful, Vito Cerretani. Vito was like a father to Jimmy even though Jimmy had a real father—Clemente "The Tailor." Clemente was a good man, and Jimmy loved him. But he idolized Vito Cerretani.

It was a priceless September afternoon in Boston. The air was crisp, and the sun was shining. The Red Sox had done their annual fall flop—finishing third in the American League East behind Baltimore and New York. The home team hadn't won a World Series since 1918. The Patriot's season would open Sunday, September 15th, against Miami. No one expected much from the Patriots, but Jimmy G loved them anyway. He loved the NFL. No matter who won, the family made money on the vigorish and the point spread. "Bee-u-tee-full," the wise guys would say after each Sunday during football season. "Fuckin' bee-u-tee-full."

Jimmy G always arrived early to meet Vito. Waiting patiently for the boss showed respect. Jimmy G believed in respect—this Thing of Ours—La Cosa Nostra, The Mob—The Mafia—whatever you wanted to call it. He loved it all. He could have gone to college—his father had wanted that. Boston College offered him a football scholarship; the University of Massachusetts and Boston University too. He had been an All-City quarterback. But he didn't want college. He wanted *the life*. He figured he could have it all and still be a good guy. Okay, so killing wasn't good—but it was necessary in *the life*. Everyone in *the life* knew that.

What everyone outside *the life* didn't know or didn't want to know was that Jimmy G killed people. He'd never been arrested for murder, and when he had been a suspect, he always had an alibi.

"I heard Jimmy G kills people."

"No, he don't."

"That's what I heard."

"Prove it."

"Can't."

"See?"

Everyone loved Jimmy G. Well, maybe not everyone.

Standing on Hanover Street in front of the European Restaurant—looking good in his black, bespoke Zegna suit, white shirt, maroon tie, and Bruno Magli loafers, Jimmy G felt like a million bucks. His Neanderthal bodyguards, Jello Damiano, and Skinny Russo were nearby, but Jimmy felt safe without them. This was his neighborhood. His home turf. Everyone knew him, and he knew everyone.

"How you doin', Jimmy G?"

"Good Vinnie. How's your mother?"

"She's good. Who you like in the Pat's game?"

"You know me. Take the points and take the money."

Life was good for Jimmy G.

❧ ❧ ❧

BANG! The noise sounded like a firecracker. Jimmy G turned his head toward the sound. *What the fuck?* He thought, seeing a cloud of grey smoke rising from the sidewalk a few yards east of the European.

Seconds later, a tall man wearing a wide-brimmed black hat and an ankle-length black trench coat emerged from the smoke. His face was hidden behind a plain-white, full-face mask with two eyeholes. The nose and mouth were sculpted without openings—the mouth turned up in a big smile. A black mustache and goatee were painted on the white surface.

The front of the specter's cape opened slowly as a sawed-off shotgun with four barrels parted the fabric. The gun was cradled in the man's right arm; his right index finger was on one of the triggers; his left hand was under the barrel. The butt rested on his hip.

BOOM! The first blast came without warning. It blew a hole in Jimmy G's chest and threw him against the brick wall of the European. The second blast blew Jimmy's handsome face through the plate glass window behind him and into the restaurant.

"Holy shit," three-hundred-pound Skinny Russo shouted, reaching for the handgun under his ill-fitting suit jacket. The shotgun roared a third time. Skinny's fat face exploded like a watermelon hitting the pavement at the end of a long drop.

"Madonna Mia!" parsnip shaped Jello Damiano exclaimed, reaching for the gun in his belt. A fourth blast blew away his hand, his belt, and his bowels.

Four shots, three dead, sixty seconds.

Pedestrians panicked—strollers scrambled—divers ducked—cars crashed—chaos —cacophony—carnage.

The man in the cape raised his left arm over his head and brought it down fast like he was hurling something to the pavement. There was another *BANG*, and another cloud of thick smoke drifted up from the sidewalk, enveloping the gunman. When the smoke was gone, so was the shooter.

Fifteen minutes later, sirens shrieked. Someone had called the cops. The panic level plummeted. People were walking, talking, and gawking.

An unmarked police car arrived and screeched to a halt. The screaming siren stopped suddenly. Two plain-clothes detectives got out and approached the massacre. One of them, Mickey O'Toole, was big and broad with a tough Irish face, highlighted by a badly broken nose. The other, Eddie Perlmutter, was of indeterminate origin. If he were a dog, he would have been a mutt—short, wiry, and unimpressive…unless you looked in his eyes and saw the craziness in them. By outward appearances, it was hard to believe that Eddie was responsible for Mickey's broken nose—or that they were best friends—but both things were true. It was also true that Eddie Perlmutter was Boston's most promoted-demoted cop with an uncanny ability to solve the most complicated homicides using the most unconventional methods. He was called "Eddie the Kid" for his expert marksmanship but was also known to fire from the hip without aiming. Either way, he didn't miss. As he stood on Hanover Street surveying the crime scene, he was confident he would figure it out. It was what he did, and he did it better than anyone.

Made in the USA
Columbia, SC
18 November 2019

83432886R00261

ARNOLD'S

LATIN PROSE COMPOSITION

REVISED BY G. G. BRADLEY

Crown 8vo, 5s.

AIDS TO WRITING LATIN PROSE

With Exercises

BY

G. G. BRADLEY, D.D.

DEAN OF WESTMINSTER

Edited and arranged by

T. L. PAPILLON, M.A.

FELLOW AND TUTOR OF NEW COLLEGE, OXFORD

LONGMANS, GREEN, AND CO.

LONDON, NEW YORK, BOMBAY, AND CALCUTTA.

A PRACTICAL INTRODUCTION

TO

LATIN PROSE COMPOSITION

BY

THOMAS KERCHEVER ARNOLD, M.A.

Edited and Revised

BY

GEORGE GRANVILLE BRADLEY, D.D.

SOMETIME DEAN OF WESTMINSTER

LATE MASTER OF UNIVERSITY COLLEGE, OXFORD
AND FORMERLY MASTER OF MARLBOROUGH COLLEGE

NEW IMPRESSION

LONGMANS, GREEN, AND CO.
39 PATERNOSTER ROW, LONDON
NEW YORK, BOMBAY, AND CALCUTTA
1908

PREFACE

Some years have passed since I was requested by the Publishers of the late Mr. T. Kerchever Arnold's educational works, to undertake the revision of his *Introduction to Latin Prose Composition*.

The wide and long sustained circulation of the book, both in England and America, was a proof that, whatever might be its defects, its author had provided something which commended itself as a practical aid to an exceedingly large class both of students and teachers of the Latin language.

The task, however, of so revising such a work as to place it on a level with the requirements of the present time I found far more serious than I had expected. The result of much labour, and of more than one unsuccessful attempt to satisfy myself, may be stated broadly as follows :—

In the first place, an Introduction has been prefixed containing three parts, two of which are new, the other much modified.

1. The first of these is an explanation of the traditional terms by which we designate the different "parts of speech" in English or Latin. The exposition is confined to the most simple and elementary points; but it is scarcely necessary to remind any experienced teacher of the extreme vagueness with which the nature of such essential distinctions is often mastered, even by those whose mental training has for years been almost confined to the study of Language.

2. This is followed by a few pages on the Analysis of the Simple and Compound Sentence. Such logical analysis of language is by this time generally accepted as the only basis of intelligent grammatical teaching, whether of our own or of

a 2

any other language. At all events, no teacher, who would care to make trial of the present work, will regret the insertion of a short explanation of the general principle on which all its exposition of syntactical questions is directly founded.

3. I have followed Mr. Arnold's example in prefixing some remarks, retaining so far as possible his own language, on the Order of Words; I have added some also on the Arrangement of Clauses in the Latin Sentence. It is desirable to point out, at the very earliest stage of the learner's progress, not only the great differences between the structure of the two languages in this respect, but also the grounds on which these differences rest, and to indicate the general laws which regulate what may appear to the uninstructed the loose and arbitrary texture of the Latin Sentence.

The matter for translation as comprised in the various Exercises has been almost entirely rewritten. I have not, after full consideration, taken what would have been the easier course, and substituted single continuous passages for a number of separate and unconnected sentences. I found that for the special purpose of the present work, dealing as it does with such manifold and various forms of expression, the employment of these latter was indispensable, and I have by long experience convinced myself of their value in teaching or studying the various turns and forms of a language which differs in such innumerable points from our own as classical Latin.

At the close of the Exercises, I have omitted Mr. Arnold's "List of Differences between English and Latin idioms." As these differences are, or should be, brought home to the reader in almost every line of the present revision of his work, such a list would either convey a false impression of general similarity with occasional disagreement, or would reach a length which would defeat its purpose. It is better that the pupil should learn from the very first, that as a general rule, Latin and English express the same or similar thoughts by a more or less different process, and that a perfectly literal translation of every word in one language by a corresponding word in another will, whether he is translating English into Latin or Latin into English, almost inevitably result in absurdity and solecism.

A few words may be added on the order in which the various subjects treated in the different Exercises are arranged. Some surprise may be caused at its want of scientific method, and apparently of definite principle. It would have been quite possible to have started with exercises on the shortest and most elementary form of the simple sentence; then to have traced its various enlargements through all the manifold uses of the pronouns, oblique cases, uses of adjectives, adverbs, participles, gerunds, and prepositions, and thus to have deferred to the second or rather final portion of the work any notice of the various forms of the compound sentence, of many uses of the infinitive, of even the most ordinary uses of the relative, and of all subordinating conjunctions. I observe that in Seyffert and Busch's last edition of Ellendt's Latin Syntax, the construction of the accusative with the infinitive is not reached till two-thirds of the work have been read, that of the "indirect question" till considerably later. But had I followed this course, the pupil must have been conducted, by the aid of a long series of elaborately constructed specimens of the Simple Sentence, through all the range of usages that could possibly be comprised within its limits. Not till this was done could he have attempted to deal with the very commonest turns of language, such as meet him in every line of natural English, and form the texture of every sentence in Caesar or in Livy. He would have wasted his strength and patience in mounting and descending ladder after ladder of artificial language before he was invited to set foot on the free and natural paths of speech. It is difficult, no doubt, to decide which among the innumerable idioms of a language so unlike our own has the first claim on the attention of the teacher; and the precise order which should be adopted is a matter less of principle than one dictated by various and complex

considerations of practical utility. But I have not hesitated
to invite the learner, who will follow the guidance of
the present work, to leave at a very early period the
artificially smoothed waters of such simple sentences as are
carefully framed with a view to exclude the most ordinary
forms of speech in both English and Latin, and to face
as soon as possible the constructions of the Infinitive Mood,
of the Relative and Interrogative Pronoun, of the Conjunctional Clause, and some of the main uses of the Subjunctive Mood, and of the Latin, as compared with the
English, Tenses. It appears to me that after thus obtaining
some firm grasp of the great lines in which the Latin language
is modelled under the influence of that great instrument of
thought, the Verb, he will be far more likely to notice
and retain a permanent impression of the usages and
mutual relations of other parts of speech, than if he had
followed step by step an opposite system under the guidance of a synthetically arranged Syntax. At the same time,
as some amount of systematic arrangement is desirable even
on practical grounds, the Exercises have been arranged, as a
glance at the Table of Contents will show, in groups of
closely related subjects. Such questions as the use of the
Cases, and of the various Pronouns, presented considerable difficulty. Placed where they are, they somewhat
interrupt the main current of the general teaching on the
structure of the Latin sentence, yet I hesitated to relegate
them to the end of the book. As it is, I have used them
largely, and I hope successfully, not only to elucidate the
subject of which they directly treat, but also to renew,
impress, and enforce the principles and details laid down
in the earlier sections. At the same time there is no reason
why the teacher should not postpone their use for a time,
and pass on to any of the groups of Exercises which follow.

It only remains that I should express my obligations, not
only to the great German Grammarians, including the recently
completed *Historische Syntax* of Dr. Draeger, to Schultz's
Synonymik and Haacke's *Stilistik*, but also to two such English

writers on Latin Grammar as Professor Kennedy and Mr. Roby. To the former, eminent alike as a teacher and a writer, I owed, as a comparatively young teacher, my first full perception of the educational value of a systematic study of Latin Syntax as based on the Analysis of the Sentence; to the second volume of Mr. Roby's valuable work I am largely indebted. I may also mention the less obvious but not less real assistance which I have received from the published works and ever ready assistance and guidance of Professor Max Müller; also from Professor Earle's treatise on the Philology of the English tongue, and from some interesting Lectures of Professor Burggraff of Liége.

I must also express my obligations for much help received in an earlier stage of the work from Mr. A. M. Bell of Balliol College; more recently from Mr. F Madan of Brasenose College, and for the great aid given me in shaping the Vocabulary and drawing up the Index, by Mr. T. W. Haddon, late Scholar of my own College.

G. G. BRADLEY.

TABLE OF CONTENTS

¹ See Preface, p. viii.

INTRODUCTION.

THE PARTS OF SPEECH.

1. By Parts of Speech we mean the various classes, or headings, under which all words used in speaking or writing may be arranged.

2. In English Grammars eight are usually enumerated, viz. :—

Noun.	Pronoun.	Adverb.	Conjunction.
Adjective.	Verb.	Preposition.	Interjection.

3. Besides these there is a ninth, the Article, definite and indefinite, *the; an, a.* The former is merely a shortened form of the demonstrative pronoun *that;* the latter two of the numeral adjective *one;* and both may be classed under the adjective.

But in Latin Grammars the list is somewhat different, and it will be more convenient to follow the usual arrangement.

4. There is no Article in Latin, and the Adjective is included under the Noun.

i. Noun { Substantive. / Adjective.		iv. Adverb.
ii. Pronoun.		v. Preposition.
iii. Verb.		vi. Conjunction.
		vii. Interjection.

As all these names will be frequently used in the following pages, it is necessary that their meaning and nature should be understood.

The Noun.

5. (i.) The NOUN is the name (*nomen*) which we give to any person, thing, or conception of the mind; for even conceptions we may regard as *things.* We may name such

A

persons or things in two different ways; nouns therefore, or *names*, may be of two kinds.

6. The **Substantive** is a name which we give to a person or thing to distinguish it from other persons and things: Caesar, table, goodness; *Caesar, mensa, virtus.*

It denotes the assemblage, or *sum-total*, of all the qualities by which we recognise such person or thing.

Hence its name (nomen *substantivum*), as a name denoting what was once called the *substantia*, or essential nature of persons and things.

It denotes also something which is looked on as having an existence (*substantia*) by itself.

7. The **Adjective** is a name which we add or apply to a person or thing, to denote some *one quality* which we attribute to it: good, white, small; *bonus, candidus, parvus.*

8. As this one quality may be shared by many persons or things, the adjective is not well fitted to stand by itself as the name for persons or things; many different persons and things might be "good," "white," or "small."

Its proper use, therefore, is either to be attached to the *nomen substantivum*, or general name of an object, so as to define its meaning more closely, as *white* horses, *good* men; equi *albi*, homines *boni;* or to be *predicated*, that is asserted, of such substantive: the men are *good;* homines sunt *boni;* in the first case it is called an *attribute*, in the second a *predicate.* Hence its name, nomen *adjectivum;* a name, that is, fitted for adding, or attaching, to another name, from *adjicere*, "to add to."

9. In Latin this *fitness for attachment* or *addition* is even more marked than in English. Latin adjectives have, what the English have not, *inflexions, i.e.* variable terminations of gender, case, and number, which vary with those of the substantive *to* which they are attached, or *of* which they are predicated. Thus *mulier superba; vir est superbus; arbores vidi alta*s. In English the adjective has no longer any inflexions: A *proud* lady, the man is *proud*, I saw *lofty* trees. We can attach the same word *proud* to *lady* and to *man;* the same word *lofty* to *tree* and to *trees.*

Pronouns.

10. (ii.) PRONOUNS are words substituted for nouns (*pro nomine*) to *indicate* or *point to* a person, thing, or quality, without naming the thing, or its quality : *I, you, he, she, it ; that, such, who,* and many others.

The noun then, and pronoun, *name* or *point to* persons, things, or the qualities of persons or things ; but,

The Verb.

11. (iii.) The VERB *makes a statement* as to them, it joins together *two* such objects of our thought.

> *Vales,* you are well ; *curro,* I run ; *vincuntur,* they are conquered.

In each of these Latin words not one but two separate conceptions are included ; " you " and the " being well," " I " and " running," " they " and " being conquered ;" of these, the first is called the *Subject,* the second the *Predicate.*

12. The Latin verb differs from the English in not requiring the aid of a separate pronoun (*ego, tu,* etc.) to make its statement. The pronoun is contained in, and expressed by, its final syllable.

> *Vivo, I* live ; *vixisti, you* have lived ; *amat, he* loves.

13. The verb then is a *saying* about persons or things (*verbum* = *Gk.* ῥῆμα : a saying, or thing said).

It makes a statement, or, as it is called, a *predication,* as to the state of, or action done either by, or to, some person or thing.

> *Valeo,* I am well ; *vinco,* I conquer ; *vincor,* I am conquered.

14. All these parts of speech have in Latin their *inflexions, i.e.* variable and movable terminations, answering to those in such English words as d*ost*, table*s*, come*s*, and admit of other changes in form (cf. *I, me ;* come, came), by the aid of which they express various relations, or notions, of *number, case, gender, degree of comparison, time, person, mood.*

In English, many, if not most, of these relations are expressed by separate words, as pronouns, prepositions, auxiliary verbs, or by the place of the word in the sentence ; thus compare,

> *Pater filium videbit.*   The father *will* see his son.
> *Patrem filius viděrat.*   The son *had seen* his father.
> *Hunc librum tibi dederam.*   *I had* given this book *to* you.

15. But the other four parts of speech are not inflected, or *declined;* they are all called particles *(particula)*, or less important *parts* of *speech,* because they are not so essential to the formation of a sentence as those already described.   The first three can form a sentence by themselves, not so the last four.

The Adverb.

16. (iv.) The ADVERB *(adverbium)* is so called, because its main use is to attend upon the *verb.*   All verbs make a statement ; the adverb qualifies the statement which the verb makes, by adding some particular as to the *manner, amount, time,* or *place* of the state or action asserted.

Fortiter *pugnavit.*	tum *excessit.*	ibi *cecidit.*
He fought *bravely.*	*then,* or *at that time,* he went out.	he fell *there,* or *in that place.*

17. But adverbs, especially those of *amount* or *degree,* may also be joined with *adjectives,* and even with other *adverbs.*

> Satis *sapiens.*   Admŏdum *negligenter.*
> *Sufficiently* wise.   *Very* carelessly.

18. Adverbs when derived from adjectives are capable of one kind of inflexion ; that which expresses " more," " most," *sapienter, sapientius, sapientissime.*

19. Observe how often the adverb may be interchanged with an adverbial *phrase; i.e.* two or more words equivalent to an adverb : negligently, *with negligence;* hastily,

in haste; then, *at that time.* The same is the case in Latin : *Tunc = eo tempore.*

Prepositions.

20. (v.) PREPOSITIONS are words which are joined with, and almost invariably *placed before (praeposita),* nouns and pronouns, to define their relation to other words in the sentence.

Ad *me vēnit.*	a *Caesare victus est.*	pro *patriā mori.*
He came *to* me.	he was conquered *by* Caesar.	to die *for* one's native land.

21. There are a great many prepositions in Latin, and the same preposition is used in various senses, *e.g., a (ab),* " from " *and* " by." They are rarely used with any but the accusative and ablative cases.

22. But the case-ending alone will often express what in English must be expressed by a preposition.

Ense me percussit.	*Romam Narbone rediit.*
He struck me *with* a sword (instrument).	He returned *to* Rome *from* Narbonne (motion from and to a town).

23. Many words used as prepositions are also used as adverbs, *i.e.* are not joined with nouns but with verbs.

Ante te *natus sum.*	*Hoc nunquam* ante videram.
I was born *before* you (prep.).	I had never *before* seen this (adverb).

24. Many also are prefixed to and compounded with verbs, to modify their meaning. Very often they convert an intransitive into a transitive verb.

Pugno, I fight; op*pugno,* I assault (a place).

The same was the case in Old English; we still use *over*come, *with*stand, *gain*say. In later English the preposition is placed after the verb : " He is *sent for,*" " I am *laughed at.*"

A list of prepositions, with the cases which they govern, or are joined with, will be found further on. (See Ex. XLIII., XLIV.)

Conjunctions.

25. (vi.) Conjunctions are indeclinable words which join together (*conjungo*) sentences or clauses,[1] and occasionally even words.

26. Their proper office is to unite two or more sentences or clauses, and to show the relation between the clauses which they unite. "You went, *but* I remained behind," the *but* expresses *opposition;* "you did this, *therefore* I will," *therefore* draws an *inference.*

27. *Obs.*—They often connect *words*, but generally the word connected represents a clause left out, *e.g.* You and I saw this = You saw this, *and* I saw this.

Sometimes however they really connect words, and words only : "This good *but* poor man would often say," or "two *and* two make four."

For the list of conjunctions and their classes see below.

Interjections.

28. (vii.) Interjections are so called because they are words inserted (*interjecta*), or *thrown in among* the other words of a sentence to express some feeling or emotion. They are either mere exclamations, as *heu, vae,* alas ! woe ! or abbreviated sentences, such as *Me Dius fidius (juvet).* Compare "good-bye" (God be with you). They do not enter into the construction of a sentence, and their *syntax* therefore presents no difficulty.

FURTHER REMARKS ON THE PARTS OF SPEECH.

29. The Noun.—(i.) Substantives are of more than one kind.

(*a.*) The **proper** name (*nomen proprium*), *i.e.* the special name appropriated to and the *property* of a single person or place : *Caius, Roma, Italia.*

(*b.*) The **common** noun or name (*nomen appellativum*), by which we can designate either a whole class, or an individual of the class: *arbor, flumen ;* tree, river. Any tree or river may bear this name. Without the help of

---

[1] See below, Intr. 78.

these words we should require a separate name for every object that we speak of.

(*c.*) **Collective** nouns, or nouns of multitude (*nomina collectiva*) are such as, though singular, yet by their nature denote a number of individuals : *Exercitus, populus, senatus ;* army, people, senate.

(*d.*) **Abstract** nouns (*nomina abstracta*) are words which denote some quality, or state, or action, as *withdrawn* from the person or thing *in which* we see it *embodied* (*concretum*), and looked on as existing *by itself*. Thus *servitium* is the state of " servitude " which we see existing in a number of *servi ; candor*, "whiteness," the quality which is denoted by the adjective *candidus*, wherever that quality is found.

30. (ii.) ADJECTIVES may be divided into—
Adjectives of **quality**, as *bonus, malus, fortis ;* good, bad, brave.

Adjectives of **quantity** and **number** (numeral): *multi, pauci, dŭcenti ;* many, few, two hundred.

There is also a large number of *pronominal* adjectives formed from or closely connected with pronouns : *meus, tuus, ullus,* etc. ; mine, thine, any, etc. These are more conveniently included under pronouns.

31. Though the adjective is especially fitted for *attaching to* or being *predicated of* substantives, yet where no ambiguity can arise it is capable of being used by itself as a substantive: *boni*, good (men) ; *bona*, good (things), the words *men* and *things* being represented by the masculine and neuter terminations of the Latin adjective ; -*i* and -*a* representing the plural of " he," " it."

32. PRONOUNS.—The personal pronouns answering to the English *I, you,* as also to *he, she, it,* are essential parts of conversation in all languages to represent the person *speaking*, the person *spoken to,* and the person or thing *spoken of.*

We have already seen that they may be expressed in Latin by the termination of the verb. Rules for the insertion of *ego, tu, is, ille,* etc., will be given below.

33. Besides these *personal* pronouns, which indicate, without again naming, the two or three persons before named, there are a large number of words closely connected with them, which are also called pronouns (or in some cases *pronominals, i.e.* words resembling pronouns) Such are—

The Reflexive and
Emphatic Pronouns . *sui, se ; ipse, egomet,* etc.,—himself, myself, etc.

The Demonstrative . . *hic ; iste, is, ille ; idem,*—this; that; the same, etc.

The Interrogative . . . *quis, qui* (adjectival), *ecquis ; quot ?* etc.,—who? what? how many?

The Relative . . . . *qui, quicunque,* etc.,—that, who, which, whoever.

The Indefinite . . . . *quidam ; quis ; aliquis,*—a certain one ; any ; some, etc.

The Possessive . . . . *meus, tuus, suus, noster,* etc.,—mine, thine, his, ours, etc.

The Reciprocal . . . . (No single word in Latin) ; each other, etc.

The majority of these are used adjectivally; but the personal pronouns of the first and second person, the reflexive (*se*), *quis* as opposed to *qui, quid* to *quod,* are substantival.

34. There are also certain **correlative** pronouns or pronominals, which are used in corresponding pairs. Such are *is . . . qui ; tantus . . . quantus ; tot . . . quot.* Their use will be explained further on. (See Ex. XII.)

35. VERBS.—The distinction between the different kinds of verbs must be carefully attended to in composition. Verbs are thus classed :—

(i.) **Intransitive** Verbs are so called because any action which they denote does not extend or pass over (*transire*) to any other person or thing besides that which forms the subject or nominative of the verb.

Spiro, I breathe ; *curro,* I run ; *cado,* I fall ; *sum,* I exist.

Any of these verbs can form a complete sentence in Latin, though not in English, in a single word.

36. Some of them, however, hardly give a *clear* sense without the aid of a noun or pronoun to complete the statement which they make; and this is one of the chief uses of the dative case. Thus *noceo,* "I am hurtful," *pāreo,* "I am obedient," give a vague sense, unless we know *to whom* "I am hurtful" or "obedient"; and these intransitive verbs (which obviously contain an idea resembling that of the adjective) are mostly joined with a *dative* never with an *accusative:* tibi *noceo;* mihi *paret.* They are often represented in English by transitive verbs: "I *hurt* you," "he *obeys* me." There are many such apparently transitive, but really intransitive, verbs in Latin. (See Ex. I. 5.)

37. (ii.) **Transitive** Verbs are those which denote an action which necessarily affects, or *passes over to,* some person or thing other than the *subject* of the verb: *interficio,* I kill; *capio,* I take. Here *I* is the *subject* of the verb, but we ask at once *whom,* or *what,* do *I* kill, or take?

38. This other person or thing, without which the statement is incomplete, is called the *object* of the verb, and is always in the *accusative* case. In English the object follows the verb, in Latin it more often precedes it.

Fratrem tuum *vidi.* I saw *your brother.*

39. (iii.) Both transitive and intransitive verbs are called **Active.** Their inflexions are similar, and both denote *action* of some kind.

For English verbs used both transitively and intransitively, as "I move," etc., see **20, 21.**

40. Many Latin transitive verbs may be used *absolutely* (*i.e.* without an expressed object).

Vinco, I conquer (my enemies), "I win the day"; *scribo,* I am writing (a letter or book).

41. (iv.) By **Passive** Verbs we mean a form or inflexion of the transitive verb which denotes that the action indicated by the verb takes effect, not on another person or thing, but on the *subject* of the verb.

Amor, I *am loved; interficitur,* he *is killed.*

I and *he* are no longer *agents* or actors, but recipients or sufferers (*patior, passivus,* adj.), and the *agent* is some one else represented in Latin by the ablative with the preposition *a, ab.*

Ab hoste *interfectus est.*   He was slain by the enemy.

42. Remember that it is only transitive verbs, *i.e.* verbs which are joined with an accusative, that have a full passive voice. We cannot say *noceor,* or *curror,* or *vivor.*

But there is a very common use of the third person singular of a passive form of intransitive verbs, without any nominative expressed, to denote that the action described by the verb is produced or effected ; *Hac* itur, there *is a going, i.e.* men go, in this direction ; *tibi* nocetur, *harm is done* to you, *i.e.* you are injured. Owing to the large number of verbs which, like *noceo,* are intransitive in Latin, this construction is of great importance.   (See 5.)

43. (v.) Besides these **active** and **passive** verbs, there is a large class of verbs called **Deponent.**

These are verbs which, though having passive *inflexions,* have laid aside (*deponere*) a passive, and assumed an active, *sense.* Of these, some are transitive, some intransitive.

Te sequor, I follow you ; *tibi irascor,* I am angry with you.

44. Some are called **Semi-deponents** ; they have an active form in the present, a passive in the past, with no change of meaning.

Gaudeo, I rejoice ; *gavisus sum. audeo,* I dare ; *ausus sum.*

45. It is important to remember that deponent verbs differ from other Latin verbs in furnishing both a past and present participle with an active sense.

Proficiscor, I set out ; *proficiscens,* and *profectus,* "setting out," and "having set out."
(See 14.)

46. (vi.) **Impersonal** Verbs are those which are not used in the first or second persons, but only in the third.

Even with the third person of such verbs, the subject or

nominative case is never a person, or even a substantive ; but either (*a*) the vague *it* (or *he*) implied in the termination : or the verb is accompanied and explained by (*b*) an infinitive mood, or (*c*) a whole clause, or (*d*) a neuter pronoun.

> *Pudet.* *It* shames me.
> Haec fecisse *piget.* *It* is painful to have done this.
> *Accĭdit* ut abessem. *It* happened that I was absent.
> Hoc *refert.* This is of importance.

(See **123**, and **202**.)

Among these must be classed the very important construction mentioned above (**42**).

47. (vii.) By **Auxiliary** Verbs we mean verbs used as aids (*auxilia*) to enable other verbs to form moods and tenses which they cannot express within the compass of a single word. Compare " I fell " with " I *have* fallen," where "have" has lost the sense of possession, and only serves as an auxiliary verb to the verb *fall*. Such verbs abound in English, because the English verb often requires the aid of another word—*may, would, should, shall, will, let,* etc.—to express what can be expressed in Latin by a change in the verb itself. Compare " I *was* loving " with *amabam;* " *let* him go " with *eat*.

In Latin, the only auxiliary verb is *esse*, " to be," assisted by the forms, *fore, forem*. This is used largely in the passive voice and future infinitive : *auditus* sum, *auditurum* fore.

48. But much resembling these auxiliary verbs are certain verbs which are closely united with the infinitive of another verb, and add to that verb various *modes* of expressing its meaning, almost as if they were additional *moods;* hence they are called,

(viii.) **Modal** Verbs. Such are those of *being able, beginning, ceasing, wishing,* etc.

> Possum, nequeo, desĭno, volo, *haec dicere.* I *am able, unable, cease, wish,* to say this.

(See **42**.)

49. (ix.) **Copulative** or **Link** Verbs are those which unite together two nouns or pronouns, one of which, the predicate, is asserted or predicated of the other, the subject.

Caesar est *Dictator.*   Caesar *is* Dictator.

Obs.—The principal of these is the verb *sum*, whose *original* meaning was "I breathe."

When *sum* means "I am," "I exist," it is called a *substantive* verb, because it expresses the idea of existence, *substantia.* (See 6.)

When it merely joins together the subject and predicate of a sentence, as above, it is called a *copulative* verb.

When it supplies the passive voice or infinitive mood with aid to form tenses, it is called an *auxiliary* verb.

50. Besides *sum* there is a large class of other verbs which have in some cases laid aside their original meaning, and are used to connect nouns. Such are *fio* (used as the passive of *facio*), *evado*, *existo*, and also the passive of verbs of *thinking*, *naming*, etc. Of course, as link verbs they couple together words which correspond as closely as possible, and the two nouns which they unite will be in the same case.

Caesar fit Dictator.   Caesar becomes Dictator.

For Verbs called **Factitive** Verbs, see **239**.

51. The verb, when its meaning is defined or limited (*finis*) by a nominative case, *i.e.* when used as a true verb, as in the first, second, or third person, is called sometimes a *finite* verb.

But sometimes the verb, to a certain extent, lays aside its true nature as the *instrument of making an assertion by joining together two objects of our thoughts*, and takes that of another part of speech, the noun, both the *substantive* and the *adjective.* The verb is used as a substantive in the *infinitive* mood, in the *gerund*, and in the two *supines.* It is used as an adjective in the *participles*, and in the *gerundive*, or *participle* in -*dus*.

These will all form subjects of Exercises.

52. **Adverbs** have been already classified. The learner must be again reminded that just as in English we use very freely a great number of *adverbial phrases* in place of

adverbs, *e.g. in silence*, for "silently," *to the benefit of*, instead of "beneficially to," the state, so he must not think that every English adverb or adverbial phrase is to be rendered literally into Latin. Full guidance, however, will be given in the following Exercises. (See, for instance, **61, 63, 64.**)

PREPOSITIONS will be classified further on. (See Exercises XLIII, XLIV.)

53. CONJUNCTIONS are divided, both in English and Latin, into two classes; *Co-ordinating* and *Subordinating* conjunctions.

54. **Co-ordinating** conjunctions join together sentences on equal terms; these sentences are of equal grammatical rank, or co-ordinate (*ordo*, rank), *i.e.* each is *grammatically* independent of the other.

You go, *and, but, therefore*, I shall follow.

55. **Subordinating** conjunctions attach to a sentence or clause another clause which holds (grammatically) a lower or subordinate position, qualifying the principal clause just as an adverb qualifies a verb. " I will do this, *if* you do;" the *if*-sentence (or clause) is equivalent to the adverb *conditionally*. (See Intr. 82.)

56. The Co-ordinating conjunctions in Latin and English are—

a. **Copulative—**
> *Et, -que, ac, atque ; nec, neque* (when used for "and not");
> *etiam, praeterea,* etc.
> And, also ; nor, and not ; moreover, etc.

b. **Disjunctive**, *i.e.* they join together the sentences, but they *disjoin* or separate from each other the thoughts conveyed : " We must do this, *or* die."
> *Aut, vel, -ve ; nec, neque ; sive, seu ; (an, -nĕ).*
> Or, either ; neither, nor ; whether, or ; (or).

c. **Adversative.** Two statements are opposed to each other—
> *Sed, autem, verum, vero, tamen.*
> But, nevertheless, notwithstanding, however, etc.

d. **Illative or Inferential.** The statement of one sentence " brings in " (*infert*) or proves the other ;

> *Ergo, igitur, itaque.* Therefore, accordingly, and so, etc.

e. Causal ;

> *Nam, namque, enim, etenim.* For.

57. Observe that Latin has a greater variety of conjunctions than English ; for our " and " it has *et, -que, atque, ac,* for our " or " *aut, vel, -ve,* as well as *an ;* and each of these words has a somewhat different meaning.[1]

58. Very often also the relative pronoun *qui* may take the place of an English co-ordinating conjunction, and be placed at the head of a sentence or clause where we should use " and," " but," " so."

> *Quae* postquam audivit. *And* after he heard *this.*

59. The Subordinating conjunctions are—

a. Final—

LATIN.	ENGLISH.
Ut, quo ; and negative *nē, quominus.*	That (*followed by* may *or* might), in order to, to *with the Infinitive ;* that not, lest, etc.

---

[1] Latin has three Copulative conjunctions to represent our "and,"— *et ; atque, ac ;* and *-que.* *Et* simply couples words and clauses ; *-que* couples two words as forming one whole, *se suaque,* etc., or connects a closely related clause ; *atque* connects with emphasis, "and also," "and I may say."

Ac, the shorter form of *atque,* must never be used before words that begin with a vowel.

Aut . . . aut, and *vel . . . vel,* both answer to the English *either . . . or,* but *aut* marks a sharp distinction : Hoc *aut* verum est *aut* falsum, This is either true or false, *i.e.* if it is true, it is not false. *Vel* (*ve*) is connected with *velle ;* and treats the difference as unimportant : "whichever you like."

> Hoc velim *vel* vi *vel* clam facias.
> I would have you do this either by force or secretly (as you prefer).

Hence *vel . . . vel* is often equivalent to *et . . . et,* and both = *alike . . . and.*

> Vir *vel* (*et*) ingenio *vel* (*et*) virtute insignis.
> A man remarkable *alike* for his ability *and* his goodness.

An is only used for "or" in questions. (See **159.**)

b. Consecutive—

LATIN.	ENGLISH.
Ut; ut non, quin.	So that, so as to; so as not to, etc.

c. Temporal—

Quum, ubi, ut; quamdiu, dum; quoad, donec, priusquam, antequam; postquam.	When, as soon as; while, as long as; until, before that; after that, etc.

d. Causal—

Quod, quia, quoniam, quandoquidem, often *quum; non quo.*	Because, since, inasmuch as, seeing that, whereas; not that, not because, etc.

e. Conditional—

Si; nisi, si non; sive, seu; also *dum, modo; dum ne, modo ne.*	If; unless, if not; whether . . . or; provided that, so long as, on the condition that, etc.

f. Comparative and Proportional—

Quam; quasi, tanquam, sicut, ut, quemadmodum, proinde ac; quo . . . eo, with comparatives.	Than; as, as if, as though, just as, in proportion as; *the* (old abl.) more . . . *the* more, etc.

g. Concessive—

Etsi, tametsi, quamquam, quamvis, licet, ut.	Although, albeit, etc.

h. Defining or Explanatory—

Quod, ut: but their use is limited in Latin, their place being largely taken by the infinitive mood.	That (He says, or knows, etc., *that* I did it. It is true *that* he did it, etc.) Used most widely in English and modern languages.

i. Interrogative (with dependent clauses)—

Cur, utrum, an, num; quemadmodum, ut; cur, quamobrem; ubi, quando.	Whether . . . or, if; how; why, wherefore; where, when.

Observe in how many different senses *ut* and *quum* are used.

60. The relative *qui* is used also very commonly in place of subordinating conjunctions: see Exercises LXIII, LXIV.

ANALYSIS OF THE LATIN SENTENCE.

61. By a **sentence**, whether in Latin or in English, we mean a grammatical combination of words, which either (1) makes a *statement,* or (2) asks a *question,* or (3) conveys a *command* or desire.

Every such sentence, however long or however short, consists of two parts :—

62. First, a **subject**—that of which something is stated, asked, or desired ; secondly, a **predicate**—that which is stated, asked, or desired in reference to that subject.

| He is well. | Is he well ? | May he be well ! |
| *Valet.* | *Valetnĕ ?* | *Valeat !* |

In each of these sentences *he* (expressed in Latin by the termination, or personal inflexion of the verb: see 12) is the *subject,* the rest is the *predicate.* (See 11.)

63. But such short sentences are rare in all languages. They are shorter in Latin than in English for the reason given in 12.

The following more ordinary form of sentence is one that occurs in Bk. i. c. 1 of Caesar *de Bello Gallico :—*

> *Hi omnes lingua, institutis, moribus, inter se differunt.* These all (*or* all of these) differ from one another in language, institutions, and habits.

Here in both languages *Hi omnes* (these all) is the *subject ;* all the rest is the *predicate.* The main part of the predicate is the verb *differunt,* the rest being *adjuncts* or additions to the verb, explaining and limiting it, telling us *from whom* all of these differ, and *in what points.*

64. A sentence of this kind, whether short (as the examples in 62) or longer (as that in 63), is called a *simple* sentence.

By a **simple sentence** we mean one which consists of a single subject and a single predicate.

65. *Obs.*—Sometimes there is a *single* predicate and *two* or *more subjects* united by conjunctions, as

> *You and I* lifted up our hands.
> *You and I* are old.

Sometimes a *single subject* with *two* or *three predicates*, as

The army *put to flight* and *killed* many of the enemy.

These are sometimes called *contracted* sentences, as they are a shortened form of such sentences as,

You lifted up your hands, *and* I lifted up my hands.

It may be better to look on them as simple sentences with a subject or predicate consisting of two or more words, united by the conjunction *and*. (See 27.)

66. In both languages the **subject** will always be a substantive of some kind, or its equivalent. The equivalent may be a substantival pronoun (33), or an adjective, participle, or adjectival pronoun used as a substantive (31), or an *infinitive mood* (51), or some combination of words, used as a substantive. (See Examples in 67.)

67. The **predicate** will always consist either of a verb, or else of some adjective,[1] substantive, or combination of words, connected with the subject by a verb expressed or understood (see 49), *e.g.*:—

Caesar vixit. Caesar *has lived.*
Sapientes sunt beatissimi. Wise men *are the happiest.*
Hic rex est. He (this man) *is king.*
Agrum colere mihi delectationi est. Cultivating the land (*or* farming) *is a delight to me.*

Obs.—Where the link verb is omitted we supply it (at least in English and Latin) in thought.

Happy the good ! *Quot homines tot sententiae.*
(There are) as many views as there are men.

68. The subject may, even in a simple sentence, be greatly *enlarged* or prolonged by the addition of *adjectives, adjectival phrases,*[2] *pronouns,* words in *apposition*, etc.

Boni *reges amantur.* *Good* kings are loved.
Caius, vir optimus et magnae auctoritatis, *interficitur.*
Caius, *an excellent man and of great influence*, is slain.

---

[1] The adjective is specially adapted for a predicate ; it may even be said that the substantive when used as a predicate is used adjectivally.
[2] By an adjectival phrase we mean some word or combination of words other than an adjective used in place of an adjective :—
vir summae fortitudinis = *vir* fortissimus.
haec res tibi magnae *erit* delectationi = gratissima.

B

69. So also the **predicate** may be enlarged and made more distinct and intelligible by the addition of oblique cases of substantives to the verb to express its nearer and remoter objects; and these substantives may have in their turn various adjuncts, such as adjectives or other substantives in apposition.

> Pater filio, *puero aetatis tenerae carissimo,* librum *pretiosissimum Romae emptum, dono* dedit.   *The father gave his* much-loved *son* of tender years *a* present of a costly *book* bought at Rome.

"The father" is the subject; all the rest is the predicate.

Obs.—The verb *dedit* says of the father that he *gave* something.   The dative case *dono,* closely combined with the verb, explains (by a special use of that case) that what he gave he gave *as,* or *for, a present.*   The dative case *filio* does the regular work of the dative, *i.e.* specifies the *remoter object* of that gift, the son who benefited by it ; the substantive and adjective in apposition, together with the adjectival phrase *aetatis tenerae,* give some further particulars as to that remoter object.

The accusative case *librum* completes the idea vaguely expressed by *dono dedit.*   It performs the proper function of the accusative case, as it completes the idea only half expressed by a transitive verb, by supplying the (nearer) object of the verb.   (See 38.)

It is in turn made more distinct by its combination with an adjective, *pretiosissimum,* and a participle combined with the local case of a noun, *Romae emptum.*   These tell us its value, and the place where it was purchased.

But the main and essential parts of the predicate are the verb *dedit* with its two accompanying cases *filio* and *librum.*

70. Again, the action described by the verb may be explained and made distinct by the addition of *adverbs,* or of substantives used **adverbially** (especially the ablative and locative cases), *adverbial phrases, participles, gerunds, gerundives,* or *adjectives* used adverbially ; *e.g.*

> Diu *vixit.*   He lived *long.*
> *Vixit* nonaginta annos.   He lived *ninety years.*
> Fame *interiit.*   He died *of famine.*
> Summa cum celeritate *venit* (= celerrime *venit*).   He came *with the utmost speed.*

Londini *vixit.* He lived *at London.*
Pugnans *interficitur.* He is killed *while fighting.*
Sui liberandi causa *pugnavit.* He fought *to free himself.*
Invitus *hoc feci.* I did this *unwillingly.*

In each of these sentences we have adverbs, or their equivalents, fulfilling the proper function of adverbs, *i.e. qualifying and explaining the action described by the verb.*

71. The verb, instead of being, as in the example above, a very important part of the predicate, may serve as little more than a **link to connect together** the subject and predicate.

Ego consul ero.   I *shall be* consul.

Here the verb *ero* is a mere link (adding however the idea of time) between the subject and predicate.
So other verbs in a less degree.

Rex Numa appellatur.   The king *is named* Numa.

(See 50.)

In such cases the predicate and subject will, as already explained, be in the same case, as it is their agreement or identity that the verb asserts.

72. The use of the **adjective**, when it stands in such sentences as the **predicate**, must be distinguished from its use as an **attribute.**   (See 8.)

Hic rex *bonus (predicate)* est.   Reges *boni (attribute)* **amantur.**

THE COMPOUND SENTENCE.

73. Simple sentences are in English and in Latin rather the exception than the rule.

In Latin, as in English, we can neither converse nor write without using sentences which are either combined with, or contain within themselves as part of their subject or predicate, other sentences or clauses.[1]

I. CO-ORDINATION.

74. Sentences are combined together by **Co-ordination.** That is, two or more sentences are placed side by side in combination with each other; they stand to each other on equal terms; one is grammatically as important as the other.   (See 54.)

75. Such sentences are connected in English and Latin by co-ordinating conjunctions, *and, but, for; et, aut, nam,* etc.

> You do this, *but* I do that;
> I shall go home, *for* I am tired;
> Either you must go, *or* I shall (go).

For a list of English and Latin co-ordinating conjunctions, see 56.

76. It has been stated that even the relative *qui,* among its other uses, is frequently used to connect two co-ordinated sentences.   (See 58.)

In English also this is the case, though more rarely;

> I met your son, who told me that you were at home.

Here *who = and he.*

---

[1] The term *clause* is used for the various *sub-sentences* which make up the whole compound sentence.

Notice again how many sentences, and even chapters, in Caesar and other Latin authors begin with a relative.

Obs.—Sometimes co-ordinate sentences are placed side by side without any conjunction.

> *Veni, vidi,vici.*   I came, I saw, I conquered.
> *Contempsi Catilinae gladios, non pertimescam tuos.*

77. The syntax of the co-ordinate sentence will cause no special difficulty.   The characteristic of a co-ordinate sentence is, that it does not *grammatically depend on another;* it is a sentence combined with another, but on an *independent footing.*   The mood and tense of its verb, the case of its noun or nouns, are in no way dependent upon any other sentence.

II. SUBORDINATION.

78. Sentences may be joined together by SUBORDINA-TION.

A **sentence** may consist of different **clauses**, each containing its own verb, so combined that we have one principal or main clause, containing the principal verb, to which other clauses stand, so far as grammar is concerned, in a *subordinate* or dependent position.

> *Hereupon the commodore,* after he had cast anchor, *sent some of his men to land,* and *ordered them* to ask whether provisions and water could be procured, if the fleet that was yet to come should need them.

Here we have what we may call a *double compound* sentence; *i.e.* two co-ordinate main clauses (in italics) connected by *and,* each with one or more subordinate clauses dependent on it.

79. Such subordinate clauses will answer to the three different parts of speech—the substantive, the adjective, and the adverb,—which form with the verb the chief component parts of a sentence.

i. Substantival.

80. They may be SUBSTANTIVAL. That is, they may stand in the relation of **substantives** to the verb of the principal clause.

The following are three clearly marked instances of different kinds of substantival clauses—

(*a*) Se regem esse *dixit.*   He said *that he was a king.*
(*b*) Quid fieret *quaesivit.*   He asked *what was being done.*
(*c*) Ut sibi ignoscerem *oravit.*   He entreated me *to pardon him.*

In each of these Latin sentences the main clause consists of a single word, the verbs *dixit, quaesivit, oravit;* but each has appended to it a subordinate clause, answering to an accusative case, and containing (*a*) a statement, (*b*) a question, (*c*) an entreaty.

ii. Adjectival.

81. Subordinate clauses may also be ADJECTIVAL. By this we mean that they may stand in the same relation to the principal clause as an **attributive adjective.** (See 8.)

They include all such "clauses" as are introduced by *qui* in its simplest use as the relative; used, that is, to define or specify some previous substantive expressed or understood.

They are called **adjectival** because they define more closely such **antecedent** substantive or pronoun, precisely as an adjective or a substantive used as an adjective, *i.e.* in apposition, would do.

For "Boni *reges amantur*" we may say "*Reges*, qui boni sunt, *amantur.*"

For "*Servorum* fidelissimum *misi*" we may say "*Servum misi*, quem fidelissimum habui."

For "*Cicero* Consul" we may say "*Cicero*, qui Consul est," or "fuit."

iii. Adverbial.

82. There also is a great variety of ADVERBIAL clauses.

By these we mean those which add to the principal clause, grammatically complete without them, some further clause expressing *end in view, result, time, cause, condition, contrast, likeness.*

These clauses play the part of **adverbs** or **adverbial phrases** to the main clause.   Compare—

> *Hoc* consulto *feci,*   with   *Hoc feci* ut tibi placerem ;
> I did this *purposely,*   with   I did this *in order that I might please you ;*

where the adverbs *consulto* and *purposely* are replaced by *adverbial clauses.*

Or take an English sentence—

I will do this conditionally.

We have here a simple sentence, in which the predicate is qualified by the adverb *conditionally.*   Substitute—

I will do this, *if* (or *on the condition that*) *you do that.*

Here we have no longer a simple but a compound sentence, the principal clause, *I will do this,* being qualified by a subordinate adverbial clause.

83. These **adverbial** clauses are divided into seven classes—

1. Final, those which denote a *purpose.*
2. Consecutive,   „   *result.*
3. Temporal,   „   *time.*
4. Causal,   „   *reason* or *cause.*
5. Conditional,   ,,   *supposition.*
6. Concessive or adversative,   *contrast.*
7. Comparative,   ,,   *comparison* or *proportion.*

84. They are connected with the main clause sometimes by subordinating conjunctions, a list of which has been given above (see 59), sometimes by the relative *qui,* the use of which is in Latin far wider and more varied than in English.

85. The following are instances :—

Final, .	. Huc veni, *ut te viderem.* I came here *in order to see you.*
Consecutive,	. Humi cecidit *ut crus frangeret.* He fell on the ground *so as to break his leg.*
Temporal,	. *Quum haec dixisset,* abire voluit. *When he had spoken thus,* he wished to depart.
Causal, .	. *Quod haec fecisti,* gratias tibi ago. I return thanks to you *for acting thus.*
Conditional,	. *Si hoc feceris* poenas dabis. *If you do this* you will be punished.
Concessive,	. *Quanquam festīno,* tamen hic morabor. *Though I am in haste,* yet I will delay here.
Comparative } or Modal, }	*Proinde ac meritus es* te utar. I will deal with you *as you have deserved.*

In each case the subordinate clause, or its substitute in English, is in italic letters, the main clause in Roman.

ORDER OF WORDS AND CLAUSES IN A LATIN SENTENCE.

86. The order of words in a Latin sentence differs, in many important respects, from the English order. There are very few sentences in which the natural order of one language corresponds to that of the other. There is much greater freedom and variety in Latin, especially as regards substantives, adjectives, pronouns, and verbs. For these parts of speech are each susceptible of a great variety of changes in their terminations, called *inflexions.* It is these inflexions, and not their place in the sentence, which mark the relations of words to other words. As we have far fewer of these inflexions in English, we are obliged to look for the precise meaning of a word, not to its *form* but to its *position.*

87. If we take the English sentence, " The soldier saw the enemy," we cannot invert the order of the two substantives, and write " The enemy saw the soldier," without entirely changing the meaning ; but in Latin we may write *miles vidit hostem, hostem vidit miles*, or *miles hostem vidit*, without any further change than that of shifting the emphasis from one word to another.

But for all this the following rules should be carefully attended to in writing Latin, and variations from them noticed in reading Latin prose authors.

ARRANGEMENT OF WORDS.

88. The subject of the sentence, the **nominative** case, stands, as in English, at the beginning of or early in the sentence.

> Caesar, or *Tum* Caesar *exercitum in Aeduorum fines* ducit.
> Compare—Thereupon Caesar leads his army into the territory of the Aedui.

89. The *verb* (or if not the verb, some important part of the predicate) comes last of all, as *ducit* in the sentence above.

> *Ea res mihi fuit* gratissima.
> That circumstance was most welcome to me.

> *Obs.—Sum*, when used as a link verb, rarely comes last.

90. But if great stress is laid on the verb it is placed at the beginning, and the subject removed to the last place.

> *Tulit* hoc vulnus graviter Cicero.   Cicero *doubtless* felt this wound deeply.
> *Est* caeleste nūmen.   There *really is*, or there exists, a heavenly power.

This position of *sum* often distinguishes its **substantive** from its **copulative** and **auxiliary** uses.   (See 49, *Obs.*)

91. For it must always be remembered that

The degree of **prominence** and **emphasis** to be given to a word is that which mainly determines its position in the sentence. And,

The two emphatic positions in a Latin sentence are the *beginning* and the *end*. By the former our attention is raised and suspended, while the full meaning of the sentence is rarely completed till the last word is reached.

Hence, from the habit of placing the most important part of the predicate, which is generally the verb, last of all, we rarely see a Latin sentence from which the last word or words can be removed *without destroying the life,* so to speak, of the whole sentence.

This can easily be illustrated from any chapter of a Latin author.

92. The more **unusual** a position is for any word, the more emphatic it is *for that word.* Thus

> *Arbores seret diligens agricola, quarum adspiciet baccam ipse* nunquam.—(*Cic.*)

Here the adverb is made emphatic by position; in English we must express the emphasis differently, as by "though the day will never come when he will see their fruit."

A word that generally stands close by another receives emphasis by *separation* from it; especially if it be thus brought near the beginning or end of a sentence.

> *Voluptatem percepi* maximam. *Propterea quod aliud iter haberent* nullum. *Aedui equites ad Caesarem* omnes *revertuntur.*

93. As regards the interior arrangement of the sentence, **governed words**, such as (1) the accusative or dative, expressive of the nearer or remoter objects of verbs, or (2) genitive or other cases governed by a noun or adjective or participle, come usually *before*, not as in English *after*, the words which govern them.

> Hunc librum filio *dedi.*
> Compare—I gave this book to my son.
> *Frater tuus* tui *est simillimus.*
> Compare—Your brother is exceedingly like you.

94. Adjectives, when used as attributes, are oftener than not placed *after* the noun with which they agree; but the pronoun *hic*, and monosyllabic pronouns and adjectives of number or quantity, *before*, as in English.

> *Vir* bonus; *civitas* opulentissima; haec *opinio;* permulti *homines.*

When a substantive is combined both with an adjective and a genitive, the usual order is this—

> *Vera animi magnitudo.* True greatness of mind.

95. A word in apposition generally stands, as does the adjective, after the word to which it relates.

> *Q. Mucius* augur; *M. Tullius Cicero* consul; *Pythagoras* philosophus.
> *Luxuria et ignavia,* pessimae artes.

96. Adverbs and their equivalents, such as ablative and other cases, and adverbial phrases, come before the verbs which they qualify.

> *Hic rex* diu *vixit.* This king lived *long.*
> *Agrum* ferro et igni *vastavit.* He laid waste the land *with fire and sword.*
> Libenter *hoc feci.* I did this *cheerfully.*
> Triginta annos *regnavit.* He reigned *thirty years.*

97. But in all these cases the usual order may be reversed to a far greater extent than in English for the sake of emphasis.

98. *Enim, vero, autem, quoque, quidem* (with the enclitics,[1] -*que*, -*ve*, *nĕ*), cannot be the first words of a clause; *quoque* and *quidem* follow the words to which they belong.

99. The negative adverbs *non, haud, neque,* are placed always before the words which they qualify; *ne quidem,* "not even," always enclose the word which they emphasise: as, *ne* hic *quidem,* "not even he."

---

[1] An enclitic is a word which does not stand by itself, but is written at the end of the word which it qualifies: -*nĕ* (interrogative), -*quĕ* = and, -*vĕ* = or, are the commonest Latin enclitics.

ARRANGEMENT OF CLAUSES.

Substantival Clauses.

100. **Substantival Clauses**, whether statements, questions, or commands, usually come before the verb on which they depend. (See 80.)

> Errare se *ait*.　He says *that he is wrong.*
> Quid fiat *dicam*.　I will tell *you what is being done.*
> (Ut) hoc facias *oro*.　I beg you *to do this.*

English and Latin here differ exactly as they do in the position of the accusative case, which in English *follows,* and in Latin *precedes,* the verb.

101. But if the dependent clause is long and important, and the principal clause short and unemphatic, the order is generally reversed.

> Respondet ille, *si velit secum colloqui,* etc. (introducing a long speech).
> Quaeris *cur hoc homine tanto opere delecter*
> Oro *ut me, sicut antea, attente audiatis.*

Adjectival Clauses.

102. The **relative clause** is placed often where it would stand in an English sentence.
But it may be placed earlier and more in the centre of the sentence than is possible in English.

> *In his,* quae nunc instant, *periculis.*
> In these dangers *which now threaten us.*

This is accounted for by the principle laid down in 91, and the relative clause often, for the same reason, precedes the main clause.

> Quam quisque norit artem, *in hac se exerceat.*
> Let each practise the profession with which he is acquainted.

Adverbial Clauses.

103. These, like the adverbs in a simple sentence, usually, unless very emphatic, come *before* the main clause.

They are placed, in fact, much as they would be in an English sentence, but with a greater tendency to place the main and more emphatic clause last. (See 91.)

104. **Temporal clauses** such as, *haec ubi audivit*, etc., together with ablative absolutes (*hoc comperto*, etc.), and participial phrases, *id veritus*, etc., often, like adverbs of time and place, *tum, ibi, deinde*, etc., form the opening word of a sentence.

So also clauses introduced by *quum* (temporal), *quoniam* (causal), *quanquam* (concessive), *si* (conditional), *sicut* (comparative), usually come before the main clause; as do final clauses (*ut . . . ne . . .*), more frequently than in English.

But **consecutive clauses** (*ut*, so that) usually, as in English, follow the main clause.

105. The following are examples of the *usual* order:—

Quum haec dixisset, *abiit* (temporal).	Having said this, he departed.
Si futurum est, *fiet* (conditional).	If it is to be, it will come to pass.
Ut sementem feceris, *ita metes* (comparative).	You will reap as you have sown.
Quoniam vir es, *congrediamur* (causal).	Since you are a man, let us close in fight.
Romani, quanquam fessi erant, *tamen obviam procedunt* (concessive).	The Romans advanced to meet (them) in spite of their fatigue.
Esse oportet, ut vivas. ⎫ Haec ne facias, *abi*. ⎭ (final).	You should eat to live. To avoid doing this, begone.
Quis fuit tam ferreus, ut mei non misereretur (consecutive).	Who was so hard-hearted as not to pity me?

106. It may be well to add that a repeated word, or a word akin to another in the sentence (such as one pronoun to another), is generally placed as near to that word as possible.

> *Nulla* virtus virtuti *contraria est.* No kind of *virtue* is opposed to *virtue.*
>
> Te-*nĕ* ego *aspicio?* Is it *you* whom *I* see?
>
> Aliis aliunde *est periculum.* Danger threatens *different* men from *different* quarters.
>
> Timor timorem *pellit. Fear* banishes *fear.*

We see that Latin has a great advantage in this respect over English.

107. Of two corresponding *clauses* or *groups* of words of parallel construction, the order of the first is often *reversed* in the second : so that two of the *antithetical* words are as *near* as possible.

> *Fragile* corpus animus *sempiternus movet. Ratio nostra* consentit ; pugnat *oratio. Quae me* moverunt, movissent *eadem te profecto.*

To many of these rules exceptions may be found. For the order in Latin is determined, as has been already said, not by any strict rules, but by considerations of **emphasis, clearness, sound, rhythm, variety,** some of which sometimes defy explanation, but which may be easily noticed and understood by any one who reads Latin with observation and intelligence.

As a general rule, **in any but the shortest clause the English order is sure to be ill adapted to a Latin sentence.**

EXERCISES.

EXERCISE I.

ELEMENTARY AND GENERAL RULES.

MOST of the following rules necessarily follow from what has been said in the Introduction. Two or three are added on constructions of exceedingly frequent occurrence.

1. A finite verb (see Intr. 51) agrees with its *subject* (or its nominative case) in *number* and *person*.

> *Avis can*it.   The bird sings.
> *Aves can*unt.   The birds sing.

2. An adjective, pronoun, or participle agrees with the substantive to which it is attached, or of which it is predicated, in *gender*, *number*, and *case*.   (Intr. 8, 9.)

> *Rex ille, vir justissimus, plurima foedera pact*us *est*.   That just king contracted many treaties.

3. When to a substantive or personal pronoun there is added a substantive explaining or describing it, the latter is said to be placed in *apposition* to the former, and must agree *in case* with the substantive to which it is added.

> Alexander, *tot regum atque populorum* victor.   Alexander, the conqueror of so many kings and nations.

Obs.—The substantive when thus used resembles an adjective. Alexander is here described by one *special quality*.   (Intr. 7.)

4. A **transitive** verb, whether active or deponent, is joined with an **accusative** of the *nearer object;* that is to say, of the *person* or *thing acted upon.*

> *Sacerdos* hostiam *cecīdit.* The priest struck down the victim.
>
> *Alius* alium *hortatur.* One man exhorts another.

This rule is invariable; **every really transitive verb governs an accusative.** (See Intr. 38.)

5. But many verbs that are transitive in English must be translated into Latin by what are really intransitive verbs, and are therefore joined with a **dative** of the person (or thing) *interested in* the action of the verb. *i.e.* the *remoter object.* (Intr. 36.) Thus—

I favour you,	tibi *faveo,*	(I am favourable *to* you.)
I obey you,	tibi *pareo,*	(I am obedient *to* you.)
I persuade you,	tibi *suadeo,*	(I am persuasive *to* you.)
I please you,	tibi *placeo,*	(I am pleasing *to* you.)
I spare you,	tibi *parco,*	(I am sparing (merciful) *to* you.)

These verbs, in the passive voice cannot be used otherwise than impersonally.

You are favoured,	tibi *favetur,*	(Favour is shown to you.)
You are spared,	tibi *parcitur*	etc.
You are pardoned,	tibi *ignoscitur.*	
You are persuaded,	tibi *persuadetur.*	
You are obeyed,	tibi *paretur.*	

6. The dative of the remoter object is sometimes, but by no means always, marked in English by the preposition *to* or *for.*

But it does not express *to* in the sense of *motion to.*

> I gave this *to* my father. *Hoc* patri meo *dedi.*

but

> I came *to* my father. Ad patrem *veni.*

For *to* in the sense of motion to a town, see **9,** *b.* *For,* when it means "in defence of," "in behalf of," is expressed by *pro.*

> Pro *patria mori.* To die *for* one's country.

7. The verb *to be*, and such verbs as *to become, to turn out, to continue,* etc., passive verbs of *being named, considered, chosen, found,* and the like, do not govern any case, but act as links between the subject and predicate, and therefore have the same case after as before them. (See Intr. 49, 50.)

> *Caius est justus.* Caius is a just man.
> *Scio Caium justum fieri.* I know that Caius is becoming just.
> *Caius imperator salutatus est.* Caius was saluted as Imperator.

8. (*a.*) With passive verbs and participles, "the thing *by which,*" or "*with which*" (the instrument), stands in the **ablative**; "the person *by whom*" (the agent), in the ablative **with the preposition** *a* or *ab.* (Intr. 41.)

> *Castra* vallo fossāque a militibus *munita sunt.* The camp has been fortified *by* the *soldiers with* a *rampart* and *ditch.*

(*b.*) But when "with" means "together or in company with" the preposition *cum* must be used.

> Cum telo *rēnit.* He came *with a weapon.*
> Cum Caesare *hoc feci.* I did this *with Caesar.*

Obs.—*Cum* is written after, and as one word with, the ablatives of the personal and reflexive pronouns (*mecum, tecum, secum, nobiscum, vobiscum*), and sometimes after the relative, as *quicum* (abl.), *quibuscum.*

9. (*a.*) The ablative also expresses the time *at* or *in* which a thing takes place, the accusative the time *during which* it lasts.

> Hoc mense *quindecim* dies *aegrotavi.* I have been ill for fifteen days in this month.
> Tres *ibi* dies *commoratus sum,* quarto die *domum redii.* I stayed there three days, I returned home on the fourth day.

(*b.*) With the proper names of **towns** the ablative expresses motion *from,* without a preposition.

> Romā *venit,* "he came from Rome," but ex *or* ab Italiā, "from Italy;" also domo *venit,* "he came from home."

C

Motion *to* a town is expressed by the accusative without a preposition.

> Neapolin *rediit,* "he returned to Naples;" but ad *or* in *Italiam,* "to Italy."

The accusatives *domum,* (to) home, and *rus,* to the country, are used in the same way as towns, without a preposition.

10. One substantive in close connexion with another which it defines is put in the **genitive** case.

> *Horti* patris.   The gardens of my father = my father's gardens.
> *Laus* ducis.   The praise of the general.
> Fortium virorum *facta.*   The deeds of brave men.

This case corresponds often to the English possessive case, the only true *case* retained by English substantives.

11. (*a.*) PRONOUNS.—When a pronoun is the nominative case to a verb, it is not expressed in Latin, except for the sake of *emphasis* or particular *distinction.*

This is because the termination of the verb contains a pronominal element; therefore, to express the pronoun is really to have the person twice repeated.   (See Intr. 12.)

*Ama-*t is a compound word = Love-he, *i.e.* he loves.   Ille *amat* means, *As for that man,* he loves.   There is a repetition of the pronoun to call special attention to the subject of the verb.

> Ego *hoc volo.   For myself* I wish this

(*b.*) When there is a distinction or contrast between persons to be expressed, the personal pronouns must be used.

> Tu *Tarentum amisisti,* ego *recēpi.   You* lost Tarentum, *I* retook it.

(*c.*) Even the *possessive* pronoun is seldom expressed when there can be no doubt as to *whose* the thing is.

> *Tum ille dextram porrigit.*   Then he (the other) holds out *his* right hand.

But it must be used when emphatic, *i.e.* = *his own,*

or when its omission would cause a doubt as to the meaning.

> Suo *se gladio vulneravit.* He wounded himself with his (own) sword.
>
> *Patrem* meum *vīdi.* I have seen my father.

(*d.*) *He, she, it, they,* and their oblique cases, when they carry no emphasis, but merely *refer* to some person or thing already named, should be translated by *is, ea, id,* not by *ille. Ille* is much more emphatic, and often means "the other" in a story where two persons are spoken of, and sometimes "that distinguished person." *Iste* is "that of yours."

(*e.*) But when *him, her, them* denote the same person as the subject of the verb, *se, sui, sibi* must be used.

> He says he (himself) will do it. *Hoc se facturum esse ait.*

The same rule applies to the possessive pronoun *suus.*

12. The relative pronoun *qui* agrees in *gender* and *number* with a substantive or demonstrative pronoun, which is usually expressed in a preceding sentence. Its *case* depends on the construction of its own clause. The substantive to which it thus *refers* (*refero, relatirum*) is called its **antecedent** (or *fore-going* substantive).

> *Ille est equus,* quem *ēmi.* Yonder is the horse which I have bought.
>
> *Pontem video,* qui *flumen jungit.* I see a bridge which spans the river.

13. The relative is often used in place of the English conjunctions *and, but, so,* etc., combined with the pronoun, *he, she, it,* etc. (See Intr. 58.)

> *Divitias optat,* quas *adepturus est nunquam.* He is praying for riches, *but* is never likely to obtain *them.*

14. PARTICIPLES.—(*a.*) There is no past participle active in Latin except with deponent verbs. (Intr. 45.)

We can say *secutus* for "having followed," from *sequor* (verb dep.) But for "having come," we must say either *quum vēnisset,* or *postquam* (*ubi*) *vēnit.*

(*b.*) With a transitive verb the **ablative absolute** of the passive participle may also be used.

Thus for " *having,*" or " *after having,* heard this," we may say either *hoc audito,* or *hoc* quum *audivisset,* or *hoc* postquam (ubi) *audivit.*

(*c.*) The participle in -*rus* is always active, and has various meanings.

> *Hoc* facturus est.   He is *going to, likely to, intending to, ready to, destined to,* do this.

15. Where in English two finite verbs are coupled by *and* we may often substitute a Latin participle in the proper case for one, and omit the *and.*

> They marvelled *and* went away.   Admirati *abiere.*
> They heard *and* wondered at him.   Auditum *admirati sunt.*

Vocabulary 1.

NOTE.—In the vocabularies hyphens (*e.g.* in *contem-no,* etc.) have not been inserted on any etymological principle, but simply to mark clearly the inflexions.

again, rursus.

always, semper.

and, et, -que, atque, ac. (See Intr. 57, *note.*)

arrive (at), I, per-vĕnio, īre, -vēni, -ventum (*ad* with *acc.*).

begin, I, in-cīpio, ĕre, -cēpi, -ceptum.

blockade, I, ob-sĭdeo, ēre, -sēdi, -sessum.

brave, fort-is, -e.

but, sed, vero.

chief, prin-ceps, -cipis, *m.*

city, urbs, urbis, *f.*

consul, cons-ul, -ŭlis.

day, di-es, -ei, *m.*[1]

daybreak, prima lux (lūcis).

despise, I, contem-no, ĕre, -psi, -ptum.

district, ag-er, -ri, *m.*

elected, I am, fi-o, ĕri, factus.

enemy, host-is, -is.

envy, I, in-vĭdeo, ēre, -vīdi, -visum (*dat.*). (See **5.**)

favour, I, făveo, ēre, fāvi, fautum (*dat.*).

fire and sword, ferrum et ign-is (*abl.* -i).[2]

fortunate, fel-ix, -īcis.

fourth, quart-us, -a, -um.

friend, amic-us, -i, *m.*

halt, I, con-sisto, ēre, -stiti.

hate, I, od-i, isse, -eram. (Perf. with pres. meaning.)

hear, I, aud-io, ire, -ivi, -ītum.

hour, hor-a, -ae, *f.*

human, hūmanus.

I, ego. (See **11.**)

if, sī.

injure, I, nŏc-eo, ēre, -ui, -ĭtum (*dat.*).

January, Januarius.

lay waste, I, vasto, are.

march (subst.), it-er, -inĕris, *n.*

messenger, nunti-us, -i, *m.*

---

[1] Occasionally fem. in sing. only.

[2] Note order. *Ferrum,* " iron," used for "sword " in metaphorical sense. (See **17.**)

mid-day, meridi-es, -ei, *m.*
month, mens-is, -is, *m.*
my, meus.   **(11, c.)**
never, nunquam.
now, jam = *by this time*, can be used of the past ; nunc, *at the present*, at the moment of speaking.   **(328, b.)**
obey, *I*, pār-eo, ēre, -ui (*dat.*). (See 5.)
people, pŏpul-us, -i, *m.*
race, gĕn-us, -ĕris, *n.*
right hand, dextr-a, -ae, *f.*
Roman, Romānus.
send (*to*), *I*, mitto, ĕre, misi, missum (*ad*).   **(6.)**
send for, arcess-o, ĕre, -īvi, -ītum (*acc.*).

show, *I*, monstro, are.
sometimes, interdum.
spare, *I*, parco, ĕre, peperci, (*dat.*). (See 5.)
speak, *I*, lŏ-quor, -qui, -cūtus.
stretch forth, *I*, por-rigo, ĕre, -rexi, -rectum.
take by assault, *I*, expugno, are.
that (*pron.*), ill-e, -a, -ud.
three, tres, tria.
to (*motion*), ad (*acc.*).   (See 6.)
town, oppid-um, -i, *n.*
you, tu, *pl.* vos.   **(11,** *a* and *b.*)
vote, suffragi-um, -i, *n.*
waste.   (See *lay.*)
way, vi-a, -ae, *f.*

Exercise 1.

1. I have been elected consul by the votes of the Roman people ; you are favoured by the enemies of the human race.   2. The town had now been blockaded for three days ; it was taken by assault on the fourth day.   3. I sent three messengers to you in the month (of) January.[1]   4. If you are (*fut.*) obeyed I shall be spared.   5. That district had been laid waste by the enemy[2] with fire and sword.   6. I am envied, but you are despised.   7. Fortune favours the brave (*pl.*), but sometimes envies the fortunate.   8. Having arrived at the city at daybreak he sent for the chiefs.   9. I never injured you, but you have always envied me, and you hate my friends.   10. Having heard this he halted for three hours, but at mid-day began his march again.   11. Having spoken thus,[3] and having stretched[4] forth his right hand he showed him the way.

---

[1] *Januarius* is properly an adjective.
[2] Plural ; the singular *hostis* is used sometimes like our "enemy," as a collective noun.   (Intr. 29, *c.*)
[3] "These things," *haec.*
[4] Abl. abs., *lit.* his right hand having been stretched out.   **(14, b.)**

EXERCISE II.

MEANING OF WORDS AND PHRASES.

THOUGH Latin words answering to all the English words in the following Exercises will be found in the Vocabularies, yet some care and thought will be necessary, even with their aid.

16. The same English word is often used in very different senses, some **literal**, some **figurative**. It is most unlikely that a single word in Latin will answer to all the various meanings of a single English word.

(*a.*) Thus we use the word " country" (connected through the French with the Latin *contra*, "opposite to us ") in a great variety of meanings : " rural districts " as opposed to " town ;" " our native land," as opposed to a foreign country ; " the territory," of any nation ; " the state," as opposed to an individual ; even " the inhabitants or citizens of a country." Each of these senses is represented by a different word in Latin. Thus :—

Rus *abiit*. He went into the *country*.
Pro patria *mori*. To die for one's (native) land or *country*.
In fines *or* in agros *Helvetiorum exercitum duxit*. He led his army into the *country* of the Helvetii.
Rei publicae (*or* civitati) *non sibi consuluit*. He consulted the interests of the *country*, not of himself.
Civibus *omnibus carus fuit*. He was dear to the whole *country* (or *nation*).

No Vocabulary or Dictionary therefore will be of any real use, unless we clearly understand the precise meaning of the English.

(*b.*) Again, we might meet with the word " world " in an English sentence ; but we cannot translate it into Latin till we know whether it means " the whole universe," or "this globe," or "the nations of the world," or "people generally," or "mankind," or "life on earth."

> *Num casu factus est* mundus ? Was the *world* (sun, moon, stars, and earth) made by chance ?
>
> *Luna circum* tellurem *movetur.* The moon moves round the *world* (this planet).
>
> Orbi terrarum (*or* omnibus gentibus) *imperabant Romani.* The Romans were rulers of the *world*.
>
> Omnes (homines) *insanire eum credunt.* The whole *world* thinks him out of his mind.
>
> *Nemo* usquam. No one in the *world*.
>
> *Multum* hominibus *nocuit.* He did *the world* much harm.
>
> *In hac* vita *nunquam eum sum visurus.* I am never likely to see him in this *world*.

With words therefore used in such different senses we must ask ourselves their precise meaning. Great assistance will be given in the present book ; but the learner cannot too soon learn to dispense with this kind of aid, and to think for himself.

17. There are a great number of **metaphorical expressions** in English which we cannot possibly render literally into Latin. We say, "His son ascended the throne," or "received the crown," or "lost his crown ;" and we might be tempted to translate such phrases literally after finding out the words for "to ascend," for "a throne," for "to receive," for "a crown," and so on.

But the fact is that these words when so combined **mean** something quite different from what they **say**, and to translate the actual words literally would be to say in Latin something quite different from the idea which the English conveys.

Filius solium ascendit, or *conscendit,* would (except in a poem) merely mean that his son "went up," or "climbed up," a throne ; *Filius coronam accepit* that he "received a (festal or other) garland." A Roman would certainly say *regnum excepit,* "received in turn (inherited) the *sovereignty.*"

Obs.—This is only a specimen of the kind of mistakes which we may make by not asking ourselves what words *mean* as well as what they say.

Compare such common expressions as "he held his peace," "he took his departure," answering to *conticuit, abiit.* Mistakes in such phrases as these are more likely to occur in translating longer passages without the aid afforded in these Exercises ; but the warning cannot be too early given.

18. There are many English words whose **derivation from Latin words** is obvious. We are apt to think that if we know the parent word in Latin we cannot do better than use it to represent the English descendant, which so much resembles it in sound and appearance ; but we can hardly have a worse ground than that of the similarity of *sound* in Latin and English words on which to form our belief that their *meaning* is identical. Most of these words have come to us through the French, *i.e.* through a language spoken by Roman soldiers and settlers, and borrowed from them by the Gauls ; the Gauls in turn communicated the dialect of Latin which they spoke to their German conquerors ; from these the Normans, a Scandinavian people, learnt, and adopted, what was to them a foreign tongue, with words from which, after conquering England, they enriched the language spoken by our English or Saxon forefathers. It would be strange if the meaning of words had not altered greatly in such a process.

When, therefore, we meet such a word as " office " in an Exercise we must beware of turning it by *officium*, which means " a duty," or an " act of kindness." We shall learn in time, by careful observation, when the English and Latin kindred words correspond in meaning, and when they differ, but we cannot too early learn that they **generally differ.**

19. Thus—

> "Acquire" is not *acquirere*, but *adipisci, consequi.*
> A man's "acts" are not *acta*, but *facta.*
> "Attain to" is not *attinere ad*, or *attingere ad*, but *pervenire ad*, or *consequi.*
> "Famous" is not *famosus*, but *praeclarus.*
> "Mortal" (wound) is not (*vulnus*) *mortale*, but *mortiferum.*
> "Nation" is not *natio*, but *civitas, populus, res publica, cives.*
> "Obtain" is not *obtinere*, but *consequi, adipisci*, etc.

"Office" is not *officium*, but *magistratus*.

"Oppress" is not *opprimere*, but *vexare*, etc.

"Perceive" is not *percipere*, but *intellegere*.

"Receive" is not *recipere*, but *accipere*.

"Ruin" (as a metaphor) is not *ruīna*, but *pernicies*, *interĭtus*, etc.

"Secure" (safe) is not *securus*, but *tutus*.

"Vile" is not *vilis*, but *turpis*.

These are only specimens. The Vocabularies will be a sufficient guide, but the learner cannot too early be on his guard against a fruitful source of blunders, or learn too soon to lay aside, as far as possible, the use of vocabularies and similar aids, and trust to his own knowledge as gained from reading Latin.

Vocabulary 2.

acquire, I, ad-ipiscor, i, -eptus. (See **19.**)

admire, I, admir-or, āri, -atus.

advantage, emolument-um, -i, *n.*

all (things), (*n. pl.*), omnia.

as regards = from (the side of), a, ab (*abl.*).

attain to = arrive at. Voc. 1. (**19.**)

both . . . and, et . . . et.

boy, pu-er, -eri.

care. (See *free.*)

country, rus, ruris, *n.*; patri-a, -ae, *f.* (See **16,** *a.*)

crown, regn-um, -i, *n.* (See **17.**)

din, strepit-us, -ūs, *m.*

do, I, făc-io, ĕre, fēci, factum.

empire, imperi-um, -i, *n.*

ever = always. Voc. 1.

famous, praeclarus.[1] (**19.**)

father, pat-er, -ris.

fight, I, pugno, āre.

for (conj.), nam, enim. (Intr. 98.)

for (prep.), pro (*abl.*). (**6.**)

forefathers, major-es,[2] -um.

foretell, I, praedi-co, -ĕre, -xi.

free from care, securus. (**19.**)

from, a, ab (*abl.*).

glory, glori-a, -ae, *f.*

great, magnus.

greatly, maxime.

Hannibal, Hannib-al, -ălis.

highest, summus.

hold, I, obtin-eo, ēre, -ui. (**19.**)

hold my peace, I, contic-esco, ĕre, -ui. (See **17,** *Obs.*)

king, rex, rēgis.

last, at, tandem.

long (adv.), diu.

made, I am being, fio. (See *become,* Voc. 1.)

means, by no, haudquaquam.

mind, anim-us, -i, *m.*

mortal (wound), morti-fer, -fera, -ferum. (**19.**)

much, multus.

native country. (See **16,** *a.*)

nation, civit-as,[3] -atis, *f.* (**19.**)

never, nunquam.

obedient to, I am, = obey. Voc. 1.

---

[1] *Famosus* means "notorious" in a bad sense, "infamous."

[2] *Patres* is never used in prose for "forefathers." Our use of "fathers" in this sense came into English from Hebrew through the Bible.

[3] *Natio* is rarely used of a civilised and organised nation; it means a people, or tribe, sprung from one race, of the same blood (*nascor*).

office, magistrat-us, -ūs, *m.*   (19.)
orator, ōrăt-or, -ōris.
pleasing (*to*), gratus (*dat.*).
ready to, I am, vŏlo, velle, vŏlui.
receive, I, ac-cipio, ĕre, -cēpi, -ceptum.   (19.)
reign, I, regno, āre.
Rome = nation of, populus Romān-us.   (See 319.)
ruin, interĭt-us, -ūs, *m.* ; clad-es, -is, *f.*   (19.)
say, I, dī-co, ĕre, -xi, -ctum.
secure = safe, tutus.   (19.)

succeed to, I, (*crown*) = *I inherit* (see 17), ex-cipio, ĕre, -cepi, -ceptum.
sword (*metaph.*), arm-a, -orum, *n.* ; ferr-um, -i, *n.*   (17.)
this, hic, haec, hoc.
time, at that, tum.   (64.)
vile, turp-is, -e.   (19.)
violence, vis, *abl.* vi, *f.*
whole, totus.
world.   (16, *b.*)
wound, vuln-us. -ĕris, *n.*
yet, tămen.

Exercise 2.

1. I was made king by the votes of the whole nation.
2. He attained to the highest offices in (his) native country.
3. I hate the din of cities; the country is always most pleasing to me.   4. Our forefathers acquired this district by the sword.   5. The whole world was at that time obedient to the empire of Rome.   6. He reigned long; the crown which he had acquired by violence he held to[1] the great advantage of the nation.   7. He was a most famous orator, and all the world admired him greatly.
8. He was most dear to the whole nation, for he was ever ready to do all things for the country.   9. He received a mortal wound (while) fighting for his native land.   10. At last he held his peace ; he had said much (*neut. pl.*), and (spoken) long.   11. He succeeded to the crown (while) a boy ; (as) king he attained to the highest glory.   12. He was now secure from all violence, yet he was by no means free from care as regards Hannibal.
13. He never attained to his father's glory, but all things that were vile he always hated.   14. He foretold the ruin of his country.

---

[1] Use *cum* with abl.

MEANING AND USE OF WORDS—*Continued.*

VERBS.

20. In translating a Verb into Latin, it is most important to be sure of the precise sense in which the verb is used.

We have in English a large number of verbs which are used in two senses, one **transitive**, the other **intransitive** or **reflexive**.

We say "he changed his seat," and "the weather is changing;" "he moved his arm," and "the stars move;" "we dispersed the mob," and "the fog dispersed;" "he turned his eyes," and "he turned to his brother;" "he collected books," and "a crowd collected;" "he joined this to that," "he joined his brother," "the two ends joined."

But in translating such verbs into Latin, we must carefully distinguish between these different senses of the same verb.

If the English transitive verb is used intransitively, or as we should say in Greek in the Middle Voice (as in "the crowd *dispersed*"), we must either (*a*) use the passive of the Latin verb, or (*b*) insert the reflexive pronoun *se*, or (*c*) use a different verb.

43

21. Thus—

(*a.*) He *changed* his seat.   *Sedem* mutavit.
       The weather *is changing,*
         or *altering.*   Mutatur *tempestas.*

       He *broke up* the crowd.   *Multitudinem* dissipavit.
       The fog *broke up.*   Dissipata est *nebula.*

       The moon *moves* round
         the earth.   *Luna circa tellurem* movetur.
       He *moved* his arm.   *Brachium* movit.

       He *rolled down* stones.   *Lapides* devolvit.
       The stones *roll down.*   Devolvuntur *lapides.*

(*b.*) He will *surrender the city.*   *Urbem* dēdet.
       The enemy will *surrender.*   Se dēdent *hostes.*

(*c.*) Riches *increase.*   Crescunt *divitiae.*
       He *increased* his wealth.   *Opes suas* auxit.
       He *collected* books.   *Libros* collēgit.
       A crowd was *collecting.*   Conveniebat *multitudo.*

22. Many English verbs, usually intransitive, become transitive by the addition of a preposition: to hope, to hope *for* (trans.); to wait, to wait *for* (trans.); to sigh (intrans.), to sigh *for* (trans.); similarly " to gaze *on*," " to look *at*," " to smile *at*," and many others.

To determine whether the preposition really belongs to the verb, the verb may be turned into the passive; if the preposition *remains attached to the verb,* we may be sure that the two words form one transitive verb.

He *waits for* his brother.   His brother *is waited for.*

To " wait for," therefore, is a compound verb; " to wait " is converted by the addition of a preposition from an intransitive to a transitive verb.

Fratrem expectat.   *Frater* expectatur.

23. Some of the commonest of such words are—

       1 aim *at* distinctions (high office).   *Honores* peto.
       I crave *for* leisure.   *Otium* desidĕro.
       I hope *for* peace.   *Pacem* spero.
       I listen *to* you.   *Te* audio.
       I look or wait *for* you.   *Te* expecto.
       I look round *for* you.   *Te* circumspicio.

I look *up* at the sky.   *Caelum* suspicio.

I pray *for* (*i.e.* desire much) this.   *Hoc* opto.

But the number of such English verbs is very large.

24. In Latin (as in older English I *forego*, I *bespeak*) an intransitive verb very often becomes transitive by composition with a preposition prefixed to the verb. (See Intr. 24.)

> *Sedeo*, I sit, ob*sideo*, I blockade (a town); *vehor*, I am carried, *or* I ride, praeter*vehor*, I ride past; *venio*, I come, con*venio*, I have an interview with, as, *ad te* vēni, *Caesar*em convēni.

25. A single Latin verb will often express an English *verbal phrase*, *i.e.* a combination of a verb with a substantive or other words. Thus—

> *Taceo*, I keep silence; *abeo*, I take my departure; *navigo*, I take, *or* have, a voyage; *insanio*, I am out of my senses; *minor*, I utter threats; *colloquor*, I have a conversation; *te libero*, I give you your liberty : *adeo mortem pertimescit*, such is his terror of death.

Vocabulary 3.

absent, I am, ab-sum, esse, etc.

besiege, obsideo.[1] (See *blockade*, Voc. 1.)

bestow (*these things on you*), *I* (haec tibi) larg-ior, īri, -ītus.

bloody, cruentus.

carry on, I = *I wage*, gĕ-ro, ĕre, -ssi, -stum.

country, in the, ruri.

crave for, I, desidero, āre. (22, 23.)

desert, I, deser-o, ĕre, -ui, -tum.

disperse, to (*intrans.*), di-labi, -lapsus. (20.)

down from, de (*abl.*).

eight, octo (*indec.*).

endeavour, I, cōnor, ari.

exile, an, ex-ul, -ūlis.

fatal,[2] funestus.

flock together, to, congregari.

friend. Voc. 1.

gate, port-a, -ae, *f.*

gather together, to, con-vĕnire, -vēni, -ventum.

Heaven (*metaph.*), **(17)**, Di Immortales. Caelum would mean "the sky."

leisure, oti-um, -i, *n.*

long (*adj. of time*), diutĭnus.

look for, I, expecto, are. (22, 23.)

look round for, I, circum-spicio, -ĕre, -spexi, -spectum. (22, 23.)

look up at, I, suspicio, ĕre, etc.

many, mult-i, -ae, -a.

mingle with, I (*intrans.*), im-misceor **(20)**, ēri, -mixtus (*dat.*).

morning, in the, mānĕ (*adv.*).

---

[1] *Obsideo* is "besiege" in the sense of blockading; *oppugno*, in that of assaulting.

[2] *Fatalis* is "destined," "fated," and may be used either in a good or bad sense. (See **18.**)

mountain, mon-s, -tis, *m.*
multitude, multitud-o, -inis, *f.*
noon.   See *mid-day*, Voc. 1.
obtain, *I*, ad-ipiscor, -ipisci, -eptus ;
  conse-quor, i, -cutus. **(19.)**
one (of), unus (e, *abl.*).
our, nost-er, -ra, -rum.
peace, pax, pacis, *f.*
pray for, *I*, (*desire much*), opto,
  āre (*acc.*).
return (*subst.*), redit-us, -ūs, *m.*
rock, sax-um, -i, *n.*
roll, I (*intrans.*), vol-vor **(21,** *a*), vi,
  volutus.
soldier, mil-es, -ĭtis.

struck (*participle*), ictus, (*fr.* ico,
  icĕre.)
surrender, *I*, (*trans.*) de-do, ĕre,
  -didi, -ditum ; (*intrans.*)me dedo.
  (21, *b.*)
swarm out of, *I*, effundor, i, effus-
  us (*abl.*).
then, tum, tunc.
towards, ad (*acc.*).
turn, *I* (*intrans.*), con-vertor, i,
  -versus. **(20.)**
vain, in, frustrā.
vast,[1] maximus ; ingeñ-s, -tis.
wait for, *I*, expecto. **(22, 23.)**
war, bell-um, -i, *n.*
world. **(16,** *b.*)

Exercise 3.

Verbs marked in *italics* are to be expressed by participles, the
conjunction that follows to be omitted **(15).**

1. We all were craving for peace, for we had carried on
a long and bloody war.   2. They at last surrendered the
city, which-had-been-besieged (*part.*) for eight months **(9,***a*).
3. He prays for peace and leisure, but[2] he is never likely[3]-
to-obtain these things.   4. All the world is looking for
war, but heaven will bestow upon us the peace for which
we pray.   5. Then he *turned* (*part.*) towards his friends,
and in vain endeavoured to look up at them.   6. He looked
round for his friends, but all for whom he looked round
(*imperf.*) had deserted him.   7. The enemy *had swarmed*
out of the gates and were mingling with our soldiers.
8. The multitude which had gathered together in the
morning dispersed before noon.   9. Many rocks were
rolling down from the mountains, and one of our guides
was struck by a vast mass, and received a mortal wound.
10. On that fatal day I craved for you, but you were
absent in the country.   11. A vast multitude had flocked
together, and was now waiting for the return of the
exiles.

---

[1] *Vastus* does not mean "vast" in size, but either "shapeless," or
"waste," "desolate," etc.   (See **18.**)
  [2] Relative neut. pl. **(13)** = "which things."
  [3] "Likely-to," participle in *-rus* of "to obtain."   (See **14,** *c.*)

EXERCISE IV.

AGREEMENT OF THE SUBJECT, OR NOMINATIVE CASE AND VERB.

26. If one verb is predicated of two or more **subjects** of **different** grammatical **persons**, it will be in the plural number, and agree with the first person rather than the second, and with the second rather than the third.

> *Et ego*[1] *et tu manus* sustulimus.   Both you and I raised our hands.
> *Et tu et frater meus manus* sustulistis.   Both you and my brother lifted up your hands.

(For the analysis of these sentences see Intr. 65.)

27. But sometimes the verb will be in the **singular** and agree with the subject *nearest itself.*

> *Et tu* ades, *et frater tuus.*   Both you and your brother are here.

28. If a single verb is predicated of several subjects of the **third person**, it may either be in the plural number, or it may agree with the substantive nearest itself.

> *Appius et soror ejus et frater meus manus* sustulerunt. Appius and his sister and my brother lifted up their hands.

But "Sustulit *manus Appius et soror ejus et frater meus,*" with the same meaning, would be good Latin.

---

[1] For "Caius and *I*," the Romans, putting "*I*" first, said "*Ego* et *Caius.*" When therefore Cardinal Wolsey said "*Ego* et *Rex meus,*" he was a good grammarian but a bad courtier. Similarly they placed the second person before the third; "Your brother and you" would be, *Et tu et frater tuus.*

29. After **disjunctive** conjunctions (Intr. 56, *b*), *neque* (*nec*) . . . *neque; aut* . . . *aut*, etc., either construction may be used.

> *Neque tu neque frater tuus* adfuistis.   Or,
> *Neque tu* adfuisti, *neque frater tuus.*   Neither you nor your brother were present.

But the latter is much more usual.

Obs.—There is therefore great freedom in all these constructions in Latin ; greater than is usual in English.[1]

30. A singular collective noun (see Intr. 29, *c*) is *occasionally* followed by a plural verb.

> *Magna pars . . . fūgēre.*   A large proportion fled.

But *much oftener,* and always if it denotes a united body which acts as one man, it is followed by a singular verb.

> *Vult populus Romanus.*   It is the wish of the Roman people, *or,* of the people of Rome.
> *Exercitus e castris* profectus est.   The army started from the camp.
> *Senatus* decrevit.   The senate decreed.

Obs.—The singular is always used with *Senatus populusque;* the two words are looked on as forming one idea.

In English there is greater freedom ; we can use the plural if we think rather of the individuals than of the body as a whole.

> The gentry *were* divided in opinion.

Vocabulary 4.

Alexander, Alexand-er, -ri.	*decree, I,* de-cerno, ĕre, -crevi, -cretum.
army, exercit-us, -ūs, *m.*	*end,* fin-is, -is, *m.* (properly, *limit*).
before (*prep.*), ante (*acc.*).	*ever,* unquam.
brother, frat-er, -ris.	*exile, I am in,* exulo, āre.
Clitus, Clit-us, -i.	*flock,* gre-x, -gis, *m.*
countryman, civ-is, -is.	

---

[1] But compare :—
> "The thought that thou art safe, and he."—COWPER.
> "For thine *is* the kingdom, the power, and the glory."

Gauls, the, Gall-i, -orum.
great.   Voc. 2.
health, I am in good, val-eo, ĕre, -ui.
home, domum (*acc.*).   (See 9, *b.*)
honour (*distinction*), hon-os, -ōris,
 m.
kindness, benefici-um, -i. *n.*
kill, I, inter-ficio, ĕre, -fĕci.
matter, a, res, rei, *f.*
next day, the, postridie.
number (*proportion or part*), par-s,
 -tis, *f.*
return, I, redeo, redīre, redii.
reward, praemi-um, -i, *n.*

safe (*unharmed*), incolum-is, -e.
senate, senat-us, -ūs, *m.*
settle, I, constit-uo, ĕre, -ui (*trans.*).
spare, I.   Voc. 1.
summer, aest-as, -ātis, *f.*
sword, gladi-us, -i, *m.*
third, terti-us, -a, -um.
time, at that, either *tum* (Voc. 2),
 or use subst., *tempest-as, -ātis, f.,*
 with *is, ea, id.*
toil, lab-or, -ōris, *m.*
wage, I, gero, ĕre, gessi, gestum.
war.   Voc. 3.
well, bĕne (*adv.*).

Exercise 4.

1. If the army and you are in good health, it is well.
2. Both you and I have waged many wars for our country.
3. The Gauls were conquered by Caesar before the end of the summer.   4. The flock returned home safe the next day.   5. Neither you nor your brother have ever done this.   6. A great number of my countrymen were at that time in exile.   7. Both you and I have been made consuls by the votes and by the kindness of the Roman people.
8. I have spared my countrymen, you the Gauls.
9. Having settled[1] these matters, he returned home on the third day.   10. Clitus was killed by Alexander with a sword.   11. The Roman people and senate decreed many honours to you and to your father.   12. Neither you nor I had looked for this reward of all our toil.

---

[1] Abl. abs.   (See **14,** *b.*)

EXERCISE V.

ACCUSATIVE WITH INFINITIVE.

ORATIO OBLIQUA.

31. The infinitive takes before it (as its *subject*) not the nominative but the *accusative*.

Frater cecĭdit. His brother fell; but—
Narrat fratrem cecidisse. He reports *that* his brother fell.

The accusative with the infinitive is especially used, where in English we use a clause beginning with "that," after (*a*) verbs of *feeling, knowing, thinking, believing, saying* (**verba sentiendi et declarandi**); and (*b*) such expressions as *it is certain, manifest, true*, etc.

In turning such sentences into Latin, *that* must be omitted; the English *nominative* turned into the *accusative;* and the English verb into the *infinitive mood.*[1]

(*a*.) *Sentimus* calere ignem. We perceive-by-our-senses *that* fire is hot.
Hostes adesse *dixit.* He said *that* the enemy was near.
Fratrem tuum fortem esse *intellego.* I perceive *that* your brother is a brave man.
Rem ita se habere *video.* I see *that* the fact is so.
Respondit se esse iturum. He answered *that* he would go.

---

[1] We are not quite without this idiom in English.
    "I saw *him to be a knave*" (= "I saw *that* he was a knave").

Such a sentence as "*narravit fratrem suum in praelio cecidisse,*" may be sometimes translated literally, "he declared (*or* reported) his brother *to have fallen* in the battle." At the same time this constant employment of the infinitive, in place of such conjunctions as the English *that,* the French *que*, the German *dass,* and even the very common Greek ὡς or ὅτι, is one of the most characteristic idioms of the Latin language. (See Intr. 59, *h*.)

(*b.*) *Manifestum est* nivem esse albam.   It is plain *that* snow
  is white.

  Constat Romam non sine labore conditam fuisse.   It is
  agreed *that* Rome was not built without toil.

The statement made by the verb in the infinitive mood
is called *indirect* predication, or **oratio obliqua**; because
the statement is not made directly (oratio *recta*), but
indirectly, *i.e.* through a verb that is itself dependent on
another verb or phrase.

32. Cautions.—(*a.*) Beware of ever using *quod* or *ut* to
represent *that* after any verb or phrase *sentiendi vel
declarandi.*

Never say "*Scio* quod *erras,*" "I know that you are
wrong;" but always, "*te errare scio.*"

(*b.*) In English we often express a statement or an
opinion as though it were a fact, but with such words as
"*he said,*" "*he thought,*" etc., inserted in a parenthesis.

  You were, *he said*, mistaken.   You were absent, *he
    thought*, from Rome.   He is, *it is plain*, quite mad.

In Latin this construction must not be used; such
expressions as "*he said,*" "*he thought,*" "*it is plain,*"
must form the principal verb or clause with the infinitive
dependent on it.

We must write—not "tu, *dixit*, errasti," but "te errare
dixit;" not "Roma, *credidit*, aberas," but "Roma te abesse
credidit."

For the use of *inquit* with *oratio recta* see **40.**

33. The English verb *say* when joined to a negative is
translated into Latin by the verb of denial, *nego.*

  He *says* that he is *not* ready.   *Se paratum esse* negat.
  He *said* he would *never* do this.   *Se hoc unquam esse fac-
    turum* negavit.
  He *says* he has done *nothing.*   *Negat se quidquam fecisse.*

34. The *pronoun*, so often *omitted* in *oratio recta* (*currit*,
(*he*) runs), must always be *inserted* in *oratio obliqua:* se
currere ait.

He, she, they must be translated by the reflexive pronoun *se* (11, *c*), whenever one of these pronouns stands for the *same person* as the *subject* of the verb of saying or thinking.

> *Hoc* se *fecisse negat.*   He says that *he* (himself) did not do this.

Eum or *illum* would be used if the second *he* denoted a different person from the first *he*. Latin is therefore much less ambiguous than English, as it carefully distinguishes the different persons denoted by *he*, etc.

Tenses of the Infinitive.

35. In translating the verb in an English *that*-clause dependent on a past tense, we must attend carefully to the following rule :—

An English *past* tense in a *that*-clause will be translated by the *present* infinitive, if the time denoted by the two verbs is the same.

> *Se in Asia* esse[1] *dixit.*   He said that he *was* in Asia. (When ?—at the time of his speaking.)

The perfect infinitive is only used if the verb in the *that*-clause denotes a time *prior* to that of the verb *sentiendi vel declarandi.*

> *Se in Asia* fuisse *dixit.*   He said that he *had been*, or *was*, in Asia. (When ?—at some time earlier than that at which he was speaking.)

36. The future infinitive is supplied by the participle in -*rus* with *esse, fore, fuisse,* and is used thus :—

> Both, He *says* that he *will go* ;
> And also, He *said* that he *would* go. }   *Se* iturum esse *or* fore { *dicit.* *dixit.*
>
> He *says* or *said* that he *would have* gone.   *Se* iturum fuisse *dicit* or *dixit.*

---

[1] Thus the present infinitive represents both the present and imperfect of the indicative,—the imperfect being the tense which denotes a past event, not merely as past, but as *contemporaneous with something else in the past.* (See below, **177**, *b.*)

Vocabulary 5.

against, contra (*acc.*).

answer, I, respon-deo, dēre, -di, -sum.

attack, I, oppugno, āre. **(24.)**

believe, I, cred-o, ĕre, -idi, -itum.

break, I (*met.*), violo, āre.

camp, castr-a, -orum, *n.*

follow, I, sequor, i, secutus sum.

general, dux, dŭcis.

gladly, libenter.

hope for, I, sper-o, āre.

interview, I have an interview with, con-venio, īre, -vēni (*trans.*). **(24.)**

law, lex, lēgis, *f.*

line (*of battle*), aci-es, -ei, *f.*

man, vir, vĭri.

now. See Voc. 1.

one and all, omnes (*placed last*). (Intr. 92, 97.)

perceive, I, intel-lĕgo, ĕre, -lexi, -lectum. **(19.)**

place, loc-us, -i, *m.*

plain (*adj.*), manifestus.

please, I, plac-eo, ēre, -ui, -itum (*dat.*). **(5.)**

Pompey, Pompe-ius, -i.

preceding, proximus.

remember, I, memin-i, isse, (*imperat.*) memento.

reply, I. See *answer.*

repose, oti-um, -i, *n.*

ride past, I, praeter-vehor, i, -vectus (*trans.*). **(24.)**

say, I. Voc. 2.

sigh for (*I crave for*), desidero, āre (*trans.*). (See **22.**)

sin, I, pecco, āre.

soon, mox, brĕvi.

take up, I, sūm-o, ĕre, -psi, -ptum.

to, ad, in (*acc.*).

train, I, exerc-eo, ēre, -ui, -itum.

year, ann-us, -i, *m.*

Exercise 5.

1. He had waged, he answered, many wars, and was now sighing for peace and repose. 2. He says that he has not sinned. 3. Both you and your brother, he replied, were in good health. 4. He perceived that the enemy[1] would soon attack the city. 5. He says that Caesar will not break the laws. 6. It is plain that the place pleases you. 7. It was plain that the place pleased you. 8. It was plain that the place had pleased you. 9. Pompey believed that his countrymen would, one and all, follow him. 10. The soldiers said that they had not taken up arms against their country and the laws. 11. Brave men, remember, are trained by toils. 12. The soldiers answered that they would have gladly attacked the town in the preceding year, but that now they hoped for repose. 13. Having returned to the camp, he said that he had ridden past the enemies' line, and had an interview with their[2] general.

---

[1] Sing. (See p. 37, note ?.)

[2] Gen. pl. of *is:* why would *suus* be wrong? (See **11,** *d* and *e.*)

EXERCISE VI.

ACCUSATIVE WITH INFINITIVE—*Continued.*

SOME of the *verba sentiendi et declarandi* have **special constructions**.

37. Thus, after the verbs *sperare* (to hope), *promittere* or *pollicēri* (to promise), *recipere* (to engage or undertake), *minari* (to threaten), *jurare* (to swear), and similar verbs referring *to the future*, the *future infinitive* is used in Latin with the *accusative* of the pronoun.

Obs.—In English we generally treat these verbs as *modal* verbs (see Intr. 48) and join them with the *present* infinitive ; in Latin, and sometimes in English, they are used as verbs of thinking or saying something future.

In English we say " he hopes *to* live," and also " he hopes *that* he *will* live ; " in Latin the latter is the regular construction.

> *Sperat plerumque adolescens diu* se victurum (esse).[1] A young man generally hopes *to live* a long time.
> *Hoc* se facturum esse *minatus est.* He threatened *to do* this.

N.B.—The verb *posse* is often used in the present infinitive after *spero*.

> *Hoc se facere* posse *sperat.* He hopes to be able to do this.

38. With active verbs that have no future in -*rus,* and generally with passive verbs, and even as a substitute for the ordinary construction, *fore ut* with a subjunctive is used.

> *Spero* fore ut deleatur *Carthago.* I hope that Carthage will be annihilated.
> *Speravit* fore ut *id sibi* contingeret. He hoped that this would fall to his lot.

---

[1] With these *compound* infinitives *esse* is often omitted.

Obs.—The *tense* of the verb after *fore ut* depends upon that of the verb of hoping, etc. ; after the present, perfect with *have*, and future, the present subjunctive is used ; after a past tense, the imperfect.

39. After *simulare*[1] (to pretend), the *accusative* of the pronoun must be expressed in Latin.

Se *furěre simulat.* He pretends *to be* mad.

40. The great exception to the construction of *verba declarandi* is *inquam, inquit,*—" say I," " says he."
Inquit always quotes the *exact words used*, and never stands first.

Domum, inquit, *redibo.* " I will," *says he*, " return home."
Domum se rediturum esse dicit *or* ait. He will, *he says*, return home.

Inquit therefore is always used with oratio *recta* ; all other words of *saying* with oratio *obliqua*.

41. The accusative with the infinitive is also used after—

(*a.*) Certain verbs of *commanding* and *wishing*, especially *jubeo, volo, cupio, prohibeo*.

(*b.*) Verbs expressing *joy, sorrow, indignation, wonder*, etc.

Milites abire *jussit.* He ordered the soldiers to go away.
Te *incolumem* rediisse *gaudeo.* I rejoice that you have returned in safety.

Vocabulary 6.

assert, I (maintain), vindĭco, āre.	*finish, I,* con-ficio, ěre, -feci, -fectum.
business, the, res, rei, *f.*	
country (**16**, *a*), ager, agri, *m.*	*foe* = *enemy.* Voc. 1.
crown. Voc. **2**, and see **17**.	*force,* vis, *f.* (*abl.* vi).
cruel, crudel-is, -e.	*freedom,* libert-as, -atis, *f.*
earlier than (= *before*), ante (*acc.*).	*greatly,* vehementer.
fifth, quint-us, -a, -um.	*highest,* summus.
find, I, in-venio, ire, -vēni, -ventum.	*home, at,* domi.
	husband, vir, viri.

---

[1] *Simulo* is used of a person who pretends that something exists which does not. *Dissimulo* of some one who tries to conceal something which does exist.

Quae *non* sunt *simulo ;* quae *sunt*, ea *dissimulantur*.

land. (See *country.*)
last, at. Voc. 2.
London, Londini-um, -i.   (9, *b.*)
long. (See *so.*)
mad, I am quite, fŭro,[1] ēre.
mind, I am out of my, insan-io, ire,
   -ivi, *or* -ii.   (25.)
nation, popul-us, -i, *m.* ; *or* civ-es,
   -ium.   (19, and p. 41, note [3].)
now. Voc. 1.
obtain. Voc. 3.   (19.)
oppress, I, vexo, are.   (19.)
presently = *soon.*
pretend, I, simulo, āre.
promise, I, polli-ceor,[2] ēri, -citus ;
   pro-mitto, ĕre, -misi, -missum.

rejoice, I, gaudeo, ēre, gavisus sum.
satisfactory, use adverbial phrase
   ex sententia, "in accordance with
   one's views."
see, I, vĭdeo, ēre, vīdi, visum.
shortly, brevi.
sister, sor-or, -oris.
so long, tamdiu.
Solon, Sol-on, -ōnis.
soon. Voc. 5.
swear, I, juro, āre.
sword, by the (*met.*).   Voc. 2.
threaten, I, minor, ari.
voyage, I have a, navigo, āre.   (25.)
win, I = *I obtain.*   Voc. 3.
yet, not, nondum.

Exercise 6.

1. Solon pretended to be out of his mind.   2. I will pretend, says he, to be out of my mind.   3. He promised to come to London shortly.   4. I hope that you will have a satisfactory voyage.   5. He hopes to obtain the crown presently.   6. He was pretending to be quite mad.   7. Caesar threatened to lay waste our country with fire and sword.   8. He replied that he had had a satisfactory voyage. 9. He swore to finish the business by force.   10. He says that he will not return home earlier than the fifth day. 11. He replied that he had not yet seen his sister, but (that he) hoped to find both her and her husband at home. 12. The army hoped that the land of the enemy would now be laid waste with fire and sword.   13. He hopes soon to attain to the highest honours, but [3] I believe that he will never win them.   14. I rejoice greatly that your nation, (which has been) so long oppressed by a cruel foe, has at last asserted its freedom by the sword.   15. I have not, says she, yet seen my sister, but I hope to find both her and her [4] husband at home.

---

[1] *Furo* is a stronger term than *insanio : furor* often means "frenzy," but it never means "fury" in the sense of mere "anger."

[2] *Promitto,* "I give forth," general word for "I give assurance for the future ;" *polliceor,* "I give something *that lies in my own power.*"

[3] See 13.   [4] *Ejus.* Why not *suum ?*

NOMINATIVE WITH INFINITIVE, MODAL VERBS, PASSIVE VERBS OF SAYING, Etc.

42. (i.) **A large number of verbs are used in Latin in close combination with an infinitive mood without any intervening accusative.** They are, in fact, a kind of *auxiliary* verb, as they cannot, as a rule, stand by themselves, or make full sense without the infinitive with which they are joined ; they are called modal because they give, as it were, a fresh mood (*modus*) to the other verb. (See Intr. 48.)

Compare the English " I can *do*," " must *do*," " ought *to do*," " wish *to do*," etc., where *do* and *to do* are both in the infinitive mood.

Such are verbs of

(a.) *Possibility* or the *reverse*.	*Possum, nequeo,* etc.
(b.) *Beginning* [1] or *ceasing.*	*Coepi, incipio, desino, desisto,* etc.
(c.) *Habit, continuance, hastening.*	*Soleo, assuesco, pergo, festino,* etc.
(d.) Many verbs of *wish*,[2] *purpose, aim, endeavour,* etc.	*Volo, nolo, malo, cupio, audeo, statuo,* etc.
(e.) *Duty.*	*Debeo.*

(ii.) When a finite verb of this kind is combined with the infinitive, the *nominative,* not the accusative, is used in the predicate.

Civis Romanus fieri, vocari, *cupio.*

I am anxious to become, *or* to be called, a citizen of Rome.

Soleo, or *incipio,* or *festino, otiosus* esse.

I am accustomed, *or* I am beginning, *or* I am making haste, to be at leisure.

Mori malo quam servus esse.

I had rather die than be a slave.

---

[1] This is sometimes expressed by the termination *-sco* of the verb : *senesco,* I begin to grow old. Such verbs are called *inchoative.*

[2] Sometimes expressed by the termination *-urio : edo,* I eat ; *esurio* I am hungry.

43. With passive verbs *sentiendi et declarandi*, such as *videor*, " I seem," *dicor*, " I am said," and similar verbs, the impersonal construction, "*it* seems," "*it* is said," is not used in Latin.

We must not say for "*It is said*, or *it seems*, that Cicero was consul that year," " *Videtur, dicitur*, Ciceronem *eo anno* consulem *fuisse*," but " *Videtur, dicitur* Cicero *eo anno* consul *fuisse*."

44. But a very common use is *ferunt, dicunt, tradunt*, they *or* men say, etc., followed by the accusative and infinitive. So that for "There is a tradition that Homer was blind," we may either say " *Traditur Homerus caecus fuisse*," or " *Tradunt Homerum caecum fuisse*," but not " *Traditur Homerum caecum fuisse*."

45. Verbs of *purposing, resolving*, and many others, are used with the infinitive and the nominative case, only when *the subject of both verbs is the same*.

> *Constituit Caesar* consul fieri.
> Caesar determined to become consul.

But

> *Constituit Caesar* ut Antonius consul fieret.
> Caesar determined that Antony should be made consul.

(See **118.**)

46.   EXCEPTIONS.

(*a*.) The past tense of such longer phrases as *mihi nuntiatum est, memoriae proditum est*, and others, is used impersonally, and is followed by the accusative and infinitive.

> *Caesari* nuntiatum est *adesse Gallos*.
> *News was brought* to Caesar that the Gauls were at hand.

(*b*.) *Videtur* can be used impersonally, but means, not " it seems," but " it seems *good*."

> *Hoc mihi facere* visum est.
> It seemed *good* to me (I resolved) to do this.

(*c.*) The impersonal verbs, *apparet* (not "it *seems*," but "it is *clear*") and *constat*, "it is agreed," are very common, and are followed by the accusative and infinitive.

(*d.*) The accusative is sometimes introduced after *volo*, even when the subject of both verbs is the same. We may say either Consul *esse vult*, "He wishes to be consul," or Se consulem *esse vult*, "It is his wish that he himself should be consul."

Vocabulary 7.

accept, I, ac-cipio, ĕre, -cepi, -ceptum.

ambassador, legat-us, -i.

ask for, I, posco, ĕre, poposci. (22,23.)

become, I, fio, ĕri, factus.

begin, I. Voc. 1.

blame, culpa, *f.*

break, I. (See *word.*)

candidate for, I am a, pet-o, ĕre, -ivi, *or* -ii, -ĭtum (*trans.*). (23.)

cease, I, de-sino, ĕre, de-sivi, *or* -sii.

chief (*man*). Voc. 1.

clear, it is, appār-et, ēre, -uit. (46, *c.*)

coward, timidus ; ignavus.

crown. Voc. 2.

deceive, I, de-cipio, ĕre, -cepi, -ceptum.

despair, I, despero, āre.

destined, fatāl-is, -e.

die, I, morior, i, mortuus[1] sum, moriturus.

either . . . or, vel . . . vel ; aut . . . aut. (See Intr. 57, *note.*)

free (*adj.*), lib-er, -era, -um.

free from, I, libero, āre.

hand, I am at, ad-sum, esse, -fui.

jury (*judges*), jud-ex, -ĭcis (*in plur.*).

keep, I (*promises*), sto, stare, steti, lit. "I stand on my promises" (*abl.*).

live, I, vi-vo, ĕre, -xi, -ctum.

member of the state, civis.

nation. Voc. 6.

offer, I, de-fero, ferre, -tuli, -latum.

office. (See **18,** and Voc. 2.)

once, at, statim.

patriot, true patriot, bonus civis : lit. "a good member of the state."

prefer, I. (See *rather.*)

private (*person*), privat-us, -i.

promise (*thing promised*), promissum (*neut. participle*), -si, *n.*

Pyrrhus, Pyrrh-us, -i.

rather, I had, or would, mālo, malle, malui.

refuse, I. (See *unwilling.*)

resolve, I, de-cerno, ĕre, -crēvi, -cretum.

rich, div-es, -itis ; *comp.* divitior (ditior), *superl.* divitissimus (ditissimus).

seem, I, videor, eri, visus.

slave, serv-us, -i ; *m.*

surrender, I. (Voc. 3, and **21,** *b.*)

than, quam.

townsman, oppidan-us, -i.

tradition, there is a, tra-do, ĕre, -didi, -ditum. (**44.**)

troublesome, molestus.

unwilling, I am, nōlo, nolle, nolui.

venture, I, audeo, ēre, ausus sum.

verdict, sententia, *f.* (*plur.*[2])

word, I break my, fidem fallo, ĕre, fefelli.

world, in the (*= of all men*), omnium hominum. (See **16,** *b.*) Why not *in mundo?*

your (*plur.*), vest-er, -ra, -rum.

---

[1] *Mortuus est* is "he is dead ;" "he died" is (*e*) *vita excessit.*

[2] Plur., because each judex gave his own *sententia*, "opinion" or "vote."

Exercise 7.

1. I had rather keep my promises than be the richest man in the world.　2. I begin to be troublesome to you.　3. Cease then to be cowards and begin to become patriots.　4. He resolved to return at once to Rome, and become a good member of the state.　5. It seems that he was unwilling to become king, and preferred to be a private person.　6. It is said that by the verdict of the jury you had been freed from all blame.　7. Having [1] resolved to be a candidate for office, I ventured to return home and ask for your votes.　8. We would rather die free than live (as) slaves.　9. There is a tradition that he refused to accept the crown (when) offered by the nation and (its) chief men.　10. It was clear [2] that the destined day was now at hand; but the townsmen were unwilling either to despair or to surrender.　11. He said that he had neither broken his word nor deceived the nation.　12. The senate [3] and people resolved that ambassadors should be sent to Pyrrhus.

---

[1] See **14**, *a*.　　　[2] Imperfect tense.　　　[3] See **30**, *Obs.*

EXERCISE VIII.

ADJECTIVES.

Agreement of Adjectives.

47. When a single adjective or participle is used as **predicate of several singular substantives,** much variety of construction is allowed.

(*a.*) If several *persons* are spoken of, the adjective is generally in the *plural,* and the masculine gender takes precedence over the feminine.

> *Et pater mihi et mater* mortui *sunt.* Both my father and mother are dead.

(*b.*) But the predicate may also agree both in *gender* and *number* with the substantive nearest to itself. Thus a brother might say for " Both my sister and I had been summoned to the praetor," either " *Et ego et soror mea ad praetorem* vocati *eramus,*" or " Vocatus *eram ad praetorem ego et soror mea,*" or even " *Et ego et soror mea ad praetorem* vocata *erat.*"

The usage therefore greatly resembles that of verbs with more than one subject (**26, 27**).

48. (*a.*) If the substantives are not persons but *things,* the adjective or participle is usually in the plural, and agrees in gender with both substantives if they are of the same gender.

> *Fides tua et pietas* laudandae *sunt.* Your good faith and dutifulness are to be praised.

But *laudanda est* would be also allowable. (See *e.*)

(*b.*) If they are of different genders the adjective is generally in the *neuter.*

> *Gloria, divitiae, honores* incerta ac caduca *sunt.* Glory, riches, and distinctions are uncertain and perishable (things).

(*c.*) Where the substantives are **abstract nouns** (Intr. 29, *d*), the neuter is common in the predicate, even if they are of the same gender.

> *Fides et pietas* laudanda *sunt.* Good faith and a sense of duty are to be praised.

For the neuter *laudanda* means *things* to be praised (as *incerta ac caduca* in *b*); the terminations of the Latin adjective, *us, a, um, i, ae, a,* etc., express the singular and plural of *man, woman, thing,* exactly as the personal terminations of the verb express the personal pronouns. (See Intr. 31.)

(*d.*) Hence *Mors est omnium* extremum, "Death is the last of all things," is as good Latin as *Mors . . .* extrema.

(*e.*) Sometimes, but more rarely, the predicate agrees in gender and number with the substantive nearest itself.

> Spernendae *igitur sunt divitiae et honores.* Riches then, and distinctions, are to be despised.
> *Mihi principatus atque imperium* delatum est. The sovereignty and chief power were offered to me.

49. Where a single adjective is used as the *attribute* of two or more substantives of different genders, it usually agrees with the one nearest itself. Either "*Terras* omnes *et maria perlustravit*," or "*Terras et maria* omnia *perlustravit*," He travelled over all lands and seas.

It is sometimes repeated with each: *terras* omnes, *maria* omnia, etc.

These rules will cause very little real difficulty, as the freedom which they allow is great. The Exercise will be mainly on what follows.

Adjectives used as Substantives.

50. When the substantive is *"man," "woman,"* or *"thing,"* it is often not expressed in Latin by a separate word, for the reason given above, 48, *c.*

> Boni[1] sapientes*que* (*ex*)[2] *civitate pelluntur.* The *good* and *wise* are being banished (literally, driven from the state).
>
> *Jam* nostri *aderant.* Our *men*, or *soldiers*, were now at hand.
>
> Hae *ita locutae sunt.* These *women* spoke thus.
>
> Omnia mea *mecum porto.* I am carrying all *my property* with me.

51. Hence many adjectives, pronominal adjectives, and participles, both singular and plural, masculine and neuter, are used precisely as substantives, and may even have other adjectives attached, or *attributed* to them.

(*a.*) Masculine—

> (Singular) *adolescens,*[3] *juvenis* (young man), *amicus, inimicus; aequalis* (a contemporary, one of the same age), *candidatus, socius.*
>
> (Plural) *nobiles,*[4] *optimates* (the aristocracy), *majores*[5] (ancestors), *posteri* (posterity), *divites* (the rich), and many others.

---

[1] *Boni* thus used means generally, "the well-affected," "the patriotic party;" opposed to *improbi*, "the disaffected

[2] The ablative may be used here without the Preposition. See Voc. 8 (*banish*).

[3] *Adolescens* denotes a younger age than *juvenis*—it embraces the period from boyhood to the prime of life; *juvenis* is used of all men fit to bear arms.

[4] *Nobiles*, "nobles," *i.e.* men whose ancestors had borne a curule office; opposed to *novi homines*, "self-made men." *Nobilis* never means "noble" in a moral sense. *Optimates*, the aristocracy, as opposed to the popular party, or *populares*.

[5] *Patres, avi,* are never used in prose for "forefathers," but denote "men of the last generation" and "of the last but one." (See p. 41, note [2].) *Minores, nepotes*, etc., are used for "posterity" only in poetry.

(*b.*) Neuter—

> *factum*, a deed ; *dictum*, a saying ; *bona*, property ; *de-cretum*, a decree ; *promissa*, promises ; *edictum*, a pro-clamation ; *senatus-consultum*, a vote or resolution of the senate, etc.

(*c.*) Also the neuter adjectives *honestum, utile, com-modum, verum*, are used in the singular, and still more in the plural, for the English abstract words, " duty," " expediency," " advantage," " truth ;" so also

> *Summum* bonum, the highest *good* or happiness.

But the abstract nouns *honestas, utilitas*, are oftener used, and always in oblique cases, and with adjectives.

52. Ambiguous expressions are rarely used in Latin ; hence " thing " is generally expressed by *res* (fem.), when the adjective alone would leave it doubtful whether men or things were meant.

Thus " of many things," *multarum rerum ;* very seldom, and only when no mistake can occur, *multorum*, which might mean, " of many men ;" so—

> *Futura*, the future ; but *rerum futurarum*, of the future : *boni*, the good, *or* well-affected ; but *bonorum hominum*, of the well-affected.

53. The neuter *plural* of Latin adjectives is constantly used in the nominative and accusative cases where we use the *singular* of an adjective or substantive.

Much, multa.	*Very little*, perpauca.
Very much, permulta.	*Everything*, omnia.
Little (few things), pauca.	*All this*, haec omnia.

So *Vera et falsa.*   Truth and falsehood.
   Vera *dicebat.*   He was speaking *the truth.*

54. The neuter adjective is used in Latin without a substantive, where we *might* substitute " *things*," but really use some more appropriate nouns, as *property, objects, possessions, performances, thoughts, reflections*, etc.

The learner must look to the *Latin Verb* to guide him to the proper English noun to insert in his translation or to omit in his composition. The Latin adjective in the neuter plural will generally be translated by a substantive kindred in meaning to the verb.

Magna *sperabat.*	His *hopes* were high.
Multa *cogitabat.*	He was revolving many *thoughts.*
Haec *sequebatur.*	He was pursuing these *objects.*
Illa *ausus est.*	He ventured on those *enterprises.*
Multa *mentitus est.*	He told many *falsehoods.*

The singular neuter of the pronoun is used in the same way.

Hoc *secutus est.*	This was his *object.*
Quid *mentitus est ?*	What *falsehood* has he told ?

These are some of the many instances in which the English substantive cannot be translated literally into Latin.

55. It follows from **51** that we can say *adolescens* optimus, an excellent *young man;* praeclara *facta*, noble *deeds;* even *inimicissimi* tui, your deadliest enemies ; the participle or adjective (even a superlative adjective) being treated as a real substantive.

But many of these words retain a double nature, and are treated sometimes as substantives, sometimes as adjectives or participles.

We can say either " Ciceronis *est amicus*," or " Ciceroni *est amicus*," either " *Multa fuere* ejus *et* praeclara *facta*," or " *Multa* ab eo praeclare *facta sunt*," for "there were many noble deeds of his;" *i.e.* we may treat *facta* as either a substantive or a participle, in which latter case it will be joined with an adverb.

This latter construction is the commoner with participles such as *facta, dicta, responsa,* etc.

Other uses of Adjectives.

56. In English we join the adjective *many* with another adjective, "many excellent men." In Latin we should insert a conjunction, " *homines multi optimique, multi* atque *optimi homines*," or ". . . *multi*, iique *optimi*."

Of course we can say " *adolescentes* multi," or " *amici* multi," because these words are used as substantives.

E

So, too, if the second adjective is so constantly united with its substantive as to form a single expression.

> Multae *naves longae.*   Many ships of war.

57. (*a.*) The superlative degree of adjectives and adverbs is often used in Latin to mark merely a high degree of a quality.

> *Optimus,* excellent; *praeclarissimus,* famous *or* noble.

Sometimes, not always, it should be translated by an English intensive adverb or phrase.

> *Hoc* molestissimum *est.*   This is exceedingly, *or* very, *or* most, troublesome.
>
> *Hoc* saepissime *dixi.*   I have said this repeatedly, *or* again and again.

(*b.*) So also the comparative degree is often used, without any direct idea of comparison, to express a *considerable, excessive,* or *too great* amount. It may then be translated by " rather," " somewhat," " too," etc., or by a simple adjective in the positive degree.

> Saepius, *somewhat* often; asperius, with *excessive* harshness; *morbus* gravior, a *serious* illness.

Vocabulary 8.

abandon, I, fall off from, de-scisco, ĕre, -scīvi (*abl.*).

accomplish, I, ef-ficio, ĕre, -feci, -fectum.

across, trans (*acc.*).

alike (*adv.*), juxta, pariter.

allowed, it is, or agreed on, constat (*impers.*).

appear (*seem*), *I,* videor, ēri, visus. (**43.**)

aristocratic party. (**51,** *a, n.*[4].)

attempt, I, conor, ari.

banish, civitate pello, expello; in exilium pello, ĕre, pepuli, pulsum, *or* ex-igo, ĕre, -egi, -actum.

broad, lātus.

change of purpose, inconstantia, *f.*

contrary, contrarius.

conversation, I have, col-loquor, ī, -locutus. (**54.**)

country, fin-es, -ium, *m.* (**16,** *a.*)

courage, virt-ūs, -ūtis, *f.*

cowardice, ignavia, *f.*

deadly. (**55.**)

decree, a, decretum. (**51,** *b.*)

defile, a, salt-us, -ūs, *m.*

deny, I, nego, are.

dictator, dictat-or, -oris.

drive on shore, I, e-jicio, ĕre, -jeci, -jectum.

drive from, I, ex-igo, ĕre, -egi, -actum.

duty, honestum. (**51,** *c.*)

each other, to, inter se.

enemy, hostis, inimicus.[1]

enterprise. (**54.**)

---

[1] *Hostis,* an enemy in war, properly " a foreigner;" *inimicus,* a personal enemy.

everything. (53.)
excellent, optimus. (57.)
faithful, fidel-is, -e.
forefathers = ancestors. (51 *a*, *n.*[5])
foretell, I, praedi-co, ĕre, -xi, -ctum.
future. (52.)
glorious, praeclarus.
grandfather, av-us, -i.
himself, ipse, a, um.
hopes, I form = I hope. (Voc. 5, and see **54**.)
ignorant of, I am, ignoro, āre (*acc.*). (22.)
interest (*subst.*), utilit-as, -atis, *f.* (51, *c.*)
join you, I, me tibi, *or* ad te ad-jun-go, ĕre, -xi, -ctum.
know, I, sc-io, scīre, -ivi, -itum.
last (*of time*), proximus.
lead, I, transdu-co, ĕre, -xi, -ctum.
list of, I write a, perscri-bo, ĕre, -psi (*trans.*).
little. (53.)
lofty, praealtus.
marsh, pal-ūs, -ūdis, *f.*
meditate on, I, cōgito, āre, de (*abl.*).
merchant vessel, navis oneraria.
mistaken, I am, erro, āre.
much. (53.)
name, good, fama, *f.*
native land. (16, *a.*)
noble, praeclarus. (51, *a*, *n.*[4].)
no one, nemo, nullius.[1]
object. (54.)
oppress, I. Voc. 6.
past, the, praeterita, *n.*, *plur.* (52.)
pathless, invius.
persecute, I, insector, ari (*dep.*).
poor, paup-er, -ĕris.

popular party, popular-es, -ium.
posterity. (51, *a.*)
praised, to be, laudand-us, -a, -um. (48, *c.*)
praiseworthy, laudabil-is, -e.
proclamation, edictum. (51, *b.*)
promises, I make, polliceor, ēri. (54.)
property. (51, *b.*)
pursue, I, sequor, i, secutus (*dep.*).
rashness, temerit-as, -atis, *f.*
resolve, I, statu-o, ĕre, -i.
rich, the. (51, *a*, and Voc. 7.)
river, flum-en, -inis, *n.*
saying, a, dictum. (55.)
scarcely, vix.
shatter, I, quasso, āre.
sink, I (*trans.*), demer-go, ĕre, -si, -sum.
sometimes. Voc. 1.
spare, I. Voc. 1.
speak, I. Voc. 1.
storm, tempest-as, -atis, *f.*
strikingly, graviter. (55.)
think, I (*reflect*), cogito, āre.
threats, I make = I threaten. Voc. 6.
throne (*metaph.*). (17.)
traditions, I hand down, trad-o, ĕre, -idi, -itum.
transact, ago, ĕre, ēgi, actum.
unhealthy, pestilen-s, -tis.
unjust, iniquus.
variance with, I am at, pugno, āre, cum (*abl.*).
venture on (*enterprises*), *I*, audeo. (54.)
violent (*storm*), maximus.
vote of the senate, senatus consul-tum. (51, *b.*)
well-affected. (50, *n.*[1].)
winter, hi-ems, -ĕmis, *f.*
youth, a, adolescens. (51, *a*, *n.*[3].)

Exercise 8.

A.

1. He said that he would never[2] banish the good and wise. 2. We are all ignorant of much. 3. He said that courage and cowardice were contrary to each other. 4. It

---

[1] *Nemo* (subst. = *ne homo*) is used in the nom. and acc. (*neminem*). In other cases the adj. (*nullius, nulli, nullo, -ā, -o*) should be substituted.
[2] See 33.

appears that he was banished with you, not by the Dictator himself, but by a praiseworthy vote of the senate. 5. He resolved to abandon the aristocratic and to join the popular party. 6. He said that rashness and change of purpose were not to be praised. 7. He was an excellent youth, and a most faithful friend to me; he had much conversation with me that day about the future. 8. Having returned to Rome he promised to transact everything[1] for his father. 9. The army was led by Hannibal through many pathless defiles, and across many broad rivers, and many lofty mountains and unhealthy[2] marshes, into the country of the enemy. 10. You will scarcely venture to deny that duty was sometimes at variance with interest. 11. I know that your forefathers ventured on many glorious enterprises. 12. He makes many promises, many threats, but I believe that he will accomplish very little.

B.

13. You, said he, were meditating on the past; I was attempting to foretell the future; I now perceive that both you and I were mistaken. 14. He tells (us) that he has been driven by these brothers, his deadly enemies, from his throne and native land; that they are persecuting with unjust[3] proclamations and decrees all the well-affected, all the wise; that no one's property or good name is[4] spared; that rich and poor are alike oppressed. 15. I hope to write a list of the many striking sayings of your grandfather. 16. These objects, said he, did our forefathers pursue; these hopes did they form; these traditions have they handed down to posterity. 17. It is allowed that many noble deeds were done by him. 18. I rejoice that you spoke little and thought much. 19. It is said that many merchant vessels were shattered and sunk, or driven on shore, by many violent storms last winter.

[1] See 6. [2] Superl. (See 57, *a*.) [3] Superl. [4] See 5.

EXERCISE IX.

ADJECTIVES—Continued, ADVERBS.

58. The adjective and the genitive case of substantives (see **214**) are both used to **define the meaning of the substantive.** So in English, "the *king's* palace," "the *royal* army." Hence the Latin adjective is often used where in English we employ the preposition "of" with a noun. Thus—

Res alienae.   The affairs *of others.*
Conditio servilis.   The condition or state *of slavery.*
Vir fortis.   A man *of courage.*

So often with proper names—

Pugna Cannensis (not *Cannarum*).   The battle *of* Cannae.
Populus Romanus (never *Romae*).   The people *of* Rome.

Obs. So "*vir* fortissimus," "a man *of* the greatest courage." In Latin this adjectival genitive of quality may be used only where an adjective is added to the substantive. We can say "*vir* summae *fortitudinis;*" not "*vir* fortitudinis." (See **303**.)

59. Sometimes we must use a Latin genitive where the adjective is wanting, or rarely used, in Latin.

Corporis, *or* animi, *dolor.*   *Bodily* or *mental* pain.
Omnium *judicio* or *sententiis.*   By a *unanimous* verdict, or *unanimously.*
In hoc omnium *luctu.*   In this *universal* mourning.
Meā unius *sententiā.*   By my *single* vote.
Post hominum *memoriam.*   Within *human* memory.

60. The Latin adjective is used in agreement with a substantive where we use a partitive substantive expressing *whole, end, middle, top,* etc., followed by the preposition "of." Thus—

Summus *mons.*   The top *of* the mountain.
In mediam *viam.*   Into the middle or centre *of* the road.
Reliquum *opus.*   The rest *of* the work.
Ima *vallis.*   The bottom *of* the valley.
Novissimum *agmen.*   The rear *of* the line of march.
Tota *Graecia.*   The whole *of* Greece.
Summa *temeritas.*   The height *of* rashness.

Obs. These adjectives, especially where, as with *summus, medius,* etc., ambiguity might arise, generally stand before the substantive, not, as the attribute usually does, after it.

61. The adjective is often used **in close connexion with a verb,** where in English we should use either an *adverb* or an *adverbial phrase, i.e.* a preposition and noun.

Invitus *haec dico.*   I say this *unwillingly,* or *with reluctance,* or *against my will.*
Tacitus *haec cogitabam.*   I was meditating *silently,* or *in silence,* on these subjects.
Imprudens *huc veni.*   I came here *unawares.*
Incolumis *redii.*   I returned *safely,* or *in safety.*
Adversos, aversos, *aggressus est.*   He attacked them *in front,* or *from behind.*
So—Absens *condemnatus est.*   He was condemned *in his absence.*
Totus *dissentio.*   I disagree *wholly,* or *entirely.*
Frequentes *convenere.*   They came together *in crowds.*
Vivus.   In his lifetime.   *Mortuus.*   After his death.
Diversi *fugere.*   They fled *in opposite directions.*

62. So the adjectives *solus (unus), primus (prior* if of two), *ultimus,* are joined *adverbially* with the verb to express "only," "first," "last," where we should add a relative clause, or an infinitive mood, and make the adjective the main predicate.

Primus *haec fecit.*   He *was* the *first* who did this, *or* to do this.
Solus *mala nostra sensit.*   He *was* the *only* person who perceived our evils.
Ultimus *venisse dicitur.*   It is said that he *was* the *last* to come.

63. Certain *substantives* also, especially those which relate to *time, age,* and *office,* are used with the verb, where in English we should use an adverbial phrase.

> *Hoc* puer, *or* adolescens, *or* senex, *didici.* I learned this lesson (**54**) *in my boyhood,* or *youth,* or *old age.*
> *Hoc* consul *vovit.* He made this vow *in his consulship,* or *as consul.*

So—*Victor.* When victorious; "in the hour of triumph."

64. A single adverb in Latin will often represent a whole adverbial phrase in English; and on the other hand an English adverb will often require a Latin phrase, or whole clause, or combination of words. (Intr. 19 and 52.) Thus—

> *Pie.* With a good conscience.
> *Divinitus.* By a supernatural interposition.
> *Omnino.* Speaking in general, as a general rule, etc.

So—Easily. *Nullo negotio.*
Indisputably. *Dubitari non potest quin . . .* (See **133.**)
Fortunately. *Opportune accidit ut . . .* (See **123.**)
Possibly. *Fieri potest ut . . .*
You are *obviously* mistaken. *Errare te* manifestum *est.*
You are *apparently* unwell. *Aegrotare* vidēris.

It must therefore never be taken for granted that an adverb in one language can be translated by the same part of speech in the other.

Vocabulary 9.

acquit, I, absol-vo, -ĕre, -vi, -utum.
attain to, I = I obtain (Voc. 3), or = *arrive at* (Voc. 1).
beautiful, pul-cher,[1] -chrior, -cherrimus.
born (partic. of *I bear*), natus (nascor, *I am born*).
boyhood, in his. (**63.**)
break (*a law*), *I.* Voc. 5.

brought up (partic. of *I bring up*), educatus (edŭco).
change, I, muto, āre. (**21.**)
clothing, vestit-us, -ūs, *m.*
companions, his, sui, suos, etc.
conscience, with a good. (**64.**)
consent (*subst.*), consens-us, -ūs, *m.*
crowds, in. (**61.**)
death, after his. (**61.**)

---

[1] *Pulcher* is "beautiful" in a general sense; *amoenus,* "lovely *to look on,*" is applied to natural objects such as a landscape or scenery.

distinction, hon-or (-os), -ōris, m.
enterprise. (54.)
entrust, I, per-mitto, ĕre, -misi, -missum,
eye, ocul-us, -i, m.
fair, amoenus. (See p. 71, n.¹.)
faith, good, fid-es, -ei, f.
farmhouse, villa, f.
food, vict-us, -ūs, m.
fortune, fortuna, f.
funeral, fun-us, -ĕris, n.
gather together, to (intrans.). Voc. 3.
highest. Voc. 6.
honour, I (of external marks of honour), orno, are.
kind of, every, omn-is, -e.
kindness, bonit-as, -atis, f.
last, the, ultimus.
late, too (adv.), sēro.
lifetime, in his. (61.)
listen to, I, aud-io, ire. (23.)
look down on, I, de-spicio (trans.), ĕre, -spexi, -spectum. (23.)
management, procurati-o, -onis, f.
marble (adj.), marmoreus.
mind, I am out of my. Voc. 6.
miraculous interposition, by a. (64.)
monument, monumentum, n.
neglect, I, negle-go, ĕre, -xi, -ctum.
next, the, proximus ; insequen-s, -tis.
office. Voc. 2.

old age, in my. (63.)
other persons, of (adj.). (58)
panic, pav-or, -oris, m.
plain, camp-us, -i, m.
poet, poët-a, -ae, m.
point out, I, monstro, āre.
post up, I, fī-go, ĕre, -xi, -xum.
reach, I, pervenio ad . . .
read through, I, per-lĕgo, ĕre, -lēgi, -lectum.
recover myself, I, me re-cipio, -cepi.
relinquish, I, o-mitto, ĕre, -misi, -missum.
safety, in. (61.)
silence, in. (61.)
speech (to soldiers, or multitude), conti-o, -onis, f.
spread beneath, I, sub-jicio (trans.), ĕre, -jeci, -jectum ; subjicior (intrans.). (20.)
state (adj.), publicus.
summit. (60.)
supply you with these things, I, haec tibi suppedito, āre.
tomb, sepulcrum, n.
troublesome, molestus.
turn to, I. Voc. 3.
unanimously. (59.)
universal. (59.)
whole of. (60.)
wholly. (61.)
write, I, scri-bo, ĕre, -psi, -ptum.
youth, in my. (63 ; also 51, n.³.)

Exercise 9.

1. He said that the management of other people's affairs was always exceedingly¹ troublesome. 2. In this universal panic your brother was the first to recover himself. 3. I obeyed, said he, the law² in my youth : I will not break it in my old age. 4. I was the first to venture on these enterprises ; I will be the last to relinquish them. 5. In his lifetime we neglected this poet ; after his death we honour him with a state funeral, a marble tomb with

---

¹ To be expressed by superlative adj. (See 57.)
² Plural. Lex (sing.) is seldom used in an abstract sense ; it means a law.

many beautiful[1] monuments, and every kind of distinction. 6. The king having been (14, *a*) the first to reach the summit of the mountain, looked down in silence on the fair plains spread beneath his eye (*pl.*).   7. He turned[2] to his companions and pointed out the farmhouse in which he had been born and brought up in his boyhood; too late, said he, has fortune changed.   8. He promised to supply the army of Rome with food and clothing.   9. I read through the whole of this proclamation in silence; it seemed to me that he who wrote and posted *it up* (when) written was out of his mind.   10. He was unanimously acquitted, and returned home in safety; the next year he attained with universal consent to the highest office in the nation.   11. The soldiers, having gathered together in crowds, listened to his speech in silence.   12. I entrust myself wholly to your good faith and kindness.   13. No one can with a good conscience deny that your brother returned home in safety by a miraculous interposition.

---

[1] Superl. **(57.)**   [2] Participle.   (See **15.**)

EXERCISE X.

THE RELATIVE.

65. In a relative or adjectival *sentence*, each *clause*[1] has its own verb, and its own independent construction. The relative pronoun *qui* is of the same gender, number, and is joined with the same person of the verb, as its *antecedent* substantive, or pronoun, in the other clause. (See **12**.)

> Arbŏres *seret diligens agricŏla*, quarum *adspiciet baccam ipse nunquam*.[2] The careful husbandman will plant *trees*, any fruit *of which* he will himself never behold.
>
> Mulierem *aspicio* quae *pisces vendit*. I see a *woman who* is selling fish.
>
> *Ubi est* puer, cui *librum dedisti?* Where is the *boy to whom* you gave the book?
>
> Adsum *qui* feci. *I, who* did the deed, am here.

For the meaning of the term *adjectival*, as applied to a clause, or to the sentence of which such a clause forms a part, see Intr. 81.

66. Where there is more than one antecedent, the rules for the number and gender of the relative are the same as those for the adjective.

> *Pater ejus et mater* qui *aderant*. His father and mother *who* were present. (**47**, *a*.)
>
> *Divitiae et honores* quae *caduca sunt*. Riches and distinctions, *which* are perishable (things). (**48**, *b*.)

67. Sometimes a *relative* refers not to a single word, but to the *whole statement* made by a clause. When this is the case, we often find *id quod*, for *quod* only. (Here *id* is in *apposition* to the former sentence.) Sometimes *quae res* is found : = "*a circumstance which*."

> *Timoleon*, id quod *difficilius putatur, sapientius tulit secundam quam adversam fortunam*. Timoleon, *though this (lit. a thing*

---

[1] For meaning of *clause*, see page 20, note.
[2] For place of *nunquam*, see Intr. 92.

74

which) is thought the more difficult (task), bore prosperity more wisely than adversity.

Multae civitates a Cyro defecerunt; quae res multorum bellorum causa fuit. Many states revolted from Cyrus ; *and this* (see **13**) (*circumstance*) was the cause of many wars.

Obs.—"*As*" is often used in English as equivalent to "*a thing which*," or "*which*," in reference to a whole clause.

"He, *as* you have heard, died at Rome." *Ille, id quod audiisti, Romae mortem obiit.*

68. A relative pronoun in the accusative case is frequently omitted in English, but never in Latin.

This is the man *I saw.* *Hic est* quem *vidi.*
He found the books *he wanted.* *Libros* quos *voluit reperit.*

69. When in English the antecedent is qualified by a superlative, the superlative is in Latin placed in the relative clause.

Volsci civitatem, quam habebant optimam, *perdiderunt.* The Volsci lost the *best* city they had.

The same place is given to any emphatic adjective, especially those of number or amount.

Equites, quos paucos *secum habuit, dimisit.* He sent away the *few* mounted men whom he had with him.

Use of *qui* with *is.*

70. The demonstrative pronoun which corresponds to *qui*, as *he* to *who,* is not *ille,* but *is.* *Ille* is only used when great emphasis is laid on the "he;" "that *well known,* or that *other* person." *Is* may be thus used of all three persons.

I am the man I always was. Is *sum* qui *semper fui.*

71. Where the antecedent and relative are in the same case, *qui* without *is* will express "he who;" where the cases are different, *is* is to be used.

Qui *haec videbant flebant.* *Those* who saw this (the spectators) wept.
Eis, qui *adstabant,* irascebatur. He was angry with *those* who stood by (the bystanders)

72. *Is, ei (ii)*, etc., often answer to our "one," "men," "a man," when used to denote a class of persons.

> Eum qui *haec facit odi.* I hate *one* who, or *a man* who does this.
>
> Eos qui *haec faciunt odi.* I hate *men* who do this.

Qui alone (**71**) will express the same phrases.

> Qui *haec faciunt, pejora facient. Men* who are doing this will do worse.

73. The oblique cases, especially the genitive and dative, of the participle are often used to represent "him who," "those who."

> Adstantium *clamore perterritus.* Alarmed by the shouts of *the bystanders, or* of *those who stood by, or* of *those standing by.*
>
> Interrogantibus *respondit.* To *those who questioned* him, or to *those questioning* him, or to *his interrogators.*

74. But we must never combine *ei, eorum, eis*, etc., with the participle to denote a class. *Eorum adstantium, eos adstantes,* is very bad Latin for "those who stood by," or "those standing by."

75. Sometimes the force of the demonstrative in *is qui,* and similar combinations, *hic qui*, etc., is emphasised by placing the relative clause first, and the demonstrative pronoun, in the other or principal clause, afterwards.

> Qui *tum te defendit,* is *hodie accusat.* He who (the very man who) then defended you is to-day accusing you. Your former advocate is your present accuser.

This construction is always to be used where a strong contrast is dwelt on.

76. Observe how often the substantive has to be expressed in Latin by a clause beginning with *qui, is qui, ea quae,* etc., *i.e.* by an *adjectival clause.* Thus—

> Qui me ceperunt, my *captors; qui me vicit,* my *conqueror;* (ea) *quae vera sunt,* the *truth.*

(See **175.**)

Is qui, with the subjunctive, will be treated further on.

Vocabulary 10.

again and again, saepe (saepissime). (**57.**)

agreement (with), I am in, consentio, īre, -si, -sum (cum, *abl.*).

assistance, I come to his, sub-vĕnio, -vēni (*dat.*).

concerning (prep.), de (*abl.*).

despise, I, de-spicio,[1] ĕre, -spexi, -spectum.

directions, in different. (**61.**)

disagree with, I, dis-sentio. (See *agreement.*)

dismayed, I am, perterr-eor, ēri, -itus.

dismiss, I, di-mitto, ĕre, -misi, -missum.

entirely. (**61.**)

first . . . then, primum . . . deinde.

foot-soldier, ped-ĕs, -ĭtis.

gladly, lĭbens (*adj.*) (**61**), *or* libenter (*adv.*).

halt, I. Voc. 1.

helplessness, in, in-ops, -ŏpis (*adj.*). (**61.**)

institution, an, institutum. (**51**, *b.*)

join him, I. (**20**, and Voc. 8.)

keep my word, I, fidem prae-sto, āre, -stiti.

know, I (a fact), scio (Voc. 8) ; (*a person*) nōvi, nôsse, nōveram (nôram).

man, the, (contemptuous), hom-o, -inis.

meet, I come to, obviam vĕnio, vēni (*dat.*).

occasion, on that, tum. (Intr. 19.)

one. (**72.**)

oppose, I, adversor, āri (*dat.*).

order, I, jubeo, ēre, jussi, jussum.

poverty, paupert-as, -ātis, *f.*

present, I am, ad-sum, -esse, -fui.

rather, I would. Voc. 7.

reluctantly. (**61.**)

repeatedly = *again and again.*

riches, diviti-ae, -arum.

ruin, exitium, *n.* (**18, 19.**)

scatter, I (intrans.), dissipor, āri. (**20.**)

seek for, I, pet-o, ĕre, -ii, *or* -ivi, -ītum.

send back, I, re-mitto, ĕre, -misi, -missum.

set at nought, I, con-temno,[1] ĕre, -tempsi, -temptum.

shout, clam-or, -oris, *m.*

slave, I am a, servio, īre, -ii, -itum.

stand by, I, ad-sto, -stare, -stĭti.

story, I tell a, narro, -are (**54.**)

suddenly, subĭto.

to-day, hodie.

to-morrow, cras.

treat lightly, I, parvi[2] facio, ĕre, feci, factum.

value highly, I, magni[2] aestimo, āre.

woman, muli-er, -ĕris.

yesterday, heri.

Exercise 10.

1. Those[3] who were in agreement with you yesterday, to-day entirely disagree (with you). 2. Both you and I despise one who[3] would rather be a slave with[4] riches than free with poverty. 3. We know that he, concerning

---

[1] *Despicio*, I look down on *as beneath myself; contemno*, I think lightly of *in itself* = *parvi facio ; sperno*, I put from me ; *aspernor*, the same, with idea of strong dislike ; *repudio*, I put from me with contempt ; *neglego*, I am indifferent to.

[2] For this genitive see **305.**

[3] The relative clause to come first, *is* to be used in the other clause (See **75.**)   [4] See **8,** *b.*

whom you have told us all this story, expects to attain
to the highest offices, the greatest distinctions; but[1] I
hope that he will never obtain them, for I know the man.
4. I who[2] repeatedly opposed you in your youth, will
gladly come to your assistance in your old age and helplessness.　5. I sent you the best and bravest foot-soldiers
that I had with me; and having promised[3] to send them
back, you reluctantly kept your word.　6. He ordered
those standing by (him) to follow him; but they were
dismayed by the shouts of those who were coming to
meet (him); first halted, and then suddenly scattered and
fled in different directions.　7. The woman for whom you
were seeking is present; I will therefore[1] hear and dismiss
her.　8. The best institutions and laws you have set at
nought, and this[4] will be your ruin to-day.　9. The
things[2] which I treated lightly in my boyhood, I value
highly in my old age.　10. I who[2] was the last to come
to your assistance on that occasion, will be the first to
join you to-morrow.

---

[1] The demonstrative and conjunction, *but*, *therefore*, etc., to be expressed by the relative.

[2] The relative clause to come first, *is* to be used in the other clause.
(See **75**.)

[3] See **14**.　　　　　　　　　　　　　　　　[4] See **67**.

*For all succeeding Exercises the Student is referred to the
General Vocabulary at the end of the Book.*

THE RELATIVE—*Continued.*

Qui in Oratio Obliqua.—Co-ordinate and other uses.

77. The verb in an **adjectival clause** is in the *indicative* mood, unless there is some special reason for the *subjunctive*.

For instance, if the verb in the principal clause is in *oratio obliqua, i.e.* is in the infinitive after a verb of *saying* or *thinking*, the verb in the *qui*-clause will be in the *subjunctive*.

Thus—*Mulierem aspicio, quae pisces* vendit. (Oratio recta.) I see a woman who is selling fish.

But—Ait *se mulierem* aspicere, *quae pisces* vendat. (Oratio obliqua.) He *says* that he sees a woman who is selling fish.

Exceptions to this rule will be explained further on.

Obs.—This idiom extends very widely in Latin. It holds good not only with relatives, but with all subordinating conjunctions, and applies not only to indirect statements, but also to indirect commands and questions. (See Exercise LVI.)

78. Besides its use in adjectival clauses, *qui* is also used very largely as a substitute for both kinds of *conjunctions.* (Intr. 53, 54, 55.)

(i.) It is often used as equivalent to the co-ordinating conjunctions *and, but, so, therefore,* etc., and a demonstrative, to connect together co-ordinate sentences and clauses. (See **13.**)

Ad regem veni, quem *cum vidissem.* . . . I came to the king, *and* when I had seen *him.* . . .

Indeed the Latin *relative* is often used where we should use the *demonstrative* only. Thus nothing is commoner than for Latin sentences to begin with—Quibus *auditis,* having heard *this;* Quod *ubi vidit,* when he saw *this;* quam *ob rem,* quocirca, *and therefore,* or, *therefore.*

This is called the *co-ordinating* use of the relative, because it links co-ordinate sentences. (Intr. 74.) The relative so used does not affect the mood of the verb any more than a demonstrative pronoun, or the conjunction *et.*

Thus, if *qui* used for "and" connects (or co-ordinates) a principal verb in *oratio obliqua* with another, it will introduce an infinitive mood.

> *Dixit proditorem esse eum* . . . quem *brevi periturum* esse. He said that he was a traitor . . . *and* that *he* would soon perish.

79. (ii.) The Latin relative is also largely used in place of many kinds of *subordinating* conjunctions; *ut,* in order that, or, so that; *quamvis,* although; *quod,* because.

The verb which follows *qui,* when so used, is in the subjunctive.

[The following Exercise will include only its adjectival use as subordinate to *oratio obliqua,* and its *co-ordinating* use as a substitute for a conjunction. Its use in the sense of "in order to," "so that," etc., will be treated further on.]

Other Uses of the Relative.

80. *"But"* after universal negatives, as *nemo, nullus, nihil,* is equivalent to "who not," and should be translated by *qui non,* or by *quin* if the relative is in the *nominative* (or occasionally the *accusative*) case. *Qui non* or *quin* will always be followed by a *subjunctive.*[1]

> Nemo *est* quin *te dementem putet.* There is no one *but* thinks you mad; or *the whole world* thinks, etc.
> Nemo *fuit* quin *viderim.* There was no one whom I did not see (but *quem non* is more usual).

---

[1] The explanation of the subjunctive will be given in its proper place. (See Qui with the Subjunctive, Exercise LXIII.)

81. It has been already said that the English relative with words such as *only, first, last,* as its antecedent, is not usually expressed in Latin by a relative clause, but by an adverbial use of the adjective.

> He was the first *who*, or *that* did this.　*Primus haec fecit.*
> (See **62.**)

82. Relative clauses in English, especially such as correspond to a clause beginning with *it*, are often expressed in Latin merely by the emphatic order of the words.

> Ab hoc homine *interfectum esse fratrem tuum negat.*　He says that *it was not* by this man *that* your brother was killed.

83. When the predicate of a relative clause is a substantive, the relative is often attracted into the gender of the predicate instead of agreeing with its antecedent.

> *Thebae,* quod *Boeotiae caput est.*　Thebes which is the capital of Boeotia.

Obs.—The same attraction takes place with demonstrative pronouns.

> Ea (not *id*) *vera est pietas.*　*That* is true piety.

Exercise 11.

In the following Exercise the italics indicate the use of the co-ordinating relative, **78** (i.).

1. He pretended that he had met the man[1] who had killed the king by poison.　2. There is no one but knows that one who does not till his land will look in vain for a harvest.　3. The exiles believed that they had reached the locality from which (whence) their forefathers were sprung.　4. I hope to avert this ruin from my country *and therefore* I am willing to venture on or endure anything.　5. He promised to lead his troops into the country of the Remi, *and* (said) that he hoped he should[2] soon recall *them* to their allegiance.　6. Having heard *this* he perceived that the ambassadors spoke the truth,[3] and that

---

[1] *Is.* (**71.**)　　[2] Fore ut. (**38.**)　　[3] That which (pl.) was true. (**76.**)

the danger was increasing.   7. He said that he had never preferred expediency to duty, *and* (that) *therefore* he would not abandon allies whom he had promised to succour. 8. Having ascertained *this* fact, he promised to break up the crowd which had gathered around the king's[1] palace. 9. He pretended that it was not for the sake of gain but of friendship that he had given me all the books which his brother had left.   10. He said that the friends for whom you were looking round were all safe, *and therefore* that he for his part was free from anxiety.   11. He pretends to reject glory, which is the most honourable reward of true virtue.   12. All the world[2] knows that the moon moves round the earth.

---

[1] Adjective. (**58.**)   [2] See **80.**

EXERCISE XII.

THE RELATIVE—*Continued*.

Correlatives.

84. The relative pronouns and pronominal words, *qui* (who), *qualis* (of what *kind*), *quantus* (of what *size*), *quot* (how many), answer respectively to the demonstratives *is* (he), *talis* (of such a *kind*), *tantus* (of such a *size*), *tot* (so many).

When they answer to these demonstratives, all **relatives** except *qui*, and even *qui* with *idem*, **are to be translated by the English "***as***."**

> Talis *est*, qualis *semper fuit.*   He is such *as* (of the same character as) he has ever been.
> Tantam[1] *habeo voluptatem*, quantam *tu.*   I have as much pleasure *as* you.
> Tot *erant milites*, quot *maris fluctus.*   The soldiers were as many *as* the waves of the sea.
> Idem *est* qui *semper fuit.*   He is the same *as* (or *that*) he has always been.
> *Res peracta est* eodem *modo* quo *antea.*   The thing has been done in the same manner *as* before.

85. When thus used, the two pronouns which correspond with each other are called **correlative**, or corresponding, words.

As with *is* and *qui*, so with the others, the relative or adjectival clause is often placed first, and the other or principal clause last.

---

[1] *Tantus* is sometimes used in a limiting sense, "just as (*only* as) much as;" tantum *faciet* quantum *coactus erit*, he will do *no more* than he is compelled (to do)

This is in accordance with the general tendency of Latin to place the most emphatic part of a sentence at or near the end. (Intr. 91.)

> Quot *adstabant homines,* tot *erant sententiae.* There were as many opinions as there were men standing by.
> Qualis *fuit domina,* talem *ancillam invenies.* You will find the maid of the *same character as* her mistress was.

86. "*Such*" in English is often used where *size* or *amount* is meant rather than *kind* or *quality.* *Such—as* should then be translated into Latin by *tantus—quantus;* not by *talis—qualis.*

We must therefore always ask ourselves whether "such" means "of such a kind" or "so great." Thus, in "the storm was *such* as I had never seen before," "such" evidently means "so violent" or "so great;" in "his manners were *such* as I had never seen," "such" evidently means "of such a kind." In the former case we must use *tantus,* in the latter *talis.*

87. When "such" means "of such a kind," the place of the pronominal adjective *talis* is often taken by the genitive of quality. (See **58.**)

> *Ejusmodi, hujusmodi, istius modi.* Of such a kind, of such a kind *as this,* of such a kind *as you speak* of.
> Hujusmodi *homines odi.* I hate such men (as these).

88. "*Such*" in English is often combined as an adverb with an adjective,—"*such* good men," "*such* a broad river." *Talis* and *tantus* cannot of course be used as adverbs. We must say—tam *bonus vir,* or talis tamque *bonus vir;* tam *latum flumen,* or tantum tamque *latum flumen,*— not, talis *bonus vir,* tale *latum flumen.*

Obs.—But *tantus* and *talis* are often combined with *hic,* sometimes with *ille;* haec *tanta multitudo, this great* number of men, or *so great,* or *such* a, multitude *as this.* So the adverb *tam.*

> Hic tam *bonus vir.* *So* good a man *as this,* or, this *good* man.

89. The same *correlative* construction is used with relatival or pronominal *adverbs,* as, *e.g.* those of place.

> *Ubi* (where) corresponds to *ibi, illic* (there), *hic* (here).
> *Unde* (whence) „ *inde* (thence), *hinc* (hence).

Quo (whither)   corresponds to *eo*, *illuc* (thither), *huc* (hither).
Qua (in the direction in which)   ,,   *eā*, *hāc* (in that or this direction).

> *Inde venisti*, unde *ego*.   You have come *from the same place as* I.
> *Eo rediit*, unde *profectus est*.   He returned *to the place from which* he had set out.

90. Observe also that with *idem*, *ac*[1] (*atque*) frequently takes the place of *qui*.

> *Eadem* ac (=quae) *tu sentio*, my views (**54**) are the same as yours.

91. With *alius, contra, aliter*, and words signifying *contrast*, *ac* (*atque*) is the rule.

> *Aliter* ac *tu sentio*.   My views are different from yours.

Sometimes *quam* is used.

> *Res contra* quam (*or* atque) *expectavi evenit*.   The matter turned out *contrary to* my expectation.

See Comparative Clauses, Ex. LXII.

92. Where a strong *difference* is pointed out, a repeated *alius* is often used; aliud *est dicere*, aliud *facere*, " there is *all the difference* between speaking and acting;" "speaking is *one thing*, acting *another*."

93. All that has been said (**77**) as to the mood of the verb in *qui*-clauses applies equally to every kind of relative clause, whether introduced by a relatival or pronominal *adjective*, such as *qualis*, etc., or by a relatival *adverb*, such as *ubi, unde*. Thus—

> *Ubi tu* es, *ibi est frater tuus*.   Your brother is in the same place as you.   (Dicit) *ubi tu* sis, *ibi esse fratrem tuum*.

So—

> *Qualis* fuerit *frater tuus, talem te esse dicunt*.   They say that you are of the same character as your brother was.

---

[1] *Ac* is never used before a vowel : see Intr. p. 14, *note*.

Exercise 12.

A.

This Exercise (A) contains examples of various *relative* constructions; instances of relative clauses in *Oratio Obliqua* will be
found in B.

1. This is the same as that. 2. You are of the same
character as I have always believed you to be. 3. All the
world knows that the past cannot be changed. 4. The
waves were such as I had never seen before. 5. He died
in the place where he had lived in boyhood. 6. He was
the first who promised to help me. 7. I will send the
most faithful slave I have with me.[1] 8. There is no one
but knows that the Gauls were conquered by Caesar.
9. The island is surrounded by the sea which you (*pl.*)
call ocean. 10. The Gauls are the same to-day as they
have ever been. 11. He was the first to deny the
existence of gods. 12. I was the last to reach Italy.
13. That expediency and honour are sometimes contrary
to each other (is a fact[2] that) all the world knows. 14. I
believe him to have been the first within human memory[3]
to perpetrate such a monstrous crime, and I hope he will
be the last to venture on anything of the kind.

This Exercise may be also varied by placing "he said" before 2, 4,
7, 10, and altering the sentence accordingly; thus:—"he said that
you *were* of the same character, as he *had* always believed you to be."

B.

1. All the world allows that you are of the same
character as your father and grandfather. 2. The scouts
having returned to the camp brought back word that the
enemy, who had flocked together in crowds the-day-before,
were now breaking up and stealing away in different
directions. 3. He said that he would never abandon such
good and kindly men, who had so often come to his aid in
adversity. 4. My objects[4] are different from yours, nor are

---

[1] 8, *Obs.*   [2] Omit in Latin and compare **82.**   [3] See **59.**
[4] Express by neut. pl. of adj. (see **54**); so with "hopes."

my hopes the same as yours.   5. He said that he himself[1] was the same as he had ever[2] been, but that both the state of the nation and the views of his countrymen had gradually changed, and that the king, the nobles, and the whole people were now exposed to dangers such as they had never before experienced.   6. Many ships of war were shattered and sunk by the violence of the storm ; a single merchantman returned in safety to the point from[3] which it had set out.

---

[1] Himself,—*quidem* after "he " (he *at least*, he *on the one hand*).
[2] Ever = always, as in the preceding Exercise, A. 10.
[3] = Whence. (89.)

EXERCISE XIII.

THE INFINITIVE AS SUBSTANTIVE.

94. The infinitive[1] mood (see Intr. 51), as doing little more than name the general action or state denoted by the verb, is used as a **verbal substantive of the neuter gender.** Thus—

Sedere me delectat. " *To sit,*" or " *sitting,*" delights me.

The English word "sitting" is here a verbal noun,[2] and must be carefully distinguished from the participle, which resembles it in form only. Compare " *sitting* rests me" with "he rested *sitting* on a bank."

95. This infinitive may be thus used as a substantive in two cases only—(1) in the *nominative,* either as subject

---

[1] The infinitive mood is so called because the verb in this form is *not defined* or restricted by inflexions denoting person or number. Were it not for its special use in Latin, already noticed, as marking statements which are made in *oratio obliqua,* it could hardly be called a *mood* at all; for it is only when so used, as answering to what in most languages is represented by a conjunction (*that,* etc.) and a finite verb, that it in any sense acts as a true verb by joining together two conceptions of the mind (see Intr. 11). By a "mood" we mean a special mode (*modus*) or manner in which a verb does this (see **147**). In its other uses, as in that mentioned in the present exercise, the infinitive can hardly be called a mood, but, as explained in **94,** a verbal noun; for it makes no statement, but merely *names* a single idea, that *state* or *action* which the verb not only names, but predicates of its subject. Compare *sedēre* with *sedeo.*

[2] The origin of this English verbal noun in *-ing* does not come within the scope of this work. From its similarity in form to the participle, it has acquired a participial construction, and we no longer say "the seeing *of* you," but " the seeing *you,*" etc. As such, it is synonymous with the ordinary, or prepositional, form of the English infinitive " to see;" but its use is much wider than that of the Latin infinitive, and even than that of the gerund. We can say "he went away without *speaking,*" "instead of *answering,*" where the Latin gerund is inadmissible (see Gerunds); and it also answers to the supine in *-um:* " he sent us out foraging," properly *a* (i.e. *an* or *on*) foraging,—*nos pabulatum emisit.*

to *est, fuit*, etc., followed by a neuter adjective, or with an impersonal verb, or verb used impersonally; (2) in the *accusative*, as subject to another infinitive, after a verb *sentiendi* vel *declarandi*.

> Nihil agere *me delectat.*   *Doing* nothing is a pleasure to me.
> *Turpe est* mentiri.   It is disgraceful *to lie*, or, *lying* is disgraceful.
> *Dixit turpe esse* mentiri.   He said that *lying* was disgraceful.

For other cases see **99.**

Obs.—The infinitive thus used may be the *antecedent* to a *relative*, which will be in the *neuter gender.*

> Laudari, quod, *or* id quod, *plerisque gratissimum est, mihi molestissimum est.*   To be praised, which is very pleasant to most men, is to me most disagreeable.

96. But though the infinitive is thus used as a substantive, it retains some part of its true nature as a verb. For—

(*a.*) It is qualified, not by an adjective, but by an adverb.

> " *Good* writing " is bene *scribere, not* bonum *scribere.*
> Bene *arare est* bene *colere.*   Good ploughing is *good* farming.

(*b.*) It is joined with or governs an accusative, or other case as its object.

> Haec *perpěti, et* patriā *carere, miserrimum est.*   To endure these things, and to be deprived of one's country, is most wretched.

(*c.*) It retains the tenses of a verb.

> *Haec facere, fecisse, facturum esse.*   The doing, the having done, the being about to do, this.

97. This infinitive is also joined with a subject, **which is always in the accusative case.**

> Te *hoc dicere mihi est gratissimum.*   *Your* saying this is most welcome to me.

Obs.—In English, when an infinitive (or a sentence introduced by "*that*") is the nominative to a verb, it generally *follows the verb*, the pronoun "*it*" being used as its representative before the verb.   "*It is* pleasant *to be praised.*" "*It* is strange *that you should say so.*" This "*it*" is not to be translated into Latin. We must write simply, Laudari *jucundum est.*   Te *hoc* dicere *mirum est.*

98. This substantival infinitive, with or without other words, will often express the nominative and accusative cases of English *abstract* nouns for which Latin either has no exact equivalent, or for which the infinitive is (often) preferred. Thus—

(*a.*) *Sibi placere,* "self-satisfaction;" *suis rebus contentum esse,* "contentment;" *mentiri,* "falsehood;" *cunctari,* "procrastination" (=cunctatio); *improbos laudare,* "praise of the bad;" *felicem esse,* "success;" *prosperis rebus uti,* "prosperity."

(*b.*) So, too, as Latin has no single word to express "happiness" or "gratitude," the infinitive is mostly used for both. Thus—

> *Beate vivere,* or *beatum esse*=*vita beata,* or happiness.
> *Gratiam habere*=*gratus animus,* or the feeling of gratitude.
> *Gratias agere,* the returning thanks, *or* expression of gratitude.
> *Gratiam debere,* the being under an obligation.
> *Gratiam referre,* the returning a favour, *or* the showing gratitude.

These are instances of the general tendency of Latin to prefer direct and simple to more general and abstract modes of expression.

99. But in all such phrases the infinitive is only used in the *nominative* or in the accusative of *oratio obliqua.* In other cases, and with the accusative after a preposition, the *gerund* (or *gerundive*) takes its place.[1] Thus—

> *Pugnare,* to fight, *or* fighting; but, pugnandi *cupidus,* desirous *of* fighting; ad pugnandum *paratus,* prepared *for* fighting; pugnando *vincemus,* we shall win the day *by* fighting.

Obs.—The *gerund* governs the substantive with which it is combined, the *gerundive* agrees with it. See Gerund and Gerundive, XLIX.

> *Gratias* agendo (Gerund).
> *Ad* agendas *gratias* (Gerundive).

---

[1] In Greek the infinitive with the article can be used in all cases,— τὸ, τοῦ, τῷ βασιλεύειν = *regnare, regnandi, regnando.*

Exercise 13.

1. It is always delightful[1] to parents that their children should be praised.   2. He said that it was disgraceful to break one's word, but keeping one's promises was always honourable.   3. Both your brother and you[2] have told many falsehoods;[3] falsehood is always vile.   4. It is one thing to be praised, another to have deserved praise. 5. To be praised by the unpatriotic is to me almost the same thing as to be blamed by patriots.   6. Feeling gratitude, says[4] he, is one thing, returning thanks another.   7. Procrastination, which in all things was dangerous, was, he[5] said, fatal in war.   8. Pardoning the wicked is almost the same thing as condemning the innocent.   9. Procrastination in showing gratitude is never praiseworthy; for myself[6] I prefer the returning kindness to being under an obligation.   10. Happiness is one thing; success and prosperity another.   11. Brave fighting, says[4] he, will to-day be the same thing as victory; by victory we shall give freedom to our country.

---

[1] The intensive superlative may be used here and with many of the other adjectives in this exercise.   (See **57**, *a.*)
[2] See **26** and *note*.   [3] See **54**.   [4] See **40**.
[5] See **32**, *b.*   [6] See **11**, *a.*

FINAL CLAUSES. *Ut, Ne, Quo.*

100. The English infinitive mood ("to do, to go,"—properly a gerundial use of the infinitive with the preposition *to*) is constantly used **to denote a purpose, or end in view** (*finis*).

But in Latin prose the infinitive mood is **never used** in this *final* sense.[1]

The English final infinitive is expressed in Latin in many ways.

"He sent ambassadors *to sue* for peace" is never expressed in Latin by "*legatos misit pacem* petere," but in various other ways, either by

    a. *legatos misit* ad pacem petendam (Gerundive),
    b.   ,,   pacis petendae causā (Gerundive).
    c.   ,,   pacem petitum (Supine),
    d.   ,,   qui pacem peterent (Relative Clause),

or, especially if the purpose or end in view is strongly dwelt on,

    e. *legatos misit,* ut pacem peterent.

The following rules, therefore, must be carefully attended to.

101. (i.) "That," when equivalent to *in order that,* and followed by *may* or *might;* also "in order to" and "to" in the same sense, followed by an English infinitive, must often be translated in Latin by *ut* with the subjunctive.

Multi alios laudant, ut *ab illis*[2] laudentur. Many men praise others, *that* they *may be praised* by them, *or, to be praised* by them, *or, in order to be praised* by them.
Multi alios laudabant, ut *ab illis* laudarentur. Many men were praising others, *in order to be praised* by them.

---

[1] Hence such parenthetic clauses as "not to mention," "so to say," "not to be tedious," must never be translated by the Latin infinitive, but by *ne dicam, ut dicam, ne longus sim.*

[2] *Illis* is here used in place of the less emphatic *iis,* as a marked distinction between *themselves* and *others* is intended. (**11,** *d.*)

(ii.) "That"=*in order that*, followed by *not*, or any negative word (the verb having *may* or *might* for its auxiliary), must be translated by *nē* (=*lest*) with the subjunctive. *Ne* expresses a *negative purpose; a purpose of preventing*, and often answers to the English phrase "to prevent," *or* "avoid."

> *Gallinae avesque reliquae pennis fovent pullos*, nē *frigŏre* laedantur. Hens and other birds cherish their young with their feathers, *that* they *may not be* hurt by the cold, or, *to prevent that* they be hurt, etc.
>
> *Gallinae avesque reliquae pennis fovebant pullos*, nē *frigore* laederentur. Hens and other birds were cherishing their young with their feathers, *that they might not* be hurt by the cold.

Notice the correspondence of tenses *laudant* . . . *laudentur; laudabant* . . . *laudarentur; fovent* . . . *laedantur; fovebant* . . . *laederentur.* (See **104**.)

102. When the dependent clause expressing purpose *i.e.* the *final* clause, contains an adjective or adverb in the comparative degree, "that" is translated by *quo=by which;* this is equivalent to *ut eo=that by this (means),* but *quo* must never be used in this sense without a comparative.

> *Medico puto aliquid dandum esse*, quo *sit* studiosior. I think that something should be given to the physician, *that* he may be *the more attentive*, or *to* make him *more attentive*.

103. *Ut* is never used with a negative in *final* clauses; "that no one," when a purpose is expressed, is never *ut nemo*, but *ne quis*. (See **109**.) When a second or third negative final clause is added, *neve* or *neu* is used instead of *neque*.

> *Hoc feci, ne tibi displicerem* neve *amicis tuis nocerem*. I did this to avoid displeasing you, or injuring your friends.

Sequence of Tenses.

The tense of the verb in a final clause will cause no difficulty. The rule is very simple. (Read the Classification of Tenses, given at 177.)

104. If the verb in the principal clause is in a *primary* tense, *i.e.* present, true perfect, or future, the verb in the *ut-*, *quo-*, or *ne-* clause will be in the present subjunctive.

> *Haec* scribo, scripsi, scribam, scripsero, *ut bono* sis *animo.*
> I *write, have written, shall write, shall have written*, this, in order that you *may* be in good spirits.

If the principal verb is in a *historic* tense, *i.e.* imperfect, aorist perfect, or pluperfect, the subordinate verb will be in the imperfect subjunctive.

> *Haec* scribebam, scripsi, scripseram, *ut bono* esses *animo.*
> I *was writing, wrote, had written*, this, in order that you *might* be in good spirits.

105. The Latin Perfect discharges the part of two English tenses, and has therefore a double construction. (See **187.**)

> Laudavi *te, ut bonus* haberere. I *praised* you that you *might* be accounted good. (Laudavi is *historical,* an **aorist** *tense.*)
> Laudavi *te, ut bonus* habeare.[1] I *have praised* you that you *may* be accounted good. (Laudavi is *primary,* a **perfect** *tense.*)

Exercise 14.

1. In order not to be driven into exile, I shall pretend to be mad. 2. That you might not be punished for this crime both your brother and you told many falsehoods. 3. He pardoned, it is said,[2] the wicked, in order to obtain a reputation for clemency. 4. He spared the best patriots when he was[3] victorious, in order that his own crimes might be forgiven. 5. He praised your countrymen again and again in their presence, in order to be praised by them in his absence. 6. The enemy will, they say,[2] be here to-morrow with[4] a vast army in order to[5] besiege

---

[1] But even in the latter case the Romans often wrote *haberere*, looking rather to the past time when the *intention was formed.*

[2] See **32,** *b ;* **43.**   [3] See **63.**   [4] **8,** *b.*   [5] Gerundive with *ad.* **100,** *a*

our city.   7. That he might not be condemned in his
absence he hastened to go to Rome.   8. It is said that he
told many falsehoods to make[1] himself seem younger than
he really was.   9. It seems that he wishes to return home
in order to[2] stand for the consulship.   10. There is a
tradition that he refused to accept the crown to avoid displeasing his brother, or injuring the lawful heir.   11. In
order to testify his zeal and loyalty he hastened in his[3]
old age to Rome, and was the very first[4] to pay his respects
to the new king.

---

[1] See **102.**   [2] **100,** *b.*   [3] See **63.**   [4] Lit., first *of all.*   See **62.**

EXERCISE XV.

Ut, Ut non, IN CONSECUTIVE CLAUSES.

106. *Ut* with the subjunctive is also used in Latin to denote, not a *purpose*, but a *consequence* or *result*.

We see the difference at once in English.

(*a.*) I ran against him *in order to throw* him down (Final) ;

(*b.*) I ran against him with *such* force *that I threw* him down (Consecutive).

In the former sentence, (*a*), nothing is said of the *result*, only the end in view, or *motive*, is mentioned. In the latter, (*b*), nothing is said of the *motive*, only the *result* is named.

It is the peculiarity of Latin that this result, even when stated as an actual fact, is described by *ut* with a verb in the *subjunctive* mood.

Tanta vis probitatis est, ut eam vel in hoste diligamus. Such is the force of honesty, that *we love* it even in an enemy.

"That we love it" is stated as a *fact*, and would be indicative in other languages, but in Latin *diligimus* would never be used after a consecutive *ut*.

107. The Latin *ut*, therefore, is used with the same construction in two different senses, but the context will almost always prevent ambiguity. In such a sentence as *puer humi prolapsus est*, ut *crus frangeret*, the boy fell down *so that he* broke (*or so as to break*) his leg, *intention* would be absurd. Very often *ut final* will correspond to some such word or phrase as *idcirco, eo consilio, ob eam causam*, etc., in the principal clause ; *ut consecutive* to *adeo*, or *tam*, or *ita*, or *tantus :* and thus the meaning of *ut* is made clear at once.

Hoc eo consilio *dixi ut tibi prodessem.* I said this *to be* of use to you, or *with the intention of being* of use.

Hoc ita *dixi, ut tibi prodessem.* I said this *so as to be* of use to you, or *in such a manner that I was of use to you.*

108. The English *as* **before the** *infinitive,* **and after** *so, such* (in Latin *tantus, talis, tam, adeo*, etc.), **must always be translated by** *ut* **with the subjunctive.**

Nemo tam *potens est, ut omnia efficere* possit. Nobody is so powerful *as to be* able to perform everything.

96

. But *ut*=" as," in comparisons, is followed in Latin, as in English, by an indicative.

> Ut *multitudo* solet, *concurrunt*. They are running together, *as* a multitude *is wont* to do.

Here *ut* introduces, not a *consecutive*, but a *comparative* clause (Intr. 85), and the construction may be compared to that of *tantus* followed by *quantus*, as opposed to *tantus* followed by *ut*.

Compare

> Talis *fuit* ut *nemo ei* crederet.   He was of *such* a character *that* no one believed him,

with

> Talis *fuit* qualem *nemo antea* viderat.   He was of *such* a character *as* no one had seen before,

and note the difference of the moods in Latin.

109. A negative *consequence* is not expressed by *ne*, but by *ut non*.

> *Tanta fuit viri moderatio*, ut *repugnanti mihi* non *irasceretur*.   The self-control of the man was so great, *that* he *was not* angry with me when I opposed him.

The following rule is therefore most important :—

That nobody	if expressing *purpose*	*ne quis*
That nothing	and followed by *may* or	*ne quid*
That no	*might* must be translated	*ne ullus*
That never	by	*ne unquam.*

But if they express *consequence*, and are followed by a simple English indicative, must be translated in Latin by	*ut nemo*
	ut nihil
	ut nullus
	ut nunquam.

In both cases alike the verb will be in the subjunctive mood.   Thus—

> The gates were shut *that no one might* leave the city (or *to prevent any one* from leaving, or *in order to* prevent any one, etc.).   *Portae clausae sunt*, ne quis *urbem relinqueret.*
> The fear of all men was so great, *that no one left* the city.   *Tantus fuit omnium metus*, ut nemo *urbem reliquerit.*

G

110. As *ne quis*="that no one" in final clauses, and *neve*, or *neu* quis="*or, and*, that no one," so also in indicative clauses,

    "and no one" is always *nec quisquam,*
    "and nothing"   „   *nec quidquam,*
    "and never"   „   *nec unquam.*

Similarly *nec ullus* (adj.), *nec usquam*, "and no where," etc.

111. Closely allied to the *consecutive* is a *limiting* force of *ut*, the negative of which is frequently translated by the English "without."

> *Ita bonus est, ut interdum peccet.* He is good *to this extent* (*or* he is *only* so far good), that he makes mistakes sometimes.
>
> *Nec perdi potes, ut non alios perdas.* Nor can you be ruined *without ruining* others.

Compare with the first example the limiting use of *tantus.* **84,** *note.*

Sequence of Tenses.   Tenses of the Subjunctive.

112. There is no such simple rule for the tense of the verb in the consecutive clause as that given for the final clause, and there is greater variety in the tenses; but in practice there will be little difficulty

Use the tense of the subjunctive mood which you would use if the verb were, as it would be in English, in the indicative.

Thus—

    "He *is* so wicked that nothing *has* ever *called* him away from crime;"

"has ever called" is the "true perfect;" write therefore,

> *Tam improbus est ut nihil eum unquam a scelere revocaverit.*

We have here a *present* tense in the principal, a true *perfect* in the consecutive clause; both are primary tenses. (See **177.**)

> *Hoc eum adeo terruit ut vix hodie prodire audeat.* This so *terrified* him that he scarcely *ventures* to come forward to-day.

Here one tense is historic, the other primary, but the English is a sufficient guide.

113. The only difficulty is the choice between the perfect and the imperfect subjunctive in the consecutive clause after an historic or *aorist* perfect in the principal clause.

The imperfect subjunctive denotes a *continuous* state, or action ; or one described as *commencing;* or as strictly *contemporaneous with* some point in past time.

The perfect subjunctive represents (*a*) a state or action as simply a fact in the past (aorist) ; or (*b*) a fact still producing a result in the mind of the speaker (perfect).

That the army *was flying*, or *began to fly* (imperfect) ; that the army *fled* (aorist) ; that the army *has fled* (perfect)—will represent the three tenses in English : the two latter would both be expressed in Latin by the words *"ut* fugerit," as opposed to *"ut* fugeret *exercitus."* (See **184, 185, 186.**)

If the verb in the consecutive clause implies continuance, or contemporaneous time in the past, use the **imperfect subjunctive.** If it denotes a **single fact**, or one looked on as **now completed**, use the perfect subjunctive. Thus—

> *Tanta* fuit *pestis ut permulti quotidie* perirent, *rex ipse morbo* absumptus sit.   The pestilence was so great that many *died* daily, and the king himself *was cut off* by the disease.
>
> *Ducis adventus adeo militum* redintegravit *animos ut impetum extemplo* { facerent. / fecerint. }   The general's arrival so restored the soldiers' spirits that they charged at once.

Facerent implies " at once began to ;" *fecerint* may either mean "charged" as a simple fact (aorist), or in vivid language "they *have* charged" (perfect), as though we saw the fact.

With the perfect (aorist), the consequence is looked upon as a single result, at once achieved, and not as spread over a space of time, for which idea the imperfect would be appropriate.

Future Subjunctive.

114. The only future subjunctive is the participle in *-rus* combined with the right tense of the verb *sum*. This must therefore be used where the *result* denoted by the consecutive clause is a future one.   Thus—

> *Nunquam posthac* pugnabimus.   We shall never fight again (after this).

But—

> *Adeo* territi sumus *ut nunquam posthac* pugnaturi simus.   We have been (*or* were) so frightened that we shall never fight again.

So—

> Dixit *se adeo* territos fuisse *ut nunquam postea* pugnaturi essent. He said that they (himself and his companions) *had been* so frightened that they *would* never fight again.

115. The pluperfect subjunctive, our "*would have,*" is represented in a consecutive clause by the participle in *-rus* with the *perfect subjunctive of sum.* Thus—

> *Nemo superfuisset.* No one would have survived.

But—

> *Tanta fuit caedes* ut . . . *nemo* superfuturus fuerit. The slaughter was such *that* no one *would have* survived.

Instances of Sequence of Tenses.

116.

Hoc ita facio, feci, faciam, *ut tibi* displiceam. *I do (am doing), have done, will do,* this so as to displease you.

Hoc ita feci, faciebam, feceram *ut tibi* displicerem. *I did, was doing, had done,* this so as (*then*) to displease you.

Hoc ita feci *ut tibi* displiceam (rare). *I did* this so as *now* to displease you.

Hoc ita feci *ut tibi* displicuerim. *I did* this so as to *have* now displeased you, *or* I did this so that (as a matter of fact) *I displeased* you.

Dixit *se hoc ita* fecisse *ut tibi* displiceret. He said that he did this so as to displease you.

Hoc ita feci *ut tibi* displiciturus sim. *I have* done this so that *I shall* displease you (or so as *to be likely to,* etc.).

Exercise 15.

1. I have lived, said[1] he, so virtuously, that I quit life with resignation. 2. He had lived, he said,[1] so virtuously, as to quit life with resignation. 3. I will endeavour, said he, to live so as to be able to quit life with resignation. 4. He said that he had lived so as to be able to quit life with resignation. 5. The charge of the enemy was so sudden that no one could find his arms or proper rank. 6. Thereupon the enemy made a sudden[2] charge in order to prevent any of our men from finding either his arms or proper rank. 7. Thereupon he[3] began to tell many[4] false-

---

[1] See **40.**   [2] Use adverb, *made suddenly a charge.*
[3] Ille (*the other*), **11,** *d.*   [4] See **54.**

hoods with the intention of preserving his life. 8. He told so many falsehoods that no one believed him then, and that no one has ever put faith in him since. 9. He was so good a king that his subjects loved him in his lifetime, sighed for him after his death, honour his name and memory to-day with grateful[1] hearts, and will never forget his virtues. 10. The waves were such as to dash over the whole of[2] the ship, and the storm was of such a kind as I had never seen before. 11. The cavalry charged so fiercely that had[3] not night interfered with the contest, the enemy would have[4] turned their backs. 12. You cannot, said he, injure your country without[5] bringing loss and ruin upon yourself and your own affairs. 13. I said this with the intention of benefiting you and yours, but the matter has so turned out that I shall injure you whom I wished to benefit, and benefit those whom I wished to injure. 14. So little did he indulge even a just resentment, that he pardoned even those who had slain his father.

---

[1] Superlative. See **57**.   [2] See **60**.
[3] *Nisi* with pluperf. subj.   [4] **115**.   [5] See **111**.

EXERCISE XVI.

Ut, Ne, INTRODUCING A SUBSTANTIVAL CLAUSE.[1]

117. One of the main difficulties in translating English into Latin is to know when to represent the English infinitive by the same mood in Latin, when to use a conjunction, such as *ut* or *ne* followed by the subjunctive.

We have already seen that the Latin infinitive takes the place of an English conjunctional or *that*-clause after verbs of *saying, thinking,* etc. (**31-32**).

On the other hand we have seen that the Latin infinitive must never be used to express either a *purpose* or a *result* (**100, 106**).

But besides these clear cases, which need cause no difficulty, many verbs which in English are followed by the infinitive require in Latin an *ut-* or *ne-* clause. These clauses, though originally *adverbial,* are virtually *substantival.*

Thus in *oro te* ut *hoc* facias, "I entreat you *to do* this," *ut hoc facias* is in the strictest sense an *adverbial* or *final* clause, "I entreat you, *with a view to your doing* this ;" but it may also be regarded as equivalent to an accusative case after *oro;* compare, pacem *oro;* and it is usual to consider those clauses whose final nature is not obvious at first sight as *substantival* clauses, and to class them as such, under the name of indirect *commands* or *entreaties,* with the indirect *statement* and indirect *question.* (See Intr. 80.)

118. The English infinitive after verbs and phrases of **entreating, commanding, decreeing, advising, striving, effecting,** must be translated into Latin by *ut,* or, if a negative is required, by *ne,* followed by the subjunctive mood.

Such verbs are nearly all the *verba* **imperandi vel efficiendi,** such as *oro, peto, precor, opto* (not *volo*), *edico, impero* (not *jubeo*), *hortor, moneo, suadeo, video* (I take care), *permitto*

---

[1] For the meaning of the term *substantival clause* see Intr. 80.

(not *sino* or *patior*), *facio, efficio, impetro* (I obtain by ask-ing), and such phrases as *id ago,* " I make it my aim ;" "*operam do,*" " I take pains."

The Sequence of Tenses, as well as the use of *ne* in negative clauses, will be that of the *final* clause (**104**). Thus—

> *Ut hostem terreret, militibus* imperavit, ut *clipeos hastis* percuterent. In order to terrify the enemy he com-manded the soldiers *to strike* their shields with their spears.

Here the first *ut* introduces an *adverbial* (final), the second a (virtually) *substantival* clause.

> *Magno opere te* hortor, ut *hos libros studiose* legas. I ear-nestly advise you *to read* these books attentively.
> *Capram* monet, ut *in pratum* descendat. He advises the she-goat *to come down* into the meadow.
> *Hoc te* rogo, ne demittas *animum.* I beg of you *not to be disheartened* (literally, not to let your mind sink).
> Effecit ne *ex urbe* exirent. He prevented *their leaving* the city.
> *Mihi* ne *quid* facerem imperavit. He ordered me *to do* nothing.

119. We must therefore never say *hoc te* facere, *or* non facere *oro, suadeo, hortor,* for—" I entreat, persuade, exhort you *to do,* or *not to do* this," but always *hoc* ut, or *hoc* ne *facias,* etc. The *ut* is sometimes omitted, especially with the 2nd pers. sing. (See **126.**)

120. But there are exceptions to the rule which must be carefully noticed. The commonest of all is *jubeo* (I bid), which takes an infinitive with the accusative.

Compare
> *Consul* militibus ut (*or* ne) *pedem* referrent imperavit
with
> *Consul* milites *pedem* referre jussit (*or* vetuit).

And the infinitive construction is usual with *volo,* and *cupio* (I wish, desire), also with *veto,* I forbid, *prohibeo,* I prevent, *conor,* I endeavour, *sino, patior,* I allow.

121. It has already been said (**45**) that some verbs of *purposing*, *resolving*, etc., take the infinitive when the subject of both verbs is the same, but an *ut-* or *ne-* clause when the subject of the second verb is different : *ego ne redirem, curavit, he* took care that *I* should not return ; *nec redire curat*, and he does not care to return. In the second example *curat* is a modal verb (**42**).

122. It is important to observe that the same verb may be used in two senses, and therefore with two constructions.

It may be used as a verb *sentiendi vel declarandi*, in which case it will take the accusative and infinitive (**31**); or it may be used as a verb *imperandi vel efficiendi* (**118**), in which case it will be followed by an *ut-* or *ne-* clause; thus—

(*a.*) *Moneo* adesse hostem.   I warn you *that* the enemy *is* at hand.
Ne *hoc* facias *moneo*.   I warn you not *to do* this.

(*b.*) *Mihi persuasum est* (**5**) finem adesse.   I was persuaded *that* the end *was* near.
Mihi persuasum est ne *hoc* facerem.   I was persuaded *not to do* this.

(*c.*) *Mihi scripsit* se venturum esse.   He wrote me word *that* he *would* come.
Mihi scripsit ne *ad se* venirem.   He wrote to me (to order or beg me) *not to come* to him.

(*d.*) *Fac* venias.   Be sure *to come.*
Fac te venisse.   Suppose yourself *to have* come.

The same verbs are used in English with a double construction ; but where we use the conjunction *" that "* Latin uses the infinitive, and Latin uses a conjunction where we use the infinitive.

123. Many **impersonal** verbs and phrases are followed by an *ut*-clause containing a verb in the subjunctive. This clause acts in place of a subject to the impersonal verb.

Accidit ut *nemo senator adesset.*   It happened that no senator was present, *or*, no senator happened to be present.
Ex quo factum est ut *bellum indiceretur.*   The consequence of *this* (**78**) was that war was declared, *or*, the result was a declaration of war.

These *ut*- clauses are properly speaking *consecutive*, as those in **117**, **118**, are properly *final;* hence *ut nemo*, not *ne quis* in the first example. (See **109**.)

The sequence of Tenses will be that of the consecutive clause.

Obs.—Never translate "it happened to him to be absent" by *accidit ei abesse*, always by *ei accidit ut abesset*, or else by *is forte abfuit*.

124. *Tantum abest*, "so far from," is always used impersonally, and is followed by two *ut*-clauses, of which one is *substantival* and subject to *abest*, the other is *adverbial*, being a consecutive clause explaining *tantum*.

> Tantum abest ut *nostra miremur* ut *nobis non satisfaciat ipse Demosthenes*. *So far are we from* admiring our own works, *that* Demosthenes himself does not satisfy us.

Ut nostra miremur; a substantival clause, standing in place of a subject to *abest*.

Ut nobis non satisfaciat ipse Demosthenes; an adverbial clause which, joined with *tantum*, qualifies *abest* like an adverb of degree or quantity.

The same idea might also be expressed by *adeo non . . . ut*, or by *non modo non . . . sed*, as,

> Adeo non *nostra miramur* ut *nobis non* satisfaciat, etc. ; or,
> Non modo non *nostra miramur*, sed *nobis non* satisfacit.

125. The following verbs and phrases are followed by *ut*, introducing a substantival clause.

(*a.*) It follows ; the next thing is, *sequitur :* or *proximum est*.
(*b.*) It happens by chance, *casu accidit*.
(*c.*) Hence it happens, *ita fit*, lit. thus it happens.
(*d.*) How happens it ? *qui fit ?*
(*e.*) It is possible, *fieri potest ut*, lit. it can happen that.
(*f.*) It is (quite) impossible, *nullo modo fieri potest ut*, lit. it cannot happen that.
(*g.*) It remains, *reliquum est, restat*.
(*h.*) So far from, *tantum abest ut—ut*.
(*i.*) I will not allow myself to, *non committam ut*.
(*j.*) He succeeded (in becoming consul), *effecit (ut consul fieret)*.
(*k.*) He contrived (not to be punished), *effecit (ne poenas daret)*.

126. *Ut* is generally omitted (especially before the 2nd person singular) when the subjunctive is combined with *oportet, necesse est, velim, nolim, licet*.

> *Hoc* facias *velim*.   I would have you do this.
> *Culpam* fateare *necesse est*.   You must needs avow your fault.

127. The ordinary construction of the case of the person after words of entreating and commanding, etc., is

(a.) Te *oro, obsecro, rogo, moneo, admoneo, hortor, adhortor, jubeo, veto, prohibeo, sino.*

(b.) Tibi *impero, praecipio, edico, mando, permitto.*

(c.) A, ab (abs) te *peto, postulo, impetro.*

(d.) *Posco, flagito, precor,* both with acc. as (a), and *a* or *ab* with abl. as (c).

128. *Jubeo* expresses our "bid," and may be used in a wide sense, and wherever in *oratio recta* we should use the imperative. *Salvere te jubeo* = salve. It may express the wish of equals, superiors, or inferiors.

Impero implies an order from a higher authority, as from a commanding officer.

Edico, a formal order from some one in office, as a Praetor, etc.

Praecipio, a direction or instruction from one of superior knowledge.

Mando, a charge or commission intrusted by any one.

Permitto differs from *sino,* as meaning rather to give leave *actively;* *sino,* not to prevent. *Permitto* sometimes means "to intrust wholly to," "hand over to."

Exercise 16.

A.

1. I entreated him not to do this,[1] but suggested to him to trust his father.   2. He exhorted the soldiers not to be disheartened on account of the late disaster.   3. He made it his aim to avoid injuring any one of his subjects, but to consult the good of the whole nation.   4. He gave orders to the soldiers to get ready for fighting, and exhorted them to fight bravely.   5. The senate passed a resolution that the consuls should hold a levy.   6. I resolved to warn your brother not to return to Rome before night.   7. And, to prevent him from telling any more falsehoods, I bade him hold his peace.   8. It happened (on) that day[2] that the consuls were about to hold a levy.   9. I prevailed on him to spare the vanquished (*pl.*), and not[3] to allow

---

[1] Co-ordinate relative.   (See **78.**)   [2] See **9,** (*a*).
[3] *Neve* or *neu.*   (See **103.**)

his (soldiers) to massacre women and children. 10. I was the first to warn him not to put faith in the falsest and most cruel of mankind. 11. You[1] and I happened that day to be in the country; the consequence[2] of this was that we have been the last[3] to hear of this disaster. 12. He said that he would never allow himself to promise to betray his allies.

B.

1. Thereupon he earnestly implored the bystanders not to obey men[4] who were ready (subj., **77**) to betray both their allies and themselves in order to avoid incurring a trifling loss. 2. He succeeded at last in persuading the Spaniards that it was quite impossible to leave the city, (which was[5]) blockaded on all sides by the enemy, unharmed. 3. He says[6] that he never asked you to pardon the guilty or condemn the innocent. 4. I will not, said he, allow myself to be the last to greet my king after so heavy a disaster. 5. The jury were at last persuaded that my brother was innocent; they could not be persuaded to acquit him by their verdict, such was their terror[7] of the mob. 6. News has been brought to me in my absence that the city has been taken: it remains (for me) to retake it by the same arts as[8] those by which I have lost it. 7. So far am I from praising and admiring that king, that it seems[9] to me that he has greatly injured not only his own subjects, but the whole human race. 8. So far am I from having said everything, that I could take up the whole of the day in speaking; but I do not wish to be tedious.[10] 9. It never before happened to me to forget a friend in his absence, and this[11] circumstance is a great consolation to me to-day.

---

[1] See **26**, note. [2] See **123**, example 2. [3] See **62**.
[4] See **72**. [5] Omit relative and use participle.
[6] See **33**. [7] See **25**, last example. [8] See **84**.
[9] See **43**. [10] See **42**, ii. [11] See **67**.

EXERCISE XVII.

Quominus, Quin. VERBS OF *Fearing* WITH *Ut, Ne.*

129. These two compound words are used as conjunctions after verbs and phrases which denote *prevention, hindrance, opposition,* etc.

Quo minus=*ut eo* (*hoc*) *minus*, "that by it the less," or "that by this means the less." *Quin*=*qui* (old abl.=*quo*), and *ne*, the old form of the negative, "that by it not."

130. *Quo minus* is generally, *quin* only, used when the verb of *preventing*, etc., is joined with a negative or virtual negative.

By a *virtual negative* we mean *vix, aegre,* "scarcely," "with difficulty," or questions expecting the answer "no," "none," "nothing."

131. *Quo minus* often answers to the English verbal noun in -*ing* combined with a preposition.

> *Naves vento tenebantur* quominus *in portum* redirent. The ships were prevented by the wind *from returning* into harbour.
> *Per te stetit* quominus vinceremus. You were the cause *of our not winning* the day.
> *Non recusabo* quominus *te in vincula* ducam. I will not object *to taking* you to prison.

In all these instances a negative *result* or *aim* (two notions so often identified in Latin) is expressed by *quominus*.

132. *Quin* is still more common than *quominus,* but is only used after negative words and phrases.

(*a.*) Nec *multum afuit* quin *interficeremur.*   And we were not far *from losing* our lives.

(*b.*) Nec *eum unquam adspexit,* quin *fratricidam compellaret.* And she never beheld him *without calling* him a fratricide.

(*c.*) Vix *inhiberi potuit,* quin *saxa jacĕret.*   He could scarcely be prevented *from throwing* stones.

(*d.*) Nullo modo *fieri potest* quin *errem.*   It is quite impossible *that I am not* mistaken, or *but that I am,* etc.

(*e.*) *Fieri* vix *potuit* quin *te accusarem.*   It was scarcely possible *for me not to* accuse you.

133. *Quin* is also used as equivalent to "*but that*" or "*that*" after verbs or phrases of *doubting,* combined with a negative, or virtual negative.

Quis dubitat quin *hoc feceris?*   Who doubts (=no one doubts) *but that* (*or* that) you did this?

134. *Quin* is also used (see **80**) as containing not a conjunction but a relative pronoun (*qui, quae, quod,* and *ne*).

Nemo est quin [=qui non] *intelligat.*   There is no one *but* (*who* does not) perceives, *or* all the world perceives.

In all these uses *quin* is joined with the subjunctive.

135. But it is also used sometimes as a direct interrogative = *qui non?*

Quin *hoc mihi das?*   *How* (or, why) do you not give me this? *i.e.* give it me ;

and sometimes as a mere emphatic particle = "nay ;" *quinetiam* = "moreover."

In these senses it can be joined with *any mood.*

136. (*a.*) *Recuso (quominus)* means properly "I protest against," "give reasons against," (*re* and *causa*) ; hence it is equivalent to our "object." It is sometimes used less emphatically as a modal verb with the infinitive (**42**) ; but the English "I refuse" in the sense "I am reluctant" is generally to be turned by *nolo,* or, if a refusal expressed in words is meant, by *nego* with future in *-rus.*

(*b.*) *Dubito* when negatived (see **130**) is followed by *quin,* but it is also used as a modal verb in the sense of " hesitate," " scruple."

Thus we sometimes find not only

Nec recuso quominus *hoc patiar.* And I do not protest *against* suffering this.

Nec dubitat quin *hoc facere audeat.* And he does not hesitate *to venture* on doing this.

but—

Neque hoc pati *recuso, nec hoc* audere *dubitat.*

137. (I.) Words and phrases followed by *quin* with the subjunctive are :—

(*a.*) All the world (believes), *nemo est quin* (*credat*).

(*b.*) Not to doubt, *non dubitare* (*quin*).

(*c.*) There is no doubt, *non est dubium* or *dubitandum* (*quin*), " it is not doubtful."

(*d.*) Who doubts ? *quis dubitat* (*quin*) ?

(*e.*) It cannot be (it is impossible) but that, *fieri non potest* (*quin*).

(*f.*) I cannot refrain from, *temperare mihi non possum* (*quin*). See (*j.*)

(*g.*) It cannot be denied, *negari non potest* (*quin*). (Rare : the infinitive is to be preferred.)

(*h.*) To be very near ; to be within a very little, *minimum abesse ; haud multum abesse* (*quin*) ; always used impersonally.

(*i.*) To leave nothing undone to, *nihil praetermittere* (*quin*).

(*j.*) I cannot but, I cannot help, *facere non possum* (*quin*).

(*k.*) To restrain, to keep back from, *retinere, tenere* (after negative words, and *aegre,* " with difficulty," *vix,* " scarcely," etc.).

(*l.*) What reason is there against ? *quid causae est* (*quin*) ?

(II.) Verbs that may be followed by *quominus.*

To frighten from, to deter, *deterrere.*

To hinder, prevent, *obstare* (dat.), *impedire* (acc.). (So *officere, obsistere, repugnare, intercedere,* etc.)

Prohibeo and *veto* mostly take the infinitive. (See **120.**)

Verbs of Fearing.

138. The construction used in Latin after verbs of *fearing* is quite different from that which follows verbs of *hoping.* (See **37.**)

With verbs of **fearing**, *that* as well as *lest* must be translated by *nē, that not* by *ut.*[1]

Such verbs are *timeo, metuo, vereor,* etc., and the same construction is used with such phrases as *periculum est (fuit), metus est,* etc.

After such verbs and phrases the English *future* and the *verbal substantive* are translated by the *present* or *imperfect* subjunctive, with *ut* or *nē.*

> *Vereor* ne *veniat.*   I fear *that* he *will* come, *or,* I fear *or* am afraid of his *coming.*
>
> *Vereor* ut *veniat.*   I fear *that* he *will not* come, *or,* I am afraid *of his not coming.*
>
> *Veritus sum* ne *or* ut *veniret.*   I feared that he *would,* or *would not* come.
>
> *Periculum erat* ne *hostes urbem expugnarent.*   There was a danger of the enemy's taking the city.

139. But where stress is laid on the idea of futurity, or the sense of *likelihood* is introduced, the subjunctive future, *i.e.* the future in *-rus* with *sum* (114), is used.

> *Vereor* ut *hoc tibi* profuturum sit.   I am afraid that this *is not likely* to do you good

Obs.—Verbs of fearing are *sometimes* used like *recuso* and *dubito* as modal verbs in close combination with the infinitive.

> *Nec* mori *timet.*   And he is not afraid of dying.

---

[1] The origin of this use of *ne* and *ut* after verbs of fearing is not quite clear. The *ne* is easily explained. "I fear, with a *wish* or *aim* that he may not come" = "I fear *lest* he come or be coming" (English subjunctive), compare the French *je crains qu'il* ne *vienne*; and thus the *ne* introduces a final clause.

On the same principle the *ut* may mean "I *am in fear,* with the desire or aim that *he may* come" = "I am afraid of his not coming," in French—je crains qu'il *ne vienne pas.*

The *ut* may also be explained as used in its interrogative sense of "how," "as to how," and thus the *ut veniat* would be a dependent interrogative clause; "I have fears *as to how* he is coming" = "that he is not coming."

This explanation is simple, but involves a totally different origin and construction from that of the *ne*-clause.

Exercise 17.

1. I never beheld him without imploring him to come to the aid of his oppressed and suffering country; but I fear that he will never listen to my prayers.   2. I cannot refrain from blaming those who were ready to hand over our lives, liberties, rights, and fortunes to our deadliest enemies.   3. All the world believes that you did wrong, and I am afraid that it is quite impossible that all mankind have been of one mind with me in a blunder.   4. He pretends that I was the cause of my countrymen not joining the cause of every patriot.   5. The soldiers could not be restrained from hurling their darts into the midst of the mob.   6. He promises to leave nothing undone to persuade your son not to hurry away from the city to the country.[1]   7. We were within a very little of being all killed, some of us pierced by the enemy's darts, others cut off either by famine or disease.   8. Nothing,[2] he said, had ever prevented him[3] from defending the freedom and privileges of his countrymen.   9. What circumstance prevented you from keeping your word, and coming to my aid with your army, as you[4] had promised to do?   10. I will no longer then protest against your desiring to become a king, but I am afraid you will not be able to obtain your desire.   11. What reason is there why he should not be ready to return in his old[5] age to the scenes which he left unwillingly in his boyhood?[5]   12. Such was his terror[6] of Caesar's victory, that he could scarcely be restrained from committing suicide.   13. He could not, he replied,[7] help waging war by land and sea.   14. News has been brought me, said he, that the general has been struck by a dart, and I fear that he has received a mortal wound.   15. Nor was he afraid, he replied, of our being able to reach Italy in[8] safety; the[9] danger was[10] of our being likely never to return.

---

[1] See **9**, *b*.   [2] See **33**.   [3] *i.e.* himself, **11**, *e*.   [4] See **67**, *Obs.*
[5] **63**.   [6] See **25**.   [7] **32**, *b*.   [8] See **61**.
[9] Lit., that (*ille*) was the danger, etc.
[10] Inf. mood, dependent on "he replied."

EXERCISE XVIII.

COMMANDS AND PROHIBITIONS.

Imperative Mood.

140. The **imperative mood** is used freely in Latin, as in English, in both commands and entreaties, in the second person singular and plural.

Ad me veni. *Come* to me.   Audite[1] *hoc. Hear* this.

141. But, especially in the singular, where one person, an equal, is addressed, there are many substitutes for so peremptory a mode of speaking. A short compound sentence containing either a subordinate or a co-ordinate clause is substituted for the simple command.

Thus: for *scribe*, scribas velim, "I would have you write" (126), is often used; or *tu*, quaeso, *ad me scribe*, or *scribe* sis (for si vis): or again, for *ad me veni*, fac, *or* cura ut, *ad me venias*, "be sure to come:" so with the plural, *vos*, oro et obsecro, *attendite*.

Obs.—The subjunctive is used for the imperative in the second person singular; but only where no definite person is addressed, but a general maxim given.

Postremus loquaris : *primus* taceas.   Be (*you*, or *a man* should be) the last to speak, the first to be silent.

---

[1] There is also a more emphatic form, *venito, venitote*, which is called the *future* imperative; it is used in both the second and third persons, and is called future from its very common use in *laws* and *wills* which concern the future, and from its often forming the *apodosis* to a future perfect clause ; *cum ego dixero, tum vos* respondetote, when I have spoken, then, *and not before*, do you reply.   But it is used also for mere emphasis : *nolitote, scitote*, are often met with.

142. In **negative commands,** or **prohibitions,** the simple imperative is little used.   Such phrases as *ne sævi, magna sacerdos* (AEN. vi.) ("be not wroth, mighty priestess"), are almost entirely confined to poetry.

In English also, though in older English, and in poetry, we find constantly "go not," "fear not," etc., yet we generally substitute the infinitive with an auxiliary verb in the imperative : *do* not go, *do* not fear.

In Latin, in addressing a single person familiarly, *ne* is often used with the *perfect* subjunctive.

> *Ne dubitaveris,* do not hesitate ; *lit.* do not (allow yourself to) *have* hesitated, *or* beware against *having* hesitated.

So—*Nihil dederis,* give nothing.

The *present* subjunctive is not used in speaking to a person ; *ne multa* discas, *sed multum* is a general maxim. (See **141,** *Obs.*)

143. But by far the more common mode of forbidding or deprecating is by a periphrasis ; using, as we do in '*do* not *do* this,' *two* verbs.

> Noli, nolite, nolitote, *hoc facere, or* cave, cavete (ne) *illud facias, faciatis.*

The *ne* is often omitted with the second person.   (See **126.**)

144. For the *first* and *third* persons (except in formal documents, see **140,** note) Latin employs the subjunctive mood in a *jussive* sense to express *exhortation, wish,* or *command,* and uses *ne* to prohibit or deprecate.

> *Moriamur, let* us die ; *pereat, may* he perish ; *abeat, let* him go ; ne sim *salvus, may* no good befall me ; ne exeat *urbe, let* him not go out of the city.   In older English and in poetry we have "*turn* we to survey," "hallowed *be* thy name."

145. "Nor," "or," "and not," with prohibitions is generally *neve* or *neu,* but *neque* is also used.

> *Hoc facito ; illud ne feceris,* neve *dixeris.*   Do this ; do not do *or* say that.
> *Sequere,* neque *retrospexeris.*   Follow *and* do *not* look behind.

146. There is also a common use of such phrases as *vidĕris,* *viderint,* in the sense of "you, they, must look to it," when the responsibility of giving an opinion is declined or postponed.

> *De hac re tu* videris, *or* viderint *sapientiores.* I leave this to you, *or* to wiser men ; do you, *or* let wiser men, decide.

This is a future perfect indicative, as in the first person *videro* is used.

Exercise 18.

1. Do not then lose (*sing.*) such an opportunity as[1] this, but rather let us, under your leadership, crush the eternal enemies of our country.   2. Do not, my countrymen, count the foes who are threatening you with massacre and slavery; let them rather meet the same lot which they are preparing for us.   3. Pardon (*sing.*) this fault of mine ; and be sure you remember that I, who have done wrong to-day, have repeatedly brought you help before.   4. Let us then refuse to be slaves, and have the courage not only to become free ourselves, but to assert our country's freedom also.   5. And therefore[2] do not object to[3] endure everything in behalf of your suffering country and your exiled friends.   6. And therefore,[2] my countrymen, do not believe that I, who have so often led you to the field of battle, am afraid to-day of fortune abandoning me.   7. Let us be the same in the field (of battle) as[4] we have ever been ; as[5] to the issue of the battle let the gods decide.

---

[1] See **88,** *Obs.*   [2] See **78.**   [3] See **136**
[4] See **84.**   [5] Prep. *de* with *abl.*

EXERCISE XIX.

REMARKS ON MOODS: THE SUBJUNCTIVE
USED INDEPENDENTLY.

147. By a *Mood*[1] we mean a special form assumed by the Verb in order to mark some special manner (*modus*) in which that connexion between a subject and predicate which every verb implies is viewed by the speaker. (Intr. 11, and see note.)

---

[1] In the words of an old grammarian (Priscian) *modi sunt diversae* inclinationes *animi* (movements, variations, swayings, of the human mind) *quas varia consequitur* declinatio (inflexion, or form). In some languages, especially those which have no written literature, the number of moods is exceedingly large, different modifications of the form of the verb being used to represent many different *moods*, or frames, or attitudes, of the mind of the speaker. Thus, in addition to those forms which denote *time* (tenses), we find separate forms or moods to express *certainty, doubt, inquiry, contingency, negation, command, desire*, etc. But in the languages of highly civilised nations economy is practised in the use of such varied forms; the intelligence of the hearer or reader is relied on, and a single form (as with the case-inflexions of nouns) is used to represent various ideas more or less related to each other. In Greek the two ideas of a command and a wish as applied to a third person are expressed by two moods, ἀπολέσθω, ἀπόλοιτο; Latin is content with one—*pereat*. Both agree with English in having no mood to distinguish a simple question from a simple statement. In modern English prose the subjunctive mood, so exceedingly common in Latin, hardly exists as a true mood, *i.e.* a separate and distinct form of the verb. We retain its use occasionally as a contingent mood after *though* and *if*, "though he *fail*," "if it *be* so;" but as a rule we either disregard those slighter, though real, shades of meaning which call for the subjunctive in Latin (as often in German and French), and are content with the indicative, or, if the difference is too great to be disregarded, we substitute for a true mood a combination of an auxiliary or modal verb with the infinitive mood—"*let* him go," "if he *were* to come," "I *would* not do this,"—exactly as we substitute a preposition with a noun for the case-inflexions of nouns. As regards therefore the use of the Latin subjunctive, the usage of English will be a most inadequate guide. It would, for instance, never lead us to suspect the necessity of such a mood in such sentences as "he was so injured that he *died*," "it happened that he *was* absent," "I fear that you *are* deceiving me," "tell me why you *did* this," "he said that the man who *did* this should die," "he is one who *will* never fail to do his duty;" yet these are among the most obvious constructions in which the use of the subjunctive is required in Latin.

116

i. Thus the **Indicative** mood is so called because it simply points out (*indĭcat*) a connexion or agreement between a subject and predicate. In itself it does nothing more than this, and is quite neutral and colourless, so to speak ; but it is capable of being joined with other words which may greatly qualify the meaning which the verb itself conveys. Thus *valet,* "he is well ;" fortasse *valet,* "perhaps he is well" (uncertainty) ; si *valet,* "*if* he is well" (contingency) ; non *valet,* "he is *not* well" (denial) ; and the addition of a particle in Latin, or an inversion of the order in English, or even the mere tone in which the verb is pronounced, may without any alteration of its form (for there is no interrogative mood in either Latin or English) enable it to ask a question, that is, to suggest instead of stating the agreement between the two essential elements of every sentence, the subject and the predicate. (Intr. 61, 62.) *Valet ? valet*ne ? "he is well ?" "is he well ?"

ii. The **Imperative** mood is a form assumed by the verb to mark that the agreement between the subject and predicate is not *stated* or *suggested* but *commanded* or *willed :* aude, audcte, "dare thou," "dare ye."

iii. The difference between these two moods is clear ; and it has already (**94**, note 1) been explained that the **Infinitive** mood is hardly in the strict sense a mood at all, being properly the verb used as a substantive, as, *sedere,* "the act of sitting ;" it is however very widely used in Latin as the mood of indirect assertion. (See **31**.)

iv. The **Subjunctive** is the mood which gives rise to the greatest difficulty in the study of Latin. Its use in that language is constant and manifold, while it hardly exists in modern English (see note, p. 116). Nor will its name (*modus* **subjunctivus** or **conjunctivus**) be a sufficient guide, for though so called on account of its being found principally in subordinate clauses, yet such clauses often require the use of the indicative, and the use of the subjunctive, as will be shown shortly, is by no means confined to them.

It perhaps was originally used as a separate form in order to add, to the simple statement made by the indicative, some further idea of *uncertainty* or *contingency.* Hence its use in Latin to express, not a fact which we *indicate,* but something which we regard rather as a mere conception of the mind, as that which we purpose or wish to be a fact, or which we refer to as the result of another fact, or as stated on other authority than our own ; and in this way it is used in Latin in a large number of sentences in which the use of any special mood would never occur to any one who was acquainted only with English.

*** These remarks will illustrate the term "modal verb" used above (**42**), and will be of use to those who wish to understand the meaning of the term Mood ; but the following Exercise will be confined to the points stated in **148-153**.

148. The Latin subjunctive is mainly used in certain classes of subordinate or *subjoined* clauses : hence its name (*subjunctivus*). But it is also used both in simple sentences, and in the main clause of a compound sentence, either to make a *statement* (*a.*), or to ask a *question* (*b.*), or to express a *command* or *desire* (*c.*).

149. (*a.*) **The subjunctive makes a statement**: but it does this in a hesitating and uncertain manner; in what is sometimes called the "potential" mood, or *modus dubitativus*, formed in English by the auxiliaries "may," "might," "would," "could," "should."

It is thus used in the present, perfect, and imperfect tenses :

i. In the first person :—

*Hoc dicere au*sim.   This I *would* venture to say.

*Vix credider*im.   I *can* scarce believe.

*Hoc affirmaver*im.   This I *would* or *may* assert.

It appears as a polite form (Gk. θέλοιμ' ἄν), in *velim*, *nolim*, joined, when the wish applies to another person, not with the infinitive, but with another subjunctive without *ut.*

*Vel*im *ad*sis.   I wish, or could wish, you *were* here (pres.).

*Vell*em *ad*esses.   I could have wished you *had been* here (used of *continuous* time in the past, or a *vain* wish in the present).

*Hoc facias vel*im.   { I wish you would } do this, *or* please do { I would have you } this.   (See **141.**)

*Vell*em *ad*fuisses.   I could have wished you had been there (once for all).

ii. In the second person :—

*Cred*as, *cred*eres.   You (that is *any one*, no definite person) would believe, would have believed.   (This is a common way of expressing "it seems, seemed as though ".)

iii. In the third person :—

Dicat (*or* dixerit) *aliquis* or *quispiam*.   Some one *may* say, *i.e.* "may perhaps say."

In all these cases we may supply a suppressed condition,—"if I were allowed," "if you should ask me," and the like.

150. (*b.*) **The subjunctive also asks a question.**

Quis credat?   Who would believe? (a virtual negative.)
*Hoc tu dicere aud*eas?   Would you dare to say this?
   (astonishment.)

So when perplexity or hesitation is implied (*modus deliberativus,* probably an interrogative form of the jussive use, 151).

*Quid faci*am?   What am I to do?
Quid faceret?   What was he to do?

Note that these are "rhetorical questions," *i.e.* they are not asked for information ; but either imply a negative answer, "no one will believe," and are virtual negatives (see 130), or are asked in mere doubt or perplexity, implying often, "I have," or "he had, no resource."

If the question were asked for information, the Latin would be *quid mihi* faciendum est? *quid ei* faciendum fuit?

151. (*c.*) **The subjunctive also is largely used in a jussive sense,** to express a *wish* or *desire.* It is thus used with or without *utinam ;* the negative wish is expressed by *ne.*

Quod Di bene vertant!   And may the Gods bring this to
   a good issue !
Quod utinam ne faciatis !   And may you never do this !
Ne *hic diutius* cunctemur.   Let us not linger any longer
   here.

(See 144.) (For *ne credideris,* "do not believe ;" *abeat,* "let him go," see 142 and 144.)

152. *Utinam* can be also used, like *vellem,* with the past : *Utinam hoc* fecerit ! "May he have done this !" But it generally, as is natural with wishes about the past, expresses a *vain* wish, and is so used with the imperf. and pluperf. subjunctive.

Utinam adesset, "would he *had been* present," contemporaneously
   with some event in past time ; *or,* continuously and extending
   (often) up to the present moment, "would he *were* present."
Utinam adfuisset, "would he had been present" (once for all).

153. It is important to remember that Latin often uses the indicative where in English we use the compound potential or subjunctive mood.

Longum est.   It *would be* tedious.
Satius, or, *melius* est. fuit.   It *would be, would have been,*
   better.
Quisquis, quicunque es.   Whoever thou *be* (subj.).

So also, the indicative is used with modal verbs, *possum, debeo,* etc.

Possum *hoc facere.* I might do this.
Potui *hoc facere.* I might have done this.
Hoc debuisti *facere.* You should (or ought to) have done this.

The possibility or duty is *asserted* by the indicative; though it is implied at the same time that the action expressed by the verb in the infinitive did not take place.

Obs.—In English, in speaking of past time we constantly say, "It would have been better to have done this," where we should more correctly say, "to do this." The present infinitive is used in Latin: *melius* fuit *hoc* facere.

Exercise 19.

1. This at least I would venture to say, that as[1] I was the first to urge you to undertake this work, so[1] I promise to be the last to advise you to abandon the undertaking. 2. What was I to do? said he, what to say? who would care to blame me because I refused to listen to such[2] abandoned men? 3. I would neither deny nor assert that he had looked forward to all this (*pl.*), but he should have provided against the country being overwhelmed by such disasters. 4. On that day my brother was reluctantly absent from the battle at your suggestion; would that he had been[3] there! For it would have been better to have fallen on the field than to have submitted to such dishonour. 5. In return[4] then for such acts of kindness I would have you not only feel but also show your gratitude. 6. I could have wished that you had sent me the best[5] soldiers that you had with you. 7. The soldiers stood (*imperf.*) drawn up in line, eager for the fight,[6] with[7] eyes fixed on the foe, clamouring for the signal; it seemed as though they were waiting for a banquet. 8. I have consulted, as[8] I ought to have done, your (*pl.*) interests rather than my own; may you not ever impute this to me as a fault!

---

[1] as . . . so, *et* . . . *et*.   [2] See **88**.   [3] Use *adsum*, **149**, i.
[4] *pro*, abl.   [5] See **69**.   [6] Gerund, **99**.
[7] Abl. abs., "their eyes being fixed."   [8] See **67**, *Obs.*

EXERCISE XX.

INTERROGATIVE SENTENCES.

I. Direct (Single and Disjunctive).

154. Interrogative sentences may be divided into two classes, Direct and Indirect.

By the **direct question** we mean a question properly so called, such as is marked by the interrogative sign in English: "Is he gone?" "Are you well?"

These sentences differ from *statements* and *commands,* inasmuch as the connexion between the subject and the predicate is not *stated,* or *desired,* but only *suggested.*

Obs.—As there is no interrogative *mood* in either Latin or English, in direct questions (other than those *rhetorical* questions already **(150)** mentioned) the **indicative** mood is used, unless for some special reason.

155. In English we mark a question by the order of the words, and sometimes by the insertion of an auxiliary verb. Compare "*Saw* ye?" "*Is* he well?" "*Did* you see?" "*Will* he come?" with "Ye *saw;*" "He *is* well;" "You saw;" "He will come;" and in French "*Va-t-il?*" with "Il va."

But in Latin, where the order of the words would have no such effect (Intr. 87), questions are usually asked by the interrogative particles -*ně* (enclitic, Intr. 98, *note*), *num, utrum, an,* or by interrogative *pronouns* or pronominal *adverbs.*

There is sometimes no definite word which marks that the speaker is putting a question. The tone, manner, and gesture of the speaker supply what in ordinary language is expressed by certain words.

(*a.*) -*ně* is used in questions that ask simply for information, and to which the answer may be either "yes" or "no."

> *Scribitne Caius?* Is Caius writing? (The person who asks the question does not expect one answer more than another.)

(*b.*) *Num*[1] expects the answer " no."

Num putas?   Do you fancy ? = Surely you don't fancy ? (expected answer " no ".)

(*c.*) *Nonne* expects the answer " yes."

Nonnĕ putas?   Don't you fancy ? = Surely you do fancy ? (expected answer " yes ".)

156. *Nĕ* is always attached to the emphatic word.

Praetoremne *accusas?*   *Is it a Praetor* whom you are accusing ?

Mene *fugis?*   *Is it* from *me* that you are flying ?

Here, as often, the English expresses emphasis by a separate clause, of which the emphatic word is the predicate, and " it " the subject ; the rest of the sentence being thrown into an adjectival clause explanatory of " it."

157. Other interrogative words are either (i.) Pronouns, or (ii.) Interrogative Particles.

Notice that pronouns are used either as substantives or as adjectives, *i.e.* as attached to substantives.

Quid *fecit ?*   What has he done ?

Quod *facinus admisit ?*   What crime has he committed ?

Also that for interrogative particles[2] a phrase or combination of words is often substituted : thus *quemadmodum?* " in what manner?" = *qui?* " how ?"

The following is a list of Interrogative Pronouns and Particles :—

(i.) PRONOUNS—

Quis? quisnam? quid? quidnam? who ? what?

Quantum? how much? (followed by *genitive, quantum* temporis ? how much time ?)

Qui? what?   *Quot?* how many ?   *Uter?* which of the two ?

Qualis? of what kind ?

Quantus? how great ?

Quot ? how many ?

---

[1] *Num* is properly " now " (*nunc*) : compare *tum* and *tunc*.

[2] These particles are in fact *adverbs*, inasmuch as they qualify the sense in which the verb is used, forming a substitute for an interrogative mood (see **147**, *note* i.) ; when used to connect a dependent with a principal clause they assume the nature of *conjunctions*. (See Intr. 25, 26.)

PRONOUNS—*continued.*

> *Quotus?* one of how many? (answer "third," "fourth," etc.)
>
> *Num quis, qua, quid* (subst.)? *num qui, quae, quod* (adj.)? *ecquis?* any?

(ii.) PARTICLES—

> *Ubi?* where? *Unde?* whence? *Quo?* whither?
> *Cur? quare?* quamobrem?** why? wherefore?
> *Quî?* how? (often in the phrase *quî fit ut?*)
> *Quam?* how? (with adj. and adv.)
> *Quomodo? quemadmodum?** how? in what manner?
> *Quantum? quantopere?* how much?
> *Quando?* when? (never *quum*.) *Quoties?* how often?
> *Quamdiu? quousque?* how long? how far?
> *Cur non? quin?* why not? how not?

Obs.—The adverb *tandem* (lit. "at last") is often joined with interrogatives in the sense of "tell me," "(who) in the world," "I ask," etc.

> *Quousque* tandem. To what point, I *ask?*
> *Quae* tandem *causa.* What *possible* cause?

Disjunctive Questions.

158. A direct question may be put in another form. In English two or more **alternative** questions may be combined by the disjunctive conjunction *or* (see Intr. 56) so that an affirmative answer to the one negatives the other or others.

> "Are you going to Germany, *or* (are you going) to Italy, *or* to France?"

These are called *alternative*, or *disjunctive*, or *double* questions.

We have here two or more simple sentences joined together by *co-ordination.* (See Intr. 74, 75.)

In English the first question has no interrogative particle (*whether* being obsolete in *direct* questions), the second and any further are introduced by "or," which however is sometimes, where the verb is suppressed, confined to the last.

> "Did you mean me, *or* think of yourself, *or* refer to some one else?"
> "Did you mean me, him, *or* yourself?"

---

* Words with an asterisk are mostly confined to *indirect* questions.

159. In Latin the **interrogative nature** of the first question will be indicated by *utrum,* or the appended "*-ne ;*" in the second, or any further question, the "*or*" will be translated by *an,* never by *aut* or *vel.*

> Utrum *hostem,* an *ducem,* an *vosmet ipsos culpatis ?* Is it the enemy, *or* your general, *or* yourselves that you blame ?
>
> *Servine estis,* an *liberi ?* Are you slaves *or* freemen ?

But in such questions there is frequently, as in English, no interrogative particle in the first question, and *or* is translated by *an,* or (more rarely by) the enclitic *-ně.*

> *Herum vidisti,* an *ancillam ?* Did you see the master *or* the maid ?
>
> *Hoc, illud*ne *fecisti ?* Did you do this *or* that ?

"*Or not ?*" in a direct question should be translated by *an non ?*

> *Ivitne,* an non ? Did he go, or not ?

160. The forms for these double questions are :—

1. *utrum,* . . . . *an, an non ?*
2. *-ne,* . . . . . *an ?*
3. —— . . . . *anne ?*

(The *line* means that the first particle is omitted.)

Num is occasionally used for *utrum* where a negative answer is expected.

161. *An* is sometimes found before a single question. But there is always an *ellipsis,* or suppression of a previous question, so that *an* means "*or* is it that ?" "can it be that ?" and hence generally expects the answer "no."

> An *servi esse vultis ?* Or is it that you wish to be slaves ?

Answers to Questions.

162. The affirmative and negative answer is rarely given in Latin so simply as by the English "yes" and "no."

Sometimes "yes" may be turned by *etiam, ita vero ;* and "no" by *minime, nequaquam, non.*

But more often some emphatic word is repeated from the interrogative sentence ; such a question as *dasne hoc mihi ?* would be answered by *do ; do vero, ac libenter quidem*

(= " yes "): or by *minime ego quidem* (= " no "), much more often than by *etiam*, or *minime* simply.

> *Visne hoc facere?* velle se, nolle se, *respondit.* Are you ready to do this? he answered " *yes*," " *no*."
>
> *Num hoc fecisti?* Have you then done this? *Negat.* He answers " no." *Feci, inquit.* He answers " yes."

Sometimes *ait* is used as opposed to *negat*.

Exercise 20.

1. Is it possible for a true patriot to refuse to obey the law[1]? 2. Where, said he, did you come from, and whither and when do you intend[2] to start hence? 3. Can we help fearing that your brother will go away into exile with reluctance? 4. What crime, what enormity, has my client[3] committed, what falsehood has he told, what, in short, has he either said or done that you, gentlemen of the jury, should be ready to inflict on him either death or exile by your verdict? 5. Will any one venture to assert that he was condemned in his absence in order to prevent his pleading his cause at home, or impressing the jury by his eloquence? 6. Was it by force of arms, or by judgment, courage, and good sense, that Rome was able to dictate terms to the rest of the world? 7. Does it seem[4] to you that death is an eternal sleep, or the beginning of another life? 8. Are you ready to show yourselves men of courage, such as the country looks for in such a crisis as this? you answer " yes "; or are you ceasing to wish to be called Roman soldiers? " no," you all reply. 9. Do you believe that the character of your countrymen is altering for the better, or for the worse? 10. Whom am I to defend? whom am I to accuse? how much longer shall I pretend to be in doubt? was it (156) by accident or design that this murder was committed? 11. What am I to believe? that the enemy or that our men won the day yesterday? Do not tell more falsehoods on such[5] an important question. 12. Was he not a prophet of such a kind that no one ever believed[6] him?

---

[1] Ex. ix. p. 72, *note* 2.   [2] Fut. in -*rus*. (**14.** *c.*)
[3] Simply *hic*, this man *by me:* never *cliens.*   [4] See **43.**   [5] **88.**
[6] Use perf., not imperf. : the *fact* is summed up. (See **113.**)

EXERCISE XXI.

INTERROGATIVE SENTENCES—*Continued*.

II. Dependent or Indirect.

163. The **dependent question** is a *subordinate clause* introduced by an interrogative word (either a pronoun or conjunction), and connected by that interrogative word with the main clause.

Quis es? who are you? *cur hoc fecisti?* why have you done this? are direct questions, and each is a simple sentence.

But *rogo quis sit, I ask* who he is; dic mihi *cur hoc feceris, tell me* why you did this, are two compound sentences. Neither *taken as a whole* is a question : the first is a *statement*, the second a *command;* but each *contains* an indirect question, *i.e.* a subordinate substantival clause, answering to an accusative case after *rogo* and *dic*, introduced in the one case by the interrogative pronoun *quis*, in the other by the interrogative conjunction *cur*.

164. The Latin verb in such subordinate clauses is invariably in the subjunctive. It is of the utmost importance to remember this, as the subjunctive mood is no longer used in such clauses in English.

Compare the English and Latin moods in—

Quis eum occīdit? Who *killed* him?
Quis eum occīderit, quaero. I ask who *killed* him.

165. The dependent interrogative clause is recognised by an interrogative word introducing it (see list in **157**); but **the principal verb** or clause on which it depends **need not be at all of an interrogative character.**

Quid faciendum sit moneo moneboque. I *warn and will warn* you what you ought to do.
Quando esset rediturus metui. I *had fears* as to when he would return.
Cur haec fecerit miror. I *wonder* why he did this.

The words in the Latin marked in italics are *interrogative* clauses; for they are connected with the main clause by the interrogative pronoun *quid* and by the interrogative adverbs, used here as conjunctions, *quando* and *cur;* but neither *moneo, metuo,* nor *miror* are verbs of *asking*.

166. Thus the dependent question may follow not only a wide range of verbs but also many phrases, such as *incertum est ; incredibile est ; difficile dictu est* (it is hard to say) ; *magni refert* (it is of great consequence), and many others.

167. A dependent question in English is constantly introduced by the conjunctions " if " and " whether;" but *si* and *sive* are never used in Latin to introduce an interrogative clause.

" If " and " whether " are represented in a single indirect question by -*ne* and *num*, occasionally by *nonne.*

Num in the *indirect* question does not, as in the *direct*, imply the answer " no " (but *nonne* still suggests an affirmative answer).

> *Epaminondas quaesivit salvusne esset clipeus.* Epaminondas asked *whether* his shield *was* safe.
>
> *Dic mihi* num *eadem quae ego* sentias. Tell me *if* you *have* the same opinion as I.
>
> *Quaesieras ex me,* nonne putarem, *etc.* You had inquired of me *whether* I *did not* suppose, etc.

Disjunctive Interrogatives.

168. The form of the *disjunctive* question is very much the same in dependent as in independent questions. The important difference is the substitution of the *subjunctive* for the *indicative* mood.

Thus, utrum *servi* estis an *liberi ?* are you slaves *or* free men ? will be altered into, utrum *servi* sitis an *liberi, nihil refert;* it matters not *whether* you *are* slaves *or* free : and in the dependent clause we may substitute for *utrum . . . an* such forms as

> *Servine sitis,* an *liberi,*
> *Servi sitis,* an *liberi,*
> *Servi sitis, liberine,*

without any difference of meaning.

Obs.—" Or not," " or no " (*annon* in *direct*), should be turned by *necne* in *indirect* questions.

> *Iturus sit,* necne, *rogabimus.* We will ask *whether or not* he means to go.

169. Notice that *an* is in indirect, as in direct, questions confined to the second place, and answers to "or," which is never to be translated, when used interrogatively, by *aut, vel,* or *seu.*

In the phrases *haud scio* an, *forsitan* (*fors sit an*), there is a suppression of a first clause : "I know not," "it is a chance" (*whether something else is the case*), or *whether* (*rather*) . . . Both are equivalent to "perhaps," and both are followed by the *subjunctive.*

> *Difficile hoc est, tamen* haud[1] scio an *fieri possit.* This is difficult, yet *perhaps* (*I incline to think that*) it is possible.

But *nescio quis* (subs.), *nescio qui* (adj.), "Some one (or other) ;" *nescio quo modo,* or *quo pacto* (adv.), "Somehow," are taken as single words, and do not affect the mood of the verb; *accurrit* nescio quis, *some one* runs up. (See Pronouns, **362.**)

170. *Forte* is not "perhaps" but "by accident," and is only used for "perchance" after *si, nisi, ne.*

Forte *cecidit* is "he fell *by chance*," not "*perhaps* he fell."

Forte *abest,* "he is *accidentally* absent" (*indicative*).

Forsitan *absit,* "*perhaps, it may be that,* he is absent" (*subjunctive*).

Nescio, *or* haud scio an, *absit,* "*perhaps* (I incline to think that) he is absent" (*subjunctive*).

Fortasse *abest,* "*perhaps* (*it is likely that*) he is absent" (*indicative*).

171. The double use in English of "if," "whether," and "or," must be carefully borne in mind.

Si,[2] *sive, seu, aut,*[3] *vel,* must never be used as *interrogatives* in Latin.

(*a.*) You shall die *if* (conditional) you do this. *Moriere* si *haec feceris* (fut. perf. ind.).

(*b.*) I ask *if* (interrogative) you did this. Num *haec feceris* (subj.) *rogo.*

(*c.*) He shall go, *whether* he likes it *or* no (alternative condition). Seu *vult* seu *nonvult, ibit.*

(*d.*) I ask *whether* he likes it *or* no (alternative question). Utrum *velit* an *nolit rogo.*

(*e.*) He is *either* a wise man *or* a fool (disjunctive sentence). Aut *sapiens est* aut *stultus.*

---

[1] *Haud* is mostly used with *scio* and with adjectives and adverbs in the sense of "far from," when a negative idea is substituted for a positive, as *haud difficilis* for *facilis,* etc.

[2] For the special use of *si,* "in hopes that," after *expecto, conor,* and similar verbs, see Conditional Clauses, **474.**

[3] For the difference between *aut* and *vel,* see Intr. 57, note.

(*f.*) I don't know *whether* he is a wise man *or* a fool
Utrum *sapiens sit* an *stultus nescio.*

Obs.—In (*a.*) and (*c.*) "if," "whether," introduce *adverbial* clauses
merely qualifying the main clause by adding a condition (Intr. 82).
In (*e.*) "either," "or," introduce two *co-ordinate* sentences. In (*b.*),
(*d.*), (*f.*), "whether," "or," introduce *substantival* clauses, equivalent
in Latin to accusative cases after *rogo* and *nescio.*

Exercise 21.

1. Whether Caesar was rightfully put to death, or foully
murdered, is open to question; it[1] is allowed by all that
he was killed on the 15th[2] of March by Brutus and
Cassius and the rest of the conspirators. 2. It is still
uncertain whether our men have won the day or no; but
whether they have won or lost it, I am certain that they
have neither been false to their allies nor to their country.
3. It is hard to say whether he injured the world[3] or
benefited it most; it is unquestionable that he was a man,
alike in his ability (*abl.*) as in his achievements, such as
we are never (Intr. 92) likely to see in this world. 4. It is
scarcely credible how often you and I have advised that
(friend) of yours[4] not[5] to break his word; but it[6] seems
likely that we shall lose our labour to-morrow, as yesterday
and the day before. 5. Be sure you write me word when
the king intends[7] to start for[8] the army; he is perhaps
lingering purposely in order to raise an army and increase
his resources; I am afraid he will not[9] effect this,[10] for
people are either alarmed or disaffected. 6. Some one has
warned me not to forget how much you once injured me
in my boyhood: whether you did so (this) or no matters
little; what[11] is of importance to me is whether you
are ready to be my friend now. 7. As[12] he felt himself
sinking (*inf.*) under a severe wound, he asked first if his
shield was safe; they answered yes; secondly, if the
enemy had been routed; they replied in the affirmative.
8. They asked if it was not better to die than to live dishonourably. 9. He was the dearest to me of my soldiers,
and perhaps the bravest of (them) all.

---

[1] *Illud, i.e.* "the following."   [2] *Idibus Martiis.*   [3] **16,** *b*
[4] See **11,** *d.*   [5] See **118.**   [6] See **43.**   [7] **14,** *c.*   [8] *Ad.*
[9] See **138.**   [10] Relative.   [11] Lit., the following (*illud*).
is of importance.   [12] *Quum* with imperf. subj.

EXERCISE XXII.

DEPENDENT INTERROGATIVE—*Continued.*

Mood and Tense.—Interrogative Clauses for English Nouns.

172. Sometimes the Latin verb in the interrogative clause is already in the subjunctive; in this case no change will take place in the mood, even if we convert the *direct* into the *indirect* question.

> *Quid* facerem ? What was I to do ? (See **150**.)
> *Quid* facerem *dubitavi.*[1] I was at a loss what to do.

In such cases the *subjunctive* answers to the English *infinitive* after an interrogative word.

> *Quid* faciam, *quando* redeam, *dubito.* I am at a loss what *to do*, when *to return*.

173. The use of the *tenses* in (dependent) interrogative clauses will cause little difficulty.

(i.) The *perfect subjunctive* is exceedingly common to express simple past time in such clauses.

> *Quid causae* fuerit *postridie intellexi.* I perceived the day after what *was* the cause (lit. "for a cause").

(ii.) But the *imperfect* must be used if the time denoted by the dependent verb is strictly contemporaneous with that of the principal verb.

> *Quid* facerent *intellexi.* I perceived what they *were* doing. (See **185**.)

(iii.) As the only *future subjunctive* in Latin is that formed by the future in -*rus*, " I ask when he *will* return " is, *quando* sit rediturus *rogo;* " I asked when he would return " is, *quando* esset rediturus *rogavi.*

The future in -*rus* expresses also the ideas of *likelihood, intention,* etc. (See **14,** *c.*)

The following remarks require careful attention both in writing Latin and in translating from Latin.

---

[1] *Quid faciendum esset* would differ slightly as expressing less perplexity, and somewhat more of deliberation.

174. Dependent interrogative *clauses introduced* by *quis* (*qui*), *qualis, quantus, quot, quando, cur,* etc., are very often used in Latin where in English we use a single word, such as *nature, character, amount, size, number, date, object, origin, motive,* etc.

Latin does not use nearly so many *abstract terms* as English. Thus—

(*a.*) Quot *essent hostes,* cur[1] *advenerint,* quantas *haberent opes,* quando *domo profecti essent, rogavit* (note carefully the *tenses*). He asked the *number* of the enemy, the *reason* of their having come, the *magnitude* of their resources, the *date* of their departure from home.

(*b.*) Quale *ac* quantum *sit periculum demonstrat.* He explains the *nature* and *extent* of the danger.

(*c.*) Qualis *sit,* quemadmodum *senex vivat, videtis.* You see the *kind* of man he is, his *manner* of life in his old age. ('63.)

(*d.*) *Haec res* quo *evasura sit, expecto.* I am waiting to see the *issue* of this matter.

(*e.*) Quam *repentinum sit hoc malum intellego,* unde *ortum sit nescio.* I perceive the *suddenness* of this danger, its *source* I know not.

This is only one of the many instances where Latin prefers simple and direct modes of expression to the more abstract and general forms of noun with which we are familiar in English. (See **54.**)

175. For the same reason, as well as from a lack of substantives in Latin to express *classes* of persons, and also of verbal substantives denoting *agents,* such English substantives must often be translated into Latin by a relative or adjectival clause. Thus:—

"Politicians," *qui in republica versantur;* "students," *qui literis dant operam;* "my father's murderers," *qui patrem meum occiderunt;* "my well-wishers," *qui me salvum volunt;* "the government," *qui reipublicae praesunt;* "his predecessors on the throne," *qui ante eum regnaverant.*

For the use or omission of *ei* with this use of *qui* see **71.**

176. The difference between these two kinds of dependent clause, the *relative* (or adjectival) and the *interrogative,* will be marked by

---

[1] In indirect clauses *cur* may be used ; but *quare, quamobrem, quam ob causam,* are more common ; and *quemadmodum* almost always takes the place of *quomodo.*

the use of the *indicative* in the one, the *subjunctive* in the other. Thus—

> (*a.*) *Hi sunt* qui *patrem tuum occid*erunt.   These are your
>   father's murderers.

Here the relative *qui* introduces an *adjectival* clause, used, as adjectives sometimes are, as a substitute for a substantive.   (See **51**.)

> (*b.*) Qui *patrem suum occid*erint, *nescit*.   He knows not who
>   were his father's murderers.

Here the interrogative *qui* (pl. of *quis*) introduces one of the three kinds of substantival clause (Intr. 80), viz., the dependent question ; the mood therefore is the subjunctive.   (See **164**.)   So—

> (*a.*) Quae *vere* sentio *dicam*, I will *utter* my real sentiments ;

here *quae* is a relative :

> (*b.*) Quae *vere* sentiam *dicam*, I will *tell you what are* my real
>   sentiments ;

here *quae* is interrogative.

The substantival nature of the dependent interrogative will explain why it generally comes before the main clause.   (See Intr. 100.)

Exercise 22.

1. I am waiting to see what is the meaning of this crowd, what will be the issue of the uproar.   2. I wish[1] you would explain to me his manner of life in boyhood ; I know pretty well the kind of man that he is now.   3. We perceived well enough that danger was at hand ; of its source, nature, character, and extent, we were ignorant. 4. Do but reflect on the greatness of your debt to your country and your forefathers ; remember who you are and the position that you occupy.   5. I knew not (*imperf.*) whither to turn, what to do, how to inflict punishment on my brother's murderers.   6. The doer of the deed I know not, but whoever he was,[2] he shall be punished.   7. The reason of politicians not agreeing with the commanders of armies is pretty clear.   8. I wonder who were the bringers of this message, whether (they were) the same as the perpetrators of the crime or no.   9. He was superior to all his predecessors on the throne in ability ; but he did not perceive the character of the man who was destined to be his successor.   10. The government was aware of the suddenness of the danger, but they did not suspect its magnitude and probable[3] duration.

---

[1] **149**, i.   [2] Mood ? (See **153**.)   [3] **173**, iii.

EXERCISE XXIII.

REMARKS ON TENSES.

177. The Latin tenses are generally divided into **Primary** and **Secondary.**

(*a.*) **Primary** tenses are those in which the point of time taken as the standard by which we reckon is the *present*, the moment at which we are speaking :

(Simultaneous) *scribo,* " I write," "am writing," *at* the present moment.

(Past) *scripsi,* " I have written," *before* the present moment (true perfect).

(Future) *scribam,* " I shall write," *after* the present moment.

(*b.*) In **Secondary** tenses (called also **Historic,** from their constant use in history or narrative) the standard of comparison is some point in *past* time :

(Simultaneous) *scribebam,* " I was writing *contemporaneously with* some time in the past.

(Past) *scripseram,* " I had written," *before* some point in the past.

(Indefinite, or aorist) *scripsi,* " I wrote," at some time or other in the past.

Obs.—It will be seen that the Latin *scripsi* belongs to both divisions ; also that it is not easy to fix its place under (*b.*). It is sometimes explained as denoting an event that *follows something else* that happened in the past.

A third division might be introduced by taking as the standard of comparison a point in *future* time :—

(Simultaneous) *scribam,* " I shall *be writing.*"

(Past) *scripsero,* " I shall *have written.*"

(Future) *scripturus ero,* " I shall be *going to* write."

The Present.

178. The **Latin present tense** corresponds to two forms of the English present ; *scribo* = " I write," and also " I am writing."

179. As in English, but far more commonly in Latin, the *present* tense is often in an animated narrative substituted for the *past.*

This *Historical present* is often in the best Latin writers intermingled with past (aorist) tenses ; and is even followed as a historic tense by the imperfect subjunctive.

> *Subito* edicunt *Consules ut ad suum vestītum Senatores* redirent.
> The Consuls suddenly *publish* (=published) an edict, that the Senators *were to* return to their usual dress.

133

The present, when thus used, may be followed either by the *present subjunctive* (according to the general rule for the sequence of tenses or by the *imperfect subjunctive* (as being itself *virtually* a past tense). (See **104.**) The latter is quite as common as the former. In English we should either say "published," or alter "were to" into "are to."

180. In describing the past, the conjunction *dum*, "while," is constantly used with a *historical present* even when all the surrounding tenses are in past time.

> *Dum Romani tempus terunt, Saguntum obsidebatur.* While the Romans *were wasting* time, Saguntum was being besieged.

This idiom is almost invariable where the *dum*-clause represents, as here, a *longer period within which* the other event is comprised.

181. To express "*I have been doing a thing for* a long time," the Romans said, "*I am doing it* for a long time already." The Greeks and French have the same idiom.[1]

> *Jam pridem* (or *jampridem*) cupio. I *have* long *desired*.
> *Vocat me alio jam dudum* (or *jamdudum*) *tacita vestra expectatio.* Your silent expectation *has* for some time *been calling* me to another point

So also they used the Imperfect for our "had (long) been."

> *Copiae quas diu comparabant.* Forces which they *had* long *been collecting*.

182. The present is used sometimes, but far less widely than in English, in an *anticipative* sense for the future.

> *Hoc ni propere fit.* Unless this *is* done at once.
> *Antequam dicere incipio.* Before I *begin* to speak.

But see below (**190**).

The Imperfect.

183. This tense is used far more widely in Latin than the English compound tense "I was doing," etc.

It denotes a time contemporaneous with some period, or surrounding, as it were, some point, in past time, and hence it has various meanings.

It is the tense of *continuous* or *incomplete*, as opposed to *momentary*, or *completed* action.

---

[1] πάλαι λέγω ; Depuis longtemps je parle.

It is the tense of *description* as opposed to mere *narrative* or *statement*.

Thus it is often used to describe the circumstances, or feelings, which accompany the main fact as stated by the verb in the (aorist) perfect :—

> *Caesar armis rem gerere* constituit, videbat *enim inimicorum in dies majorem fieri exercitum,* reputabat*que,* etc.

We should use the same tense in all three verbs ; *resolved, saw, reflected ;* but the two last explain the *continued* feeling which accounted for the *single fact* of his decision.

184. For the same reason, the imperfect often expresses ideas equivalent to " *began to,*" " *proceeded to,*" " *continued to,*" " *tried to,*" " *were in the habit of,*" " *used to,*" " *were wont to,*" sometimes even to the English " *would.*" It must therefore often be used where we loosely use *the* (aorist) *past tense,* and we must always ask ourselves the precise meaning of the English past tense before we translate it.

> *Barbari saxa ingentia* devolvebant. The barbarians *began to* (or *proceeded to*) roll down huge stones.
>
> Stabat *imperator immotus.* The general *continued to* stand motionless (or *was seen to stand,* as if in a picture).
>
> *Haec fere pueri* discebamus. When we were boys we *used to* learn (or *we learned*) something of this kind.
>
> *Hujusmodi homines adolescens* admirabar. These were the men whom I admired (or *would admire*) in my youth.

185. This meaning of the imperfect extends to the subjunctive mood, and must be kept in mind in translating subordinate clauses.

" I asked why he did it " is generally *cur id* fecerit *quaesivi.* (See **173.**) But if we mean " why he *was doing it then*" we must say *cur id* faceret *quaesivi.*

It will also explain the difference between the imperfect and perfect subjunctive after *ut* consecutive. (See **113.**)

These different shades of meaning as regards past time are rarely distinguished in English.

186. What is called the *Historic Infinitive* is often used as a substitute for the imperfect, especially when a *series of actions* is described, and is always joined with the nominative.

> *Interim quotidie Caesar Aeduos frumentum,* . . . flagitare ; . . . *diem ex die* ducere *Aedui* . . . dicere, etc. (Caesar, *de B. G.* i. 16.) Meanwhile Caesar *was* daily *importuning* the Aedui for provisions ; they *kept putting* off day after day, asserting, etc.

The Perfect.

187. The **Latin perfect** represents two English tenses. (See 105, 177.) *Feci* is both " I did," and " I have done."

"I did" is the *preterite* or *aorist*. It is the ordinary tense used in simply narrating or mentioning a past event.

"I have done" is the true *perfect*, or tense of *completed action*. It represents an act as past in itself; but in *its result* as coming down to the present. "I *have been* young, and now am old." We should say of a recent event, with the result still fresh on the mind, " My friend has been killed ;" we should not say, " Cain has killed Abel."

In Latin the same word *dixi* may mean "I have spoken," *i.e.* "I have finished my speech," or "I spoke." *Vixerunt*, "they lived," or "they have lived," *i.e.* "are *now dead*."

The context will generally make it quite clear in which sense the Latin tense is used.

Obs.—The English auxiliary *am, are*, etc., with a passive verb, may mislead. "All *are* slain" may be either *occisi sunt*, or *occiduntur*, according to the context.

188. Sometimes the verb *habeo*, "I have," or "possess," is used, especially with verbs of knowledge, etc., in combination with a participle in a use approaching that of the English auxiliary "have."

Hoc compertum, cognitum, exploratum habeo. *I have* found out, ascertained, made sure of this.

Hunc hominem jamdiu notum habeo. I *have known* this man long.

Future.

189. Latin differs exceedingly from English in the use of the future. It has **three future tenses :**—*scribam, scripsero, scripturus sum.*

Fut. i. *Scribam* is properly, I shall *be writing* (*at* some time in the future).

Fut. ii. *Scripsero*, I shall *have written* (*before* some time in the future).

Fut. iii. *Scripturus sum*, I am *about* to, or *likely* to, write; *intending* to, etc. (See 14, *c*.)

Obs.—Fut. i. and iii. are both represented in the subjunctive mood by the future in *-rus*, Fut. ii. by the perfect subjunctive *scripserim*.

We must carefully distinguish between Fut. i. and ii. in all subordinate clauses where the principal verb is in the future.

190. A **Latin future** is constantly to be substituted for the English loosely-used present.

There was no true future in Old English, and we are obliged to use the auxiliaries *shall* and *will.* We still say, "I *return* home to-morrow," for "*cras domum* redibo," or "*rediturus sum.*"

(i.) An English *present* tense after *relatives,* or *"when," "if," "as long as," "before,"* etc., is to be translated by a *future perfect,* when the action expressed by it is still *future,* but *prior to* something still more future.

> *Si te* rogavero *aliquid, nonne respondebis?* If I *put* any question to you, will you not answer?
>
> *Quum Tullius rure* redierit, *mittam eum ad te.* When Tullius *returns* from the country, I will send him to you.
>
> *Quodcunque* imperatum erit, *fiet.* Whatever *is* ordered shall be done.

The Latin idiom is correct, as the one action must, though now future, be completed (future *perfect*) before the other begins.

(ii.) When the two actions or states are *simultaneous,* but still future, the Latin Future i. is used for an English present.

> *Dum hic* ero *te amabo.* As long as I *am* here I shall love you.
>
> *Facito hoc, ubi* voles. Do this when you *please.*
>
> *Tum, qui* poterunt, *veniant.* Then let those come who *have the power.*

Obs.—Sometimes the English perfect is used for the Latin future perfect.

> *Quae quum* fecero, *Romam ibo.* When I *have* done this, I shall go to Rome.

191. This **future perfect,** though rarely met with in the form "shall have" in ordinary English, is exceedingly common in Latin. It is sometimes found even in the principal clause as a substitute for the first future.

> Respiravero, *si te videro.* If once I *have* seen (*or* see) you, I *shall* breathe freely : lit. *shall have* breathed ; implying that the relief will be instantaneous.

For *videro, viderint,* see **146.**

Pluperfect.

192. The pluperfect does not differ materially from the corresponding English tense, " I *had* done, or seen," etc.

But it is used in Latin after relatives and conjunctions to denote *frequency* or *repetition* in past tense.

> *Quum eo* venerat, *loco delectabatur.* *As often as* he came there, he was charmed with the situation.
> *Quos* viderat *ad se vocabat.* *Whomever* he saw he summoned to him.

For the use of these *imperfects* see **184.**

Tenses of the Infinitive.

193. (i.) In the infinitive mood the *present* (*laudare,* etc.) answers to both the *present* and *imperfect* of the indicative.

It expresses time *contemporaneous* with that of the verb on which it depends.

> *Dico,* or *dixi, me otiosum* esse.   I say, *or* said, that I *am,* *or was,* at leisure.   (See **35.**)

(ii.) The *perfect* infinitive (*scripsisse*) answers to the *aorist perfect, true perfect,* and *pluperfect,* of the indicative.

It denotes time *prior* to that of the verb on which it depends.

> *Dico me otiosum* fuisse.   I say that I *was, have been, had been* at leisure.

The context must decide between the three meanings.

(iii.) The *future* infinitive is formed by the participle in *-rus.*

> *Dicit, dixit se* venturum esse.   He says, said, that he *will* or *would* come.

Where there is no participle in *-rus,* and in the passive voice, the periphrasis of *fore ut* must be used.

> *Spero* fore ut *convalescat,* fore ut *urbs capiatur.*   I hope that he *will* get well, that the city *will* be taken.
> *Speravi* fore ut *convalesceret,* fore ut *urbs caperetur.*   I hoped that he *would* get well, that the city *would be* taken.

(iv.) With *passive* verbs the place of the missing *future infinitive* is often supplied by the supine in *-um*, with the impersonal infinitive *iri.*

> *Credidit urbem* expugnatum iri. He believed (lit. that *there was a going* (Intr. 42) to take the city) that the city *would be* taken.

Urbem is governed by the supine which has an active force, and is itself the accusative of *motion to*, after *iri.*

(v.) A *potential* future infinitive is formed for past time, thus :—

> *Credo hoc te* facturum fuisse. I believe you *would have* done this.
> *Credo* futurum fuisse *ut urbs expugnaretur.* I believe the city *would have* been taken.

194. As these remarks are somewhat long, it will be well before doing the exercise to study very carefully the use of the tenses in the following examples on the most important constructions.

1. *Dum haec inter se* loquuntur, advesperascebat.
2. *Jamdiu te* expecto . . . expectabam.
3. Dixi, *judices; vos, cum* consedero, *judicate.*
4. *Signum pugnandi* datum est; stabant *immoti milites,* respicere, circumspicere; *hostes quoque parumper* cunctati sunt; *mox signa* inferre; *et jam prope intra teli jactum* aderant, *cum subito in conspectum* veniunt *socii.*
5. *Si mihi* pares, *salvus eris.*
6. *Si mihi* parebis, *salvus eris.*
7. *Si mihi* parueris, *salvus eris.*
8. *Si hoc* feceris, *moriere.*
9. *Veniam, si* potero.
10. *Si hostem videro,* vicero.
11. *Tui, dum* vivam, *nunquam obliviscar.*
12. *Quemcunque* ceperat *trucidari* jubebat.
13. *Polliceor me, quum haec* scripserim, *rediturum esse.*
14. *Pollicitus est se, quum haec* scripsisset, *rediturum esse.*

Obs.—In the two last examples the 2d future indicative is represented by the *perfect* and *pluperfect* subjunctive; these two tenses represent its force in the subjunctive mood after present and past time respectively.

Exercise 23.

A.

1. I have long been anxious to know the reason of your being so afraid of the nation forgetting[1] you.   2. Both my father and I had for some time been anxious to ascertain your opinion on this question.   3. When you come to Marseilles, I wish[2] you would ask your brother the reason of my having received no letter from him.   4. My speech is over, gentlemen, and I have sat down, as[3] you see of yourselves; do you decide on this question.   For myself, I hope, and have long been hoping, that my client will be acquitted by your unanimous[4] verdict.   5. While the Medes were making these preparations, the Greeks had already met at the Isthmus.   6. Up to extreme old age your father would learn something fresh daily.   7. As often as the enemy stormed a town belonging[5] to this ill-starred race, they would spare none; women, children, old men, infants, were butchered, without[6] any distinction being made either of age or sex.

B.

1. He promises to present the man[7] who shall be the first to scale the wall, with a crown of gold.[8]   2. When I have returned from Rome, I will tell you[9] why I sent for you.   3. The Gauls had long been refusing[10] either to go to meet our ambassadors, or to accept the terms which Caesar was offering.   4. Suddenly the enemy came to a halt, but while they[11] were losing time, our men raised[12] a cheer, and charged into the centre of the line of their

---

[1] **138.**   [2] See **149,** i   [3] See **67,** *Obs.*
[4] See **59.** The "your" may either agree with "verdict" or with "all."
[5] Genitive, = "of."
[6] Abl. abs., "no distinction made."   [7] See **72.**
[8] See **58.**   In English we may use either the genitive, or "golden," or turn "gold" into an adjective, by placing it before "crown."
[9] Of course dative : "you" is the remoter object of "tell."
[10] See **136,** *a.* *Nego* here, because their refusal was expressed in words.
[11] Use *illi*, to distinguish the enemy from our men.   (See **70.**
[12] Se **186.**

infantry.   5. The general had for some time seen that his men were hard pressed by the superior numbers of the enemy, who hurled darts, slingstones, and arrows, and strove to force our men from the hill.   6. I have done my speech, judges : when you[1] have given your verdict it will be clear whether the defendant is going to return home with impunity, or to be punished for his many crimes.

---

[1] *Vos,* to be placed first.   (See **11,** *a, b.*)

EXERCISE XXIV.

HOW TO TRANSLATE *Can, Could. May, Might, Shall, Must, etc.*

195. The ideas of **possibility, permission, duty, necessity,** are expressed in English by auxiliary verbs, "can," "may," "ought," "should," "must," etc. (Intr. 47.)

Obs.—These words have, in modern English, owing to their constant use as mere auxiliaries, ceased to be used as independent verbs. In Latin no verb has been reduced to this merely auxiliary state, though the verb *sum* is largely used as an auxiliary. (Intr. 49, *Obs.*)

The same ideas are expressed in Latin, partly (1) by the modal verbs (see **42**) *possum* and *debeo;* partly (2) by the impersonal verbs *licet, oportet, decet,* and the impersonal phrase *necesse est, fuit,* etc.; and largely (3) by the so-called participle in -*dus.*

N.B.—In all these cases the difference between the use of the tenses in Latin and English will require great care.

196. Possibility is expressed by the modal verb *possum.*
- (*a.*) *Hoc facere* possum, potero. I *can* do this (*now, or in the future*).
- (*b.*) *Hoc facere* poteram, potui, I *might have done* this (*past*).

Obs.—*Fecisse,* the literal translation of our "have done," would be quite wrong, for it would mean "*have finished* doing."

197. Permission is expressed by the impersonal verb *licet* with the *dative* and *infinitive.*
- (*a.*) *Hoc* mihi *facere* licet, *or* licebit. I *may* do this (*now or hereafter*).
- (*b.*) *Hoc* mihi *facere* licebat, licuit. I *might have done* this (*past*).

Here again notice *facere* in (*b.*).

Licet is also used occasionally with the subjunctive.

Hoc facias *licet.* You may do this. (See **126**.)

Obs. 1.—"*May*," "*might*," must be translated by *possum* or *licet* according as they mean " I have the *power*," or " have *permission.*"

Obs. 2.—A very common construction is :

Hoc tibi per me *facere* licuit. You might have done this, so far as *I was concerned*, or, *I should have allowed* you to do this.

Hoc per me *facias* licebit. I shall *leave you free* to do this.

198. To express **duty, obligation,** "ought," " should," etc., three constructions may be used :—

(i.) The personal verb *debeo.*

(*a.*) *Hoc facere* debes, debebis. You *ought* to do this, you *should* do this (*present* and *future*).

(*b.*) *Hoc facere* debuisti, debebas. You ought to, *or* should, *have done,* this (*past*).

(ii.) The impersonal verb *oportet*[1] with the accusative and infinitive.

(*a.*) *Hoc te facere* oport-et, -ebit.

(*b.*) *Hoc te facere* oport-ebat, -uit.

Obs.—*Oportet* is also used with the subjunctive.

Hoc faceres *oportuit.* You should have done this.

(iii.) (Commonest of all.) The *participle in -dus;* used either impersonally (*gerund*) with intransitive, or as an adjective (*gerundive*) with transitive verbs. (See Exercises XLIX. and L. on Gerund and Gerundive.)

The **person on whom the duty lies** is in the dative.

Gerundive—

(*a.*) *Haec tibi* facienda *sunt, erunt.* You ought *to do* this, (*present* and *future*).

(*b.*) *Haec tibi* facienda *erant, fuerunt.* You ought *to have done* this (*past*).

Gerund—

(*a.*) *Tibi* currendum *est.* You must run.

(*b.*) *Tibi* currendum *fuit.* You ought *to have* run.

---

[1] *Oportet* expresses a duty as binding *on oneself*; *debeo* the same duty, but rather as owed *to others,* "I am bound to," "under an obligation to." The participle in *-dus* includes both *duty* and *necessity*, and is far commoner than either *oportet* or *necesse est.*

199. To express **necessity**, use either, as above, the participle in -*dus*, which implies both *duty* and *necessity*—

(*a.*) *Tibi* moriendum est, erit, You *must* die, you will *have* to die ;

(*b.*) *Tibi* moriendum fuit, erat, You *had* to die ;

Or, more rarely and to imply *absolute* (properly *logical*) necessity.

(*a.*) *Tibi mori* (sometimes *moriare*) necesse[1] *est, erit.*

(*b.*) *Tibi mori* (sometimes *morerere*) necesse *erat, fuit.*

200. There are no words in Latin answering to the words "possible," "impossible," "possibility," "impossibility." They must be translated by substantival *clauses* subordinate to the impersonal phrase *fieri potest* with *ut* or *quin.* (See **125**, *e ;* **132**, *d.*)

There was *no possibility* of our escaping. Non fieri potuit *ut effugeremus.*

·It is *impossible* for us not to believe this. Non fieri potest *quin hoc credamus.*

Or by a personal use of *possum,*

Non *effugere* poteramus. Non possumus *hoc non credere.*

Obs.—*Potest* can be only used impersonally with passive and impersonal verbs. "It is possible to perceive this" is not "*hoc* intellegere *potest,*" but "*hoc* intellegi potest."

201. The case of the predicate after *licet* and *necesse est* should be carefully noticed.

Aliis licet ignavis *esse, vobis necesse est* viris fortibus *esse.* Others may be cowards, you must needs (*or* perforce) be brave men.

This is in accordance with the natural construction of link verbs. (See Intr. 71.)

202. The use of the infinitive mood with such impersonal verbs as *constat, apparet,* "it is evident" (not "it seems"), etc., has been pointed out (**46**, *c*).

It is also used with impersonals, denoting a *feeling* or *emotion.* Me *piget, pudet, taedet, delectat, poenitet,* mihi *libet.* Thus, *haec* me fecisse *pudet, poenitet, taedet.* I am ashamed, I repent, am weary, *of having done* this.

---

[1] *Necesse est* expresses either a purely logical necessity concerning things or ideas, in which case it takes the *accusative* and infinitive, *bis bina quattuor esse necesse est,* "twice two *must needs* be four ;" or the same idea of the inevitable as applied to a person, when it takes *dative* and infinitive, or subjunctive, *haec tibi pati,* (or *haec patiare*) *necesse est.*

Also with *pertinet ad, interest* and *refert,* "it is of importance," and with (*mihi*) *placet, videtur,* "it seems *good* that," (not *it seems that*). With the last two the *ut*-clause is also used.

Mitti *legatos,*
Ut mitterentur *legati,* { *senatui placuit, visum est.* It was resolved by, *or* it seemed good to, the Senate that ambassadors should be sent. (See **46**, *b.*)

Exercise 24.

1. We ought long ago to have listened to the teaching of so great a philosopher[1] as this. 2. Was it not your duty to sacrifice your own life and your own interests to the welfare of the nation? 3. The conquered and the coward (*pl.*) may be slaves, the asserters of their country's freedom must needs be free. 4. I blush at having persuaded you to abandon this noble undertaking. 5. You had my leave to warn your friends and relations not to run headlong into such danger and ruin. 6. It was impossible for a citizen of Rome[2] to consent to obey a despot of this kind. 7. You might have seen what the enemy was doing, but perhaps you preferred to be improvident and blind. 8. This (is what) you ought to have done; you might have fallen fighting in battle; and you were bound to die a thousand deaths rather than sacrifice the nation to your own interests. 9. Are you not ashamed of having in your old age, in order to please your worst enemies, been false to your friends, and betrayed your country? 10. Do[3] not be afraid; I shall leave you to come to Rome as often as you please; and when you come[4] there[5] be sure you stay in my house if you can. 11. Twice two must needs be four; it does not follow[6] that we must all consult always our own interest.

---

[1] 88, *Obs.* [2] 58. [3] 143. [4] Tense? (See **190**, i.
[5] For "and there" use "whither," *quo.* (See **78**.)
[6] *Non idcirco,* lit. "we must not for that reason."

EXERCISE XXV.

CASES.

General Remarks.

203. There is nothing in which Latin differs more from English than in what are called its *cases.*

By **Case** we mean such a change in the form of a noun (substantive, adjective, pronoun, or participle) as marks its relation to other words in a sentence.

204. These changes consist in the substitution of one *movable* and *variable termination* for another. Thus *Petrus Petro carus est*, Peter is dear *to* Peter ; *Petrus dominum secutus est*, Peter followed *his master.* We have here three different cases, *Petrus, Petro, dominum,* but the same change of meaning, which Latin represents by different terminations, *Petro, dominum,* we express in English,[1] not by a change in the termination of the word, but by introducing the preposition *to* in the one case, and by the order of the words in the other ; instead of saying *Petrus dominum secutus est*, we place Peter *before,* master *after,* the verb. (See Intr. 14.)

205. In Latin the order of the words will tell us little or nothing of the relation of a noun to the rest of the sentence ; the exact relation of the noun is marked by its case ; but as there are only six or at most seven cases, and the number of relations which language has to express is far greater than six or seven, the case-system is largely assisted by a great number of *prepositions*, which help to give precision and clearness to the meaning of the case.

206. The word " case" is an English form of a Latin word, *casus* (Gk. πτῶσις), used by grammarians to denote a *falling*, or deviation, from what they held to be the true or proper form of the word. The nominative was called, fancifully enough, the *casus rectus*, as that form of the word which stood *upright*, or in its natural position. The other cases were called *casus obliqui*, as *slanting* or falling over from this position ; and by *declinatio*, or " declension," was meant the whole system of these deviations, or, as we call them, *inflexions*.

---

[1] The English language once possessed, as German does still, a case-system ; but this only survives in the strictly *possessive* case, " Queen's speech," etc., and in certain pronouns *he, him ; who, whose, whom*, etc.

146

207. The Latin cases are six in number; the **Nominative, Accusative, Dative, Ablative, Genitive, Vocative.** Besides these there is a case, nearly obsolete in the classical period of Latin, the **Locative.**

208. (i.) The **Nominative** indicates the subject of the verb.

Without such subject, expressed or understood, a verb is meaningless. The nearest approach to the absence of a nominative is in such impersonal forms of intransitive verbs as *curritur*, "there is a running," *pugnatum est*, "there was fighting." (See Intr. 42.)

It was called the *casus nominativus*, as denoting the *name* of a person or thing—*Caesar, Roma, domus.*

209. (ii.) The **Accusative** completes the meaning of a transitive verb by denoting the immediate object of its action. Te *video*, I see *you*. (Intr. 37, 38.)

It was called the *casus accusativus*, interpreted as being that which we use to name a person whom we blame. But the original name (αἰτιατική) was probably given to it as denoting the αἰτία, or cause of the action of the transitive verb.

In English it is usually marked by following the verb, as the nominative by preceding it. "The sun illuminates the world;" "the world feels the sunlight."

In Latin it more often precedes the verb.

Its sense, possibly its earliest, of *motion towards* is still marked by its use after prepositions, implying this idea, *ad, in, sub*, and by its use with the names of towns to denote the same idea without a preposition: *Romam ibo*, I shall go *to* Rome.

It is used also as the subject of verbs in the infinitive mood, te *hoc dicere, "that you* should say this."

210. (iii.) The **Dative** is mainly used to represent the remoter object, or the person or thing *interested in* the action of the verb.

It was called the *casus dativus* (πτῶσις δοτική) as that used when we name a person *to whom* anything is *given*.

For the great importance and wide use of the Dative with intransitive verbs which are represented in English by verbs really or apparently transitive, see Intr. 36.

These three cases then, the *nominative, accusative,* and *dative,* are most intimately connected with the *verb,* as representing the one its *subject*, the other two the *objects* to which its action is *primarily* and *secondarily* directed.

211. (iv.) The **Ablative** is also closely connected with the verb, but in a different manner; it is an *adverbial* case, *i.e.* it is, like the adverb, an attendant on, or *satellite* of, the verb.   It gives further particulars as to the mode of action of the verb in addition to those supplied by its nearer and remoter object.   (See Intr. 16.)   Its functions are very wide, for it can express the *source, cause, instrument, time, place, manner, circumstances,* of the action of the verb, as well as the point *from* which *motion* takes place.

> Horā *eum* septimā *vidi.*   I saw him *at* the seventh hour.
> Ense *eum interfeci.*   I slew him *with* a sword.
> Romā *profectus* est.   He set out *from* Rome.

These are only three examples of the many and various senses in which this case is used. ·

It was called the *casus ablativus* (πτῶσις ἀφαιρετική) as indicating, among its other meanings, the person *from* whom anything is *taken;* or the place *from* which it is removed.

212. (v.) The **Locative** case (*locus*), answering to the question, *where ? at what place ?* remains, as distinct from the ablative, only in certain words.

> *Romae* (-ai), *at* Rome ; *Londini, at* London.

(Compare *ibi, ubi,* there, where ?)   It also is therefore an *adverbial* case.

213. All these cases then are closely connected with the verb.   The nominative sets, so to speak, the verb in motion : its movement is completed and directed by the other cases.

214. (vi.) The **Genitive**, on the other hand, is an attendant on *nouns* rather than on *verbs.*   The main use of a noun in the genitive is to define or qualify another noun (substantive, pronoun, adjective, or participle), to which it is closely attached, or of which it is predicated.

Compare " Gallos *vicit* " with " Gallorum *victor,*" " te *amat* " with " tui *est amantissimus.*"

Hence its extremely common use as a substitute for the adjective.

Vir summae virtutis = *vir* optimus.

Its use in combination with verbs (*memini, obliviscor, indigeo*) is quite exceptional.   (See **228**, *Obs.*)

It was called the casus *genitivus* as representing descent or race, regis *filius;* but the Greek πτῶσις γενική probably meant the *defining* case, that which added the γένος or class to which a word belonged. It was also sometimes called *possessivus*, sometimes *patricius:* Philippi *filius.*

215. (vii.) The **Vocative** case, *vocativus* (κλητική), is the form used in addressing a person : fili, *my son.*   As a mere *interjection* (Intr. 28) it does not affect the syntax of the sentence.

The Nominative.

216. There is no special difficulty in the syntax of the nominative.

The accusative after the active verb (the *object*) becomes the nominative (the *subject*) to the passive verb.

Brutus Caesarem *interfecit.*   Brutus killed Caesar.   But, Caesar *a Bruto interfectus est.*   Caesar was killed by Brutus. Urbem *obsidere coeperunt ;* urbs *obsideri coepta est.*

(With passive verbs the passive of the verb *coepi* is used.)

Obs.—It is often advisable in translating from Latin into English, and *vice versa*, to substitute one voice for the other.   Thus, to prevent ambiguity, "I know that Brutus killed Caesar" should be translated by *scio Caesarem a Bruto interfectum esse*, not by *Caesarem Brutum interfecisse.   Aio te, Aeacida, Romanos vincere posse* is an instance of oracular ambiguity, which should be carefully avoided in writing Latin.

217. It has been already explained that many English *transitive* verbs are represented in Latin by *intransitive* verbs, *i.e.* verbs which complete their sense, not by the aid of the *accusative*, but by that of the *dative*.   (See Intr. 36.)

The passive voice of such verbs can only be used *impersonally* (see 5) ; hence the *nominative* of an English sentence is often represented in Latin by the *dative,* combined with a passive verb used impersonally.

Nemini *a nobis nocetur.*   *No one* is hurt by us.

Puero *imperatum est ut regem excitaret.*   *The servant* was ordered to wake the king.

Tibi *a nullo creditur.*[1]   *You* are believed by no one.

Gloriae tuae *invidētur.*   *Your glory* is envied.

Obs.—The same impersonal construction is used in the passive with those intransitive verbs which complete their sense by a preposition and substantive.

Ad *urbem pervenimus.*   We reached the city.

Jam *ad urbem* perventum est.   The city was now reached.

218. This impersonal construction constantly represents the nominative of an English abstract or verbal noun.[2]

In urbe maxime trepidatum est.   The *greatest confusion* reigned in the city.

Ad arma subito concursum est.   There was *a sudden rush* to arms.

Acriter pugnatum est.   The *fighting* was *fierce.*

Satis ambulatum est.   We have had enough of *walking.*

Obs.—In such phrases the English *adjective* will be represented by a Latin *adverb.*

219. With this impersonal construction of the passive when used in the infinitive, *potest, potuit,* etc., are used impersonally (never otherwise, see **200,** *Obs.*) ; as also an impersonal passive form of some modal verbs, as *coeptum est, desitum est.*

Huic culpae ignosci potest.   It is possible to pardon this fault.

Resisti non potuit.   Resistance was impossible.

Jam pugnari coeptum (desitum) est.   The fighting has now begun (ceased).

220. The use of the nominative with the infinitive when combined with a modal verb has been pointed out: *otiosus esse cupio, debeo, incipio,* etc. (see **42**), I desire, am bound, begin, etc., to be at leisure. So also its use with *videor, credor, narror,* etc. : *videor, credor, dicor servus fuisse, it* seems, is believed, said, etc., *that I* was a slave. (See **43.**)

These points, as well as the indefinite and unexpressed nominative with impersonal verbs and such phrases as *credunt, dicunt,* etc. (**44**) have been already mentioned ; so that the following exercises will be mainly recapitulatory.

---

[1] *i.e.* "You are believed *in,* or *trusted,* by no one." *Credo* in this sense is intransitive and governs a dative ; in the sense of "I believe" or "think," it follows the usual construction of *verba sentiendi.* "You are believed by no one to have done this" would be *a nullo hoc fecisse crederis.* (See **43.**)   [2] See Intr. **42.**

Exercise 25.

A.

1. Your goodness will be envied.   2. Liars are never believed.   3. But for you[1] (*pl.*), do you not want to be free ?   4. Do not become slaves ; slaves will be no more pardoned than freemen.   5. It seemed that you made no answer to his[2] question.   6. So far from being hated by us, you are even favoured.   7. For myself,[3] it seems to me that I have acted rightly ; but you possibly take a different view.   8. I will ask which of the two is favoured by the king.   9. The fighting has been fierce to-day ; the contest will be longer and more desperate to-morrow.

B.

1. Thereupon a sudden[4] cry arose in the rear, and a strange[4] confusion reigned along[5] the whole line of march. 2. When I said "yes" you believed me ; I cannot understand why you refuse to trust my word when I say "no." 3. When[6] a boy I was with difficulty persuaded not to become a sailor, and face the violence of the sea, the winds, and storms : as an old man I prefer sitting at leisure at home to either sailing or travelling : you perhaps have the same views.[7]   4. You ought to have been content with such good fortune as this, and never (110) to have made it your aim to endanger everything by making excessive demands.[7]   5. So far from cruelty having been shown in our case, a revolt and rebellion on the part of our forefathers has been twice over pardoned by England.   6. It seems that your brother was a brave man, but it is pretty well allowed[8] that he showed himself rash and improvident in this matter.   7. It seems that he was the first of[9] that nation to wish to become our fellow-subject, and it is said that he was the last who preserved in old age the memory of (their) ancient liberties.

---

[1] "But for you," *Vos vero ;* "for" = "as for," and is simply emphatic. The emphasis is given in Latin by the *use* and place of *vos.*   (11, *a.*)
[2] To him questioning.   [3] *Equidem.*
[4] Adjectives will become adverbs.   (See **218**, *Obs.*)
[5] "Along" may be expressed by the ablative of place.
[6] See **63**.   [8] = agreed on.
[7] "Views," etc., not to be expressed. see **54**: cf. **91**.   [9] *ex.*

EXERCISE XXVI.

APPOSITION.

Apposition is not confined to the nominative; but it is more often used with the nominative and accusative than with other cases.

The general rule was given in **3**; see also **227**.

221. The substantive in apposition stands in the relation of an adjective to the substantive with which it is combined; in *Thebae, Boeotiae caput*, the words in apposition define *Thebes* by adding the special quality of its being *the capital of Boeotia*.

> *Te* ducem *sequimur.* We follow you *as*,[1] or *in the capacity of,* our leader.

Hence if the substantive be *feminine,* use the *feminine form,* whenever it exists, of the substantive *in apposition.*

> *Usus,* magister *egregius.* Experience, an admirable teacher.
> But—*Philosophia,* magistra *morum.* Philosophy, the teacher of morals.

222. Where a geographical expression, such as " city," " island," " promontory," is defined in English by *of,* with a proper name, apposition is used in Latin. Thus—

> *Urbs* Veii, the city *of* Veii; *insula* Cyprus, the island *of* Cyprus; *Athenas,* urbem *inclytam,* the renowned city *of* Athens.

Obs.—A similar explanatory " of " may be represented in Latin by the word *res* in apposition to another substantive.

> *Libertas,* res *pretiosissima.* The precious possession *of* freedom.

---

[1] We must always ask what *as* means. " We follow you as (= as *though*) a God " is, *te* quasi *Deum sequimur.*

223. Certain substantives are regularly used in apposition as adjectives.

> *Cum filio* adolescentulo. With a son *in early youth.*
> *Cum exercitu* tirone. With a *newly levied* army.
> Nemo [1] *pictor,* no painter ; always nemo (never *nullus*) *Romanus,* no Roman.

224. The Romans did not combine, as we do, an adjective of praise or blame with a proper name (rarely with a word denoting a person) unless by way of *cognomen* or *title,* as *C. Laelius Sapiens.*

They substituted *vir* (or *homo*) with an adjective, in apposition.

> " The learned Cato " is " *Cato,* vir *doctissimus.*"
> " Your gallant *or* excellent brother" is " *Frater tuus,* vir *fortissimus, optimus.*"
> "The abandoned Catiline" is " *Catilina,* homo *perditissimus.*" (See **57,** *a.*)

Obs. 1.—This appositional use of *vir* or *homo* with an adjective often supplies the place of the absent participle of *esse.*

> *Haec ille,* homo [2] *innocentissimus, perpessus est.* This is what he, *being (i.e. in spite of being)* a perfectly innocent man, endured.

Obs. 2.—Sometimes it represents our "*so* good, bad, etc., *as.*"

> *Te* hominem [3] levissimum, *or, te,* virum optimum *odit.* He hates so trifling a person, so good a man, as you ; *or* one so good, etc., as you.

225. The substantive or adjective is often used in apposition with an unexpressed personal pronoun.

> Mater *te appello.* I your mother call you ; *or* it is your mother who calls you.
> Omnes *adsumus.* All *of us* are here.
> Quot *estis?* How many *of you* are there ? Trecenti *adsumus.* "There are three hundred *of us* here." (See **297.**)
> *Hoc facitis* Romani. This is what *you* Romans do.

---

[1] *Nemo* is a substantive : *nullus,* which supplies *nemo* with genitive, ablative, and often dative, an adjective.

[2] The word in apposition generally follows, unless unusual emphasis is to be conveyed. *Rex* comes before the proper name as applied to hereditary kings, *pro rege Deiotaro.*

[3] *Homo* is "a human being" as opposed to an animal or a God : *vir,* "a man" as opposed to a woman or child. Hence *homo* is joined with adjectives of either praise or blame ; *vir* with adjectives of strong praise, *fortissimus, optimus,* etc.

226. The predicate agrees with the principal substantive unless that be the name of a town in the plural, when it naturally agrees with the singular word *urbs* or *oppidum*, etc., in apposition.   Thus—

> Brutus et Cassius, *spes nostra*, occiderunt.   Brutus and Cassius, our (only) hope, have fallen.
>
> But—Thebae, *Boeotiae caput, paene* deletum est.   Thebes, the capital of Boeotia, was nearly annihilated.

227. Single words are used appositionally in all cases ; phrases, *i.e.* combinations of words, only in the nominative and accusative ; in other cases, and with prepositions, a *qui*-clause is substituted.

Extincto Pompeio, quod *hujus reipublicae lumen fuit.*

Ad Leucopetram, quod *agri Rhegini promontorium est.*

Notice in each case the attraction of the relative to the gender of the predicate.   (See **83.**)

Exercise 26.

1. Philosophy, he says, was (**32**) the inventor of law,[1] the teacher of morals and discipline.   2. There is a tradition that Apiolae, a city of extreme[2] antiquity, was taken in this campaign.   3. It is said that your gallant father Flaminius founded in his consulship the flourishing colony of Placentia.   4. Do not, says he, I earnestly implore you, my countrymen, throw away the precious jewels of freedom and honour, to humour a tyrant's caprice.   5. The soldier, in spite of his entire innocence, was thrown into prison; the gallant centurion was butchered then and there. 6. There is a story that this ill-starred king was the first of his race to visit the island of Sicily, and the first to have beheld from a distance the beautiful city of Syracuse. 7. I should scarcely believe that so shrewd a man as your father would have put confidence in these[3] promises of his.

---

[1] See p. 72, n. 2.

[2] Use adjective "most ancient" for adjectival phrase (p. 17, *n.* 2, and see **214**).

[3] "In him making (*participle*) these promises." (**54.**)

ACCUSATIVE.

228. The **accusative** has been already defined as **the case of the direct** or **nearer object of the transitive verb.**

It may be said that the direct object of every such verb, including deponents and impersonals, is a word in this case, and in this only.

Te *video*, te *sequimur*, te *piget*, or *poenitet*.

Obs.—The apparent exceptions are not really exceptions. When we say that in Latin the words *parco*, I obey, *utor*, I use, *memini*, I remember, govern a *dative*, *ablative*, and *genitive* respectively, we really mean that the Romans put the ideas which we express by these three verbs into a different shape to that which we employ ; and that in neither of the three they made use of a transitive verb, combined with its nearer object. In the first case we say, " I obey *you ;*" they said, tibi *parco*, " I am obedient *to* you." In the second we say, " I use *you ;*" they said, *utor* vobis, " I serve *myself with* you." In the third we say, " I remember *you ;*" they said. tui *memini*, " I am mindful *of* you." In a precisely similar way, where the Romans said *te sequimur*, the Greeks said σοὶ ἑπόμεθα, " we are followers *to* you." They looked, that is, on the person followed as *nearly interested in*, but not, as the Romans did, as the *direct object of*, the action described by the verb (ἑπόμεθα).

229. Many intransitive verbs in Latin, as in English, become transitive, when compounded with a preposition. (See Intr. 24, and also **24.**)

This is especially the case with verbs that express some bodily movement or action ; often the compound verb has a special meaning.[1]

Urbem oppugno, expugno, obsideo, circumsedeo. I assault, storm, blockade, invest, a city.

Caesarem convenio, circumvenio. I have an interview with, overreach *or* defraud, Caesar.

---

[1] *Praestare*, when it means "to excel," is generally used with a dat., though sometimes with an acc. ; but with *se*, *praestare* is common as a factitive verb. (See **239.**) *Invictum se a laboribus* praestitit, he *showed* himself invincible by (*or* on the side of) toils.

Compare "I *outran* him," "I *overcame* him," etc.
Most of these verbs are used freely in the passive. *A te circumventus sum.* I was defrauded by you.

Obs.—Transducere, transjicere (trajicere) are used with a double accusative.

> Copias Hellespontum *transduxit.*
> Copiae Rhenum *trajectae sunt.*

So also—*Transjecto Rheno,* abl. abs.

230. Certain verbs of **teaching** (*doceo*), **concealing** (*celo*) **demanding** (*posco, flagito*), **asking questions** (*rogo, interrogo*), may be joined with two accusatives, one of the *person*, another of the *thing.*

> *Quis mūsicam* docuit *Epaminondam?* Who taught Epaminondas music?
> *Nihil nos* cēlat. He conceals nothing *from* us.
> *Verres părentes pretium pro sepulturā līberûm* poscebat. Verres used to demand *of* parents a payment for the burial of their children.
> *Meliora deos* flagito. I implore better things *of* the gods (**127**).
> *Racilius me primum* rogavit *sententiam.*[1] I was the first whom Racilius asked for his opinion.

231. But this construction is commonest with the neuter pronouns *hoc, illud, nihil;* otherwise *very frequently* (and with some verbs *always*) either the *person* or the *thing* is governed by a *preposition.*

Thus, though *doceo* always takes the accusative of the *person*, unlike *dico, narro,* etc. (tibi *hoc dico,* te *hoc doceo*), yet *doceo,* to give information, prefers the ablative with *de* for the *thing told.* After *peto* and *postulo, sometimes* after the other verbs of *begging,* the *person* is put in the *abl.* with *a:* and after *rogo, interrŏgo,* etc., the *thing* often stands in the *abl.* with *de.*

> *Haec* abs te *poposci.* I have made this request of you.
> De his rebus *Caesarem docet.* He informs Caesar of these facts.
> De hac re *te celatum volo.* I wish you kept in the dark about this.

---

[1] *Sententiam rogare* is a technical expression "to ask a senator for his opinion and vote," and the acc. is preserved in the passive: *primus* sententiam *rogatus sum,* "I was asked *my opinion* first."

But—Hoc te *celatum nolim.*   I should be sorry for you to be kept etc.

Aliud te *precamur.*   We pray you for something else.

But—*Haec omnia* a te *precamur.*   We pray for all these things from you.

Hóc *te rogo.*[1]   I ask you this question.

But—De hac re *te rogo.*   I ask you about this.   (See **127.**)

Haec a vobis *postulamus atque petimus.*   We demand and claim this of you.

232. Some verbs really intransitive are used occasionally in a transitive sense; such are *horreo* (oftener *perhorresco*), "I shudder," used for "I fear," and such figurative expressions as *sitio,* "I am thirsty," used as "I thirst *for,*" with accusative.   But these constructions are far commoner in poetry than in prose.   Compare—

Pars stupet *innuptae* donum exitiale *Minervae.*—VIRG.

233. The accusative after passive verbs of *the thing put on,* or of the *part affected,* is originally an accusative of the object combined with what is called in Greek a *middle* verb.

Longam *indutus* vestem.   Having *put on himself* a long garment.

Trajectus femur *tragula.*   *Having his* thigh *pierced* with a dart.

It is exceedingly common in poetry, both with participles and even with adjectives :—

Os *impressa toro,* with her face pressed upon the couch ;

Os humeros*que Deo similis,* like a God in face and shoulders ;

and is extended, with the aid of the *cognate accusative* (see **236**), into a general accusative of reference : as caetera *fulvus,* tawny *elsewhere.* But it is a rare construction in classical prose.

234. The accusative of the person is used after the impersonal verbs

> *Decet* atque *dedecet,*
> *piget, pudet, poenitet,*
> *taedet* atque *miseret.*

The last five are joined with a genitive of the cause or object of the feeling denoted.

Eum facti sui neque pudet neque poenitet.   He feels neither shame nor remorse for his deed.

---

[1] The verb "I ask" (a question), may be turned either by *rogo, interrogo,* with the accusative of the person, or by *quaero* with the prep. *ab, a : ex, e.*   "I asked him why," etc., may be turned either by *tum* eum *interrogavi cur* . . ., or by *tum* ab, *or* ex, eo *quaesivi cur.*

235. The accusative of *motion towards* is found mostly with prepositions, *ad, in, sub*, etc. ; it is also found as expressing the purpose of motion with the supine in *-um*, a verbal noun preserving its active force (see **402**) :—

Me has injurias questum *mittunt*, they send me to complain of these wrongs ;

Sperat rem confectum iri (see **193**, iv.), he hopes that the affair will be finished ;

also with certain phrases, as Venum *dare*, to sell ; infitias *eo*, I deny ; and with the accusative of motion to a *town, small island*, and the words *domum* (home), *rus, foras* (out of doors), etc. (See below, **313**.)

Exercise 27.

1. As the army mounted up the highest part of the ridge, the barbarians attacked its flanks with undiminished vigour. 2. I have repeatedly warned your brother not to conceal anything from your excellent father. 3. You ought to have been the first to have encountered death, and to have shown yourself the brave son of a gallant father, not to have been the first to have been horrified at a trifling danger. 4. If Caesar leads (**190**, i.) his troops across the Rhine there will be the greatest agitation throughout the whole of Germany. 5. Our spies have given us much information as to the situation and size of the citadel; it seems that they wish to keep us in the dark as to[1] the amount and character of the garrison. 6. Having [2] perceived that all was lost, the general rode in headlong flight past the fatal marsh (*pl.*), and reached the citadel in safety. 7. In order to avoid the heavy burden of administering the government he pleaded his age and bodily [3] weakness. 8. Many have coasted along distant lands; it is believed that he [4] was the first to sail round the globe. 9. I should be sorry for you to be kept in the dark about my journey, but this request I make of you, not to forget me in my absence. 10. About part of his project he told me everything ; the rest he kept secret even from his brother.

---

[1] "What is the amount," etc.   (See **174**.)

[2] See **14**, *a*.   [3] See **59**.

[4] "He" is emphatic = "this man" (*hic*).

ACCUSATIVE II.

Cognate and Predicative.

236. Another use of the accusative is called the **Cognate** accusative.

Even intransitive verbs such as "I run," "I live," denote some *action*. The result, or range, of this action, added to define the meaning more clearly, is sometimes treated as a *direct object* to the verb, and placed in the accusative case.

Hunc cursum *cucurri.* I ran this race.
Multa proelia *pugnavi.* I have fought many battles.

Thus we say in English, "I struck him *a blow.*"

It is called the cognate accusative because the substantive is either in form or meaning kindred (*cognatus*) to the verb.

237. The substantive when so used has generally, not always, an adjective or its equivalent attached to it.

Longam vitam *vixi.* Long is the life I have led.
Has *notavi* notas. I set down these marks.

But its commonest use in prose is with neuter pronouns, *hoc, illud, idem,* and with neuter plural adjectives, as *pauca, multa,* etc., and the word *nihil.* Hoc *laetor,* illud *glorior* (instead of, hac re *laetor,* de illa re *glorior*), "this is the meaning of my joy;" "this is my boast." So—

Illud *tibi assentior,* in this I agree with you. Nihil *mihi succenset,* he is in no way angry with me. Idem *gloriatur,* he makes the same boast. Multa *peccat,* he commits many sins. (See 54.)

With these verbs the accusative of a substantive could not be used.

238. This accusative is the origin of many constructions :—

(i.) The adverbial use of *multum, minimum, nescio quid, quantum.*

(ii.) The *poetical* use of the neuter singular and plural of many adjectives : dulce *ridentem,* sweetly smiling ; and even in prose : majus *exclámat,* he raises a louder cry.

(iii.) Such adverbial expressions as id *temporis,* at that time ; *cum* id aetatis *puero,* with a boy of that age ; tuam vicem *doleo,* I grieve for your sake.

(iv.) It is no doubt the origin of the accusative of *space,* of *time,* and of *distance.* Tres annos *absum,* I have been away *for* three years ; tria millia (*passuum*) *processi,* I advanced three miles.

239. The **Predicative**[1] accusative is quite different from the cognate. It is an additional accusative necessary to complete the meaning of a large class of transitive verbs, which in the passive are little more than link verbs, and have therefore the same case before and after them. (See Intr. 49.)

Ego mater tua *appellor.* I am called your mother.
Me matrem tuam *appellant.* They call me your mother.

These verbs, as "containing the idea of *making* by deed, word, or thought,"[2] are called *factitive* verbs.

Me consulem creant. They make me consul.
Se virum bonum praestitit. He proved himself a good man.

240. To this belong such phrases as

Haec res me sollicitum habuit. This made me anxious.
Mare infestum habuit. He infested, *or* beset, the sea.
Haec missa facio. I dismiss these matters.

And even such uses as—

Hoc cognitum, compertum, *mihi* persuasum, *habeo.* I am certain, assured, convinced of this. (See **188.**)

Obs. 1. We may compare the accusative after *volo* in such phrases as *te* salvum *volo,* I wish for your safety ; *tibi* consultum *volo,* I wish your good consulted, where the link verb *esse* is rarely found.

---

[1] The *exclamatory* use of the accusative may be classed under the head of the predicative,—*miserum hominem! O spem vanissimam!* "wretched that he is !" "how vain the hope !" It may be compared with a similar use of the infinitive, —*te,* sometimes *te-ne, hoc* dicere !

[2] Dr. Kennedy's Latin Grammar.

Obs. 2.—In place of this accusative other phrases are common. [Verbs of *thinking*, etc., are rarely treated as factitive verbs.]

I consider you *as my friend.　Te* amicorum in numero *habeo.*
I look on this *as certain.　Hoc* pro certo *habeo.*
I behaved *as a citizen.　Me* pro cive *gessi.* (See **221** and *note.*)

241. The English verb " I show " is used in a sense which cannot be expressed in Latin by *monstro* or *ostendo.*
" He *showed* himself a man of courage," or " he *showed* courage " is *virum fortem se praestitit,* or *praebuit;* or *fortissime se gessit;* or *fortissimus extitit.*

Exercise 28.

Before doing this Exercise read carefully **54**; also, for the different senses of " such," **86**.

1. And perhaps he is himself going to commit the same fault as his ancestors have repeatedly committed. 2. He makes many complaints, many lamentations; at this one thing he rejoices, that[1] you are ready to make him your friend. 3. For myself, I fear he will keep the whole army anxious for his[2] safety, such is his want of caution and prudence. 4. England had long covered the sea with her fleets; she now ventured at last to carry her soldiers across the Channel and land them on the continent. 5. The rest of her allies Rome left alone; the interests of Hiero, the most loyal of them all, she steadily consulted. 6. Whether he showed himself wise or foolish I know not, but a boy of that age will not be allowed to become a soldier; this at least I hold as certain. 7. This is the life that I have led, judges; you possibly feel pity for such a life; for myself I would[3] venture to make this boast, that I feel neither shame,[4] nor weariness, nor remorse for it. 8. He behaved so well at this trying crisis that I hardly know whether to admire his courage most or his prudence.

---

[1] See **41,** *b.*　　[2] **11,** *e.*　　[3] See **149,** i.　　[4] **234.**

EXERCISE XXIX.

DATIVE.

I. Dative with Verbs.

242. The general meaning of the **Dative** has been explained above (**210**). It expresses the person or thing *interested in,* or *affected by,* the state or action described by the verb, otherwise than as the direct object.

As the accusative answers the question, *whom? what?* so the dative answers the question, *to* or *for* whom or what?

243. In English the difference is often obliterated. "He built *me* a house;" "he saddled *him* the horse;" "I paid *them* their debt;" "I told *him* my story"—are equally correct sentences with "He built a house *for* me;" "I told my story *to* Caesar." etc. **In translating therefore into Latin we must look to the meaning rather than to the form of the word,** and use the dative of the *recipient,* or *person affected,* with verbs of *giving, telling* (except *doceo*), and even with those of *taking away.*

> *Multa* ei *pollicitus sum.*   I have made *him* many promises.
> *Poenas* mihi *persolvet.*   He shall pay *me* the penalty.
> *Omnia* nobis *ademisti.*[1]   You have taken *from us* everything.

244. A very large number of verbs which in English are, or appear to be, transitive, are in Latin intransitive, and complete their meaning not by an accusative but by a dative. (See **228**, *Obs.*) Such are—

(*a.*) Verbs of **aiding, favouring, obeying, pleasing, profiting,** etc.

> *Opitulor, subvenio, faveo, studeo, pareo, obedio, placeo, prosum.*

---

[1] Compare the French *arracher à,* "to tear *from.*"

(*b.*) Verbs of **injuring, opposing, displeasing.**

Noceo, adversor, obsto, repugno, displiceo, etc.

(*c.*) Verbs of **commanding, persuading, trusting, distrusting, sparing, envying, being angry.**

> *Impero, praecipio, suadeo, fido, diffido, parco, ignosco, invideo, irascor, succenseo,* etc.

(*Confido* takes dative of *person*, ablative of *thing* relied on.)

> *Fortibus* favet *fortuna.* It is the brave whom [1] fortune *favours.*
>
> *Haec res omnibus hominibus* nocet. This fact *injures* the whole world.
>
> *Legibus* paruit *consul.* He *obeyed* the law in his consulship.
>
> *Victis victor* pepercit. He *spared* the vanquished in the hour of victory.
>
> *Non tibi sed exercitu meo* confisus sum. It was not on you but on my army that *I relied.*

Obs.—It has already been said that these verbs must be used impersonally in the passive.

> *Mihi repugnatur.* I am resisted.
> *Tibi diffiditur.* You are distrusted. (See **217.**)

245. But certain verbs of this class are transitive in Latin also.

> *Juvo, adjuvo ; delecto ; laedo, offendo :*
> *Jubeo, hortor ; veto, prohibeo ; rego, guberno.*

Libris me delecto. I amuse myself with books.
Offendit *neminem.* He offends nobody.
Haec laedunt *oculos.* These things hurt the eye.
Fortuna fortes adjŭvat. Fortune helps the bold.

246. The impersonal verbs *accidit, contingit, expedit, libet, licet, placet,* are joined with a dative, not, as *oportet,* and those enumerated in **234,** with an accusative.

> *Hoc* tibi *dicere libet.* It is your pleasure, suits your fancy, to say this.

---

[1] See **156,** *Obs.*

247. Many Latin verbs require, to complete their sense, both an accusative and a dative, arranged however in a way quite different to that of nouns joined with the corresponding verb in English.

> Mortem mihi *minatus est.*   He threatened me *with* death.
> Pecuniam nobis *imperavit.*   He ordered us *to supply,* or exacted from us, money.
> Frumentum iis *suppeditavit.*   He supplied them *with* corn.
> Vitam vobis *adimunt.*   They are robbing you *of* life.
> Facta sua nulli *probavit.*   He won no one's approval *for* his acts.
> Hanc rem tibi *permisi* or *mandavi.*   I intrusted you *with* this.
> Haec peccata mihi *condonavit.*   He pardoned me *for* these offences.

248. Many transitive Latin verbs, as *metuo, consulo, caveo, prospicio, credo,* etc., are also used intransitively with a dative in a different sense to that which they bear with the accusative.

Compare, te *metuo, timeo,* with *nihil* tibi *metuo,* etc., I have no fears for you. Te *consulo,* I ask *your opinion;* tibi *consulo,*[1] I attend to, consult, *your interests.* Te (or *a te*) *caveo,* I am on my guard *against* you; tibi *caveo,* I am taking care *for your interests.* Tempestatem *prospicio,* I *foresee* a storm; saluti tuae *provideo,* I provide *for your safety.* Te *credo hoc fecisse,* I believe you to have done this; tibi *hoc* facienti *credo,* I believe you (trust you) while you do this. Culpā *văcat,* he is *free from* crime; philosophiae *văcat,* he *has time for* (he studies) philosophy.

249. *Tempero* and *moderor* in the sense of "to govern" or "direct" have the *accusative;* when they mean "to set limits to" they have the *dative. Temperare ab* aliquā re is "to *abstain* from," and hence (also with the dative), "to *spare.*"

> Hanc civitatem *leges moderantur.* This state is *governed* by law. (**216,** *Obs.*)
> *Fac* animo *modereris.* Be sure you *restrain* your feelings, or temper.
> Ab inermibus *or* inermibus (dative) *temperatum est.* The unarmed were spared. (The past participle of *parco* is rare.)

---

[1] A very common phrase is *tibi consultum* or *cautum volo.* (See **240,** *Obs.* 1.)

250. *Dono, circumdo,* and some other verbs, take either a *dative* of the *person* and an *accusative* of the *thing*, or an *accusative* of the *person* and an *ablative* of the *thing*.

> *Circumdat* urbem muro ; or, *circumdat* murum urbi. He surrounds the city with a wall.
>
> Ciceroni immortalitatem *donavit ;* or, Ciceronem immortalitate *donavit.* (The Roman people) conferred immortality on Cicero.

So *induit* se veste, *or* vestem sibi *induit* (*exuit*), he puts on (or off) his dress.

Exercise 29.

A.

1. I have long been warning you whom it is your duty to guard against, whom to fear. 2. I know that one so good as[1] your father will always provide for his children's safety. 3. It is impossible[2] to get any one's approval for such[3] a crime as this. 4. On my asking[4] what I was to do, whether and how and when[5] I had offended him, he made no reply (25). 5. Is it[6] your country's interest, or your own that you (*pl.*) wish consulted ? 6. I pardoned him for many offences; he ought not to have shown such cruelty toward you. 7. In his[7] youth I was his opponent; in his age and weakness I am ready to assist him. 8. I foresee many political storms, but I fear neither for the nation's safety nor for my own.

B.

1. It is said that he wrenched the bloody dagger from the assassin, raised[8] it aloft, and flung it away on the ground. 2. Do not (*pl.*) taunt with his lowly birth one who has done such good service to his country. 3. It matters not whether[9] you cherish anger against me or not; I have no fears for my own safety; you may[10] henceforth threaten me with death daily, if you please.[11] 4. You

---

[1] See **224**, *Obs.* 2.   [2] See **125**, *e, f.*   [3] **88**, *Obs.*
[4] "To me asking," *participle.*   [5] Why not *quum ?* (See **157**, ii.)
[6] See **156**.   [7] **63**.   [8] Participle passive. (**15**.)
[9] See **168**.   [10] Future of *licet.* (See **197**.)   [11] See **190**, ii.

were believed, and must have[1] been believed, for all were agreed (*imperf.*) that you had never broken your word. 5. He complained that the office with which the nation had just intrusted[2] him had not only been shared with others, but would be entirely taken away from him, by this law.   6. You have deprived us of our liberties and rights in our absence (61), and perhaps to-morrow you intend[3] to wrench from us our lives and fortunes.   7. The soldiers were all slain to a man, but the unarmed were spared.[4] 8. We are all of us[5] ignorant of the reason[6] for so gentle a prince as ours exacting from his subjects such enormous quantities of corn and money.   9. He never spared any one[7] who had withstood him, or pardoned any who had injured him.   10. I have always wished your interests protected; but I did not wish one so incautious[8] and rash as you consulted on (*de*) this matter.

---

[1] Use participle in -*dus*. (199.)   [2] Mood?   (See 77.)
[3] 14, *c.*   [4] See 249.   [5] See 225.
[6] See 174, *a.*   [7] Use *nemo unquam.*   (See 110.)
[8] Use *incautus* (224, *Obs.* 2).

EXERCISE XXX.

DATIVE—*Continued.*

II. Dative with Verbs.

251. The verb *sum* can of course never be trarsitive, and therefore its sense is naturally completed by the dative; we can say,

> Erat ei *domi filia, he had* a daughter at home;·

and most of its compounds, ad*sum*, de*sum*, inter*sum*, ob*sum*, prae*sum*, pro*sum*, super*sum*, are joined with a dative.

> Mihi *adfuit*, his rebus *non interfuit.* He gave me the benefit[1] of his presence, he took no part in these matters.

Obs.—Insum is oftener than not followed by the preposition *in*, *absum* by *a, ab*.

252. The dative is used with a very large number of verbs compounded with prepositions, such as—

> *ad, ante, cum (con-),*
> *in, inter, ob,*
> *post, sub,* and *prae.*

Also with the adverbs *bene, satis, male.* These verbs may be divided into four classes.

253. (i.) Many are intransitive and take the dative alone.

As, among many others—

> *Assentari*, to flatter; im*minere*, to hang over, threaten (*intrans.*); con*fidere* (see **282**, *Obs.*), to trust in; in*stare*, in*sistere* (sometimes with *acc.*), to press on, urge; inter*cedere*, to put a veto on; ob*stare*, re*pugnare*, to resist; oc*currere*, *obviam ire*, to meet; ob*sequi*, to comply with; satis*facere*, to satisfy; male-*dicere*, to abuse. (See **244**.)

---

[1] A very common meaning of *adsum* with dative, "I am at hand *to aid.*"

137

(ii.) Others are transitive, and complete their meaning with both the accusative and the dative.

> Te illi *posthabeo.*   I place you behind him (=illum tibi *antepono*), I prefer him to you.
> Se periculis *objecit.*   He exposed himself to dangers.
> Mortem sibi *conscivit.* } He committed suicide, "laid violent
> Vim sibi *intulit.*   } hands on himself."
> Te exercitui *praefecerunt.*   They have placed you at the head of the army.
> Bellum nobis *indixit, intulit.*   He declared, he made, war against us.

(iii.) Some are simply transitive verbs and take the accusative.   (See **229.**)

> Ad*ūlari*, to fawn upon ; *aversari*, to loathe ; at*tingĕre*, to touch lightly ; al*loqui*, to speak (kindly) to ; ir*ridēre*, to deride (sometimes dat., as also *adūlari*).

(iv.) Others require a preposition, in place of the dative.

> *Haec res* ad me (*never* mihi) *pertinet*, or *attinet*.   This concerns *me.*
> *Hoc* mecum *communicavit.*   He imparted this *to me.*
> Ad scelus *nos impellit.*   He is urging us *to crime.*
> Ad urbem *pervenit.*   He reached *the city.*
> In rempublicam *incumbere.*   To devote one's-self *to the nation, or* the national cause.

No universal rule can be given, and the usage of Latin authors must be carefully watched.

Exercise 30.

1. Possibly one so base as you[1] will not hesitate to prefer slavery to honour.   2. He says[2] that as a young man he took no part in that contest.   3. He promises never to fail his friends.   4. To my question who was at the head of the army he made no reply.   5. All of us know well the baseness of failing[3] our friends in a trying crisis.   6. I pledge myself not to be wanting either[4] to the time, or to the general, or to the opportunity; but possibly fortune is opposing our designs.   7. It is said that Marcellus wept over the fair city of Syracuse.[5]

---

[1] **224,** *Obs.* 2 ; *tu* should be expressed.   (See **334,** ii.)
[2] See **33.**
[3] See **94, 95.**
[4] "Either," "or," after *not* will be *neque.*
[5] See **222.**

8. For myself, I can scarcely believe[1] that so gentle a prince as ours could have acted so sternly. 9. In the face of these dangers which are threatening the country, let all of us devote ourselves to the national cause. 10. It concerns his reputation immensely for us to be assured whether he fell in battle or laid violent hands on himself. 11. You ought to have gone out to meet your gallant brother; you preferred to sit safely at home. 12. I would fain know whether he is going to declare and make war on his country, or to sacrifice his own interests to the nation. 13. To prevent his urging others to a like crime I reluctantly laid the matter before the magistrates. 14. He never consented either to fawn upon the powerful, or to flatter the mob; he always relied on himself, and would[2] expose himself to any danger. 15. Famine is threatening us daily; the townsmen are urging the governor to surrender the city to the enemy; he refuses[3] to impart his resolution to me, and I am at a loss what to do.

---

[1] **149,** i.   [2] Imperfect.   (See **184.**)   [3] See **136,** *a.*

DATIVE—*Continued.*

III. The Dative with Adjectives and Adverbs.

254. The dative is used not only with *verbs*, but also with **adjectives** (and even **adverbs**), to mark the person or thing *affected by the quality* which the adjective denotes.

Such are adjectives which signify *advantage, likeness, agreeableness, usefulness, fitness, facility*, etc. (with their *opposites*). So—

> *Res* populo[1] *grata.* A circumstance pleasing to the people.
> *Puer* patri *similis.* A child like his father.
> *Consilium* omnibus *utile.* A policy useful to all.
> *Tempora* virtutibus *infesta.* A time fatal to virtues.
> Convenienter naturae *vivendum est.* We should live agreeably to nature.

In all these cases the dative answers the question, *to* or *for* whom, or what? and the English will be a sufficient guide.

255. But the construction is not invariable.

Thus, *similis* takes the genitive of a *pronoun*, and usually of a *person* ("the counterpart," or "in the likeness," *of*). So—

> Pompeii, tui, *similis.* Resembling Pompey, *or* you.
> Veri *simile.* Probable.
> *Nulla res similis* sui *manet.* Nothing remains like itself.

So also—*Hoc quidem vitium non proprium* senectutis *est.* This vice is not the special property of old age.

Obs.—Many of these take different constructions : *utilis, aptus, idoneus,* ad *rem ; benevŏlus* erga, or in, *aliquem ; alienus* ab *aliquā re : assuetus, assuefactus,* "accustomed to," are joined with the ablative, *insuetus* with the genitive.

256. *Aequalis, affīnis, vicīnus, finitimus, propinquus, amicus, inimicus,* when used as *substantives*, are joined with the genitive, or a possessive pronoun (*meus, tuus,* etc.).

---

[1] Or *in vulgus ;* the form *vulgo* is only used as an adverb.

Propior, nearer, *proximus*, nearest, take the *dative*, but sometimes the *accusative*, especially in their literal sense. Their adverbs *prope, propius, proxime*, take the accusative.

> *Hi homines* prope te *sedebant.* These men were sitting near you.

Thus, nobis *vicini*, "near us," but, *vicini* nostri, "*our* neighbours;" *Ciceron-is* or *-i inimicissimi*, Cicero's worst foes.

The construction therefore varies according as they are regarded as adjectives or substantives. (See **55**.)

Exercise 31.

1. I could not doubt that falsehood was most inconsistent with your brother's character. 2. All of us are apt to love those[1] like ourselves. 3. I fear that in so trying a time as[2] this so trifling a person[3] as your friend will not be likely to[4] turn out like his illustrious father. 4. This[5] circumstance was most acceptable to the mass of the people, but at the same time[6] most distasteful to the king. 5. He had long been an opponent of his father's policy, whom in (*abl.*) almost every point he himself most closely resembled. 6. He was both a relation of my father and his close friend from boyhood; he was also[6] extremely well disposed to myself. 7. For happiness, said he, which[7] all of us value above every blessing, is common to kings and herdsmen, rich and poor. 8. To others he was, it seemed,[8] most kindly disposed, but he was, I suspect,[8] his own worst enemy. 9. He is a man far removed from all suspicion of bribery, but I fear that he will not be acquitted by such an unprincipled judge as this. 10. It was, he used to say,[9] the special peculiarity of kings to envy men[10] who had done[11] them[12] the best service.

---

[1] See 346.	[2] 88, *Obs.*	[3] 224, *Obs.* 2.	[4] 139.
[9] Relative. (See 78.)	[6] *Idem.*	[7] 95, *Obs.*	[8] 32, *b*, and 43.
Tense? (184.)	[10] 72.	[11] Mood? (See 77.)	[12] *se.* (See 349.)

DATIVE—*Continued.*

IV. Special Uses of the Dative.

257. The following idiomatic uses of the dative should be carefully noticed.

The dative is used where we should use a *possessive pronoun* or the *genitive.*

It thus gives *greater prominence* to the person mentioned.

> *Tum* Pompeio *ad pedes se projecere.* Then they threw themselves at *Pompey's* feet.
> *Hoc* mihi *spem minuit.* This lowered *my* hopes.
> *Gladium* ei *e manibus extorsit.* He forced the sword out of *his* hands.
> *Hoc* omnibus *est in ore.* This is on *every one's* lips.

258. The dative of the person interested is sometimes used where we should use the preposition " by," answering to the ablative of the agent

(i.) It is joined with the participle in *-dus,* when used to imply duty or necessity. The person on whom the duty lies is in the dative. (See **198,** iii.)

> *Hoc* tibi *faciendum fuit.* " This ought to have been done *by* you."

(ii.) The dative is used with other passive participles where the agent is looked on rather as the *person interested* than as the actual *agent ;* especially with verbs of *seeing, thinking, hearing, planning,* etc.

> *Haec omnia* mihi perspecta *et* considerata *sunt.* All these points have been studied and weighed *by* me, lit. *for me, in my eyes.*
> *Hoc mihi* probatum *ac* laudatum *est.* This has won my approval and praise = been approved of and praised *by* me.

259. The last idiomatic use of the dative is that in which it is used to express a *result* or *aim;* two ideas often blended in Latin. (See **106.**)

> *Receptui canere.* To sound the trumpet *for* retreat.
> *Hunc locum* domicilio *eligo.* I choose this place *for* my habitation.[1]

It is much used with *sum, do, duco, verto, eligo;* and (especially with military terms, as *auxilio, subsidio*) with verbs of motion; and is generally combined with the ordinary dative. Thus—

> *Haec res* ei magno *fuit* dedecori. This was (*or* proved) a great disgrace to him.
> *Ipse* sibi odio *erit.* He will be odious (*or,* an object of dislike) to himself = be *hated by* himself.
> *Noli hanc rem* mihi vitio *vertere.* Do not impute this to me *as a fault.*
> *Quae res* saluti nobis *fuit.* And this fact saved us, *proved* our *safety.*
> *Caesarem oravit, ut* sibi auxilio *copias adduceret.* He begged Caesar to bring up troops *to his aid.*

Obs. Hence such verbs as "*proves,*" "*serves,*" etc., may often be translated by *sum* with the *dative;* and an adjective after "*to be*" may often be translated into Latin by the *dative* of a substantive.

260. The following phrases are very commonly used with an additional dative of the *person interested.*

(1.) With *auxilio* (to the assistance);

> *Come,* věnire, vēni, ventum.
> *Send,* mittere, mīsi, missum.
> *Set out,* prŏficisci, profectus.

(2.) With *culpae, vitio, crimini;*

> *To impute as a fault,* culpae dăre : *with* acc. of thing; *or* vitio vertĕre, *with* acc. of thing.

(3.) *To give as a present,* dono, *or* muneri, dare, *with* acc. of thing.
> *To consider a source of gain,* habere quaestui.
> *To be very dishonourable or discreditable to,* magno esse dedecori. (*Obs.* 1.)
> *To be hated by; to be hateful,* odio esse. (*Obs.* 2.)
> *To be a hindrance,* impedimento esse.
> *To be creditable, or honourable,* honori esse.

---

[1] *Te* ducem eliga*mus,* apposition with a *person,* "*as* or *for* our leader," see **239** : *hunc locum* domicilio *eligo,* dative with a *thing,* "*as* or *for* our habitation."

To be hurtful; to be detrimental, detrīmento, *or* damno esse.
To be painful to, dolori esse.
To be a proof, argumento, documento esse.
To profit, to be profitable to, bono esse.
To bring punishment, fraudi esse.
To be a reproach; to be disgraceful, opprobrio esse.

Obs. 1.—The English adverb *very* will be represented in Latin by the adjective *magno* or *summo;* "how" by *quanto.*

Quanto *hoc tibi sit* dedecori *vides.* You see *how* disgraceful this is to you.

Obs. 2.—The phrase " *odio esse* " forms a passive voice to *odi.* Thus Hannibal, when at the close of his life he expresses to Antiochus his hatred to the Romans, says (Livy xxxv. 19) :—

Odi odioque sum Romanis. I hate the Romans and am *hated by them.*

261. The dative in the predicate with *licet,* etc., has been noticed **(201).**

Liceat nobis quietis *esse.* Let us be allowed to be at rest.

So *sometimes* after *nomen est,* etc.

Puero cognomen Iulo *additur.* The surname of Iulus is added to the boy.

But *Iulus* would be equally good Latin.

Exercise 32.

In these Exercises words and phrases marked * will be found in **260.**

A.

1. He promises to come shortly to the assistance * of your countrymen. 2. Thereupon he forced the bloody dagger out of the assassin's [1] hand. 3. I fear that these things will not prove very creditable * to you. 4. I don't quite understand what your friends [2] mean (by it). 5. It is very honourable * to you to have been engaged in such (86) a battle. 6. Such (87) superstition is undoubtedly a reproach * to a man. 7. I fear that this will prove both detrimental * and dishonourable * to the government. 8. Cassius was wont to ask [3] who had gained by the result.

---

[1] Genitive not to be used. (See **257.**)   [2] **338,** *Obs.* 2.
[3] Frequentative form, *rogito.* Tense ? (See **184.**)

9. It is vile to consider politics a source * of gain.   10. I would fain inquire what place you have chosen for your dwelling.   11. I am afraid that this will be very painful * and disgraceful * to you.   12. I will warn the boy what (*quantus*) a reproach * it is to break one's word.   13. He promised to give them the island of Cyprus as a present. 14. I hope that he will perceive how odious * cruelty is to all men.   15. Then the ambassadors of the Gauls threw themselves at Caesar's feet.   16. It seems that he hates * our nation and is hated * by us.   17. I hope soon to come to your aid with three legions.

B.

1. He gives his word to take care that the ambassadors shall be allowed to depart home in safety.   2. To this prince, owing to a temperament (which was) almost intolerable to the rest of the world, (men) had given the name of the Proud.   3. And this circumstance is a proof * that no [1] Roman took part in that contest.   4. So many and so great are your illustrious brother's (224) achievements that they have by this time been heard of, praised and read of by the whole world.   5. We know that the name of deserters is hated * and considered execrable by all the world; but we earnestly implore that this our change of sides may bring us neither punishment * nor credit. *   6. Not even (Intr. 99) in a time of universal [2] repose were we allowed to enjoy repose.   7. I can scarcely believe that so monstrous a design as this has been heard of and approved by you.   8. This circumstance, which is now in every one's mouth, he communicated to me yesterday ; I suspect it concerns you more than me.   9. When my colleague comes [3] to my assistance * I can [4] supply you with provisions and arms.

---

[1] See 223.   [2] See 59.   [3] See 190.   [4] Tense ? (190, ii.)

THE ABLATIVE.

262. The **Ablative** is more than any other an **adverbial** case; (read carefully **211**). It answers the questions *whence? by what means? how? from what cause? in what manner? when?* and *where?*

Its various meanings may be thus classified :—

(i.) Removal, or departure; *from (casus* ablativus). (Answers the question *whence*.)

(ii.) Instrumentality ; *by, with*.

(iii.) Accompaniment; *with*, etc.

(iv.) Locality ; *at* or *in* a *place* or *time*. (Answers the question *where* or *when*.)

Obs.—It therefore represents four distinct cases, the last of which certainly, others in all probability, once existed as separate forms.

263. (i.) Ablative of **removal** or **departure** from.

In most instances, either by itself, or with the prepositions *a, ab; ex, e; de*, it corresponds to the English *from*.

It is so used with verbs expressing literal motion.

Troja *profecti sunt*. They set out *from* Troy. (Name of *town*, see **9**.)

A *Pyrrho*, ex *Africa, legati veniunt*. Ambassadors come *from* Pyrrhus *from* Africa.

264. It is thus used also with many other verbs without, as well as with, a preposition. The preposition is mostly omitted where no merely bodily motion is implied.

Abstinere injuria, to abstain *from* wrong ; *abire* magistratu, go *out of* office ; *desistĕre* conatu, to abandon or cease *from* an attempt ; *cedĕre* patria, to leave his native land ; *pellĕre* civitate, to banish.

So also with verbs implying " freeing from," and " depriving."

Solvit te his legibus *Senatus*. The Senate exempts you *from* those laws.

Līberat te aere alieno. He sets you free *from* debt.

But very often the preposition is used.

Discedant ab *armis*. Let them depart *from* arms.

Abhorret ab *ejusmodi* culpā. He is far removed *from* such blame.

176

265. Not only verbs but **adjectives**[1] signifying *want* or *freedom from* are joined with the *ablative*, or sometimes the *ablative* with *a* or *ab*.

Metu *vacuus*. Free *from* fear. (Compare culpā *vacat*, he is free *from* fault.)
Loca sunt ab arbitris *libera*. The locality is free *from* witnesses.
Ab *ejusmodi* scelere *alienissimus*. Quite incapable *of* (removed *from*) such a crime.

266. (ii.) The ablative of **source** or **origin**, a very similar sense to that of *departure* from, is used mostly, though not always, without the preposition.

Consulari familiā *ortus*. Sprung *from* a consular family.
Homo optimis parentibus *natus*. A man *of* excellent parentage.

Obs.—Ortus, oriundus, when used of *remote* ancestors, are joined with the preposition *ab*.

267. (iii.) The ablative of **instrument**, and also that of (iv.) **cause,** may be considered as nearly related to that of *origin*.

Cornibus *tauri se tutantur*. Bulls protect themselves *with* their horns.
Jam vires lassitudine *deficiebant*. Their strength was now beginning to fail *through* (or *from*) weariness.

(v.) With the **agent,** *i.e.* a *person* as opposed to a *thing*, the preposition is necessary.

Clitus ab Alexandro gladio *interfectus est*. (See 8, *a*.)

Obs.—A secondary agent, *i.e.* a *person* used as an instrument, is expressed by *per* (or *operā* with the genitive or the possessive pronoun).

Haec per exploratores *cognita sunt*. These facts were ascertained by means of reconnoiterers.
Tuā operā. By your instrumentality.

So *propter* and *ob* are still more often used than the ablative to express the *cause*. The ablative is mostly confined to a bodily, or mental, or other property of the *subject of the verb*. Tua fortitudine *hoc meruisti;* but, propter tuam fortitudinem *hoc decrevit senatus*.

---

[1] In the same way *adverbs* are constantly joined with adjectives. (Intr. 17.) Compare also the use of the dative, **254.**

268. (vi.) The ablative of **manner** is nearly related to that of *instrument* and *cause*, and is very widely used.

> *Hac ratione, hoc modo,* by this means, *in* this manner; *summo opere,* earnestly; *casu, by* chance; *nullo modo, by* no means; *consilio, by* design; *jure,* rightly; *injuriā,* unjustly; *nescio quo pacto, in* some way or other; and many others.

Obs.—Many of these are used exactly as adverbs; they only differ from adverbs as being more obviously, what other adverbs were originally, *oblique cases* of substantives.

The preposition *in* is never used in Latin before words signifying *manner :* thus, never "*in hoc modo.*"

269. (vii.) The ablative of **accompaniment**[1] when applied to *things* can hardly be distinguished from that of *manner.* The rule is to use the preposition *cum* unless an emphatic adjective is added.

We can say, Summā *haec diligentiā feci,* "I have done this with the *greatest* care," and we *may,* but need not, insert *cum.* But we cannot say, *Haec* diligentiā *feci,* "I have done this with care ;" nor *lacrimis,* for "with tears."

> Cum *dignitate mori satius est quam* cum *ignominia vivere.* It is better to die *with* honour than to live *under* disgrace.

Obs.—With the following phrases *cum* is never used.

> *Hoc consilio, with* this intention ; *aequo animo, with* calmness, *or* resignation ; *jussu tuo, by* your command ; *injussu Caesaris, without* Caesar's permission ; *bonā tuā veniā, with* your kind permission ; *nullo negotio,* without trouble. But cum *emolumento,* or cum *damno, meo, to* my advantage, or loss.

270. Where however the English *with* is used in the literal sense of (viii.) "**in company with**," the preposition is required[2] both with persons and things.

> Cum *fratre meo veni.* I came *with* my brother.
> Cum *telo venit.* He came *with* a weapon.
> *Te*cum, *me*cum, *nobis*cum, *vobis*cum, *ibit.* He will go with you, me, us, you. (8, *Obs.*)

---

[1] The English preposition *with* marks the connexion between the different senses of *instrument, manner,* and *accompaniment.* "I killed him *with* a sword," "I did it *with* ease," "I spoke *with* sorrow," "I came *with* you."

[2] In military language, an army is sometimes looked on as standing in an *instrumental* relation to its general : *Dux* reliquo exercitu *contra hostem proficiscitur;* but even here the *cum* is mostly inserted.

271. Under this head of *accompaniment* is to be classed (ix.) the *ablative* of **quality**.

> Eximiā *fuit corporis* pulchritudine.   He was a man of great personal beauty.

Obs.—Here again the adjective is necessary.   See below, Gen. of Quality, **303.**

We have thus far had instances of the ablative used to denote *removal from, origin, instrument, cause, agent, manner*, and *accompaniment* of circumstances, things, persons, and qualities.

Exercise 33

A.

1. He replied that nearly the whole of the army was annihilated, and[1] that it made no difference whether it had been overwhelmed by famine, or by pestilence, or by the enemy. 2. Having been chosen king not only by his own soldiers, but also by the popular[2] vote,[3] he aimed at establishing and securing by the arts of peace a throne gained by the sword[4] and violence. 3. Sprung as he was from an illustrious family, he entered public life as[5] a young man, and retired at last from office as an old one. 4. Freed from the fear of foreign war, the nation was now[6] able to drive traitors from its territory, and show its gratitude to patriots. 5. Whether[7] your unprincipled relation has abandoned this attempt, or intends (14, *c*) to persevere in it, I know not; but whether[7] he means to take one course[8] or the other, it seems to me that he is not yet willing to abstain from wrong. 6. So far is my unfortunate brother from having been freed from debt, that he is even now leaving his country for[9] no other cause.

---

[1] Why not *et nihil?* (See **110.**)   [2] "Of the people."   (See **59.**)
[3] Plural.   Compare p. **72**, *n.* 2.   [4] Why not *gladio?*   (See **17.**)
[5] " As " not to be expressed; why would *velut, quasi,* be wrong ?
[6] *Jam ; nunc* is " at *this present* moment."
[7] " Whether." (See **171.**)   [8] = to do this, or that.
[9] *Propter* (acc.).

B.

1. I would fain ask, with your kind permission, whether it [1] was by accident, or by design that you acted [2] thus. 2. We set forth from home with tears, with wailing, and with the deepest anxiety; we reached the end of our journey relieved of a load of cares, free from fear, and amidst great and universal rejoicing. 3. He is a man of the most spotless character, and so far removed from such a crime that for my part, I wonder [3] how he can have been suspected of such monstrous impiety. 4. We had rather die with honour than live as slaves (42, ii.); but we refuse to perish in this manner for the sake of such [4] a person as this. 5. I might have [5] faced death itself without trouble, but I cannot endure such a heavy disaster as this [6] with resignation. 6. He was so transported with passion that he threatened not only his brother, but all the bystanders, with death.

---

[1] See **156.**

[2] =did this; avoid using *agere* for "to act," and notice the real meanings of *agere*.   [3] Mood? (See **106.**)

[4] See **87.** *Talis* is rarely used contemptuously.

[5] See **196.**   [6] **88,** *Obs.*

ABLATIVE—*Continued.*

272. Other senses of the ablative belong to it as having taken the place in a great degree of the nearly obsolete **locative** case, answering, not the question *whence?*, but *where?*

Obs.—This case, which ended in *i*, so often resembled *in form* the ablative after the latter had lost its final letter *d*, that at last the ablative added to its many other meanings those which properly belonged to the locative, and the same case came to represent *whence* and *where*.

Local uses of the ablative may include those which denote *at a place*, and *at a time*. (See **9,** *a*, and below, **311** and **320.**)

Pericles Athenis *vixit.* Die septimo *venit.*

273. Such too are the phrases, *terrā marique*, by sea and land ; *dextrā*, (or *a dextrā*), *sinistrā*, on the right, left, hand ; *bello et pace*, in war and peace ; *nocte, hieme, primā luce*, etc. ; so also *aeger* pedibus, suffering in the feet ; altero *saucius* brachio, wounded in one arm.

Obs.—The preposition *in* sometimes makes a slight difference in the meaning ; *tali tempore*, simply, *at* such a time, or moment ; *in tali tempore, considering the circumstances of* such a time, or emergency, *in spite of*, or *in the face of*, such a crisis.

For the Ablative Absolute, which includes the ideas both of *time* and *accompanying circumstances*, see Exercise LIII.

274. With the *local* ablative may be compared the ablative of **respect** or **limitation**; the English *in*, in the sense of "in so far as concerns," etc.

Specie, in appearance ; *re, re ipsā*, in reality ; *nomine*, in name.
Lingua, moribus, *armorum* genere *inter se discrepabant.* They differed from one another *in* language, habits, and *in* the nature of their arms.

Obs.—To this use of the ablative belongs the supine in *-u*.
Horrendum dictu. Dreadful *in the telling.* (See **404.**)

275. The ablative of **comparison** (or *difference from*) belongs (probably) to the ablative of *departure from*.

In English, a comparative adjective or adverb is connected by the conjunction *than* (originally *then*) with the clause or word with which the comparison is made : He is older *than* he was ; He is more *than* twenty years old.

In Latin also, *quam* is the regular particle of comparison. As it is a *conjunction*, and not a *preposition*, things compared by *quam* will be in the same case.

> *Europa minor est,* quam *Asiă.* Europe is smaller than Asia.
> *Dixit Europam minorem esse* quam *Asiam.* He said that Europe was smaller than Asia.
> *A nullo libentius* quam *a te litteras accipio.* I receive a letter from no one with more pleasure than from you.

276. But in Latin, where two nouns are closely compared with one another, the ablative of comparison, or thing *differed from,* is widely used; an idiom quite unlike English.

> Hoc homine *nihil contemptius esse potest.* Nothing can be more despicable *than* this man.
> *Haec nonne* luce *clariora sunt?* Are not these things clearer *than* the daylight ?

We should probably say "*so* despicable *as*," "*as* clear *as*."

Obs.—This construction however is only used when the comparative adjective is in the nominative, or the accusative after a verb *sentiendi vel declarandi.* It is exceedingly common in *negative* and *interrogative* sentences, as above.

277. The ablative of comparison is largely used after comparative adjectives and adverbs, with such words as *spes, opinio, fama, expectatio,* even *justum* and *aequum.*

> Spe *omnium* celerius *venit.* He came sooner than any one had hoped.
> *Ne* plus justo *dolueris.* Do not feel *undue* pain.

278. "Superior *to*," "inferior *to*," may be expressed in Latin by this ablative.

> *Omnia* virtute inferiora *ducit.* He counts everything *inferior to* · (of lower rank than) goodness.
> *Negant quenquam* te fortiorem *esse.* They say that no one is *your superior* in courage.

Nemo tibi virtute praestat would be also good Latin for " no one is, *etc.*"

279. Another ablative often joined with comparatives is that of the **measure of difference**, and is clearly *instrumental.*

> Multo *me doctior.*   *Greatly* my superior in learning.
> *Homo* paulo *sapientior.*   A man of *somewhat* more wisdom than is common ; " of fair, *or* average, wisdom."
> *Senatus* paulo *frequentior.*   A *somewhat* crowded senate.

Caution.—These ablative forms, *paulo, multo, eo, tanto,* etc., must never be used with adjectives or adverbs in the positive degree.   Compare the use of *quo* (**102**).

But they may be used with words which, though not comparative in form, imply comparison.

> *Paulo* ante.   A little before, *or* earlier.
> *Multo tibi* praestat.   He is much superior to you.

280. The ablative of **price**, " for," " at such a rate," may be either local (*at*), or instrumental (*by means of*).

It is used with verbs of **buying** and **selling**, etc., *emere, vendere,* etc.

> *Viginti* talentis *unam orationem Isocrates* vendidit.   Isocrates sold one oration *for* twenty talents.

So with verbs of exchanging.

> *Pacem* bello *mutavit.*   He exchanged peace *for* war.

Obs.—The adjectives *magno, parvo, nimio, quanto,* etc., are generally used by themselves, the substantive *pretio* being understood.

> *Venditori expĕdit rem* vēnire *quam* plurimo.   It is for the interest of the seller that the thing should be sold for, *or* at, as high a price as possible.
> *Multo* sanguine *victoria nobis stetit,* or, *constitit.*   The victory cost us much blood.

Verbs of *valuing, esteeming,* etc., as distinct from actual *buying,* take the genitive.   (See **305**.)

Exercise 34.

1. It is pretty well agreed on by all of you that the sun is many times[1] larger than the moon. 2. I have known this man from boyhood; I believe him to be greatly your superior both in courage and learning. 3. The king himself, while he was[2] fighting in front of the foremost line of battle, was wounded in the head. In spite of this[3] great confusion and universal panic, he refused to withdraw from the contest. 4. By this means he became rightly dear to the nation,[4] and reached the extremity of old age in name a private citizen, in reality almost the parent of his country. 5. And[5] this crime must be at once atoned for by your blood, for your[6] guilty deeds are clear and plain as[7] this sun-light, and[8] it is quite impossible that any member of the nation can wish you pardoned. 6. It seems[9] to me, said he, that all of you are soldiers in name, deserters and brigands in reality. 7. The battle[10] was now much more desperate; on the left our men were beginning to fail through weariness; the general, himself wounded in one arm, was the first to become aware of this. 8. You might[11] but lately have exchanged war for peace; too late (*adv.*) to-day are you repenting of your blunder. 9. I was anxious yesterday for your safety; but the matter has turned out much better than I had looked for. 10. How much better would[12] it have been in the presence of such a crisis to have held all considerations inferior to the national safety.

---

[1] "*Parts.*" For case, see **279.**   [2] See **180.**   [3] **88,** *Obs.*
[4] Or country. (See **16,** *a.*)   [5] Intr. 58.   [6] Iste. (See **338.**)
[7] See **276.**   [8] = nor is it possible. (See **110,** and **125,** *f.*)
[9] **43.**   [10] **218**   [11] **196, 197.**   [12] **153.**

ABLATIVE—*Continued.*

281. The ablative is also used to complete the sense of certain **deponent** verbs.

Fungor, fruor, ūtor (with their compounds), *pŏtior, vescor, dignor, glorior,* take the *ablative.*

> *Hannibal, cum* victoriā *posset* uti, frui *maluit.* Hannibal at a time when [1] (although) he might have used his victory preferred enjoying it.
>
> *Mortis* periculo defuncti *sumus.* We have got over the danger of death.
>
> *Nostri* victoriā potiti *sunt.* Our soldiers gained the victory.

Obs.—This ablative is of course not that of the *nearer object;* but these deponent verbs resemble in their use Greek verbs of the *middle voice. Utor,* I serve myself *with; fruor,* I enjoy myself *with; vescor,* I feed myself *on; potior,* I make myself powerful *with; fungor,* I discharge myself *from; dignor,* I hold myself worthy *at such a price; glorior,* I glorify myself *with:* so that the ablative is in each case used in one or other of its regular *adverbial* uses. (See **228,** *Obs.*)

282. Of these verbs, *potior* sometimes takes the genitive, "I am master *of." Utor* is freely used with adverbs ; *male, perverse, immoderate, utor,* "I make a bad, or immoderate use of," = "I abuse." The Latin adverb must be substituted for the English adjective.

> *Te* familiariter, *te* amico usus sum. I was on intimate terms with you, I found a friend in you.

Obs.—*Gloriari* is used also with *in* and *de; niti,* "to lean, or rely on," with and without *in. Confido* with dat. of person (always dat. of personal pronoun), ablative of thing. Tibi *confisus sum; exercitūs* virtute *confido.* (**244,** *c.*)

---

[1] Or, "*instead of* using his victory preferred to enjoy it."

283. Compare also with the English idiom the use of the ablative to complete the sense of certain transitive verbs.

> Honore, praemio, *te affeci.*   I conferred on you a distinction, a reward.
> Poenā, supplicio, *eum afficiam.*   I will inflict punishment on him (= *poenas de eo sumam*).
> Honoribus *te cumulavimus.*   We have heaped or showered honours on you.
> Omni observantia *eum prosecutus sum.*   I have paid him every kind of respect.   (Cf. **247.**)

284. Verbs of *abounding, filling, loading,* etc., and their opposites, such as verbs of *being without, depriving of, emptying of,* are joined with the *ablative.*

Such verbs are *circumfluere* (divitiis), *complēre, onerare, refercire, cumulare* (honoribus), *carēre, egēre, vacare* (culpā) *orbare, privare, fraudare.*

> *Flumen piscibus* abundat.   The river is *full of* fish.
> *Mortui cura et dolore* carent.   The dead are *free from* anxiety and pain.

But of these *egeo* and *indigeo* (especially the latter) govern the *genitive* also ; as also *complēre, replēre.*

> *Res maxime necessariae non tam* artis *indigent quam* labōris. The most necessary things do not require skill so much as labour.

Obs.—In verbs of *abounding,* etc., the ablative is no doubt *instrumental.* Its original sense with verbs of *want* is more doubtful: probably that of *separation,* freedom *from.*

285. The ablative is joined also with adjectives, in many of its various senses.   (See **265.**)
Dignus, indignus, contentus, praeditus, frētus are followed by an ablative without a preposition.

> *Vir omni honore* dignus.   A man worthy of every distinction.
> *Divitiis opibusque* fretus.   Relying on his wealth and resources.

Be careful not to use a genitive after *dignus.*

286. The ablative of the noun, and occasionally of the participle, is also used with *opus* (and *usus*) when they bear the sense of *need of.*

> *Ubi res adsunt, quid mihi* verbis *opus est?* When facts are here, what need have I of *words?*
>
> *Ait sibi* consulto *opus esse.* He says he has need of *deliberation.*

Sometimes the thing needed is the subject to *opus est.*

> Dux *nobis et* auctor *opus est.* We need a leader and adviser.

This indeed is the rule with neuter pronouns and adjectives :—
Quae *nobis opus sunt;* pauca *tibi opus sunt; omnia,* quae *ad vitam opus sunt,* "all the necessaries of life." The infinitive is also used :—

> *Quid haec* scribere *opus est?* What need is there to write this?

Obs.—Opus properly means " work (to be done)," and the ablative is the ablative of respect,—" there is work to be done for me *in consultation.*"

Exercise 35.

A.

1. I have now lived long on most intimate terms with your son; it seems to me that he resembles his father in ability and character, rather than in either features or personal appearance. 2. Do[1] not deprive (*pl.*) of well-earned distinction and praise one who has made so good,[2] so sensible, a use of the favours of heaven. 3. I cannot[3] but believe that it is[4] by your instrumentality that I have got over this great danger. 4. All of us, your well-wishers, make this one prayer, that you may be permitted to discharge the duties of your office with[5] honour and advantage to yourself; we all rely on your honesty and self-control, and are all proud of your friendship. 5. Relying on your support, I have ventured to inflict severe punishment on the rebels. 6. He always put confidence in himself, and in[6] spite of humble means and scanty fare preferred contentment (**98,** *a*) to resting[7] on other men's resources. 7. He preferred dispensing with all the necessaries of life (as) a free man, to abounding in riches in the condition of a slave.

---

[1] 143. [2] 282. [3] 137, *j.*
[4] See 82. The periphrasis *factum esse ut* may be used for emphasis.
[5] 269. [6] 273, *Obs.* [7] See 94.

B.

1. He promises to supply us with everything that is [1] necessary. 2. We have need of deliberation rather than haste, for I fear that this victory has already cost us too much. 3. In my youth I enjoyed the friendship of your illustrious father; he was a man of remarkable abilities, and of the highest character. 4. He hopes to visit with condign punishment the murderers of his father and the conspirators against their sovereign. 5. I fear that he seems far from worthy of all [2] the compassion and indulgence of which he stands in need to-day. 6. Nothing can ever be imagined more happy than my father's lot in life; he discharged the duties of the highest office without [3] failing to enjoy the charms of family life. 7. Relying on your good-will, I have not hesitated [4] to avail myself of the letter which you sent me by [5] my son. 8. Can any one be more worthy of honour, more unworthy of punishment, than this man?

[1] Mood, see **77**.

[2] Tantus . . . quantus.

[3] See **111**, "so discharged as to enjoy."

[4] See **136**, *b.*

[5] **267**, *Obs.*

GENITIVE.

Two of the main uses of the Genitive, or *defining* case, are—

The **Possessive**; where the genitive denotes the person or thing to which some other person or thing belongs.

The **Partitive**; where the genitive denotes the relation of a whole to a part.

I. Possessive Genitive.

287. The **Genitive** differs from all other cases (including the obsolete **Locative**) in being **rarely used with verbs.** The proper office of a noun in the genitive is to define, or give the *genus* of, another noun. (See **214.**)

288. It does this in various ways; and the relation between one noun and another, as denoted in the Latin genitive, may be very variously expressed in English : by the *possessive case*, by various *prepositions*, and by the *adjective.* Thus—

> *Libri* Ciceronis, Cicero's books ; hominum *optimus*, the best *of* men ; mortis *fuga*, flight *from* death ; Helvetiorum *injuriae* populi Romani, the wrongs done *by* the Helvetii *to* the people of Rome ; mortis *remedium*, a remedy *against* death ; *fossa* quindecim pedum, a bridge fifteen feet *wide ;* legum *obedientia*, obedience *to* law ; corporis *robur*, *bodily* strength ; amissi filii *dolor*, pain *for* the loss of his son.

In these instances the genitives express a close connexion between two substantives ; but a connexion of very different kinds ; in all **the word in the genitive explains and defines the other word.**

289. As being most properly that case in which one noun is attached, or annexed, to another, which it explains, it may be called the **adjectival case**, and in fact often corresponds exactly to the adjective.   (See 58.)

> Caesaris *causā*, meā *causā*, on behalf of Caesar, on my behalf; tuā *operā*, illius *operā*, with your, *or* his, aid ; so Sullani *milites* = Sullae *milites.*

290. Of these, the strictly **possessive** use will cause no difficulty; it answers to the English possessive case in *s* (the only real *case* remaining in the English substantive), to the preposition *of*, to the *possessive pronoun*, and to the *adjective.*

> Pompeii *aequalis ac* meus.   *Pompey's* contemporary and *my own.*
> Noster *atque* omnium *parens.*   *Our own,* and the *universal* parent.
> *Sceptrum* regis (*or* regium).   The *king's* sceptre.
> *Illud* Platonis.   That saying *of* Plato.

Obs.—Under this may be classed such expressions as tui *similis*, Ciceronis *inimicissimi* (see **256**); also Pompeii *causā, gratiā,* in the interest *of*, for the sake *of*, Pompey (*meā, tuā,* not *mei, tui*) ; and even sui juris, suae ditionis *facere,* to *bring under* his own jurisdiction, *or* power.

291. To this possessive and adjectival genitive belongs also the following construction :—

The **genitive singular** of a *substantive*, especially when it can denote a class (as *puer, rex*) or of an *adjective* used as a substantive (*stultus, sapiens*), or of an *abstract noun* (*levitas, stultitia*) or of a *pronoun,* is often used as a predicate with a copulative verb to denote such English ideas as " property," " duty," " part," " mark," etc.

Obs. 1.—This construction takes the place of the neuter adjective, especially in adjectives of one termination.
"It is foolish" *may* be translated *stultum est;* but *stulti* is much more usual ; "it is wise" is always *sapientis,* or *sapientiae, est,* never *sapiens,* which might mean " a wise *man.*" **Latin is rarely ambiguous.**

Obs. 2.—In the place of the personal pronouns the neuter of the possessive is used.

Meum (*not* mei) *est,* it is *my part,* or *duty,* or it is *for me to.* etc.

Obs. 3.—The same construction is used after verbs *sentiendi* et *declarandi.*

Hoc sapientis esse *dixit.* This, he said, was the wise course, (lit. *the part* of a wise man).

Obs. 4.—This genitive may be translated into English in various ways : and therefore there are various English phrases that may be reduced to this construction.

Such phrases are: *it is characteristic of; it is incumbent on; it is for* (the rich, etc.) ; *it is not every one* who ; *any man* may ; *it demands or requires; it betrays, shows,* etc. ; *it belongs to ; it depends upon ; it tends to,* etc.

292. Examples—

1. Imbecilli animi *est superstitio.* Superstition is a *mark* of (or *betrays*) a weak mind.
2. Judicis *est legibus parere.* It is the *part* (or *duty*) of a judge to obey the law.
3. Ingenii *hoc* magni *est.* This *requires* great abilities.
4. Cujusvis hominis *est errare.* Any man *may* err.
5. Meum *est.* It is my *business,* or *duty.*
6. Summae *est* dementiae. *It is* the height of madness.
7. *Tempori cedere semper* sapientis *est habitum.* It has always been held *a wise thing* to yield to circumstances, *or* to temporise.
8. *Hoc* dementiae *esse* summae *dixit.* He said that this *showed* the height of madness.
9. *Hoc* sui *esse* arbitrii *negavit.* He said that this did not *depend upon* his own decision.

Obs.—To this belongs a phrase common in Livy—

Hoc evertendae *esse* reipublicae,[1] *dixit.* He said that this *tended to* the destruction of the constitution.

Exercise 36.

1. Whether you (*pl.*) will be[2] slaves or free, depends upon your own decision.   2. We know that any man may err, but it is foolish to forget that error is one thing, persistency (**98,** *a*) in error another.   3. He brought under his own jurisdiction, sooner than he had hoped, the privileges and liberty of all his countrymen.   4. Living[3]

- The various meanings of this phrase *res publica* (often written as one word) should be carefully noticed. It should never be translated by "republic," but by "the constitution," "the nation," "politics," "public life," etc., according to the context, and should never be used in the plural unless when it means more than one "state" or "nation."

[2] **173,** iii.   [3] See **94.**

for the day only, (and) making no provision for the future was, he said,[1] rather the characteristic of barbarians than of a free nation.   5. Your father's contemporaries were,[2] he said, his own, and none (110) of them had[2] been dearer to him than your uncle.   6. In my absence I did not cease to do everything in your interest and (that) of your excellent brother.   7. A sensible man will[3] yield, says he, to circumstances, but it is the height of folly to pay attention to threats of this kind.   8. Whether we have won the day or no (168, *Obs.*) I hardly dare[4] say; it is, I know,[5] a soldier's duty to wait for his general's orders.   9. It will be[6] for others to draw up and bring forward laws, it is our part to obey the law.   10. You were, he said, evading the law which you had[7] yourself got enacted; a course which, he believed, tended to[8] the overthrow of the constitution.

---

[1] **32**, *b.*
[2] " Were." For tenses, see **193**, i., ii.
[3] = it is the part of a, etc.
[4] Subjunctive.   (**149**, i.)
[5] See **32**, *b.*
[6] **291**, *Obs.* 4.
[7] Mood?   (See **77**.)
[8] **292**, *Obs.*

GENITIVE—*Continued.*

The Partitive Genitive.

293. A word in the genitive often stands to another word in the relation, not of a possessor, but of a **whole** to a **part.** This is called the **partitive genitive,** and is very widely used.

This genitive answers to the English "*of*," after substantives denoting a part, in such phrases as *magna pars* exercitūs, and is used, like that preposition, with *superlative adjectives* and *adverbs*, with interrogative and other *pronouns*, with *numerals*, and with any word which can denote in any way *a part of a larger whole*, such as *nemo, quisquam, multi, pauci, uterque, quisque,* etc. Thus—

> *Unus*[1] *omnium* infelicissimus, the most unfortunate *of* all mankind ; *tu* maxime *omnium*, you most *of* all ; uter *restrum*, which *of* you two ; multi *horum*, many *of* these ; duo horum, two *of* these ; quotusquisque *philosophorum*, how few (*of*) philosophers.

294. A more idiomatic use of this genitive is with the **neuter singular** of adjectives and pronouns expressing *quantity* or *degree*, and with *nihil, satis, parum*. These are used as **quasi-substantives**, and are joined with the genitive of substantives and adjectives, an idiom not unknown in English, but exceedingly common in Latin.

Compare Latin and English in—

> Quantum *voluptatis*, how much pleasure ; plus *detrimenti*, greater loss ; nihil *praemii*, no reward ; satis, *or* parum, *virium*, sufficient, *or* insufficient strength ; quid *novi ?* what news ? nimium *temporis*, too much time ; hoc *emolumenti*, this (*of*) gain.

Obs.—This genitive is even used with **adverbs**: tum *temporis*, at that time ; eo *audaciae*, to such a pitch of boldness ; ubi *gentium*, where in the world ? and in such adverbial phrases as *cum id* aetatis *puero, ad id* locorum, up to that point (of time). (See **238**, iii.)

---

[1] Note this **intensive** use of *unus* with the superlative.

295. Cautions in the use of the partitive genitive.

(*a*) It is not used with adjectives where the genitive has no separate form for the neuter gender : write *nihil humile*, not *nihil humilis*, for " nothing degrading."

(*b*) It is not used with adjectives expressing the *whole, middle*, etc. : *tota, media*, urbs, not urbis *totum, medium*, for " the whole," " middle of the city " (**60**).

(*c*) It is not used with words joined with *prepositions*, or with other cases than the *nominative* and *accusative*.

> *Ad multam noctem.* To a late hour, not *ad multum noctis.*
> *Tanto sanguine*, not *tanto sanguinis.* At the cost of (**280**) so much blood.

296. With **numerals**, and words expressing *number*, as *nemo, multi, unus, pauci*, etc., and even with superlatives, the ablative with *ex, e, de*, or *inter* with the accusative, is often substituted ; *multi, nemo, unus* e vobis, for *unus*, etc. vestrum.

Obs.—Where *the whole* is a numeral, or contains a numeral or adjective expressing number or quantity, the preposition is always used.

> De tot millibus *vix pauci superfuere.* Of so many thousands scarcely a few survived.

297. Further Cautions.—The *partitive genitive* is only used to denote a larger amount than the word with which it is joined.

If the two words denote the **same persons,** or the **same amount,** *apposition* is used. (Nos) *omnes*, " all *of* us " (*i.e.* " we all"). *Equites*, qui *pauci aderant*, the cavalry, few *of* whom were there (lit. who were there *in small numbers*). (See **225** and **69**.)

298. (*a*) *Uterque* is used as a substantive with pronouns ; but with substantives it is treated as an adjective.

> *Uterque* vestrum ; but frater *uterque.*

(*b*) To the partitive genitive belong the phrases :—

> *Nihil* reliqui fecit. He left nothing remaining.
> *Nihil* pensi habuit. He cared not at all.
> *Quid hoc* rei *est ?* What is the meaning of this ?

Exercise 37.

1. There was[1] nothing mean in this sovereign, nothing base, nothing degrading; little learning (but[2]) fair ability, some experience of life and a dash of eloquence, much good sense, abundance of honesty and strength of mind. 2. Of the many[3] contemporaries of your father and myself, I incline to think that no one was more deserving than he of universal praise and respect. 3. Which of you two has entailed greater loss and[4] injury on the nation it is hard to say; I hope and trust that you will[5] both before long repent your crimes. 4. Fate has left us nothing except either to die[6] with honour or to live under disgrace. 5. The battle[7] has been most disastrous; very few of us out of so many thousands survive, the rest are[8] either slain or taken prisoners, so that I greatly fear that (138) all is lost. 6. Where in the world are we to[9] find a man like him[10]; it would[11] be tedious to enumerate, or express in words his many[12] good qualities; and[13] would that he had been[14] here to-day! 7. So much blood has this victory cost us that for myself I doubt whether the conquerors or the conquered have sustained[15] most loss.

---

[1] Either *sum* or *insum*.   [2] Express by order of words. (Intr. 107.)

[3] Use *tot*. (Compare the use of *tantus*, 88, *Obs.*)

[4] Repeat "greater;" this repetition of a word already used is very common in Latin in place of a conjunction.

[5] The fut. in *-rus* of *poenitet* rare. What is the substitute? (193, iii.)

[6] *Ut* with subj., compare 125, *g*.   [7] See 218.

[8] See 187, *Obs.*   [9] See 150.

[10] Use *ille*, why? (339, iii.)   [11] Mood. (153.)

[12] *Tot*.   [13] *Qui*. (78.)

[14] See 152.   [15] *Accipio*.

EXERCISE XXXVIII.

GENITIVE—*Continued.*

Subjective and Objective Genitive.

299. The Genitive case always implies a **close relation** between the noun in that case and another noun.

(i.) Sometimes that relation is such that, if the other noun were converted into a **verb**, the word in the genitive would become the *subject* to the verb.

Thus *post fugam* Pompeii might be expressed by *postquam fugit* Pompeius.

This is called the **subjective genitive**.

(ii.) Sometimes the genitive as clearly represents the *object* of a verb.

Thus, *propter* mortis *timorem=quod* mortem *timuit.* This is called the **objective genitive**.

Obs.—Both of these genitives may be combined in a single phrase.

Helvetiorum *injuriae* populi Romani. The wrongs inflicted *by* the Helvetii *on* Rome.

In such phrases the *subjective* genitive is placed first.

We may compare the English, "a *criminal's* fear *of* death," or the French, "le danger *de la mer*," "le danger *du vaisseau*," the danger *of* the sea, the ship's danger.

300. The **objective genitive** is very common in Latin. It represents not only the *accusative,* as the nearer object to a transitive verb, but also the *dative* as completing the sense of intransitive verbs; and even such combinations of a *preposition* with an *accusative,* or *ablative,* case, as are used to complete the sense of many verbs. It represents therefore many English phrases besides the possessive case and the preposition *of.*

Instances are—Litterarum *studium* (*studere* litteris), devotion *to* literature ; doloris *remedium* (dolori *mederi*), a remedy *against* pain ; rei publicae *dissensio* (de r. p. *dissentire*), a disagreement *on* political matters, *or* a political disagreement; Pyrrhi regis *bellum* (cum Pyrrho *bellum gerere*), the war *with,* or *against,* King Pyrrhus ; sui *fiducia* (sibi *confidere*), confidence *in* one's-self. So also, legum *obedientia,* submission *to* law ; Deorum *opinio,* an impression *about* the gods, and many others.

196

301. This objective genitive is combined not only as above with substantives, but also with many **adjectives**.

(i.) Thus, adjectives which signify *desire, knowledge, recollection, fear, participation,* and their *opposites;* certain *verbals* in *-ax,* and many adjectives that express *fulness* or *emptiness,* are followed by a genitive.

> *Rerum novarum* cupidus, desirous *of* change ; *militiae* ignarus, ignorant *of* warfare ; *imperii* capax, with a capacity *for* rule.

These adjectives have an *incomplete meaning,* and may be compared with transitive verbs, as they require a noun to define and complete their meaning.

(ii.) Many of them, such as *cupidus, ignarus, memor,* etc., answer to English adjectives which are followed by the preposition *of,* and will cause no difficulty ; with others the Latin genitive represents (as with substantives) various English prepositions and constructions.

> Rei publicae *peritus, imperitissimus, rudis.* Skilled, most un-skilled, unversed, *in* the management of the state.
> Pugnandi *insuetus.* Unaccustomed *to* fighting.
> Litterarum *studiosissimus.* Most devoted *to* literature.
> Hujus sceleris *particeps, expers, affinis.* With part *in,* free *from,* connected *with,* this guilt.
> Beneficii *immemor.* Apt *to forget* a favour.

Obs.—Plenus takes both ablative and genitive, oftener the former ; *prudens* and *rudis,* sometimes *in* with ablative.

Certiorem facere=to inform, has a double construction.

> (English) He has informed me *of* his plan.
> (Latin)   *Certiorem me* sui consilii *fecit;* or, *Certiorem me* de suo consilio *fecit.*

302. The objective genitive is combined with the **present participle** of transitive verbs, when the latter is used as an adjective, *i.e.* to denote a *permanent quality,* not a *single act.*

> Thus regnum *appetens*="*while* aspiring to the crown," but—
> regni *appetens*=aspiring to kingly power (*habitually,* or by character).

Such participles are, *amans, patiens, diligens,* etc. (cf. also juris *consultus,* one consulted *on* law).

These present participles, when thus used, admit, as adjectives, of degrees of comparison, *tui amantissimus,* etc.

Exercise 38.

1. He was always most devoted to literature, at the same time (366) most uncomplaining under toil, cold, heat, want of food and of sleep ; for myself, my fear[1] is that he consents to allow himself too little repose and rest. 2. Such was the soldiers' ardour for the fight,[2] such the universal enthusiasm, that they refused to obey the orders of their general, (though) thoroughly versed in warfare of the kind, and as,[3] full of self-confidence and contempt for the enemy, and cheering each other on, they advanced as [3] to certain victory, they fell unawares into an ambuscade. 3. In spite of the greatest disagreement on politics, the friendship[4] which existed[5] between your gallant father and myself remained firm longer[6] than either (*et*) he or I had hoped.   4. He had[7] enough and to spare of wealth, but he was at the same[8] time most inexperienced in political life, with but little desire for fame, praise, influence, or power, and very averse to (265) all competition for office[9] or distinction.[9]   5. But these[10] men (though) they-have-borne[11] no part in all these toils, craving only for pleasure and repose, most indifferent to the public interest, devoted to feasting and gluttony, have reached such a pitch of shamelessness, that they have ventured in my hearing to taunt with luxury an army that-has-borne-uncomplainingly[12] all the hardships of a prolonged warfare.

---

[1] *Illud vereor.*   (See **341.**)   [2] Gerund, **99.**
[3] Note carefully the different meanings of "as."   *As* he does this (time), dum *haec facit.*   *As* (though) to victory (comparison), *tanquam* . . .   I did this *as* a boy, puer *hoc faciebam.*   (**63.**)
[4] Insert *tamen,* "yet."
[5] "Which *was* to me *with* your," etc.   (Intr. 49, *Obs.*)
[6] See **277.**   [7] See **251.**   [8] *Idem.*   (See **366,** ii.)
[9] Plural.   Latin would not represent either word here by an *abstract term* in the singular.   [10] *Isti.*   (See **338,** *Obs.* 2.)
[11] Use adjective *expers* (**301,** ii.) in apposition with "these men."
[12] Use a single word, "most uncomplaining under."

GENITIVE—*Continued.*

Quality and Definition.

303. The resemblance of the Latin genitive to the adjective is to be further noticed in its next use, the **genitive** of **quality**.

(i.) A Latin substantive in the genitive is often added to another substantive, in the same manner as in English a substantive with "of" prefixed, to denote some quality, either *predicated* of, or attached as an *attribute* to, that substantive. (Intr. 7, 8.)

> *Vir est* priscae severitatis. He is a man *of* old-fashioned austerity.
> *Vir* summae fortitudinis. A man *of* the greatest courage.

(ii.) But this Latin substantive in the genitive has invariably an **adjective** attached to it. "A man of courage" is not *homo* fortitudinis, but *homo* fortis; a man of good sense, *homo* prudens, *not* prudentiae.

This use of the genitive resembles that of the ablative of quality (271), but—

Obs. 1.—If the qualifying substantive denotes *number, amount, precise dimensions, age,* or *time,* the **genitive** is always used.

> Septuaginta navium *classis,* a fleet of seventy ships; viginti pedum *erat agger,* the embankment was twenty feet high; *puer* tredecim annorum, a boy thirteen years old; provectae, exactae, aetatis *homo,* a man advanced, far advanced, in years; tot annorum *felicitas,* so many *years of* good fortune; quindecim dierum *supplicatio,* a thanksgiving of fifteen days' duration.

Obs. 2.—The **Genitive** is used mainly to express *permanent* and *inherent* qualities : optimae spei *adolescens,* a youth of the highest promise ; the **Ablative** both these and *external* characteristics of dress or appearance : *canis capillis, veste sordida;* not *canorum capillorum,* etc. So also the ablative is used for any state or feeling of the *moment: fac* bono sis animo, " Be of good cheer."

199

304. A word in the genitive is sometimes added to another substantive to *explain*, or *define*, or *restrict* its sense: *Virtus* justitiae, the virtue *of* justice; *gloriae praemium*, a reward *consisting in* glory. This is called the **genitive of definition.**

Cautions.—The resemblance of these uses of the Latin genitive to those of the English preposition *of* is obvious, but it must be remembered that—

(i.) After such words as *urbs*, *insula*, etc., apposition is used, not the **defining** genitive, to express the English *of* with the proper name.

> *Urbs* Saguntum, the city *of* Saguntum : *insula* Britannia, the island *of* Britain. (See **222.**)

(ii.) With the names of **towns** or **countries** the Latin **adjective** is used in place of the **possessive** genitive where we use "of."

> *Res* Romanae, the affairs *of* Rome ; *civis* Thebanus, a citizen *of* Thebes. (See **98.**)

(iii.) Remember also : *media* urbs, the middle *of* the city (**295,** *b*), *quot estis?* how many *of* you are there? (**297**), and avoid here the **partitive** genitive.

Exercise 39.

1. It is said that serpents of vast size are found in the island of Lemnos.   2. No one denies that he was a man of courage ;[1] the real question is, whether he was (one) of good sense,[1] and experience.[1]   3. It seems that your son is a boy of the highest promise, and of great influence with[2] those of his own age.   4. After three days'[3] procrastination he at last set out with a fleet of thirty ships ; but being[4] far advanced in life was scarcely competent to carry out so toilsome a task.   5. I would have[5] you therefore be of good cheer, and do not on account of a short-lived panic throw away the result of so many years of toil.   6. He is a person[6] of old-world, as all of us know, and perhaps of excessive, rigour : but at the same time a man[6]

---

[1] What part of speech? (**303,** ii.)   [2] Apud (*acc.*).
[3] **303,** *Obs.* 1.   [4] Turn by *homo* in app. (See **224,** *Obs.* 1.)
[5] *Fac* or *velim*. (**141.**)
[6] *Homo*, in a neutral sense, with either good or bad qualities ; *Vir*, with marked social virtues. (See **224,** *Obs.* 2, *note*).

of justice and honesty, and of the most spotless life.
7. Gallant fighting[1] and an honourable death in the field
becomes citizens of Rome; let the few therefore of us[2]
who survive show ourselves worthy alike of our ancestors
and of the nation of Rome. 8. It seemed that there
stood by him in his sleep an old man far advanced in
years, with white hair, and kindly countenance, who bade
him be of good cheer and hope for the best,[3] for (that) he
would reach in safety the island of Corcyra after a voyage
of some[4] days.

---

[1] 96, *a*.   [2] 297.   [3] Neut. plur.   [4] *aliquot*.

EXERCISE XL.

GENITIVE—*Continued.*

Genitive with Verbs.

THE genitive is also used to complete or define the sense not only of nouns but of certain **verbs**.

305. (i.) The **genitive** of **price**[1] is thus used with verbs of **valuing** and **buying**, etc., especially the former.

Magni, maximi, pluris ; parvi, minoris, minimi ; tanti, quanti, nihili, are used with *factitive* verbs such as *facio, habeo, aestimo,* etc., sometimes with *emo* and *vendo.*

Te quotidie pluris facio. I *value* you *more highly* every day.

Rempublicam nihili habet, *salutem suam* maximi. *He sets no value* on the national cause, *the highest* on his own safety.

Emit *hortos* tanti quanti *Pythius voluit.* He bought the pleasure-grounds *at the full* (or, *exactly at the*) *price* that Pythius wished for.

Obs.—This genitive of value is also used as a predicate with **link** verbs, such as *sum, fio.*

Tua mihi amicitia pluris est *quam ceterorum omnium plausus.* Your friendship is of more value to me than the applause of all the world besides.

306. (ii.) Verbs of **accusing, condemning, acquitting,** such as *accusare, arguere, reum facere, condemnare, absolvere,* take a genitive defining the **charge**.

Proditionis accusare, reum facere. To accuse, to prosecute, *for* treachery.

Furti *ac* repetundarum *condemnatus est.* He was condemned *for,* found guilty *of,* theft and extortion.

Parricidii *eum incusat.* He taxes him *with* parricide.

Sacrilegii *absolutus est.* He was acquitted *of* sacrilege.

---

[1] The origin of this genitive is doubtful ; it may possibly have originated with the locative in -*i* (*at* a price), and in course of time been transferred to other genitives ; but is more probably adjectival.

This construction may be explained by the omission of *crimine*, "on the charge," or *nomine*, "under the title," which are sometimes expressed.

Obs.—Instead of the *genitive*, the *ablative* with *de* is very common.

> De *pecuniis repetundis damnari.*   To be condemned *for* extortion.
> *Aliquem* de ambĭtu *reum facere.*   To bring an action against a man *for* bribery.

So—De *vi*, de *sacrilegio*, de *caede*, de *veneficiis*, etc., *se purgare.*   To clear one's-self *of* assault, sacrilege, murder, poisoning.

But—Inter sicarios *accusatus est.*   He was accused *of assassination.*

307. The **punishment** stands sometimes in the *genitive*; far oftener in the *ablative*.

> Capitis, *or* capite, *damnatus est.*   He was capitally condemned, *i.e. to* death or exile.
> Octupli *condemnatus est.*   He was condemned to pay eightfold.

But—Morte, exilio *condemnatus (multatus) est.*   He was condemned *to* (punished with) death, exile.

308. The genitive is also used to complete the sense of verbs of **compassionating, remembering, reminding, forgetting.**

Such are *misereor, memini, commonefacere, oblivisci.*

But—(*a*) Verbs of reminding, *admoneo*, etc., take an accusative of the thing as well as of the person, with *neuter pronouns*; hoc, illud,[1] te admoneo.

(*b*) *Memini*, an accusative with a person, in the sense of "I still remember him;" rarely otherwise in *prose*. *Recordor*, "I recall to my thoughts," is almost invariably used with the accusative.

(*c*) *Miserari*, "to express pity for," "to bemoan the lot of," an accusative.

Thus—

> Ciceronem *memini;* rerum praeteritarum (the past) *memini.*
> Nostri *miserere*, take pity on us ; casum nostrum *miserabatur*, he bemoaned our disaster.

But—Illud *nos admonuit*, he reminded us of that ; *nos* officii nostri *commonefecit*, he reminded us of our duty.

Obs.—Even an impersonal phrase equivalent to a verb of remembering is followed by a similar genitive.

> Venit mihi in mentem *ejus diei.*   I have a recollection of that day.

---

[1] This may be looked on as a cognate accusative (**236, 237**).

The Genitive with Impersonal Verbs.

309. The impersonals, *pudet*, *piget*, *poenitet*, *taedet*, *miseret*, take an **accusative** of the *person feeling*, a **genitive** of what *causes* the feeling.

> Ignavum *poenitebit aliquando* ignaviae.   The slothful man will one day repent of his sloth.
>
> Me *non solum piget* stultitiae meae, *sed etiam pudet*.   I am not only sorry for my folly, but also ashamed of it.
>
> *Taedet* me vitae.   I am weary of my life.
>
> Tui me *miseret;* mei *piget*.   I pity you ; I am vexed with myself.

What causes the feeling may also be a *verb* (in the *infinitive*, or in an *indicative* clause with *quod*).

> *Taedet* eadem audire *milites*.   The soldiers are tired of hearing the same thing.
>
> *Poenitet nos* $\begin{cases} haec \text{ fecisse.} \\ \text{quod } haec \text{ fecimus.} \end{cases}$ *We are sorry that we acted so.*

Obs. 1.—The neuter pronouns *hoc, illud, quod*, are used in place of the genitive with these verbs. Hoc *pudet*, illud *poenitet*. (Cf. **308**, *a*.)

Obs. 2.—The genitive with *pudet* is also used for the person *before whom* the shame is felt.

> *Pudet me* veteranorum militum.   I blush *before* the veterans.

310. The construction of the impersonals *interest* and *rēfert* requires attention.

(i.) The *person* to whom it is of importance is put in the *genitive* with *interest ;* but *possessive pronouns, meus, tuus, suus, noster, vester,* etc., are used in the *ablative feminine*.

> *Interest* omnium *recte facere*.   It is the interest *of all* to do right.
>
> *Quid* nostrā *interest ?*   Of what importance is it *to us ?* (or, What does it signify to us ?)

(ii.) The *thing* that is of importance may be either (*a*) an *infinitive* (*with* or *without* accusative) or (*b*) a *neuter pronoun* (*hoc, id, illud, quod*), or a *clause* introduced either (*c*) by an *interrogative* pronoun or particle, followed by the *subjunctive* mood, or (*d*) by *ut, nē*.

(iii.) The *degree of importance* is expressed either by the *genitive* of price (*magni, tanti, pluris*), or by an *adverb* or *neuter adjective* (*magnopere, vehementer, magis, parum : multum, plus, nihil, nimium, quantum*, etc.)

(iv.) The *thing* with reference to which it is of importance is sometimes indicated by *ad*.

Examples.—The following examples should therefore be well studied and analysed :—

> *a. Magni interest ad laudem civitatis haec vos facere.* Your *doing* this is of great importance *to the credit* of the state.
>
> *b.* Multum *interest quos quisque audiat quotidie.* It is of *great* consequence whom a man listens to every day.
>
> *c. Illud*[1] *mea* pluris *interest te* ut videam. It is of more consequence *to me* that I should see you.
>
> *d.* Vestrā *interest, commilitones, ne imperatorem pessimi* faciant. It is of importance *to you*, my comrades, *that* the worst sort should *not* elect your commander.
>
> *f. Hoc et* tuā *et* rei publicae *interest.* This concerns both *yourself* and the *nation.*
>
> *c. Nihil* meā *interest* quanti *me* facias. Your *estimate* of me is of no concern to me.

The constructions of *refert, it concerns,* are similar to those of *interest,* except that *refert* is rarely used with a genitive of the person concerned, but with the feminine possessive, or *ad.*

Exercise 40.

1. He was a man of moderate abilities, but of the highest character, and in the greatest crisis of a perilous war he was valued more highly in his old age than any[2] of (his) juniors. 2. He was a man of long-tried honour and rare incorruptibility, yet at that time he was taxed with avarice, suspected of bribery, and prosecuted for extortion; you all know that he was unanimously acquitted of that charge; but who[3] is there of you but remembers the (that) day on which he refused to deprecate the undeserved disgrace of condemnation, and not only cleared himself of that indictment, but exposed the malice and falsehoods of his accusers? None[4] of those who were present in the court that day will easily forget his magnificent address; nothing ever made a deeper impression on his audience.[5] 3. The whole nation has long[6] been weary of the war, regrets its own rashness, and blushes for the

---

[1] The substantival *ut*-clause is especially common after *illud* or *hoc* at the beginning of the sentence.

[2] *Quisquam.* (See **358, ii.**)

[3] To whom of you does not, etc., **308,** *Obs.*   [4] *Nemo.*

[5] " The mind (*pl.*) of his audience." Either genitive participle of, or relative clause with, *audio.* (**73, 76.**)

[6] Tense ? (See **181.**)

folly and incompetence of its general.   4. I remember
well the man [1] whom you mention ; he was a person of
very low origin, of advanced age, with white hair, mean
dress, of uncultivated and rustic demeanour ; but no one
was ever more skilled in (301, ii.) the science of war, and
his being made general [2] at such an emergency was of
the utmost importance to the welfare of the state.   5. It
makes no difference to us, who are waiting for your verdict,
whether the defendant be acquitted or condemned ; but
it is of general interest that he should not in his absence
and unheard be sentenced to either exile or death.

---

[1] *Ille*. (339, iii.)   [2] **310, ii.** *a.*

PLACE, SPACE.

Locative Case.

IN answer to the questions, *where? whither? whence?* we employ in English the prepositions *at* or *in, to, from,* etc.

In Latin all these questions can sometimes be answered merely by **case-endings**; but a **preposition** is often necessary.

311. Place at which; answer to "**where?**"

This is generally expressed by the *local* **ablative** (**272, 273**) with or even without a **preposition**. Thus, in *Italia,* in *urbe;* and so generally where an adjective is attached; but mediā *urbe,* totā *Italiā.*

Obs.—Of course other prepositions of place are used with their proper cases. Thus—

Ad[1] *urbem est.* He is *in the neighbourhood* of (outside) the city.
Ad (*sometimes* apud) *Cannas pugnatum est.* There was a battle *at (near)* Cannae.

312. But with **towns** and **small islands** as opposed to countries, the old rule is as follows:—

If the name of a town, *at which* anything is or happens, is a *singular* noun of the *first* or *second* declension, it is put in the **genitive**; if not, in the **ablative**.

Vixi Romae, Tarenti, Athenis, Rhodi, Tiburĕ (or *Tiburi*). I have lived at Rome, Tarentum, Athens, Rhodes, Tibur.

The explanation of this is that *Romae* (for older form *Romai*) *Tarenti, Rhodi,* are remains of the locative case in *i,* which in other declensions was supplanted by the ablative. (*Tiburi, Carthagini* are perhaps old ablatives.) In the plural the two cases coincide.

Other instances of this case are *domi,* at home; *humi* on the ground; *belli, militiae,* in war (only used in contrast with *domi*). *Ruri,* in the country, *vesperi,* in the evening, may be old ablatives.

Obs.—*Pendēre* animi, "to be in suspense," as also the genitive of *value* (**305**), may be locative cases.

---

[1] This is often used of Roman generals, who could not enter the city without laying down their *imperium.*

313. Place to which—whither ?

As a rule the **prepositions** *ad, in,* etc., are used with the accusative ; but

With the names of **towns**, etc., as above, the **accusative** is used without a preposition: thus, In *or* ad *Italiam, Africam, urbem, navem,* but, Syracusas, Romam, etc., *rediit.*

Obs.—The same construction is used with *domus* and *rus :* domum *rediit ;* rus *fugit.*

314. Place from which—whence ?

As a rule the **ablative** is used, joined with the **prepositions** *e, ex, a (ab)* : a *Pyrrho,* ex *Italia,* ab *Africa,* e *nave,* ab *urbe.*

But with *towns,* etc., the **ablative** alone is generally used, as also with *domus* and *rus.*

> Romā *scribit,* he writes *from* Rome ; *Tarquinios* Corintho *fugit,* he fled, *or* went into exile, *to* Tarquinii *from* Corinth : so, rure, *or* ruri *rediit.*

These rules are quite simple, but the following idiom must be carefully observed.

315. We cannot, in Latin, say, as in English, "He came to his father *at* Rome," or "from Carthage *in* Africa." With verbs of motion, all such phrases must follow the rules for motion *to* or *from,* given above. Thus—

> He returned home from his friends *at* Corinth. *Corintho ab amicis domum rediit.*
> He sent a despatch to the Senate *at* Rome. *Romam ad Senatum literas misit.*
> He returned to his friends *in* Africa. In *Africam ad amicos rediit.*

In such sentences Latin connects both nouns closely with the verb of motion.

316. None of the rules given above apply to the names of towns when joined with adjectives.

(i.) We cannot say *totius,* or *toti,*[1] *Corinthi,* for "*in* the whole of Corinth," but must use with both words the **local ablative**, *tota* Corintho. (**311.**)

---

[1] This is because the old locative case no longer exists in any but certain words.

(ii.) When *urbs*, or *oppidum*, comes before the proper name, the preposition must be used.

> In *urbe Londino*, in the city *of* London ; ad *urbem Athenas*, ex *urbe Roma.* (See 222.)

(iii.) With *domus* the **locative** construction is extended to *possessive pronouns*. With other adjectives the preposition is used.

> *Domi* meae (or *apud me*) *commoratus est.* He stayed at *my* house.

But—In *veteri domo*, ad *veterem domum*. In, or to, his *old* home.

317. When an adjective is joined with the name of a town, the construction resembles that used with the names of persons. (See 224.)

The name of the town is placed first, in either the *locative*, *accusative*, or *ablative*, according to the meaning ; then follows the word *urbs* or *oppidum* combined with the adjective, with or without a preposition according to the rules already given. Thus—

> *Archias Antiochiae natus est*, celebri *quondam* urbe (local ablative). Archias was born in the once famous city of Antioch.
> *Athenas*, in urbem praeclarissimam *veni*. I reached the illustrious city of Athens.
> *Syracusis*, ex urbe opulentissima, *profectus est.* He set out from the flourishing city of Syracuse.

318. (i.) **Space covered** (answer to the question **how far ?**) is generally expressed by the **accusative**.

> *Tridui* iter *processit.* He advanced a three days' march.
> *Ab officio cave* transversum, *ut aiunt*, digitum *discedas.* Do not swerve "a finger's breadth" from your duty.

(ii.) For **distance from** (question, **how far off ?**) either the **accusative** or **ablative** is used. (**238, iv.**, and **279**.)

> *Ariovistus vix* plus duo milia *passuum* (*or* duobus milibus) *aberat.* Ariovistus was at a distance of scarcely more than two miles.

Obs.—After *plus*, *amplius*, *minus*, *quam* is rarely used with numerals, but the case of the numeral is unaffected by the comparative.

(iii.) **Dimension** is generally in the **accusative**.

> *Milites aggĕrem latum* pedes trecentos *exstruxerunt.* The soldiers threw up a mound three hundred feet broad (*or* in breadth).

Occasionally the **genitive** of quality, or description, is used and the adjective omitted : *fossa* quindecim pedum, a ditch fifteen feet *deep.* (See **303,** *Obs.* 1.)

319. In English the name of a town or country is often personified and used for the nation or people : "Spain," "France," "England," etc. This is much rarer in Latin prose. (Cf. **17**, and end of **174**.)

O

"The war between *Rome* and *Carthage*" is *Bellum, quod* populus Romanus *cum* Carthaginiensibus *gessit.*

For "Rome" in this sense we may use *Populus Romanus, res publica Romana,* or *Romani,* but rarely *Roma.*

Exercise 41.

1. After living[1] many[2] years at Veii, a town at that period of great population[3] and vast resources, he removed thence late in life to the city[4] of Rome, which was at a distance of about fourteen miles from his old home. 2. His parents, sprung originally from Syracuse, had been[5] long resident at Carthage; he himself was sent[6] in boyhood to his uncle at Utica, and was absent from home for full three years; but after his[7] return to his mother, now[8] a widow, at Carthage, he passed the rest of his youth at his own home. 3. The enemy (*pl.*) was now[8] scarcely a single day's march off; the walls of the fortress, scarcely twenty feet high, surrounded by a ditch of (a depth of) less than six feet, were falling into ruin from age; Doria, after waiting[1] six days in vain for reinforcements, sent a despatch by[9] a spy to the governor at Pisa, earnestly imploring[10] him not to waste time any longer, but to bring up troops to[11] his aid without delay. 4. Born and brought up in the vast and populous city of London, I have never before had permission to exchange the din and throng of the city even[12] for the repose and peace and solitude of rural life; but now I hope shortly to travel to my son at Rome,

---

[1] "After living," *i.e.* "having lived." (**14,** *a.*)
[2] Case ? (See **321.**)
[3] May be turned either by "flourishing (superlative of *florens*) with a multitude of citizens and vast resources," or "most populous and wealthy."
[4] *Urbs* may be removed into the relative clause, "which city."
[5] Tense ? (See **181.**)
[6] Participle, and omit "and." (**15.**)
[7] Use verb and *postquam.* (**14,** *a.*)
[8] Why not *nunc ?* (See **328,** *b.*)
[9] Why not *ab ?* (See **267,** *Obs.*)
[10] "(in) which he implored." Why not participle ? (See **411.**)
[11] For construction see **259.** Is "his" *ei* or *sibi ?* (See **353.**)
[12] = not even. (Intr. **99.**)

and from Italy to sail, before the middle of winter, to the city of Constantinople, which I have long been eager to visit; you, I fancy,[1] will winter at Malta, an island[2] which I am not likely ever to see. In the beginning of spring I have decided to stay in the lovely city of Naples, and to betake myself to my old home at London in the month of May or June. 5. Caesar shows himself, I fancy, scarcely less tenacious of his purpose at home than in the field; it is said[3] that he is outside the city waiting for his triumph, and wishes to address the people. 6. Exasperated and provoked by the wrongs and insults of Napoleon, Spain turned at last to England her ancient foe.

---

[1] See **32**, *b*.   [2] " Which island."   [3] See **43**, **44**.

EXERCISE XLII.

EXPRESSIONS OF TIME.

320. In answer to the question **when? at what time?** the **local ablative** (272) is used with words which in themselves denote *time*.

Vere, auctumno, nocte, solis occasu, primā luce, etc.

With words which do not *in themselves* denote time, the preposition *in* is mostly inserted, unless an adjective is attached : in *bello*, in time of war ; but *bello Punico secundo*, in the second Punic war. (Cf. **311.**) But the rule is not universal.

Obs.—*In tempore* means at the *right* moment, but *Alcibiadis temporibus*, at the *time* (in the *days*) of Alcibiades.

For the difference made by the preposition *in*, see **273,** *Obs.*

321. In answer to the question **how long?** the **accusative** is used. (See **238, iv.**)

> Multos *jam* annos *hic domicilium habeo.* I have now been living (**181**) here *for* many years.

Obs. 1.—Sometimes the idea of duration is emphasised by the addition of *per.*

> Per *totam noctem,* per *hiemem.*

Obs. 2.—The answer to **for how long past?** is often expressed by an *ordinal* adjective (of course in the singular).

> *Annum jam* (or, *hunc*) vicesimum *regnat.* He has been king *for the last* twenty years.

322. In answer to **how long before? how long after?** two constructions may be used.

(*a*) The word, or words, expressing the length of time may be in the ablative of *measure of difference* (**279**), and *post* or *ante* may be used as **adverbs.** Or

(*b*) *Post* and *ante* may be used as **prepositions** with the accusative of the amount of time.

For example, for the phrase "the fleet returned after three years," we may write either, tribus *post* annis (tertio *post* anno) *classis rediit,* or *post* tres annos, etc. There is the same variety in English : "Three years *after,* the fleet returned" is English, though "After three years" is less ambiguous.

Obs.—Even when joined with this ablative, *post, ante,* may still govern a case. We may say for "a few days before his death," either "*paucis diebus* ante *ejus* mortem," or "*paucis* ante *diebus,* quam *e vita excessit.*"

212

323. The following examples may be noticed :—

(*a*) " Three hundred and two years after the foundation of Rome."

    1. Anno trecentesimo altero *quam Roma condita est.*   Or,

    2. Post trecentesimum alterum annum *quam Roma condita est.*

(*b*) *Pridie quam excessit e vitâ.*   The day before his death.
    Postridie quam a vobis discessi.   The day after I left you.
    Postero anno quam, etc.   The year after, etc.
    Priore anno quam, etc.   The year before, etc.

(*c*) (He did it) *three years* after *he (had) returned.*

    1. *Post* tres annos (*or* tertium annum) }
    2. Tertio anno[1]   } *quam* redierat.
    3. Tribus *post* annis (*or* tertio anno) *quam* redierat.
    4. Tertio anno, *quo* redierat.   (Rare.)

324. How long ago ?, reckoning from the present time, is answered by *abhinc* with the **accusative** ; the *abhinc* always coming first.

    Abhinc annos *quatuor Virgilium vidi.*   I saw Virgil four years ago.

325. Within, or **in, what time ?** is answered by the **ablative,** or the preposition *intra* with the accusative.

The singular of the *Ordinal* (" second," " third," etc.) often takes the place of the plural of the *Cardinal* (" two," " three").

    Vix decem annis, *or* decimo anno, *or* intra decimum annum, *urbem capiemus.*   We shall scarcely take the city *in*, or *for*, or *within*, ten years.

Obs.—His tribus diebus, in or *for* the last three days (from the *present* time) ; *illis, etc.,* from a *past* time ; *hoc biennio*, within two years from this time.

326. *In* with the **accusative** denotes a time *for* which provision or arrangement or calculations are made.

    In diem *vivere*, to live *for* the day (only) ; in sex dies *indutiae*, a truce *for* six days ; ad cœnam me in posterum diem *invitavit*, he invited me to supper *for* the next day : (*ad*, an exact date in the future); *ad calendas solvam*, I will pay *on*, or *by*, the 1st ; *ad tempus*, at the appointed time, punctually.
    Ex, ab, starting from the time at which a period begins.   Ex *eo die ad extremum usque vitae diem.*

---

[1] It might be supposed that "*tertio anno quam* (or *quo*) *redierat*" would mean "after two completed years from his return, and before the completion of the third." This however does not appear to be so. "*Octavo mense, quam cœptum oppugnari, captum Saguntum,*" etc. (LIV.): ἐν ὀκτὼ μησί (POLYB.) ; " *Tyrus septimo mense capta est* " (CURT.) ; πολιορκῶν ἑπτὰ μῆνας (PLUT.).

327. In answer to the question **how old** ? the usual construction is *natus* with the accusative.

> Annos *quinque et octoginta* natus *excessit e vita.*   He died
>   at the age of eighty-five.

But *quum* annos *quinque et octoginta* haberet, or *quum* annum octogesimum quintum *ageret*, would be equally good Latin.

The adjectival genitive (**303**, *Obs.* 1) may also be used : *puer quindecim* annorum.

"Under, over, twenty years," may be expressed by *minor (major) viginti* annis, or annos *natus minor (major) viginti*, and by several other curious variations, such as—

> *Minor viginti* annis *natu.*—Cic.
> *Minor* decem annorum.—Livy.

" When under," etc., by *quum nondum viginti haberet annos.*

Notes on Adverbs of Time.

328. The correct use of certain adverbs of time is important.

(*a*) "**No longer**" is only *non diutius* when a long time has already passed, otherwise *non jam ;* "no one any longer" is *nemo jam*, or (with *and*) *nec quisquam jam.*

(*b*) **Now.** *Nunc* is "at the present moment," or "as things are now." It cannot be used of the past. "Caesar *was now* tired of war" is, jam *Caesarem belli taedebat.* Occasionally, if the "now" of the past is very precise, *tum. Jam* can be used also of the future : *quid hoc rei sit,* jam *intelleges,* "you will *soon* be aware of the meaning of this."

(*c*) "**Daily.**" *Quotidie* as a rule ; *in dies* only with comparatives, or verbs of *increasing* or the reverse ; *in singulos dies* is more emphatic : *Diem de die,* day after day ; *de nocte,* after night has begun. *Diurnus* (adj.) is "daily" as opposed to *nocturnus ; quotidianus* is "daily" in the sense of "every-day."

(*d*) "**Not yet**" is *nondum, necdum ;* "no one yet" *nemo unquam*, or, where the present is opposed to the future, *adhuc nemo.*

" **Still** " (=even now) is *etiam nunc.*

(*e*) *Jam diu* is "now for a long while" simply ; *jam pridem* looks back rather to the *beginning* of the time that is past ; *jam dudum* "for *some,* or a considerable, time."

(*f*) **Again.** *Rursus,* "once more ;" *iterum,* "a *second* time," opposed to *semel* or *primum ; de integro,* "afresh" as though the former action had not taken place ; "again and again," *saepe, saepissime.* (**57**, *a.*)

Exercise 42.

1. Mithridates, who in a single day had butchered so many citizens of Rome, had now been on the throne two-and-twenty years from that date.   2. It seems that here too the swallows are absent in the winter months; I at least have seen not a single[1] one for the last three weeks. 3. He died at the age of three-and-thirty; when less than thirty years old he had already performed achievements unequalled[2] by any either of his predecessors or successors. 4. The famine is becoming sorer daily; exhausted by daily toil (*pl.*) we shall soon be compelled[3] to discontinue the sallies which up to this day we have made both by night[4] and by day.   Day after day we look in vain for the arrival of our troops.   5. He promised to be by my side by the first of June; for the last ten years I have never so much as once known[5] him to be present in good time.   6. Nearly three years ago I said that I had never yet seen any one[6] who surpassed[7] your brother in character or ability, but in the last two years he seems to be growing daily sterner and harsher, and I no longer estimate him so highly as I did before.   7. I saw your father about three weeks after[8] his return from India.   Years[9] had not yet dulled the keenness of his intellect or the vigour of his spirit; in spite of his advancing years he had commanded an army within the last six months, and was just preparing to be a candidate for office.   8. Misled by a mistake in the date,[10] I thought you had stayed at Athens more than six months.   9. I have spoken enough on this question, and will detain you no longer; six months ago I might[11] have spoken longer.[12]

---

[1] "= not even one."   (Intr. 99.)
[2] "Such as (86) not even one (had performed)."
[3] "The sallies must be," etc., part. in -*dus*.   (See 199.)
[4] Use adjectives.   (328, *c*.)
[5] *Cognosco*, "I find or ascertain."   [6] 328, *d*.
[7] Mood?   (77.)   [8] See 323, *c*.
[9] *i.e.* age.   [10] Genitive.   (300.)
[11] See 196, *b*.   [12] "Said more."   (53.)

PREPOSITIONS.

Prepositions with Accusative.

329. With the use of **Cases** is closely connected that of *Prepositions.*

(i.) **Prepositions** are indeclinable words which, besides other uses, are placed before substantives and pronouns to define their relation to other words. (Intr. 20-24.)

(ii.) Their use therefore is precisely the same as that of the *case-endings* (see **203**), but as the number of cases is not nearly sufficient to mark all the different relations of a noun to other words, prepositions[1] are used to aid the cases in making their meaning more definite and clear. Thus, to take the simplest instance, the use of the preposition distinguishes the relation of the *agent* from that of the *instrument* (**267**).

(iii.) In Latin, as in modern languages, they come, as a rule, before[2] the noun, and are used almost exclusively with the *accusative* and *ablative* cases.

Obs.—The ablatives *gratiā, causā*, are used as *quasi-prepositions* with the *genitive*, and resemble such English *prepositional phrases* as "in consequence of," "in spite of," etc.

330. The following prepositions are used with the *accusative* :—

(Those marked with an asterisk are used also as *adverbs, i.e.* without being attached to a noun, but as qualifying a *verb* or *adjective.*)

> *ante*, apud, ad, adversus*,*
> *circum*, circa*, citra*, cis,*
> *erga, contra*, inter, extra*,*
> *infra*, intra*, juxta*, ob,*

---

[1] Prepositions were doubtless originally adverbs formed from nouns and pronouns; in some languages, as occasionally in Latin, they follow the noun ; the case-endings may have had their origin in prepositional words added to the noun, cf. where*of*, where*by*, there*fore*, etc.

[2] For the position of *cum* in tecu*m*, etc., see **8**, *Obs.*; *tenus* also follows its noun (*Alpibus* tenus, *as far as* the Alps), as does *versus*, and occasionally *propter* and others.

penes, pone*, post* and *præter,*
prope*, propter*, per, secundum,
supra*, versus, ultra*, trans.

The following are joined with the *accusative* when they express *motion towards;* otherwise with the *ablative :—*

sub and *subter*, super*, in.*

The following are followed by the *ablative :—*

a (ab, abs), with *cum* and *de,*
coram*, pro with *ex* or *e,*
tenus, sine, also *prae ;*

and where *place at,* not *motion towards* is denoted—

sub and *subter*, super*, in.*

331. Their meanings are so various that no attempt will be made to illustrate more than some of the most important.

The *local* meaning is the earliest, but from this many others are deduced.

1. **Ad,** "towards," "to," used after verbs of motion, and transferred to various other senses.

(a) Ad *te scripsi* (to) ; (b) ad *hæc respondit,* "in answer to ;" (c) ad *Cannas,* "in the neighbourhood of," "near ;" (d) *hoc* ad *nos conservandos pertinet,* "this *tends to* our preservation ;" (e) *dies* ad *urbis interitum fatalis,* "the day destined *to* the ruin of the city" (*final*) ; (f) ad *unum,* "to a man" = all.

2. **Adversus,** "opposite to."

(a) Adversus *castra nostra ;* (b) "against," "with," adversus *te contendam* = *contra te* or *tecum;* (c) "in answer to" (a speech), adversus *hæc respondit.*

3. **Ante,** "before" (*place*), ante *aciem :* but mostly "*time,*" ante *me,* "before my time ;" often used adverbially ; see **322.**

4. **Apud,** "close by :" apud *Cannas,* "near, or at, Cannae," but mostly in such phrases as :

(a) Apud *me,* "in my house ;" (b) apud *Xenophontem,* "in (the *writings* of) Xenophon ;" (c) apud *vos concionatus est,* "he made a speech *in your hearing ;*" (d) apud *me,* "in my judgment ; " apud *me plus valet,* "has more influence *with* me."

5. **Circum, circa,** "round :" circa *tellurem,* "round the earth ;" circa *viam,* "on *both sides* of, *along,* the road ;" often used adverbially ; *circa* and *circiter,* "about," with numerals.

6. **Cis, citra ; trans,** " this side," " the other side :" cis, citra, trans, *flumen Rhenum.*

7. **Contra,** " facing :" contra *urbem ;* oftener " against," contra *rempublicam facere,* " to act unconstitutionally ;" contra *nos bellum gerit* = *nobiscum,* contra (praeter) *spem, opinionem,* etc.

8. **Erga** (local sense obsolete) : erga *me benevolentissimus,* " full of kindness *towards* me."

9. **Extra,** " outside of :" extra *urbem ;* extra *culpam,* "*free from* blame ;" extra *ordinem,* " out of his proper order ;" " extraordinarily."

10. **Inter,** " amongst :" inter *hostium tela :* " between," inter *me ac vos hoc* (or *illud*) *interest :* " this difference between ;" inter *se diligunt* (reciprocal), " they love *each other.*"

11. **Infra,** " below :" infra *montes.*

12. **Intra,** " within :" intra *teli jactum,* " within the cast of a javelin ;" intra *diem decimum* (325).

13. **Juxta,** " close to," " near :" juxta *murum ;* often adverbially, juxta *constiti ;* sometimes = pariter, and joined with *ac.*

14. **Ob,** " before, opposite to :" ob *oculos ;* " on account of," ob *delictum, quam* ob *rem* = " wherefore (therefore)."

15. **Penes,** " in the power of :" penes *te hoc est,* " this *depends on* you."

16. **Per,** " through," (place and time).
   (a) Per *provinciam ;* (b) per *hos dies,* " during the last few days " (325, *Obs.*) ; (c) " (causal)," per *me licet,* " you have my leave, you may (do it) as far as I am concerned ;" (d) (instrument *or* secondary agent), per *speculatores,* " by means of spies ;" (e) (manner), per *vim,* " by violence, *violently.*"

17. **Post,** " behind," " after," = **pone.**
   (a) Post *tergum ;* (b) (time), post *hominum memoriam,* " since the dawn of history," "*within* human memory ;" often adverbial (see 322).

18. **Praeter,** " past."
   (a) Praeter *castra ;* (b) " beyond," " more than," praeter *ceteros ;* (c) " contrary to " = *contra,* praeter *spem ;* (d) " except," praeter *te unum omnes.*

19. **Prope (propius, proxime),** " near to :" prope *me,* propius *urbem,* (often adverbial).

20. **Propter,** " close to."
   (a) Propter *murum ;* (b) " on account of," propter *se,* " for its own sake ;" " thanks to," propter *te salvus sum* = *tua opera.*

21. **Secundum**, "along" (following).

    (*a*) Secundum *flumen*; (*b*) secundum *naturam*, "in accordance with;" (*c*) secundum *pugnam*, "next to, *immediately after*, the fight" (time); (*d*) secundum *Deos*, "next to the Gods."

22. **Versus**, only with *domum* and *towns*; placed *after* the substantive: *Romam* versus, "in the direction of Rome."

23. **Ultra**, "beyond."

    (*a*) Ultra *flumen*; (*b*) ultra *vires*, "beyond his strength."

In, sub, super, *with accusative.*

24. **In**, "into," "to."

    (*a*) *Athenas* in *Graeciam exulatum abiit*, "went into exile at Athens in Greece" (315); *exercitum* in *naves imponere*, in *terram exponere*, "to embark," "disembark," an army; in *orbem se colligunt*, "form a circle (for defence);" (*b*) (*time*), in *quartum diem* in *hortos* ad *caenam invitavit*, (326) "*to* supper *in* his grounds *four days* from that time;" in *praesens*, "for the present;" in *dies*, "daily;" in *posterum*, "for the future;" (*c*) "against," in *me invectus* est, "inveighed *against* me;" (*d*) "towards," in *rempublicam merita*, "services *to* the nation" (but *de r. p.* mereri); (*e*) (*manner*), "after;" in hunc modum *locutus est*.

25. **Sub** ("motion"), "up to."

    (*a*) Sub *ipsos muros adequitant*, "they ride *close up* to the walls;" (*b*) (*time*), "just *before;*" sub *lucem;* sub *haec*, "just *after* this."

26. **Super**, "above."

    (*a*) Super *ipsum*, "(next) above *the host* at table;" (*b*) *alii* super *alios*, "one *after* another."

Exercise 43.

1. Next to heaven,[1] I ascribed this[2] great favour mainly to you and your children. 2. I hope that when once[3] he has reached Rome he will stay in my house. 3. It seems that this year is destined for the ruin of the nation. 4. He is generally believed to be free from blame, and no one supposes that such[4] a good patriot would have[5] done

---

[1] Why not *caelum?* (See **17**.)   [2] **88**, *Obs.*
[3] Express "once" by the right tense. (**190**, ii., *Obs.*)
[4] **88**.   [5] **193**, v.

anything unconstitutionally.   5. He drew up his line on the other side the Danube; our men, who had now for some time been[1] marching along the river, halted close to the other bank opposite the enemies' camp.   6. You had my leave to return home to your friends in London. Whether you have gone[2] away or no depends on yourself. 7. There is this difference between you and others: with them (**339,** iv.) my client has, thanks to his many[3] services to the nation, great weight; with you, for the same reason, he has absolutely none.   8. It seems that he invited your son to supper with him three days from that time at his house; since that date none of his friends have seen him anywhere.   9. The enemy had now disembarked, and had come within the reach of missiles; our men hurled[4] their javelins and tried to pass by between them and the river.   10. Such was their joy for the present, such their hopes[5] for the future, that no one suspected the real state of the case.[6]   11. Having inveighed against me with the utmost fury, he sat down; in answer to his long speech I made a very few[7] remarks. 12. Having ridden past the many[8] tall trees which stood along the road, I halted at last close to the gate.

---

[1] **181.**   [2] See **171.**   [3] *So* many, *tot.*   (Cf. **88,** *Obs.*)
[4] Historic infinitive.   (See **186.**)
[5] Singular.   In Latin prose *spes* is very rarely used in the plural.
[6] " What was really happening" *(fio),* see **174** ; or "*that* which etc.)" see **176.**
[7] " Said very little."   (See **53, 54.**)
[8] See **56,** also **69.**

PREPOSITIONS WITH THE ABLATIVE.

332. Here also the **local** meaning is the earliest.

A (before consonants and *j*, otherwise) **ab.**

(*a*) " From," ab *Africa; (b) (time)*, a *puero*, " from boyhood : " ab *urbe conditā*, " from (*after*) the foundation of the city ;" (*c*) "from the side of" = " on," a *dextro cornu* : a *fronte*, " in front ;" so, (*d*) a *senatu stare*, "to take the *side of* the senate ;" (*e*) *securus* ab *hoste*, " free from care *as to* the enemy ;" a *re frumentariā laborare*, "to be in distress *for* provisions ;" (*f*) a *te incipiam*, " I will begin *with* you ;" (*g*) *confestim* a *praelio*, "immediately *after* the battle." Cf. (*b*).

Cum, " with " (opposed to *sine*).

(*a*) "In company with," tecum *Romam redii;* hence " having," " wearing," cum *gladio*, cum *sordida veste ;* even, cum *febri*, "suffering from ;" so, cum *imperio esse*, "to be invested with military power."

(*b*) "With," of friendly, or unfriendly, relations : tecum *mihi amicitia, certamen,* etc., *est :* tecum (or *contra te*) *bellum gero ;* hoc mecum *communicavit*, "he imparted this *to* me."

(*c*) Accompanying circumstances, or results : *maximo* cum *damno meo*, " *to* my great loss."

De, " down from."

(*a*) De *moenibus deturbare*, "to drive in confusion *from* the walls ;" (*b*) de *spe dejicere*, "to disappoint ;" (*c*) " from," *homo* de *plebe*, "a man *of* (taken *from*) the people ;" (*d*) "concerning," etc., de *te actum est*, "it is *all over with* (concerning) you ;" (*e*) ("time," **328**, *c*), de *viā languere*, "to be tired *after* a journey ;" (*f*) de *industriā*, "on purpose ;" (*g*) *bene mereri* de . . . , "to deserve well *of*," " to serve ;" (*h*) *poenas sumere* de . . . , "to punish."

Ex (before all letters), **e** (only before consonants), "out of ;" many uses.

Ex *equo pugnare*, " *on* horseback ;" e *rebus futuris pendēre*, " to depend *upon* the future ;" ex *sententiā*, "*according to* one's wish *or* views ;" e *republicā* (opposed to *contra r. p.*), " *in accordance* with the constitution :" ex *improviso*, "unexpectedly," etc.

5. **In,** "in," also "among," etc.

(*a*) In *bonis ducere*, "to reckon *among* blessings ;" (*b*) (*time*), in *deliberando*, "whilst deliberating ;" (*c*) *quae* in *oculis sunt*, "*before* our eyes ;" (*d*) in *armis esse*, "*under* arms ;" (*e*) *quid* in *nobis fecit?* "*as* concerns, or, *with* us ;" (*f*) in *te nihil potestatis habet*, "no power *over* you ;" (*g*) *quantum* in *me est*, "to the utmost of my power ;" (*h*) (of circumstances), *satis ut* in *re trepida impavidus*, "with fair courage *considering* the critical state of things ;" (*i*) "in spite of, in face of," in *tanto discrimine*.   (See **273**, *Obs*.)

6. **Prae,** "in front of ;" commonest uses metaphorical.

(*a*) Prae *se ferre*, "to *avow*," "make no secret of ;" (*b*) "as a *preventive* cause," prae *clamore vix audiri potuit*, he could scarcely be heard *for* the shouting = "his voice *was drowned in* the shouting."

7. **Pro,** also "in front of."

(*a*) Pro *tribunali dicere*, "to speak (in front of) *from* the magistrate's tribunal ;" (*b*) "in defence of," pro *aris et focis :* (*c*) "in place of," "as good as," *unus ille mihi* pro *exercitu est ;* (*d*) "as," pro *certo habere*, "to feel sure of ;" (*e*) "in proportion to," pro *meritis ejus gratiam reddere ;* (*f*) "in accordance with," pro *prudentiā tuā ;* (*g*) "in virtue of," pro *potestate ;* (*h*) "in proportion to ;" with comparatives, *caedes minor quam* pro *tantā victoria*, "small in *proportion to* the greatness of the victory."

8. **Sine,** "without," but not nearly so often used as the English preposition.   Its place is taken by many constructions.

Nullo negotio, "*without* trouble ;" *re infecta*, "*without* result ;" *nullo repugnante*, "*without* resistance ;" *imprudens*, "*without* being aware."   (See **425**.)

Compare also—

Stetit impavidus neque *loco cessit*.   He stood, etc., *without* yielding ground ;

or—*Non potes mihi nocere* quin *tibi ipsi* noceas.   You cannot hurt me *without* injuring yourself.

333. There is nothing difficult in the use of the other prepositions.

Tenus is used occasionally with the genitive, and follows its noun ; it should be noticed in such forms as *hac*tenus, *aliquate*nus, and *verbo* tenus, "as far as words go."

Sub must never be used with the ablative after verbs of *motion towards ;* its metaphorical use, "under a leader *or* king," is rare in Latin ; "*under* his guidance" is *eo duce*.

Exercise 44.

1. In the midst of this dire confusion and tumult, the emperor was seen with his staff on the left wing. He was now[1] free from care as to the enemy's cavalry, and his words of encouragement were drowned in shouts of joy and triumph. 2. I fear that[2] it is all over with our army : for[3] ten successive days there has been the greatest want of provisions; in front, in flank, in rear, enemies are threatening (them); all the neighbouring tribes are in arms : on no side is there any prospect of aid : yet, for myself,[4] in the face of these great dangers, I am unwilling wholly to despair. 3. Immediately after the battle they bring out[5] and slay the prisoners : they begin with the general; none[6] are spared; all are butchered to a man. 4. I will begin, then,[7] with you : you pretend that your countrymen are fighting for their homes and hearths; and yet[8] you avow that they have repeatedly made raids upon our territory, and wasted our land with fire and sword without provocation or resistance. 5. I have known this young man from a boy : both his father and he have again and again in your father's lifetime stayed under my roof; and I consider him wanting in nothing either in point of knowledge or natural powers. 6. In virtue of the power with which my countrymen have intrusted me, I intend to reward all who have deserved well of the nation : the rest I shall punish in proportion to their crimes. 7. I will aid you to the utmost[9] of my power; but I fear that it is all over with your hopes. 8. I should be sorry to disappoint you, but I fear that your brother has returned without result. 9. Considering the greatness of the danger, he showed great courage, and we ought all to show him gratitude in proportion to his many services to us and to the nation. 10. We should[10] all of us look at what is before our eyes; to depend on the future is useless.

---

[1] See **328**, *b*.   [2] **138**.   [3] Turn in two ways. (See **321**, *Obs.* 2.)
[4] **334**, i.   [5] Accusative of passive participle. (See **15**.)
[6] Use *nemo ;* case ?   [7] Why not *tum ?* = "therefore." (Intr. 56, *d*.)
[8] Use *idem*. (See **366**, ii.)   [9] (See **332**, 5, *g*.)   Tense ?   (See **190**, ii.)
[10] *Oportet*. (See **198**, ii.)

EXERCISES ON PRONOUNS.

*_** *The following Exercises—XLV. to XLVIII.—may either be done consecutively, in the order in which they stand, or any one of them may be taken singly at any time after the first twenty-four Exercises have been done.*

EXERCISE XLV.

PRONOUNS.

Personal and Demonstrative.

334. It has already been stated that the English pronouns, *I, you, he, we,* etc., when used as subjects to a verb, are, in the absence of any special emphasis, sufficiently expressed by the termination of the Latin verb. (See 11, *a, b.*)

But many causes will account for their insertion.

(i.) *Ego* often begins a sentence in which the speaker is giving an account of his own conduct or feelings.

Ego *cum primum ad rempublicam accessi.* (*For myself*) when first I entered on political life.

(ii.) *Tu* (especially) is often used indignantly.

An tu *Praetorem accusas?* Or is it that you (*one like you*) are bringing a charge against a Praetor?

(iii.) *Ego, tu,* and even *ille,* are often inserted without any special emphasis side by side with the oblique case of another pronoun. (Intr. 106.)

His ego *periculis me objeci:* te ille *semper contempsit.* These were the dangers to which I exposed myself; he always had a contempt for you.

(iv.) They, especially *ille,* are often joined closely with *quidem,* and inserted in a clause where an admission is made in contrast with a statement which follows.

Vir optimus ille *quidem, sed mediocri ingenio.* He was an excellent man, but of moderate abilities.

224

The following are the main uses of the **Demonstrative Pronouns**, those which **point out** (*demonstro*), without naming, the person or thing of which we are speaking.

Is, ille, hic, iste.

335. Latin has many words which answer to our "he," "she," "they," in addition to the termination of the third person. In "*he* says that *he* has not done wrong," the second "he" might be expressed in Latin by *negat* se, eum, hunc, istum, *or* illum *peccâsse*, according to the precise meaning of *he* in the English sentence. The first "he" might be either unexpressed as above, or translated by *is, hic, iste, ille,* according to circumstances.

336. Is is the pronoun of **mere reference**. It is regularly used, especially in the oblique cases, for "he," "she," "him," "her," "it," as an unemphatic pronoun referring to some person or thing *already mentioned, or to be mentioned.*

Is is, in all cases, the regular pronoun corresponding to *qui*. The other demonstrative pronouns have each a special force of their own, in addition to that of mere reference to some person or thing indicated.

337. Hic is the demonstrative of the *first person.* "*This* person, or thing, *near me*" (the speaker).

> *Haec patria,* this *our* country ; *haec vita,* this *present* life ; *haec omnia,* everything *around* us ; *piget haec perpeti,* it is painful to endure the *present state of things ; his sex diebus,* in *the* last six days ; *his cognitis,* after learning *this (which I have just related).*

338. Iste on the other hand is the demonstrative of the *second person* (the person addressed), "that *near you.*"

> *Cur ista quaeris?* why do *you* put *that,* or *this,* question ? *opinio* ista, that belief *of yours ; Epicurus* iste, *your friend* Epicurus ; *casus* iste, *your present* disaster.

Obs. 1.—In the language of the law-court *hic* is often opposed to *iste. Hic* then means "the man near me," "my *client*[1] and friend here," and is opposed to *iste,* "the man near you," "my opponent," "the *defendant.*" "*Iste*" has this meaning because the jury are addressed, and the accused sat near the seats of the jury ; so *iste* has its proper meaning, "the man *beside you.*"

---

[1] *Cliens* is never used in this sense ; either *hic,* or, if more emphatic, hic *cujus causam suscepi,* hic *quem defendo,* etc.

Obs. 2.—This meaning "that of yours" often, but by no means always, gives *iste* a meaning of contempt : ista *novimus*, we know *that story; isti*, those *friends of yours* (whom *I* think lightly of).

339. Ille is the demonstrative of the *third person*, other than those present, or engaged in conversation : "that *yonder*," "that *out there*." Hence come various uses.

(i.) The remote in *time* as opposed to the present : "Illis *temporibus*, "in those days ;" *antiquitas* illa, "the far-off past," "the good old times."

(ii.) The "distinguished," as opposed to the common : *Cato* ille, "the great Cato."

(iii.) The *emphatic* "he," the "he" of whom we are all thinking or speaking ; whom we all know ; *ille* is substituted for *is*, where a well-known person is meant, even with *qui;* illi *qui, those* (whom we all know) who, not merely "*men* who."

(iv.) So, "he" in the sense of "the other" of two parties ; often substituted for a proper name in a narrative.

340. Hic and **ille** are often opposed to each other.

(i.) Of two persons or things already mentioned. *hic* relates to the *nearer*, the *latter; ille* to the *more remote*, the *former*.

> *Romulum Numa excepit;* hic *pace*, ille *bello melior fuit*. To Romulus succeeded Numa ; the *latter* excelled in peace, the *former* in war.

(ii.) So, of persons or things already mentioned or implied.

> *Neque* hoc *neque* illud. Neither the *one* nor the *other*.
> *Et* hic *et* ille (= *uterque*). Both one and the *other*.

(iii.) Sometimes they answer to "some," "others."

> Hi *pacem, bellum* illi *volunt*.

341. *Illud* is often used to introduce an emphatic statement, or a quotation.

> Illud *vereor, ne fames in urbe sit*. My real fear is, or, what I fear is, lest there should be a famine in the city.
> *Notum* illud *Catonis*. The *saying* of Cato is well-known.

It will sometimes answer to the English "this," "the following."

> *Ne* illud *quidem intellegunt* . . . They do not even perceive *this*, that . . .

342. *Is*, as the **pronoun of reference**, is the regular correlative to *qui*, and is used with all three persons.

Read again **70-76**, and explain the following examples :—

(*a.*) Qui *hoc fecerint* (**190**, i.) *poenas dabunt.*

(*b.*) *De* eis qui *hoc fecerint, poenas sumam.*

(*c.*) *Qui olim terrarum orbi imperavimus,* ei (ii) *hodie servimus.*

(*d.*) *In* eos qui defecerant *saevitum est.* The *rebels*[1] (**175**) were treated with severity.

343. For the difference between *cum ea res est, qui nos semper contempserit* (subjunctive), and the same sentence with *contempsit,* see **506.**

It will be enough to say here that

Is *sum qui* feci, is, "I am the man *who did* (it)."

Non is *sum qui* faciam, is, "I am not *such* a person *as to do* it," "one to do it."

344. *Et is, isque, idque,* etc., are often added with some detail to which attention is drawn.

Decem capti sunt, et ii *Romani.*   Ten men have been taken, and *those too* Romans.

Litteris operam dedi, idque *a puero.*   I have been a student, and *that* from my boyhood.

345. The pronoun "that," "those," is most rarely used, as it is constantly in English, to represent with a genitive case a noun already mentioned.

"Our own children are dearer to us than *those* of our friends," is, *nostri nobis liberi cariores sunt quam* amicorum ; never, *ei* (*ii*) *amicorum.*

If the second substantive represented by "those" is in a different case it is repeated.

Liberi nostri amicorum liberis *cariores sunt.*

346. So also it must be again noticed (see **74**) that neither *is* nor *ille* can be used like the Greek article, or the English demonstrative, to define a participle, adjective, or phrase.

"He ordered *those* near him" is not eos *prope se,* but eos qui *prope se erant* or *stabant;* "to *those* questioning him" is not iis *interrogantibus,* but either *interrogantibus,* or *eis* qui *interrogabant;* "those like ourselves" is not *eos nostri similes,* but *nostri similes,* or *eos qui nostri sunt similes.*

---

[1] Observe that the Latin substantives in *-tor, -sor,* express a more permanent and inherent quality than the English in *-er: gubernator* is not the "steerer" of the moment, but the *professional pilot. Defector* is first used in Tacitus.

347. When *is, hic,* or *qui,* etc., stands as the *subject* of the verb "to be," or some link verb, the pronoun generally agrees with the predicate where we might have expected it to be *neuter.* (See **83.**)

> Ea *demum est vera felicitas.* This and this only is true good fortune.

N.B.—*Felicitas* never means "happiness" (see **98,** *b*), but "good luck" or "fortune ;" note also the use of *demum:* this "at length," "nothing *till we come to* this."

348. Both *ille* and *is* sometimes represent the English "article" *the,* itself a shortened demonstrative.

> I remember *the* day on which. *Venit mihi in mentem diei* illius, *quo.*
> The friendship which existed between you and me. Ea *quae mihi tecum erat amicitia.*

So "*the* saying of Cato ;" see above, **341.**

Exercise 45.

1. Those friends of yours are in the habit of finding fault with the men, the institutions, the manners, of the present[1] day, and of sighing for, and sounding the praises of, the good old times ; possibly you yourself have sometimes fallen into that mistake. 2. There is the greatest disagreement on[2] political matters in my house; one party wishes everything changed, the other nothing. For myself, I believe neither of the two parties to be in the right. 3. He[3] always showed himself proof against these perils, these bugbears ; do[4] not you then appear unworthy of your noble forefathers. 4. Of this at least I am convinced, that that belief of yours as to[2] the antiquity of this custom is groundless; it is for you to consider[5] its origin.[6] 5. The saying of Caesar is pretty well known, that chance has the greatest influence in war. 6. When just on the point of pleading his cause, my client was

---

[1] See **337.** Repeat the pronoun with each word. (See **49.**)
[2] See **300.**   [3] **334,** iii.   [4] See **143.**
[5] See **146.**   [6] See **174.** *e.*

ready to be reconciled with the defendant, and this design [1] he shortly accomplished against my will, and in the teeth of all his friends. 7. To the question why he preferred being an exile to living in his own home, the other replied that he could not return yet without violating the law, (and) must [2] wait for the king's death. 8. This only, it is said,[3] is true wisdom : to command one's-self. 9. I value my own reputation more highly than you (do) yours, but I am ready to sacrifice my freedom to that of the nation. 10. I who [4] twenty years ago never quailed even before the bravest foe, now in the face [5] of an inconsiderable danger am alarmed for my own safety and that of my children. 11. To those who asked why they refused to comply with the royal caprice, they replied that they were not men [6] to quail before pain or danger. 12. You have been praised by an excellent man, it is true,[7] but by one most unversed in these matters.

---

[1] *Id quod.* (See **67.**)   [2] **198**, iii.
[3] See **32** *b*, and **44.**   [4] See **75**, and **342**, *c.*
[5] **273**, *Obs.*   [6] See **343**.   [7] **334**, iv.

EXERCISE XLVI.

PRONOUNS—*Continued.*

Reflexive and Emphatic Pronouns—*Se, suus, ipse.*

349. **Se, sese, sui, sibi,** as also the possessive **suus,** are used where the person whom they denote is the same as the grammatical subject of the sentence in which they occur, *i.e.* as the nominative to the principal verb.

They are used of the **third person** only. In the first and second, *me* (*memet*), *te* (*temet*), are used with *ipse.* (See **356.**)

> *Brutus pugione* se *interfecit* suo. Brutus killed *himself* with *his* dagger.
> *An* temet ipse *contemnis?* Is it that you despise *yourself?*

Obs.—*Suus* is not expressed wherever we use *his, theirs, etc.,* but only for emphasis, or to avoid ambiguity.

> *Animum advertit,* "he turned *his* attention;" *filii mortem deplorabat,* "he was lamenting *his* son's death."

But it is often used emphatically, as opposed to *alienus; suo tempore,* "at the time that suited himself;" or in combination with *quisque, suam quisque virtutem laudant;* and always in the phrase *sua sponte. Sui* is often used for a man's "friends," "party," "followers," or even "countrymen:" *ad suos rediit.*

350. *Se* (*suus*), when used as the subject to a verb in the **infinitive,** refers to the *subject* of the verb on which the infinitive verb depends.

This use will cause no difficulty, though the English idiom is different.

> *Ait* se *haec vidisse.* He says *he* saw this. (See **34.**)

Obs.—Where there is no danger of ambiguity, the *se* may refer to the *object* of the principal verb.

> *Reliquos* sese *convertere cogunt.* The rest they compel to turn.
> *Diffidentem rebus* suis *confirmavit.* He cheered him while distrusting (against his distrust of) his own position.

For the insertion of *se* after verbs of *promising,* etc., see **37.**

230

351. Sometimes, as with the English "one's self," "one's own," the subject must be supplied from the context ; Latin, like English, having no such indefinite word as the Greek τις, or the French *on*.

Alienis injuriis vehementius quam suis *commoveri.* The being more deeply moved by other men's wrongs than by *one's own*.

So *sui poenitere, sibi placere,* "self-reproach," "self-satisfaction."

352. Very common uses of *se, suus,* are—*sua sponte,* of his own accord; *secum habere,* to keep to one's-self ; *fiducia sui,* self-confidence ; *per se, propter se, pro se quisque* ("each in turn"); *sui compos,* master of himself, his reason ; *quantum in se fuit,* to the utmost of his power.

These phrases are freely used without any reference in the *se* to any other than the nearest word.

Tum illum vix jam sui *compotem esse videt.* Then he sees that he (the other) is scarcely any longer master of himself.

Haec omnia per se *ac* propter se *expetenda esse ait.* All these things are, he says, desirable *in themselves* and *for their own sake*.

Obs.—So *se, suus,* are constantly combined with *quisque,* either in a different case or with a different construction.

Milites ad sua quemque *signa redire jussit . . .,* "to *their respective,* or *several,* standards."

353. In dependent clauses introduced by *qui* or a conjunction no precise or mechanical rule for the use of *se* (suus) can be given ; but

(i.) In **adjectival** clauses *se generally* refers to the subject of the verb in its own clause.

Milites, qui se sua*que omnia nosti tradiderant, laudare noluit.* He objected to praise soldiers who had surrendered *themselves* and all that belonged to *them* to the enemy.

(ii.) In all other subordinate clauses *se generally* refers to the subject, not of its own, but of the principal clause.

Cicero effecerat, ut *Q. Curius consilia Catilinae* sibi *proderet.* Cicero had contrived that Q. Curius should betray to *him* (Cicero) the designs of Catiline.

But neither rule is universal ; sometimes in subordinate clauses *ipse* represents the subject of the principal, *se, suus,* that of the dependent verbs ; the general rule is the opposite of this.

354. Sometimes, and constantly with *inter, se* supplies the place of the **reciprocal pronoun,** which is wanting in Latin.

Furtim inter se *aspiciebant.* They would look stealthily at *each other*.

Otherwise *alius alium.* (See **371,** iv.)

355. Ipse can be used of any person (with *ego, tu,* etc.) and in any case; it may also emphasise *se* and *suus,* and is joined freely with substantives.

> *Quid* ipsi *sentiatis velim fateamini.*   I would fain have you confess *your own* sentiments.

It answers to various English expressions.

(*a.*) Ipsis *sub moenibus, close* beneath the walls (place).
(*b.*) *Illo* ipso *die,* on that *very* day (time).
(*c.*) *Adventu* ipso *hostes terruit,* "by his *mere* arrival."
(*d.*) Ipse *hoc vidi,* "with my own eyes," or, as with *inveni,* "unaided," or "of my own accord;" sometimes "on my part."

Obs. 1.—*Ipse* is often inserted in Latin for the sake of clearness or contrast where we should hardly express it.

> *Dimissis suis* ipse *navem conscendit.*   He dismissed his followers and embarked.

Obs. 2.—It very often denotes the leading person, the host as opposed to the guests, "the master" as opposed to "the disciples."

356. (i.) When used to emphasise *suus* ("own"), it is added to it in the possessive genitive, singular or plural as the sense requires.

> *Mea* ipsius *culpā, vestra* ipsorum *culpā.*   Through *my* own, *or your* own, fault.

(ii.) When *ipse* emphasises the oblique case of *se* or a personal pronoun ("self," "selves"), it sometimes agrees with that case—

> *Nos* ipsos *omnes natura diligimus.*   We all of us instinctively love ourselves ;

but more commonly it is used in the nominative as subject to the verb—

> *Me,* or *memet,* ipse *consolor.*   I console *myself.*
> *Virtus per se et propter se* ipsa *expetenda est.*   Goodness is desirable in itself and for its own sake.

The most emphatic combination is *egomet* ipse, *temet,* or *semet,* ipse, *vosmet* ipsi, etc.

Exercise 46.

1. Many evils and troubles befall us through our own fault, and it[1] is often men's lot to atone for the offences of their boyhood in mature life.   2. Having thus spoken, he sent back the officers to their several regiments, and then, telling[2] the cavalry to wait for his arrival under shelter of the rising ground, he started at full gallop

---

[1] "It" emphatic. **(341.)**   [2] Why not present participle? (See **411.**)

and encouraged by voice and gesture the infantry, who
had retreated quite up to the camp, to turn back[1] and
follow him.   3. You are one whom your countrymen
will intrust[2] with office from the mere impression of
your goodness.   4. It is a king's duty (291) to have
regard not only to himself, but to his successors.   5. I
heard him with my own ears deploring the untimely
death of his son, a calamity which[3] you pretend that he
treated very lightly.   6. We ought, says he, to be scarcely
more touched by our own sorrows than by those of our
friends.   7. Having returned to his countrymen, he proceeded[4] to appeal to them not to surrender him at the
conqueror's bidding to men who were[5] his and their[6]
deadliest enemies, to his father's murderers and their[6]
betrayers, but rather to brave[1] the worst, and perish in
the field.   8. He intends, he says, to lead his men out to
fight[7] at his own time, not at that of the Germans.
9. Any one[8] may be dissatisfied with himself and his
own generation; but it requires[8] great wisdom to perceive how we can retrieve the evils of the past, and treat
with success the national wounds.   10. To those who
asked what advantage he had reaped from such numerous
friends, he replied that friendship was to be cultivated in
itself[9] and for its own sake.   11. Taking[10] his seat, he
sent[1] for the ambassadors of the allies, and asked them
why they were ready to desert him, and betray their own
liberties at such a crisis.

---

[1] Participle, see **15**, (for mood of "follow" and "perish" see **118**).
[2] Mood? (**343**.)   [3] "Which calamity."
[4] See **184**.   [5] Mood? (**77**.)
[6] Use *ipse* for "their" in both places.   [7] *Ad* with Gerund.
[8] See **292**, 4, and **291**, *Obs*. 4.   [9] See **352**
[10] Use *consido*.   Why not present participle?   (See **411**.)

Indefinite Pronouns—*Quisquam, aliquis,* etc.

THERE are many pronouns which may be called **indefinite demonstratives** in Latin; but their main distinctions are easily pointed out. We may divide them into (1) those that are of a **negative** as well as of an indefinite nature ("Any"), and (2) those that are mainly **affirmative** ("Some").

357. "**Any**," after *si, nisi, num, ne, quo, quanto,* is the very indefinite **quis** (qui, when used as an adjective, *i.e.* as attached to a substantive).

> Si quis *ita fecerit, poenas dabit.* If *any one* does (191, i.) so, he will be punished.
> Num quis *irascitur infantibus?* Does *anybody* feel anger towards infants?
> Ne quis *aedes intret, januam claudimus.* We shut the door to prevent (101, ii.) *any one* from entering the house.
> Quo quis *versutior, eo suspectior.* The more shrewd a man (*any one*) is, the more is he suspected.

N.B.—*Quis* in this sense can never begin a sentence.

Obs.—In place of *quis*, in all but the last sentence, *quisquam* might be used. "Does any one *at all*, any *though it be but one*, feel anger?"

358. (i.) A more emphatic "**any**" is **quisquam** (subst.), (**ullus**, adj.). It is used after a negative **particle** (*nec, vix, etc.*), or a **verb** of denying, forbidding, preventing, or a

234

question implying a negative, or **si**, where the negative sense of "any" is emphasised.

> *Haec aio*, nec quisquam *negat*. This I say, *and no one* denies it.
>
> *Negant se* cujusquam *imperio esse obtemperaturos.* They refuse to (**136**, *a*) obey *any one's* command.
>
> *Et est* quisquam ? And is there *any one ?* (It is implied that there is no one.)
>
> *Vetat lex* ullam rem *esse* cujusquam, *qui legibus parere nolit.*[1] The law forbids that *anything* should belong to *any one* who refuses to obey the laws.

Obs.—*Nec quisquam* is always used (not *et nemo*) for "and no one." (See **110.**)

(ii.) As *quisquam* (*ullus*)="any *at all*," it is naturally used in *comparisons*.

> *Fortior erat* quam *amicorum* quisquam. He was braver *than any* of his friends.
>
> *Solis candor illustrior est* quam ullius *ignis*. The brightness of the sun is more intense than that of *any* fire.

359. "**Any**," in the *affirmative* sense of "any one (or thing) *you please*," almost equivalent to "every," is **quivis** or **quilibet.**

> Quodlibet *pro patria, parentibus, amicis adire periculum oportet.* We ought to encounter *any* danger (*i.e. all* dangers) for our country, our parents, and our friends.
>
> *Mihi* quidvis *satis est. Anything* is enough for me.

Obs.—*Quivis* expresses a more deliberate, *quilibet* a more blind or capricious choice (*voluntas* compared with *libido*).

360. "**Some**" is *aliquis* (-*qui*), *quispiam, quidam, nescio quis.* We might say for "some one spoke," *locutus est* aliquis, quidam, nescio quis, according to our precise meaning.

(i.) **Aliquis** (-**qui**) is "some,"[2] "some one," as opposed to "none," "no one."

> *Dixerit* aliquis. *Some* one (no *definite person* thought of) will say (have said).
>
> *Senes quibus* aliquid *roboris supererat.* Old men who had still *some* strength remaining.

---

[1] For mood of *nolit* see **77** with *Obs.*

[2] Hence with *sine* in a negative sentence *aliqui*, "some," is used, just as with *sine* in a positive sentence *ullus.* "any :" *nemo est sine* aliqua *virtute*, there is no one without *some* virtue (or other) : *homo est sine* ulla *virtute*, he is a man without *any* virtue.

(ii.) **Quispiam** is not so often used, and is vaguer.

Dicet quispiam.   *Some one* will say.

(iii.) "Some," when used in an emphatic and yet indefinite sense is often *sunt qui, erant qui,* with the **subjunctive.**

Sunt qui dicant. Some say.   *Erant qui dicerent.* Some said.

(iv.) **Nonnulli** is "some few," "more than one," as opposed to "one" or "none."

> *Disertos cognovi* nonnullos, *eloquentem* neminem. I have met with *several* clever speakers, but not a single man of eloquence.

361. Quidam is "a certain one," or simply "a." It expresses some **definite** person (and therefore differs from *aliquis*) sufficiently known to the speaker for the purpose in hand, but not further described.

> Quidam *ex* (or *de*) *plebe orationem habuit.*   *A* man of the commons made a speech.
>
> Quodam *tempore.* At *a certain* time (I need not go on to give the date).
>
> *Civis* quidam *Romanus.* A (certain) citizen of Rome.

Obs. 1.—*Quidam* also is very commonly used to qualify a strong expression, or to introduce some metaphorical language; it corresponds in use to *ut dicam,* "so to speak." (**100,** note [1].)

> *Erat in eo viro divina* quaedam *ingenii* vis. There existed in that man *almost* a divine, or, a *really* heroic, force of character.
>
> *Progreditur respublica naturali* quodam *itinere et cursu.* The state advances *in a natural* path and progress.

Obs. 2.—As the English language **admits of the use of metaphorical expressions** much more readily than the Latin, the Latin *quidam,* or some qualifying phrase (*tanquam,* "as if," etc.), will often be used where no answering phrase is required in English.

362. Nescio quis (qui) is also used as a single word with the **indicative,** or even without a verb (*c.g. contra* nescio quem). (See **169.**) It does not merely decline to name, as *quidam* does, but asserts ignorance. When used of a person it is often therefore contemptuous.

> *Alcidamas* quidam, "one Alcidamas," whom I *need not* stop to describe further.

But—*Alcidamas* nescio quis, "an *obscure person* called Alcidamas."

363. The phrases *nescio quid, nescio quo modo, quo pacto* (also *quodam modo*), are used where there is anything expressed that is not easily defined or accounted for.

> *Inest* nescio quid *in animo ac sensu meo.* There is something (*which I cannot define*) in my mind and feelings.
>
> *Boni sunt* nescio quomodo *tardiores.* Good people are *somehow or other* rather sluggish.
>
> Nescio quo pacto *evenit ut* . . . . *Somehow or other* it happened that . . . .

364. Quicunque, quisquis (substantive), "whoever," though occasionally used as indefinite demonstratives, as a rule are indefinite **relatives**, and as such are followed by a dependent verb in the **indicative**; by the subjunctive only when required on other grounds.

> *Cras tibi* quodcunque voles *dicere licebit.* To-morrow you may say *whatever you like.* (**190,** ii.)
>
> Quisquis *huc* venerit, *vapulabit. Whoever comes* (**190,** i.) here shall be beaten.

Caution.—Beware of thinking that *quicunque* governs a subjunctive. (**153.**)

Exercise 47.

1. Do not,[1] says he, be angry with any one, not to mention[2] your own brother, without adequate grounds. 2. Scarcely any one[3] can realise the extent and nature of this disaster, and perhaps[4] it can never be retrieved. 3. Your present disaster might have[5] befallen any one, but it seems to me that you have been somehow more unlucky than any of your contemporaries. 4. No one ever attained to any such goodness without, so[6] to speak, some divine inspiration, and no one ever sank to such a depth of wickedness without any consciousness of his own guilt. 5. Some believed that after the defeat of Cannae the very name of Rome[7] would disappear, and no one imagined

---

[1] Use *cave.* (**143.**)

[2] *Ne dicam* (the *dicam* does not govern the case of "brother"). (See **100,** note.)

[3] **291,** *Obs.* 4.   [4] = "which perhaps." (See **169.**)

[5] See **196.**   [6] **361,** *Obs.*   [7] Adjective. (**58** and **319.**)

that the nation would have [1] so soon recovered from so crushing a calamity.   6. It seems to me, to express [2] myself with more accuracy, that this nation has long been advancing in learning and civilisation, not of its own impulse, but by [3] what I may call an engrafted training. 7. Some one of his countrymen once said that my client was naturally disposed to laziness and timidity; to me it seems that he is daily becoming somehow braver, firmer, and more uncomplaining under any toil or danger. 8. In the [4] army that was investing Veii was a [5] Roman citizen who had been induced to have a conference with one or other of the townsmen.   He [6] warned him that such a terrible disaster was threatening the army and people of Rome, that scarcely a soul was likely to return home in safety.

---

[1] See **193**, v.   [2] See **100**, note.   [3] *Quidam.* (See **361**, *Obs.* i)
[4] See **348**.   [5] **361**.   [6] **339**, iv.

. *The next Exercise* (XLVIII.) *is on certain words nearly allied to Pronouns (sometimes called* **Pronominalia**)*, and is divided into two parts,* **A** *and* **B***.*

EXERCISE XLVIII.

A

PRONOUNS.

Idem, alius, alter, ceteri.

365. Idem. It has been already said (84) that " the same *as*" is usually expressed in Latin by *idem qui,* occasionally by *idem atque,* or (before consonants only) *ac.* (90.)

> *Idem sum* qui *semper fui.* I am the same *as* (or *that*) I have always been.
> *Eadem vos* quae, *or* atque, *ego sentitis.* Your views are the same *as* mine.

366. *Idem* has two idiomatic uses.

(i.) It joins together two *similar* ideas in the sense of " also," " at the same time."

> *Quicquid honestum est,* idem *est utile.* Whatever is right, is *also* expedient.

It is sometimes repeated :—

> Idem *vir fortissimus,* idem *orator eloquentissimus. At once a* man of the highest courage and the most eloquent of speakers.

(ii.) It also unites two *contrasted* statements as regards a common subject.

> *Accusat me Antonius,* idem *laudat.* "Antonius accuses and *at the same time, or not the less, or in the same breath,* praises me."

367. Alius. To express " different *from,* or *to,*" *alius ac, atque,* is used. (91.)

> *Alio ac tu est ingenio.* He is of a different disposition to you.

So with the adverb *aliter ;* so also with *pariter, juxta,* etc.

> *Aliter* atque *sentit loquitur.* His language is different to his (real) sentiments.

239

368. *Alius,* "other" (of any number), is opposed to **alter**, "other of two," or "second" or "one" of two, as opposed to the other.

> *Consulum* alter *domi,* alter *militiae, famam sibi paravit.* One of the consuls won glory at home, *the other* in war.   (**312.**)
> *Duorum fratrum* alter *mortuus est.* One of the two brothers is dead.
> *Amicus est tanquam* alter *idem.* A friend is a *second* self. (**361,** *Obs.* 2.)
> *Dies unus,* alter, *plures intercesserant.* One. two, several, days had passed.

369. A repeated **alius** is used in *four* common constructions.

(i.) In a distributive sense, "some . . . some . . . others."

> *Tum* alii *Romam versus, in Etruriam* alii, alii *in Campaniam, domum reliqui dilabuntur.* Thereupon they disperse, some towards Rome, some, etc.

Of course, of *two* persons, *alter . . . alter,* or *unus . . . alter,* will be used for "one . . . the other," sometimes *hic . . . ille.* (See **340.**)

370. (ii.) When used as a predicate in separate clauses, a repeated *alius* marks an essential difference.   (**92.**)

> Aliud *est maledicere, accusare* aliud.   There is a vast difference between reviling (**94**) and accusing.
> Aliud *loquitur,* aliud *facit.*   His language is irreconcilable with his actions.

371. (iii.) When *alius* is repeated *in different cases* in the same clause, it answers to a common use of the English "different," "various."

> *Hi omnes* alius aliā *ratione rempublicam auxerunt.*   All of these by *different* methods promoted the interests of the nation.

So with **adverbs**: alii aliunde *congregantur;* omnes alius aliter *sentire videmini.*   "They flock together from *various* quarters;" "all of you, it seems, have *different* views."

Obs.—The *singular* of the doubled *alius* is generally used in apposition with a *plural* subject.

Caution.—Avoid using *diversus* or *varius* in this sense. *Diversus* is rather "opposite ;" *varius,* "varying."

> Diversi fugiunt, is, speaking strictly, "fly in *opposite* directions."

(iv.) Sometimes a repeated *alius* (or of *two* persons *alter*) supplies the place of the **reciprocal** "each other." (**354.**)

> *Tum omnes* alius alium *intuebamur.* Thereupon all of us began to look at *each other.*
>
> *At fratres* alter alterum *adhortari.* . . . But the (two) brothers began to encourage *each other*, etc.

372. Ceteri is "the rest;" as is **reliqu-us, -i.**

Reliqui is opposed to "the mass," those who (or that which) *remain* after many have been deducted.

Ceteri, "the rest," as *contrasted* with some one or more already named, or indicated.

Thus either *ceteri* or *alter* will answer to our "others," "your neighbours," "fellow-creatures," as opposed to "yourself."

> *Qui* ceteros, *or* alterum, *odit, ipse eis,* or *ei, odio erit.* He who hates his neighbours will be hated by them.

Obs. 1.—*Ceteri* has no singular masculine nominative; in other forms it may be used in the singular, but only with collective nouns: *cetera multitudo.*

Obs. 2.—Note the phrase, *nec quidquam nobis Fortuna* reliqui fecit *nisi ut serviamus.* (All else is lost,) and Fate has left us nothing but slavery. (**298,** *b.*)

Exercise 48.

A.

1. Human beings pursue various objects; of these brothers, the one devoted himself to the same tastes and studies as his distinguished father, the other entered political life in quite early manhood. 2. Your judgment (**91**) in this matter has been quite different to mine. You might[1] have shown[2] yourself a true patriot, and lived in freedom in a free country; you preferred riches and pleasure[3] to the toil and danger which freedom involves. 3. All of[4] these men in different modes did good service to the human race; all of them preferred being of use to their neighbours to studying their own interest. 4. We form different aims; some are devoted to wealth, others to pleasure; others place happiness in holding[5] office,[3] in

---

[1] **196.** [2] **241.**
[3] *Plural,* as also for "toil," "danger," "office;" why? Latin uses *abstract* terms much less than English. (See **174.**)
[4] **297.** [5] Gerundive. (**389.**)

Q

power, in the administration of the state, others again[1] in popularity, interest, influence.   5. Hearing this, the soldiers began to look[2] at each other, and to wonder silently what the general wished them to do, and why he was angry with them rather than with himself.   6. You pay me compliments in every other (**377**) word, at the same time you tax me with the foulest treachery.   I would have[3] you remember that speaking the truth is one thing, speaking pleasantly another.   7. The enemy now fled[2] in opposite directions; of the fugitives the greater part were slain, the rest threw down their arms[4] and were taken[5] prisoners to a man.   Few asked for quarter, none obtained it.   8. We, most of us, came to a stand, looking silently at each other, and wondering which of us would be[6] the first to speak.   But Laelius and I held our peace, each waiting for the other.   9. After raising[7] two armies, they attack the enemies' camp with one, with the other they guard the city.   The former (*pl.*) returned without success, and a sudden panic attacked the latter; thus in both directions the campaign was most disastrous.

---

[1] *Denique*=lastly, used often in enumerations.
[2] Historic inf.   (See **186**.)   [3] **149**, i.   [4] Abl. abs.   (See **15**.)
[5] Present, **179.**   [6] **173**, iii. and 62.   [7] Abl. abs.

B

PRONOUNS—*Continued.*

Quisque, uterque, singuli, etc.

373. Quisque is "each," "any," or "every one," of a large number. It so far (in classical prose) resembles an *enclitic* (p. 27, *n.*) that it always comes *after* the word to which it most nearly belongs.

Such words are **relative, interrogative,** and **reflexive** pronouns, **superlatives, comparatives, ordinal** numerals, and **ut.**

It is very rarely used in the plural in prose, but often stands in the singular in apposition to a plural noun. (Cf. *alius* and *alter*, **371,** *Obs.*, and **371,** iv.).

Romani *domum, cum suā* quisque *praedā, redeunt.*

In the neuter, *quidque* is substantival, *quodque* adjectival.

It is sometimes emphasised by prefixing *unus : unus quisque*, "each and every one."

374. With **pronouns** its use is simple, if its proper place in the sentence is remembered.

> *Milites,* quem quisque *viderat, trucidabant.* The soldiers would butcher whomever *any* of them saw. **(192.)**
>
> *Non meum est statuere* quid cuique *debeas.* It is not for me **(291,** *Obs.* 2) to determine your debt to *each.*
>
> Suum cuique *tribuito.* Give to *every one* his due.

Its other uses are more idiomatic.

375. It is used with **superlative** (most rarely with positive) adjectives, almost always in the *singular,*[1] to express "all," or "every."

> *Haec* optimus[2] quisque *sentit.* These are the views of *all good men,* or, *of every good man.*

Beware of *bonus quisque*, or, *optimi quique.*

---

[1] In the *neuter* the plural is occasionally used, *fortissima quaeque consilia tutissima sunt ;* masculine and feminine most rarely.

[2] This phrase is generally used in a *political* sense, = all good patriots, all the "well-disposed."

376. (i.) If the superlative is *repeated*, we have one of the Latin modes of expressing *proportion.*

> Optimum *quidque* rarissimum *est.* Things, or all things, are rare in *proportion to* their excellence.

(ii.) The same idea is sometimes expressed by *quisque* with *ut* and *ita.*

> Ut quisque *est* sollertissimus, ita *ferme laboris est* patientissimus. *In proportion to* a man's skill is, as a rule, his readiness to endure toil.

(iii.) Sometimes by *quisque* with *quo, eo, quanto, tanto,* and a **comparative.**

> Quo quisque *est* sollertior, eo *est laboris* patientior.
>
> *Quo,* "in proportion," *quanto,* "in *exact* proportion."

377. *Quisque* is also joined with **ordinal numerals** : *quinto quoque anno,* "every five years ;" *decimus quisque,* "every tenth man ;" *quotusquisque,* "how few" (lit. each, one only *of how large a number,* —"the thousandth," or "ten-thousandth," that you meet).

> *Primum quidque videamus.* Let us look at each *in turn,* take each (in turn) as first.
>
> *Primo quoque tempore.* At the earliest opportunity possible.

It is also joined with *ut* in a *frequentative* sense.

> Ut cujusque *sors exciderat, alacer arma capiebat.* As each man's lot fell in turn, he took up arms with enthusiasm. (See **192.**)

378. (i.) **Uterque** is "both," in the sense of "each *of two,*" and denotes two things or persons as looked on *separately.*

> *Propter* utramque *causam.* For *both* reasons, *i.e.* for *each of the two.*

Ambo is "both," but it is used of two individuals as forming *one whole ;* "both together."

> Qui utrumque *probat,* ambobus *debet uti.* He who approves of *each* of these (separately) is bound to use them *both* (together).
>
> So *alter ambove,* "one or both."

(ii.) *Uterque* (like *nemo*) is used with the genitive of *pronouns.* but in apposition with *substantives.*

> Horum *utrumque,* "each of these ;" so vestrum *uterque,* but filius *uterque ;* so horum *nemo,* but *nemo* pictor.

(iii.) *Uterque* is used in Latin after *interest inter,* where we should use "the two."

> *Quantum inter* rem utramque *intersit, vides.* You see the great difference between the *two things.*

(iv.) *Uterque* can be used in the **plural** only where it denotes not two single things or persons, but each of two *parties* or *classes* already represented by a plural word.

Stabant instructi acie Romani Samnitesque ; *par* utrisque *pugnandi studium* (each felt the same ardour for the fight).

379. As *uterque* unites two, and = *unus* et *alter*, so **utervis, uterlibet**, disjoin them, and = *unus* vel *alter*, "whichever of the two you "like," *i.e.* excluding the other. (See **359**, *Obs.*)

Uter is generally interrogative (occasionally a relative) ; it is often repeated.

Uter utri *plus nocuerit, dubito.* I doubt which of the two injured the other most.

380. Singuli (-ae, -a) is **only used in the plural**, and has two main uses.

(*a*) A distributive numeral, "one apiece," "one each." (See **532**.)

Cum singulis *vestimentis exeant.* Let them go out each with one set of garments.

Ejusmodi homines vix singuli singulis *saeculis nascuntur.* Such men come into the world scarcely once in a century (*one in each* century).

(*b*) As opposed to **universi**, "the mass," "all," looked on as forming one class, *singuli* denotes "individuals ;" "one by one."

Romanos singulos *diligimus*, universos *aversamur.* While we feel affection for *individual* Romans, we loathe the *nation*, or "them as a nation."

Nec vero universo *solum hominum generi, sed etiam* singulis *provisum est.* Nor is it only mankind *in general* (as a whole), but the *individual* that has been cared for.

381. "A single person," where the *single* is emphatic, may be turned by *unus aliquis : ad* unum aliquem *regnum detulerunt*, "offered the crown to a single person ;" "not a single,"=an emphatic "no one," is *ne unus quidem*.

Obs.—Singularis is generally used of *qualities*, and denotes "rare," "remarkable."

Exercise 48.

B.

1. As a society we praise the poet whom as individuals we neglected.   2. All true patriots and wise men are on our side, and we would fain have those whom we love and admire hold the same sentiments as ourselves.   3. Men are valued by their countrymen in proportion[1] to their public usefulness; this man was at once a brave[2] soldier and a consummate statesman; for both reasons therefore he enjoyed the highest praise and distinction.   4. It is often the case that men are talkative and obstinate in exact[3] proportion to their folly and inexperience.   5. It is a hackneyed saying that all weak characters[4] crave for different things at different times.   6. It was now evident that the enemy intended[5] to attack our camp at the first possible opening, but that at the same time they would wait for a favourable opportunity.   7. We are one by one deserting and abandoning the man who saved us all.   8. All good patriots are, I believe,[6] convinced of this,[7] that it is quite impossible for us to effect anything by hesitation (**94, 99**), procrastination, and hanging back; so that I feel[8] sure that there is need of haste rather than of deliberation.   9. He found a difficulty in persuading his countrymen that[9] their enemies and allies were powerless separately, most powerful in combination.   10. Thereupon all, each in turn, answered his questions; this done,[10] the greater part besought the senate, appealing[11] to the whole body and to individuals, that one or both the consuls should at the earliest opportunity bring them relief.

---

[1] May be done in two ways. (See **376,** ii. and iii.)
[2] **57,** *a.*   [3] **376,** iii.
[4] " Characters " is of course not to be expressed literally in Latin, it = men. (See **174,** end.)   [5] **14,** *c.*
[6] **32,** *b.*   [7] **341.**   [8] Mood ? (**106.**)
[9] See **122,** *b.*   [10] Abl. abs.   [11] Past participle of *obtestor*. (See **413.**)

Gerund, Gerundive, Supines, *and* Participles.

These, like the infinitive mood (see **94**, and note), are all **verbal nouns** (Intr. 5). They are all derived directly from the verb ; but they are none of them true verbs, for they cannot by themselves make a statement or predication (Intr. 11). But they retain in other respects more or less of the nature of the verb from which they are formed, combined with that of either the **substantive** or the **adjective**.

EXERCISE XLIX.

GERUND AND GERUNDIVE.[1]

Nominative Case.

THE GERUND.

382. The **Gerund** is a verbal substantive in *-ndum*, formed from the present tense of the verb.[2]

It has no plural, but is declined throughout the singular like other neuter substantives in *-um*. Its cases are determined by the same rules as those of other substantives, and are often combined with prepositions : regnandi *studium*, "the desire of reigning ;" ad regnandum *natus*, "born to rule," *or* "a born ruler."

383. But it resembles a verb in so far as it is (*a*) qualified by adverbs, not by adjectives, and is (*b*) followed by the same case as the verb from which it is derived : ad bene *vivendum*, *parcendo* hostibus, orbem *terrarum subigendo*.

---

[1] These are names given by grammarians to a substantival and an adjectival form of what is often called the *participle in -dus*, sometimes the *future participle passive*. Their origin and precise nature are much disputed. Whether the Gerund arose out of the Gerundive, or *vice versa*, is a question which lies outside the scope of this work ; it will be taken for granted here that by the **Gerund** is meant the whole substantival declension, *including the nominative*, of the singular neuter form, *faciendum, -i, -o ;* by the **Gerundive** the whole adjectival declension, as seen in *facien-dus, -da, -dum* (when attached to, or predicated of, a noun), through all cases and genders, and in both numbers.

[2] The word Gerund is derived from this active sense, as expressing the *action* of the verb (*a gerendo, gerundo*), the verb *agere* being already appropriated to the term *active verbs*. Most grammarians limit the term Gerund to the oblique cases ; it is perhaps more reasonable to include the nominative.

247

384. The **gerund** therefore, like the **infinitive** mood, corresponds to the English verbal substantive in *-ing:* "for *living* well," "by *sparing* the enemy," "by *subduing* the world," (see **94**); sometimes to the English infinitive in the form "*to* do," "*to* see," properly itself a gerundial infinitive.

But as the Latin infinitive is not used as a substantive in the genitive, dative, or ablative, or with prepositions, its place is taken by the gerund in *-ndi, -ndo, -ndum.* (See Examples in **99**.)

385. In the nominative (and accusative in *oratio obliqua*) the two verbal nouns, the **infinitive** and **gerund**, exist side by side, but their uses are quite different.

(*a*) The **nominative gerund** has *laid aside* its power [1] of governing an accusative of the nearer object, and has acquired **the sense of duty, necessity, obligation.**

(*b*) Thus *currere* = running, and we can say, currere *mihi jucundum est, running* is delightful to me ; but we do not use *currendum* in the same sense ; for *mihi* currendum *est* (*lit.* there is *a running* for me), is only used in the sense of " I *must* run."[2]

386. But this use of the *nominative* of the gerund is only found with **intransitive** verbs, or **transitive** verbs used **absolutely.** (Intr. 40.)

We cannot say, hostes *nobis vincendum est*, we must conquer *the enemy,* but must use the **gerundive**, hostes . . . vincendi sunt ; but we can say, *vincendum est*, we must *win the day;* and we can say *hostibus parcendum est*, we ought to spare the enemy, or *occasione utendum fuit*, the opportunity should have been used, for *parco* and *utor* are *intransitive* verbs. (See **228**, *Obs.*)

387. The **person** on whom the duty lies is in the **dative.**

But with verbs which are combined with a *dative* as their object, the ablative with *a, ab*, should be substituted **to avoid ambiguity :** civibus a te *consulendum est*, you must consult the interests of your countrymen ; *tibi* would leave the meaning doubtful ; but, *suo* cuique *judicio utendum est*, each should follow his own judgment.

Obs.—The gerund therefore, though properly **active**, has sometimes the construction of **passive** verbs.

---

[1] There are still traces of this construction in classical Latin :—

     Aeternas poenas *in morte timendum est.*—Lucretius.
     Quam (viam) *nobis quoque ingrediendum sit.*—Cicero.

[2] The reader may be referred to a very interesting discussion of the whole question in Mr. Roby's preface to the second volume of his *Latin Grammar.*

388. By the aid of the gerund and the verb *sum*, a whole conjugation can be formed to express the idea of what *is, was, will be*, etc., a duty or necessity.

Mihi, tibi, ei, etc., *scribendum* est, fuit, erit. I, you, he, etc., *must* write, *should have* written, *shall* or *will* have to write.

So also—Ne *nobis moriendum* sit. To prevent our *having to* die.

Or—*Dixit sibi scribendum* esse, fuisse. He said that he *had*, had *had*, to write.

Obs.—This is the commonest of all modes of expressing duty, obligation, etc., commoner even than *oportet, debeo*, or *necesse est*. (See **198**, iii.)

The Gerundive.

389. When we wish to use a transitive verb *with its direct object expressed*, we cannot use the gerund, but must have recourse to the **gerundive**.

The **gerundive** is a verbal *adjective* in *-ndus*, and as such is used in agreement with (Intr. 9) substantives and pronouns.

Though probably not originally passive, it has assumed a passive meaning; the object of the transitive verb will therefore, where a duty is asserted, be in the nominative, and the gerundive be used as a *predicative adjective*.

The person on whom the duty falls will still be in the *dative*.

Hostes tibi timendi *erant*. You *ought to have* feared the enemy.

390. In the **nominative** (and accusative of *oratio obliqua*), the gerundive, like the gerund, denotes *necessity* or *duty;* in **other cases** it, like the gerund, denotes merely the *action of the verb*, the English verbal in *-ing*.

Nom. Amici tibi consolandi sunt. You *ought to* console your friends.

Gen. Tui consolandi causā. For the sake of *consoling* you.

391. The use of the gerundive is confined to **transitive** verbs, including **deponents**.

N.B.—We cannot say *tu parcendus eras*, "you ought to have been spared," but we can say *gloria consequenda est*.

With verbs which govern any case but the accusative, the **gerund** must be used, not the **gerundive**.

Tibi parcendum[1] *erat, tibi persuadendi causā*.

---

[1] Such exceptional uses as haec *utenda, fruenda, pudenda*, etc., *sunt*, are to be accounted for by the fact that in older Latin these verbs were occasionally transitive, *i.e.* were used with the accusative; it is better to write, his rebus *utendum est*.

Obs.—The difference will be shown by the double use of *consulo.* Just as *consulo* Caium, means, "I ask Caius for advice," *consulo* Caio, "I consult the interests of Caius," so we must say—

> Caius *consulendus est.*   Caius must be consulted.
> But—Caio *consulendum est.*   The interests of Caius must be consulted.

So also tibi *credendum fuit;* haec *credenda sunt,* for, "you ought to have been believed (trusted);" "these (statements) ought to be believed." (See **248.**)

Compare the impersonal use of the passive voice of intransitive verbs.   (217.)

392. As with the gerund, a whole conjugation may be formed by the *gerundive* and verb *sum.*

> *Hostes tum* debellandi fuere.   The enemy *should have been* conquered then.
> *Dixit rem* perficiendam fuisse.   He said that the matter *should* have (=ought to have) been finished.

393. The gerundive is sometimes used as an *attributive* adjective with a sense of *necessity, fitness,* etc., even in the *oblique cases.*

> *Cum haud* irridendo *hoste pugnavi.*   I have fought with no *despicable* foe (no fit object for ridicule).

394. Caution.—Neither gerund nor gerundive denotes **possibility**; our "is to be" requires caution, as it may mean either *possibility* or *duty.*

"Your son was not to be persuaded" is not *filio tuo non fuit* persuadendum (=your son *should* not have been persuaded), but, *filio tuo persuaderi* non potuit.

But sometimes with *a negative* word it approaches the idea of possibility.

> *Calamitas* vix toleranda.   A scarcely *endurable* calamity.

Exercise 49.

The Gerund and Gerundive to be used exclusively for "ought,"
"should," etc.

1. He ought voluntarily to have endured exile, or else died on the field of battle, or done anything[1] rather than this. 2. Ought we not to return thanks to men to whom we are under an obligation ? 3. The soldiers should have been ordered[2] to cease from slaughter, and to slay no unarmed person ; women at least and children ought to have been spared, to say nothing[3] of the sick and wounded. 4. I do not object to your exposing your own person to danger, but you ought in the present emergency to be careful for your soldiers' safety. 5. This is what one so sensible[4] as yourself should have done, and not left that undone. 6. Seeing[5] that he must either retreat, or come into collision on the morrow with a far from contemptible enemy, he decided on forming line and fighting at once. 7. Nor should we listen to men (72) who tell us that we ought to be angry with a friend who refuses[6] to flatter and fawn upon us. 8. Your son was unwise enough[7] not to be persuaded to confess that the matter should or could be forgotten. 9. We shall all have to die one day : when[8] and how each will have to meet the common and universal doom, is beyond[9] the power of the wisest of mankind to foresee or to foretell. 10. It seems that you have one and all come to me in[10] the king's palace from two motives, partly for the sake of consulting me, partly to clear yourselves ;[11] you must therefore seize the opportunity, and plead your cause while the king is present (*abl. abs.*).

---

[1] **359.**   [2] Do in two ways, *i.e.* use both *jubeo* and *impero*. (See **120.**)
[3] Use *ne dicam* (**100,** note) ; it is used almost as an adverb, *i.e.* any case may be used by the side of the *dicam* (**364,** Ex. *note*[1]).
[4] **224,** *Obs.* 2.   [5] *Quum videret.* (See **429.**)
[6] Mood ? (See **77.**)
[7] Turn "your son, being most unwise, was not," etc. (**224,** *Obs.* 1.)
[8] Not *quum*. (See **157,** ii.)
[9] "Not even the wisest of mankind can," etc.
[10] See **315.**   [11] See **399,** *Obs.* 1.

GERUND AND GERUNDIVE—*Continued.*

Oblique Cases.

395. In other cases than the nominative (and accusative of *oratio obliqua*) neither the Gerund nor (with few exceptions) the Gerundive conveys any sense of *duty, necessity*, etc.

They merely denote the **general action** of the verb, and correspond to the infinitive mood used as a noun, and to the English verbal substantive in *-ing*. (See **384, 390,** and **99**.)

When thus used, the **gerund** retains its proper verbal power of governing an accusative (**385**); we can say "patres vestros *videndi*," of seeing your fathers; "vera *judicando*," by forming a right decision; but oftener than not, and especially in the *accusative* and *dative*, it gives place to the **gerundive**. Thus—

Acc. *Ad Gallos insequendos* is far more common than *ad Gallos insequendum*, which is scarcely ever used.

Dat. Bello *gerendo* is always used, rather than, bellum *gerendo*.

Abl. *Epistolā scribendā* is commoner than *epistolam scribendo*.

Gen. *Epistolae scribendae* is commoner than *epistolam scribendi*.

Of course with **intransitive** verbs the **gerund** is invariably used. (**391**.)

Ad succurrendum miseris, parcendo feminis, hostibus persuadendi, etc., never *ad miseros succurrendos, parcendis feminis*, etc. So, *miseris succurritur* not *miseri succurruntur*, etc.

396. The **accusative** of both the gerund and gerundive is used with *ad*, as a substitute for a separate **final** *clause*, with *ut, quo,* etc. (See 100.)

" To," " in order to," " for the purpose of," is constantly thus expressed; sometimes also by the **genitive** with *causā* or *gratiā*.

> *Gerund.*—Ad *consultand*um, or *consultand*i causa, *huc venimus.* We have come here *to deliberate.*
>
> *Gerundive.*—Ad *pacem petendam*, or, *pacis petendae* causā *missi sumus.* We have been sent for the purpose of asking for peace.

Sometimes we find the participle in -rus : *consultaturi adsumus,* we are here *to deliberate.*

Its use with other prepositions is rare : inter *ludendum*, ob *judicandum:* " in the midst of play," " for the sake of giving a verdict."

397. The **dative** of both forms is used after certain verbs and adjectives such as *praeficere, praeesse, dare operam, impar,* etc., and also in the sense of *aim* or *purpose.*

> *Gerund.*—Legendo *dabat operam.* He was giving his attention *to* reading.
>
> *Gerundive.*—Bello gerendo *me praefecistis.* You made me preside *over* the carrying on the war.
>
> *Gerundive.*— *Comitia* consulibus creandis. The meeting *for* the election of consuls.

Note also, solvendo *non esse,* not to be *able to* pay (one's debts). The **gerundive** is almost invariably preferred with transitive verbs.

398. The use of the **ablative** is mainly *instrumental* and *causal.*

With transitive verbs the **gerundive** is more common (except with neuter pronouns) than the **gerund;** aliquid *agendo* (by doing *something*); but, bello *trahendo vinces* (by prolonging the war).

Obs.—It is also occasionally used with the preposition *in;* but it is *not* used with *pro* and *sine* to represent our " instead of," " without," followed by the verbal substantive ; you cannot say pro *sequendo,* sine *sequendo* for " instead of," *or* " without following." (See **332.** 8.)

399. The **genitive** of both gerund and gerundive is used in most of the senses of the genitive ; with transitive verbs the latter is to be preferred, unless **ambiguity,** or a recurrence of the same sound, would arise. Thus *discendi* aliquid (*alicujus* **would be ambiguous**); vera *judicandi;* patres vestros *videndi causā* (to avoid *vestrorum vidend*orum).

Obs. 1.—The genitive *singular* of the gerundive is used with *sui,* even when it denotes a number of persons: *sui* purgandi *causa* adsunt, they are here to clear *themselves,* so *vestri, nostri.*

Obs. 2.—Notice such phrases as *respirandi spatium,* a breathing space; *sui colligendi facultas,* an opportunity of rallying; *pacis faciendae auctor et princeps fui,* I was the suggestor of, and the leader in making peace. The idiom *hoc conservandae libertatis est,* this tends to the preservation of freedom, has been noticed above. (**292,** *Obs.*)

400. The accusative of the gerundive is used **predicatively** (**239**) in a *final* sense in combination with certain verbs: *do,* I give, *curo,* I take care of, *suscipio,* I undertake, etc.

> *Obsides Aeduis* custodiendos *tradit.* He hands over the hostages to the Aedui, to keep in guard.
> *Agros eis* habitandos *dedit.* He gave them lands *to dwell in.*
> *Caesar pontem* faciendum *curavit.* Caesar *had a* bridge made.

It thus retains the idea of **obligation,** and often answers to the English infinitive (*to* keep, etc.), itself originally a dative of aim or purpose.

Exercise 50.

1. These men came, it is said, to our camp for the purpose of praising themselves[1] and accusing you (*pl.*); they are now intent on pacifying you, and clearing themselves of a most serious indictment. 2. The matter must on no account be postponed; you must on this very day come to a decision, as to whether it tends to the destruction or to the preservation of the constitution. 3. Such gentleness and clemency did he show in the very hour of triumph, that it may be questioned whether he won greater[2] popularity by pardoning his enemies or by relieving his friends. 4. There can be no question that

---

[1] **399,** *Obs.* 1. [2] *Plus.* (See **294.**)

in point[1] of consulting his country's interests rather than
his own, of sacrificing his own convenience (*pl.*) to that[2]
of his friends, of keeping in check alike his temper and
his tongue, this young man far outdid all[3] the old.   5. All
the spoil which the defendant had obtained by sacking
temples, by confiscating the property of individuals, and
by levying contributions on so many communities, he
secretly had[4] carried out of the country.   6. It was by
venturing on something, he said, and by pressing on, not
by delay and hanging back, nor by much[5] discussion and
little action, that they had effected what they had hitherto
achieved.[6]   7. It was I who suggested the following up
the enemy (*sing.*), in order to leave[7] him no breathing
space, no[8] opportunity of rallying, or of ascertaining the
nature[9] or number of his assailants. ·

---

[1] Simply abl. of limitation, or reference. (**274.**)   [2] See **345.**
[3] Use *quisque*. (**375.**)   [4] *Curo.* (**400.**)
[5] "Much," "little," with gerund.   (See **53.**)
[6] Repeat the same verb ; mood ?   (See **77.**)
[7] Use the passive.   (**216.**)
[8] Use *ullus* after *ne*, as more emphatic than *qui*.   (See **357, 358.**)
[9] See **174.**

THE SUPINES.

401. The so-called **Supines** in -um and -u are the accusative and ablative cases of a **verbal substantive** of the fourth declension.

This substantive is formed in the same manner as the passive participle (*auditus, factus*, etc.), and the name *supine* is a Latin translation of the Greek ὕπτιος (on his back), which, by a metaphor borrowed from wrestlers, was fancifully applied to the passive as distinguished from the active voice. Neither, however, of the supines has a really passive signification.

402. The **Supine** in -um is used only in combination with *verbs of motion*. It expresses the purpose, design, or *final cause*, of the motion. It is thus included among the various Latin modes of expressing purpose or design mentioned in 100.

It so far keeps its verbal nature as to govern the case of the verb from which it is formed.

> *Pacem nos* flagitatum *venerunt* (**230**). They have come to importune us for peace.
> *Pabulatum emisit milites.* He sent his soldiers out to forage, *or* "a foraging" (a = an, on).

Obs.—This *supine* is one of the few instances of *motion towards* being expressed by the accusative without a preposition. (See **235**.)

403. It is used with *ire* (to go) oftener than with any other verb, and forms with this sometimes a kind of additional tense, though rarely, if ever, in Caesar or Cicero: "I am on the way to," "I set about." It thus gives the action an intensive force, sometimes almost equal to our "goes out of his way to."

> *Video te patris tui injurias* ultum ire. I observe that you are *on the way to* avenge the wrongs done to your father.
> *Fortunas suas* perditum it. He is *on the way to* ruin his own fortunes.
> *Sibi* nocitum it. He is *on the way to* damage himself.

Obs.—Its use with the impersonal passive of *iri* to supply the place of the absent **passive infinitive future** has been noticed (**193**, iv.).

> *Injurias patris ultum iri dixit.* He said that the wrongs done to his father would be avenged.

404. The **Supine** in -u is the **ablative** of a similar verbal substantive.   It is in fact an ablative of *limitation* (274). It is mostly confined to forms derived from verbs of **speaking** and of the **senses**, such as *dictu, memoratu, auditu, visu,* etc., but includes *factu* and *natu.*

It is only used with **adjectives** (mostly such as express *difficulty and ease, credibility and the reverse*), and a few **substantives** resembling adjectives, such as *fas, nefas, scelus,* and the **verb** *pudet.*

> Difficile *est* dictu *quanto simus in odio.*   It is *hard to say* how hated we are.
> Nefas *est* dictu *talem senectutem miseram fuisse.*   It is *sacrilege to say* that such an old age was wretched.

Note that the *supine* in -*u* does not, as that in -*um*, govern a case ; but it may, as in these two examples, have either an interrogative clause (165), or an infinitive dependent upon it.

It may be compared with the Greek infinitive active καλός ἰδεῖν. or the English "fair *to see.*"

Exercise 51.

1. Ambassadors came from the Athenians to Philip at Olynthus[1] to complain of wrongs done to their countrymen.   2. He started to his father at Marseilles from his uncle at Narbonne to see the games, but within the last[2] few days was killed, either by an assassin, or by brigands, while[3] on his journey.   3. Do you (*pl.*) remain within the camp in order to take food and rest and all else that you require ; let us, who are less exhausted with fighting—for did we not arrive fresh and untouched immediately after the contest?—go out to get food and forage.   4. We have come to deprecate your (*pl.*) anger, and to entreat for peace; we earnestly hope that we shall obtain what (*pl.*) we seek for.   5. He sent ambassadors to the senate to congratulate Rome[4] on her victory.   6. It sounds incredible how repeatedly and how urgently I have warned[5] you to place no reliance in that man.   7. It is not easy to say whether this man should be spared, and be[6] sent away with his companions, or whether he should at once be either slain or cast into prison.

---

[1] For this and the " *at's* " in the next sentence, see **315**.
[2] See **325**, *Obs.*   [3] Either *dum* (see **180**), or present participle (**410**).
[4] Why not *Roma ?*   (See **319**.)
[5] Mood ?   (See **165, 166.**)   [6] *ipse.*   (See **355**, *Obs.* 1.)

EXERCISE LII.

PARTICIPLES.

General Remarks.

405. Participles are verbal adjectives, or rather **verbs used as adjectives.**[1]

Hence their name, *participia*, as sharing in (*participari*) the nature of two parts of speech. They differ from the Gerundive as they may govern all cases precisely as finite **verbs**, and also as representing more distinctly *tense* and *voice ;* but they are inflected as **adjectives**, and, as adjectives, are both *attached to*, and, as in compound tenses, *predicated of*, substantives and pronouns. (See Intr. 8.)

> *Res* abstrusa *ac* recondita (attribute). A deep and mysterious question.
>
> *Multi* occisi *sunt* (predicate). Many were slain.

406. (i.) But their most characteristic use is that in which they stand in **apposition to the subject or object of a verb**, and form as in English, but to a still greater extent, a substitute for a *subordinate clause*, either adjectival or adverbial. (Intr. 81, 82.) Thus—

> *Caesar haec* veritus. Caesar fearing (= *who*, or *as he*, feared) this.
>
> *Haec* scribens *interpellatus sum.* I was interrupted *while*[2] *I was* writing this.
>
> *Urbem* oppugnaturus *constitit.* He halted *when*[2] *he was* on the point of assaulting the city.
>
> *Nobiles, imperio suo jamdiu* repugnantes, *uno praelio oppressit.* He crushed in a single battle the nobles, *who had* long been contesting his sovereignty.

---

[1] The **action** or **state** which the verb in its finite form (*i.e.* when used as a true verb) *predicates*, is looked on as a **quality** embodied in, and attached by language, or *attributed*, to some person or thing. "Caesar seeing this, etc.,"—we add to our general idea of Caesar the special quality of *seeing this.*

[2] In English the temporal conjunctions *when, while,* can *apparently* be closely connected with participles, "when coming," "while writing." These are really elliptical expressions, "when (he was) a (on) *coming*," "while (he was) *a writing ;*" and the apparent *participle* was originally a verbal noun. In Latin such combinations as "*dum scribens,*" "*quum veniens,*" are of course absolutely inadmissible.

258

(ii.) Sometimes the Latin participle represents not a *subordinate*, but a *co-ordinate*, clause.   (Intr. 74, 75.)

Militem arreptum *trahebat.*   He *seized* the soldier, *and* began to drag him off.   (See 15.)

Patrem secutus *ad Hispaniam navigavit.*   He *followed* his father, *and* sailed to Spain.

407. Some participles are used precisely as **adjectives**, and as such admit of comparative and superlative degrees.

(i.) Such past participles as *doctus, erudītus, paratus, erectus,* etc., are constantly so used.

(ii.) So also such present participles as *abstinens, amans, appetens, fidens, florens, nocens,* etc. ; these when transitive are often joined with the genitive in place of the accusative : patriae *amantissimus.* (See **302.**)

(iii.) Some even, as adjectives, admit the negative prefix *in-*, which is never joined with the verb : in*nocens,* im*potens,* in*sipiens,* in*domitus,* in*victus,* in*tactus.*

Obs.—At the same time, though this use of the participle is common in both languages, we must be cautious in translating English *participial adjectives* literally : "a *threatening* letter," is "*literae* minaces ;" "a *moving* speech," "*oratio* flebilis ;" "a *smiling* landscape," "*aspectus* amoenus ;" "*burning* heat," "*aestus* fervidus."

408. Others, like adjectives, are used exactly as **substantives**: *adolescens, infans, senatus-consultum, candidatus, praefectus,* etc.   (See 51.)

Such are—*Institutum,* "fixed course," "principle" (sing.), "institutions" (pl.) ; *acta,* "measures," "proceedings ;" *facta,* "deeds ;" *merita* (*in*), "services" (towards) ; *peccatum, delictum,* "wrong-doing," "crime ;" the *future participle* is only so used in the word *futur-um* (-*a*, pl.).

Obs.—It has already been said that many of these still retain their true participial, *i.e. verbal,* construction : *multa* ab eo *praeclare facta.* (See **55.**)   But we may also say *merita* ejus, *facta, acta, dicta, praecepta, delicta,* ejus, etc.

409. There are in Latin **three** participles, exclusive of the **gerundive**, which is not here included among the participles as it cannot govern a case.

Active verbs have **two** : *Dicens* (pres.), *dicturus* (fut.).

Deponent verbs have **three** : *Sequens* (pres.), *secutus* (past), *secuturus* (fut.).

Passive verbs have **one** : *Dictus* (past).

Obs.—This last has occasionally a middle signification.   (See **233** and **413.**)

Present Participle.

410. This participle is always **active.** When used as a participle (not as a mere adjective) it denotes **uncompleted action contemporaneous with** that of the verb to whose subject or object it is in apposition.

> *Haec dixit* moriens. He said this *while dying.*
>
> *Provincia* decedens[1] *Rhodum praetervectus sum. In the act of* (or, *while*) returning home from my province, I sailed past Rhodes.
>
> *Ad mortem* eunti *obviam factus sum.* I met him *as he was going to death.*

Obs.—Thus after "to hear," and "to see," the present participle is used when the actual presence of the hearer or seer is emphasised.

> I heard you say. *Audivi te* dicentem.[2]
>
> He saw the house blaze. *Aedes* flammantes *vidit.*

411. Hence (especially in the **nominative**) its meaning is far more limited than that of the English present participle, which is often used *vaguely,* as regards even time, and *widely* to represent other conjunctions than those of mere time. Thus—

> "*Mounting* (*i.e.* after mounting) his horse he galloped off to the camp ;" "*arriving* (*i.e.* having arrived) in Italy he caught a fever ;" "*hearing* this (*i.e.* in consequence of hearing), he ordered an inquiry ;" "*throwing* themselves at his feet (*i.e.* having thrown) they made a long speech."

In all these cases the Latin present participle would be entirely wrong ; *equum conscendens* would mean that he galloped to the camp while *in the act of* mounting ; *in Italiam perveniens,* that the fever was caught at *the moment of reaching* Italy ; *haec audiens,* that the inquiry was ordered *while he* was listening to a story ; *se projicientes,* that they made a long speech *whilst* in the very act of falling prostrate ; —all of which would of course be wrong or absurd.

In the first three instances *quum* should be used with the pluperfect subjunctive : quum *equum* conscendisset ; quum pervenisset ; quum *haec* audivisset (or *his auditis*) ; and in the last the passive, or rather *middle,* past participle,—*ad pedes ejus* projecti.

---

[1] *Decedere* is the technical word for *to return home* from holding the government of a province.

[2] Sometimes, *audivi te,* cum diceres. (See **429.**)

412. So too, when the English present participle, while expressing time **contemporaneous with a verb in the past,** implies also a *cause, quum* with the **imperfect subjunctive** should be used.

"Caesar, *hoping* soon to win the day, led out his men," should be, *Caesar,* quum *se brevi victurum esse* speraret, *suos eduxit;* not *Caesar* sperans, etc.

Though this rule should be strictly observed, it is not without exceptions, especially in Caesar.

Obs.—The present participle sometimes represents a *concessive* or *though*-clause. (Intr. 59, *g.*)

> *Re* consentientes, *verbis,* or *vocabulis, discrepamus.* *Though* we agree (*while* agreeing) in substance, we differ in words.

413. On the other hand, the **past participles of deponent** and **semi-deponent verbs** (Intr. 44), such as *veritus, ratus, ausus, confisus, diffisus, usus, progressus* (advancing), *aversatus* (expressing disgust at), *indignatus* (feeling indignation at), and those of passive verbs used in a *middle* or *reflexive* sense, as *conversus* (turning), *projectus* (throwing himself), *humi provolutus* (rolling on the ground), are used much in the same sense as the English participles "fearing," "thinking," "venturing," "trusting," "advancing."

"Caesar *fearing* this" should be either, *Caesar haec* veritus, or, *Caesar* quum *haec* timeret; "*turning* to his friends" should be either, quum *ad suos* se convertisset, or, *ad suos* conversus.

414. But the oblique cases, especially the **dative** and **genitive**, are used with greater freedom, and often take the place of an adjectival (or adverbial) clause, or of a substantive. (See **73.**)

> *Verum* (or *vera*) dicentibus *facile cedam.* I will always yield *to those who* speak the truth; or, to men *if* they speak the truth.
>
> Pugnantium *clamore perterritus.* Alarmed by the shouts of the *combatants,* or of those *who* were fighting.
>
> *Nescio quem prope* adstantem *interrogavi.* I questioned some one *who* was standing by.

Obs.—Even here a relative clause is equally common, and in the nominative, "men doing this," or "those who do this," should be translated by *qui hoc faciunt; hoc* facientes *laudantur* would mean, not "*men who* do this are praised," but "*they* are praised *while doing* this," and ii *hoc facientes,* in imitation of "those doing this" (οἱ ταῦτα ποιοῦντες) is not Latin at all. (See **346.**)

415. These two oblique cases of the present participle very often take the place of an **English noun**.

(*a.*) Interroganti *mihi respondit.*   He replied to my *question.*

So—*Haec* interroganti *hoc respondit.*   To this *question* he made this *answer.*

(*b.*) Lugentium *lacrimae,* tears of *mourning.*   Gratulantium *clamores,* shouts of *congratulation.*

(*c.*) Notice also, *vox ejus* morientis, his *dying* voice or words ; adhortantis *verba,* his *cheering* words, or words of *encouragement.*

Caution.—Beware of such Latin as luctūs *lacrimae, voces* doloris, etc.

Past Participle.

416. The **past participle** belongs entirely, except in *deponent* verbs, to the **passive voice**.   We cannot say *adventus,* " having arrived," *auditus,* " having heard," but must use *quum.*   (See Elementary Rules, 14.)

The use of this participle to form the compound tenses of the passive is obvious ; its use with *habeo* (*hoc* cognitum *habeo*) has been pointed out (**188**) ; also the phrases, *tibi* consultum *volo,* " I wish your interests consulted" (**240**, *Obs.*), and, properato, *or* consulto, *opus est,* "there is need of haste *or* deliberation." (**286**.)

417. (i.) The passive participle combined with a substantive often answers to an English verbal or abstract noun, connected with another noun by the preposition *of,* and used to denote a fact in the past.

Post urbem conditam.   After the *foundation of* the city.

Violati foederis *poenas dabis.*   You shall be punished for the *violation,* or breach, *of* the treaty.

Nuntiata *clades.*   The *news of* the disaster.

(ii.) Occasionally the **gerundive** is used in a similar way as almost the equivalent of a present passive participle.

Qui violandis legatis *interfuere.*   Those who took part in the *outrage on the* ambassadors.

Obs.—We have here (and in 415) another instance of the comparative **poverty of Latin in substantives**, especially in those of an *abstract* and *generalising* nature. (See 54, 174.)

Future Participles.

418. The **future participle** in *-rus* is always **active**; for its various meanings besides those of mere futurity, see **14, c.** It forms (with *sum*) a substitute for the **future subjunctive (114)** and for the **future infinitive (193, iii.)** The following examples will recall some of its more idiomatic uses.

> (*a.*) *Hoc se unquam* facturum *fuisse negat.* He says he *would* never *have done* this. (**193, v.**)
>
> (*b.*) *Nunquam* futurum fuisse *ut urbs caperetur respondit.* He replied that the city *would* never *have been* taken.
>
> (*c.*) *Vereor ne domum nunquam sis rediturus.* I fear that you are never *destined to* return home. (**139.**)
>
> (*d.*) *Plura locuturos dimisit.* He sent them away, as they were on *the point of* speaking further.
>
> (*e.*) *Adeo territi sunt ut arma facile tradituri fuerint.* They were so terrified that they *would have* easily delivered up their arms. (**115.**)
>
> (*f.*) *Hic mansurus fui.* Here I *intended*, or *was prepared*, to remain.
>
> (*g.*) *Fiet, quod futurum est.* That which *is to be*, will be.

Exercise 52.

The asterisk* means that the participle is to take the place of the *relative* or *conjunction.*

1. Are we[1] then to spare those who* resist (us), and hurl darts at us? 2. Are we to spare these men even though* they resist us? 3. I heard you ask more than once whether we were going to return to[2] my home, or to go to your father in London. 4. I heard the whole city ring with the shouts of joy and triumph. 5. Returning in his old age from India, he died in his own house; his sons and grandsons stood round his sick-bed, gazed sadly (61) on his dying countenance, and retained in their memories his prophetic words. 6. To my complaint that he had broken his word, he said that he had done nothing of the kind, but was ready to pay the penalty of having caused[4] such a loss. 7. I saw the soldiers brandishing

---

[1] Gerund with *erit.* (See **388.**)   [3] **415, c.**
[2] **316, iii.**   [4] = of the causing of . . . (**417.**)

their weapons throughout the city; I heard the voices of joy and triumph; I recognised the clear proofs of the announcement of a victory.· 8. Throwing themselves at the king's[1] feet, they solemnly appealed to him not to give over to certain destruction men who* were not guilty up to that time, and who* were likely to be of the utmost value to the nation one day. 9. Embarking at Naples, and fearing for the safety of himself and his family,[2] he took refuge with my father at Marseilles. 10. His words alike of praise (**415,** *c*) and of rebuke were drowned in shouts of indignation, and in groans and outcries of disapproval. 11. Distrusting my own sense of hearing, I asked some[3] one who* was standing nearer you whether I had heard aright; he answered my question in the affirmative.[4] 12. Are you not ashamed[5] and sorry[5] for the abandonment of your undertaking, the desertion of your friend, and the violation of your word?

---

[1] See **257.**
[2] *Sui*, **349,** *Obs.*
[3] *Nescio quis*, **362.**
[4] See **162.**
[5] **202.**

THE ABLATIVE ABSOLUTE.

ONE of the commonest uses of the Latin participle is that called the **Ablative Absolute.**

419. A **participle** and **substantive** (or pronoun) joined together in the ablative, and standing by themselves, often in a Latin sentence form a substitute for a **subordinate clause.** *Caesar*, acceptis litteris, *proficisci constituit. Acceptis litteris* is here the exact equivalent of such a clause as *quum litteras accepisset.*

420. (i.) This ablative absolute is represented in English, sometimes by a participle in apposition, "receiving" or "having received;" sometimes by such phrases as "on," "after," "in consequence of," "in spite of," "without," "instead of," followed by a verbal substantive, as that in -*ing*; sometimes by a subordinate clause introduced by "after that," "when," "while," "because," "although," "if," etc., sometimes by a co-ordinate clause (**406,** ii.); **very rarely by the almost obsolete English absolute case,** once a dative, now a nominative: "this said," "this done."

Thus—(ii.) *His auditis,* having heard, or, hearing this; *te praesente,* in your presence; *me invito,* against my will; *hoc comperto scelere, in consequence of* discovering this crime; *te repugnante, in spite* of, in the teeth of, your resistance; *illo manente, as long* as he remains; *Antonio oppresso, if* Antony is crushed; *his dictis abiit, this said,* he went off; *patefacta porta erupit,* he had the gate opened *and* sallied forth.

421. The ablative, therefore, is occasionally that of mere *time,* as *regnante Tiberio,* "in the reign of Tiberius," but much oftener of *attendant circumstances* and *cause.*

Owing to the absence of a past participle active in Latin, the use of this idiom, as of the *quum* clause, is exceedingly frequent.

It is a good rule never to translate it into English by an absolute case, or by a clause beginning with "when."

422. Cautions.—The **ablative absolute,** however, is not always admissible.

(*a.*) It can of course only be used in the passive with *transitive* verbs (**416**). You cannot say *Caesare pervento* for "Caesar having arrived," or *Caesare persuaso* for "Caesar having been persuaded," but *Caesar* quum *pervenisset, Caesari* quum *persuasum esset.*

(*b.*) It must never be used if the person denoted by its substantive or pronoun is either the subject or object of the principal verb of the clause.

"Caesar having taken the *enemy* massacred *them*" is not captis hostibus *Caesar eos trucidavit,* but *Caesar captos hostes trucidavit.* "As I was reading this I saw you" is not, me *haec* legente *te vidi,* but *haec* legens *te vidi.*

423. (*c.*) It *need* not be used when a past participle active is supplied by a deponent verb.

Haec locutus is as good Latin as *his dictis.*

(*d.*) It is *rarely* used to represent more than a substantive and verb, or verb with its accusative : *haec me dicente;* but for so long a combination as *Caesare a militibus imperatore salutato,* a *quum-*clause should be substituted.

(*e.*) Its use with a **future** participle is very rare in the best *prose.* The phrase *Caesare venturo* is from Horace.

424. Sometimes (as the verb *sum* has no participle) the place of the participle is taken by an **adjective** or **substantive,** which is joined in a predicative sense with another substantive or pronoun.

> *Me* invito, against my will ; *te* duce, with you for leader (under your leadership (**333**)) ; *me* auctore, at my suggestion ; salvis *legibus,* without violating the law ; honestis *judicibus,* if the judges are honourable men.

Obs.—Sometimes the participle is used alone with a dependent clause.

> Missis *qui rogarent.* Having sent people to ask.
> Comperto *eum aegrotare.* Having ascertained that he was ill.

425. With a **negative** the ablative absolute often represents the English "without" joined to the verbal noun. (See **398,** *Obs.*) Thus—

> *Te* non *adjuvante, without* your assistance ; nullo *expectato duce, without* waiting for any guide ; *re infecta, without* success ; nullo *respondente, without* receiving an answer from any one ; *causā* incognitā, *without* hearing the case ; indictā *causā* condemnatur, he is condemned *without* pleading his cause.

426. The proper place for the ablative absolute is early in, or quite at the beginning of, a sentence. (Intr. 104.) It is only when extremely emphatic that it comes last. (Intr. 92.)

Exercise 53.

N.B.— 1. " And " enclosed in brackets is to be omitted and a participial construction substituted. (**406,** ii.)
  2. The asterisk* marks the use of the participle as in Ex. 52.

1. Thereupon, after saluting the enemies' general, he turned to his companions, (and) setting spurs to his horse, rode past the ranks of the Germans without either waiting for his staff or receiving an answer[1] from any one.   2. It was at my suggestion, to prevent your voice and strength failing you, that you suspended for a while the speech which* you had begun.   3. For myself, fearing that glory and the pursuit of honour had but little effect with you, I abandoned such topics[2] (and) tried to work upon your feelings by a different method.   4. All this he did at the instigation of your brother, without either receiving or hoping for any reward.   5. It was most fortunate for me that, fighting[3] as I did against your wishes and advice, not to say in spite of your opposition and resistance, I gained the victory without the loss of a single[4] soldier, and with few wounded.   6. After attacking the camp for several hours, the barbarians were so exhausted by the heat and with thirst and fatigue, that having lost more than 1200 men they abandoned[5] the attempt and returned[5] home without success.   7. It was at your suggestion, not only against my will, but in spite of my opposition, resistance, and appeals to heaven and earth, that your countrymen were persuaded to condemn a whole people without a hearing.   8. This I am persuaded of, that you will not pass this law without violating the constitution.   9. As I was thus speaking, the news of the enemies' arrival, and the handing in of a despatch from the king, filled my

---

[1] = or any one replying.
[3] Present participle. (**412,** *Obs.*)
[5] Use different tenses. (See **113.**)

[2] Simply *ista*. (**54.**)
[4] See **381.**

audience[1] with mingled rage and panic; but some,[2] judging that haste was necessary, seized their arms (and) hastened to go down to meet the foe.   10. So long as you survive and are unharmed, I feel sure that my children will never be orphans.   11. Under your leadership I was prepared (418, *f*) to take up arms, but hearing[3] that you were ill, I resolved to remain behind at home without[4] taking part in that contest.

---

[1] "The minds (*animi*) of my audience." (See **17,** *Obs.*)
[2] Use *erant qui.* (**360,** iii.)   [3] **424,** *Obs.*
[4] Use "and not to," *neque.* (**332. S.**

EXERCISE LIV.

TEMPORAL CLAUSES.

427. **Temporal** clauses are those which qualify the statement made by the verb in the main clause, in some particular as to **previous, contemporaneous,** or **subsequent time.** They are therefore *adverbial* clauses. (See Intr. 82.)

They are introduced in Latin and English by various temporal **conjunctions,** such as those given in Intr. 59, *c,* and others.

Obs.—Their place is often taken by the participial constructions given in the last two exercises, *e.g. haec locutus, his dictis* are exactly equivalent to *haec* quum *dixisset.*

428. Of those conjunctions which answer to the English "when," all but *quum (cum)* are as a rule used with the **indicative** mood, precisely as in English.

Thus in past time—

> *Quae postquam (postea quam), ubi, simul atque,*[1] audivit (or audiverat), *abiit.* "When he heard (or had heard) this he took his departure," or "*no sooner* had he heard this *than,*" etc.

Obs. 1.—This use of *audivit* (aor.) in place of the more strictly correct *audierat* is even more common in Latin than in English.

So also with **present** and **future** time—*Quae simul atque* audit, *abit; quae postquam, ubi, quoties, simul atque,* audierit (190, i.) *abibit.*

Obs. 2.—Though the indicative is the rule with these conjunctions, the **subjunctive** must be used if the principal verb is in **oratio obliqua** : dicunt *eum, postquam haec* audiverit, abiisse. (**77.**)

---

[1] *Simul ac* only before consonants.

Quum.

429. The exception to the rule is *quum*, or *cum*, the commonest of all these conjunctions. With the **imperfect** or **pluperfect** tenses *quum* is joined with the **subjunctive**.

> *Caesar*, quum *haec* videret, *milites impetum facere jussit.*
> Caesar, seeing this, ordered his troops to charge.
> *Legati*, quum *haec non* impetrassent, *domum redierunt.*
> The ambassadors having failed (*or* on failing) to obtain this, returned home.

The reason of this is that, while the other conjunctions express the relation of *time*, and time only, *quum* introduces the **circumstances** which **led up to**, or **accompanied**, the fact stated by the principal verb. These circumstances are looked on as not merely preceding, or accompanying, but as affecting and *accounting for* the fact, like our own participial construction : "*seeing that* I could be of no use, I went away."

Now whenever *quum* (conjunction formed from *qui*) implies in any way *cause* (or *contrast*) the tendency is to use the subjunctive, precisely as with the relative itself (see **501**). Hence in describing *past* events *quum* is habitually joined with the subjunctive mood, as the previous circumstance introduced is looked on as more or less influencing, or even causing, the main event which followed it, even when such causal relation is scarcely discernible ; hence such a sentence as—

> Quum *in portum* venisset, vitā *excessit.* He died *after* reaching the harbour.

430. Sometimes *quum* expresses more clearly still the idea of **cause**.

> *Quae* quum *ita se* habeant, *or* haberent. *Seeing that*, or *as* the case stands, or stood, thus ; *this being the case.*

In this purely causal sense it is regularly joined with the subjunctive mood in **all** tenses.

431. Sometimes also *quum*, without laying aside the idea of time, answers almost to "although," and points a **contrast**, *i.e.* is used as almost a *concessive* conjunction. (Intr. 59, *g.*) It is then also joined with the **subjunctive**.

> Quum *liber esse* posset, *servire maluit.* At a time when, or *although*, he might have been free, he preferred to be a slave.
> Quum *dicere* deberet, conticuit. At a time when, or *although*, he ought to have spoken, he held his peace.

Obs.—This is an obvious mode of turning the English "instead of" with the verbal noun in *-ing* (see **398**): "Instead of being free," "instead of speaking."

It can, however, only be used where the neglect of a *duty* or *opportunity* is implied, otherwise we may use *adeo non . . . ut,* or *non modo non . . . sed.* (See **124**.)

Quum *with the Indicative.*

432. *Quum* however is frequently used with the **indicative.** Thus, if simply temporal, it is regularly used with the indicative of the *present* or *future* tenses.

> Quum *in portum* dico, *in urbem dico.* When I say into the harbour, I say into the city; *or*, In saying into the harbour, I say into the city.
>
> *Poenam lues* quum venerit (**190**, i.) *solvendi dies.* You shall pay the penalty when the day of payment *comes.*

Obs.—So also *Decem sunt anni,* or *decimus hic est annus,* quum *haec* facis. You *have been* doing this (**181**) for the last ten years.

433. It is used also with the indicative even of **past** time in certain cases.

(*a*) When two clauses mark strictly *contemporaneous* events. This is often impressed on the reader by the presence of a *tum* in the principal clause.

> Quum *tu ibi* eras, tum *ego domi eram.* At the time, *or* at the moment, when you were there, I was at home.

As the cause must come *before* the effect, the presence of *tum* excludes from the *quum* any notion of *causal* circumstances, and fixes it down to a purely temporal meaning.

434. (*b*) In a **frequentative** sense, where a number of repeated acts are described, *quum* in the sense of "whenever," "as often as," is joined with the indicative.

If the principal verb is in past time, *quum (cum)* is used with the **pluperfect**; if in present time, with the **perfect**.

> Cum *rosam* viderat, *tum ver esse* arbitrabatur (**184**). *Whenever* he saw the rose in bloom (year after year), he judged that it was spring-time.
>
> Cum *ad villam* veni, *hoc ipsum nihil agere* me delectat. *As often as* I come to my country-house, this mere doing nothing (**94**) has a charm for me.

Obs.—The same construction is used with *si quando, ubi, ut quis-que,* and the *relative qui, quicunque.*

> Ut quisque *huc* venerat, *haec* loquebatur.   *Whenever* any one *came* here, he *would* use this language.
> Quos *cessare* viderat, *verbis* castigabat.   *Whomever* he *saw* hanging back he *made a point* of rebuking.

But in Livy often, in Tacitus regularly, the subjunctive is used, in accordance with the Greek use of the optative.

> *Id fetialis* ubi dixisset, *hastam* immittebat.   As soon as (*in every case*) the herald had uttered this, he would launch a spear, etc.

N.B.—*Quoties* is only used where the idea of " *every* time that " is strongly emphasised.

435. (*c*) The indicative is also used where, by an inverted construction, what would otherwise be the principal assertion is stated in a subordinate clause introduced by *quum.*

> *Jam ver appetebat,* quum *Hannibal ex hibernis* movit.[1] Spring was already approaching, when Hannibal left his winter quarters.

This sentence would stand with the same sense almost more naturally—

> Vere jam appetente *Hannibal ex hibernis movit.*

The indicative is natural, for *quum* here = "and suddenly," "and at once," and may be compared with the co-ordinating use of *qui*. (See **78.**)

Exercise 54.

The asterisk * means that one of the various constructions of *quum* is to be used.   Where " and " is in brackets use the participial construction (**406,** ii.).

1. This * being the case, he was reluctant to leave the city, and openly refused,[2] in the governor's presence, to do so.   2. As* I was wearied with my journey, I determined (**45**) on staying at home the whole day and doing nothing.   3. No sooner was he made aware, by the hoisting of a flag from the summit of the citadel, that the advanced guard of the enemy was approaching, than, taking advantage[3] of the darkness[4] of the night, he caused a gate to

---

[1] A military term : *castra* must be supplied.
[2] See **136.**   [3] *Utor* (**413.**)   [4] = night and darkness.

be thrown open (and) sallied out boldly into their midst. 4. No sooner had he heard of the landing of the enemies' forces, than, instead of remaining quietly at home, he determined on taking up arms and doing his utmost[1] to repel the invasion. 5. Seeing * that his prayers and entreaties were of no avail with the king, he brought his speech to an end; no sooner was he (*qui*) silent, than the door was opened (and) two soldiers were introduced each[2] with a sword. 6. At the moment when * the enemy was entering the gates of your crushed and ruined city, not one of you so much as heaved a groan; when * even worse than this (*pl.*) befalls you, who will[3] pity you? you will bewail, I fear, your[4] destiny in vain. 7. Whenever * he heard anything of this kind, he would instantly say that the story was invented by some neighbour. 8. Whomever he saw applauding the conqueror he would blame, and exhort not to congratulate their country's enemies. 9. For the last five years the enemy has been[5] sweeping in triumph through the whole of Italy, slaughtering our armies, destroying our strongholds, setting fire to our towns, devastating and ravaging our fields, shaking the allegiance of our allies, when * suddenly the aspect of affairs is changed, (and) he sends ambassadors, and pretends to sigh for peace, tranquillity, and friendship with[6] our nation.

---

[1] See **332. 5,** *g.*   [2] Why not *quisque?* **(378.)**   [3] **309.**
[4] *Iste.* **(338.)**   [5] **432,** *Obs.*   [6] Genitive. **(288.)**

S

TEMPORAL CLAUSES—*Continued.*

Dum, donec, priusquam, etc.

436. The other temporal conjunctions will cause little difficulty, if the remarks on Tenses are carefully read, especially those in 190.

The general rule is that **the indicative is used unless** (*a*) **the clause falls under oratio obliqua (77), or** (*b*) **some other idea than that of time** is introduced. Thus—

437. *Dum,* as also *donec, quamdiu, quoad* in the sense of "while," "as long as," where they connect together two periods of time *of equal length,* are used with the **indicative** in various tenses.

> *Haec feci,* dum licuit. I did this as long as I was permitted.
>
> *Vivet ejus memoria,* dum erit *haec civitas.* His memory will live as long as this country *exists.*

Obs.—Quamdiu implies a *long* period ; *donec* generally in prose "until," or "up to *the last moment* that;" *quoad* also "to the last moment that," but not limited to *time: quoad potui,* "to the utmost extent of my power" = *quantum in me fuit.* (**332. 5.**)

438. But *when* dum,[1] " while," denotes a longer period, **during part of which** something else has happened, it is joined with the **present indicative** (historic) even when past time is referred to (see 180), and even in *oratio obliqua.*

> *Allatum est praedatores,* dum *latius* vagantur, *ab hostibus interceptos fuisse.* News was brought that the plunderers, while they *were* wandering too far, had been cut off by the enemy.

---

[1] " While " is constantly used in English without any idea of *time,* simply to place two statements side by side, generally with the idea of *contrast,* "while you hate him, we love him." *Dum* is never used in this sense in Latin : we must write either, *tu quidem eum odisti, nos vero amamus* ; or simply, *tu eum odisti, nos amamus.* (See also **406**, *note* [2].)

439. When *dum* is used for "so long as," in the sense of "if," "provided that," it invariably takes the **subjunctive**, and with negative clauses is joined with *ne*.[1]

> *Veniant igitur*, dum ne *nos* interpellent. Let them come then, provided they don't interrupt us.

440. When *dum, donec, quoad* mean "until," their mood is determined by the rule in **436**. If nothing more than **time** is indicated they take the **indicative** (except in *oratio obliqua*).

> *Mane hic*, dum *ego* rediero, redibo, *or even* redeo. Remain here till I return. (**182** and **190**.)
>
> *In senatu fuit* quoad (*or* donec) *senatus* dimissus est. He was (as we should say) in the House, till the moment when it was adjourned.

441. But if some further idea of *expectation, purpose,* or *watching* is introduced, the **subjunctive** is used, as the mood proper to **final** clauses.

> *Num expectatis* dum *testimonium* dicat? Are you waiting till he gives his evidence? *i.e. with a view* of hearing him.

Thus—*Epaminondas ferrum in corpore retinuit*, quoad *renuntiatum est vicisse Boeotios.* Epaminondas retained the spear in his body, till it was reported to him that the Bœotians were victorious.

Here the two facts are related as connected together in time, but by nothing else.

Esset in place of *est* would imply that he retained the spear *with the purpose of* waiting till the news should be brought.

> *Differant*, donec *ira* defervescat. Let them put off till their anger cools; *i.e.* let them put off with the *purpose* that their anger may cool, *till they feel* their anger cool.

Defervescet would mean simply till the *time when* their anger shall be cooling; *deferbuerit*, "has cooled." (**190**, i. ii.)

442. *Antequam* and *priusquam* follow the same principle. To denote simple *priority of time* the indicative is used.

> *Quarto* ante *die* quam *huc* veni. Four days (**323**, *n.*) before I came here.

---

[1] *Modo ne* is often used in the same sense : literally "only let (them) not."

But when the idea of an *end in view, motive,* or *result prevented,* is added to that of time, the subjunctive of **final** and **consecutive** clauses (see 106) is invariably used.

> Priusquam *e pavore* reciperent *animos, impetum fecerunt hostes.* The enemy made a charge before they *could recover* from the panic, *i.e.* to *prevent them* from recovering (*end in view*).
> Priusquam pugnaretur *nox intervenit.* Before the fight *could begin* night interposed (*result prevented*).

The subjunctive is also used in general maxims, especially when the second person is used in an indefinite sense. (141, *Obs.*)

> *Priusquam* incipias, *consulto opus est.* Before *men* begin, they require deliberation.

Obs.—In these wider senses *priusquam* is more common than *antequam.*

443. *Priusquam* (as *antequam*) is properly a *phrase* of two words, which may be placed in separate clauses, especially in negative sentences.

(i.) So used, they are often equivalent to *not . . . until.*

> *Non* prius *respondebo* quam *tacueris.* I will *not* answer *until* you are silent.

(ii.) They may also sometimes translate *without.* (See 425.)

> Prius *ire noluit* quam *judicum sententias audivisset.* He refused to go *without hearing* the verdict of the jury. (*Audivisset* is *virtual oratio obliqua,* "*said he* would not go." See 448.)

Obs.—"Not until" is often expressed by *tum demum* (or *denique*).

> Tum demum *respondebo,* quum *tacueris.* I will *not* answer *till* you are silent.

Exercise 55.

The asterisk * means that *dum* is to be used in one of its various constructions. ** *Antequam* or *priusquam* is to be used.

1. I am ready to pay you the greatest possible honour, so* long as you are ready to estimate at its proper value all the slander and detraction of my rivals. 2. The[1] launching of this handful of cavalry against the enemies' left wing caused such universal panic that, while* the king was inquiring of his staff what was happening, even the centre began[2] to fall into confusion; before

---

[1] 417.   [2] "Even in the centre confusion began." (See 219.)

worse[1] befell us, night intervened, so that fighting ceased[2] on both sides.   3. And now before we could reap the fruit of a contest which had cost us so much bloodshed, a second army came on the scene, so that, while* our general was sleeping in his tent, the battle had to be[3] begun anew.   4. He will be dear to his countrymen as long* as this nation exists, nor will his memory die out of the hearts of men till** all things are (190) forgotten. 5. He did not enter political life till[4] by the death[5] of his father he was able, as[6] he had long desired, to join the ranks[7] of the aristocratic party.   6. Let them venture on anything,[8] provided* they do not injure the influence and authority of those with whom rests the administration of the nation.   7. As long[9] as I believed you to be studying these matters for their own sake, so long I honoured you highly; now I estimate you at your true value.   8. As long* as those who are to[10] command our armies are chosen either by chance, or on grounds of interest, the nation can never be served successfully.

---

[1] Neut. pl.   [2] Impersonal construction. (219.)
[3] Gerundive : tense of *sum* as in 115.   [4] See 443, *Obs.*
[5] Abl. abs. with *mortuus.*   [6] 67.
[7] Why not *ordines?*   (See 17.)   [8] See 359.
[9] *Quamdiu* (437, *Obs.*), *tamdiu.*   [10] 418, *q.*

EXERCISE LVI.

SUBORDINATE CLAUSES IN *ORATIO OBLIQUA.*

444. It has been already said (**77**) that **in all subordinate clauses in** *oratio obliqua,* **whether introduced by a** *relative* **or a** *conjunction,* **the subjunctive mood takes the place of the indicative.**

This usage is so unlike English that it is constantly overlooked by the young scholar.

In English, if we alter "the man who does this *is* foolish" into "*he says that* the man who does this is foolish ;" or, if to "as soon as they saw the enemy they *fled*," we prefix the words, "*they say that,*" no change takes place in the mood of either of the verbs.

In Latin not only does the principal verb, "*is,*" "*fled,*" pass in such cases into the *infinitive* mood, but it carries with it, so to speak, all verbs really subordinate to it into a fresh mood, the *subjunctive.*

Oratio recta.	*Oratio obliqua.*
Stultus est, *qui hoc* facit.	(Ait) *stultum* esse, *qui hoc* faciat.
Simul atque hostem viderunt, fugēre.	(Dicunt eos) *simul atque hostem* viderint, fugisse.
Qui hoc fecerint,[1] *poenas* dabunt.	(Dixit) *eos qui hoc* fecissent, *poenas* daturos esse.

445. The same rule applies to indirect or dependent *questions* and *commands* as much as to indirect *statements,* for the term *oratio obliqua* in its full sense includes all three kinds of such substantival sentences. (Intr. 80.)

Oratio recta.	*Oratio obliqua.*
QUESTION.	
Cur priusquam vidistis *hostem, pedem retulistis ?*	(Rogavit) *cur priusquam* vidissent *hostem, pedem retulissent.*
COMMAND.	
Qui adsunt, *me sequantur.*	(Jussit) *eos qui* adessent, *se sequi.*

---

[1] For the tense of *fecerit* see **190**, ii. This *future perfect* will be represented after a past verb of *saying* by the *pluperfect subjunctive.* (See **471,** *Obs.*)

446. It will be remembered therefore that rules as to *postquam, quod, quanquam,* etc., being joined with the indicative, do not apply to clauses that are dependent on any form of *oratio obliqua;* in such clauses the **indicative is inadmissible.**

447. The principle is the same throughout. Let A be the author of the book, or the speaker ; B any one else *through* whom A makes any statement, or whom he mentions as asking or commanding something : no verb that forms any part of what B says will be in the indicative mood. In the examples (**444, 445**) *all* on the left hand, but on the right hand only *ait, dicunt, rogavit, jussit,* are A's words ; the rest of each sentence expresses the ideas of the subject of each of those verbs, or of B, and the **indicative therefore is excluded.**

Obs.—Indeed, the *tendency* is to introduce the subjunctive into the subordinate clause when the principal verb is in the infinitive or subjunctive for *any* cause : and though such *assimilation* does not amount to a rule, it will sometimes help to account for unexpected subjunctives.

> *Hoc feci, ut eos qui me* sequerentur, *incolumes praestarem.* I did this to secure the safety of my followers.

Virtual *Oratio obliqua.*

448. The subjunctive also takes the place of the indicative, not only where the form of the sentence shows that the writer is reporting what *some one else* said, thought, asked, or ordered, but where in the absence of any verb *declarandi, sentiendi, rogandi,* or *praecipiendi* we have ourselves to supply the idea, "as he said," or even "as I thought."

It is a short mode of distinguishing what the writer or speaker (A) states on his own responsibility, from that for which he declines to be responsible, and which he tacitly shifts to B.

Thus in the fable, "The vulture invited the little birds to a feast which he was going to give them," "*quod illis daturus* erat" would mean that he really *was* going to give them the feast : but "*quod illis daturus* esset" would only mean that *he said* he was going to do so. So with the verbs of *accusing,* the charge often stands with *quod* in the *subjunctive,* because the *accusers are made to assert* that the crime has been committed ; the *indicative* would make the historian or speaker assert, and be *responsible for,* the truth of the charge.

This has been happily named the subjunctive of *virtual oratio obliqua.*[1]

> *Socrates accusatus est quod* corrumperet *juventutem.* Socrates was accused of corrupting the young men.

Quod corrumperet throws the responsibility of the charge on the accuser. *Corrumpebat* would imply that the historian agreed with the charge

This construction is especially common with *quod*-clauses. (See below, **484.**)

Exceptions.

449. Sometimes the subordinate clause, though *grammatically* subordinate to a verb in *oratio obliqua*, is really an explanatory parenthesis inserted by the writer, and is therefore in the indicative.

> *Themistocles certiorem eum fecit, id agi, ut pons,* quem ille in Hellesponto fecerat, *dissolveretur.* Themistocles sent him word that it was intended to break down the bridge, which he (Xerxes) had made over the Hellespont.

The words "*quem ille in Hellesponto* fecerat" are inserted by the historian, they do not belong to the words reported as used by Themistocles. They belong to A, not to B. (**447.**)

Similarly, in such a sentence as "he ordered him to send for the troops who were in the rear," the *who*-clause would be in the *subjunctive* if it were part of the order given, in the *indicative* if a mere definition of the troops were meant, and inserted as such by the *historian*.

Exercise 56.

1. Then turning to Cortes, he made a vehement attack upon the Spaniards, who, without any[2] adequate justification, were invading his territory, and were either inviting or compelling his subjects to rebel. 2. He gave orders not to spare a single (**358**) person who had been present at the massacre of the prisoners, or the outrage on the ambassadors. 3. Then the gallant and undaunted chief, though surrounded on all sides by armed men, turned to the

---

[1] Dr. Kennedy. Such curious constructions as *quod religionibus impediri se* diceret, for *quod* impediretur, though by no means uncommon, will not be noticed here.

[2] See p. 235, *note 2.*

conqueror and denounced the cowardice of his countrymen, who by surrendering him to the Spaniards had flung away the priceless possessions[1] of freedom and of honour. 4. He promised not to leave the city till they had brought safely within the walls all who had survived from the massacre of yesterday.   5. He asked the many[2] bystanders whether those who wished for their king's safety were ready to follow him, and using[3] all speed to inflict chastisement on those who had violated their allegiance and their oath.   6. On reaching the summit of the mountain he called to him his staff, and pointed out the streams which (he said) flowed down towards Italy. 7. He said that he would not allow himself to put faith in men who had not only showed themselves cowardly and disloyal, but were still, in the face of such a political emergency, on the point[4] of sacrificing everything to their own comfort and interest.

---

[1] See **222**, *Obs.*
[3] Abl. abs. of *adhibeor.*

[2] See **69**.
[4] Either fut. in *-rus*, or *in eo esse ut.*

EXERCISE LVII.

CONDITIONAL CLAUSES.

Rules for Mood and Tense after *si.*

450. Conditional clauses are those which are introduced by the Latin and English conjunctions *si,* "if," etc., enumerated in Intr. 59, *e.* Their *adverbial* relation to the principal clause is explained in Intr. 82.

The use of the right **mood** and right **tense** in such clauses will require some care, owing mainly to the almost entire obliteration in English of the *subjunctive mood*, and the want of a true future tense. **(190.)**

A. Mood after *si.*

451. The construction of such clauses, as regards the **mood** to be used after *si,* will be perfectly clear if the following **observations** and **rules** are borne in mind.

Obs.—In all conditional or hypothetical sentences, *i.e.* such compound *sentences* as contain an *if*-clause, or its equivalent, it is quite true that the *truth* of any assertion made in the principal clause depends upon that of the condition contained in the *if*-clause ; as a matter of *reasoning* or *inference*, the principal clause, called also the *apodosis*, is dependent on the subordinate clause, or *protasis.*

Thus, in "*if* it has lightened there will be thunder," that "there will be thunder" is dependent, as an *inference,* on whether or no "it has lightened."

But *grammatically* "there will be thunder" is the principal clause, *qualified* by the secondary or subordinate clause, "if it has lightened."

It is this *grammatical* relation, and this only, which we need consider in writing grammatically, and we shall find that in **conditional sentences the mood of the verb in the si-clause will depend, as a rule, on that of the verb in the main clause.**

The following two Rules must be carefully observed.

452. RULE I.—If the verb in the principal clause is in the **indicative** or **imperative** mood, the verb in the conditional clause will be in the **indicative.**

Si hoc dicis, erras ; *si abire* vis, abi. If you *say* this you *are* wrong ; if you *wish* to depart, *depart.*

282

Obs. 1.—Dismiss all idea that *si* "governs a subjunctive" because it *suggests a doubt,* and the subjunctive mood implies a doubt. The word *si* ("if") in its very nature implies doubt ; but the mood with which it is joined depends upon the nature of the whole sentence, and this is decided by that of the *principal,* not of the subordinate, clause. If the principal verb is in the **indicative** or **imperative,** this shows that the whole sentence belongs to the sphere of **practical** and **real** life, and the indicative is the appropriate mood for the *qualifying si*-clause, as well as for the main clause.

Obs. 2.—Nor does the **mood** of the *si*-clause depend upon the *likelihood, unlikelihood, possibility,* or *the reverse,* of the supposition made ; but simply on *the mood* (that is to say, the general tone) *of the principal clause.* Cicero says, *excitate eum, si* potestis, *ab inferis ;* he did not think it possible that they could raise a man from the dead ; yet he says *si potestis,* not *si possitis.*[1]

Caution.—Beware then of such Latin as—

> *Si hoc* dicas, *errabis.*   If you *were to* say so, you *will* be wrong.

The Latin here is as unnatural as the English ; half the sentence belongs to one sphere of thought, the *practical,* "you *will,*" etc., half to that of mere *conception,* "if you *were* to," etc.   (But see **463,** *b.*)

453. RULE II.—If the verb in the principal clause is in the **subjunctive** mood, the verb in the *si*-clause will be also in the **subjunctive.**

> *Si hoc* dicas, erres.   If you *were* to say this, or, *were* you to say this, you *would* be wrong.

Erres is in the subjunctive mood because it does not say "you *are* wrong," but only that you *would* be in certain imagined conditions, on a certain *hypothesis ;* it shows that the whole sentence has left the sphere of *fact* and *practice* to which the **indicative** and **imperative** belong, and entered that of *conception* or *imagination.* The *si*-clause therefore will, as the subordinate clause, follow the mood of the

---

[1] Cicero says, Parcite *Lentuli dignitati,* si *ipse famae suae unquam* pepercit. This is in accordance with Rule I. Of course Cicero did not mean that Lentulus *had* shown tenderness to his own reputation, but the very reverse, yet he uses the indicative after *si.* So he says, *Si es Romae, vix enim puto,* sin es, . . . he uses the *indicative* because he goes on to make a *practical request.* The indicative mood is, so to speak, *colourless ;* it makes a statement (Intr. 11) : but colour may be given to the statement it makes by another word. Fortasse *hoc dicit ;* si *hoc dicit :* the *doubt* and *condition* are expressed by *fortasse* and *si,* the verb is left unaltered.

ruling or principal clause, and may be called a *hypothetical* as distinct from a *conditional* clause.[1]

> Si *hoc* dixisses, erravisses. If you had said this, *or*, had you said this, you *would have* been wrong.

If these two RULES, I. and II., are observed, few mistakes will arise as to the **mood** of the Latin verb.

Exercise A (page 286) should now be done.

B. Tense after *si*.

454. Under RULE I. the main difficulty as regards **tense** will be in the use of the **future**.

(i.) Read carefully 190 and examples 5-10 in **194**, and you will see that the best mode of translating

> "If you *do* this you *will* be punished," is, *hoc si* feceris, *poenas dabis.*

Si facis would be "if you are now doing," or, "intending to do" (an *anticipative* use, **182**) ; *si facies*, "if you shall *be doing*," *i.e.* at the time (**189**) ; but *si* facias **would be entirely wrong**, "if you *were* to do this, you *will* be punished."

(ii.) Remember also that, if a **command** regards the *future*, as most commands do, the **future** must be used with *si*. "Come (to-morrow) if you *can*" will be, *veni* (*cras*) *si* poteris, because "can" is really future time, and contemporaneous with the tense denoted by "come ;" *potes* would mean, "if you can *now*."

> *Obs.*—This future is especially common with *volo* and *possum.*
>
> *Cras veniant* (imperative) or *venient* (fut.), si *salvi esse* volent. Let them come, *or*, they will come, to-morrow if they (then) *wish* for safety.

455. Remember also the idiomatic use of the Latin **pluperfect indicative** with *si* to express *repetition* or *frequency;* it corresponds with the **imperfect** in the principal clause. (See **192** and **434**.)

> *Si quem cessare* viderat, *non verbis solum sed etiam verberibus* castigabat. If he *saw* that any one was hanging back, he *would correct* him, not with words only, but with stripes.

---

[1] The word "*condition*" would be used in such practical matters as a *treaty* or *lease*, etc. ; "*hypothesis*" we apply to an assumption in science on the truth of which we base an unproved theory. The *apodosis* to the *condition* is naturally in the **indicative**, to the *hypothesis* in the **subjunctive**.

456. Under RULE II., the only difficulty as regards Tenses will be in the use of the **imperfect subjunctive,** as distinct from that of the **pluperfect** and **present** of the same mood

(i.) The **imperfect** represents in the subjunctive, as in the indicative, *continuous action* in the past (183) ; the **pluperfect** simply past time.

> *Hoc si* dixisses, erravisses. *Had* you (*before* some past time) said this, you would *have been* wrong (once for all).
> But—*Hoc si* diceres, errares. Had you *been saying* this (*during* some past time), you would (*during that time*) *have been* in the wrong.

(ii.) But sometimes the imperfect subjunctive extends up to the *present* moment, and *hoc si diceres, errares,* means, "Had you been saying this *now,* you would have been *now* wrong."
The meaning of the imperfect subjunctive in a Latin sentence must therefore sometimes be decided by the **context.**

457. The more ordinary form in speaking *hypothetically* of the **present** is, *hoc si* dicas, erres ; but, especially when we wish strongly to imply that the supposition is false, we may use in Latin, as in English, a **past** form. But this use of the **imperfect** can never, either in suppositions or wishes, extend to the **future.**

> *Utinam* adsit. Would he *were* here (*now,* or *for the future*).
> *Utinam* adesset. Would he *had been* here (either *yesterday,* or even *to-day*).
> *Si* adsit. If he *were* here (*to-day,* or *in the future*).
> *Si* adesset. *Had* he *been* here, or *were* he but here (*previously,* or *to-day*).

458. The sense sometimes calls for a difference of *tense* in the two clauses.

> *Ego nisi* peperissem, *Roma non* oppugnaretur. Had I not become a mother, Rome would not now be under siege.

Peperissem, *merely past time,* oppugnaretur, a *continued* state, extending to the present moment.

Caution.—Remember that *si* is never used in Latin as an **interrogative** particle. "He asked him *if* he was well," is, *ex eo,* num *valeret, quaesivit.* (167.)

♠ *Obs.*—*Si* begins a sentence less commonly in Latin than in English. It often follows a name or pronoun : *Caesar* si, etc., *Ego* si, etc. Often *quod* is prefixed to connect it with the previous sentence : *quod si=* "*but if,*" sometimes "*and if,*" properly "*as to which,* if."

459. The following examples should be carefully studied.

RULE I.

Si quid habebat, dabat. If he (*during* a past time) had anything, he gave it, or *would give* it (habitually).

Si quid habuit, dedit. If he (*at a past* time) had anything, he gave it (aorist).

Si quem viderat, irascebatur. If he saw any one (*frequentative,* **434,** *Obs.*) he *would* get angry.

Si opus erit, *or* fuerit (see **190**), adero. I will be there if need *arises.*

RULE II.

Tum *si hoc* dixissem, *non* auditus fuissem. If I had said this then, I should not have found a hearing (aorist).

Tum *si hoc* dicerem, *non* audirer. If I had said (*i.e.* been saying, **183**), I should not have found (been *likely to* find) a hearing.

Si hoc dicam, *non* audiar. If I *were* to say this (*now,* or at any *future* time), I should not be listened to.

Si hoc dicerem *non* audirer. If I were to say (or *had been* saying) this *now,* I should not be (or *have been*) listened to (as I am).

Exercise 57.

A.

Mainly on the **Moods** to be used with *Si.*

1. If you love me, be sure to send a letter to me at Rome. 2. If you are at home—I am not yet sure whether[1] you have returned—I hope soon to receive a letter from you. 3. Were your country to use this language to[2] you, would she not have a claim to obtain her request? 4. If I am speaking falsely, Metellus, refute me; if I am speaking the truth, why do you hesitate[3] to put confidence in me? 5. Were virtue denied this reward, yet she would be satisfied with her own self.[4] 6. Time[5] would fail me were I to try to reckon up all his services to the nation. 7. If ever any[6] one was indifferent to empty fame and vulgar[7] gossip, it[8] is I. 8. If any one were to make this request of you, he would be justly ridiculed. 9. If you

---

[1] **167.** [2] " *With* you" (*tecum*). [3] **136,** *b.*
[4] See **356,** ii. [5] " The day," *dies.* [6] See **357.**
[7] Gen. of *vulgus.* (See **59.**) [8] "I am *he*," *is.* (See **70.**)

are desirous to enter political life, do not[1] hesitate to count me among your friends. 10. Had he been a man of[2] courage, he would never have declined this contest. 11. If you have any regard, either for your own safety or your private property, do not[3] delay your reconciliation with the conqueror. 12. But if you are aiming at the crown, why do you use the language of a citizen,[4] and pretend[5] to sacrifice everything to the judgment and inclination of your countrymen ?

B.

On the Moods and Tenses used with *Si*.

1. If the enemy had with a veteran army invaded our territory, and routed our army of recruits, no[6] German would have survived to-day. 2. If I either decline the contest, or show[7] myself a coward and a laggard, then you may[8] taunt me if you will, with my lowly birth, then call[9] me, if you choose, the basest and meanest of mankind. 3. If once[10] Napoleon throws his army across the Rhine, I am afraid that[11] no one will be able to stand in his way on this side the Vistula. 4. If we have had[12] enough of fighting to-day, let us recall the soldiers to their several (352, *Obs.*) standards, and hope for better things for[13] the morrow ; if to-morrow resistance[14] is manifestly no longer possible, let us yield, however[15] reluctantly, to necessity, and bid each take care[16] of himself. 5. If, when you have got to Rome, you care[17] to receive a letter from me, mind you are the first[18] to write to me. 6. When once Italy is reached,[19] I will either lead you (*pl.*), said he, at once to Rome, if you wish, or having let you

---

[1] See **142**.   [2] **303**, ii.   [3] *Care.* (**143**.)
[4] Adj. *civilis.* (See **58**.)   [5] **39**.   [6] See **223**.
[7] *Praebeo.* (**241**.)   [8] *Licet* with subj. (**197**.)
[9] Fut. imperat. of *dico* (p. 113, *n.*).
[10] Need not be expressed otherwise than by the right tense. (**190**, i.)
[11] *Ut quisquam.* (See **138**.)   [12] See **218**.
[13] *In.* (See **326**.)   [14] **219**.
[15] *Quamvis.* (**480**, *Obs.*)   [16] Use *consulo.* (**248**.)
[17] *Volo.*   [18] *Prior.* (See **62**.)   [19] **217**, *Obs.*

sack such[1] wealthy cities as Milan and Genoa, will send you home, if you prefer it, laden with plunder and spoil. 7. If they saw any of our soldiers running forward from (*ex*) the line of march, or left behind by his comrades, they would all hurl their darts at him. 8. It is haste,[2] said he, not deliberation, that we need; had we used it[3] earlier, we should have had[4] no war to-day. 9. These men, had you permitted it, would have been alive to-day, and been maintaining with the sword the national cause. 10. Had you asked me yesterday if I feared so worthless a person as your brother, I should have answered no; to-day the news of this defeat makes[5] me so anxious, that, were you to ask the same question, I should answer yes.

---

[1] Apposition, *urbs* used as *homo* in **224,** *Obs.* 2.   (See **317.**)
[2] Use *properatum*, and see **286.**   [3] Relative.
[4] Use *sum.* (**251.**)   [5] See **240.**

CONDITIONAL CLAUSES—*Continued.*

Exceptional Constructions of *si.*

460. **Exceptions** will be found to RULES I. and II. as given above in 452 and 453 ; these exceptions, however, are in many cases part of the regular construction of Latin, and are always easily accounted for.

461. **Apparent Exceptions.**—With the **modal verbs** *possum, debeo, oportet,* etc., and with **periphrastic tenses,** formed either by the *gerund* or *gerundive* (to express *duty,* etc.), or by the *future participle* (to express *intention,* etc.), with the verb *sum,* the **indicative** is regularly used in the *apodosis* or principal clause in place of the **subjunctive.** (153.)

The place of these modal verbs and participial phrases is taken in English by the auxiliary verbs *may, might, would, should, must, ought, am to, have to,* etc., which often form a substitute for our nearly obsolete subjunctive mood. Thus—

Quid, si hostes ad urbem veniant, *facturi* estis ? In case the enemy *should* come to the city, what *would you* do ?=what *do* you intend to do ?

Hunc hominem, si ulla in te esse *pietas, colere* debebas. If you *had had* any natural affection (*as you had not*), you *ought to have* respected this man.

Deleri totus exercitus potuit, *si fugientes persecuti victores* essent. The whole army *might* have been destroyed, if the victors had pursued the fugitives (*which they did not*).

Hos nisi manu misisset, *tormentis etiam dedendi* fuerunt. If he had not set these men free, they *must have been* given up to torture.

Bonus vates poteras esse, *si voluisses.* You *might have been* a good prophet, had you cared to be one.

Aliter si fecisses, *idem* eventurum fuit. Had you acted otherwise, the result *would have been* the same.

These are exceptions to, but not real violations of, RULE I. Thus *facturi estis* is another form of expressing *faciatis, colere debebas* of *coluisses.* These *modal* verbs, and the other periphrastic forms, supply the Latin verb with, as it were, fresh *moods,* or *modes of*

T

statement. (See **42**.) They add an assertion of **intention, duty, probability**, etc., to the idea conveyed by the verb.

Thus in, *Si quis haec* loquatur, *vix* puto *eum impetraturum esse*, "if any one were to use this language, I scarcely think he would obtain his request," the *vix puto*, etc., is equivalent to a subjunctive mood, *vix impetret*.

So *facturus fui* is almost equivalent to *fecissem*, *culpari potui* to *culpatus fuissem*.

462. Nor is, *Si hoc* dixi, nolim *dictum*, "If I said this, I am sorry," a violation of RULE II., for *nolim* is only a polite form of the indicative. (See **149**, i.)

So, *moriar*, *nisi hoc verum* est (may I perish, if this is not true), is no real violation of RULE I., for *moriar* is practically an *imperative*, not "I should die," but "let me die ;" nor is, *Si in hoc* erravi, *quis mihi* irascatur (if I have done wrong in this, who would be angry with me?) a violation of RULE II., for the question is a *virtual* negative, equivalent to *nemo mihi* irascetur. (See **150**.)

463. Real Exceptions.—Sometimes, however, RULES I. and II. are really violated.

> (*a*) Perieram *nisi tu* accurrisses. I should have perished
>   if you had not run to my assistance.

Compare the English "*I had perished had you not run up.*"[1]

> (*b*) *Si fractus* illabatur *orbis*, *impavidum* ferient *ruinae.*
>   Were the globe to be rent and fall upon him, the
>   fragments *will* strike but not dismay him.

In the first example (*a*) what is *unreal* (he had not perished) is stated *as though it were real*, for the sake of making the language more emphatic : " I *all but* perished."

The second (*b*) is from the *poet* Horace, who in *ferient* passes from the ordinary form of the conditional sentence to that of strong assertion or *prophecy*. These idioms, at all events the second, should never be imitated by the young composer.

Exercise 58 A should now be done (page 293).

Nisi, si non, sin, si minus ; sive, seu.

464. The rules for **mood** and **tense** are the same as those given for *si*.

---

* In using this pluperfect we are really, though unconsciously, using the now obsolete form of the English subjunctive.

Nisi, " if not," " unless," negatives a *whole clause ;* with *si non* the negative applies to a *single word*.

> *Morietur*, nisi *medicum adhibuerit*.   Unless he calls in, or, if he
>   does not call in, a physician he will die.
> *Morietur*, si *medicum* non *adhibuerit*.   He will die, if he *fails*-to-
>   call-in a physician.

465. *Sin (si ne.* properly " if not ")=" but if," and is used to introduce a fresh *si*-clause, *contrary* in sense to one already expressed or implied.   If the fresh clause is *negative, si non* with a verb, or simply *si minus*, takes the place of *sin*.

> *Si luna clara est, domo exeunt*, sin *obscurior, domi manent*.   If
>   the moon is bright, they leave their houses, *but if* it is at all
>   dim (**57**, *b*), they stay at home.
> *Si haec fecerit, gaudebo*, $\left\{\begin{array}{l}\text{si non } fecerit,\\ \text{si minus,}\end{array}\right\}$ *aequo animo feram*.   If
>   he *does* this, I shall be glad ; if he *does not* (or *if not*), I shall
>   take it quietly.

466. *Si, nisi, si non, si minus*, are sometimes like some other conjunctions (Intr. 27) joined with single words in place of clauses.

> (*a*) *Juravit se*, nisi victorem, *nunquam rediturum*.   He swore
>   never to return, unless victorious.
> (*b*) *Nihil aliud discere est*, nisi recordari.   Learning is nothing
>   else than recollecting.
> (*c*) *Cum spe*, si non *optimā*, at *aliquā* tamen *vivere*.   To live with
>   some hopes, if not the highest.   (Note *order of English*.)

Caution.—It is only in such phrases, where it emphasises a single word, that *at tamen* should be used ; it should **never begin a sentence**, as it so often does in later Latin.

467. Sive, *seu*, though translated by " whether," " or," are never used as *interrogatives*, never, that is, as identical with *utrum, an*.   (See **171.**)   They introduce two or more alternative *conditions*, between which the speaker makes no choice ; they affect the principal clause, or *apodosis*, equally.

> Sive *adhibueris medicum*, sive *non adhibueris*, convalesces.
>   You will get well, *whether* you call in a physician *or* no,
>   *i.e. if* you do, and *if* you do not.

The rules for the **mood** are the same as the two given for *si* (**452, 453**).

> *Seu* legit, *seu* scribit, *nihil temporis* terit.   Whether he *reads* or
>   *writes*, he *wastes* no time.   (RULE I.)
> *Seu* legat, *seu* scribat, *nihil temporis* terat.   Whether he *were to*
>   *read*, or *were to write*, he *would waste* no time.   (RULE II.)

Caution.—Great care must be taken to distinguish *sive
. . . sive, seu . . . seu,* from *utrum . . . an,* and *aut . . . aut.*

(*a*) *Sive . . . seu* introduce **adverbial** clauses (conditional).
(*b*) *Utrum . an* „   **substantival** clauses (interrogative).
(*c*) *Aut . . . aut* „   **co-ordinate** clauses.

(*a*) Seu *legit,* seu *scribit, nihil temporis terit.* *Whether* he reads
     or writes, he wastes no time.
(*b*) Utrum *legat* an *scribat nescio.* I do not know *whether* he is
     reading *or* writing.
(*c*) Aut *legit* aut *scribit.* He is *either* reading *or* writing.

The manner, therefore, in which "whether" and "or" are to be
translated into Latin depends entirely on the sense in which they are
used, that is, on the nature of the clause which they introduce. (See
171.)

468. *Dum, modo (dum modo), ita . . . ut* (consecutive),
when used in the sense of "provided that," "on the condition that," will cause no difficulty, as they are invariably
used with the **subjunctive.**

(*a*) *Oderint* dum *metuant;* (*b*) *maneat,* modo *taceat* (jussive);
(*c*) ita *maneat* ut[1] *mihi pareat,* ut ne quid *me invito faciat.*

(*a*) is " Let them hate me, so long as they fear me ;" (*b*) "let him
remain on condition of being silent ;" (*c*) "let him remain on condition that he obeys me, (and) does nothing against my will."

But *ita . . . ut (comparative*=as) is sometimes used in a similar
sense with the **indicative.**

Ita vivam ut te amo. May I die if I do not love you ; *lit.* may
     I live *so far* (only) *as* I love you.

Exercise 58.

A.

Exceptional uses of the Mood with *Si.*

1. Had he listened to your warnings, had he endured
everything in silence, the result would have been the
same then as to-day.   2. Had you been in office during

---

[1] The *ut* here is of course consecutive, "so as to," and hence
equivalent to a *condition ;* but it approaches also a *final* sense "with
the intention of ;" hence the *ne* in the next clause. Cf. the Greek
ὥστε, ὥστε μή.

(in) the same year as my father, had you encountered the same political storms as he did, you would have shewn,[1] if not[2] as great self-control, yet as much good sense as he did.   3. Had I said this with the intention of being of use to, and of pleasing, him, yet I should have had to put up with his abuse and insults.   4. Had your father said this with the intention of displeasing you, yet you should have remembered that he was your father, and have endured his angry mood calmly and in silence.   5. This is the course, which, had I been born in the same position as you, I should have had to take; but happily I have never had to undertake such a task.   6. Had the son been of the same character as the father, I might have touched his heart by prayer[3] and entreaty; but in truth he is so inhuman, so cruel, that, had all mankind endeavoured to soften him, no one would[4] have prevailed.   7. If you wish to see me before I leave the city, I would have[5] you write to your father not[6] to summon me to the army till you have come to Rome.   8. If you have been persuaded[6] to pardon him his offences, and not to exact punishment for so many crimes, would any[7] one impute that to you as a fault, or taunt you with your clemency and gentleness?   It might perhaps have been[8] better not to have listened to prayer; but error is one thing, wrong-doing another.

B.

Nisi, si non, sin ; sive, seu.

1. If you fail to return at the end of a week, you will greatly injure your own[9] cause.   2. I should not have written thus[10] had not I been convinced that your father took the same view on this question as I.   3. He was a man of the highest ability, the highest character, of respectable, if humble origin.   4. If I obtain my request,

---

[1] Use *adhibeo*, I employ. call in.   [2] See **466.**   [3] Gerund.
[4] See **115.**   [5] **141.**   [6] **122,** *c, b.*   [7] **358.**   [8] **153.**
[9] See **356,** i.
[10] *Haec.* So *haec,* or *hoc, facere,* is "to act *thus,*" never *ita agere.*

I shall be most grateful; if not, I will do my best[1] to bear it with resignation.   5. In the morning he [2] promised and bound himself by oath never to return from the field, unless victorious; yet [3] in the evening I saw him with my [4] own eyes walking in the park, with countenance unmoved and calm, if not cheerful.   6. Let him speak out his whole mind, his whole wishes; provided that he is silent for the future, it matters little what he says at present.   7. You shall obtain your request, but only on [5] condition that you depart at once, and never more return. 8. Whether you were absent intentionally, or by chance, concerns yourself, and is of no small importance to your own reputation; what [6] we have to decide is whether you were absent [7] or present; if you were absent [7] during [8] the battle, whether it happened by design or by mere chance, you will be condemned, and that[9] deservedly, by a unanimous verdict, for you ought never to have[10] left the camp. 9. Whether you will do me this favour or not, I do not yet know, but whether you consent to do it or no, I shall always be grateful to you for [11] your many kind deeds, and will show my gratitude if I can.   10. Whether this bill is constitutional   or   unconstitutional   may   be   questioned; but whether it is constitutional or unconstitutional, I venture to say this, that if not indispensable, it is so beneficial, so useful to the nation in the face[12] of the present crisis, that it has been approved of by every patriot.

---

[1] See **332**, 5, *g.* (p. 222).   [2] *Iste.* (See **338**, *Obs.* 2.)
[3] *Idem* for "yet him." (See **366**, ii.)   [4] *Ipse.* (**355**, *d.*)
[5] *Ita . . ut.* (**468**, *c.*)   [6] **341.**
[7,7] Tenses? one the mere fact, the other continuous time. (**173.**)
[8] "Then . . . when the fight was going on." (**218.**) Mood ? (See **433**.)
[9] *Idque.* (See **344.**)   [10] Tense ? (**198**, i., ii., *b.*)
[11] *Propter tot.*   [12] **273.** *Obs.*

EXERCISE LIX.

CONDITIONAL CLAUSES—*Continued.*

Si-clause in Oratio obliqua.

469. If a verb of *saying* or *thinking* is inserted before the **principal** clause of a conditional sentence, the verb of that clause will of course pass from the **indicative** or **subjunctive** mood into the **infinitive** (**31**), which represents the English finite verb with "that" prefixed.

(i.) With the apodosis, or main clause, of sentences under RULE I., this will give no difficulty; in those that fall under RULE II., the subjunctive, answering to the English *would, would have,* will be (somewhat roughly) represented by the future in *-rus* with *esse* and *fuisse* respectively.   (See **36.**)

Amem (I would love) will be represented by (*dico*) *me amaturum esse.*

Amarem and *amavissem* (I would have loved), by (*dico*) *me amaturum fuisse.*

(ii.) The verb in the *si*-clause will, in all such cases, be in the **subjunctive** mood; the indicative has no proper place in any clause dependent on a verb in *oratio obliqua.* (**444.**)

470. (i.) Thus with sentences under RULE I.   (**452.**)

Oratio recta.		Oratio obliqua.
(*a*) *Si hoc* dico, erro,	will become	(*dicit*) me, *si hoc* dicam. errare.
(*b*) *Si hoc* dicebam, errabam	,,	(*dicit*) me, *si hoc* dicerem, erravisse.
(*c*) *Si hoc* dixi erravi	,,	(*dicit*) me, *si hoc dixerim,* erravisse.
(*d*) *Si hoc* dicam (fut.) errabo	,,	(*dicit*) me, *si hoc* dicam, erraturum esse.

(ii.) If, as in narrative is more usual, the verb of saying is in a **historic** tense.   (**177,** *b.*)

Oratio obliqua.

(*a*) and (*b*) will become (*dixit*) me, *si hoc* dicerem, errare.

(*c*)   ,,   (*dixit*) me, *si hoc* dixissem, erravisse (*or* dixerim).

(*d*)   ,,   (*dixit*) me, *si hoc* dicerem, erraturum esse.

295

471. But when, as is more usual, the **future perfect** is used in the protasis to a future clause, care must be taken.

Oratio recta.	*Oratio obliqua.*
Si hoc dixero, erràbo, will become	(dicit) *me, si hoc* dixerim, erraturum esse, but
	(dixit) *me, si hoc* dixissem, *erraturum esse.*

That is, after a past verb, expressed or implied, of *narrating*, the **future perfect** of *oratio recta* passes into the **pluperfect**, after a *present* verb into the **perfect**, subjunctive.

Obs.—The *future perfect* of the indicative of *oratio recta* has a **double** sense, *future* and *past (shall have)* ; both cannot be represented in the subjunctive ; accordingly Latin represents only the **past** sense, English sometimes only the future, sometimes the past very vaguely.

Oratio recta.	*Oratio obliqua*
Eng. If [1]*once* he *does* this he *shall,* or *will,* die.	**He said that** if he *should* once do, or once *did,* this, he *should,* or *would,* die.
Lat. Si hoc fecerit, *morietur.*	*Eum si hoc* fecisset, *moriturum fore.*
Or *Ei, si ,, ,, moriendum erit.*	*Ei, si ,, ,, moriendum fore.*

472. With sentences under RULE II. (453) there will be no change in the mood of the *si*-clause ; the tense will of course vary with that of the verb of *saying* or *thinking.*

Oratio recta.	*Oratio obliqua.*
Si hoc dicam, errem, will become	(*dicit*) *me, si hoc* dicam, erraturum esse.
	(*dixit*) *me, si hoc* dicerem, erraturum esse.

Si hoc dicerem, errarem ; $\begin{Bmatrix} dicit \\ dixit \end{Bmatrix}$ *me si hoc* dicerem, erraturum fuisse. If I had *been saying* this, I should have been in error.

Si hoc dixissem, erravissem ; $\begin{Bmatrix} dicit \\ dixit \end{Bmatrix}$ *me si hoc* dixissem, erraturum fuisse. If I *had said,* etc.

---

[1] Remember how often our "*if once*" is expressed by the Latin future perfect (*semel* need rarely be inserted), and this tense and its representatives in the subjunctive must always be used if the time indicated is. though still future, prior to that of the principal verb.

473. The periphrasis for the future, and contingent future, **passive** must not be forgotten. (**193**, iii. and v.)

(a) "He said that the city *would be taken*, if Caesar *did* not come to its aid." (*Dixit*) *urbem, nisi* subvenisset *Caesar,* captum iri, *or,* fore ut *urbs caperetur* (*captam fore* is found, but rarely).

(*Nisi subveniret* would mean, *were* coming, or *were ready* to come.)

(b) "He said that the city would *have been* taken if Caesar had not come to its aid," or "*but for* Caesar *having* come," etc. (Dixit) *Caesar nisi* subvenisset, futurum fuisse ut *urbs caperetur.*

In *oratio recta* we should have (a) *urbs, nisi* subvenerit *Caesar,* capietur, (b) *urbs* capta fuisset, or *capi* potuit (see **461**), *nisi* subvenisset *Caesar.*

474. Such apparent violations of RULE I. as (a) *mortem mihi* denuntiavit *pater, si* pugnassem, (b) expectabat *Caesar, si hostes* posset *opprimere,* are both instances of **virtual** *oratio obliqua.* (See **449**.)

(a) is "My father threatened me with death, *if I should fight,* or *fought;*" (b) "Caesar was waiting, *in hopes of being able* to crush the enemy."

In (a) *si pugnassem* is not really the *protasis* or adverbial clause to *denuntiavit,* which is quite unqualified : it belongs really to a suppressed clause contained in *mortem,* such as *fore ut perirem;* it is therefore a perfectly regular instance of a *si*-clause in *oratio obliqua :* "He *said* that I should die if I fought" (his words were "*si pugnaveris moriere*").

In (b) *si posset* does not qualify *expectabat,* which is quite unqualified. It is used in the sense "in hopes that," and it answers to a suppressed clause expressing what *was in Caesar's mind,* "intending to use the chance, in case," etc. It is therefore virtual *oratio obliqua,* and the mood is quite regular.

475. How to express "would have" in the **principal clause** of a conditional sentence after consecutive *ut,* or a dependent interrogation.

The **pluperfect subjunctive** is not used, but gives place to the **perfect subjunctive** of the modal verb *possum* or of the periphrasis formed by the future in -*rus,* or gerund or gerundive with *sum.* (**461**.)

Quid tu, *si tum adesses,* dixisses, will become *rogo, quid tu, si tum adesses,* dicturus fueris.

Si *id fecissem,* periissem, will become *ut* ("so that") *si id fecissem,* periturus fuerim, *or* pereundum *mihi* fuerit. (**115**.)

Some additional examples of more or less **exceptional** constructions are added for careful observation.

1. Debuisti *enim, etiam* si *falso in suspicionem* venisses. *mihi ignoscere.* You ought to *have* forgiven me, or it *would have* been your duty to forgive me, even if you had been falsely suspected. (**461.**)

2. *Atrox certamen* aderat, ni *Fabius rem* expedisset. A desperate contest was at hand (*would have* taken place) had not Fabius solved the difficulty. (**463.**)

3. *Ibi* erat *mansurus,* si *ire* perrexisset. It was there he *would have* stayed, had he continued his journey. (**461.**)

4. *Quid enim futurum* fuit, si *res agitari coepta* esset. For what *would have* happened, if once the question had begun to be discussed. (**461.**)

5. *Neque hostem sustinere* poterant, ni *cohortes illae se* objecissent. And they *could not have* maintained themselves against the enemy, but for those cohorts' exposure of themselves. (**461.**)

6. *Virgines* si effugissent, impleturae *urbem tumultu* erant. Had the maidens escaped, they *would have* spread disorder through the whole city. (**461.**)

7. *Praeclare* viceramus, nisi *fugientem Antonium* recepisset *Lepidus.* We *should have* won a splendid victory, had not Lepidus given a reception to Antony when in full flight. (**463.**)

8. Si *in hoc* erravi, *id mihi* velim *ignoscas.* If I have blundered in this, I beg you to forgive me. (**462.**)

9. *Circumfunduntur hostes,* si *quem aditum reperire* possent. The enemy swarm (historic pres.) round, *in hopes of* finding some means of approach (*with the view of breaking* in, if), etc. (**474.**)

10. *Praemium proposuit,* si *quis ducem interfecisset.* He offered a prize, *i.e. said that* he would give a prize, in case any one should kill the leader. (**474.**)

11. *Nuntium ad te misi,* si *forte non* audisses. I sent you a messenger, in case you had not heard. (We must supply *ut audires,* etc.) (**474.**)

12. *Non recusavit quo minus vel extremo spiritu,* si *quam opem reipublicae ferre* posset, *experiretur.* He did not flinch from trying even with his latest breath whether he could not give some aid to his country—*lit.* from making the experiment *in hopes that* he could . . . (**474.**)

Exercise 59

A.

1. Did you imagine that, if all the rest were cut off either by the sword or by famine, you alone would be saved ?   2. He feared, he said, that unless he consented to do everything that the king should command, he would never be allowed to return to his native land.   3. He will bear, he says, cheerfully his own destitution and that[1] of his family, if once he be freed from this degrading suspicion. 4. He warned them of the extent[2] and suddenness[2] of the crisis, that they could win the day if they were ready to show themselves brave men and worthy of their forefathers, but that if they hesitated or hung back, all the neighbouring tribes would soon be in arms.   5. He felt convinced of this, that if once he crushed the barbarians who had long been[3] infesting the mountains, the way to Italy would be open to himself and his soldiers.   6. He said that he would never have imparted this story to you, had he not when[4] leaving home promised his father to conceal nothing from such dear friends as[5] yourselves.   7. He felt convinced, he said, that unless they had placed so experienced a general as yourself at the head of a veteran army, the city would have been stormed within a week.   8. He said he would never have pardoned you so monstrous a crime, had not your aged father thrown[6] himself at his feet and implored him to spare you.

B.

The following Exercise is recapitulatory ; the sentences contain various kinds of *if*-clauses.

1. If you are at Rome, I scarcely imagine you are, but if you are, please write at once.   2. If the enemy reaches the city, there will be reason[7] to fear a dreadful massacre. 3. I sent you a letter of Caesar's, in case you wished to

---

[1] See **345**.   [2] See **174**, *b* and *e*.
[3] Tense? (See **181**.) Mood? (See **444, 449**)   [4] See **406**, *note* [2].
[5] **224**, *Obs.* 2.   [6] See **257**. Use passive (or middle) participle.
[7] "must (*tense ?*) be feared."

read it.   4. He declared that it was absolutely impossible for the Germans to win the day, if they engaged in battle before the new moon.   5. If you are ready to make some exertion, you will take the city.   6. If you once exert yourselves, you will take the city.   7. He said that if they once exerted themselves, they would take the city.   8. As the neighbouring tribes were all jealous of his fame, he felt that if he and his people surrendered their arms, their doom[1] was certain.   9. If anything falls out amiss,[2] we shall make you responsible.   10. He threatened him with violence and every species[3] of punishment, if he entered the senate-house.   11. It was certainly[4] a wonderful speech; I could not imitate it if I would; perhaps I would not if I could.   12. The Dictator announced a heavy penalty in case any one should fight without his permission.   13. They feared that if they once departed without success, they would lose everything for the sake of which they had taken up arms.   14. They now at last perceived that if, at his suggestion, they had consented to abandon the popular party, and join the nobles, they would have lost all their privileges and their freedom, if not their lives.   15. If you do this, you will possibly incur some loss; if you do not you will undoubtedly have acted dishonourably; it is for[5] you to decide which of the two you prefer to do.   16. If any one evades military service, he shall be declared infamous; if any one has fears for his own safety, let him at once lay down his arms, and leave his native land safe and sound.

---

[1] " were doomed to certain destruction."
[2] *Secus*, otherwise than *well*.   [3] Simply *omnis*.
[4] *Sane*, " certainly," in the sense of making an *admission*.
[5] **291**, *Obs.* 2.

CONCESSIVE CLAUSES.

Quanquam, quamvis, etc.

476. By **concessive clauses** we mean such adverbial clauses as are introduced in English by " although " and the like, in Latin by the conjunctions *etsi (tametsi, etiam si)*; *quanquam, quamvis, licet.* (See Intr. 59, *g*.)

Such clauses are called *concessive* because they admit or *concede* something, in spite of which the statement made in the main clause is true ; its truth is emphasised by the contrast.

477. Their syntax is not difficult.

Rule.—When the point conceded in the concessive clause is **admitted as a fact** the **indicative** is used; otherwise, when only conceded **for the sake of argument**, the **subjunctive.**

The difference is still occasionally marked in English : " though he *is* guilty," " though he *be* guilty ;" " though he *was* guilty," " though he *were* guilty ;" but the nearly obsolete use of the English subjunctive is a precarious guide.

(*a*) In the sense of the Latin **indicative** we constantly use such phrases as, *in spite of*, or *notwithstanding*, his guilt, *or*, guilty *as* he is, etc.

(*b*) In that of the **subjunctive**, *whatever* his guilt=*however* guilty he is (be), *were* he guilty, etc.

478. *Etsi (tametsi)*, when it contrasts one *fact* with another *fact*, is joined with the **indicative.**

> Etsi *mons Cevenna iter* impediebat, *tamen ad fines Arvernorum pervenit.* Although the Cevennes were in the way of his march (or *in spite of . . . being* in the way) he reached the territory of the Arverni.

But when both the concession and the other statement are purely **imaginary**, the **subjunctive** is used.

> *Ego* etsi abessem, *tamen cum ceteris me condemnasses?* Though I *had been absent (all the* time), *would* you yet *have* condemned me with all the rest ?

That is, the *etsi* clause follows the mood, as a rule, of the main clause, precisely as the *si*-clause, of which it is only another form.

479. *Quanquam* (a doubled *quam*), which contrasts one
fact with another, naturally takes the **indicative.** It
should never be joined with the subjunctive unless in
oratio obliqua.

> *Romani* quanquam *itinere et aestu fessi* erant, *tamen obviam
> hostibus* procedunt. Though the Romans were fatigued with
> the march and the heat, yet they advanced (historic present)
> to meet the enemy.

Observe how often *tamen,* "yet," "still," is inserted in the main
clause to mark the contrast; but *at tamen* should never be used
except with single words. (See **466.**)

Obs.—*Quanquam* is often used *co-ordinately* [1] to introduce an entirely fresh sentence in contrast with what precedes it, and is then =
"and yet ;" cf. the co-ordinate use of *quum.* (**435.**)

480. (i.) *Quamvis,* on the other hand, **requires a subjunctive.**

> *Quamvis* sit *magna expectatio, tamen eam vinces.* Although
> expectations are (*or,* may be) great, you will surpass
> them (or, *however* great are (*be*) the expectations formed
> of you).

Quamvis = *quam vis,* [2] "as you will," must have a subjunctive from
the nature of the case, as the above sentence would originally be,
"*Let* expectations *be* as great *as you please,* you will surpass them."

Obs.—*Quamvis,* like *nisi* (**466**), is sometimes joined closely with a
single word (*quamvis* audax, "however bold," "whatever his boldness "), without a verb.

(ii.) *Licet,* "although," is simply the impersonal **verb,**
" it is granted " (**197**). It should therefore never be used
with the indicative.

> Licet *undique pericula* impendeant, *tamen subibo.* *Though*
> dangers threaten me on every side, I will face them.

481. As in English, so in Latin, the same idea as is
denoted by the concessive conjunctions "although"
quanquam, etc., may be expressed in many other ways.

---

[1] Cf. the opening of the fine passage in Georgic I. 469—
　　　　"Tempore *quanquam* illo," etc.

[2] *Quamvis* is properly a separate clause, "*as* you *choose,*" and the
subjunctive is *jussive* (**144**) ; it is sometimes even inflected : *quam* volet
cunctetur, (lit.) let him delay *as much as he chooses.* But in later Latin
its origin, and that of *licet,* became obliterated, and they were used
freely with the indicative, *quanquam* with the subjunctive.

Thus " Though he is an excellent man, he does wrong sometimes," may be translated not only by, Quanquam *homo optimus est*, tamen *interdum peccat*, but by (*a*) *Homo optimus* ille quidem, sed *interdum* peccat (**334**, iv.) ; or (*b*) Ut (" granted that") sit *homo ille optimus*, *tamen interdum peccat;* or (*c*) Ita *homo optimus est* ut *interdum* peccet, *i.e.* " *so far only*," etc. (**111**) ; or (*d*) *Sit* (jussive) *homo ille optimus*, *tamen interdum peccat;* or (*e*) very commonly by the use of *sane* in one clause, followed by an *adversative conjunction* (Intr. 56, *c*) in the other,—*res* sane *difficilis, sed tamen investiganda*, " *though a* difficult question, *yet still* one that demands investigation ;" or (*f*) by the mere participle,—*hoc crimine* absolutus, *furti tamen condemnatus est*, " *though* acquitted on this charge he was found guilty of theft." (**406.**)

For the use of *qui*   for " although " see **509**, *b*.
  „   *quum*   „   **431.**
  „   *sicut* . . . *ita*   „   **492** (i.).

Exercise 60.

1. Though he feels neither remorse nor shame for this deed, yet he shall pay me the penalty of his crime. 2. Even though it were quite impossible to pardon his fault, yet you ought[1] to have taken into account his many services to the nation. 3. Whatever his guilt,[2] whatever his criminality, no one has a right to indict him in his absence and to condemn him unheard. 4. Entirely guilty as he is, and absolutely deserving of condign punishment, yet I cannot help comparing his present fallen and low condition with his former good fortune · and renown. 5. Miserable as it is for an innocent man to be suspected and charged, yet it is better for the innocent to be acquitted than for the guilty not to be accused. 6. However criminal he had been, however worthy of every kind of punishment, yet it would have[3] been better for ten guilty persons to be acquitted, than for one innocent to be found guilty. 7. In spite of his having had the sovereignty and supreme power offered and intrusted to him by the unanimous vote[4] of his countrymen, he long refused to take any part in politics, and was the only person in my day who attained to the highest distinctions

---

[1] Gerundive. (**389.**)   [2] Use adjective. (**477**, *b*.)
[3] Mood ? (**153.**)   [4] Number ?

against his will, and almost under compulsion. 8. Though[1] freed from this apprehension, I was soon suspected of a darker[2] crime, and perhaps but for your having come to my aid, might have fallen a victim[3] to the hatred and schemes of my enemies. 9. Many[4] as are the evils that you have endured, you will one day, I still believe,[5] not only enjoy good fortune, but a rarer gift,[6] happiness.

---

[1] **481,** *f.*   [2] Metaphor. (See Vocab.)

[3] Metaphor; (**17**)="been crushed by."

[4] "Although . . . so many" (*tot*, **477,** *a*).   [5] **32,** *b.*

[6] "Gift," metaphor; "that which (**67**) more rarely falls to men's lot.

EXERCISE LXI.

CAUSAL AND EXPLANATORY CLAUSES.

482. By these are meant such **subordinate**[1] adverbial clauses as give a **reason** or **explanation** of the statement, etc., made by the verb in the principal clause. They are introduced in English by "because," "inasmuch as," "seeing that," "whereas," "considering that," etc. (Intr. 59, *d*.)

483. The conjunctions *quod, quia,* "because," *quoniam* (i.e. *quum jam*), *quandoquidem,* "since," are followed by an **indicative** mood.

> *Vos, inquit,* quoniam *jam nox* est, *domum discedite.* Do you, says he, *since* it is now night, depart home.

Obs.—These conjunctions are all formed from the *relative*, and like the relative (**84**) often have a *demonstrative* particle or phrase corresponding to them in the other clause. Cf. *tamen* in concessive, *idcirco* in final, clauses, etc. (See **107**.)

> Idcirco, eo, hanc ob causam, etc., *ad te scribo* quod *me id facere jussisti.* The *reason* of my writing is *that* you told me to do so. *Nullam aliam* ob causam . . . *quam* quod, etc. The one and only *cause* or *motive* . . . is *that*, etc.

484. All of these conjunctions however may be joined with the **subjunctive**, on either of two grounds.

(*a*) The principal clause may be in *oratio obliqua.* (**446**.)

> *Jussit eos,* quoniam *nox* esset, *discedere.*

(*b*) The *quod*-clause may be in *virtual oratio obliqua.* (See **448**.)

That is, we may supply in thought the words "as he (they) said," or "thought," after the causal conjunction ; or translate *quod* by "asserting that," "under the impression that," "in the belief that."

> *Abire voluit,* quoniam *nox* esset. Since it was, *as he said*, night.

---

[1] The connexion of cause and effect may be stated by a *co-ordinate* clause with causal or inferential conjunctions (Intr. 56, *d* and *e*) : *Rediisti: gaudeo* igitur ; or *gaudeo: rediisti* enim ; but the construction of such co-ordinate conjunctions presents no difficulty, as they have no effect on the mood of the verb.

Obs.—This use of the subjunctive in a *quod*-clause is exceedingly common after words of *praising, blaming, accusing, admiring, complaining, wondering.*

> *Rex civibus odio erat,* quod *leges* violasset.   The king was hated by his subjects, because (*they felt that*) he had broken the law, or, *as* having, *or*, for having (*as they thought*), broken the law.

Violarat would be a statement made and accredited by the historian. "for having (as he had) broken the law."
It is naturally most common after verbs of *complaining, blaming,* etc.

> *Mihi irascitur,* quod *eum* neglexerim.   Because (*as he says* or *fancies*) I have neglected him, *as* having neglected him.

The responsibility of the statement is shifted from the speaker or writer to the subject of the principal verb. (See 448.)

485. When a reason is mentioned only to be set aside, *non quo,* "not that," *non quin,* "not but what," are used, always with the **subjunctive.**

Sometimes the reason *accepted* follows, with *sed quod* and the **indicative.**

> Non quo *tui me* taedeat, or, non quin *me* ames, sed quod *abire* cupio.   *Not that* I am tired of you, or *not but what* you love me (or, *not that* you *don't*), *but because* I am anxious to depart.

Quum with the subjunctive is often causal (see **430**).   So also is *qui* (see **509**).

486. *Quod* ("that") often answers to the English "the fact *that*," or, "*of*," and is used to **explain** the object or subject of a verb, especially in apposition with a neuter pronoun.

> *Magnum est hoc,* quod *victor victis* pepercit.   This is no small thing, I mean *the fact of* his having spared the vanquished when victorious.
> *Omitto illud,* quod *regem patriamque* prodidit.[1]   I pass over *the fact of* his having betrayed his king and country; or simply, "his *betrayal* of," etc.

---

[1] Sometimes a kind of *virtual oratio obliqua* is used, where there is only a single speaker, who looks on himself as, so to speak, *two persons:* *Omitto . . . quod prodiderit,* I pass over *my belief that* he betrayed.

Obs.—This *quod* with the indicative (or subjunctive) will be found very useful in translating the English verbal **substantive** of the present or perfect tense, *e.g.* "your *saying* or *having said* this," and such **abstract nouns** as "circumstance," "fact," "reason," "reflexion."

Of course it cannot be used for "that" after verbs **sentiendi et declarandi.** (See **32**, *a*.) *Illud* dico, quod *patriam prodidisti* would mean, not, "I *say that* you have betrayed your country," but, "I *mean the fact* of your having betrayed," etc.

487. Notice also the phrases—

    (*a*) *Peropportune* accidit quod *venisti.* Your *coming* was *very fortunate* (only substituted for *ut* (**123**) when an *adverb* is joined with *accidit*).

    (*b*) Accedit quod *domi non est.* There is the *additional reason* that he is not at home.

    (*c*) Quod scribis *eum rediisse, num verum sit dubito.* As to your *writing* to say that he has returned, I doubt its truth.

Obs.—With verbs of **rejoicing**, etc., there is no perceptible difference between the infinitive (**41**, *b*) and the *quod*-clause : Te rediisse *gaudeo* = quod rediisti *gaudeo.* The latter emphasises the *fact* of the return.

Exercise 61.

1. The reason of my somewhat disliking in my youth one so attached to me as[1] your excellent relative, was my being unable to bear his want of steadiness and principle. 2. I am hated by every[2] bad citizen for having been the very last to uphold the national cause, and because I have constantly disdained to flatter the conqueror. 3. I received[3] the thanks of parliament and the nation for having been alone[4] in not despairing of the commonwealth. 4. It was scarcely possible[5] for you not to incur the hatred[6] of your countrymen,—not that you had been guilty of betraying your country, but because you had the courage to be the advocate of a burdensome and distasteful, however[7] necessary, peace. 5. All honoured your gallant father for having sacrificed the unanimous offer[8] of a throne to the true and more substantial glory of

---

[1] **224**, and *Obs.* 2.   [2] **375.**
[3] = "thanks were returned to me by . . ."   [4] See **62**, and **484**, *Obs.*
[5] **132**, *e.*   [6] *Pl.*, why? Because "countrymen" is plural.
[7] Use either *ille quidem* (**481**, *a*) or *si . . . at tamen* (**466**, *c*) or *quamvis.* (**480**, *Obs.*)
[8] Same construction as that in **417.**

giving[1] freedom to his country.   6. Though the whole
world is angry with me for having pardoned (as they
say[2]) my father's murderers, yet I shall never be ashamed
of the reflexion[3] of having spared the vanquished in the
hour of victory.   7. As for your having still a grudge
against me, under the impression[2] that six years ago I
injured you in your absence, and sacrificed your interests
to my own gain (*pl.*), my only motive in wishing to
refute such a charge is because I count your friendship
worth seeking.   8. And now, in spite of his being incapable of any such baseness, he was the object of universal
unpopularity, as having[2] supplied the enemy with funds,
and treated the office with which the nation had intrusted
him as a source of disgraceful gain; though no one was
ever more incapable of so black a crime.

---

[1] Same construction as that in **417**.   [2] See **484**, *b*.
[3] **486**, *Obs.* and *note*.

EXERCISE LXII.

COMPARATIVE CLAUSES.

Proportion.

488. By **comparative clauses** we mean here such adverbial clauses (Intr. 82-84) as express *likeness, agreement,* or the *opposite,* with what is stated, asked, or ordered, in the principal clause.

He acted *as I had ordered him;* why was he treated worse *than he deserved?* Do *as I bid you;* he behaved *as though he were mad;* are instances of such clauses in English.

In Latin the number of **conjunctions** or **conjunctional phrases** used to introduce such clauses is very large ; *ut (sicut), quemadmodum, atque (ac), quam, quasi, velut* (si), *tanquam* (si), *quasi, ac si.* (Intr. 59, *f.*)

They correspond also to a number of **demonstrative adverbs** or phrases, which stand to them in the same relation as *is* to *qui, tantus* to *quantus, idcirco,* or *adeo,* to *ut, tamen* to *quanquam,* etc.

Such are *ita, sic, pro eo, perinde, pariter, potius, aliter, secus,* etc.

489. All such clauses, both in English and Latin, fall naturally into **two classes.**

Class I.—Those in which the **comparison** made in the subordinate clause is *stated,* or *predicated,* as something *real,* as for example :—

He was punished *as he deserved.* *Perinde ac meritus* est, *poenas persolvit.*

Class II.—Those in which such **comparison** is introduced as a mere *conception* of the mind, something *imaginary* or *unreal,* not stated as a *fact;* as—

He was punished *as though he had deserved it.* *Perinde ac si,* or *ut si,* or *quasi, meritus* esset, *poenas persolvit.*

In CLASS I. the **indicative** is the rule (except in *oratio obliqua*), in CLASS II. the **subjunctive.**

Class I.—Comparative Clauses with the Indicative.

490. Observe that the ideas of *likeness, equality, difference,* etc., which are often expressed by *adverbial* or *conjunctional* clauses, may be otherwise expressed both in English and Latin.

(i.) In Latin the place of the **conjunction** is often taken by the **relative**, *i.e.* we have an adjectival (correlative) instead of an adverbial clause.

> Tanta *est tempestas* quantam *numquam antea vidi.* The storm is greater *than I ever saw before,* or, is unparalleled in my experience. (See **84, 85.**)

(ii.) In Latin, but to a far greater extent in English, the place of the adverbial **clause** of comparison is taken by an adverbial **phrase** included in a simple sentence. (Intr. 70.)

Thus in the compound sentence, " he was punished *as he deserved,*" the adverbial clause may in both languages be expressed in three different ways : (1) by an *adverbial* clause ; (2) by an *adjectival* clause ; (3) by an *adverbial phrase,* or an *adverb.*

> (1) *Perinde* ac meritus est *poenas persolvit.* He was punished *as he deserved.*
>
> (2) *Poenas* quas debuit *persolvit.* He paid the penalty *which he merited.*
>
> (3) Pro meritis, *or* merito, *or* pro scelere, *poenas persolvit.* He was punished *in accordance with his guilt,* or, *deservedly.*

In English one of the last of these modes, the *adverbial phrase,* is far commoner than in Latin, and must constantly be translated by a Latin *adverbial clause.*

General Rule.

491. In Class I.—To express (*a*) **likeness**, *ut* (" as ") corresponds to *ita, sic,* sometimes to *perinde; atque* (*ac*) corresponds to *perinde, pariter, aeque, juxta, pro eo,* etc.

To express (*b*) **difference**, *atque* (*ac*) corresponds to *aliter, secus; ac* and *quam* to *contra; quam* to *potius,* and other *comparatives.*

> (*a*) Ut *sunt,* ita *nominantur senes.* Their title " old men" *corresponds* to the fact.
> Pro eo ac, *or* perinde ac, *debui, feci.* I have acted *in accordance with my duty.*
>
> (*b*) Aliter ac, *or* non perinde ac, *meriti sumus, laudamur.* We are not praised *in proportion to our deserts.*
> Contra quam *pollicitus es fecisti.* You have acted *in violation of your promises.*

Obs. 1.—Note the recurrence of the **indicative** mood, and the constant substitution of the English **adverbial** and other **phrases** for the Latin **adverbial clause.**

Obs. 2.—A very strong contrast may be marked by a double *aliter.*

Aliter *tum locutus es,* aliter *te geris hodie.* Your behaviour to-day is *most inconsistent with* your language at that time.

Special Idioms.

492. Ut as a comparative conjunction (="as") has many uses.

(i.) Sometimes with *ita, ut* (or *sicut*) marks a contrast, "as, or *while* (p. 274, *note*) one fact is true, so, *on the other hand,* is another," and is virtually *concessive.*

Ut *fortasse honestum est hoc,* sic *parum utile.* *Though* this is perhaps right, *yet* it is scarcely expedient.

(ii.) Sometimes, with *ita,* it is used in a *restrictive* sense, and is virtually *conditional.*

Ita *vivam* ut *te amo.* May I live *so far only* as I love you, *i.e.* May I die *if I do not love you.* (**468,** *ad fin.*)

(iii.) Without *ita,* it introduces a *general remark* in accordance with which a particular fact is noticed.

Tum rex, ut erat natura benignus, *omnibus veniam dedit.* Thereupon the king, *in accordance*[1] *with* the kindness of his nature, forgave them all.

(iv.) It introduces, as the English "as," parenthetic clauses : *ut fit,* "as (often) happens," *ut aiunt,* "as the proverb says."

But such parentheses as, *ut credo, ut arbitror, ut videtur,* are far rarer in Latin than in English, and are used in an *apologetic* and self-depreciatory sense, "*as at least* I think," or else are *ironical,* as is almost invariably the parenthetic *credo.* (See **32,** *b.*)

(v.) It is used even *without any verb* in two senses.

(*a*) "As you would expect."

Magnus pavor, ut *in re improvisa, fuit.* The panic was great, *as was natural* in so unexpected an occurrence.

(*b*) In a *restrictive* sense, "*so far as* could be expected."

Satis intrepide, ut *in re improvisa, se gessit.* He showed considerable presence of mind, *considering* the unexpected nature of the occurrence.

---

[1] The same idea might be expressed by *quā erat animi benignitate,* or *pro solitā ejus benignitate,* or *homo naturā benignissimus.* All these are substitutes for the much needed present participle of *esse.* (**224,** *Obs.* 1.)

493. Quam (see **275**) generally introduces a clause of the same construction as that of the main clause.

Nec ultra saeviit *quam satis* erat.   Nor did he show more severity than was necessary,—any needless severity.
Nos potius hostem aggrediamur quam *ipsi cum* propulsemus.   Let us take an aggressive, rather than a merely defensive, attitude.

But where **design** or **result** is indicated, a subjunctive is of course necessary.

Nihil ultra commotus est quam ut *abire eos* juberet.   He was only so far moved as to bid them depart.

Obs. 1.—A subjunctive clause is used where a course is mentioned only to be rejected.

Omnia potius tentanda quam hoc faciamus.   We ought to try any course *rather than* (allow ourselves to) *act thus.*

With *tam, quam* expresses equality [1] of *degree.*

Tam *timidus hodie est* quam *tum fuit audax.*   He is as cowardly to-day as he was then over bold.

Obs. 2.—When two **adjectives** or **adverbs** are contrasted by the comparative degree followed by *quam*, Latin often uses the comparative degree with *both.*

Pestilentia minacior fuit quam perniciosior.   The pestilence was more alarming than fatal.
Hoc bellum fortius quam felicius *gessistis.*   You have carried on this war with more courage than good fortune.

494. Quum, tum.   These are often used, in the sense of "whereas," "so especially," to unite two clauses, of which the *tum*-clause is always the most *emphatic in sense*, as well as the main clause in grammar.

Quum *omnis servitus misera est,* tum *haec omnium est miserrima.*   *As* all slavery is wretched, *so* is this the most wretched of all, *or*, all slavery is wretched, *but* this, etc.

Obs.—The indicative is used with *quum* when the **time of the two verbs is the same**; but when the *quum*-clause denotes a time **prior to**

---

[1] In Livy the comparative clause is often introduced in a way impossible to imitate in English.

Cujus rei non tam *ausim tantum virum insimulare . . .* quam *ea suspicio haud sane purgata est.   Though* I would not venture *. . . yet* that suspicion, etc.

that of the *tum*-clause the usual idiom is followed, and the subjunctive used even though a fact is asserted in the former.   (See **429**.)

Cum te semper amavi, *tum mei amantissimum* cognovi. Not only have I always felt affection for you, but I have found you most affectionate towards myself.

But—*Cum te semper* dilexerim, *tum hodie multo plus* diligo.   I have always loved you, but I love you far more now.

Class II.—Comparative Clauses with the Subjunctive.

495. In comparisons made with an **unreal** or **imaginary** case, the adverbial clause is introduced by *velut, tanquam* (often with *si* added), *ut si, quasi, ac si*.   The corresponding demonstratives are *sic, ita, perinde, proinde, non secus*, or such phrases as *similes sunt, similiter faciunt*, etc.   The **subjunctive** is always used in the adverbial clause.

Sic *eum ames velim* ut si *frater* esset *tuus*.   I would have you love him *as if* he were your own brother.

Ita *se gessit* quasi *consul* esset.   He behaved as *though he* were consul.

496. These conjunctions are often used with a **single word** (substantive, adjective, or participle) or a **phrase**.

Eum tanquam hostem, *or* tanquam patriae proditorem, *odi*.   I hate him as (though he were) an enemy, *or*, a traitor.

They are constantly so used in Latin to **qualify a strong expression** or **metaphor**, and must often be inserted where there is nothing answering to them in English, where metaphors are much more freely used.   (See **17**.)

"The soul flies forth from the *prison-house* of the body." *E corpore*, velut e carcere, *evolat animus*.

Neve te obrui, tanquam fluctu, sic *magnitudine negotii, sinas*. And do not suffer yourself to be overwhelmed by *the tide of business*.

In the same sense *quidam* (**361**, *Obs*. 1, 2), *quodammodo*, and *ut dicam* are often used.

497. Proportional clauses.—Such ideas as are expressed in English by a clause introduced by "in proportion as," or by the phrase "in proportion to," or by a double *the* with the comparative ("*the* more . . . *the* more"), may be best translated into Latin by one of two constructions.

(*a*) *Ut quisque* with a *superlative* in one clause may correspond to *ita* with a *superlative* in another (**376**. or (*b*) *Tanto*, or *eo*, the ablative of *measure of difference* (279), joined with a *comparative* adjective, or adverb, in one clause, may correspond to *quanto*, or *quo* with a *comparative* in another.

(a) Ut quisque *est vir* optimus, ita difficillime *alios esse improbos suspicatur. In proportion to* a man's excellence is his difficulty in suspecting others to be evil-minded, *or, the* better a man is, *the* greater his difficulty in, etc., *or,* those whose character is *the highest* will find *most difficulty*, etc.

(b) Quo *quisque est vir* melior, eo difficilius, etc.

The same constructions would express such a sentence as, "A man's readiness to suspect others is *in inverse proportion to* his own goodness."

Obs.—Tanto . . . quanto mark a more *precise* correspondence than *eo . . . quo.* The latter is identical with the English *the . . . the;* "the" is the old ablative of the *demonstrative* pronoun, which in the form *that* came into use as a relative earlier than the *interrogative* "who," "which."

Exercise 62.

The asterisk (*) indicates that the *Phrases* are to be translated by a Latin *clause.* (See 490, ii.)

1. The soldiers having now reached the summit of the mountain, and seeing a vast level plain, fertile territory, and rich cities, spread beneath their eyes, crowded round their leader, and as though they had already triumphed over every obstacle, congratulated him on the conquest [1] of Italy.   2. He behaved far differently to what I hoped and you expected.   For in violation * of his repeated promises,[2] as though he made no account of the ancient tie which had long existed between his own father and mine, instead[3] of coming to my aid in my adversity, he has rejected up to this day my friendship, and has paid no attention to my more than once repeated and solemn appeals.[4]   3. May each and every one of you, when the hour of battle arrives, conduct himself in accordance * with his duty, and may each fare in accordance * with his deserts.   4. Let us endure everything rather than act in this matter contrary to * our promises.   5. We should [5] abide by the

---

[1] See 417, i.

[2] 491, *b ;* "repeated" will of course be turned by an *adverb.*

[3] See 398, *Obs.*, and use one of the constructions given in 124.

[4] *i.e.* "to me more than once solemnly *appealing*." (415.)

[5] Gerund, and for second clause see 493, *Obs.* 1.

most oppressive conditions, rather than break our word
and brand our country with dishonour.   6. Then, with his
usual [1] passionateness and want of self-control, he orders
the ambassadors to be brought before him ; as though their
mere sight had added fuel to his fury,[2] after roaring out that
their king had acted in defiance * of his promise and oath,
he ordered them to be dragged to prison.   The next day
he showed more gentleness than was consistent [3] with the
ferocity of his language of the day before, and, after apolo-
gising for his outrage on the rights of hospitality, invited
them to a banquet on [4] the next day as though he had done
nothing strange [5] or unusual.   Their answer showed [6]
more daring, considering the [7] perilous ground on which
they stood, than caution.   7. Then, putting spurs to his
horse, he dashed, with his usual [8] eagerness for battle, into
the thick of the contest, as though it were the part of a
good general to act with spirit [9] rather than with deliberation.   8. The longer the war is protracted, the more
oppressive will be the conditions of peace which will be
imposed upon us ; do not wonder then at the reason [10] of
the truest patriots being the most ardent advocates of peace.
9. The more hidden a danger is, the greater will be the
difficulty [11] in avoiding it, and those [12] among our enemies
(*gen.*) are likely to be the most formidable who are readiest
in dissembling their ill-will.   10. And it seemed to me that,
considering the importance [13] of the matter, he spoke with
some want of energy, as though he were ashamed to speak
in the presence of the conqueror with greater warmth and
emotion than became [3] either his former rank or his recent
disaster.

---

[1] 492, iii.   [2] Participle of *ardeo*. (**415.**)
[3] *Quam pro*. (See **332, 7,** *h.*)   [4] **326.**   [5] *Novus*. Case ? (See **294.**)
[6] "Showed." Avoid *ostendit*. (See **241.**) "They answered with more
daring (*adv.*) than caution." (**493,** *Obs.* 2.)
   [7] "Ground," etc., a mere metaphor. (See **273,** *Obs.*, and **492, v.** *b.*)
   [8] Use *ut* with *semper*. (**492, iii.**)
   [9] Two comparative adverbs. (Intr. 19.)   [10] *Cur*. (See **174,** *a.*)
[11] Substitute *adverb*. "will be avoided *with greater difficulty*."
[12] Use *ut quisque*. (**497,** *a.*)   [13] Simply *tanta res*.

EXERCISE LXIII.

Qui WITH THE SUBJUNCTIVE.

498. (i.) **Recapitulatory.**—It has been already said that **qui**, when used simply as the **relative** pronoun, to introduce what are called **adjectival** clauses (Intr. 81), is regularly followed by the **indicative** mood. (See **77.**)

> Qui *boni* sunt, *iidem sunt beati.* Those who are good are *also* happy. (**366, i.**)

Obs.—Here *qui* is used in its widest and most *indefinite* sense, =*quicunque*, but for all that is joined with the **indicative** in classical Latin, as is *quicunque.* (**364.**)

(ii.) It has been also pointed out, that if such adjectival clauses are subordinate to a verb in *oratio obliqua*, the mood must be the **subjunctive.** (**444.**)

The same principle applies equally to **virtual** *oratio obliqua.* (**448.**)

> *Omnia, quae pater suus* reliquisset, *mihi legavit.* He bequeathed to me everything which his father *had left.*

Legavit is, "he bequeathed in the *terms of his* will," *quae reliquisset,* "which the will *spoke of* as left by his father."

But in such cases the subjunctive is used, not as *governed* by *qui*, but on the general principle that in *all* clauses subordinate to *oratio obliqua*, whether adjectival or adverbial, the **indicative is inadmissible.**

499. Qui also, in its **co-ordinating** use, when it stands in the place of an English *conjunction* and demonstrative *pronoun*, or even of the latter alone, can of course have no effect on the mood of the verb, which will depend entirely on the nature of the clause which it introduces.

> *Fratrem tuum, virum praeclarissimum, vidi,* qui *brevi consul* fiet, *or,* qui *utinam brevi consul* fiat, *or,* quem *brevi consulem* factum iri *spero.* (See **78.**)

500. But there are many cases in which *qui*, even in *oratio recta*, must be joined not with the indicative but with the **subjunctive.**

This is because *qui*, while in form a mere relative, yet in addition to referring to some antecedent word often conveys some additional idea of either *purpose, result, cause,* or *contrast.* It then takes the place of such conjunctions as *ut, quia, quanquam*, and introduces clauses which, though in form **adjectival**, are **adverbial** in sense; and in proportion to its departure from its proper nature as a pure relative, is the urgency with which it calls for a **subjunctive** mood to mark the amount of that departure.

501. RULE.—Whenever *qui* is used in a **final** or **consecutive** sense, it is *invariably*, and whenever in a **causal** or **concessive** sense, it is *generally*, followed by the **subjunctive**.

Qui final.

502. (i.) *Qui* may express a **purpose**; it is then equivalent to *ut is*, and is always followed by a **subjunctive**.

> *Legatos misit*, qui *pacem* peterent.   He sent ambassadors *to sue* for peace (lit. *who were to sue* for peace; jussive, see 151).
> *Equites in castris reliquit*, qui erumperent.   He left cavalry behind in the camp, *to make* a charge.

With this compare *qui* with *indicative*.

> *Legatos misit*, qui *pacem* petierunt.   He sent ambassadors, *who sued* for peace.
> *Equites in castris reliquit*, qui eruperunt.   He left cavalry behind in the camp, *who made* a charge.

In these cases *qui* is equivalent to *et ii*, "and they," and therefore has no effect on the mood.

It will be seen at once that the difference of meaning between two such uses of *qui* is very great.

Qui consecutive.

503. (ii.) *Qui* may express a **consequence**, and *sometimes* even be translated by a *consecutive phrase* in English; but whenever the English "who" or "that" implies "*such as to*," "*of such a kind as to*," *qui* must be joined with the **subjunctive**.

> *Darius exercitum*, quem *immensa planities vix caperet*, *comparavit*.   "Which could not be contained," = "*such as was not to be* contained within," etc.

*** This use of *qui* extends very widely; the commonest of the less apparent examples of this meaning may be thus arranged.

504. The **subjunctive** is used after *sunt qui, erant qui* (= "some") *reperiuntur qui, quotusquisque est qui,* and such **negative** and **interrogative** forms as *nemo est qui, quis est qui? neminem habeo qui,* etc. Thus—

> *Erant qui* putarent. Some fancied (there were people *of such a kind as to* fancy).
>
> *Nihil est quod dicere* velim. There is nothing that I care to say (*of such a kind as for me to*, etc.).
>
> *Quotusquisque est (invenitur) qui haec facere* audeat. How few there are (are met with) who venture to do this (one of how great a number ["one in a thousand," "*the thousandth*"] is he *who is such* as to, etc.).

Hence the use of the subjunctive after *quin* (= qui ne [*non*]).

> *Nemo est* quin *sciat.* All the world knows (**134**), *i.e.* there is no one *of such a kind as not* to know.

Obs.—When *est, sunt,* etc., are joined in an affirmative clause with a *numeral* or *plural* adjective of *number* the **indicative** is used.

> Multi, trecenti, duo, quidam, *sunt qui haec* dicunt. There are *many, three hundred, two, certain,* persons who say this.

Qui is here used in its proper relatival sense, "the people *who say this* are three hundred, etc."

But after *solus, unus,* used as predicates, with *sum* as link verb, the **subjunctive** is used.

> Solus *es* cui *omnes* pareamus. You are the only person whom all of us obey (somewhat more emphatic than, tibi soli *paremus omnes.*)

505. Qui is also used with the subjunctive—

(i.) After *dignus* or *indignus.*

> *Dignus est qui* ametur. He deserves to be loved (*lit.* He is worthy *that he should* be loved).
>
> *Indignus erat cui summus honos* tribueretur. He was not a proper person *to receive* the highest mark of distinction.

(ii.) After **comparatives** followed by *quam.*

> *Quae beneficia majora sunt quam quibus gratiam referre* possim. These favours are greater than I can requite (*too great for me to* requite).

(iii.) After **negative** and **interrogative** clauses, *qui* may take the place of *ut* in correspondence with *tam, sic, adeo,* and even *tantus.*

> Quis tam, or nemo tam, *ferreus est* qui *haec* faciat. Who is *or* no one is, *so* hard-hearted *as to do* this.
>
> Nulla *vis* tanta *est* quae *hoc* efficiat. No force is *so great as* to produce this result.

But you cannot say with an *affirmative* clause, *hic homo tam ferreus est* qui . . . , but must use *ut.*

506. Is is largely used (both affirmatively and negatively) with *qui* in a consecutive sense.

Non is *sum* qui *haec* faciam. I am not the man *to do* this, *or*, I am not one *to do* this.

Ea *est Romana gens* quae *victa quiescere* nesciat.[1] The race of Romans *is one* (of a kind) *that* knows not how to rest under defeat.

The difference between *is qui* with an **indicative** and *is qui* with a **subjunctive** must be carefully noticed, as it is one which is often not at all marked in English.

(*a*) When *is* and *qui* denote *identity*, the **indicative** is always used (in *oratio recta*).

Is *sum* qui feci. I am the man who did this.
Cum eo *hoste pugnamus* cui *nullo modo parcendum* est. We are fighting with an enemy who ought in no wise to be spared.

In both these cases *is* and *qui* are *co-extensive;* the *qui-* and *cui-*clauses apply to the person denoted by *is* and *eo*, and to *no one else.*

(*b*) But when the *qui*-clause is used *generically*, denotes a *larger class* to which we say that the *is* belongs, the **subjunctive** is used.

When we say, *non* is *sum* qui *haec* faciam, we mean, "I do not *belong to the larger* class (or *genus*) of men who do this."

By *cum* eo *pugnamus hoste* cui *nullo modo parcendum* sit, we mean, "we are fighting with a foe who is *one of those who* ought in nowise to be spared;" not a single person who *in himself* does not deserve quarter (**indicative**), but *one of those who do* not deserve quarter. In such sentences therefore we may use either mood according to the precise meaning of the English ; the **subjunctive** is far more common.

507. *Qui* also, like consecutive *ut*,[2] is used in a *corrective* or *limiting* sense.

Nemo, quod sciam ; *nemo*, qui *quidem* paulo *prudentior* sit. No one *to my knowledge*; no one, *at all events* no sensible man. (57, *b*.)

Obs.—But *quantum* scio, *quod* attinet *ad;* because the word *quantum* and the phrase *quod attinet ad* express limitation by their own meaning, and do not need a change of mood.

508. All that has been said of the **final** and **consecutive** use of *qui* applies equally to relatival **adverbs**, *ubi*, *unde*,

---

[1] *Nesciat* is here a *modal verb* (**42**), equivalent to *non possit*, or *nequeat*. Compare the English "I can," properly "I know" (ken).
[2] Compare—Ita *sapiens est ut interdum erret*. He is wise *with this limitation, that* he sometimes makes a mistake ; and see **111**.

cur, etc., when used as final or consecutive **conjunctions.**[1]

Massilium ivit ubi *exularet.*   He went   Marseilles *to live*
        in exile *there.*
Cupit habere unde *solvat.*   He wishes to have *means to* pay.
Nihil est cur *irascare.*   You have no *reason to be* angry

Exercise 63.

1. Caesar, seeing that the tide of battle[2] was turning,
and that he must take advantage of the critical[3] moment,
sent forward all his cavalry to attack the enemies' infantry in the rear; he himself, with the rest of his soldiers,
whom wounds, heat, and fatigue left[4] scarcely capable of
supporting their arms, hastened to charge them in front.
2. He was one who was worthy of every kind of distinction, for no one, within my knowledge, has governed the
nation in this generation, whose public services have been
equal to his, and who has been satisfied with so moderate
a reward of his exertions.   How few there are who have
been, or will be, like him.   3. The chiefs of the enemy
easily perceived that in the recent rebellion and mutiny
their offences had been too great[5] to be pardoned; at the
same time (366, ii.). in spite of this great defeat, they
were too high-spirited to ask for mercy, and too powerful
to obtain it.   4. He is not, so far as I know, one who
hesitates to follow his own line in a discussion, or prefers
to bow to the opinion[6] of others.   5. Who is there in the
whole world so stony-hearted as not to be ashamed of
having, in order to please his worst enemies, abandoned
his friends, and of having betrayed his country to win the
favour of its most ancient foes ?   6. We have[7] to carry on
war with an enemy who has no respect for any treaty, or
armistice, or promise, or agreement; unless we conquer him
in the field, there will be nothing which can keep him back
from our shores, or repel him from our walls and homes.

---

[1] When used, that is, not to qualify the verb, or predicate, of a simple
sentence, but to connect together two clauses. (Intr. 16 and 25.) Mr.
Roby uses the term *connective adverbs.*
[2] Use the phrase *res inclinatur.*   Why would the use of this English
metaphor be less admissible in Latin?
[3] Simply *tempus.*   [4] Use *possum* with *prae.* (**332, 6, b.**)
[5] Use *majora delinquere*, or *peccare.* (See **54.**)
[6] *Auctoritas.*   As an opinion which claims to *have weight.*
[7] Gerundive.

EXERCISE LXIV.

Qui—CAUSAL AND CONCESSIVE.

509. Qui is also used both in a **causal** and a **concessive** sense; and in each of these is joined with the **subjunctive** on the principle stated in 500.

> (a) *Me miserum,* qui *haec non* viderim! Unhappy that I am (**239**, *note* [1]) *in not having seen this.*

Here *qui* is obviously **causal** = quod *haec non* vidi.

> (b) *Ego,* qui *serus* advenissem, *non tamen desperandum esse arbitratus sum.* For myself, *though I had arrived late* (or *in spite of my having*, etc.), yet 1 did not think I need despair.

Here *qui* is as obviously **concessive** = quanquam *serus* adveneram.

510. But in neither of these senses is the subjunctive (though it should be used by the young scholar) so invariable after *qui* as in its *consecutive* and *final* uses.

The writer sometimes prefers to emphasise the **reality** of the statement which *qui* introduces, and to leave the reader to infer the relation of **cause** or **contrast** in which it stands to the other clause.

Gratiam tibi habeo, qui *vitam meam* servasti, is as good Latin as, though less usual than, *gratiam . . . servaveris,* for, "I am grateful to you, *for* you have saved my life."

So, *Caesar fertur in caelum,* qui *contra te bellum* comparavit, "Caesar is extolled to the skies (by you), *although he* (or, *and yet he*) levied war against you :" *comparaverit* would be more usual, but the indicative **emphasises the fact**, and leaves the reader to draw the **contrast**.

511. An exceedingly common use of *qui* with the **subjunctive** in either its causal or concessive sense is to represent the **circumstances** *under,* or *in spite of,* which the action of the principal verb takes place.

It corresponds therefore exactly to the use of *quum* (**429**) or to the *abl. abs.* (**420**), or the *past participle of deponent* verbs (**413**), and to a common use of the English participle (**411**).

> *Tum Caesar,* qui *haec omnia explorata* haberet, *redire statuit.*
> Then (or thereupon) Caesar, *having* full knowledge of all this, etc.
> *Tum ille,* qui *homo* esset *justissimus,* etc. Then he (the other) *being* a just man, etc.

X

Obs.—Where a concessive sense, or *adversative* circumstances, are implied, this is generally made clear by a *tamen* in the main clause, cf. the use of *idcirco, adeo,* etc., to mark the precise sense of *ut.* (**107.**)

> *Tum Caesar, qui hoc intellegeret,* tamen *redire statuit.* Then Caesar, *in spite of his* being aware of this, yet, etc.

512. The **causal** force of *qui* is sometimes made more clear by prefixing *quippe,* sometimes *utpote,* or *ut.*

In Cicero *quippe qui* (=*for* or *because* he, etc.) is always followed by the subjunctive.

> *Eum semper pro amico habui,* quippe quem scirem *mei esse amantissimum.* I always looked on him as a friend, *for* I knew that he bore me the warmest affection.

In Sallust and Livy *quippe qui* is used with the indicative as though=*quod,* but *ut qui* with the subjunctive is very common in Livy.

> *Nec consul,* ut qui *id ipsum* quaesisset, *moram certamini fecit.* Nor did the Consul, *as* this was the very object at which he had aimed, delay the contest.

513. When *qui,* or *quicunque,* expresses an action **repeated in past time**, a difference of usage is found in the best Latin writers.

(1) In Cicero and Caesar it is followed by an **indicative** of the pluperfect.
(2) In Livy, by a **subjunctive**.

> *Quicunque* venerat, *damnabatur.*—(*Cicero* and *Caesar.*) Whoever came (*from time to time*), was condemned.
> *Quocunque eques impetum* tulisset, *Romani cedebant.*—(*Livy.*) Wherever the rider charged, the Romans yielded. Cicero or Caesar would have written *tulerat.*

This difference has been already noticed under Temporal Clauses (**434**). Nor in the best writers is *qui* used with a subjunctive, because it means "any[1] who," "all who," **498,** *Obs.;* this usage came in, as in the *frequentative* sense, under the influence of Greek.

Exercise 64.

The asterisk* indicates that *qui* causal or concessive is to be used.

1. Thereupon the messenger, seeing* that it was im-

---

[1] In Livy's description of Hannibal's character, *id quod gerendis rebus* superesset, *quieti datum* (Bk. xxi. 4), "*Any* time that remained (or *might* remain) after active work was done, was given to repose," the mood of *superesse* is no doubt due to Greek influence.

possible by fair[1] words to succeed in persuading the
Spaniards not to advance further, aimed at producing[2]
the same effect by menaces (*gerund*), and appeals to fear.
The forces, he said,[3] which were gathering and concealed
on the other side of the mountain, were too numerous
(505, ii.) to be counted, while[4] those who were already
assembled, and were visible close at hand, were veteran
soldiers, too brave and well trained to be routed, as[5] the
Spaniards seemed to hope, in the first onset of a single
fight. 2. Who is there of you, who in any way is
worthy of this assembly and this nation, that does not
cherish and value highly the memories[6] of the heroes[7]
of the past, even though he has never seen them.*
3. There are things which I fear still[8] more; in his
absence his brother, since* his influence with that faction
is unrivalled, will be still more formidable; as long as
he lives, will the party[9] of disorder, do you[3] suppose,
ever lack a standard round which to rally? 4. Thereupon he dismissed the council, and ordered the Indian[10]
chiefs to be brought before him; the unhappy men, as*
they had no suspicion or fear of his intentions,[11] hurry in
joyfully,[12] for there was none among[13] them who had
any fears either for[14] his freedom or his safety, or was
aware of the extent[15] of the danger which threatened
them, or of the[15] character of the host with whom he was
to have an interview. Even he, though* he blushed at no
treachery, and felt remorse for no crime, was, it seemed,
somewhat touched by the confidence and friendliness of
those whom he (felt[16] that he) was on the point of betraying.

---

[1] " By pleading gently."   [2] *Idem efficere.* (See **54.**)
[3] Beware of this parenthesis. (**32,** *b.*)
[4] Why not *dum?* (**438,** note): *et* or *vero* would do.
[5] **67,** *Obs.*   [6] *Memoria* is never used in the pl., cf. *spes.*
[7] Why not *heros?* a Greek word=demigod : say of "illustrious
men, and those (**344**) ancient (ones)."   [8] Rarely expressed in Latin.
[9] Use *perditi*, or *improbi, cives;* the latter is Cicero's usual term as
opposed to the *boni*, or *optimus quisque.*
[10] "Of the Indians."   [11] " As to what he would do." (**173, iii. ; 174.**)
[12] Adj. (**61.**)   [13] Gen. or *ex.* (**296.**)   [14] **248.**
[15] **174.**   [16] See **448.**

REPORTED SPEECHES IN *ORATIO OBLIQUA*

Preliminary.

514. In reporting another person's language two methods may be used.

(i.) The historian may name the speaker, and give what purport to be the words he used in the precise form in which he spoke them, as (*e.g.*) in a play of Shakespeare,

> To this Caesar replied, "I will come if you are ready to follow."

In such professedly *verbatim* reports the whole speech may be spoken of as being in *oratio recta*, as coming, as it were, *directly* from the lips of the speaker.

(ii.) This method is used in Latin, sometimes in a formal report of **long speeches** in the senate or elsewhere, sometimes in reporting a **short saying**, if very memorable or striking. In the latter case it is marked, as by *inverted commas* in English, so by the insertion of *inquit* after the first or second word of the speech or saying. Such speeches should never be preceded, as in English, by verbs like *dixit, ait, respondit*, etc., which are as a rule reserved for the second and more usual mode of reporting, the *indirect* rather than the *direct*.

"I will come, he said," "I will come, he replied," must be translated either by "se venturum esse *dixit, respondit*," or by "veniam, *inquit*." (See **40**.)

515. But the more usual method in Latin, more common even than it is in English, is not to profess to give the speaker's words in the form in which they were spoken, but to insert (or imply)[1] a verb of *saying, asking*, etc., and then to report what was said, or its substance, in the third person, that is, in **oratio obliqua**. All the principal verbs will now be dependent on a verb of *saying*, expressed or understood. Thus, instead of Caesar's own words, "I will go, if you are ready to follow," we should have "Caesar replied that *he* would go, if *he* were ready to follow."

---

[1] The actual verb is often omitted, the infinitive or subjunctive moods being sufficient evidence of the construction.

> *Legatos ad Caesarem mittunt:* "*sese paratos esse portas aperire.*"
> They send ambassadors to Caesar: (*saying*), We are ready to open the gates.

> *Colonis triste responsum redditum est: facesserent propere ex urbe.*
> The colonists received a severe answer: "Begone at once from the city."

516. The great difference between the two methods will be seen at a glance.

Oratio recta.	*Oratio obliqua.*
Tum Caesar, ibo, inquit, *si* tu me *sequi* vis.	*Tum Caesar*, iturum se respondit *si* ille se *sequi* vellet.

Obs.—This method of reporting speeches, or even reflexions, in the third person is common in English (as for instance in reporting speeches in Parliament), but far more common in Latin, and should often be used in translating into Latin what in English is reported in the more *dramatic* form of *oratio recta.*

The following are the principal rules for the conversion of *oratio recta* into *oratio obliqua.*

Pronouns.

517. The **first** and **second** person will entirely disappear; both will be converted into the **third**.

(*a*) *Ego, meus, nos, noster*, will become *se*,[1] *suus* (in the nominative *ipse*).

(*b*) *Tu, vos, tuus, vester*, will become *ille, illi, illius, illorum, ipsius,* etc.

Tu Tarentum amisisti; ego recepi, will become, *respondit* illum *Tarentum amisisse*, se *recepisse;* or better (**216**, *Obs.*), ab illo *amissum esse Tarentum*, a se *receptum.*

Nostram patriam civitati vestrae anteponimus, will become, suam se[1] *patriam* illorum *civitati anteponere.*

So *hic* and *iste* will give place to *ille* and *is.*

Obs. 1.—Latin has here a great advantage over English ; " I and you" have alike, in English *oratio obliqua*, to be expressed by *he;* hence constant obscurity. In Latin the " I " will become *se*, the "you" *ille.*

Obs. 2.—*Ille* will be in very constant use in place of *is*, as it is more distinctive, and opposes the *other party* to the speaker ; sometimes as in English, a proper name will be introduced.

Adverbs.

518. As speeches are generally reported in *past* or *historic* time, **adverbs** of **present** time must be changed into those of **past** time. *Nunc, hodie*, will become *jam, tunc, illo die*, etc. So with **place**, *hic* will become *ibi*, etc.

---

[1] The insertion of the *se* will often be necessary where no pronoun is required in *oratio recta :* compare *tibi parco* with *dixit* se *ei parcere.*

But all these changes are common to Latin with English. "*I* say that *I* will speak to *you now* and *here*" would in English be converted into "*He* said that *he* would speak to *them then* and *there*."

The rules more peculiar to Latin are connected with the use of **Moods** in **principal** and **subordinate** clauses.

Principal Clauses.

519. In all these the **indicative** will entirely disappear.

Statements and **denials** made in Latin by a verb in the **indicative** will of course pass into the **infinitive**. *Nihil dolco,* " I feel no pain," will become, *nihil se dolere,* " he felt no pain ; " *hoc faciam,* will become, *id se facturum esse,* etc.

Obs. 1.—This infinitive will even follow *qui* if strictly **co-ordinate**.

Adsunt *hostes,* instat Catilina, qui *brevi scelerum poenas* dabit.
Adesse *hostes,* instare Catilinam, quem *brevi scelerum poenas* daturum esse. (**499.**)

Obs. 2.—Statements (hypothetical) made in the **subjunctive**, because qualified by a *si*-clause, will pass from the

Present subjunctive into the future in *-rus* with *esse* or *fore.*
Imperfect or pluperfect subjunctive into the future in *-rus* with *fuisse.* (See **469,** i.)
Thus, *Rideat si adsit* into *risurum cum fore, si adesset.*
Rideret si adesset } into *risurum cum fuisse, si adesset,* or,
Risisset si adfuisset } *adfuisset.*

520. Questions asked by the speaker in the **indicative** mood will pass into the **subjunctive**; and if, as is usual, the narrative is in past time, from the **present** into the **imperfect** tense.

Nonne auditis ? will become, *nonne* audirent ?
Quid vultis ? *quid* optatis ? will become, *Quid* vellent ? *quid* optarent ?

Questions already in the **subjunctive** (**150**) will remain in the **subjunctive** ; the *tense* only being altered if, as is usual, it is necessary, and of course the *person.*

Quid faciam ? " what *am I* to do ?" will become, *quid* faceret ? " what *was he* to do ?"
Quo eamus ? "whither *are we* to go ?" will become, *quo* irent ? " whither *were they* to go ?"

521. But questions that do not expect an answer (**rhetorical** questions, 150), especially those in the **first** and **third persons**, will pass from the **indicative** or **subjunctive** to the **infinitive**, for such questions are really **denials** in disguise.

> Ecquis *unquam ejusmodi monstrum* vidit? "did any one ever see such a monster?" will become, Ecquem *unquam ejusmodi monstrum* vidisse?
>
> *Num* haec *tolerare* debemus? will become, *Num* illa se *tolerare* debere?

So *quo* eamus? will often become, *quo* sibi eundum esse? for the meaning is often merely, "we have *no place* to go to."

522. Commands, prohibitions, and **wishes,** expressed by the **imperative** or **subjunctive,** will pass into the **subjunctive** with the necessary alteration of **tense** and **person.**

Oratio recta.	*Oratio obliqua.*
Festinate; utinam salvi sitis.	*Festinarent; utinam* salvi essent.
Nolite cunctari; ne despexeris.	*Ne cunctarentur; ne* despiceret.

Obs.—The **hortative** 1st person (and even other forms of command) will be easily converted into a statement by the aid of the **gerund** or **gerundive.**

> *Nihil temere* agamus.   *Nihil* sibi *temere* agendum esse.

Subordinate Clauses.

523. Moods.—The indicative will entirely disappear.

Even the exceptional indicative after *qui* mentioned in **449** will hardly find place in the report of a speech of any length.

RULE.—**Subordinate** clauses, whether introduced by the **relative** (except where strictly **co-ordinate**) or by any subordinating **conjunction** (except occasionally *dum*), will always be in the **subjunctive.**

This has been fully explained before. (See **444.**)

524. Tenses.—As reported speeches are usually part of a narrative of **past** events, the most usual and regular tenses in subordinate clauses will be the **imperfect** and **pluperfect** subjunctive.

(i.) The **imperfect,** as the tense of *time contemporaneous with a date now past,* will take the place of the **present, imperfect,** and even the **future i.** of *oratio recta.*

> *Qui* adsunt, *fugiant,* will become *qui* adessent, *fugerent.*
> *Idcirco fugi, quod* timebam   ,,   *fugisse se, quod* timeret.
> *Qui hoc* dicet, *errabit*   ,,   *qui id,* or *illud,* diceret, *erraturum esse.*

(ii.) But **future ii.** (future perfect) will be changed into the **pluperfect**. (See **471**, *Obs.*)

Qui hoc dixerit, *errabit* will become *qui illud* dixisset, *erraturum esse.*

(iii.) The **perfect** as well as the **pluperfect** will generally be represented by the **pluperfect** subjunctive.

Hic est locus quem ostendi.   *Illum esse locum quem* ostendisset.

525. But though the exclusive use of the **imperfect** and **pluperfect** subjunctive would be grammatically correct, yet the **present, perfect,** and **future perfect** are very often introduced into *oratio obliqua* (just as in *oratio recta* the *historic present* often takes the place of the *[aorist] perfect*), in order to give greater *liveliness* to the reported speech by representing parts of it in the actual tense used, as though the speaker were *in our presence.*

Indignum videri ab iis se obsideri quorum exercitus saepe fuderint. They *said* that it *seemed* degrading to be besieged by men whose armies they had (lit. *have*) often routed.

In *oratio recta* the word used would have been *fudimus* —" *we have* routed."

There are few reported speeches in Caesar or Livy in which this rhetorical use of present for past, perfect for pluperfect, tenses will not be found.

526. The following examples should be carefully studied :—

1. " Your children have gone ; when will they return ? (rhetorical question), try to avenge them." [1]

Oratio recta.	*Oratio obliqua.*
Profecti sunt liberi vestri ; quando redituri sunt ? vos, quantum potestis, ultum ite.	Jam liberos illorum profectos esse ; quando redituros fore ? quantum possent ultum irent.

---

[1] In English *oratio obliqua* the passages would run thus :—

" *Their* children *had* gone ; when *would* they return ? *Let them* try to avenge them."

" Away then with such follies ! *Did they* not see that *their* liberty and lives were *that* day at stake? Why *did they* obey a few centurions, still fewer tribunes, who *could* do nothing against *their* will ? When *would they* dare to demand redress? It *was* of the utmost importance what *they did. Let them* awake at last and follow *him,* remembering the ancestors from whom *they were* sprung. If *they* let slip this opportunity, *they would* deservedly be slaves, and no one *would* give *them* a thought, or compassionate *their* present condition."

2. Away then with such follies !   Do you not see that your liberty and lives are at stake to-day ? why do you obey a few centurions, still fewer tribunes, who can do nothing against your will?   When will you dare to demand redress !   It is of the utmost importance what you do.   Awake at last, and follow me !   remember the ancestors from whom you are sprung.   If you let slip this opportunity, you will deservedly be slaves, and no one will give you a thought, or compassionate your present condition.[1]

Oratio recta.	*Oratio obliqua.*
Pellantur igitur, inquit, *ineptiae istae ; nonne videtis de libertate, de vitis vestris, agi hodie? Cur paucis centurionibus, paucioribus tribunis, qui nihil invitis vobis facere possunt dicto audientes estis? quando remedia exposcere audebitis? Maximi quid faciatis refert. Expergiscimini aliquando ; majorum quibus orti estis reminiscimini : me sequimini. Hanc occasionem si praetermiseritis, merito servibitis, nec quisquam vel rationem vestri habebit, vel istius fortunae miserebitur.*	Pellerentur *igitur ineptiae* illae ; *nonne* viderent *de libertate* ipsorum, *de vitis,* eo die *agi? Cur paucis centurionibus, paucioribus tribunis, qui* invitis illis *nihil facere* possent, *dicto audientes* essent? *quando remedia* exposcere ausuros? *maximi* referre *quid* facerent. Expergiscerentur *aliquando, et* se sequerentur. *Majorum quibus orti* essent reminiscerentur. Eam *occasionem si praetermisissent, merito* servituros esse, *nec* quenquam *vel rationem* eorum habiturum fore, *vel fortunae* illius miseriturum.

Caesar and Livy will furnish abundant instances for practice, and the learner should translate every "reported speech" in either, into English oratio recta.

Exercise 65.

A.

The following sentences are all to be converted into *oratio obliqua ;* the tenses to be altered throughout from *primary* to *historic.* (See **177.**)   It may be well to begin by converting the sentences into *English oratio obliqua.*

1.   Can any[2] one endure this ? ought we to abandon this great undertaking ? it would have been better to have fallen on the field with honour, than to submit to such slavery.   2.   Do not delay then ; a few soldiers will suffice ; we have no other allies anywhere, no other hopes, whither can we turn if you think of abandoning us ? but if you wish[3] for our safety, you must away[4] with all

---

[1] See **526,** *note.*
[3] See **240,** *Obs.* 1.

[2]   Use *ecquis.*
[4] Use *pello.* (See **526.** 2.)

niceties of argument;[1] it is haste, not deliberation, that is needed. 3. What are you doing? what are you wishing for? are you waiting till the enemy is at hand, till you hear their shouts, till you see their standards? Even now[2] resistance is possible, provided you do not linger or hesitate. 4. It is possible that I on my part[3] have made the same mistake as you; if the case is so, I pray, forget the past,[4] and in union with your king consult the national interests. Is there any thing in the world which we ought to value more highly? 5. What am I to do? whither to turn? do you bid me to go to meet the enemy? I would do so most gladly, if it could be done without ruin to the nation. But what could be more foolish, what more fatal, than with[5] an army of recruits to engage in conflict with veteran soldiers[6] trained in twenty years of battle?[7] 6. How many of you are there? whence do you come? what do you demand or hope for? when do you expect to[8] be allowed to enjoy freedom, (and) to return home? Possibly the time is even now at hand, provided you do not let slip the opportunity, or injure your cause by putting off the contest. But if you refuse to take up arms till[9] I assist you, you will ruin the common cause, and sigh in vain for the[10] freedom which brave men assert by arms.

B.

To be translated into *oratio obliqua:* a Spaniard speaks.

In vain therefore do you appeal to Spain;[11] it makes no difference whether you intend to make an alliance with the rebels, or to threaten them with war. I shall neither rely on your friendship, nor do I dread your enmity. For what could be more despicable than your policy and schemes, seeing that within the last five years you

---

[1] Gerund.   [2] See **518**.   [3] See **355**, *d.*
[4] "What is past."   [5] **270**, *note* [2].   [6] Sing.
[7] "Battles of twenty years." (See **303**, *Obs.* 1.)
[8] *Fore ut,* etc. (**193**, iii.)   [9] *Prius . . . quam.* (**443**, i.)
[10] **348**.   [11] **319**.

have thrice abandoned your allies, twice joined your enemies like[1] deserters, and have not now sent ambassadors to me to sue for a peace of which you are so unworthy, till[2] you had made sure that, unless with our[3] aid you can get over this danger, you are doomed to infallible destruction? Would any one have put trust in such allies? would any one in the future feel gratitude to such friends? If you wish to find a remedy and shelter against[4] your present[5] dangers, return home; lay down your arms; throw open the gates of your cities and strongholds, place yourselves entirely at the mercy of the sovereign against whom you have been so long waging an unnatural war. Possibly I may be touched by your prayers; I shall pay no attention to your envoys and orations.

---

[1] *Velut.* [2] **443,** *Obs.*
[3] Use for clearness the proper noun and abl. abs., "The Spaniards helping." (**517,** *Obs.* 2.)
[4] See **300.** [5] *Hic* in *oratio recta.* (**337.**)

EXERCISE LXVI.

NUMERALS.

Numerals form in Latin, as in English, a special class of **adjectives**; in certain cases, as in the plural of *mille* (*duo civium* milia,[1] cf. hundreds, thousands), they have a **substantival** character, and they are all accompanied by appropriate **adverbs.**

Their two main classes are, as in English, **Cardinal** and **Ordinal.**

527. Cardinal (*cardo*, hinge), or primary, numerals answer the question "how many?" *quot?*

Unus, duo, tres, quattuor; undecim, duodecim, tredecim (decem et tres); duodeviginti (decem et octo), undeviginti (decem et novem); viginti, unus et viginti (viginti unus), duodetriginta (28), quadraginta, nonaginta octo (octo et nonaginta), centum (et) unus (101); ducenti, -ae, -a, trecenti, -ae, -a, quadringenti, quingenti, ses-(sex-)centi, septingenti, octingenti, nongenti, mille (substantive), *duo milia, unum et viginti milia, centum milia, quingenta milia, decies centena milia* (1,000,000).

The full list will be found in any Grammar; those enumerated are examples given for special reasons, the alternative forms are added in brackets.

528. The **first three** are (as in many kindred languages) declinable; the rest, including *viginti*, are indeclinable up to *ducenti, -ae, -a*: this, and the series of hundreds, are plural declinable adjectives; *mille* is indeclinable in the singular, *exercitus* mille *militum*, "an army *of* 1000," but declined in the plural (*cum duobus* milibus) as a **substantive.**

As in English so in Latin, from 20 to 100 a compound number may be arranged in two ways, "one-and-twenty" or "twenty-one;" above 100 the higher number stands first; 28,455 is, *duodetriginta milia quadringenti quinquaginta (et) quinque (et* is rarely expressed).

---

[1] The second *l* is usually omitted in the plural, as coming before *i*.

Unus.

529. The English numeral " **one** " gave rise to the indefinite article *an*, *a*, (not probably to the indefinite "one" in "one knows," etc.) The uses of *unus* in Latin are very different ; thus (*a*) our "none" is *ne* "not" and *unus* "one," but *non unus* is the very opposite of *nullus;* it means "*more than* one ; " non uno *praelio devictus sum:* "not one" is *ne unus quidem*, or even *nemo unus.* So (*b*) *unus* is a strong form of *solus:* unus *hoc fecisti*, "you are the *only* one who has done this." (*c*) It is used to strengthen *quisque, unus quisque*, each one, "each and every" (373), and (*d*) to emphasise **superlatives** : the Latin superlative often not retaining its full force (57, *a*). Thus *Ducem praestantissimum amisimus*, "we have lost *one of our* best leaders, or *a distinguished* leader," but *Ducem* unum *praestantissimum*, "we have lost *the very best* of our leaders." (*e*) It often, however, represents the English "one of" (a class) without any stress on the numeral : unus *ex captivis*, "*one of* the prisoners." (*f*) In the predicate it often answers to our "belonging to the class of :" unus ex *fortunatis hominibus esse videtur*, "he seems to be one of (*i.e.* to belong to the number of) fortune's favourites." (*g*) "One, two, three, several." is in Latin, *unus, alter, tertius, plures.* "One or two" is *unus vel (aut) alter, unus alterve.*

Ordinal Numerals.

530. These answer to the question "in what order?" *quotus ?*

They are all *declinable adjectives;* only a few will be enumerated. *Primus (prior)* ; *secundus* or *alter ; tertius decimus* (13th), *duodevicesimus (octavus decimus)* (18th), *unus (primus) et vicesimus* (21st), *alter (secundus) et tricesimus (tricesimus alter)* (32nd,) *undetricesimus* (29th), *quadragesimus* (40th), *quintus et nonagesimus (nonagesimus quintus)* (95th), *centesimus primus (primus et centesimus)* (101st), *millesimus, bis millesimus* (2000th), *decies millesimus* (10,000th), *semel et vicies millesimus* (21,000th), etc.

531. Notice that (*a*), as in English, the two first **ordinals** are not derived from the corresponding **cardinals** : and that *alter*, as "other" in older English, is largely used for "second." *Secundus* is rather " following " next in *time* or in *rank.*

" *Alter idem* " is " a second self," *altero tanto*, " by as much again."

(*b*) *Unus* often takes the place of our "first" in enumerating.

> *Hujus rei tres sunt causae*, una, altera (or alia), tertia ; "*first*, second, third."

(*c*) The **ordinal** is often used in reckoning time.

> Undevicesimum *jam annum bellum* gerebatur. The war had now gone on *for* 19 *years.* (See 321, *Obs.* 2.)

(*d*) "After," "since," with an ordinal is expressed by *ab.*

> *Anno* ab *urbe condita millesimo.*   In the 1000th year (*or* the
> year 1000) after the foundation of the city.   (See **323**, *a.*)

(*e*) The ordinal is always used in giving *dates*, as in the last example.

532. Another class is the **Distributives**, answering to the question "how many at a time?" *quoteni?* or "how many each?" "*by twos*," "*two each.*"   Among these are—

> *Singuli, bini, seni* (6); *terni deni* (13); *viceni singuli* (21);
> *centeni, singula milia, centena milia.*

(*a*) *Ex* singulis, *or* binis, *familiis* singulos, binos, ternos, *obsides elegimus.*   We selected *one, two,* or *three,* hostages from *each separate* household, or *each pair* of households.

(*b*) They are also used as **cardinal** numerals with names that have no singular, *uni, -ae, -a* taking the place of *singuli.*

> *In* unis *aedibus* binae *fuere nuptiae.*   There were *two* weddings in *one* house.

(*c*) For the special uses of *singuli* as opposed to *universi* and *singularis* (*imperium singulare* is used for "a *personal* despotism)," see **380**.

Obs.—The distributive numerals are used with **multiplicatives**.   (See below.)

533. The numeral **adverbs** are those that answer to the question "how often?" "how many times?" *quoties,* (*quotiens*)?   Such are—

> *Semel, bis, ter, sexies,* ter *decies, vicies, bis et vicies, tricies,* etc.
> Once,   twice,   13 times.   20 times.   30 times.

(*a*) These are both adverbs **of time**, and also simple *multiplicatives;* cf. the English six *times,* ten *times.*

> *Sexies consul factus est.*   He was made consul *six times* (but *sextum, for* the *sixth time*).
> *Quinquies tantum quam quantum licuit civitatibus imperavit.*   He ordered the states to furnish *five times as much as* was legal.

(*b*) They are coupled with *distributives* in the multiplication table.

> *Bis bina sunt quattuor.*   Twice *two* is four.

(*c*) With *semel* as an adverb of *time, iterum* is used in place of *bis. Iterum* means *not* "again," but "for a second time;" *semel atque iterum* is not "once and again," in the sense of "frequently," but "once and even *twice;*" "once and again," "more than once," is *semel ac saepius;* "again and again," *saepissime.*

534. Ordinal adverbs of time are *primum, iterum, tertium,* etc.; these answer to the English "for the first, second, third, time," etc.

> Iterum, quartum, *Consul factus* est.　He was made Consul for the second *or* fourth time.
>
> *Tum* primum *justo praelio interfuit.*　That was the first occasion on which he took part in a regular engagement.

Obs.—"In the first place." "secondly," "lastly." is expressed in a narrative or argument, *primo* (*-um*, *deinde* (*deinceps*), *tum*, or *post, denique, postremo, ad extremum; denique* is often inserted in an emphatic and final clause.

535. Fractions are expressed thus:—(*a*) One-half, *dimidium* or *dimidia pars.* (*b*) Others, where the *numerator* is 1, by ordinals with *pars*: $\frac{1}{3}$. tertia pars, $\frac{1}{1000}$, *millesima pars;* "tithes," *decumae* (*sc.* partes). (*c*) $\frac{2}{3}$. *duae partes;* $\frac{3}{4}$, *tres partes;* $\frac{3}{5}$, *tres quintae* (*sc.* partes). (*d*) *Dimidio plures,* "half as many again;" *duplo plures,* "twice as many."

> Dimidium *exercitus* quam quod, *or* quantum *acceperat, reduxit.* He brought back half the army which he had received.

536. The following are the common modes of expressing numbers.

(*a*) *Nostrorum,* or, *e nostris, decem, triginta, ducenti, ad mille* ducenti (1200, *ad* is here *adverbial* and governs no case), *tria milia quingenti* (3500) *interfecti sunt.*

(*b*) *Nostrorum,* sometimes *nostri* (the numeral being occasionally used in *apposition*), duo milia *caesa,* or *caesi* (*milia* being treated sometimes as masculine where men are concerned), *aut desiderati sunt* (were missing).

(*c*) *Milites praemisit ducentos viginti; pedites ad mille ducentos cum amplius*[1] *mille equitum praemisit,* or *peditum tria milia ducentos,* etc.

Obs.—Large *indefinite* numbers are expressed by sex-(ses-)centi, -a, -ae: sexcenta *alia,* "a hundred other things;" milies *mori praestat,* "'twere better to die a *thousand* deaths;" ne millesimam *quidem* partem intelligo, "I don't understand a *particle* (of what he says)."

Exercise 66.

A.

1. In his ninety-second[2] year he was still[3] able to answer those who[4] asked his opinion. 2. I ask first

---

[1] Remember that with numbers *quam* is rarely expressed after *plus, amplius,* etc. (**318,** *Obs.*)

[2] Either *anno aetatis,* or as in **327.**

[3] "Still" need not be expressed.　　　　[4] Part. pres. (**414.**)

whence you come, secondly, whither you are going, thirdly, why you are armed, lastly, why you are in my house.   3. The generals met at the river side, each with an interpreter and ten soldiers.   4. One, two, three days had now passed, yet[1] no agreement had been come to as regards the conditions of peace.   5. In prosperity I thought your father one of Fortune's favourites, in these dark[2] days I see that he belongs, and always has belonged, to the class of great men.[3]   6. He stayed at Milan, one of the richest and most populous of cities, one or two days; yet out of 100,000 citizens, not one thanked him for the preservation[4] of the city and the repulse of the enemy from its walls, and perhaps[5] not one single soul felt the gratitude which he owed.   7. There has been a disastrous[6] battle; 2,500[7] of our men have been slain; it is said that half as many again are taken prisoners, and that one or two[8] of the four generals are missing.   8. We have lost an excellent man; if not the very best of his class, yet at all events one of those who come but once[9] in a generation.   9. I have received two[10] letters from you to-day, one yesterday; the rest I have looked for in vain; though I have waited for them one or two days, and sent to inquire,[11] not once,[12] but twice.   10. This is the nineteenth day from the commencement of the siege.   The commander of the garrison is demanding two hostages from every[13] household, to prevent[14] any rising on the part of the townspeople, who are mostly[15] armed, and who outnumber his troops by two to one.

---

[1] *Nec tamen quidquam.* (See **110.**)   [2] Simply *tempora.*
[3] Use *vir* with *summus.* (See **224,** *note* [3].)   [4] See **417,** i.
[5] Use *haud scio an.* (**169.**)   [6] Impersonal, **218,** *Obs.*
[7] **536,** *a.*   [8] Ex, e. (**296,** *Obs.*)   [9] **380,** *a.*
[10] **532,** *b.*   [11] Supine of *sciscitari.* (**402.**)
[12] **533,** *c.*   [13] **532,** *a.*
[14] "That no (**103**) rising *of* . . . may take place."
[15] Use *plerique* in app., often so used where *the whole* and a *part* are not contrasted. (**297.**)

Exercise 66.

B.

At the age of scarcely nineteen he had again and again taken part in regular engagements, and had more than once slain an enemy in single combat, and was now[1] on the point[2] of engaging an army half as large again as that which he[3] commanded. Yet in the face of such a crisis, he did not hesitate to detach more than 1600 infantry to defend[4] his allies against an irruption of the Indians, although two-thirds of his army consisted of recruits,[5] who[6] were now to fight their first battle. But he preferred to die a thousand[7] deaths, rather than turn his back on a barbarian foe, who if once he won[8] the day would, he well[9] knew, afflict his country with every kind of wrong.

---

[1] **328.** *b.*　　　　[2] **418,** *d.*　　　　[3] **355,** *Obs.* 1.
[4] " To repel (gerundive) from his allies."　[5] *Tiro miles,* sing. **(223.)**
[6] Part. in *-rus.* **(406.)**　　　　[7] **536,** *Obs.*
[8] Mood and tense ? **(471,** *Obs.*)　　[9] **32,** *b.*

Y

THE ROMAN CALENDAR.

537. The Roman months consisted (after the reform of the Calendar by Julius Caesar) of the same number of days as the English months; but the days were numbered quite differently.

538. The *first* day of the month was called *Kalendae* (the **Kalends**); the **Nones** (*Nonae*) fell on the *fifth* or *seventh*; the **Ides** (Id-us, -uum, f.) were always eight days after the **Nones**, that is, the *thirteenth* or *fifteenth*.

> "In March, July, October, May,
> The Nones were on the seventh day."

(The **Ides** therefore on the 15th.)

To these names of days, the names of the month were attached as *adjectives:*[1] *ad Kalendas* Maias, "*by* the 1st *of May*" (326); *In Nonas* Junias, "*for* the 5th *of June;*" *Idus* Martiae, "the 15th *of March.*"

539. From these three fixed points the other days of the month were reckoned *backwards*, and *inclusively, i.e.* both days were counted in.

Days between the Kalends and the Nones were reckoned by their distance from the **Nones**; those between the Nones and the Ides by their distance from the **Ides**; those after the Ides by their distance from the **Kalends** of the *following month.*

To suit this Roman way of reckoning, we must subtract the given day from the *number of the day* on which the Nones or Ides fall *increased by one.* If the day be one

---

[1] These forms are, Januarius, Februarius, Martius, Aprilis, Maius, Junius, Quintilis (*or* Julius), Sextilis (*or* Augustus), Septem-, Octo-, Novem-, Decem-, bris.

The months of July and August were called *Quintīlis, Sextīlis,* respectively (=the *fifth* and *sixth* month, reckoning from *March*, the old beginning of the year), till those names were exchanged for *Julius* and *Augustus* in honour of the two first Caesars.

before the Kalends, we must subtract from *the last day* of the month *increased by two*, as the Kalends fall within the next month.

Thus take the 3rd, 9th, 23rd of June:—

(1) In June the Nones are on the *fifth ;* therefore three must be subtracted from $(5+1=)$ *six ;* and the remainder being 3, the day is "the *third* day before the *Nones* of June."

(2) In June the Nones being on the fifth, the Ides are on the *thirteenth,* and the subtraction must be from *fourteen*. Hence subtract 9 from 14; the remainder being 5, the day is the *fifth* day before the Ides of June.

(3) Since June has *thirty* days, we must subtract from thirty-two. Hence subtract 23 from 32; the remainder being 9, the day is the *ninth* day before the *Kalends of July.*

So December 30th is not the *second,* but the *third* day before the Kalends of January.

540. The names for days are thus expressed in Latin.

"On the third before the Kalends of March" is by rule "*die tertio* ante Kalendas Martias," which was shortened by the omission of *die* and *ante* into "*tertio Kalendas Martias,*" or iii. *Kal. Mart.*

But another form is used (almost exclusively) by *Cicero* and *Livy;* this form is "*ante diem tertium Kalendas Martias,*" shortened into "a. d. iii.[1] *Kal. Mart.*"

This *ante-diem* came to be treated as an indeclinable substantive, and the prepositions *ad, in, ex* were prefixed to it, as to other substantives of time.

The last day of the month is *pridie Kalendarum* or *pridie Kalendas.*

The following are examples.

1. *Natus est Augustus* ix. Kal. Oct. (nono Kalendas Octobres), *i.e. on the 23rd of September.*
2. Kalendis Augustis *natus est Claudius,* iii. Id. Oct. (tertio Idus Octobres) *excessit*. (1st of August and October 13th.)
3. *Meministi me* a. d. xii. Kal. Nov. *sententiam dicere in Senatu ?* Do you remember my speaking in the Senate *on the 21st of October ?*

---

[1] For an explanation of this form see ROBY, *L. G.* vol. i. p. 454.

4. *Quattuor dierum supplicatio indicta est* ex a. d. v. Id. Oct.
A four days' public thanksgiving has been proclaimed *from
the 11th of October.*

5. *Consul comitia* in a. d. iii. Non. Sext. *edixit.* The Consul fixed
the 3rd of August for the elections.

6. In ante dies octavum et septimum Kalendas Octobres *comitiis
dicta dies.* The date fixed for the elections is *the 24th and
25th of September.*

Exercise 67.

1. We have been looking for you day [1] after day from
the third of March to the tenth of April : your father and
I [2] begin to fear that something has happened amiss.
2. Your father parted from us at [3] Rhodes on the 14th of
July : he seemed to be suffering seriously both from sea-
sickness and home-sickness; we have not [4] yet received
any letter from him, but we hope that he will reach home
safe and sound by [5] the twelfth of August. The day after [6]
he left us we heard that he ought [7] to have started three
days earlier [8] if he wished [9] to be at home in good time.
3. You promised six months ago to stay in my house [10]
from the 3rd to the 21st of April. I hope that you will
do your utmost to keep your word ; you have been looked
for now these ten [11] days. 4. Instead [12] of keeping his
word by starting to his father at Rome on the last day of
August, he preferred to linger in the fair city [13] of Naples
for over twenty days. He scarcely reached home by the
25th of September ; a circumstance [14] of which, as [15] it
was fatal also to his own prospects and his father's good
name, he repented, I believe, from that day [16] to the latest
day of his life.

---

[1] **328**, *c.*　　　[2] See **26**, *note.*　　　[3] See **315**.
[4] *Nullus adhuc.* (See **328**, *d.*)　　　[5] *Ad.* (**326**.)
[6] **323**, *b.*　　　[7] Gerund.　(**388**.)　　　[8] *Ante* with abl. (**322**, *a.*)
[9] Mood? (**444**.)　　　[10] **316**, iii.　　　[11] **321**, *Obs.* 2.
[12] **431**, *Obs.*　　　[13] **317**.　　　[14] *Quae res.* (**67**.)
[15] *Quum.* (**430**.)　　　[16] **326**.

SUPPLEMENTARY EXERCISES.

541. The following Supplementary Exercises are added, partly for the purpose of enlarging the range of practice in applying the rules and remarks contained in the earlier portion of the book, partly also with a view of introducing a few specimens of continuous passages adapted to at least the standard of an ordinary Entrance or " Pass " Examination at the Universities or elsewhere.

The last Exercise (No. 15) is recapitulatory, and consists of a hundred short sentences bearing mainly on the same portion of the work (Exercises i.-xxiii.). Reference here and in other Exercises is frequently made to later sections. The sentences, though necessarily limited in their range, will be found to illustrate a large number of the most fundamental points of difference between the Latin and English languages.

Obs.—In attempting any more continuous passage it should be borne in mind that the connexion in thought between each fresh sentence and that which precedes it is much oftener indicated by some word or phrase in Latin than it is in English. Hence in writing Latin we must often insert some **co-ordinating conjunction** (Intr. 56), answering to "moreover," "but," "for," "therefore," etc., which is wanting in the English, or change "not" into "nor," or the **demonstrative** into the **relative**. (See **78.**)

No. 1.

To follow Exercises 1 and 2.

1. Not even[1] the vilest of mankind would have envied his own father.   2. Yesterday he returned from Naples, to-morrow he is to[2] set out from Italy to Spain.   3. No one in the world is more secure against[3] violence, for no one[4] ever consulted to such[5] a degree the interests of the country.   4. Having obtained the throne by violence, he yet became before long[6] most dear to the whole nation, for no one ever less consulted his own interests.   5. On the fourth day after his father's death he ascended the throne, on the fifth he was saluted Emperor by the soldiers, on the sixth, having led his army into the enemies' country, he was wounded by his own sword while he was mounting[7] his horse.   6. No one was ever more famous, and no one ever attained to higher (*greater*) rank, or acquired such (**87**) wealth ; yet he was dear to few, hated by many, and no one ever did his country greater harm.   7. You are obeyed by no one, yet your father was the ruler[8] of a mighty nation.   8. That[9] deed of yours will never be pardoned by your countrymen.

---

[1] Intr. 99.   [2] Fut. in *-rus.* **14,** *c.*   [3] *a, ab.*
[4] *neque enim quisquam* (see 110); *non* is but rarely used before *enim.*
[5] *tantum,* adv.   [6] =" soon."   [7] Tense ? See 180. Cf. **411.**
[8] *impero, -are.*   See 25.   [9] *iste.* **11,** *d.*

No. 2.

To follow Exercise 3.

1. For three days[1] we waited for you (*pl.*) and hoped in vain for your arrival : on the fourth day the Indians, who were blockading our camp, dispersed and[2] took their departure ; a[3] circumstance which gave us freedom from long-continued fear and anxiety.   2. You (*pl.*) crave for freedom, and are going[4] to fight for[5] your native land, for your altars and hearths ; these (men) pray for peace, and are afraid of the hardships and toils of war.   You I honour, them[6] I despise.   3. Your riches increase daily, but they neither increase your leisure, nor bring you (**243**) either happiness or peace of mind.   4. Your native land, which was once the ruler of many nations, is now most cruelly oppressed by the vilest enemy, whom lately she both despised and hated.   5. I am waiting here in vain for the arrival of the soldiers whom I sent for yesterday, the enemies' forces are increasing daily, and we shall soon despair of peace.   6. By a bloody and long-continued war we have freed our country, and repelled from our walls a haughty foe ; we now pray for peace.   7. Having[7] advanced into the thick[8] of the battle he received a mortal wound ; while[9] dying, he foretold the ruin of his nation and the triumph of the enemy.

---

[1] 9, *a.*   [2] 15.   [3] See 67.   [4] 14, *c.*
[5] *pro.*   Se 6.   [6] *ille.* 11, *d.*   [7] 14, *a.*   [8] " midst of."   See 60.
                                    [9] See 406, *note* 2.

No. 3.

To follow Exercise 4.

1. Both your brother and you were at that time in exile; my father and I were at home, exposed to the fury and cruelty of our deadliest[1] enemies. We had provoked no one either by words or acts, yet we endured much, and long and sorely[2] sighed in vain for freedom and safety; now you and I are secure and free from care, and no[3] one will any longer[4] inflict on us injury or wrong. 2. Freed from the barbarous tyranny of an alien race, we have spared those[5] who had most cruelly oppressed our country, (and) we have pardoned those who in the face[6] of national ruin had neglected[7] the welfare of the nation, and were consulting merely their own interests; but neither you nor I will any longer[8] consent to forgive the offences of these[9] men, or to listen to those who, having obtained rank and riches by the vilest arts, are now urging upon us a dishonourable peace.

---

[1] 55.	[2] *multum diuque.*	[3] 110.	[4] *jam.* See 328, *a.*
[5] *is.* 70.	[6] *in* (abl.). 273, *Obs.*	[7] Abl. abs. 14, *b.*	
[8] *diutius.* See 328, *a.*		[9] *iste,* contemptuous. See 338, *Obs.* 2.	

No. 4.

To follow Exercises 5 and 6.

1. You and I were, he replied, in the country with[1] your brother, but would return to Naples on the first[2] of August; I believe that he made[3] a great mistake, and that[4] not designedly but by pure[5] accident, for I do not imagine that he would have endeavoured to deceive a friend and guest; but we shall, it is plain, be looked for in vain both by your father and my relations. 2. He ascertained that the weather had changed,[6] and that the crowd, which had gathered together in the morning, would soon disperse; he hoped therefore before night to be able to leave his house, and reach our camp in safety; having arrived there[7] he wished to have an interview with Caesar, whom he had long been pretending to wish to join, and from whom he was anxious to obtain[8] safety and assistance. For he hoped by his[9] aid to attain to the highest rank and office in his[9] own nation.

---

[1] *i.e.* "in the house of," *apud.* 331, 4 *a.*	[2] *Kalendis Sextilibus.* See 538.
[3] Use *multum* or *vehementer* with a verb. 25.	[4] *neque id.* Cf. 344.
[5] Use two adverbs with *ac.* See Vocab., under *chance.*	
[6] Abl. abs. 14 and 15.	[7] "Whither when he had arrived." 14, *a.*
[8] *i.e.* "by asking." See Vocab.	[9] See 11, *d* and *e*; "aid" is *opera.*

No. 5.

To follow Exercise 7.

1. News was now brought to me that my brother, having been struck by a javelin, and exhausted by many[1] serious wounds, was no longer able either to keep[2] the saddle, or lead his men[3] against the enemy. Having[4] heard this, I was much affected, for I could neither hurry to him as[5] I wished to do, nor did I hope that he would be able any longer to keep the enemy in check. It seemed moreover, that the soldiers who were with[6] me were losing heart, and it was said that the enemy was expecting large reinforcements before night, and would soon take the aggressive. I resolved therefore to try to finish the matter by a single charge. 2. Your brother was, he said, a man of[7] a kindly heart, and abounded[8] in wealth and resources, and he was sure that he would never desert his friends, nor wish such a blow to be inflicted on his own relations. 3. It seems that he had resolved to become consul in that year, but that he pretended to be craving for repose and quiet. 4. He was unwilling, he replied, to despair, but would rather be in exile than be a slave.

---

[1] See below, 56.   [2] *in equo haerere.*   [3] *sui.*   [4] Intr. 58.
[5] 67.   [6] 8, *Obs.*   [7] Abl. 271.   [8] *circumfluo.* 284.

No. 6.

To follow Exercises 7 and 8.

1. He talked very little about the past; about the future his hopes were high, but he perceived that he was at variance on this question[1] with many excellent men, and he preferred being[2] silent to disagreeing[2] with these, and agreeing[2] with his own enemies, and his country's foes; neither you nor I can think that he was mistaken, for we know that his good sense, honesty, and courage were worthy of all praise. 2. He promised to send me[3] a letter on the 15th of March,[4] and made many other fine pretences,[5] but he has neither kept his promises, nor does he any longer venture to make a secret of having purposely broken his word. 3. He threatens, they say, to take from me all the distinctions which I have obtained from the Senate and people of Rome; for myself,[6] I hardly think he will succeed in this[7] design. 4. He would rather, he replied, obey the most unjust laws, than be at variance with true patriots, and disagree with every sensible[8] man. 5. We scarcely dare to hope that your brother will return to Rome and imitate the noble acts of his forefathers, but all his contemporaries can guarantee[9] that he will never desert his friends, or break his word, or join the enemies of his native land.

---

[1] *in hac causa,* lit. "in this *suit.*"   [2] Infinitive in each case. See 94, and 42.
[3] *ad me.* See 6.   [4] See 538.   [5] See 54.
[6] *ego* or *equidem,* 11, *a.*   [7] *qui* (see Intr. 58), early in the clause.
[8] Superlative with *quisque.* 375.   [9] Use *spondeo.*

No. 7.
To follow Exercise 9.

1. You (*pl.*) have come here[1] manifestly with reluctance, and you say that you will not[2] wait any longer for the arrival of your friends. who will, you think,[3] be far from[4] secure in our camp. For myself, I have promised you again and again to say nothing about the past, and I have resolved both to pardon you, and to spare them. But you apparently expect that in the hour of triumph, I shall break my word, and act[5] towards[6] you and them with the height of treachery. I know that you can scarcely believe that I am speaking the truth, and that you are silently despairing both of your own and your children's safety. What falsehood[7] have I ever told? When have I ever broken my word? 2. It is said that the king himself was the only one of[8] the whole of his army to ride in safety past the fatal marsh (*pl.*), and the first to reach the foot of the mountains, whence on the next day he mournfully and reluctantly led back his troops and never[9] again ventured to form such high hopes or embark[10] on such great enterprises. It seemed that as[11] he had been the first to hope for the best,[12] so he was the first to abandon his undertaking ; he preferred to appear fickle and cowardly rather than to bring ruin and destruction on his country.

---

[1] Why not *hic?* *huc* after verbs of motion.   [2] 33.   [3] 32, *b.*
[4] *parum*, "but little."   [5] *utor*, "employ treachery" (with abl.).
[6] *in vobis*, "in your case."   [7] See **54.**   [8] *e, ex,* "out of."
[9] *nec unquam postea.* Never join *et* with *nunquam*, or any negative word. **110.**
[10] Metaphor. Use *moliri,* and see **54.**   [11] *sicut . . . ita,* or *et . . . et.*   [12] Neut. pl.

No. 8.
To follow Exercises 10 and 11.

1. As[1] I was making my way through the lowest part of the valley, I fell unawares into an ambush of brigands. My captors[2] had, it seemed, been long expecting my arrival, and having seized[3] and made[3] me fast with chains, and dragged me from the road[4] into the neighbouring forest, they again and again threatened me with (**247**) torture and death. At last, when I promised to send a large amount[5] of gold within four days, my chains[6] were struck off and I was set at liberty, and in company[7] with two armed guards, returned to the place[8] whence I had set out. 2. He had now, he said, ceased to hope for much, for he had lost (he said) the best friends he had,[9] and was going to live with men who had always been his deadly enemies, by whom he had been both accused and condemned in his absence, and who had reluctantly spared his life. 3. Your accusers[10] will, I expect, reach the city to-morrow ; I hope that you will be (**193, iv.**) unanimously acquitted. 4. You[11] who once set at nought bodily (**59**) pain (*pl.*), are now apparently dismayed by it. It is[12] with reluctance that I say this of (*de*) the son of so great a man. 5. You obviously treat lightly the affairs of others ; I hope that you will value highly the good opinion of your countrymen.

---

[1] *dum* with pres. See **180.**   [2] 76.   [3] Acc. of participle pass. **15.**
[4] *de via.*   [5] *pondus, n.*   [6] Abl. abs.
[7] 8, *b.*   [8] *eo, unde.* See **89.**   [9] Mood? See **77.**
[10] 14, *c.* Not *accusator.* See **76.**   [11] See **75.**   [12] See **82.**

No. 9.

To follow Exercises 12 and 13.

1. It is generally[1] agreed among historians that this king, trained by toil (*pl.*) and accustomed to bear with patience the frowns[2] of fortune, showed[3] in the midst of disaster (*pl.*) and ruin the same character as in prosperity. As he had been the first to help his country in its hour[4] of distress, so he was the last to despair of it (when) conquered and downtrodden. But he preferred being an exile in his old age to living in safety at home, and obeying one whom the rest of the world, almost without exception, believed to be likely to keep his word. 2. There is all the difference between returning thanks and showing gratitude. As I was the last to believe that you would have set at nought honour, honesty, and the good opinion of your countrymen, so to-day I refuse to think that you have proved[6] to be of such a character as the rest of the world represent[7] you to be ; and it is with reluctance that I yield to those who deny that you are the same man as I once fancied you to be

---

[1] *satis* or *fere.*   [2] Metaphor, "adverse fortune."
[3] See 241.   [4] Simply part. pres. of *laboro, -are.*
[5] See 14, c.   [6] Use *existo.* See 241.   [7] "assert."

No. 10.

To follow Exercises 14 and 15.

On the next day the king, to avoid wearying by a long march his soldiers (who were) exhausted with a long and indecisive battle, kept his men within their lines. Meantime the enemy having sent for reinforcements were waiting for an attack (on the part) of our men, so that they seemed by no means desirous of fighting. After noonday the king, seeing[1] that the strength and spirits of his men were now so much restored, that they were likely to shrink from no danger, and stood (up) prepared for fighting,[2] threw open[3] two gates, and having made a sudden[4] sally surprised the enemy (who were taken) unawares and looking for nothing of the[5] kind. Great numbers they surround[6] and slay, and so great was the slaughter that out of (*ex*) more than[7] 3000 soldiers scarcely 500 escaped unwounded, and that, had[8] not night interposed, not even these would have survived. So (entirely) in short did fortune change (sides), that those who quite lately[9] were on the point of winning the day, were now stealing away and praying for night and darkness, and those who but lately[10] were despairing of their safety, and looking for death or slavery, were exulting in victory and freedom.

---

[1] See 412.   [2] 99.   [3] Abl. abs.   [4] Use adverb.   [5] 87.
[6] 14, c.   [7] 318, *Obs.*   [8] *nisi* with pl.-perf. subj.   [9] *paulo ante.*   [10] *modo.*

No. 11.

To follow Exercise 16.

Thereupon, he sent[1] for their chief men, and exhorted them not to be disheartened on account of such a serious disaster. He had warned them, he said,[2] that the enemy was at hand, but it had been impossible to persuade them not to put faith in idle rumours and fictitious messages. The Indians earnestly implored him to forgive them[3] for this great error ; they succeeded at last by their prayers or tears in persuading him that they would never again[4] allow themselves to be so easily overreached and entrapped (*caught*). While[5] they were thus[6] conversing, it happened that a[7] prisoner was brought to Cortes, who professed to be one[8] of the king's[9] bodyguard. The general ordered his[10] fetters to be struck off and himself to be set at liberty, and sent him back with a letter to the king. He did this with the intention of appearing to be anxious for a truce ; but so far was he from wishing for anything[11] of the kind that he was ready to reject any[12] conditions, and preferred to put the fortune of war a second time to the test (rather) than to accept from the king even the most honourable peace.

---

1 Acc. part. pass. 15.	2 Avoid parenthesis. 32.	3 Pronoun? See 353, ii. and 247.
4 *postea*.	5 *dum :* tense? 180.	6 *haec*. 7 *quidam*. 361.
8 *unus e.* See 529, *e.*	9 Adj. 58.	10 Relative. 78.
11 *quisquam*. 358.		12 359.

No. 12.

To follow Exercises 17 and 18.

I am afraid that this letter will not reach you across the enemies' lines. We have now been[1] invested here for a whole month (321), and[2] I cannot help beginning to despair of the whole state[3] of affairs. The numbers[4] of the enemy are such as we had never dreamed of,[5] and as[6] all the roads are closed, no supplies can be brought up ; scarcely any letters reach us, so that it is impossible to doubt that we are involved in very serious danger. Do you therefore not hesitate to write to the general to hasten to bring us assistance, and do not allow yourself to think that I am writing thus with the intention of calling[7] him away from his great designs and bringing him here for the sake of our safety. I fear that the enemy (if once) victorious here, will soon become formidable to him also, and I do not think that we can be crushed without[8] drawing others into the same ruin.

---

1 Tense? 181.	2 *neque,* etc. ; cf. 110.	3 *summa res.*
4 *multitudo* (sing.).	5 Metaphor, "fancied would come together."	
6 Abl. abs. 420.	7 Part. pass. 15.	8 See 111.

No. 13.
To follow Exercises 19 and 20.

Are we to say that Caesar was foully[1] murdered or that he was rightfully[2] slain? That either one[3] or the other is true is most certain. Do you (*sing.*) then choose whichever[4] you like; but do not say now this, now that, and[5] do not to-day look on Brutus as a patriot, to-morrow as an assassin. Did Caesar pay the penalty of his crimes? You answer "No;" then let his slayers be either banished or put[6] to death as traitors. Or[7] did Brutus speak the truth,[8] when (while) raising aloft the bloody dagger, he exclaimed that the nation's freedom was recovered? "Yes," you reply. Then why do you heap abuse on one to whom alone[9] you are indebted for your freedom? Or[7] do you think that what Brutus did was in[10] itself right and a benefit[11] to the nation, but that he himself acted criminally, and should be punished[12] with banishment, or imprisonment, or death? For myself I decline to meddle with so nice[13] a question : I leave it to philosophers (**146**).

1 "criminally."
2 "*jure caesus*," a legal phrase answering to our "justifiable homicide."
3 *hic. ille.* See 340, ii. 4 *utervis.* 379. 5 **145**.
6 "He is put to death, etc.," *more majorum in eum animadvertitur*, a euphemism for scourging and beheading. 7 *An.* 161. 8 *tum . . . quum.* 433, *a.* 9 *unus.* 529, *b.*
10 *per se.* 11 Use *utilis*, avoid *beneficium* in this sense.
12 Gerundive of *multo, -are*, with abl. 13 *subtilis*, or *difficilis.*

No. 14.
To follow Exercises 21 and 22.

The king summoned his staff and set before them the nature and extent of the danger, the numbers of the enemy, the magnitude of their resources, their aims,[1] designs,[1] and hopes. For my part, said he, I will utter my real sentiments and will not hide the fact[2] that I have no doubt that both all (of) you and I myself are to-day involved in the greatest danger. I know that it is difficult to say[3] whether the reinforcements which we look for will ever reach us, or whether we shall perish first[4] overwhelmed by the weapons of this enormous[5] host But whether we are[6] to live or die, I venture to feel sure of this at least, that no one of us will allow himself to think it a light[7] matter, whether our countrymen are to be grateful to us in our graves[8] or to scorn (despise) us in our lives; so that we need only deliberate on one single question, by what[9] course of action or of endurance we shall best serve (**332, 3,** *g*) our common country. Possibly we can consult our own safety by remaining here, sheltered and preserved by these walls; and perhaps this[10] is the safer plan; but it sometimes happens that the most daring[11] course is the safest; and I hope to persuade you that it will so turn out to-day.

1 **174.** Use the verbs *peto*, and *mol-ior, -iri.* 2 *illud.* **341.** 3 Supine in -*u.* **404.**
4 *prius.* 5 Simply *tantus.* **88.** 6 Fut. in -*rus.* 7 *parvi facere.* **305, i.**
8 Metaphor, use *mortuus.* **61.** 9 "By doing what, enduring what." **398.**
10 Relative. 11 See **375**, *note* 1.

No. 15.

The following Exercise is mainly recapitulatory ; it, or any part of it, may follow Sections 1-194.

1. The whole world knows why you are envied.   2. He asked if you had ever spared a single enemy.   3. He hoped, he said, that the matter would turn out contrary to his expectations.[1]   4. Have you not come from the same place [2] as I ?   5. He was the first to reach the summit of the mountain, the last to descend.   6. He was revolving many thoughts (64) in silence.   7. He said that he was no longer [3] such as he had once been.   8. There had been, he replied, as many opinions as there were men standing by.   9. It seems that you were the first within human memory to venture on this enterprise.   10. Having promised to settle these matters, he held his peace.   11. In my youth I travelled over many lands and seas, in my old age I remain at home.   12. He came home with a weapon intending [4] to kill your father ; fortunately [5] no one was at home.   13. It seemed that he was returning thanks unwillingly ; but it is most certain that he feels grateful.   14. All the world knows that you are under an obligation to me, no one believes that you will show gratitude.   15. I who was once your advocate am to-day your accuser.   16. So alarmed was he by the shouts of the bystanders that he could scarcely answer his questioners.[6]   17. Both you and I have lost an excellent friend, whom we are never likely to see again in this world.   18. Neither you nor I are likely to believe that the world was made by chance.   19. I know not whether you wish to be a friend [7] to me or an enemy.   20. I did this with the intention of pleasing you ; I earnestly beg you therefore not to be angry.   21. He wrote me word [8] not to leave the city ; I happened by chance to have [9] already set out.   22. I know not whether I am likely to deter him from [10] injuring his friends.   23. I fear that we have lost the city ; it remains to see if we can retake it.   24. Three months [11] ago the city [12] of Veii was invested by the troops of Rome ; it has now been (181) long blockaded, it will soon be assaulted, and there is danger,[13] they say, of its being stormed.   25. The weather was now changing, and the sailors were dreading the violence of the winds.   26. I have silently resolved to be at leisure to-morrow, but perhaps this is [14] impossible.   27. I asked him first (534, *Obs.*) if he had committed that monstrous crime ; he answered " Yes ;" secondly, why he had acted so ; next, when ; lastly, with what weapon.   28. He turned to his companions [15] and asked them when they intended to return home.   29. That your friend is fortunate is indisputable (64) ; I

---

[1] See 91. Mood, 77, *Obs.*   [2] 89.   [3] *jam.* 328, *a.*
[4] 14, *c.*   [5] 64.   [6] 73.
[7] 46, *d.*   [8] 122, *c.*   [9] 123.
[10] 137, ii.   [11] 324.   [12] 222.
[13] 138.   [14] 169.   [15] 349, *Obs.*

entirely disagree with those who say that he is happy ; happiness [1] is
one thing, prosperity another.   30. Having started with his followers
(**349**, *Obs.*) the next day, he fell unawares into an ambush ; most
fortunately [2] I came to his assistance, and attacked the enemy from [3]
behind.   31. Both he and you, it is plain, were persuaded to believe
men who were deceiving you.   32. I fear that in his old age he no
longer has the same views as in his youth.   33. You ask me if [4] he
is of the same character as his brother, I unwillingly answer " No." [5]
34. I earnestly implored him to warn his father not to put confidence
in that man.   35. Perceiving (*quum*, **412**) that he was unwilling to
trust me, I ceased to urge him to go with me.   36. Be sure you come
to me at Rome (**315**) that we may both [6] have an interview with
Caesar.   37. So cowardly and mean-spirited was he, that I think I
have never seen any one like him. [7]   38. I have stayed here so long
that I begin to believe I shall never go away.   39. So dear was he to
his friends that they never ceased to sigh for him in his absence, to
admire him when present.   40. What was I to do ? whither to turn ?
I could have wished you had stood by me ; but both my friends and
you were absent.   41. It would be tedious to tell all this [8] story,
but I cannot help praising one of (*ex*) his exploits.   42. Do not believe, judges, that I am of the character [9] which this man attributes [10]
to me.   43. It is of great consequence whether (**166**) you inflict punishment on men who deserve punishment, or on the innocent.   44.
Whether you have devoted me to death or [11] not, I know not, nor does
it matter much.   45. Do you not perceive that it is absolutely impossible for the privileges and liberty of the nation to be outraged by you
with impunity.   46. I asked him if he wished to make me responsible
for a brother's [12] crime.   He answered in the affirmative.   47. He
asked if I was willing to aid men who were aiming at giving freedom
to their oppressed and down-trodden country.   48. A (*is*) massacre
followed, the like of which [13] I had never seen ; of such an extent
and character that I can hardly dare to recall to mind the scene. [14]   49. I
have spoken thus with the intention of persuading him to pardon you :
whether he will do so or not is uncertain.   50. He succeeded [15] in
persuading the king to forgive [16] him this great error.   51. It has
repeatedly fallen to my lot to be suspected of many crimes ; I have
never before been condemned in my absence and unheard.   52. Possibly your countrymen, freed from an alien despotism, are going
to offer you the supreme power ; what they doubt is (**341**) whether
you will accept it.   53. He said that he had never taken any part [17]
in politics, or made it his aim (**118**) to attain to any distinctions, or to
acquire rank or riches.   54. You are, I see, victorious and most fortunate ;
that you enjoy happiness I do not allow.   55. I might have [18] said

---

[1] 98, *a*, *b*.	[2] 64.	[3] 61.
[4] 167.	[5] 162.	[6] *ambo.* 378,
[7] 255.	[8] 54.	[9] *talis.* 84.
[10] "pretends (*fingit*) that I am."	[11] 168, *Obs.*	[12] Adj. 58.
[13] "(one) like which." 255.	[14] " The things which I saw." 176.	
[15] 125, *j.*	[16] 247.	
[17] Use either *versari in republica* or *rempublicam attingere.*		[18] **196**, *b.*

much more on (*de*) the vileness of these men ; but I do not wish to be either tedious or burdensome to you. 56. More than once (**533, c**) he took advantage of my gentleness and clemency; in my absence, he loaded me with abuse and insults. 57. I fear that our soldiers have been incapable of sustaining the onset of such[1] a well-trained host. 58. Thrice with his army of recruits[2] he advanced against the enemy; thrice he retreated ; at last his soldiers dispersed, and fled in opposite directions. 59. He was at last persuaded to spare the innocent (*pl.*) and unarmed ; but he long refused to do so. 60. As a young man, he attained to the height of fame, in his old age he was undeservedly disgraced. 61. Overreached and deceived by men[3] who pretended to be his friends, he could no longer put confidence in those who wished his interest consulted (**240, *Obs.* 1**). 62. It is almost incredible (**166**) how seldom it has been my lot to see so famous a person. 63. Do not object[4] to be free. Let cowards act so, and those who dread death. 64. The manner[5] of his death I have never heard, all the world knows that he is dead. 65. Having returned home in his old age, he became dear to many excellent members of the state. 66. So far from hating him, I am anxious to defend him against[6] his deadliest enemies. 67. I could never see your brother without[7] calling to mind his dead father's countenance. 68. I cannot help wondering at the reason[8] of your having come here. 69. He swore (**37**) to confess to no one the motive[8] of his having told these falsehoods. 70. It is almost incredible (**166**) how often he has been warned against[9] doing anything of this kind (**87**). 71. I was so foolish as to be almost persuaded (**5**) to turn back[10] to the place from whence (**89**) I had set out. 72. No one in the world (**16, b**) could have spoken with more prudence,[11] or more candour. 73. What you have done is possibly (**64**) in accordance[12] with law, I greatly doubt[13] whether it is constitutional.[14] 74. Do you think that such a man as this[15] can be restrained from[16] using violence? 75. I know that this is right and honourable, whether it is expedient or no I leave[17] to wiser men to decide. 76. You pretend to be a citizen of Rome ; for myself I cannot help[18] suspecting that you are not only a foreigner, but one of the soldiers of Carthage. 77. It is impossible to doubt (**200, *Obs.***) that he has injured the nation ; whether he has done this accidentally or designedly, I leave to himself to decide. 78. I was the last to perceive what you were aiming at ; I shall be the first to oppose you in that aim[19] (**415**). 79. He bade the soldiers drag their own (**356, i.**) general to execution; reluctantly and mournfully they obeyed his orders (**415, a**). 80. Do you go to meet the enemy in front (**61**), I will charge him from behind, and off his guard. 81. The whole world knows now-a-days that the earth moves round the sun ; it is (**82**) into the nature,[20] properties, and

---

[1] 88.	[2] See 223.	[3] 72.
[4] *recuso* with inf. 136.	[5] 174, *c.*	[6] *ab.*
[7] 132, *b.*	[8] 174, *a.*	[9] 118.
[10] *revertor*, "I turn back," return without completing my intended journey.		
[11] Adv. *prudenter*. 64.	[12] 331, 21.	[13] *vehementer*.
[14] 332, 4.	[15] 87.	[16] 131.
[17] 146.	[18] 137, *j.*	[19] "aiming at that." 415
[20] See 174. Use *quid, quale*, etc.		

magnitude of the sun that philosophers are inquiring. 82. I never feared that you were not (138) going to consult my interest; the real[1] danger was that fortune would change. 83. So changed was your brother's face and features that I hardly knew that he was the same person that I knew in my youth. 84. To-morrow we are to fight; be sure to (141) take part in the contest, if you can (190, ii.). 85. What was I to do (150)? what to say? whither to turn? no one was coming to my aid; it seemed that the whole world thought me out of my mind. 86. He was unanimously (59) acquitted, but at the same time (366, ii.) universally condemned. 87. Your father refused to leave his own house; would he had been here (152) to-day. 88. The weather, I fancy, will change to-morrow; be sure, therefore, to cross the channel to-day. 89. Let us no longer obey a master of this kind, it would be better to die a thousand[2] deaths than endure such disgrace. 90. The whole of the city echoed with voices of weeping[3] and mourning; you would have thought[4] that there was no one but had lost a parent or children. 91. So earnestly did he implore me to spare the unarmed that I could no longer withstand his entreaties.[5] 92. Having communicated[6] this matter to me, he warned me to be on my guard[7] against an[8] enemy of my brother. 93. To this advice[5] of his I replied that I had no fears for myself, but was anxious to provide[7] for the safety of my friends. 94. I have been informed, said he, by[9] my scouts that you have long been (181) supplying[10] the enemy with corn. 95. It seems that you are threatening[10] us with imprisonment and death; perhaps[11] it would have been better (153) to provide for your own safety. 96. It is said that he intrusted[10] you with the whole of this matter; perhaps he relied[12] on you too much. 97. Three days[13] ago, I asked when you were to come here; it seemed that no one knew. 98. Your father happened[14] that day to be absent; he hoped to return within a[15] week. 99. In the study of nature your son has made great progress; in everything that relates to literature I incline to think that many of his contemporaries have outstripped him. 100. It is uncertain whether at that[16] time he preferred to be a politician or a student (175).

---

1 341.　　　　　　　2 536, *Obs.*　　　　3 415, *b.*
4 149, ii.　　　　　5 415.　　　　　　6 253, iv.
7 248 (for this and next sentence).　　　8 361.
9 *Per.* 267, *Obs.*　　10 247.　　　　　11 *haud scio an.* 170.
12 244, *c.*　　　　　13 324　　　　　　14 123.
15 "the seventh day." 325.　　　　　　16 *tum temporis.* 294, *Obs.*

GENERAL VOCABULARY.

Caution.—It should be understood that the Latin words given in this Vocabulary are not necessarily equivalent to the English when the latter are used with a meaning and context different to that in which they occur in the Exercises. (See 17-19.)

Figures refer to sections, except where p. (= *page*) *or Ex.* (= *Exercise*) *is prefixed.*

abandon, I (*a person*), deser-o,[1] ĕre, -ui, -tum; de-sum, esse, -fui (*dat.*, **251**); destitu-o, ĕre, -i; de-scisco, ĕre, scivi, ab *or abl.* (*fall off from a party*).

abandon, I (*a thing or work*), o-mitto, ĕre, -misi, -missum (see note under *undone, I leave*); de-sisto, ĕre, -stiti, ab, *or abl.*

abandoned (*wicked*), perditus.

abandonment of, *the*, use o-mitto, ĕre, etc. (**417, i.**)

abide by, I, sto, are (*abl.*).

ability, or *abilities*, ingenium, *n.* (*sing.*).

able, I am, possum, posse, potui.

abound in, I, circum-fluo, ĕre, -fluxi. (**284.**)

about (*adv.*), circa, circiter; fere, ferme.

about (*prep.*), de. (**332, 3, *d.***)

absence, in my. (**61**, and **420, ii.**)

absent, I am, absum, esse; *from*, a, ab.

absolutely, plane; *or superl. of adj.*

absolutely impossible. (**125, *f.***)

abstain from, I. (**264.**)

abundance of, plurimum. (**294.**)

abuse, maledicta, *n. pl.* (**51, *b.***)

accept, I, ac-cipio, ĕre, -cepi, -ceptum.

acceptable to, gratus. (See note under *delightful.*)

accident, cas-us, -ūs, *m.*

accident, by, casu; fortuito. (**268.**)

accomplish, I, ef- *or* con-ficio, ĕre, etc.

accordance with, *in*, perinde ac, etc. (**491,** *a*); pro (**332, 7,** *f.*).

account of, *on*, propter (*acc.*).

account, *on no*, nullo modo; minime.

account, *I take into*, rationem habeo (*gen.*).

accuracy, *with more*, verius. (Intr. 52.)

accuse, I, accuso, are.

accuser, = *he who accuses.* (**76.**)

accustomed, I am, soleo, ēre, solitus.

achievements, res gestae.

achievements, *I perform*, res gero, ĕre, gessi, gestum.

acquire, I, ad-ipiscor, i, -eptus. (See **19.**)

acquit, I, absol-vo, ĕre, -vi, -utum. (**306.**)

across, trans (*acc.*).

act, I (*behave*), me gero, ĕre.

act rightly, I, recte facio.

act thus, *i*, haec facio.

action, by, agendo, aliquid (**398**): *nom.* agere (**95, 99**).

acts, facta, *n. pl.* (**51, *b.***)

address (= *speech*), orati-o, -onis, *f.*

address (*the people*), I, verba (apud populum) facio.

adequate, justus.

---

[1] *Relinquo*, I abandon, in neutral and general sense of "leaving;" *desero*, I quit a place or person where or with whom duty bids me stay; *destituo*, I leave "in the lurch" one who without me will be unaided; *desum*, I fail to be present where my presence is desirable or right; *deficio* (*ab* or acc.), "I fail" or "fall off from," those whom I have hitherto stood by.

administering the government, rei
  publicae procurati-o, -onis, *f.* ;
  rempublicam gubernare.
administration, procurati-o, -onis, *f.*
admire, I, admiror, ari.
advance, I, pro-cedo, ĕre, -cessi,
  -cessum ; pro-gredior, i, -gressus.
advance in learning, I, doctior fio.
advanced (age), provecta (aetas).
  (See 303, *Obs.* 1.)
advanced in life or years. (303,
  Obs. 1.)
advanced guard, primum agm-en,
  -inis, *n.*
advantage, emolumentum, *n.*
advantage, to your. (269, *Obs.*)
advantage, what? quid emolumenti?
  (294.)
adverse, adversus (*adj.*).
adversity, res adversae.
*advice, against your, turn by pres.
  part. of* dissuadeo, ēre. (See
  420, ii.)
advise, I, moneo.
advocate of (peace), auctor.
advocate of, I am an, suadeo, ēre,
  with acc. of thing. (See 247.)
advocate, I am your, te defendo,
  ĕre.
affair, res, rei, *f.*
affected (agitated), I am, com-move-
  or, ēri, -motus.
affirmative, to reply in the. (162.)
afflict with, I, afficio, ĕre. (283.)
afraid, I am, timeo.
afraid of, I am, = *I fear* (25), per-
  timesco, ĕre, -timui (*acc., or* ne,
  ut, 138).
after (prep.), post (*acc.*). (See
  322, 323.)
after (with verbal subst.), use quum.
  (429.)
again, rursus. (328, *f.*)
again (with neg.), posthac ; postea.
again and again, saepe, saepissime.
  (57, *a ; see also* 533, *c.*)
against, contra (*acc.*).
against (my wishes) = "*in spite of.*"
  (420, ii.)

age (time of life), aet-as, -atis, *f.*
age (of things), vetust-as, -atis, *f.*
age, old, senect-us, -utis, *f.*
age, of that. (238, iii.)
age, those of his own, aequales.
  (51, *a.*)
age of, at the. (327.)
aged, exactae aetatis. (303, *Obs.* 1.)
aggressive, I take the, ultro arma
  or bellum, infero.
agitation, there is, trepidatur. (218.)
ago. (324.)
agree with, I do not, parum (*but
  little*) consen-tio, ire, -si (cum).
agreed by (all), it is, constat inter
  (*acc.*).
agreed on by, it is, con-vēnit, -vēnit,
  inter.
agreement, an, pactum, *n.*
agreement is come to, an, convēnit
  (*impers.*).
agreement with, I am in, consen-tio,
  īre, -si, -sum, cum (*abl.*).
aid, auxilium, *n.*
aid, I, opem fero (*dat.*).
aid, I come to your, tibi subvenio.
aid or assistance, I come to your
  (Ex. 32). (260, 1.)
aid, by your, operā tuā.
aim at, I, or I form aims, pet-o,
  ĕre, -ivi, -ii (-isti), -ītum ; appeto, ĕre, etc. (*trans.*).
*aim at (doing, etc.), I, or I make it
  my aim*, id ago, ēgi, ut. (118.)
alarmed, I am, timeo, ēre.
alarmed (anxious) for, I am, metuo
  (*with dat.,* 248).
Alexander, Alexan-der, -dri.
alien (adj.), externus.
alien (subst.), peregrin-us, -i, *m.*
alike (adv.), juxta, pariter.
alike . . . and ; or . . . as, sicut . . .
  ita ; vel . . . vel (p. 14, *n.*).
alive, I am, vivo, ĕre.
all, omnis, *also* cunctus, universus.[1]
all (things), n. pl. of omn-is, -e.
all is lost, de summa re actum
  est.
allegiance, fid-es, -ei, *f.*

---

[1] *Universi*, all as a body, opposed to *singuli ; omnes*, all without exception, opposed
to *nemo* or to *unus ; cuncti*, a stronger *omnes*, "all together ;" *omnis* (sing.), every kind
of ; *cunctus* (sing.), all as a whole, nearly = *totus*, the whole as opposed to a part.

alliance with, I *make*, societatem ineo ire, -ivi, -ii, cum.

allow, I (*let*), per-mitto, ĕre, -misi, -missum (*dat.*, **128**, *end*).

allow, I (*grant*), concedo, ĕre.

allow, I (*confess, admit*), fateor, ēri, fassus ; con-cedo, ĕre, -cessi.

allow myself to, I will not, non committam ut. (**125**, *i.*)

allowed, I am, licet mihi. (**197**.)

allowed, it is, admitted, or agreed on, constat (*impers.*); *allowed by*, constat inter (*acc.*). (**46**, *c.*)

ally, an, soci-us, -i, *m.*

almost, fere,[1] paene, prope.

aloft, alte.

alone in doing this, I am, solus *or* unus (**529**, *b*), hoc facio. (**62**.)

along. (**331**, 5 *and* 21.)

already, jam.

also, quoque (Intr. 9S) ; *or (sometimes*), idem, idemque. (**366**, i.)

altars and hearths, arae atque foci.

altering, I am (intrans.), mutor, ari. (**21**, *a.*)

always, semper.

ambassador, legat-us, -i, *m.*

ambush, ambuscade, insidiae, *f. pl.*

amiss, secus.

among, inter (*acc.*).

ancestors, major-es, -um. (**51**, *a*, *n.5*.)

ancient, pristinus,[2] vet-us, -eris ; vetustus, a, um, *superl.* vetustissimus ; antiquus. (See *note.*)

and, et, -que, atque, ac (p. 14, *note ;* see also **110**).

anew, de integro. (**328**, *f.*)

anger, ira, *f. ; I cherish*, suc-censeo, ēre, -censui, -censum (*dat.*).

angry with, I am, ira-scor, i, -tus (*dat.*).

angry mood, iracundia, *f.*

angry outcries. (See *outcries*.)

annihilate, I, del-eo, ēre, -ēvi, -ētum.

announcement, of, use nuntio, are. (**417**, i.)

another (a second), alt-er, *gen.* -erius. (**368**.)

answer, I, respon-deo, ēre, -di, -sum.

answer, I make no, = I *answer nothing*. (**54** and **237**.)

answer to, in. (**331**, I. *b*, and 2. *c.*)

antiquity (of a thing existing), vetust-as, -atis, *f.*

anxiety, sollicitud-o. -inis, *f.*

anxiety, free from, securus.

anxious for, I feel, dif-fido, ĕre, -fisus (*dat.*).

anxious to, I am, cupio, ĕre (*inf.*).

any (after negat.), *any one, anything*, quisquam, quidquam, ullus. (See **358**.)

any? (impassioned interrogative), ecqui, ecquis.

any longer, ultra. (See also **328**, *a.*)

any man may, cujusvis est. (**292**, 4.)

any one (in final and consec. clauses). (**109**.)

anything (you please), quidvis, *gen.* cujusvis. (**359**.)

anywhere (after negat.), usquam.

Apiolae, Apiolae, arum.

apologise for, I, veniam peto, *with* quod *or gen. of participle*.

apparently. (**64**.)

appeal to, I, obtestor, ari (*acc.*) : *to you, not to*, te obtestor, ari, ne. (See **118**.)

appeal to you, I solemnly, fidem tuam imploro, are, ut *or* ne.

appeal to fear, to, deterr-eo, ēre, -ui. (**25**.)

appear (seem), I, videor, ēri, visus. (**43**.)

applaud, I, plau-do, ĕre, -si, -sum (*dat.*).

apprehension, met-us, -ūs, *m.*

---

[1] *Fere (ferme* in Livy) is "more or less," "about :" *paene, prope*, less than but bordering on. Hence *quod fere fit*, as *generally* happens ; but, *prope divinus, all but* divine, "heroic."

[2] *Antiquus*, old and no longer existing; *vetus* (fem. and neut., often borrowed from *vetustus*), old and still existing. Thus *domus antiqua*, "what was long ago my home ;" *domus (vetus or) vetusta*, "what has long been my home :" *mos antiquus*, an old custom now obsolete ; *veteri more*, in accordance with long-established custom. *Antiquus* = "of the good old times," often used in praise. *Priscus* = "old-fashioned," "rarely seen now ;" *pristinus*, simply " arlier," as opposed to " the present."

approach, I, advento, are.
approval for this, I get your, hoc tibi probo. (247.)
approved of (by you), it is, (tibi) probatur. (258, ii.)
apt to, I am, = I am wont, soleo.
ardently, vehement-er, -ius, -issime.
ardour for, studium, *n. (with gen.).* (300.)
argue, I, dis-sero, ĕre, -serui.
aright, recte
aristocratic party, the, optimat-es, -um *or* -ium, *m. pl.* (See 51, *a, and note.*)
arm (one), bracchium, *n.* (alter-um, 368).
armed, armatus.
arms, arma, *n. pl.*
armistice, an, indutiae, *f. pl.*
army, exercit-us, -ūs, *m.*
arrival, advent-us, -ūs, *m.*
arrive (at), I, per-vĕnio, ire, -vēni, -ventum (ad *with acc.*).
arrow, sagitta, *f.*
art, ars, artis, *f.*
as, or as . . . so, sicut (*with* ita *in main clause*); et . . . et.
as (as though), tanquam. (496.)
as (= while), dum. (180.)
as often as, quoties ; cum. (See 192, 434.)
as regards, or as to (= about), de (*abl.*). (332, 3.)
as to (free from care as to), ab (332, 1, *e*) ; *(from the side of, as regards),* ibid.
as to (inf.) (See 108.)
ascend the throne, I (see 17), rex fio, *or* regnum accipio.
ascertain, I, cog-nosco, ĕre, -novi, -nitum ; certior fio.
ascribe to you, I, tibi acceptum refero. (See *indebted to you.*)
ask (you), I (a question), te rogo, interrogo ; ex, abs, te quae-ro, ĕre, -sivi. (See p. 157, *note.*)
ask (you), I (request, beg), te rogo, oro, are ; abs te pet-o, ĕre, -ivi, -ii, -itum (ut). (See 127, *c.*)
ask for, I, posco, ĕre, poposci.
ask your opinion, I, te consul-o, ĕre, -ui, -tum. (248.)

aspect of affairs, the, rerum faci-es, -ei, *f.*
assailants, = those who assail (ag-gredior). (See 175.)
assassin, sicari-us, -i, *m.*
assault, I. (See *attack.*)
assemble, to (intrans.), convenire.
assembly, convent-us, -ūs, *m.*
assert, I (pretend), dictito, are.
assert, I (as a fact), affirmo, are.
assert, I would. (149, i.)
assert, I (maintain), vindico, are.
assert my country's freedom, I, patriam in libertatem vindico.
assertors of (freedom), = those who have asserted, etc. (175.)
assist, I, adjuvo, are. (245.)
assistance, I bring you, tibi opem fero.
assistance, I come to his, subvenio, ire, etc. (*dat.*).
assured, I am. (240.)
Athenians, Atheniens-es, -ium.
atone for, I, luo, ĕre ; poenas do (*gen.*).
attached to me, mei amantissimus. (302.)
attack, I (general sense), ag-gredior, -i, -gressus (*acc.*) ; *(a city or place),* oppugno, are (see 24) ; *(suddenly),* ad-orior, iri, -ortus.
attack, I (in words), in-vehor, i, -vectus, in (*acc.*).
attack, to (of a pestilence, panic), inva-dĕre, -si, -sum.
attain to, I (= arrive at), pervenio ad. (19.)
attain to, I (= obtain), adipiscor. (19.)
attempt, I, conor, ari ; id ago ut.
attempt (subst.), inceptum, *n.* ; conat-us, -ūs, *m.*
authority, potest-as, -atis. (See *influence,* note.)
avail myself of, I, utor, i, usus (*abl.*).
avail with, I am of no, nihil valeo apud. (331, 4, *d.*)
avarice, avaritia, *f.*
avert from, I, prohib-eo, ēre, -ui, -itum, ab.
avoid, I (a burden, etc.), de-fugio, ĕre, -fūgi.

avoid, I (*a danger*), vito, are.
avoid, to (= *in order not to, etc.*).
  (**101**, ii. ; cf. **109.**)
avow, I, prae me fero.
aware of, I am, or become, sen-tio,
  ire, -si, -sum.

backs, they turn their, terga dant,
  děderunt.
band, man-us, -ūs, *f.*
banish, I, civitate pello, expello ;
  in exilium pello, ěre, pepuli,
  pulsum, *or* exigo, ěre, exēgi, ex-
  actum : *banishment*, exilium, *n.*
bank, ripa, *f.*
banquet, a, epul-ae, -arum, *f.*
barbarian, a, barbar-us, -i, *m.*
barbarous, *superl. of* crudelis.
  (**57**, *a.*)
base (*adj.*), turpis.
baseness, turpitud-o,-inis, *f.* ; *the
  baseness of*, = *how base it is.*
  (**174**, *e.*)
battle, proelium, *n.*
battle, in, in acie.
bear, I, fero, ferre, tuli, latum.
beautiful, pul-cher,-chrior,-cherri-
  mus. (See Voc. 9, *n.*)
because, quia, quod, etc. (Intr.
  59, *d.*)
become, I, fio, fieri, factus.
becomes (*us*), *it*, (nos) decet (**234**) ;
  or gen. with est. (**291**, *Obs.* 4.)
befall, to, accĭ-děre, -di (*dat.*).
before (*adv.*), antea ; antehac ;
  ante (**322**) ; (*prep.*), ante (*acc.*).
before long, = *soon* or *shortly.*
beg, I, rogo, oro, etc. (See *ask.*)
begin, I, in-cipio, ěre, -cēpi, -cep-
  tum ; coepi (I *begin*) (*mostly
  modal*), coeptum est (**219**) ; *often
  expressed by imperf. tense* (**184**) ;
  begin anew, redintegro, are
  (*acc.*) ; *begin with.* (**332**. 1, *f.*)
beginning, the, initium, *n.*
behalf of, on, pro (*abl.*).
behave, I, me gero, ěre, gessi, gestum (*with adv.*). (See **241.**)
behold, I, a-spicio, ěre,-spexi,-spec-
  tum.
belief, a, opini-o, -onis, *f.*

believe, I, cred-o, ěre, -idi, -itum :
  with dat. = *I trust.* (**248.**)
belong to the class of, I, unus sum
  ex. (**529**, *f.*)
beneficial, salutaris ; utilis.
benefit you, I, tibi prosum, pro-
  desse, profui.
beseech, I, oro, are. (**118.**)
besiege, I (*blockade*), ob-sideo, ēre,
  -sedi, sessum ; (*by actual attack*),
  oppugno, are.
best, the very. (**529**, *d.*)
bestow (*these things on you*), I, haec
  tibi larg-ior, īri, -itus.
betake myself to, I, me confero ad.
betray, I, pro-do, ěre, -didi,
  -ditum ; *betrayers*, = *those who
  had betrayed.* (See **175.**)
better, for the, in melius.
better, it would have been, satius,
  melius fuit. (**153.**)
between. (**331**, 10.)
bewail, I, comploro, are.
bid, I, ju-beo, ēre, -ssi, -ssum.
  (**120.**)
bidding, at the, jussu. (**269**, *Obs.*)
Bill, a, rogati-o,-onis, *f.*
bind myself, I, me obstrin-go, ěre,
  -xi.
black (*metaph. of crime*), *simply*
  tantus ; *or* tam atrox.
blame, culpa, *f.*
blame, I, vitupero, are ; reprehen-
  do, ěre, -di, -sum.
blessing, a, bonum, *n.* (**51**, *c.*)
blind, caecus.
blockade, I. (See *besiege.*)
blood, sangui-s, -nis, *m.* ; cru-or,
  ōris, *m.* ; *so much.* (**295**, *c.*)
bloodshed, caed-es, -is, *f.*
bloody, cruentus.
blow, a (*metaph.*), calamit-as, -atis, *f.*
blunder, err-or, -oris, *m.*
blush at, or for, I, me pudet, *with
  inf.* (**202**) *or gen.* (**309**).
boast, I make a, glorior, ari.
body, the whole, universi. (**380**, *b.*)
  (See note under *all.*)
body-guard, a, satell-es, -itis, *m.*
boldly, audacter ; ferociter ; *often
  adj.* (**61**), ferox.[1]

---

[1] *Ferox* is not used in the sense of "ferocious ;" it denotes "high spirit" carried to
excess.

book, *a*, lib-er, -ri, *m.*
born, natus (nascor).
born and brought up, natus educatusque.
both, uterque ; ambo. (See **378.**)
both . . . and, et . . . et, vel . . . vel (p. 14, *n.*).
bound, *I am* (*in duty*) (p. 143, *note*).
bow to, *I* (*metaph.*), obsequor, i (*dat.*).
boy, pu-er, -eri.
boy, *from a*, or *from boyhood*, a puero ; *when used of more than one*, a pueris.
boyhood, *in.* (**63.**)
brand (*you*) *with dishonour*, *I*, ignominiae notam (tibi) in-uro, ĕre, -ussi, -ustum.
brandish, *I*, jacto, are.
brave (*adj.*), fort-is, -e ; *adv.* fortiter.
brave the worst, *I*, ultima ex-perior, iri, -pertus.
break, *I* (*metaph.*), violo, are.
break my word, *I*, fidem fallo, ĕre, fefelli, falsum.
break up, *I* (*trans.*), dissipo, are.
break up, *I* (*intrans.*), dissipor, ari.
breathing space. (**399.** *Obs.* **2.**)
bribery, ambit-us, -ūs,[1] *m.*
brigand, *a*, latr-o, -onis, *m.*
bring, *I*, duco, ĕre, duxi, ductum.
bring (*you this*), *I*, hoc tibi af-fero, ferre, attuli, allatum.
bring back word, *I*, renuntio, are.
bring (*a person*) *before you*, *I*, ad te ad-duco, ĕre, etc.
bring credit to, = *be creditable to.* (**260,** 3)
bring forward, *I* (*a law*), fero, ferre, tuli.
bring help, *I*, opem fero, ferre, etc.
bring loss on you, *I*, tibi damnum in-fero, ferre, -tuli, illatum.
bring out (*persons*), *I*, pro-duco, ĕre.
bring (*cause*) *punishment to.* (**260,** 3.)

bring (*my speech*) *to an end*, *I*, finem facio *with gen. of gerund.*
bring under, *I*, facio, *with gen. of* jus (juris), *or* arbitrium. (See **290,** *Obs.*)
bring up, *I* (*of supplies, etc.*), sub-ve-ho, ĕre, -xi, -ctum ; sup-porto, are ; *of soldiers*, adduco, ĕre.
bringer of a message, *I am the*, nuntio, are.
broad, latus.
brother, frat-er, -ris.
brought up (= *bred*), educatus (educo, are).
bugbears, terrores, *m. pl.* ; terricula, *n. pl.* (Livy).
burden (*of administering*), *use* res laboriosissima *in appos.* (**222,** *Obs.*)
burdensome, molestus ; gravis.
business, *the*, res, rei, *f.*
but, sed ; verum (*emphatic*).
butcher, *I*, trucīdo, are.
bystander, *bystanders*, *use* adsto *or* circumsto. (See **71, 73, 175.**)

calamity, calamit-as, -atis, *f.*
call away, *I*, avoco, are
call to me, *I*, ad me voco, convoco, are ; *call to mind*, *see* recall.
called, *I am*, vocor, ari. (**7.**)
calm (*adj.*), tranquillus.
calmly, aequo animo.
camp, castr-a, -orum, *n. pl.*
campaign, = *year*, ann-us, -i, *m.*
campaign was disastrous, *was prosperous*, res infeliciter (-issime), prospere, gesta est.
can, I, possum, posse, potui.
candid, liber.
candidate for, *I am a*, pet-o, ĕre, -ivi, -ii, -ītum. (**22, 23.**)
Cannae, *of*, Cannensis. (**58.**)
cannot, *I*, nequ-eo, ire, -ivi, -ii.
caprice, libid-o, -inis, *f.*
care, cura, *f.*
care, *free from*, securus.
care to, *I*, volo, velle, volui.
careful for (*your safety*), *I am*, tibi caveo. (**248.**)

---

[1] *Ambio*, lit. " I go round," or " I canvass ;" hence for illegal canvassing or bribery.

carry across, I, transporto, are. (229, *Obs.*)

carry on, I, = I *wage,* gero, ĕre, gessi, gestum.

carry out, I, exsequor ; conficio.

carry out of the country, I, exporto, are.

Carthage, C[K]arthag-o, *loc.* -ini.

case, in our, in nobis ("*in us*").

case, it is the, fit ut. (123.)

cast, I, conjicio, ĕre, etc.

catch, I, capio.

cause, a, causa, *f.*

cause (*loss*), I, infero, ferre, etc.

cause (*panic*), I, injicio, ĕre, etc., *with acc. and dat.*

cause of, I am the, per me fit ut, stat quominus. (131.)

cause to be thrown open, I. (See I *open.*)

caution, want of, temeritas, -atis, *f.*

caution, with, caut-e, -ius.

cavalry, equit-es, -um, *m. pl.*

cease, I, de-sino, ĕre, -ivi, -ii, -itum; or de-sisto, ĕre, -stiti.

certain, certus.

certain (*victory*), exploratus.

certain, as, pro certo. (240, *Obs.*)

certain, I am, certo (*adv.*) scio, -ire.

certainly (= I grant that), sane.

centre of, the. (60.)

centre (*of army*), media (60) aci-es, -ei.

centurion, centuri-o, -onis, *m.*

chain (*general term*), vinculum, *n.,* and see *fetters.*

Chance (*personified*), Fortuna, *f.*

chance, by mere, forte ac casu. (268.)

change, I (*trans.*), muto, commuto, are (see 20, 21) ; (*intrans.*), mutor, ari.

change of purpose, inconstantia, *f.*

change of sides, transĭti-o, -onis, *f.*

channel, fretum, *n.*

character, often turned (*as in Ex.* 22) *by a dependent clause.* (See 174.)

character (*natural*), ingenium,[1] *n.*

character (*good*), virt-us, -utis, *f.* (See *note.*)

character (*mode of life*), mor-es, -um, *m.* (See *note.*)

character, highest, optimi mores ; virtus summa.

character, of the same, as, talis, . . . qualis. (See 84.)

characteristic of, it is the. (291, *Obs.* 4.)

charge, a (*of troops*), impet-us, ūs, *m.*

charge, I make a, inva-do, ĕre, -si, -sum (in) ; impetum facio (in).

charged, I am (*with*), in crimen venio (*gen.*).

charm (*subst.*), dulced-o, -inis, *f.*

chastisement on, I inflict, animad-vert-o, ĕre, -i, in (*acc.*).

check, I keep in (*temper, etc.*), moderor, ari (249) ; (*troops*), con-tin-eo, ēre, -ui.

cheer, a, clam-or, -oris, *m.*

cheer, I am of good. (303, *Obs.* 2.)

cheer on, I, hortor, ari ; adhortor.

cheerful, hilaris.

cheerfully, facile.

cherish, I, tueor, ēri.

choose to, I (*or like*), mihi libet. (246.)

choose (*for*), I, e-ligo, ĕre, -legi, -lectum. (See 259, *note.*)

chief, a (*chieftain*), regul-us, -i.

chief (*chief man*), a, prin-ceps, -cipis.

child, a, pu-er, -eri.

children (*offspring*), liber-i, -orum.

circumstance, res, rei, *f.*

circumstances (*I yield to*), temp-us, -oris, *n.* (292, 7.)

citadel, arx, arcis, *f.*

city, urb-s, -is, *f.*

civilisation, I advance in, humani-or fio.

---

[1] *Ingenium* (*ingigno*), "natural gifts," mostly used of *intellectual* as *indoles* of natural *moral* gifts : *ingenium moresque* sometimes expresses the whole idea of "character" as natural and acquired by habit. *Ingenium* often = "abilities," "genius," as distinct from *indoles* or *virtus.* It is never used in the plural of a single person : once Cicero joins the two words, *summa ingenii indoles,* "the highest natural gifts." When "character" = good character, *virtus* should be used.

claim, I have a, debeo.
clamour for, I, flagito, are (*acc.*).
class, gen-us, -ĕris, *n. ; of his class,* sui generis.
clear, certus ; manifestus.
clear as, as, clari-or, -us. (**276.**)
clear, it is, appar-et, ēre, -uit (see **46,** *c*); *or* manifestum est.
clear (myself) of, I, (me) purgo, are, de (**306,** *Obs.*), *or with abl. simply.*
clemency, clementia, *f. ; adj.* clemens.
client, my, hic. (**338,** *Obs.* 1.)
Clitus, Clit-us, -i.
close (friend), superl. of amicus. (**55.**)
close, I (shut up), interclu-do, ĕre, -si, -sum.
close at hand, prope ; haud procul.
close to. (**331,** 13 *or* 19.)
closely resembling, use superl. of similis.
clothing, vestīt-us, ūs, *m.*
coast along, I, (nave) praeter-ve-hor, i, -vectus (*acc.*). *With* praetervehor, nave *and* equo *are often omitted.*
cold (subst.), frig-us, -oris, *n.*
colleague, collēga, -ae, *m.*
*collision (with), I come into,*con-fligo, ĕre, -flixi, -flictum (cum).
colony, colonia, *f.*
combination, in, conjuncti.
comfort, commoda, *n. pl.*
command (an army), I, praesum (*dat.,* **251**) ; duco.
command myself, I, mihi impero, are.
commander (of garrison, etc.), praelectus. (**408.**)
commanders (general sense), =those who lead (duco).
commencement of, initium, *n. or part. pass. of* incipio. (See **417,** i.)
commit, I (a crime), com-mitto, ĕre, etc. ; facio.
commit a fault, I, pecco, are. (**25.**)
common (belonging to many), communis ; *common to you and me,* communis tibi mecum.
commonwealth, respublica.

communicate to, I (=I impart to), communico, are, cum. (**253,** iv.)
community (civil), civit-as, -atis, *f.*
companions, his, sui. (**349,** *Obs.*)
compare, I, con-fero, ferre (cum).
compassion, misericordia, *f.*
compel, I, cogo, ĕre, coēgi, coactum.
competent, I am, =I am able.
competition for, contenti-o, -onis, *f. (with gen.,* **300**).
complain, make complaints, I, queror, i, questus ; conqueror.
compliments to, I pay, collaudo. (**25.**)
comply with, I, ob-sequor (*dat.*). (See **253,** i.)
compulsion, under, coactus (cogo).
comrades, his. (See *companions.*)
conceal, I, celo, are. (See **230.**)
concerning (prep.), de (*abl.*).
concerns, it, pertinet (**253,** iv.) ad ; *used with inf.*
condemn, I, condemno, are. (**306, 307.**)
condemnation, condemnati-o, -onis, *f.*
condign (punishment), gravissimus.
condition (lot), fortuna, *f.; (term),* conditi-o, -onis, *f.; condition of slavery.* (**58.**)
conduct myself (of soldiers), I, rem gero.
conference (with), I have a, col-lo-quor, i, -locutus, (cum).
confess, I, fateor, ēri, fassus : confiteor, ēri, -fessus.
confidence, fiducia, *f.; I put confidence in,* con-fido, ĕre, -fisus (**282,** *Obs.*) ; fidem (tibi) habeo.
confiscate, I, publico, are.
confusion, trepidati-o, -onis, *f.*
confusion reigns, etc. ; use impers. pass. of trepido, are. (See **218.**)
congratulate you on this, I, hoc (*acc.*), hanc rem, *or* ob hanc rem, *or* de hac re, tibi gratulor, ari.
conquer, I, vinco, ĕre, vici, victum.
conqueror, the, vict-or, -oris.
conscience, with a good. (See **64.**)
consciousness, sens-us, -ūs, *m.*
consent (subst.), consens-us, -ūs, *m.*
consent to, I (modal verb), volo.
consider, I, arbitror, ari. (See note under *fancy.*)

considerations, all, = *everything.*
(53, 54.)

considering, ut in (492, v. *b*):
considering the greatness of, ut in
with tantus. (332, 5, *h.*)

consist of, I, consto, are, e, ex.

consolation, is a great, magno est
solatio (*dat.*). (260, 3.)

conspire, I (against), conjuro, are
(contra) (*acc.*).

conspirator, turn by qui *with verb.*
(175.)

Constantinople, Constantinopolis,
acc. -im, *loc.* -i.

constantly, semper *or* nunquam non.

constitution, the, respublica. (See
292, *Obs. and note.*)

constitutional ; unconstitutional, e
republica (332, 4) ; contra rempublicam.

consul, cons-ul, -ulis.

consulship, consulat-us, -ūs, *m.*

consult, I (= *I ask the opinion of*),
consul-o, ĕre, -ui, -tum (*with acc.*).

consult the good or interest of, I,
consulo, *with dat.* (See 248.)

consummate. (See *statesman.*)

contemporary, a, aequalis. (51, *a.*)

contempt for, contemptus, -ūs, *m.*
(*with gen.,* 300.)

contemptible, far from, haud (169,
n.) contemnendus (393).

content with, I am, contentus sum
(*abl.*).

contest, a, certam-en, inis, *n.* ; or
use impers. pass. of certo, are.
(218.)

continent, the, continen-s, -tis (*sc.*
terra).

contrary (adj.), contrarius.

contrary to, contra quam. (491, *b.*)

convenience, commoda, *n. pl.*

conversation, I have, col-loquor, i,
-locutus.

converse (with), I, colloquor, i (cum)
(*of two or more,* inter se, 354).

convinced, I am, = *I am persuaded.*
(See 122, *b.*)

convinced of this, I am, or *feel,* hoc
mihi persuasum habeo. (240.)

corn, frumentum, *n.*

Cortes, Cortesi-us, -i.

cost, I, consto (280, *Obs.*) ; *costs too
much, it,* nimio constat.

council, a, consilium, *n.*

count, I (number), numero, are.

count, I (= *I hold*), habeo ; duco.

count among, I. (240, *Obs. 2.*)

countenance, vult-us, ūs, *m.*

country (one's), patria, *f.* (see 16,
a) ; (*the*), respublica.

country (territory), fin-es, -ium, *m.*
(See 16, *a.*)

country (as distinct from the town),
rus, ruris, *n.* (see 16, *a*) ; *in the
country,* ruri.

countryman, civ-is, -is.

courage, virt-us, -utis, *f.* ; constantia, *f.* ; fortitud-o, -inis, *f.*

courage, a man of. (58, *Obs.*)

courage, I show. (241.)

courage to, I have the, = *I venture* (25) ; audeo, ere, ausus.

course, I take this, haec facio ; hanc
rationem ineo.

course which, a, id quod. (67.)

court, the, judicium, *n.*

cover, I (with armies or fleets), infestum habeo. (240.)

coward, timidus, ignavus ; *cowards,*
ignavi.

cowardice, ignavia, *f.* ; timidit-as,
-atis, *f.*

cowardly, ignavus ; timidus.

crave for, I, desidero, are (*acc.*)
(*mostly for what I have had and
have lost*) ; *in Ex.* 48 B *use*
appeto, ĕre.

craving (partic.) for, appetens (*with
gen.*). (302.)

credible, it is scarcely, vix credi
potest. (200, *Obs.*)

credit, a, or *creditable, it is.* (260, 3.)

crime, a, facin-us, -oris, *n.* ; flagitium, *n.* ; scelus,[1] -eris, *n.* ; delictum, *n.* (See *note.*)

---

[1] *Scelus,* a crime ; offence against a fellow-creature, ἀδίκημα ; also the guilt which causes overt crimes, ἀδικία ; *vitium,* a fault, that which marks imperfection ; *peccatum,* a sin or offence which deserves blame or punishment ; *delictum,* an omission, or contravention, of some duty ; *flagitium,* a crime as a breach of duty towards oneself ; *facinus,* an act of heinous crime (sometimes a great exploit) ; *nequitia,* wickedness in the sense of "worthlessness.'

criminal, sceleratus.
criminally, nefarie.
crisis, a, discrim-en, -inis, *n.* ;
　temp-us, oris, *n.*
critical moment (such a), use simply
　tempus, *or* occasio.
cross, I, trajicio, ĕre.
crowd, a, multitud-o, -inis, *f.*
crowd, to (intrans.), congregari.
crowds, in. (**61.**)
crown (kingly), regnum, *n.* (See **17.**)
crown (circlet), corona, *f.*
cruel, crudelis, e.
cruelly, crudel-iter, -ius, -issime.
cruelty, crudelit-as, -atis, *f.* ; *I show*,
　saev-io, ire, -ii, itum.
crush, I, op-primo, ĕre, -pressi,
　-pressum ; *crushed (pass. part.)*,
　oppressus.
crushing (calamity), use tantus *or*
　tantus tamque gravis.
cry, I raise a, conclamo, are.
cultivated, to be (= sought for),
　expetendus.
custom, a, mos, moris, *m.*
cut off, I (destroy), ab-sumo, ĕre, etc.
cut off (destroyed), I am, intereo, ire.

dagger, pugi-o, -onis, *m.*
daily, quotidie ; *with comparatives*
　and certain verbs, in dies. (See
　328, c.)
danger, periculum, *n.*
danger was (of), the. (**138.**)
dangerous, periculosus.
Danube, the, Danubius, *m.*
dare, see *venture: daring (adj.)*,
　audax.
daringly, audacit(act)-er, -ius.
dark (metaph. applied to crime),
　atrox.
dark, I keep you in the, te celo, are
　(*acc.*, **230**, *or* de ; **231**).
darkness, tenebrae, *f. pl.*
dart, a, jaculum, *n.* ; telum, *n.*
dash (of), a, non nihil. (**294.**)
dash into, I, me im-mitto, ĕre, -misi, *in.*
dash over, I (intrans., see **20, 21**),
　in-fundor, i, -fusus (*dat.*).
date, temp-us, -oris, *n.*

day, di-es, -ei, *m.*
day after day. (**328, c.**)
day before, the, pridie.
day before, of the, hesternus.
day, for the, in diem.
day, in my, = *in my time (pl.).*
daybreak, prima lux (lucis).
deadly (hostile), infensus.
deadly (enemy). (See **55.**)
dear, car-us, -ior, -issimus.
dear friends, homines amicissimi.
　(**224,** *Obs.* 2.)
death, mor-s, -tis, *f.* ; *after his.* (**61.**)
debt, aes alienum ; *gen.* aeris
　alieni, *n.*
deceive, I, decipio, ĕre.
decide (resolve), to, or on, I, statuo ;
　constituo. (**45.**)
decide (pass judgment), I, or *I*
　decide on (a fact), judico, are.
decide (let others, etc.) (**146.**)
decision, I come to a, decerno, ĕre.
decision, depends on my. (**292, 9.**)
declare (war), I, indi-co, ĕre, -xi,
　-ctum. (**253, ii.**)
decline, I (trans.), detrecto, are.
decline (to), I (modal), nolo.
decree, I, de-cerno, ĕre, -crēvi,
　-cretum.
decree, a, decretum, *n.* (See **51, b.**)
deed. (See **51, b.**)
deep (of feelings), gravis.
deeper (impression). See *impression.*
defeat, clad-es, -is, *f.* ; *of Cannae,*
　Cannensis (*adj.*, **58**).
defend, I, defen-do, ĕre, -di, -sum.
defendant, the, iste. (**338,** *Obs.*)
defiance of, in, contra, contra quam.
　(**491,** *b.*)
defile, a, salt-us, -ūs, *m.*
degrading, indignus (*unmerited*) ;
　humilis (*abject*).
delay (to), I, cunctor, ari.
delay, by, gerund of cunctor. (**99.**)
delay, without, confestim.
deliberate, I, delibero, are.
deliberation, need of. (**286.**)
deliberation, with, consult-o, -ius
　(*adv.*).
delightful, jucundus.[1]

---

[1] *Jucundus (juvicundus)*, that which causes joy or delight ; *gratus*, what s acceptable, deserves gratitude ; *ista veritas etiamsi jucunda non est, mihi tamen grata est.* —
(Cicero.)

demand, I, postulo,[1] are. (**127,** c.)

demand (exact) this from you, I, hoc tibi impero, are.

demeanour, habit-us, -ūs, *m.* (*sc.* corporis).

denied this, I am. hoc (*abl.*) careo, ēre.

denounce, I (upbraid), in-crepo, are, -crepui.*

deny, I, nego, are.

depart, I (= go away), ab-eo, ire, -ii ; dis-cedo, ēre, -cessi.

departure, I take my. (**25.**)

depend on, I, pendeo, ēre, e, ex.

depends on you, this. (**331,** 15.)

deplore, I, deploro, are.

deprecate, I, deprecor, ari.

deprive of, I, privo, are (**264**) : ad-imo, ēre, -emi, -emptum (**243**).

depth of, of the, use gen. (**318,** end.)

depth of, such a, use tantus ; *or eo with gen.* (**294,** *Obs.*)

descend, I, descend-o, ēre, -i.

desert, I, deser-o, ēre, -ui, -tum ; destitu-o, ēre, -i. (See note under *abandon.*)

deserter, transfūg-a, ae, *m.*

desertion, use desero, ēre. (**417,** i.)

deserts, in accordance with his. (**490,** ii. 3.)

deserve, I, mereor, meritus ; *also* mere-o, ēre, -ui.

deserve well of, I. (**332,** 3, *g.*)

deservedly, merito.

deserving of, dignus. (**285.**)

design (subst.), consilium, *n.* ; *by design,* or *designedly (abl.)* (**268**) ; consulto (*adv.*).

desire, I, am desirous to, cupio, ēre, ivi (ii) ; studeo, ēre (*inf.*).

desire (subst.), = that which (you) desire. (**76.**)

desire for, with little, parum appetens (*with gen.,* **302**).

despair, I, despero, are ; *of,* de (*abl.*).

despatch, a, litterae, *f. pl.*

desperately, atro-citer, -cius.

despicable. (See **276.**)

despise, I, contem-no, ēre, -psi, -ptum : de-spicio, ēre, -spexi, -spectum. (See Voc. 10, *note.*)

despot, domin-us, -i.

despotism. dominium, *n.*

destitution, egest-as, -atis, *f.*

destined, fatalis, e (see Voc. 3. n.) ; *for* or *to,* ad. (**331,** 1. *e.*)

destiny, fatum, *n.*

destroy, I, exsci-ndo, ēre, -di, -ssum.

destruction (general sense), exitium, *n.* ; pernici-es, -ei, *f.* ; (*massacre*), interneci-o,- onis, *f.*

destruction of (tends to the). (See . 292, *Obs.*)

detach (troops), I, = I send.

detain, I, re-tineo, ēre, -tinui.

determine on, I, decerno, ēre (*inf.*, **45**).

detraction, obtrectati-o, -onis, *f.*

detrimental, it is. (**260,** 3.)

devastate, I, vasto, are.

devote myself to, I, operam do (*dat.*): or (*stronger*), in-cumbo, ēre, -cubui, in. (**253,** iv.)

devoted to, studiosus (*gen.,* **301,** ii.).

dictate terms to you, I, leges tibi impono.

dictator, dictat-or, -oris.

die, I, mor-ior, -i (-tuus est), vitā excessit. (See Voc. 7, *note.*)

die out of, to (metaphor), ex-cīdĕre, -cīdi, e, ex.

difference between, there is this (**331.** 10); *there is all the.* (**92.**)

difference, it makes no, nihil interest (**166**); *to us,* nostrā (**310,** i.).

different, alius ; *to,* ac. (**91** ; see also **92,** and **370, 371.**)

different times, at, alius alio tempore. (**371.**)

differently to, aliter ac. (**491,** b.)

difficult, difficilis.

difficulty in persuading, I find a, = *I persuade this* (illud) *with difficulty* (aegre).

difficulty, with, aegre ; vix ; difficulter, *comp.* difficilius.

din, strepit-us, -ūs, *m.*

dire, use tantus.

directions, in both, utrimque ; *in different, opposite,* diversi. (**61** ; and see also **371,** and *caution.*)

---

[1] *Posco,* I " call for," make a sharp, peremptory demand ; often used of what is unjust *postulo.* I claim in accordance with, or as though in accordance with, what is right.

disaffected, I am, male sentio.

disagree with, I, dissen-tio, ire, -si ab *or* cum.

disagreement on, dissensi-o, -onis, *f.* (*with gen.*, **300**).

disappear, I (=*I am destroyed*), ex-tinguor, i, -tinctus.

disappoint, I. (**332, 3,** *b.*)

disapproval (*expressed by clamour*), acclamo,[1] are. (**415,** *b.*)

disaster, cas-us,[2] -us, *m.*; calamit-as, -atis, *f.*

disastrous, most, use the adv., infeliciter, -issime. (**218,** *Obs.*)

discharge the duties of, I, fung-or, i, -ctus. (**281.**)

discipline, disciplina, *f.*

discontinue, I, inter-mitto, ĕre, misi. (*See note under undone, I leave.*)

discussion, by, in, gerund of dissero, ĕre. (**99.**)

disdain to, I, dedignor, ari.

disease, a, morbus, i, *m.*

disembark, I. (**331, 24,** *a.*)

disgrace, ignominia, *f.*

disgraceful, turpis, e. (See **57.**)

disgraceful, it is. (**260, 3,** and *Obs.* 1.)

disheartened, I am. (See **118,** *example.*)

dishonour (*subst.*), ignominia, *f.*

dishonourable, inhonest-us; *adv.*, -e.

dishonourable, it is. (**260, 3.**)

dislike, I somewhat, haud multum amo.

disloyal, infidus.

dismayed, I am, perterreor, ēri.

dismiss, I, dimitto, ere.

dispense with, I, careo, ĕre (**284**); *or* carere volo.

disperse, to (*intrans.*), di-labi, -lapsus. (See **20.**)

displease, I, displiceo, ēre (*dat.*).

disposed to (*a quality*), *use comparative of adj.* (**57,** *b.*)

dissatisfied with oneself, one is, sui poenitet.

dissemble, I (=*I hide*), dissimulo, are.

distance, from a, e longinquo.

distance from, I am at a, absum. (**318.**)

distant, longinquus.

distasteful, ingratus.

distinction (*mark of difference*), discrim-en, -inis, *n.*

distinction (*honourable*), hon-os, -oris, *m.*

distinguished (*adj.*), praeclarus (*sup.*, **224**).

district, ag-er, -ri, *m.*

distrust, I, dif-fido, ĕre, -fisus. (**244,** *c.*)

ditch, fossa, *f.*

divine, divinus.

do, I, facio, ĕre, feci, factum.

doer, the, = *he who committed,* facio, committo.

doom, fatum, *n.*

doomed to, I am, destīnor, ari, *with dat. or* ad.

doors, for-es, -um, *f.*

Doria, Doria, *f.*

doubt, I am in (=*I doubt*), dubito, are.

down from, de (*abl.*).

down-trodden, afflictus.

drag (*to prison*), *I,* tra-ho, ĕre, -xi, -ctum, in.

draw, I (=*I drag*), traho, ĕre.

draw up, I (*a law*), scribo.

draw up, I (*soldiers*), instru-o, ĕre, -xi, -ctum.

dread, I, reformido, are.

dreadful, atrox.

dress, vest-is, -is, *f.* (**303,** *Obs.* 2.)

drive from, I, ex-igo, ĕre, -ēgi, -actum; pello, ĕre, pepuli, pulsum.

drive on shore, to, ejicĕre, ejēci, ejectum.

drowned (*metaph. of words*). (**332, 6,** *b.*)

dull, I, hebĕto, are; afficio.

duration (*its future*), = *how lasting* (diuturnus) *it will, or would, be.* (**174.**)

duty, it is my, debeo. (**198.**)

duty of, it is the, use gen. (**291.**)

---

[1] *Acclamo* always in Cicero of disapproval; in later writers, of approval.

[2] *Casus,* properly an accident, that which *falls* out, is mostly used in a bad sense, as misfortune or disaster; but is not so strong a word as *calamitas.*

duty (as opposed to expediency), honest-as, -atis, *f.* ; *or* honesta, *n. pl.* (51, *c*)

dwelling, domicilium, *n.*

each and every, unus quisque. (529, *c.*)

each other, one another, alius alium ; *of two,* alter alterum (see 371, iv.) ; inter se (354).

eager for, cupidus (*gen.,* 301, i.).

eager to, I am, gest-io, ire, -ii.

early manhood. (See *manhood.*)

earlier (adv.), maturius.

earlier than (=*before*), ante. (331, 3.)

earliest, =*first.*

earnestly, magnopere.

earnestly implore, I, oro atque obsecro (127, *a*). *Notice double phrase equivalent to English ad- verb.*

ears, with my own. (355. *d.*)

earth, the, tell-us, -uris, *f.*

easy, facilis.

easily (readily), facile ; nullo ne- gotio (*without effort*).

echo with, to, person-are, -ui (*abl.*).

effect, I, efficio, ĕre.

effect on, I have but little, parum valeo apud.

eight, octo (*indecl.*).

eighteenth. (530.)

either . . . or, aut . . . aut : vel . . . vel (p. 14, *note*).

elected, I am, fi-o, -ĕri, factus.

eloquence, eloquentia, *f.*

else, or, aut (p. 14, *n.*).

embark, I (intrans.), navem con- scend-o, ĕre, -i.

emergency, temp-us, -oris, *n.; in the present,* see, for *in,* 273, *Obs.,* and for *present,* 337.

emotion, with, commot-e, -ius.

Emperor, Imperat-or, -oris.

empire, imperium, *n.*

empty, inanis.

enacted, I get (a law), per-fero, -ferre, -tuli.

encamp, I, castra pono, ĕre.

encourage, I, co-, *or* ad-hortor, ari (*acc. and* ut, 118).

encouragement, words of, adhor- tantis vox. (415, *c.*)

encounter, I (death), oppeto, ere, -ii, -ivi, -itum ; *evil,* exper-ior, iri, -tus.

end, fin-is, -is, *m.* (*rarely f.*).

endanger, I, periclitor, ari (*dep.*).

endeavour, I, conor, ari.

endure, I, per-fero, ferre, -tuli.

enemy (private), inimicus.

enemy (public), host-is, -is.

energy, with some want of, paulo (279) remissius.

engage (an enemy), I, con-gredior, i, -gressus, cum.

engage in, I (= *I take part in*), intersum 251) ; *in battle,* prae- lium committo, ĕre ; *in conflict,* manus conser-o, ĕre, -ui, -tum.

England (the people), Angli. (See 319.)

engrafted, insitivus.

enjoy, I, fru-or, i, -etus (281) ; *the friendship of,* amico utor (282) ; *praise, etc.,* flor-eo, ĕre, -ui (*abl.*).

enjoy happiness, I, beatus sum.

enmity, inimicitia, *f.*

enormity, flagitium, *n.* (See note under *crime.*)

enormous, such, tantus.

enough and to spare, satis super- que (*with gen.,* 294).

entail this upon you, I, hoc tibi in- or af-fero. (252.)

enter, I, in-gredior, i, -gressus ; venio, ire, in.

enter political life, I. (See *politi- cal life.*)

enterprise. (See 54.)

enthusiasm, alacrit-as, atis, *f.*

entire innocence. (See *innocence.*)

entirely, totus (*with verbs,* 61) ; *for adjs., use superl.*

entreat, I, oro, are. (127, *a.*)

entreat for, earnestly, I, flagito, are. (127, *d.*)

entreaty, obsecrati-o, -onis, *f*

entrust, I. (See *intrust.*)

enumerate, I, enumero, are.

envoy (embassy), legati-o, -onis, *f.*

envy, I, in-video, ēre, -vidi, -visum (*dat.*). (See 5.)

equal to, use tantus . . . quantus. (490, i.)

err, I, erro, errare.

error, err-or, -oris, *m. ; or* errare.[1]
(94, 99.)

escape, *I*, ef-fugio, ĕre, -fūgi.

establish, *I*, stabil-io, ire, -īvi.

estimate, *I*, aestimo, are.   (305.)

eternal, sempiternus.

evade (*shirk*), *I*, subterfugio, ĕre
(*acc.*) ; *a law*, legi fraudem facio.

even, etiam ; quoque (*enclitic*) ;
before adj., vel ; *not even*, ne . . .
quidem. (Intr. 99.)

even now (*i.e. at the present time*),
hodie.

evening, *in the*, vesperi.

events, *at all*, certe.   (See note
under *least*, *at.*)

ever (*always*), semper ; *with negat.*
(= *at any time*), unquam.

every (= *all*, *pl.*), omnis ; *everything*, omnia, *n. pl.*   (53.)

evident, *it was*, (satis) apparebat.
(46, *c.*)

evil, *an*, incommodum, *n.* ; malum,
n.   (51, *b*

exact from, *I* (*make requisition of*),
impero, are.   (247.)

exact (*punishment*), *I*, sum-o, ĕre,
-psi, ab, de *or* ex.

exasperate, *I*, irrīto, are.

excellent, optimus, a, um (see 57,
a) ; *for use with proper noun or
person see* 224.

except to, nisi ut.

exception, *without*, = *all.*

excessive, nimius.

exchange for, *I*, muto, are ; per-
muto, are.   (See 280.)

exclaim, *I*, ex- *or* con-clamo, are.

execrable (*by*), *considered*, execra-
bilis (*with dat.*).

execution (*punishment*), supplicium,
n.

exertion, *I make* (*some*), (paulum)
ad-nitor, i, -nisus.

exertions, = *toils.*

exhausted, fatigatus ; confectus ; *I
am*, *or become*, fatigor, ari.

exhort, *I*, hortor, ari.   (118.)

exile, *an*, ex-ul, -ulis.

exile, *I am driven into*, in exilium
pellor. (See *banish.*)

exile, *I am in*, or *I endure*, exŭlo,
are.

exist, *I*, sum, esse, fui. (Intr. 49, *Obs.*)

existence, *use* sum (*no Latin subst.*) ;
est Deus = *God exists.*

expect, *I*, expecto, are.

expedient, utilis.

expediency, utilit-as, -atis, *f.*

experience, *I*, exper-ior, iri, -tus.

experience of life, rerum peritia, *f.*

experienced (*adj.*), (rerum) peritus.
(301, ii.)

explain, *I*, expono, ĕre, etc.

exploit, res gesta.

expose, *I* (*to danger, etc.*), ob-jicio,
ĕre.   (253, ii.)

expose, *I* (*confute*), coargu-o, ĕre, -i.

express myself, *to*, ut dicam.   (100,
note.)

extent.   (174, *b.*)

extortion, res repetundae, *f. pl.*

extreme, extremus.

extremely, *use superl. of adj.*

extremity of, extremus (*adj.*).   (60.)

exult in, *I*, exulto, are (*abl.*).

eye, ocul-us, -i, *m.*

eyes, *with my own*, ipse (355, *d*) ;
before our (332, 5, *c*).

face, *I* (*meet*), obviam eo, ire
(*dat.*).

face, *I* (*put to the proof*), ex-perior,
iri, -pertus.

face, faci-es, ei, *f. ; in the face of*,
in (*with abl.*, 273, *Obs.*)

fact, *a*, res, rei, *f.*

faction, *a*, facti-o, -onis, *f.*

fail, *I* (*am wanting to*), deficio, ĕre
(*used absolutely or with acc.*) ;
desum (*dat.*, 251).   (See note
under *abandon.*)

fain, *I would; or I would fain have
(done)*, velim, vellem. (See 149, i.)

fair (*adj.*), pulcher ; amoenus.
(Voc. 9, *note.*)

fair (= *fair amount of*), satis.
(294.)

faith, *good*, fid-es, -ei, *f.*

faith in you, *I put*, fidem tibi
habeo.

faithful, fidelis, e.

---

[1] *Errare*, error generally, in the abstract ; *error*, an error or blunder.

fall, I (*in battle*), pereo, ire, ii.

fall into, I, in-cido, ĕre, -cĭdi, in (*acc.*) ; *or* praecipito, are (*fall headlong*) ; *into ruin,* corru-o, ĕre, -i.

fallen, afflictus.

falls out, it, accĭdit ut.

falls to (*my*) *lot.* (See *lot.*)

false (*of persons*), mend-ax, -acis ; (*of things*), falsus ; fictus.

false to, I am, de-sum (*dat.,* 251). (See note under *abandon.*)

falsehood, a, mendacium, *n.*

falsehood (*abstract*), mentiri. (98, *a.*)

falsehood, I tell a ; I speak falsely, ment-ior, iri, -itus. (54.)

fame, gloria, *f.*

family, familia, *f. ; his family,* sui. (349, *Obs.*)

family (*adj.*), domesticus.

famine, fam-es, -is, *f.*

famous, praeclarus. (19.)

fancy, I, puto,[1] are ; opĭnor, ari.

far, by, multo. (279.)

far from (*adv.*), parum.

far removed from, alienus (*superl.*) ab.

fare (*subst.*), vict-us, -ūs, *m.*

fare, I, mihi evĕnit (*impers.*).

farmhouse, villa, *f.*

fatal, pernicios-us, -issimus ; funestus. (Voc. 3, *note.*)

Fate, Fortuna (*personified*).

father, pat-er, -ris.

fatigue, lassitud-o, -inis, *f.*

fault, culpa, *f.*

fault, I commit a, pecco, are. (25.)

favour (*kindness*), *a,* beneficium, *n.*

favour, I, făveo, ēre, făvi, fautum (*dat.,* 5).

favour, I do you this, hoc (*acc.,* 237) tibi gratificor, ari.

favour, I win your, apud te gratiam ineo, ire.

favourable (*suitable*), idoneus.

fawn upon, I, adulor, ari. (253, iii.)

fear, met-us, -ūs, *m.* ; tim-or, -oris, *m.*

fear, I,[2] metu-o, ĕre, -i ; vereor, ēri, verĭtus (see 138, 139) ; *I fear, or have fears, for,* metuo *with dat.* (248).

fear for my safety, I, saluti meae dif-fido, ĕre, -fisus.

feasting (*subst.*), epulae, *f. pl.*

features, vult-us, -ūs (*sing.*).

feel, I, sen-tio, ire, -si, -sum.

feelings, anim-us, -i, *m.*

fellow-subject, civ-is, -is, *m.*

ferocity (*of an act*), atrocit-as, -atis, *f.*

fertile, fertilis, e.

fetters, catenae, *f. pl.*

few, pauci, ae, a ; perpauci (*very few*).

fickle, lĕvis.

fictitious, fictus.

field of battle, aci-es,[3] -ei, *f.*

field, in the (*in war*), militiae, *opposed to* domi. (312.)

fiercely (*boldly*), ferociter ; acriter.

fifth, quintus.

fight, I, pugno, are ; *a battle,* praelium com-mitto, ĕre, -misi, -missum.

fill with (*panic*), *I,* in-cutio, ĕre, -cussi, -cussum. (Ex. 53, note.)

find, I, reper-io, ire, -i, -tum (*by search*) ; in-venio, ire, -vēni, -ventum (*by chance*).

find fault with, I, vitupero, are.

fine, pulcher. (Voc. 9, *note.*)

finish, I, con-ficio, ĕre, -feci, -fectum.

fire and sword, ferrum et ign-is (*abl.* -i). (See Voc. 1, *note.*)

firm, constans.

first (*adv.*); *first . . . then ; first . . . secondly, etc.* (534, and *Obs.*)

---

[1] *Puto,* "I incline to think," "I fancy," "I suspect," I think without having as yet any full clearly reasoned grounds for thinking ; *opinor,* "I conjecture," with still less clear grounds ; *reor,* rather "I calculate." "I come to a conclusion ; "*arbitror,* I form my own personal judgment ; *censeo,* I form and express a clear view or judgment.

[2] *Timere,* the feeling of fear, causing a wish to fly ; *metuĕre,* the sense of danger, causing us to take precautions ; *verēri,* often, to look on with respect or awe.

[3] *Acies,* the *edge* or *line* of battle, often answers to the English "field," or even "battle."

first of June, the, kalendae Juniae (538) ; *by the* (326).
first to, first who. (62.)
five, quinque.
fix (my eyes) on, I, defi-go, ĕre, -xi, -xum, in (*acc.*).
flag, signum, *n.*
flank, a, lat-us, -ĕris, *n. ; in.* (332, 1, c.)
flatter, I, assentor, ari. (253, i.)
fleet, a, class-is, -is, *f.*
flight, fuga, *f.*
fling away, I, pro- or ab-jicio, ĕre, -jeci, -jectum.
flock (subst.), grex, gregis, *m*
flock together, to, congregari.
flourishing, opulentus (*use superl.,* 57, a).
flow down. I, de-fluo, ĕre, -fluxi.
fly, I, fugio, ĕre, fūgi.
foe, host-is, -is, *m.*
follow, I, sequor, i, secutus ; *follow up,* insector, ari (*acc.*).
follow that, it does not, non idcirco.
folly, stultitia, *f. ; or use adj.* stultus. (376.)
food, vict-us, ūs, *m.*
food, I get (of soldiers), frumentor, ari.
food, I take, cibum capio.
food, want of, inedia, *f.*
foolish, insipiens ; *it is foolish.* (291, Obs. 1.)
foot of (a mountain) īmus. (60.)
foot-soldier, ped-es, itis.
for (prep.), pro. (See 6 and 332, 7, b.)
for (conj.), nam ; enim (Intr. 98) ; quippe. (See also Intr. 56, e.)
for some time (past), jamdudum. (181.)
forage, I get, pabulor, ari.
force, vis, *f.* (*abl.* vi).
force of arms, by, vi et armis.
force from, I, deturbo, are, de (*abl.*) : *force out of* (=*wrench from*), extor-queo, ĕre, -si, -tum. (257.)
forces (troops), copiae, *f. pl.*
forefathers, major-es, -um. (See Voc. 2, *n.*, and p. 63, *note* 5.)
foreign, externus.
foreigner, a (opposed to civis), peregrin-us, -i, *m*
foremost, primus.

foresee, I, praesentio ; pro-spicio, ĕre, -spexi, -spectum, pro-video, -vidi, -visum. (248.)
forest, a, silva, *f.*
foretell, I, praedī-co, ĕre, -xi, -ctum ; praesagio, ire.
forget, I, obliviscor, i, oblītus (*gen.,* 308).
forgive, I, ignosco, ĕre, -novi, -notum (*dat.,* see 5) ; veniam do (*dat. of person, gen. of thing*) ; or condono, are (*dat. of person, acc. of thing*).
forgotten, I become, or I am, in oblivionem vĕnio, ire, vēni.
form line (of battle), I, aciem instruo, ĕre, -xi, -ctum.
former, pristinus (see note under *ancient*), *often joined with* ille. (339, i.)
formidable, formidandus (393) ; *comp.* magis formidandus.
fortress, arx, arcis, *f.*
fortunate, fel-ix, -īcis.
fortunate, it was most, peroppor-tune accidit ut. (123.)
fortune, fortuna, *f. ; fortunes,* for-tunae, *pl.*
fortune, good, felicit-as, -atis. *f.*
Fortune's favourites. (529, *f.*)
foul, foedus.
foully, nefarie.
found, I (a colony), de-duco, ĕre, -duxi, -ductum.
fourteen, quattuordecim.
fourth, quartus.
free (adj.), liber, a, um ; *free from,* vacuus (265) ; *free from blame,* extra culpam (331, 9) ; *free from care,* securus (19).
free, I ; I give freedom to ; or I set at liberty (from), libero, are, ab or *abl.* (264) ; *freed from, I am,* liberor, ari, etc.
freedom, libert-as, -atis, *f.*
freedom, in, liber. (61.)
fresh, recens.
friend, amic-us, -i (51 a, and 55, 256) ; *close friend,* amicissimus.
friend here, my ; your friend there. (338, Obs. 1 and 2.)
friend, I make my, amicorum in numero habeo. (240, Obs. 2.)

friendliness, benevolentia, *f.*

friendship, amicitia, *f.* ; *friendship of*, *I enjoy the*, amico utor. (282.)

from, a, ab (*abl.*). (332, 1.)

front, in, a fronte (332, 1, *c*); adversus, *adj* (see 61) ; *in the front of* (=*before*), ante (331, 3).

fuel, I add (*metaph.*), faces subjicio, ĕre (*dat.*)

fugitives, use pres. part. of fugio.

full (= *the whole of*), totus. (60.)

full of, plenus (*abl.*).

funds, pecuniae, *f. pl.*

funeral, fun-us, -eris, *n.*

further, ultra.

jury, ira, *f.*, *not* furor. (Voc. 6, *note ;* see also Ex. 62, *note.*)

fury, with the utmost, vehementissime.

future, the, futura, *n. pl.* (52, 408.)

future, in, or *for, the*, in futurum ; in posterum. (331, 24, *b.*)

gain, emolumentum, *n.* ; utilit-as, -atis, *f.* ; (*for*) *a source of gain*, quaestui. (260, 3.)

gain by, I, = *it is profitable to me.* (260, 3.)

gained, partus (pario, peperi, *I produce*).

gallant, fortis (*superl.*) ; for usage with *proper noun* or *word denoting a person*, see **224.**

gallantly, fortiter.

gallop, at full, equo concitato.

games, the, ludi, *m. pl.*

garrison, praesidium, *n.*

gate, porta, *f.*

gather (*together*), *to* (*intrans.*), convĕnire, -vēni, -ventum ; congregari. (20.)

Gauls, the, Gall-i, -orum.

gaze on, I, intu-eor, -ēri.

general, a, dux, ducis.

general (*adj.*), = *of all.* (59.)

generally (*believed*), = *by most men.*

generation, a, aet-as, -atis, *f.*

Genoa, Genua, *f.*

gentle, mitis ; mitissimi ingenii (303, i.); *so gentle as* (224, *Obs.* 2).

gentlemen of the jury, judices.

gentleness, lenit-as, -atis, *f. ; I show*

gentleness (241) ; *such*, tam *or* adeo mitis, etc.

gently, leniter.

German, a, German-us, -i.

Germany, Germania, *f.*

gesture, gest-us, -ūs, *m.*

get over (*danger*), *I*, fungor, i, -ctus, *or* defungor. (281.)

get ready for, I, me paro, are, ad *with gerund.* (396.)

get to, I. (See *I reach.*)

give, I, do, dăre, dĕdi, dătum ; *a verdict*, sententiam dico, ĕre : *a name*, nomen in-do, ere, -didi, -ditum : *my word* (*formally*), fidem interpono, ĕre.

gladly, libenter ; *or use adj.*, libens. (61.)

globe, the, orbis terrarum, *m.*

glorious, praeclarus.

glory, gloria, *f.*

gluttony, gula, *f.* (*lit. the gullet*).

go away, I, ab-eo, ire, -ii, -iturus.

go down to meet, I, obviam (*dat.*) descend-o, ĕre, -i.

go out, I, ex-cedo, ĕre, -cessi ; exeo, ire, -ivi, -ii (*abl. with* or *without*, e, ex).

God, De-us, -i, *nom. pl.* Di.

gold, of, aureus.

good fortune, I enjoy, felix sum.

good name, existimati-o, -onis, *f.*; fama, *f.*

good old times. (339, i.)

good sense, prudentia, *f.*

good-will, benevolentia, *f.*

goodness, virt-us, -utis, *f.*

gossip, rumusculi, *m. pl.* (*diminutive of contempt*).

govern, I, praesum. (251.)

government, the. (175.)

governor (*of city*), praefect-us, -i.

gradually, paulatim.

grandfather, av-us, -i.

grandson, nepo-s, -tis.

gratitude, I show, gratiam re-fero, -ttuli ; *I feel*, habeo. (98. *b.*)

grateful, gratus ; *I am most grateful*, maximam habeo gratiam. (98, *b.*)

great, magnus, *comp.* major, *superl.* maximus ; *great men*, summi viri ; viri praestantissimi.

greater (= *more of*), plus. (294.)

greatly, magnopere ; vehementer ; maxime ; *with comparatives*, multo. (279.)

greatness of (your) debt = *how much (you) owe* (debeo). (174.)

Greeks, the, Graec-i, -orum.

greet, I, saluto, are.

groans (angry), convīcium, *n.* (*sing.*).

ground, on the, humi. (312.)

ground, perilous, on which they stood, tale tempus ; tantum periculum. (See Ex. 62, *note.*)

groundless, falsus.

grounds (= *reason*), causa, *f.; on grounds of*, propter. (331, 19, *b.*)

grow, I, = *become.*

grudge against you, I have a, tibi succens-eo, ēre, -ui.

guard, a, custo-s, -dis, *m.*

guard, off his, incautus. (61.)

guard, I, custod-io, ire, -ivi, -ii, -itum ; *guard against*, caveo, ēre, cavi, cautum. (248.)

guest, a, hosp-es, -itis.

guide, dux, ducis.

guilt, scel-us, -eris, *n.* (See note under *crime.*)

guilty, nocen-s, -tis.

guilty deed, a, facin-us, -oris, *n.* (See note under *crime.*)

guilty, I find, condemno, are; *I am found*, condemnor.

guilty of, I am (not), (non) id committo ut.

habit of, I am in the, soleo, ēre, solitus (*inf.*).

hackneyed, tritus, *lit.* "*well worn*" (tero).

hair, white, cani capilli (*pl.*).

half as many, large, again. (535, *d.*)

halt, I, or come to a halt, con sisto, ēre, -stiti.

hand, a, man-us, -ūs, *f.*

hand, I am at, ad-sum, -esse, -fui.

hand in, I, af-fero, ferre.

hand over to, I, per-mitto, ēre, -misi. (128.)

handful of = *so small a band of.*

hang back, I, cesso,[1] arc.

happens, it, accidit, ēre. (123.)

happily (see 64), deorum beneficio or peropportune accidit.

happiness, vita beata ; beate vivere ; beatum esse (98, *b*) ; *I enjoy* beatus sum.

happy, beatus.

hard pressed, I am, premor, i.

hard to say, difficile dictu. (404.)

hardly, vix.

hardship, incommodum, *n. ; hardships*, molestiae, *pl.*

harm, I do. (See *injure.*)

harsh, asper, asperior, asperrimus.

harvest, mess-is, -is, *f.*

haste (subs.), celerit-as, -atis, *f. ; there is need of haste*, properato opus est. (See 286 and 416.)

hasten, I, propero, are ; *absolutely or with inf.* ; contend-o, ēre.

hate, I, od-i, -isse, -eram (*perf. with pres. meaning*) ; *am hated.* odio sum. (260, *Obs.* 2.)

hatred, odium, *n.*

haughty, superbus. (57, *a.*)

have you, I would. (149, i.)

he himself, ipse (355) ; *he* (11, *a, d; see* Ex. 45).

head, cap-ut, -itis, *n.*

head of, I am the, prae-sum. (251.)

headlong, prae-ceps, -cipitis (*adj.*).

health, I am in good, valeo, ēre, -ui.

heap (abuse) on you, I, te (maledictis) onero, are.

hear, I, or hear of, aud-io, ire, -ivi, -ītum ; accipio, ēre.

heard of by, have been. (258, ii.)

hearing, in my, use abl. abs., *pres. partic.* (420, ii.); *without a hearing* (425).

hearing, sense of, aur-es, -ium, *f. pl.*

heart (affections, spirit), anim-us, -i, *m.* ; (*disposition*), ingenium, *n.*

heat, aest-us, -ūs, *m.*

h eave a groan, I, ingem-isco, ēre, -ui.

Heaven (metaph.), Di immortales. (See 17.)

---

[1] *Cesso*, I hang back from something which I have begun or have to do ; *differo*, I put off action, adjourn it to another time ; *cunctor*, I delay from caution or indecision.

heaven and earth, I appeal to, deorum hominumque fidem imploro.

heavy, gravis ; *or, in metaphorical sense only,* laboriosus (*use superl.,* 57, *a*).

height of, summus. (60.)

heir, the, haer-es, -edis.

help, I can (*not*). (137, I, *j.*)

help you, I, auxilio tibi sum. (259, 260, I) ; tibi opem fero.

helplessness, in, in-ops, -opis (*adj.*). (See 61.)

henceforth, jam.

herdsman, bubulc-us, -i, *m.*

here, hic.

here, I am, ad-sum, -esse, -fui.

hesitate to, I, dubito, are, *inf.* (136, *b.*)

hidden, occultus.

hide, I (*by silence*), dissimulo, are (p. 55, *note*).

high, altus ; *high hopes.* (See 54.)

high-spirited, ferox. (See note under *boldly.*)

highest, summus.

highly (*I honour*). (See *I honour.*)

hill, coll-is, -is, *m.*

himself, ipse, a, um. (355.)

his, ejus ; illius ; suus. (See 11, *c, d* and *e,* and Pronouns I.)

his own (*enemy*), sibi, *or* sui (55), ipse (inimicus).

historian, rerum script-or, -oris.

hoist (*a flag*), *I,* e-do, ĕre, -didi, -ditum.

hold, I, obtin-eo, ĕre, -ui (19); habeo.

hold, I (*think*), duco, ĕre, duxi, ductum ; *hold* (*count*) *as,* habeo (240); habeo pro (240, *Obs.* 2).

hold my peace, I, contic-esco, ĕre, -ui. (See 17, *Obs.*)

home, at, domi (312) ; *at his own home* (316, iii.); *from home* (*with verb of motion*), domo (9, *b*); *home* (*I return*), domum (9, *b*).

home-sickness, suorum desiderium.

homes and hearths, for, pro aris et focis.

honest, probus.

honesty, probit-as,[1] -atis, *f.*

honour (*good faith*), fid-es, -ei, *f.*

honour (*distinction*), hon-os, -oris, *m.*

honour (*self-respect*), dignit-as, -atis, *f.*

honour (*as opposed to expediency*), honest-as, -atis, *f.* (51, *c* ; see note under *honesty.*)

honour, I pay (*you*), or *I honour* (*you*), honorem (tibi) habeo ; te in honore habeo ; *honour highly,* in summo honore habeo.

honour (*with*) *I* (*publicly*), orno, are (*abl.*) ; *or* pro-sequor, i, -secutus.

honourable, honestus ; *to be honourable* (*creditable to*), honori esse. (260, 3.)

hope for, I, spero, are. (23.)

hopes, spes,[2] spei, *f.* ; *I form hopes,* spero. (54.)

horrified at, I am, per-horresco, ĕre, -horrui.

hospitality, rights of, jus hospitii.

host, a (opp. to *guest*), hosp-es, -itis, *m.*

host, a, multitud-o. -inis, *f.*

hostage, obs-es, -idis.

hour, hora, *f.*; *of victory.* (63.)

house, in my, apud me (331, 4, *a*) ; domi meae (316, iii.).

household, a, familia, *f.*

how. (See 157, ii.)

how (*disgraceful, etc.*) (260, *Obs.* 1.)

how much (*adv.*), quantum.

how much (*with comparat.*), quanto.

how often, quoties. (157, ii.)

human, humanus ; *or gen. pl. of* homo. (59.)

human beings, homines.

humble means, tenuis fortuna.

humble origin, of, humili loco natus.

humour, I, gratificor, ari (*dat.*).

hundred thousand, a. (527.)

---

[1] *Honestas* is not "honesty," but the *abstract term* for what is honourable (*honestum*) in a general sense.

[2] *Spes* is one of the few words in which Latin goes further in forming an abstract noun than English : it is rarely used in the plural of the "hopes" of a single person, or even of many. Cf. *ingenium, memoria.*

hurl, I, con-jicio, ĕre, -jēci, -jec-
tum ; *at,* in (*acc.*).
hurry away from, I, avolo, are.
hurry to, I, conten-do, ĕre, -di
(ad) ; festino, are.
husband, vir, viri.

I, ego.　(See **11,** *a* and *b ;* also
334.)
idle (vain), vanus.
if, si. (See Conditional Clauses and
171.)
if not . . . yet. (**466,** *c.*)
ignorant of, I am, ignoro,[1] are
(*trans.*) ; nescio, ire.　(**174,** *e.*)
ill, I am, aegroto, are.
ill-starred, infelix, *comp.* infelicior.
(**57,** *b.*)
illustrious,　praeclarus　(*superl.*) ;
praestans (*superl.*).　(**57,** *a.*)
ill-will, malevolentia, *f.*
imagine, I (think), puto, are.　(See
note under *fancy.*).
imagine, I (conceive), animo concipio, ĕre.
imitate, I, imitor, ari.
immediately after.　(**332,** I, *g, or*
331, 21, *c.*)
immensely, quam plurimum.
impart (to), I, communico, are
(cum).　(**253,** iv.)
impiety, impiet-as, -atis, *f.*
implore, I, obsecro, are.
importance of the matter, the, tanta
res.
importance to me, it is of, meā
interest (**310**) ; *of the utmost importance to* (= *with reference to*).
(**310,** iii. and iv.)
important, gravis.
impose upon you (conditions), I, tibi
impono, ĕre.
impossible, it is, or *it is quite.* (**125,** *f.*)
*impress (affect) you, I ; make an
impression on you,* te, *or oftener*
animum tuum, moveo *or* com-
moveo, ĕre, -mōvi, -mōtum ;
*where more than one person is
implied, pl.* animos.

impression (of), opini-o, -onis, *f.*
imprisonment, vincula, *n. pl.*
improvident, improvidus.
impulse, of its own, sua sponte.
(See note under *voluntarily.*)
impunity, with, impune (*adv.*).
impute this to you as a fault, I,
hoc tibi vitio ver-to, ĕre, -ti,
-sum ; culpae do, dăre, dedi,
datum.　(**260,** 2.)
in ; in a time of, in (*abl.*).　(See
332, 5 ; **273,** *Obs.*)
incapable of, I am (morally), ab-
horreo, ēre, ab ; alienissimus
sum ab.　(See *unable.*)
inclination, volunt-as, -atis, *f.*
incline to think that, I.　(**169.**)
incompetence (ignorance), inscītia, *f.*
inconsiderable (of danger), parum
gravis.
inconsistent with, alienus ab.
incorruptibility, integrit-as, -atis, *f.*
increase, I (trans.), au-geo, ēre, -xi,
-ctum.
increase, I (intrans.), cresco, ĕre,
crevi.
incur, I, incurro, ĕre, in (*acc.*) ;
incur loss, damnum capio, ĕre,
cēpi.
indebted to you for this, I am, hoc
tibi acceptum re-fero, -ferre,
-ttuli (*metaph. from account-book*).
indecisive, an-ceps, -cipitis.
India, India, *f.* ; *an Indian,* Ind-us, i.
indict, I, reum facio ; accuso.
(**306.**)
indictment, crim-en, -inis, *n.*
indifferent to, neglegens (*with gen.,*
301) ; *I am indifferent to,* parvi
or nihili (**305**) facio.
indignation, use indignor, ari.　(**415,**
b.)
indispensable, necessarius.
individuals ; as individuals, singuli.
(**380,** *b.*)
induced, I am, mihi persuadetur.
(**244,** *Obs.*)
indulge, I, indul-geo, ēre, -si (*dat.*).
indulgence (forgiveness), venia, *f.*

---

[1] *Nescio,* "I am absolutely ignorant of," opposed to *scio ; ignoro,* "I have not made
myself acquainted with," opposed to *novi ; illum ignoro* (not *nescio*), I do not know
him.

inexperience, use adj., imperitus. (376, iii.).
infallible, certissimus.
infamous, I am declared, ignominiā notor, ari.
infant, infan-s, -tis.
infantry, pedit-es, -um.
inferior to. (278.)
infest, I, infestum habeo. (240.)
inflict (loss) on (you), I (damno te) afficio, ĕre. (283.)
inflict death on you (judicially), I, morte te multo, are.
inflict punishment on, I, poenas sum-o, ĕre, -psi, -ptum, de (abl.).
influence, auctorit-as,[1] -atis, *f.*
influence with, I have (much, etc.), possum apud. (331, 4, d.)
information, I give, doceo. (231.)
inhuman, inhumanus.
injure, I, noc-eo, ĕre, -ui, -itum (dat.).
injury (harm), damnum, *n.* (See note under *wrong.*)
innocence, entire, use superl. of innocens, and see 224, *Obs.* 1.
innocent, I am, extra culpam sum. (331, 9.)
innocent, the, innocentes. (50.)
inquire, I, quaero, ĕre, a *or* ex ; (te) rogo, inter-rogo, are (231, note) ; percunctor, ari (acc.).
inspiration, afflat-us, -ūs, *m.*
instantly, continuo.
instead of (doing, etc.), adeo non . . . ut ; non modo . . . sed ; tantum abfuit ut . . . ut (124) ; *or* quum posset, deberet (431, Obs.).
instigation, use auctor (424), *or* suadeo, moneo (420, ii.).
institution, an, institutum. (51, b.)
instrumentality, by your. (267, Obs.)
insult, an, contumelia, *f.*
intellect, men-s, -tis, *f.*
intend to, I, use fut. in -rus. (See 14, c.)
intent on, I am, do operam. (397.)

intention of, with the. (107.)
intentionally, consulto ; consilio. (268.)
interest, gratia, *f.* (See note under *influence.*)
interest (advantage), utilit-as, -atis, *f.* (51, c.)
interest or interests of, I consult, consulo, ĕre *with dat.* (See 248.)
interest of, in the, causā. (290, Obs.)
interfere with, I, inter-venio, ire, vēni (dat.).
interpose, I (intrans.), = *interfere.*
interposition, miraculous. (64.)
interpreter, interpr-es, -etis.
intervene, I, inter-venio, ire, -vēni.
interview with, I have an, con-venio, ire, -vēni (trans., 24 and 229) ; col-loquor, i, -locutus (cum).
intimate terms with, I live on. (282.)
into, in. (331, 24.)
intolerable (to). almost, vix ferendus. (394 and 258, i.)
intrust, I, per-mitto, ĕre, -misi, -missum ; mando, are. (See 247 and 128.)
invade, I, bellum, *or* arma, in-fero, ferre, -tuli, illatum, in (acc., 331, 24, c).
invasion, use bellum infero (pass. part., 417, i.).
invest (a city), I, circum-sedeo, ĕre (trans., 229).
inveigh against, I. (331, 24, c.)
invent, I (fabricate), fingo, ĕre, finxi, fictum.
inventor, invent-or, -oris : *fem. form* inventr-ix. -icis.
invite, I, invito, are. (331, 24. b.)
involved in, I am, versor, ari, in (abl.).
involves, it (implies), habet.
irruption, an, incursi-o, -onis, *f.*
island, insula, *f.*
issue, the, event-us, -ūs, *m.* ; but see 174, d.

---

[1] *Auctoritas,* moral influence as distinct from authority in the sense of *power ; potestas,* legal or legitimate authority or power ; *imperium,* military authority or power ; *potentia,* "power," "might," in a more general sense ; *regnum,* kingly or despotic power ; *gratia,* "interest" with the powerful ; *favor,* "popularity" with the masses.

Isthmus, the, Isthm-us, -i, *f.*
Italy, Italia, *f.*
itself, ipse, a, um. **(355.)**

January, Januarius. (See Voc. 1, *note.*)
javelin (Roman soldiers'), pilum, *n.*
jealous of you, I am, tibi in-video, ēre, -vīdi.
jewel (metaph.), res *sufficient.* **(222,** *Obs.*)
join (you), I (intrans.), me (tibi, or ad te), adjun-go, ēre, -xi, -ctum ; *the ranks of,* ad.
journey, a, it-er, -ineris, *n. ; I am on a journey,* iter facio.
joy, laetitia, *f. ; shouts of joy,* lae-tantium (laetor) clamor. (See **415,** *b,* and the *caution.*)
joyful, laetus.
judge, I (think), reor, ratus sum. (See note under *fancy.*)
judgment (decision), judicium, *n.*
judgment (will), arbitrium, *n.*
judgment (good), consilium, *n.*
judgment is different, my, aliter judico. **(54.)**
June (month of), (mensis) Junius : *first of,* kalendae Juniae. **(538.)**
juniors, juniores ; natu minores.
jury (judges), judices. (Voc. 7, *note* **2.**)
just (adj.), justus
just (lately), nuperrime (nuper).
just (then), jam tum.
justification, causa, *f.*
justly, jure. (See note under *rightly.*)

keenness, aci-es, -ei, *f. (lit. edge).*
keep, I (promises), sto, stare, stěti *(abl.).*
keep (within), I, contin-eo, ēre, -ui (intra).
keep anxious about, I, sollicitum habeo de. **(240.)**
keep back from, I, prohibeo, ēre ; arceo, ēre *(abl.).*
keep in the dark, or secret, I, celo. **(230, 231.)**

keep my word, I, fidem prae-sto, are, -stiti.
kill, I, inter-ficio,[1] ēre, -feci, -fectum; occī-do, ēre, -di, -sum.
kind deed, a, beneficium, *n. ;* offi-cium, *n.*
kind of, every, omnis, e.
kind of man, the, use qualis. **(174,** *c.*)
kind, of this, hujusmodi ;[2] *of the, of that kind ; that kind of,* ejusmodi.[2] (See **87.**)
kindly (adj.), benignus ; humanus.
kindly disposed to, bene-volus, -vol-entior, in. **(255,** *Obs.*)
kindness, bonit-as, -atis, *f.; (act of),* beneficium, *n. ; I return* (see *gratitude*).
king, rex, regis ; *king's,* regius *(adj.,* **58**).
know, I, scio, ire *(a fact)* ; nōvi, nōsse, nōveram (nōram) *(a person)* ; notum habeo **(188).**
knowledge (learning), doctrina, *f.*
knowledge, to, or within, my. **(507.)**

lack, I, mihi deest. **(251.)**
laden, onustus.
laggard, a, ignavus.
lamentations, I make, lamentor, ari.
land, terra, *f. ;* ag-er, ri, *m.*
land, our (territory), agri nostri. (See *country* and **16,** *a.*)
land on, I (trans.), ex-pono, ēre, -posui, -positum, in *(abl.).*
landing of, the, partic. of expono. **(417, i.)**
language (conversation), serm-o, onis, *m.*
language, I use this, haec loquor, i. (See **25** and **54.**)
large. (See *great.*)
last (to), the, ultimus. **(62.)**
last (of past time), proximus *; for, or within, the last (days, etc.)* **(325,** *Obs.*)
last, at, tandem ; demum.
lasting, diuturnus.
late (recent), recen-s, -tis.

---

[1] *Interficere,* general word for to kill : *occidere,* to kill with a weapon, as in war : *necare,* to put to death cruelly ; *trucidare,* to murder inhumanly, to "butcher."
[2] *Hujusmodi, ejusmodi.* etc., are constantly used contemptuously ; *talis* rarely so. (Ex. 33 B, *n.* 4.)

late in life, jam senex (63) ; provecta jam aetate (*abl. abs.*).

late, too (*adv.*), sero.

lately, nuper, *superl.*, nuperrime ;
but lately, paulo ante. (279,
caution.)

launch against, I, im-mitto, ĕre,
in (*acc.*).

law, a, lex, legis, *f.* (Ex. 9, *n.* 2.)

lawful, legitimus.

lay before, I, defero, ferre, ad.

lay down my arms, I (*disband or
surrender*), ab armis dis-cedo, ĕre,
-cessi.

lay violent hands on myself, I.
(253, ii.)

lay waste, I. (See *waste.*)

lazy, ignavus.

lead, I, duco, ĕre, duxi, ductum.

lead a life, I. (237.)

lead across, or through, I, trans-
duco, ĕre, -duxi. (229, *Obs.*)

lead back, I, reduco, ĕre.

lead out, I, educo, ĕre.

leadership. (424.)

learn, I, disco, ĕre, didici.

learn fresh (*additional*), I, ad-disco,
ĕre, -didici.

learning, doctrina. f. ; but *I advance
in learning*, doctior fio ; and see
279 for *superior in learning.*

least, at, saltem ; *I at least*, ego certe.[1]

leave, I, or leave behind, re-linquo,
ĕre, -liqui, -lictum (see note
under *abandon*); (*a place*), ex-
cedo, ĕre, *abl. or* ex: proficiscor,
i, -fectus (*abl.*, see 314); *leave my
country* (264).

leave you (*free*) *to, I.* (197, *Obs.* 2.)

leave alone, I, missum, am, um,
facio. (240.)

leave nothing, I (298, *b*); *leave nothing undone* (137, *i.*).

leave, you have my. (331, 16, *c.*)

left (*adj.*), sinist-er, -ra, -rum.

legion, a, legi-o, -onis, *f.*   •

leisure, otium, *n. ; at leisure*, otiosus
(*adj.*).

Lemnos, Lemn-os, *gen.* -i.

less (*adv.*) minus ; *less than* (*with
numerals*). (318, *Obs.*)

let (*you*), I, (tibi) tra-do, ĕre, -didi,
ditum *with gerundive*. (400.)

let slip, I (*an opportunity*), desum.
(251.)

letter, a, litter-ae, -arum, *f. ; from*,
a, ab.

level plain, planiti-es, -ei, *f.*

levy (*subst.*), delect-us, -ūs, *m. ; I
hold a levy*, delectum habeo.

levy contributions on you, I, pecunias
tibi impero, are.

liar, a, mend-ax, -acis (*adj.*).

liberties, libert-as, -atis, *f.* (sing.);
=*exemptions*, immunitat-es, -um,
f. pl.

life, vita, *f.*

lifetime, in his (61); *in your father's*,
=*your father being alive* (vivus),
abl. abs. (424).

like (*adj.*), similis. (254, 255.)

likely to, *use partic. in* -rus. (14, *c.*)

line (*of battle*), aci-es, -ei, *f.* (see
note under *field*); *line of march*,
agm-en, -inis, *n. ; lines* (*fortified*),
munimenta, *n. pl. ; line* (*metaph.
for* "*opinion*"), judicium, *n.*

linger, I, cunctor, ari.

list of, I write a, per-scribo, ĕre
(*trans.*).

listen to, I, audio, ire. (23.)

listen to, I (*comply with or obey*),
obtempero, are. (See *obey*,
note) ; *listen to prayer*, exoror.

literature, litterae, *f. pl.*

little (see 53); *little of*, parum (294).

live, I, vivo, ĕre, vixi, victum.

load, I, onero, are.

load, a, ŏn-us, -eris, *n.*

locality, loc-a, -orum, *n.*

lofty, praealtus.

London, Londinium, *n.*

long (*in distance*), longus ; *in time*,
diutinus,[2] diuturnus.

long (*adv.*), diu, or jam diu : *long
ago*, jam pridem ; *long continued*,
diutinus ; *long tried*, spectatus.
(57, *a.*)

---

[1] *Certe*, when it follows a word, means "at least," and is equivalent to *saltem*, more
emphatic than *quidem.*

[2] *Diuturnus*, long, lasting, of long standing : *diutinus* long continued, in a bad
sense, "wearisome."

longer (*adv.*), diutius ; *no longer, or any longer* (*after a negative*), jam or diutius (**328,** *a*); *how much longer ?* quousque, *or* quousque tandem (**157,** *Obs.*)

look at, I, specto, are (see note under *see*) ; intueor, ēri (*perf. rare*).

look down on, I, de-spicio, ĕre, -spexi, -spectum (*trans.*).

look for, I, (*wait for*), expecto, are. (**23.**)

look for (*in vain*), I, desidero, are.

look forward to, I, provideo, ēre (*acc.*).

look round for, I, circum-spicio, ĕre, -spexi. (**22, 23.**)

look up at, I, suspicio, ĕre.

looked for, than I had, spe, *or* expectatione, meā. (**277.**)

lose, I, a-mitto, ĕre, -misi, -missum.

lose, I (*opportunity*), de-sum, esse. (**251.**)

lose heart, I, animo deficio, ĕre ; *of more than one person,* animis.

lose my labour I (= *I effect nothing*), nihil ago.

lose time, I, tempus tero, ĕre, trivi, tritum.

lose the day, I (= *I am conquered*), vincor, i, victus.

loss, damnum, *n.* ; detrimentum, *n.*

loss of, without the, use a-mitto, ĕre. (**425.**)

loss what to do, I am at a. (**172.**)

lost, all is, de summa re actum est.

lot (*metaph.*), *lot in life,* fortuna, *f.*

lot, it falls to (*my*), (mihi) contingit :[1] *it is men's lot to,* hominibus . . . ut. (**123.**)

love, I, di-ligo, ĕre, -lexi, -lectum ; amo,[2] are.

lovely, pulcherrimus.

low, abjectus ; *very low,* infimus. (**57,** *a.*)

low, or lowly, birth, ignobilitas, -atis, *f.*

lowest part of, īmus. (**60.**)

loyal, fidelis.

loyalty, fid-es, -ei, *f.*

luxury, luxuria, *f.*

mad, I am (*quite*), furo, ĕre. (See Voc. 6, *n.*)

made, I am being, fio, fieri, factus.

magnificent, praeclarissimus.

magnitude, use quantus. (**174,** *a.*)

mainly, potissimum.

maintain, I, sustin-eo, ēre, -ui.

make, I, facio, ĕre, feci, factum , *make war,* infero, ferre (**253,** ii.); *make my way,* iter facio.

make fast (*bind*), I, constri-ngo, ĕre, -nxi, -ctus.

malice, malitia ;[3] malevolentia.

Malta, Melita, *f.*

man, vir, viri ; hom-o, -inis (for the difference see p. 153, *note,* 3) ; *to a man* (**331,** i., *f.*).

management, procuratio, -onis, *f.*

manhood, in quite early, admodum adolescens. (**63,** and p. 63, *note* 3.)

manifestly, = *obviously.* (**64.**)

mankind, homines ; *or* genus humanum.

manliness, with, viril-iter, -ius.

manner, in this. (**268** and *Obs.*)

manner of life. (**174,** *c.*)

manners, mor-es, -um, *m. pl.*

many, mult-i, -ae, -a.

marble (*adj.*), marmoreus.

march, a, it-er, -ineris, *n.*

march, I, iter facio.

Marseilles, Massilia, *f.*

marsh, pal-us, -udis, *f.*

mass, a, mol-es, -is, *f.*

mass (*of the people*), vulg-us, -i, *n.* ; *for dat. in* vulgus, **254,** *note.*

massacre, caed-es, -is, *f.*; *I am present at the, use gerundive.* (**417,** ii.)

---

[1] *Contingit,* "happens" by a natural process ; oftener, but not always, of what is desirable : *accidit,* "happens," "falls out," by chance, often, but not always, of what is undesirable : *usu venit,* "falls within my experience :" *evenit,* "happens," "turns out," as the result of previous circumstances.

[2] *Amare* expresses greater warmth of feeling than *diligere:* it is "to love passionately," "to be enamoured of."

[3] *Malevolentia,* ill-will ; *malitia,* the same feeling shown in underhand attacks or schemes ; *malignitas,* ill-will shown in a desire to defraud, "niggardliness."

massacre, I, trucīdo, are. (See *kill.*)
master, a, domin-us, -i, *m.*
matter, a, res, rei, *f.*
matters little, it, parvi rēfert (**310** *at end*) ; *it matters not,* nihil refert (*ibid.*).
mature life, in, jam adultus. (**63.**)
May (month of), (mensis) Maius. (**538,** *n.*)
may, I. (**197** and *Obs.*)
mean (adj.). sordidus ; abjectus.
mean, what I, you, etc. ; or what is the meaning (**174**) *of,* quid mihi velim, tibi velis, ətc. (**163**).
means, by no, nequaquam ; haudquaquam ; nullo modo ; minime.
means, by this. (**268.**)
means, humble, tenuis fortuna.
meantime, interea.
meddle with, I, at-tingo, ĕre -tigi, -tactus.
Medes, the, Medi, -orum.
meditate on, I, cogito, are de (*abl.*).
meet, I. obviam fio (*dat.*); *I come, go, go down, to meet,* obviam venio, ire ; eo, ire ; descendo, ĕre.
meet, I (endure), ex-perior, iri, -pertus.
meet (doom), I, ob-eo, ire, -ii (*acc.*).
meet (together) at, to, convĕnire ad. (**331,** i. c.)
member of the nation, or state, civ-is, -is, *m.*
memory, memoria, *f.*
menace (with), I, denuntio, are (*acc. of thing, dat. of person*) ; *for menaces use gerund.* (**99.**)
mention, I, mentionem facio (*gen.*).
mention, not to, ne dicam. (**100,** *note.*)
merchant vessel, navis oneraria.
mercy, misericordia, *f.* ; *I place myself entirely at your,* totum me tibi trado ac permitto.
mere (from the), ipse (*use abl. of cause,* or propter : see also **355,** *c*): *merely, = only: "mere"* and *"merely" are often expressed by emphatic order simply.*
message, a, nuntium, *n.*
messenger, nunti-us, -i, *m.*
method, rati-o, -onis, *f.*
mid-day, meridi-es, -ei, *m.*

middle of, midst of. (**60.**)
midst of, in the. (**332,** 5, *h.*)
mighty, superl. of magnus.
Milan, Mediolanum, *n.*
mile, a, mille, *pl.* milia, *sc.* passuum (1000 *paces of 5 feet*).
mind, animus, -i, *m.* ; (= *intellect*), men-s, -tis, *f. ; his whole mind,* = *all that he thinks* (sentio, ire).
mind (verb imperat.), fac, cura, ut. (**141.**)
mind, I am out of my, insan-io, ire, -ivi, -ii. (See **25.**)
mind, I am of one (with), consentio, ire, -sensi (cum).
mingle with, I (intrans.), im-misceor, (**20**), ēri, -mixtus (*dat.*).
mingled . . . and, et . . . et.
miraculous interposition, by a. (**64.**)
miserable, mis-er, -era, -erum.
mislead, I, decipio, ĕre, etc.
missile, a, telum, *n.*
missing, I am, desideror, ari.
mistake, a, err-or, -oris, *m.* ; *in, gen.* (**300.**)
mistake, I make a ; am mistaken, erro, are.
Mithridates, Mithridat-es, -is.
mob, multitud-o, -inis, *f.*
mode, rati-o, -onis, *f.*
moderate (not too great), modicus ; mediocris (*"middling"*).
moment when, at the. (**433.**)
money, pecunia, *f.*
monstrous (wicked), nefarius.
monument, monumentum, *n.*
moon, luna, *f.*
morals, mor-es, -um, *m.*
more (adv.), plus ; magis : *as subst.* (**294**), plus, *n. pl.* (**54**) plura ; *more than (= rather than),* magis quam ; *more than once,* see once.
more (never), posthac.
moreover, praeterea.
morning, in the, māne (*adv.*).
morrow, the (still in future), dies crastinus ; *on the morrow (of a past date),* die postero.
mortal (wound), morti-fer, -fera, -ferum. (**18, 19.**)
most (used loosely in comparing two only), plus. (See *more.*)

most men, plerique.

motive, from, or *with, a, use* ob
(331, 14) *and* causa, *f. ; my only
motive is* (483, *Obs.*). (See also
107.)

mount up, I, ascend-o, ĕre, -i.

mountain, mon-s, -tis, *m.*

mournfully, maestus. (61.)

mouth, in every one's. (257.)

move, I (*intrans.*), moveor, ēri,
motus. (20.)

much, multus, a, um ; *as subst.* (see
53) ; = *much of* (294) ; *with comparat.,* multo (279).

multitude, multitud-o, -inis, *f.*

murder, a, caed-es, -is, *f.*

murder, I, neco, are.

murderer. (See 175.)

must be, use part. in -dus. (198,
iii.)

mutiny, sediti-o, -onis, *f.*

my, meus. (See 11, *c.*)

myself (*emphatic*), ipse (355, *d*) ;
(*reflexive*), me, me ipsum (356,
ii.); *for myself,* ego, *or* equidem
(11, *a,* and 334, i.).

name, a, nom-en, -inis, *n. ; in name*
(*nominally*). (274.)

name, good, fama, *f.*

Naples, Neapol-is, -is, *loc.* -i.

Narbonne, Narbo, -onis, *m.*

nation, popul-us, -i, *m. ;* civit-as,
-atis, *f.. or* civ-es, -ium ; respublica. (See 19, and Voc. 2, *n.*)

national, communis ; *or gen. of*
respublica. (58.)

national cause, the, respublica ;
communis rei p. causa.

natural powers, natura, *f.,* and see
note under *character.*

naturally (*by nature*), naturā.

nature, use qualis *or* quis. (174, *b.*)

native land, or *country* (see 16, *a*) :
I leave my, patriā cedo (264).

nearly, prope, paene. (See note
under *almost.*)

necessary, necessarius ; *is necessary.*
(See 286.)

necessaries (*of life*). (286.)

necessity (=*emergency*), temp-us,
-oris, *n.*

need of ; is needed, etc., opus. (286.)

needs must, necesse est. (201, and
p. 144, *note.*)

neglect, I, negle-go, ĕre, -xi, -ctum.

neighbour (*actual*), vicin-us, -i ; *in
sense of "fellow man,"* or *"men,"*
alter ; ceteri. (372.)

neighbouring, finitimus.

neither . . . nor, neque . . . neque.

neither of the two. (340, ii.)

never, nunquam ; *and never,* nec
unquam. (110.)

new, novus.

news of, the, use nuntio, are (417
i.) ; *news has been brought* (46, *a*).

next, the, proximus ; insequen-s,
-tis ; *next* (*day*), posterus ; *or* (*on
the*), postridie (*adv.*).

next to (*prep.*). (331, 21, *c.*)

niceties (*of argument*), argutiae, *f. pl.*

night, nox, noctis, *f.*

nineteen, undeviginti. (527.)

ninety-second. (See 530 and 531.)

no (162) ; *I say* or *answer "no,"*
nego, are.

no, none (*adj.*), nullus.

no (*not*) *more* (*adv.*) *than,* nihilo
magis quam.

no one, none, nemo, *gen.* nullius
(see 223, *note*) ; *and no one, none,*
nec quisquam (110).

no sooner . . . than, ubi primum ;
simul atque. (428.)

noble (*morally*), praeclarus (p. 63,
note 4) ; pulcherrimus (57, *a*) ;
*for usage with proper nouns and
persons see* 224.

nobles. (51, *a,* and *note.*)

noon, noon-day. (See *mid-day.*)

nor, neque ; *in final clauses,* neu.

not yet, nondum.

nothing, nihil.

now, jam (=*by this time, can be
used of the past*) ; nunc (*at the
present, at the moment of speaking*) ; hodie (*to-day*).

now . . . long, jamdiu ; jampridem.
(181.)

now . . . now, modo . . . modo.

number (*proportion or part*), par-s,
-tis, *f.*

number of, the (*interrog.*). (174, *a.*)

numbers, great, multi ; complures ;
superior, multitud-o. -inis, *f.*

numerous, *more,* plures ; *such numerous,* tot.

oath, jusjurandum, jurisjurandi, *n.*
obedient to, I am, = *obey.*
obey, I, pär-eo,[1] ēre, -ui *(dat.*, **5**) ; obtempero, are *(dat.)* ; *the orders of,* dicto audiens sum *(dat.*).
object, I, recuso, are (**136**, *a*); *I do not* (**131**).
object (subst.), *objects,* (see **54**); *object of unpopularity with you, I am,* invidiā flagro, are, apud vos.
obligation, I am under, gratiam debeo. (**98**, *b.*)
obstacle, (id) quod obstat.
obstinate, pertin-ax, *comp.* -acior.
obtain, I, adipiscor,[2] i, adeptus ; con-sequor, ī, -secutus (**18**, **19**) ; *a request,* impetro, are.
obviously. (**64.**)
occasion, on that, tum. (Intr. **19.**)
occupy, I (hold), ten-eo, ēre, -ui.
ocean, ocean-us, -i, *m.*
off (at a distance of), I am, absum. (**318.**)
offence, an, peccatum, *n.* (**408.**)
offend, I (annoy), offen-do, ĕre, -di, -sum. (**245.**)
offer, I, de-fero, -ferre, -tuli, -latum ; *offer (terms),* fero.
office, magistrat-us, -ūs (**18**, **19**) ; *I am in,* in magistratu sum ; *I hold,* m. habeo ; obtineo.
officers, the (military), tribuni (militum) centurionesque.
often, saepe ; *so often,* toties.
old. (See *ancient,* and note.)
old age, senect-us, -utis, *f.* ; *in my.* (**63.**)
old man, sen-ex, -is.
old-world, old-fashioned, priscus ; antiquus. (See note under *ancient.*)

oldest, natu maximus.
once, semel ; *often exp. by tense of verb* (**471**, *note*) ; *more than once,* semel ac saepius. (**533**, *c.*)
once (formerly), quondam : olim.[3]
once, at (immediately), statim.
once, at (at the same time), use idem. (**366**, i.)
one (numeral), unus ; *of,* ex '**529**, *e*) ; *one of the best* (**529**, *d*) *one or two; one, two, several.* (**529**, *g.*)
one (indefinite), one who (see **72**) ; *one so* (**224**, *Obs.* 2).
one, not, nemo (**223**, *note*), ne unus quidem (**529**, *a*).
one, . . . the other. (**368.**)
one and all, cuncti (see under *all*) ; omnes *(placed last).*
one by one, singuli. (**380**, *b.*)
one day (= at some time or other), aliquando. (See note under *once.*)
one thing . . . another, it is. (**92.**)
only, solum, modo, tantum *(placed after the word qualified)* ; *this and only this* (**347**, *example*) ; *not only,* non solum, non modo.
onset, impet-us, -ūs, *m.*
open, I ; throw open ; open wide ; cause to be opened, pate-facio, ĕre, -feci, -factum.
open, to be, patēre *(no fut. in* -rus **193**, iii.).
open to question, is, = *can be doubted,* dubitari potest.
opening, first possible. (**377.**)
openly, palam.
opinion, good, existimati-o, -onis, *f.*
opinion on, your, = *what you think of* (censeo, ēre, de).
opponent, I am an. See *I oppose.*
opportunity, occasi-o, -onis, *f.* ; facult-as, -atis, *f.* ; *first possible.* (**377.**)

---

[1] *Pareo,* the general word for "I obey," applied often to habitual obedience of any kind : *obtempero,* I obey as from a sense of reason and right ; *oboedio,* I obey a single command ; *obsequor,* "I comply with," "I suit myself to ;" *dicto audiens sum,* I render implicit obedience, as that of a soldier.

[2] *Nanciscor,* I obtain, often without effort, by circumstances or chance ; *consequor,* I obtain a thing which I follow after as a good ; *adipiscor.* I obtain after effort : *impetro,* by entreaty.

[3] *Olim (ille, olle),* at a distant *point,* in the past or (sometimes) in the future : *quondam (quidam),* only of the past, and generally during some *space* of time in the past; *aliquando,* at some time or other, past, present or future, opposed to "never."

oppose, I, adversor, ari (*dat.*, **244**, *b*); ob-sto, are, -stiti (**253**, i.).

opposite to. (**331**, 2.)

opposition, in spite of your, use partic. of adversor, ari. (**420**, ii.)

oppress, I, vexo, are. (**19.**)

oppressive, iniquus.

or, aut, vel (see p. 14, *note*); *in final and consec. clauses*, **103**, **110**; *interrog.*, **159**, **160** ; **168**, *and Obs.*

orator, orat-or, -oris.

order, I, jubeo, ēre, jussi, jussum. (**120**, **128**.)

orders, jussa, *n. pl.* (**51**, *b.*)

orders, I give, impero, are ; edico, ĕre, etc. (**127**, *b*, and **128**.)

origin (extraction), gen-us, -eris, *n.* ; *of humble origin*, humili loco natus.

originally (sprung). (See *sprung*.)

orphan, orbus, a, um.

other, the (of two), ille (**339**, iv.) ; alter (**368**); *others*, alii, *or* (= *other men, the rest*) ceteri (**372**) ; *it is for, use gen.* (**291**, *Obs.* 4).

other men's, or persons', alienus (*adj.*, **58**).

ought, I. (**198.**)

our, nost-er, -ra, -rum.

our men, nostri. (**50.**)

out of, e, ex (**332**, 5), *or* de (*abl.*).

outcries, angry, maledicta, *n. pl.* (**408.**)

outdo, I (far), (facile) vinco, -ĕre, supero, are.

outnumber, we, plures sumus quam.

outrage on, the, use gerundive or partic. of violo. (**417**, ii. *or* i.)

outside (the city). (**311**, *Obs.*)

outstrip, I, = *outdo.*

over (more than), plus. (**318**, *Obs.*).

over with, all. (**332**, 3, *d.*)

over-reach, I, circum-venio, ire, -vēni. (**229.**)

overwhelm, I, obru-o, ĕre, -i, -tum ; op-primo, ĕre, -pressi, -pressum.

owe, I, debeo. ēre.

owing to, propter (*acc.*, **331**, 20, *b*).

own, his, suus (**11**, *c*); *my own*, meus.

pacify, I, placo, are.

pain, dol-or, -oris, *m.*

painful, is. (**260**, 3.)

palace, dom-us, -ūs, *f.* ; *the king's*, domus regia. (**58.**)

panic, pav-or, -oris, *m.*

pardon, I, ig-nosco, ĕre, -novi, -notum (*dat.*, 5) ; *pardon (you) for (this)* , hoc tibi condono, are (**247**) ; *I wish you pardoned ;* tibi ignotum volo (**240**, *Obs.* 1) ; *by pardoning, gerund of* ignosco (**99**).

parent, paren-s, -tis.

park (pleasure grounds), horti, *m. pl.*

Parliament = Senate.

part, for my, equidem. (See also **334**, i.)

part, it is our. (**291**, *Obs.* 2.)

part, the greater, plerique.

part from, I, discedo, ĕre, ab.

part in, I take, me im-misceo, ēre, -miscui, -mixtum (*dat.*); *a battle*, intersum (*dat.*); *politics*, attingo.

part in, without, exper-s, -tis (*gen.*, **301**, ii.).

partly, partim.

party, the (popular), pars, -tis, and see *popular* and *aristocratic.*

party, one . . . the other. (**340**, iii.)

pass (a law), I, perfero, ferre.

pass (time), I, dēgo, ĕre, dēgi ; ago, ĕre.

pass, to (intrans., of intervals of time), inter-cedĕre, -cessit.

pass by, I, praeter-eo, ire, -ii.

passion (anger), ira, *f.*

passionate, iracundus.

passionateness, iracundia, *f.*

past (adj.), praeteritus ; *the past*, praeterita (**52**) ; tempus prae-teritum.

pathless, invius.

patience, with, aequo animo, *or* patienter.

patriot, true patriot, bonus civis ; civis optimus ; *patriots, every patriot, all true patriots;* optimus quisque (**375**, *and note*); *best patriot*, optimus civis.

pay attention to, I, rationem habeo (*with gen.*): *pay (you) honour ;* honorem (tibi) habeo ; *pay my respects to*, saluto, are (*acc.*) ; *pay the penalty* (**243**, and see *penalty*).

peace, pax, pacis, *f.*

peace (*of mind*), securit-as, -atis, *f.*

peculiarity, special, proprium, *n.* (255.)

penalty, poena, *f. ;* supplicium, *n.; I pay the penalty of,* poenas do (*gen.*). (See note under *punishment.*)

people (= *men*), homines ; *a people* (= *nation*), popul-us, -i, *m.*

perceive, I, intel-lego, ĕre, -lexi, -lectum. (19.)

perhaps, nescio an (see 169), *or* haud scio an (*the latter should always be used before an adj. when no verb is expressed*) ; fortasse ; forsitan (170).

perilous, periculosus. (57, *a.*)

period, at that. (294, *Obs.*)

perish, I, pereo. ire.

permission, with your kind ; without his. (269, *Obs.*)

*permit,*I, per me licet (331, 15, *c*) : *I am permitted,* mihi licet (197).

perpetrate, I, com-, *or* ad-, mitto, ĕre ; facio, ĕre.

perpetrator (*of*), = *he who perpetrated.* (175.)

persecute, I, insector, ari (*dep.*).

persevere or *persist,* I, persevero. are.

person, a, homo, -inis. (224, *Obs.* 2 *and note,* and Ex. 39, *note.*)

person, a single (*after a negat.*), quisquam. (358, i.)

person (*your own*), caput, *n.*

personal appearance, corporis (59) habit-us, -ūs.

persuade, I, persua-deo, ēre, -si, -sum (5) ; *I cannot be persuaded,* persuaderi mihi non potest. (219, see also 122, *b.*)

pestilence, pestilentia, *f.*

philosopher, philosoph-us, -i.

philosophy, philosophia, *f.*

pierce, I, con-fodio, ĕre, -fōdi, -fossum.

pitch of, to such a, eo (*gen.*, 294, *Obs.*).

pity for, I feel, me miseret (*gen.*, 309).

place, loc-us, -i, *m. ; in the place* (*where*), ibi; *to the* (. . . *whence*), eo. (89.)

place, I, pono, ĕre.

plain, camp-us, -i, *m.*

plain (*adj.*), manifestus ; *as plain as,* manifestior. (276.)

plan, consilium, *n.*

plead (*as excuse*), I, excuso, are ; = *negotiate,* ago, ere ; *my cause,* causam oro, are. dico, ĕre.

pleasantly (*I speak*), jucunda. *n. pl.*

please, I (*you*), plac-eo, ēre, -ui. -itum (*dat.*, 5).

please, I (= *it pleases me*), mihi libet, libuit *or* libitum est (246); *if you please,* si libet.

pleasing to, gratus (*dat.*).

pleasure, volupt-as, -atis, *f.* (*often in pl., when used for pleasure in the abstract*).

pledge myself, I, spondeo, ēre, spopondi.

plunder, praeda, *f.*

poet, poeta, *m.*

point (*in every*), res (*pl.*).

point of, in. (332, 1, *e.*)

point of, on the, use fut. in -rus (189, iii.) ; *when on the, partic. in* -rus (418, *d*).

point (*whence*), *to the,* eo. (89.)

point out, I, monstro, are ; ostend-o, ĕre, -i.

poison, venenum, *n.*

policy, consilia, *n. pl.*

political, gen. of res publica (see 59); *for political storms,* in republica.

political life, res publica ; *I enter political life ;* ad rem p. me confero, ferre; *or* ac-cedo, ĕre, -cessi.

politicians. (175.)

politics, respublica (*never pl.*).

poor, paup-er, -eris : *the poor,* pauper-es, -um. (51, *a.*)

popular (*party*), popularis : *or the popular party,* popular-es, -ium. *m. pl.* (p. 63, *note* 4).

popularity, fav-or, -oris, *m.* (See note under *influence.*)

populous, frequen-s, -tissimus.

position, loc-us, -i, *m.*

possible (*with superlatives*), vel.

possible, it is. (125, *e.*)

possibly, use potest fieri ut. (64 and 125, *e.*)

post up, I, figo, ĕre, fixi, fixum.

posterity. (See **51**, *a, and note.*)

postpone, I, differo, ferre. (See note under *hang back.*)

poverty, paupert-as, -atis, *f.*

power, potentia, *f. ;* potest-as, -atis, *f.* (See note under *influence.*)

power, under his own, gen. of ditio sua, arbitrium suum. (**290**, *Obs.*)

powerful, potens; *the powerful*, potentissimus quisque (*sing.*, **375**); *I am most powerful*, plurimum possum.

powerless, I am, nihil possum.

praise (*subst.*), lau-s, -dis, *f.*

praise, I, laudo, are.

praised, to be (*adj.*), laudandus.

praiseworthy, laudabilis.

pray for, I (*I desire much*), opto, are (*acc.*) ; *I make one prayer*, unum opto.

prayers, prec-es, -um, *f.*

preceding, proximus.

precious, pretiosus (*superl.*, **57**, *a*).

predecessors. (**175**.)

prefer, I (*modal verb*), malo, malle, malui. (**42**, i. *d*, and ii.)

prefer (*him to you*), I, (eum tibi) prae-, *or* ante-pono, ĕre, -posui, -positum (**253**, ii.) ; *or* prae-fero, ferre, -tuli.

preparations, I make, paro, are. (**54**.)

prepare (*trans.*), I (*for or against you*), (tibi) in-tendo, ĕre, -tendi.

preparing to, use partic. in -rus. (**14**, *c*.)

presence, in his, my, etc., praesens. (**61**, *or* **420**, ii.)

presence of, in the (*prep.*), in (**273**, *Obs.*) ; coram (*abl. of persons*).

present (*adj.*), hic (**337**) ; *but your present*, iste (**338**).

present, I am, ad-sum, -esse, -fui ; *present at*, intersum. (**251**.)

present, at, or for the, in praesens. (**331**, 24, *b*.)

present, as a. (**260**, 3.)

present you with this, I, hoc (*abl.*) te (*acc.*) dono, are.

presently, mox ; brevi.

preservation of, the, use conservo, are. (**399**, *Obs.* 2 ; **292**, *Obs.*)

preserve, I, servo, are ; conservo, are.

press on, I, insto, are ; *by pressing on, gerund* (**99**.)

pretend, I, simulo, are (**39**) ; dictito,[1] are (*assert*) ; fingo, ĕre, finxi, fictum.

pretty (*adv.*) ; *pretty well*, satis.

prevail by prayer, I, impetro, are, *upon*, ab. (**127**, *c.*)

prevent, I (*from*), ob-sto, -stare, -stiti (*dat.*), quominus. (**137**, II.)

prevent, to (*in order that . . . not*), ne. (**101**, ii.)

priceless, pretiosissimus.

prince, rex, regis.

principle, want of, levit-as, -atis, *f.*

prison, vincula, *n. pl.*

prisoner, captiv-us, -i, *m. ; I am being taken*, capior, i, captus.

private (*person*), privatus ; *private property*, res familiaris.

privilege, a, jus, juris, *n.*

procrastinate, I, differo, ferre, distuli. (See note under *hang back.*)

procrastination, cunctati-o, -onis, *f. ; or use verb*, cunctor. (**98**, *a.*)

profess, I, pro-fiteor, ēri, -fessus.

progress in, I make (*much, more*), (multum, plus) proficio, ĕre, in (*abl.*).

project (*subst.*), consilium, *n.*

prolonged, diutinus.

promise, I, pollic-eor, ēri, -itus ; promitto, ĕre, -misi, -missum. (**37**.) (Voc. 6, *n.*)

promise, a, promissum, *n.* (**51**, *b*) ; *of good, or the highest* (**303**, *Obs.* 2) ; *I make promises*, polliceor (**54**).

proof, indicium, *n. ; is a proof.* (**260**, 3.)

proof against, invictus ab, *or* adversus (*acc.*).

---

[1] For *simulo* see p. 55, *note*. When the pretence is applied to words rather than to conduct, *dictito* (a frequentative form of *dico*) is common in the sense of "I assert, allege." *Fingo*, and still more *mentior*, emphasises the falsehood of the allegation.

proper, suus, a, um.

property, bona, *n. pl.* (51, *b*) ; fortunae, *f. pl.* ; res, rei, *f.*

prophet, vat-es, -is, *m.*

prophetic, = *of him foretelling the future.*

proportion to, in (332, 7, *h* ; 376) : *exact proportion to* (*with verbs of valuing*), tanti . . . quanti.

prosecuted for, *I am*, reus fio ; accusor. (306.)

prospect, or *prospects*, spes, spei, *f.* (*sing.*) (See note under *hope.*)

prosperity, res prosperae, *or* secundae.

protect your interests, *I*, tibi (248) caveo, ēre, cavi, cautum, *wish* . . . *protected* (240, *Obs.* 1).

protest against, *I.* (136, *a.*)

protract, *I* (*war*), traho, ĕre.

proud, superbus.

proud of, *I am*, glorior, ari. (281 *and* 282, *Obs.*)

prove, *I* (*intrans.*). (259, *Obs.*)

provide against, *I*, caveo, ēre, cāvi, cautum, ne, *or*, *with subst.*, *acc.*

provide for, *I*, pro-video, ēre, -vīdi, -visum. (248.)

provided that, modo, modo ne. (468.)

provision, *I make no*, nihil provideo ; *for.* (331, 24, *b.*)

provisions (*for army*), frumentum, *n.*; res frumentaria.

provocation, *without*, = *no one provoking*, abl. abs. (See 332, S, *and* 425.)

provoke, *I*, lacess-o, ēre, -ivi, or -i, -itum ; irrīto, are.

prudence, prudentia, *f.*

prudence, *want of*, imprudentia, *f.*

public (*services*), = *to the people* ; *public interest*, respublica ; *public life*, see *political life.*

punish, *I*, poenas sumo, ĕre, de (332, 3, *h*) ; *am punished for*, poenas do, dāre, *with gen. of the crime.*

punishment, poena,[1] *f.* ; supplicium, *n.* (*heavy*); *to bring punishment*, fraudi esse. (260, 3.)

purpose, *a*, propositum, *n.* (51, *b*) ; consilium, *n.*

purposely, consulto.

pursue, *I*, sequor, i, secutus.

pursuit, studium, *n.*

put off, *I*, differo, ferre, distuli.

put to death, *I*, caedo, ĕre, cecīdi, caesum: (See also under *kill.*)

put to the test, *I*, periclitor, ari (*dep.*).

put up with, *I*, tolero, are (*acc.*).

Pyrrhus, Pyrrh-us, -i.

quail before, *I*, pertim-esco, ĕre, -ui (*acc.*).

qualities, *good*, virtut-es, -um, *f. pl.*

quantity, vis, *acc.* vim. (See also 174.)

quarter, *I ask for*, ut mihi parcatur precor, -ari ; mortem *or* victoris iram deprecor ; *I obtain*, ut mihi parcatur impetro, are ; *or* mihi parcitur.

question, *I* (*ask*), interrogo, are (231, *note*) ; *it is questioned* (*doubted*), dubitatur : *may be*, dubitari potest.

question, *my*, *his*, *the* ; *to my*, *etc.*, *pres. part. of* interrogo (415, *a*, *and* 346) ; *the real question* (see *real*).

question, *a* (*matter*), res, rei, *f.*

quiet (*subst.*), tranquillit-as, atis, *f.*

quietly, use *adj.* (61), securus.

quit, *I*, exce-do, ĕre, -ssi, -ssum (*with or without* e, ex, 314).

quite, *not*, parum ; vix.

quite up to, ad *with* ipse. (Cf. 355, *a.*)

race (*nation*), gen-s, -tis *f.* ; *the human race*, hominum (59), *or* humanum, gen-us, -eris, *n.*

rage, ira, *f.*

raid upon, *I make a*, incursionem facio in (*acc.*).

raise, *I*, tollo, ĕre, sustuli, sublatum; (*an army*) (exercitum) comparo, are : (*a cheer*) (clamorem) tollo.

raise up, *I*, attollo, ĕre, sustuli, sublatum.

---

rally, I (intrans.), me col-ligo, ĕre, -lēgi ; *to rally (of a number)*, concurrĕre.

rank (position), stat-us, -ūs, *m. ; (of army)*, ord-o, -inis, *m. ; ranks (metaph. of a party)*, part-es, -ium, *f. pl. ; high rank*, dignit-as, -atis, *f.*

rare (remarkable), singularis.

rarely, raro, *comp.* rarius.

rash, temerarius.

rashness, temerit-as, -atis, *f.*

rather (adv.), potius.

rather, I had, or I would, malo, malle, malui.

ravage, I, populor, ari *(dep.)*.

reach, I, pervĕnio ad (253, iv.) ; *reach such a pitch of*, eo (294, *Obs.*) procedo, ĕre ; *to reach (of letters)*, perferri ad.

reach (of darts), the, jact-us, -ūs, *m.*

read through, or of, I, per-lego, ĕre, -lēgi, -lectum.

ready to, I am, volo, velle, volui *(modal); or use fut. in* -rus. (14, *c.*)

real (question) is, the, illud (341) quaeritur (218).

realise, I (conceive), animo, *or* mente, concipio, ĕre.

reality, in ; really, re ; re ipsā ; re verā. (274.)

reap (gain), I, per-cipio, ĕre ; *the fruit of*, fructum percipio *(gen.)*.

rear, tergum, *n. ; in the*, a tergo (332, I, *c*), *or* aversus (See 61.)

reason, a, causa, *f. ; for (both) reasons* (378, i.) ; *what reason?* (137, 1, *l*) ; *the reason (of)* ; quas ob causas *or* cur (174, *a*) ; *the reason (of)* . . . *was* (483, *Obs.*).

rebel[1] *a*, qui contra regem arma sumpsit. (175.)

rebel to (I invite), = *to rebellion*.

rebellion (renewal of war after submission), rebelli-o, -onis, *f. ; (revolt)*, defecti-o, -onis, *f.*

rebuke (subs.), use increpo, are. (415, *b* and *c*.)

recall (to), I, revoco, are (ad) ; *to mind*, in animum.

receive, I, ac-cipio, ĕre, -cēpi, -ceptum (19) ; *without receiving* (425, 420, i.).

recent, recens.

reckon up, I, enumero, are.

recognise, I, cognosco, ĕre.

reconciled with you, I am, tecum in gratiam red-eo, ire, ii.

reconciliation (you delay your), = *to be reconciled with.*

recover, I (trans.), recupero, are ; recipio, ĕre ; *recover myself*, me recipio ; *recover (intrans.) from*, emer-go, ĕre, -si, -surus, e, ex.

recruit, a, tir-o, -onis ; *army of recruits.* (223.)

reflect on, I, recordor, ari.

refrain from, I. (137, I, *f.*)

refuge with, I take, con-fugio, ĕre, -fūgi, ad.

refuse, I, nŏlo. (136, *a.*)

refute, I (an opponent), redarguo, ĕre ; *a charge*, diluo, ĕre ; *a me* removeo, ēre.

regard for or to, I have, rationem habeo *(gen.)*.

regiment, use cohor-s, -tis, *f.*

regret, I, me pud-et, ēre, -uit. (309.)

regular engagement, a, justum praelium.

reign, I, regno, are.

reinforcements, subsidia, *n. pl.*

reject, I, repudio, are.

rejoice, I, gaudeo, ēre, gavisus. (Intr. 44.)

rejoicing (subst.), laetitia, *f.*

relates to, spectat ad.

relation, a, propinqu-us, -i. *m.* (256.)

reliance on (you), I place, fidem (tibi) habeo.

relief, I bring you, tibi succurr-o, ĕre, -i.

relieve, I, sublevo, are (acc.) ; *relieve of*, levo, are (abl. of thing).

relinquish, I, o-mitto, ere, -misi, -missum. (See note under *undone, I leave.*)

reluctant, I am, nolo, nolle.

reluctantly ; with reluctance. (61.)

rely on, I, con-fido, ĕre, -fisus (282, *Obs.*, 244, *c*); fidem habeo *(dat.)*.

---

[1] A "rebel" might also be "*qui a fide descivit or defecit ;*" or *rem publicam* might be substituted for *regem.*

relying on (*adj.*), fretus. (285.)

remain behind, I, re-maneo, ēre, -mansi.

remain firm, I, permaneo, ēre.

remains, it, restat ut. (See 125, *g.*)

remarkable, singularis.

remember, I, memin-i, -isse (*imperative* memento ; *for pres. subj.* meminerim).

Remi, the, Rem-i, -orum.

remorse for, I feel, me (234) poenit-et, ēre, -uit (*gen.,* 309).

remove (*my home*), I, commigro, are (*intrans.*).

removed from, I am, far. (264.)

renown, gloria, *f.*

repeatedly, saepe; saepissime (57, *a*); persaepe.

repel, I, propulso, are ; *from,* ab.

repent of, I, me poenit-et, -ēre, -uit. (309.)

reply, I, respond-eo, ēre, -i.

repose, otium, *n. ; I enjoy,* otiosus sum.

reproach, it is a. (260, 3.)

reputation, existimati-o, -onis, *f. ;* fama, *f. ; reputation for,* lau-s, -dis, *f.* (*gen.*).

request, I make a, peto, ēre (127, *c*), posco, ēre, poposci (231.) (See note under *demand*) ; *I make this,* hoc (*acc.*) peto ; *my request,* quae peto. (175.)

require, I, *use* opus. (286.)

resemble (*closely*), I, similis (*superl.*) sum. (255.)

resentment, dol-or, -oris, *m.*

resident, I am, domicilium habeo ; *at.* (312.)

resignation, with, aequo animo.

resist, I, repugno, are. (*dat.*)

resistance, use inf. pass. of resisto, ēre (219), *in spite of resistance,* resisto *or* repugno (420, ii.).

resolution (*design*), consilium, *n.*

resolution, I pass a, decerno, ēre.

resolve, I, statu-o, ēre, -i ; decerno, ēre, -crevi, -cretum. (45.)

resources, op-es, -um, *f.*

respect, observantia, *f.*

respectable, honestus.

responsible (*for*), *I make you,* rationem a te reposco, ēre (*with gen.*)

rest, qui-es, -ētis, *f.*

rest (*of*), *the,* ceteri ; *or* (372) reli-qu-us, -i (*in agreement,* 60, *or with gen.*) ; *rest of the world.* (See *world.*)

rest on, I, ni-tor, i, -sus (*abl.,* 282, *Obs.*).

rest with, to, penes (331, 15) esse.

restore, I (*strength, etc.*), redintegro, are.

restrained from, to be. (137, 1, *k.*)

result, res, rei, *f. ;* (*of toil*), fruct-us, -ūs, *m. ; the result is, was, etc.,* evĕnit, evēnit, eventurum ; *without result.* (332, 8.)

retain, I, re-tineo, ēre, -tinui.

retake, I, re-cipio, ēre, -cepi, -ceptum.

retire from, I, abeo, ire. (264.)

retreat, I, me recipio, ēre ; pedem refero, ferre.

retrieve, I, sano, are.

return (*subst.*), redit-us, -ūs, *m.*

return, I (*intrans.*), red-eo, ire, -ii, -iturus.

return kindness, I, gratiam refero. (98, *b.*)

revolt, a, defecti-o, -onis, *f.*

reward, praemium, *n. (prize*) ; merc-es, -ēdis, *f. ;* fruct-us, -us, *m. (fruit*).

reward, I, praemiis afficio.

rich (*of persons*), div-es, -itis, divit- (dit-)ior, -issimus ; *of cities,* opulentus ; *the rich* (51, *a*).

riches, diviti-ae, -arum.

ride past, I, (equo) praeter-vehor, i, -vectus (*trans.,* 24) ; cf. *coast along.*

ridge, jugum, *n.*

ridiculed, I am, irrideor, ēri. (253, iii.)

right (*subst.*), jus, juris, *n. ; I have a right,* debeo, ēre : *I am in the right,* vere, recte, sentio, ire.

right hand, dextra, *f.*

rightly, rightfully, jure.[1] (268.)

rigour, severit-as, -atis, *f.*

ring with, to (*echo with*), person-are, -ui (*abl.*).

---

[1] *Jure* is "rightly" in the sense of "rightfully," "deservedly ;" *recte,* "correctly," "accurately ;" *rite,* in accordance with religious usage or ceremonial.

rising, *a*, sediti-o, -onis, *f.*
rising ground, tumul-us, -i, *m.* (*use pl.*).
rival, invid-us, -i, *m.*
river, flum-en, -inis, *n.* ; fluvi-us, -i, *m.*
road, *a*, via,
roar out, *I*, vociferor, ari ; magnā voce conclamo, are.
rock, saxum, *n.*
roll, *I* (*intrans.*), volvor, i, volu-tus. (**21**, *a.*)
Rome (*the city*), Roma, *f.* ; (*the nation*) populus Romanus. (**319**.)
roof, *under my.* (**331**, 4, *a.*)
round (*prep.*), circa or circum (*acc.*, **331**, 5) ; *round which* (*standard*), quo (**508**).
rout, *I*, fundo, ĕre, fudi, fusum.
royal, regius.
ruin, interit[1]-us, -ūs, *m.* ; exitium, *n.* ; pernici-es, -ei, *f.* ; clad-es, -is, *f.* ; calamit-as, -atis, *f.* ; *without ruin to*, *use* salvus (*abl. abs.*, **424**).
ruin, *I*, pessum do, dăre (Sallust) ; *ruined*, afflictus (affligo).
ruler of, *I am*, impero, are (*dat.*).
rumour, rum-or, -oris, *m.*
run forward, *I*, pro-curro, ĕre, -curri.
run into, *I*, incurro, ĕre (in, *acc.*).
rural, rusticus.
rustic (*adj.*), agrestis.

sack (*a city*) *I*, di-ripio, ĕre, -ripui, -reptum.
sacrifice to (*metaph.*), *I = I place behind*, post-habeo. (**253**, ii.)
sad, maestus.
safe, tutus ; incolumis (*safe and sound*) ; salvus (*of things as well as persons*). *For adv. use* tutus *or* incolumis. (**61**.)
safety, sal-us, -utis, *f.* ; *in safety*, tuto (*adv.*) ; incolumis (*adj.*, **61**) ; *I wish for your safety*, te salvum volo. (**240**, *Obs.* 1.)
sail, *I*, navigo, are ; *sail round*, circumnavigo, are (*trans.*)

sailor, naut-a, -ae, *m.*
sake of, *for the*, causā, or gratiā, *with gen. or pronominal adj.* (**289**); *or with gerund* (**396**) ; *for its own sake*, propter se (**331**, 20, *b*).
sally, *a*, erupti-o, -onis, *f.* ; *I make a*, eruptionem facio. ĕre.
sally out, *I*, e-rumpo, ĕre, -rupi.
salute, *I*, saluto, are.
same as, *the.* (**84**, **365**.)
satisfactory. (See Voc. 6.)
satisfied with, contentus (*abl.*, **285**).
save you, *I*, tibi salutem affero, ferre.
say, *I*, dico, ĕre, dixi, dictum ; *said he* (*parenthetic*) (**40**) ; *it is said* (**44**). (See also under *speak.*)
saying, *a*, dictum (see **51**, *b*, **55**); *the saying*, illud (**341**).
scale, *I*, conscen-do, ĕre, -di.
scanty, exiguus.
scarcely, vix.*
scatter, *to*, (*intrans.*), dissipari. (**20**, **21**, *a.*)
scene, *I come on the*, intervenio, ire.
scenes (*places*), loc-i, -orum, *m.*
schemes, insidiae, *f.* ; art-es, -ium, *f.*
science of war, res militaris.
scout, *a*, explorat-or, -oris.
sea, mar-e, -is, *n.* ; *by sea and land*, terra marique (*note the order*).
sea-sickness, nausea, *f.*
second, alter (**531**, *a*) ; (*for*) *a second time*, iterum (**533**, *c*) ; *secondly*, deinde (**534**, *Obs.*).
secret from, *I keep*, celo, are (**230**) ; *I make a secret of*, dissimulo, are (*with constr. of* simulo, **39**).
secretly, secreto (*adv.*)
secure (*safe*), tutus. (**19**.)
secure, *I* (*make secure*), confirmo, are.
see, *I*, video,[2] ĕre, vīdi, visum ; (*as a spectator*) specto, are; (*in sense of perceive*), intel-lego, ĕre, -lexi, -lectum ; *I am seen*, con-spicior, i, -spectus.

---

[1] *Ruina* is the fall (literal) of a building, etc., and is only occasionally used in a metaphorical sense. (See 17-19.)
[2] *Videre*, the general word, to see ; *spectare*, to look long at, to watch as a spectacle ; *cernere*, to see clearly, to discern ; *conspicere*, to get sight of ; *aspicere*, to turn the eye towards ; *intueri*, to gaze at earnestly or steadfastly.

seek for, I, pet-o, ĕre, -ii, -ivi, -ītum.

seem, I, videor, ēri, visus **(43)** ; *it seems as though* **(149,** ii.**).**

seize, I, comprehen-do, ĕre. -di, -sum ; (*an opportunity*), utor, i, usus. **(281.)**

seldom, raro.

self-confidence, sui fiducia, *f.* **(300.)**

self-control, ˊmodestia ; (animi) moderati-o, -onis, *f.*

self-control, want of, impotentia, *f.; adj.* impotens, *adv.* impotenter.

Senate, the, Senat-us, -ūs, *m.*

Senate House, the, Curia, *f.*

send, I, mitto, ĕre, misi, missum ; *to,* ad **(6)** ; *send back* (*to*), remitto, ĕre (ad) ; *send for,* arcess-o, ĕre, -ivi, -ītum (*acc.*).

sense, good, prudentia, *f.*

sensible, or *of sense,* pruden-s, -tior, -tissimus ; *one so sensible as* **(224,** *Obs.* 2) ; *adv.,* prudenter.

sentenced to, I am, multor, ari. **(307.)**

sentiments, I hold the same, eadem **(365)** sentio **(54).**

separately, singuli. **(380,** *b.***)**

serious, grav-is, -ior, -issimus.

serpent, serpen-s, -tis, *f.*

served, the nation is, respublica geritur, gesta est.

service, military, militia, *f.*

service to, I do (*good, the best, such good*), (bene, optime, tam bene) mereor, ēri, meritus, de **(332,** 3, *g*) ; but *services to,* merita **(51,** *b*) in **(331,** 24, *d*).

set (*spurs*), *I,* subdo, ĕre (*dat.*).

set at liberty, I, libero, are.

set at naught, I, con-temno, ĕre, -tempsi, -temptum (see Voc. 10, *n.*) ; parvi, minimi, nihili, facio or habeo **(305).**

set before (*you*), *I,* (tibi) expo-no, ĕre, -sui, -situm.

set fire to, I, incen-do, ĕre, -di, -sum (*acc.*).

set out, I, pro-ficiscor, i, -fectus.

settle, I, constit-uo, ĕre, -ui (*trans.*).

several (= *some*), aliquot (*indecl.*) ; = *respective,* suus *with* quisque. **(352,** *Obs.***)**

severe, gravis.

sex, sex-us, -ūs, *m.*

shake, I (*trans.*), labefacto, are.

shamelessness, impudentia, *f.*

share (*with*), *I,* communico, are (cum, ˙253, iv.).

shatter, I, quasso, are.

shelter, I, tego, ĕre, texi, tectum.

shelter, perfugium, *n.; under shelter of,* tectus (*abl.*).

shew, I. (See *show.*)

shield, scutum, *n.*

ship of war, a, navis longa ; *merchant ship,* navis oneraria.

short, in, denique.

short-lived (*panic*) = *of the shortest time.* **(303,** *Obs.* 1.**)**

shortly, brevi.

shout, a, clam-or, -oris, *m.*

show, I (*point out*), monstro, are ; *I show* (*display*) *clemency, etc.,* or, *I show myself* (*prove*) (see **241**) ; *I show such cruelty to,* adeo saevio, ire, in (*abl.*) ; *show gratitude* (**98,** *b*).

shrewd, acutus (*superl.* **57,** *a.*).

shrink from, I, detrecto, are (*acc.*).

sick, aeg-er, -ra, -rum ; *I am sick,* aegroto, are ; *his sick-bed,* = *him whilst sick and failing.*

side (*of a river*), ripa, *f.*

side, I am by your, tibi praesto (*adv.*) sum ; *on your,* a te sto, are, stĕti. **(332,** i., *d.***)**

side, on no, nusquam ; nec usquam ; *on this side* (*of*), *prep.,* cis **(331,** 6) ; *on the other,* ultra **(331,** 23) ; *on all sides,* undique.

sigh for, I (*metaph.*), desidero, are (*trans.,* **22, 23**).

signal, a, signum, *n.*

silence, in. **(61.)**

silent, I am, taceo, ēre.

sin, I, pecco. are.

since, (*adv.*), postea ; *as prep.,* = *from.* **(326.)**

single combat, in, comminus.

single, a, unus ; *not a single ; not one :* ne unus quidem. **(529,** *a.***)**

sink, I (*trans.*), demer-go, ĕre, -si, -sum ; *intrans.* (*metaph.*), descend-o, ĕre, -i : *I am sinking* (*fainting*) *under,* exanimor, ari (*abl.,* **267**).

sister, sor-or, -oris.
sit, *I*, sĕdeo, ĕre, sēdi ; *sit down*, con-sido, ĕre, -sēdi.
situation, sit-us, -ūs, *m.*
six, sex ; *sixth*, sextus.
size, magnitud-o, -inis, *f. ;* and see **174.**
slander, maledicta, *n. pl.* (**51,** *b.*)
slaughter, *I, use* occidione oc-cīdo, ĕre, -cīdi, -cīsum.
slave, serv-us, -i, *m.; I am a slave,* serv-io, ire, -ii, -ītum.
slavery, servĭt-us, -utis, *f.*
slay, *I.* (See *kill.*)
sleep, *I*, dorm-io, ire, -ivi, -ii, -itum; *in his sleep, use pres. partic.*
sleep, somn-us, -i, *m.*
sleep, *want of*, vigiliae, *f. pl.*
slingstone, *a*, glan-s, -dis, *f.*
so, ita : *with verbs,* adeo ; *so little,* adeo non : *with adjs. and advs. only,* tam : *so = accordingly,* itaque : *so great, so many* (**84**) : *so small,* tantulus: *so far from,* tantum abest ut (**124**): *so, or as, long as, abl. abs.* (**420,** ii.) (See also **224,** *Obs.* 2.)
society, *as a.* (**380,** *b.*)
soften (*metaph.*), *I*, exoro, are.
solemnly appeal, I. (See *appeal.*)
soldier, mil-es, -itis.
solitude (*of a place*), infrequentia, *f.*
Solon, Sol-on, -onis.
some (*some one*), aliquis (**360**); nescio quis (**362**); *some . . others,* alii . . . alii (**369**).
some (*amount of*), aliquantum (*gen.,* **294**) ; *for some time,* aliquantum temporis.
somehow. (**363.**)
something (*opposed to nothing*), aliquid (**360**).
sometimes, nonnunquam ;[1] interdum.
son, fili-us, -i.

soon, mox ; brevi ; jam (**328,** *b*) ; *sooner than he had hoped*=*quicker* (celerius) *than his own hope* (**277**).
sore (*of famine*), gravis.
sorrows, incommoda, *n. pl.*, aerumnae (*stronger*).
sorry, I should be, nolim. (**231,** *example.*)
soul, (*not*) *a,* quisquam (**358,** i.); *in Livy* unus *is sometimes added ;* ne unus quidem. (**529,** *a.*)
sound your praises, I, laudibus te fero, ferre.
sounds incredible, it, incredibile dictu est. (**404.**)
source of (*metaph.*), *the, use* unde (**174,** *e*); *a source of* (*gain*) (**260,** 3).
sovereign (*king*), rex.
sovereignty, principat-us, -ūs, *m.*
Spaniard, a, Hispan-us, -i ; *Spain* (= *the nation*), Hispani. (**319.**)
spare, I, parco, ĕrc, peperci (*dat.,* **5**) ; *for perf. pass.* temperatum est (**249**).
speak, I, loquor[2], i, locutus ; dico, ĕre ; *I speak out,* eloquor, i ; *in speaking, abl. of gerund.*
special peculiarity of. (See *peculiarity.*)
speech, a, orati-o, -onis, *f.* ; *if to soldiers or multitude,* conti-o, -onis, *f.; my speech is over ; I have done my speech,* dixi. (**187.**)
speed, celerit-as, -atis, *f.*
spirit, anim-us, -i, *m. ; of more than one person,* animi ; *with spirit,* ferociter. (See note under *boldly.*)
spite of, in, in (**273,** *Obs.*) ; *of your resistance, etc.*), *abl. abs.* (**420,** ii.); *in spite of his innocence* (**224,** *Obs.* 1).
spoil, praeda, *f.*
spotless, integer, integerrimus ; innocen-s, -tior, -tissimus.

---

[1] *Nonnunquam,* "fairly often ; " approaches *saepius. Interdum,* "now and then," more rarely than *nonnunquam. Aliquando,* "on certain occasions," opposed to "never," almost = *raro.*

[2] *Dico*, I "speak" or "say," *i.e.* I give expression to thoughts or views which I have formed : *loquor,* I "speak," use the organs of speech to utter articulate words. Hence *dico* = I make a formal speech *loquor* = I utter informal or casual words.

spread beneath, I (trans.), sub-jicio, ĕre, -jeci, -jectum; *intrans.,* sub-jicior, i. (20.)

spring, the, ver, vēris, *n.*

spring, I (am sprung), orior, īri, ortus; *sprung from,* ortus (*abl.*); *originally sprung from,* oriundus ab.

spur, calc-ar, -aris, *n.* ; *I put spurs to,* calcaria subdo, ĕre (*dat.*).

spy, a, speculat-or, -oris, *m.*

staff (military), legati, *m. pl.*

stand, I, sto, stare, stĕti; *stand by,* ad-sto, -stare, -stiti (*dat.*); *stand round,* circum-sto, are, -steti (*acc.*).

stand for, I, (am a candidate for), peto, ĕre (*acc.*).

stand in need of, I, indigeo, ēre. (284.)

stand in your way, I, tibi obsto, are. (253, i.)

standard, a, signum, *n.*; vexillum, *n.*

start (set out), I, pro-ficiscor, i, -fectus, -fecturus.

state (condition), stat-us, -ūs, *m.*

state (adj.), publicus.

statesman, a consummate, reipublicae gubernandae peritissimus. (301, ii.)

stay with, I (I visit), commoror, ari apud (331, 4, *a*) ; deverto, ĕre (*reflexive*), apud; *I stay at home,* domi maneo, ēre.

steadily, turn by *did not cease to* (desisto, ĕre, -stiti).

steadiness, want of, inconstantia, *f.*

steal away, I (intrans.), di-labor, i, lapsus.

stern, severus.

sternly, I act, saevio, ire. (25.)

still (adv.), adhuc ; etiam nunc (*of the present*) ; etiam tum *(past or fut.*).

stony-hearted, ferreus.

storm, tempest-as, -atis, *f.*

storm, I (take by storm), expugno, are.

story, a, res, rei, *f.*; and see **54** ; *there is a story,* ferunt (**44**).

strangely, nescio quo pacto. (See **169.**)

stream, riv-us, -i, *m.* ; see *river.*

strength, vir-es, -ium, *f. pl.; strength of mind,* constantia, *f.*

stretch forth, I, por-rigo, ĕre, -rexi, -rectum.

strike off, I, excu-tio, ĕre, -ssi, -ssum.

strikingly, graviter.

strive, I (to), conor, ari (*modal*).

stronghold, arx, arcis, *f.*

struck (partic.), ictus (ico, ĕre) ; *I am struck,* per-cutior, i, -cussus.

study, a, ar-s, -tis, *f.* ; *study (of),* cogniti-o, -onis, *f.*

study, I, operam do (*dat.*) ; *study my own interest,* mihi (**248**) con-sulo, ĕre.

subject, a, civ-is, -is, *m.*

submit to, I, per-fero, -ferre (*acc.*).

substantial, solidus, *comp.* magis solidus.

succeed in, I (a design, etc.), per-ficio, ĕre (*trans.*); efficio *with* ut. (**125,** *j.*)

succeed to, I (the throne), (regnum) ex-cipio, ĕre, -cēpi, -ceptum (**17**); *I succeed you,* tibi suc-cedo, ĕre, -cessi, -cessum.

success (**98,** *a*) ; *without success,* in-fecta re (**332,** 8 ; **425**).

successfully, prospere.

successive, continuus.

successors (his), =*those who reigned after (him)* ; or *those who are to (fut. in -rus) succeed (him).* (See **175, 342,** *n.*)

succour, I, subvenio, ire (*dat.*).

such (=*of such a kind*), talis ; (=*so great*), tantus ; *as,* qualis *or* quantus (see **86**) : *such . . . as this,* hujusmodi (**87**), *or* hic talis, hic tantus (**88,** *Obs.*): *such as to, of such a kind that* (**108**) : *such (adv.), such a (with adj.),* tam ; talis (*or tantus*) tamque (**88**): *where English subst. is expressed by Latin verb, use* adeo ; *I show such cruelty,* adeo saevio.

sudden, subitus ; repentinus (*unexpected*).

suddenly, subĭto.

suddenness of, the, = *how sudden it was.* (**174,** *e.*)

suffer from, I, laboro, are (*abl.*).

suffering (*adj.*), afflictus (affligo).

sufficient, justus ; satis, *with gen.*

suffices, it, satis est.

suggest, I, auctor sum (**399**, *Obs.* 2) ; admoneo, ēre (**127**, *a*).

suggestion, at (*my*), (me) auctore (*abl. abs.*, **424**).

suicide, I commit, mortem mihi conscisco, ēre, -scivi. (**253**, ii.)

summer, aest-as, -atis, *f.*

summit. (**60**.)

summon, I, voco, are ; *to*, ad.

sun, sol, solis, *m.*

sunlight, lux, lucis, *f.* (solis *may be added*).

superior to, I am, = I surpass ; (in courage, etc.), *use comparat. of adj.* (**278, 279**); *superior numbers* (*see numbers*).

superstition, superstiti-o, -onis, *f.*

supper, caena, *f.; to*, ad (**331**, 24, *b*, *example*).

supplies, commeat-us, -ūs, *m.* (*sing. and pl.*)

supply with, I, suppedito, are. (**247**.)

support (*subst.*), subsidium, *n.*

support (*my*) *arms, I*, arma fero, ferre.

suppose, I, puto, are. (See note under *fancy*.)

supreme power, imperium, *n.*

sure, I am or feel, certo scio ; pro certo habeo ; *I have made sure of*, compertum habeo (**188**) : *be sure to*, fac, cura (ut). (See **141**.)

surpass, I, supero, are.

surprise (*as a foe*), *I*, opprimo, ēre.

surrender, I (*trans.*), de-do, ēre, -didi, -ditum ; (*intrans.*), me dedo (see 21, *b*); *I surrender my arms*, arma trado, ēre.

surround, to, circumvēnire (*trans.*): *surrounded, use pres. partic. of* circumsto, are (*abl. abs.*, **420**, ii.); *surrounded* (*by defences*), cinctus (cingo) : *to be surrounded* (*as by water*), circum-fundi, -fusus.

survive, I, supersum ; *from*, e, ex : *so long as you survive*, te superstite (*abl. abs.*, **424**).

suspect, I, suspicor, ari ; = *I think*, puto, are (see note under *fancy*); *I am* (*become*) *suspected of*, in suspicionem vĕnio, ire (*gen.*).

suspend, I, inter-mitto, ĕre. (See note under *undone, I leave*.)

suspicion, suspici-o, -onis, *f.; I have no, = I suspect nothing.* (**54**.)

sustain (*onset*), *I*, sustineo, ēre.

swallow, a, hirund-o, -inis, *f.*

swarm out of, to, ef-fundi, -fusus (*abl.*).

swear, I, juro, are.

sweep, I (*metaph.*), volito, are.

sword, gladius, -i, *m.; in metaphorical sense*, arma, *n. pl.*; ferrum, *n.; with fire and sword*, ferro et igni ; *by sword and violence*, vi et armis : *note the order.*

Syracuse, Syracusae, *f.*

take, I (*a city*), capio, ēre ; *by assault*, expugno, are.

take advantage of, I, utor, i, usus. (**281**.)

take care that, I, facio ut. (**118**.)

take from you, I, tibi ad-imo, ĕre, -ēmi, -emptum. (**243**.)

take part in, I. (See *part in*.)

take place, to, fieri.

take prisoner, I, capio, ēre.

take the same view, I. (See *view*.)

take up, I (*arms*), sum-o, ĕre, -psi, -ptum, = *I spend*, consumo, ĕre.

talk, I, loquor, i, locutus.

talkative, loqu-ax, -acior.

tall, procĕrus.

task, op-us, -ĕris, *n.*

taste, a, studium, *n.*

taunt you with, I, tibi ob-jicio, ĕre, -jeci. (**247**.)

tax with, I, incuso,[1] are , insimulo, are (*acc. of person, gen. of thing*).

teacher, magist-er, -ri : *fem. form*, magistra.

teaching, the, praecepta, *pl.*

tear, a, lacrima, *f.*

tedious, longus.

teeth of, in the. (**420**, ii.)

tell, I (*bid*), jubeo, ēre. (**120**.)

---

[1] *Incuso*, "I tax with," "charge with," but informally, not as *accuso* with gen. "bring a charge in court." *Insimulo*, "I hint charges without proof." *Arguo*, "I try to prove guilty."

tell (a story), *I*, narro, are.

temper, anim-us, i, *m*.

temperament, indol-es, -is, *f*. (See note under *character*.)

temple, templum, *n*.

ten, decem ; *(a-piece)*, deni. (532.)

tenacious of, tenax. (301, i.)

tends to, *use gen. with* est. (292, *Obs*.)

tent, tabernaculum, *n*.

terms, condition-es, -um, *f. pl*.

terrible, *so*, tantus.

territory, fin-es, -ium, *m*.

terror, *I am in such*, adeo pertim-esco, ĕre, -ui.

testify, *I (show)*, declaro, are.

than, quam ; *or abl*. (275. 493.)

thank you (for), *I*, gratias (tibi) ago, ob *or* pro.

thanks, *I return*, gratias ago (98, *b*) ; *"thanks to"*, propter (331, 20, *b*).

that(demonstrative), ille, a, ud (339).

that, *after verbs of saying* (see Oratio Obliqua) : = *in order that*, *(so) that* (see Final, Consecutive, Clauses).

themselves (reflexive), se (ipsos) (356, ii.) ; *emphatic*, ipsi (355).

then, tum, tunc ; *then and there*, illico. (See also *therefore*.)

thence, inde.

there, ibi ; illic ; *after verb of motion*, eo, illuc.

therefore, igitur ; *in narrative*, itaque.

thereupon, tum.

thick of, *the*, = *the midst of*. (60.)

think, *I (reflect)*, cogito, are.

third, tertius (*adj*.).

thirst, sit-is, -is, *f*., *abl*. siti.

thirty, triginta (*indecl*.).

this, hic, haec, hoc. (337.)

thoroughly (with adj.), *use superl*.

though, *use pres. part*. (412, *Obs*.)

thousand (subst.), mille, *pl*. milia ; *to die a thousand deaths*, = *a thousand times*, milies (*adv*.).

threaten, *I*, insto, are ; *of things*, immineo, ĕre ; impend-eo, ĕre, -i (253, i.) ; *I threaten with*, minor, ari, minitor, ari. denuntio, are (247) ; *threaten*, *to*, minor, ari. (See 37.)

threats, minae, *f. pl.* ; *I make threats*, = *I threaten* (minor).

three, tres, tria ; *three days (space of)*, triduum, *n.* ; *three years*, triennium, *n*.

thrice, ter.

throne, regnum, *n*., *or* imperium, *n.* ; *I am on the throne*, regno, are. (See 17.)

throng, multitud-o, -inis, *f*.

throughout, per (*acc.*) ; *throughout (the city)*, = *in the whole (abl.)*.

throw, *I*, conjicio, ĕre, -jeci, -jectum ; *into*, in (*acc.*) ; *myself (at the feet of)*, me projicio, ĕre (257) ; *throw across*, trajicio, ĕre ; *throw away*, projicio, ĕre ; *throw down (arms)*, abjicio, ĕre.

tie (subst.), necessitud-o, -inis, *f*.

till, *I*, col-o, ĕre, -ui, cultum.

till (440, 441) ; *not till* (443, *Obs*.).

time, temp-us, -oris, *n.* ; *at that time*, tum ; eā tempestate ; tum temporis (294, *Obs*.) ; *at his own time* (349, *Obs*.) ; *in good time*, ad tempus (326).

timid, timidus.

to, ad (331, 1) ; in (331, 24). (See 6.)

to-day, hodie.

toil, lab-or, -oris, *m*.

toilsome, = *of such toil*. (303, i.)

tomb, sepulcrum, *n*.

to-morrow, cras.

tongue, lingua, *f*.

too (also), quoque. (Intr. 98.)

too, with adjectives. (See 57, *b*.)

too little (of), parum. (294.)

too much, 294 ; *it costs*, nimio (280, *Obs*.).

torture, cruciat-us, -ūs, *m*.

touch (his heart), *I*, (animum ejus) flecto, ĕre ; *I am touched by*, moveor, ēri (*abl*.).

towards, ad (331, 1, 22) ; *with countries*, *towns*, *and* domum.

town, oppidum, *n*.

townsman, oppidan-us, -i.

traditions, *I hand down*, **trado**, ĕre ; *there is a tradition*. (44.)

train, *I*, exerc-eo, ēre, -ui, -itum : exercito, are ; *trained in*, exercitatus (*abl*.).

training, disciplina, *f*.

traitors, cives impii.

transact, I, ago, ĕre, ēgi, actum.

tranquillity, otium, *n.*

transported, I am (metaph.), exar-
desco, ĕre, -si (*lit. I become hot*).

travel, I, iter facio ; = *go abroad,*
peregrinor, ari ; *travel over,* per-
lustro, are (*acc.*).

treachery, perfidia, *f.*

treat as a source of gain, I. (260, 3.)

treat lightly, I, parvi facio. (305.)

treat with success (heal), I, medeor,
ēri (*dat.*).

treaty, a, foed-us, -ĕris, *n.*

tree, a, arb-or, -ŏris, *f.*

tribe, a, nati-o, -onis, *f.* ; gen-s,
-tis, *f.* (Voc. 2, *note.*)

trifling, (adj.), levissimus (57, *a*) ;
inconstan-s, -tissimus. (See 224.)

triumph (success), victoria, *f. ; (a
Roman general's),* triumph-us, -i
(see note under *I triumph*) ; *in
triumph,* victor (63) ; *in the very
hour of,* in ipsā victoriā ; *shouts
of triumph,* exultantium clamor
(415, *b*).

triumph, I (metaph.), exulto,[1] are ;
triumph over, supero, are (*acc.*).

troops, copiae, *f.* ; milit-es, -um, *m.*

trouble, without, nullo negotio (269,
Obs.) ; *troubles,* molestiae, *f. pl.* ;
troublesome, molestus.

truce, a, indutiae, *f. pl.*

true, verus ; *it is true, use* ille (334,
iv.) ; *truest patriot* (see *patriot*).

trust (that), I, con-fido, ĕre, -fisus ;
trust your word, fidem tibi habeo.

truth, the, vera, *n. pl.* (53) ; *but in
truth (opposed to a supposition),*
nunc vero.

try (to), I, conor, ari.

trying, (adj.), difficilis. (57, *a*.)

tumult, tumult-us, -ūs, *m.*

turn, I (trans.), vert-o, ĕre, -i ; *my
back on you,* tergum tibi verto.

turn, I (intrans.), vertor, i, versus ;
convertor, i (20) ; *to,* ad ; *turn
back,* re-vertor, i.

turn, each in, pro se quisque. (352.)

turn out, I (prove), eva-do, ĕre, -si
(Intr. 50) ; *it turns out,* evĕnit ;
usu vĕnit (see note under *lot*) ;
turns out so, eo evadit.

twelve hundred, mille ducenti.
(527, 528.)

twentieth, vicesimus.

twenty, viginti (*indecl.*).

twice over, semel atque iterum ;
twice two, bis bina.

two, du-o, -ae, -o ; *two a-piece,* bini
(532, *a*) ; *two-thirds,* duae partes
(535, *c*) ; *two years (space of),*
biennium, *n.*

tyrant, tyrann-us, -i.

tyranny, dominati-o, onis, *f.*

unable to, I am, nequ-eo, -ivi, -ii ;
non possum.

unanimous; unanimously, use omnis.
(59.)

unarmed, inermis.

unawares, imprudens (*adj.,* 61).

uncertain, it is, incertum est. (166.)

uncle, avuncul-us, -i.

uncomplaining under, patiens (57,
a), *with gen.* (302).

unconstitutional, unconstitutionally,
contra rempublicam. (331, 7.)

uncultivated, rudis.

undaunted, intrepidus *(for usage
with proper nouns and persons,
see* 224.)

under (disgrace), cum. (269.)

understand, I, intel-lego, ĕre, -lexi,
-lectum.

undertake, I, suscipio, ĕre.

undertaking, an, inceptum, *n.*
(51, *b*.)

undeserved, immeritus.

undiminished, = the same as before.
(84.)

undone, I leave, o-mitto,[2] ĕre, -misi,
-missum.

undoubtedly, = indisputably. (64.)

unequalled, tantus . . . quantus
(followed by nemo *etc.).* (See
490, i.)

unhappy, mis-er, -era, -erum.

---

[1] *Triumpho* is rarely used metaphorically, or in any other sense than that of cele-
brating a *triumphus, i.e.* of a general entering the city in triumphal procession.

[2] *Omitto* is I give up, or do not begin, something, *designedly; intermitto,* I leave
alone *for a time : praetermitto,* I pass by, omit, *undesignedly.*

unharmed, incolumis.
unhealthy, pestilentus.
unheard, indictā causā (abl. abs.).
union, in, conjuncti.
universal, use omnis. (59.)
unjust, iniquus.
unlucky, infel-ix, -icior.
unmoved, immotus.
unnatural, nefarius.
unpatriotic, the, mali, or improbi, cives. (50, note.)
unpopularity, invidia, f. ; object of (see object).
unprincipled, nequ-am, -ior, -issimus (lit. worthless) : see 224.
unquestionable, it is, = it cannot be doubted. (See 137.)
unrivalled. (358, ii., or 490, i.`
until. (See till.)
untimely, immaturus.
untouched, integ-er, -ra, -rum.
unusual, inusitatus.
unversed in, imperitus (gen., 301, ii.).
unwilling, I am, nolo, nolle, nolui.
unwillingly. (61.)
unwise, insipiens.
unwounded, integer.
up to, ad ; up to this day, ad hunc usque diem.
uphold, I, sus-tineo, ēre, -tinui.
uproar, tumult-us, -us, m.
urge, I (to do), sua-deo, ēre, -si ; insto, are (both with dat. and ut or ne) : urge to (crime), ad (scelus) impello, ēre, -puli : urge this upon you, hoc tibi suadeo ; hujus rei auctor tibi ac suasor sum.
urgently, vehementer.
use of, I make, utor, i, usus. (282.)
use to, I am of, prosum. (251.)
usefulness, public, use verb (376, ii. iii.), reipublicae (plus, maxime) prosum.
useless, is, nihil prodest.
utmost (to), I will do my, quantum in me est or erit (332, 5, g), with ful.
utmost value. (See value.)

vain, in, frustra,[1] nequidquam.

valley, a, vall-is, -is, f.
value (to), I am of (the utmost), (maxime) prosum. (251.)
value highly, more highly, I, magni, pluris, aestimo, are ; facio, ēre : I am valued, fio, fieri ; by, apud : I estimate you at your proper value, tanti te quanti debeo facio (see 305) : I value above, = prefer to (253, i.).
vanquish, I, vinco, ēre, vīci, victum.
variance with, to be at, pugnare cum (abl.).
various. (371.)
vast, maximus ; ingen-s, -tis. (See Voc. 3, n.)
vehement, use adv. vehement-er, -issime.
Veii, Veii, m. pl.
venture, I, audeo, ēre, ausus ; by venturing on something, audendo aliquid. (99, 360, i.)
verdict, sententia, f. (use pl. : see Voc. 7, n. 2) ; I give my, dico, ēre.
versed in, peritus (gen., 301, ii.).
very, this, hic ipse (see 355, b) : for very, with adjs. see 57, a.
veteran (adj.), veteranus.
victorious, when he was, victor (subst., 63).
victory, victoria, f. ; vincĕre. (98, a.)
view (opinion), sententia, f.
view, I take the same, idem, eadem, sentio, quod, quae, or ac (365) ; a different, aliter sentio ac (367.)
rigour (spirit), ferocia, f. ; (force), vis, acc. vim, f.
vile, turpis, e. (19.)
vileness, turpitud-o, -inis, f.
violating, without, use salvus (424.)
violation of, partic. of violo, are (417, i.) ; in violation of, contra quam (491, b).
violence, vis, abl. vi, f.
virtue, virt-us, -utis, f. ; in virtue of, pro (332, 7, g.)
virtuously, honeste.
visible, I am, appareo, ēre,
visit, I, vis-o, ēre, -i.

---

[1] Frustra, "in vain," of the person who fails in his object ; nequidquam, "in vain," of the attempt which has produced no result.

voice, vox, vocis, *f.*
voluntarily, ultro.[1]
vote (*of elector*), suffragium, *n.* ; (*of judge or senator*), sententia, *f.*
voyage, navigati-o, -onis, *f.* ; *I have, or make, a,* navigo, are.

wage, I, gero, ĕre, gessi, gestum ; *with*, cum *or* contra.
wailing, plorat-us, -ūs, *m.*
wait (for), I, expecto, are (*acc.*, **22**); *wait to see* (**174**, *d* ; **474** *b.*)
walk (*take a walk*) *in, I*, inambulo, are (*abl.*).
wall (*general term*), mur-us, -i, *m.* ; *walls* (*of city or fortress*), moenia, *n. pl.*, 3rd *decl.*
want (*of*), *there has been the greatest*, maxime laboratum est (ab, **332**, 1, *e*) : *want of caution, etc.*, see *caution, etc.*
want (*to*), *I*, volo, velle, volui.
wanting to, I am (*I fail*), de-sum, esse, -fui (**251**) : *wanting in* (*nothing*), (nihil) mihi deest.
war, bellum, *n.* ; *I make war against*, bellum, *or* arma, infero, ferre (**253**, ii.) ; *I declare*, indīco, ĕre (*ibid.*): *ship of war* (see *ship*).
warfare, militia, *f.*
warmth, with, vehementer.
warn, I, mon-eo, ēre, -ui, -itum ; admoneo, ēre (**127**, *a*): *warnings*, (**415**, *a*).
waste, I lay, populor, ari ; vasto, are ; *waste* (*time*), tero, ĕre.
wave, a, fluct-us, -ūs, *m.*
way, via, *f.*
weak (*morally*), levis; *weak characters* (**375**).
weakness, infirmit-as, -atis, *f.* ; *in his weakness*, imbecillus (*adj.*, **61**).
wealth, divitiae, *f. pl.*
wealthy (*of cities*), opulentus.
weapon, a, telum, *n.*
weariness, lassitud-o, -inis, *f.* ; *I feel weariness of,* = *am weary of.*
weary, I (*trans.*), fatigo, are : *I am wearied with*, langueo, ēre de (**332**, 3, *e*), *or* e, ex.

weary of, I am, me taedet, ēre, pertaesum est. (**309**.)
weather, the, tempest-as, -atis, *f.*
week, substitute approximate number of days ; at the end of a, within a, = *after, before, the* 7*th day.*
weep over, I, illacrimo, are (*dat.*).
weight, I have great, no, multum, nihil, valeo (apud.) (**331**, 4, *d.*)
welfare, sal·us, -utis, *f.*
well (*adv.*), bene ; *well enough*, satis: *I know well*, certo scio ; *well known*, satis notus.
well-disposed to, bene-volus, -volentior in or erga. (**255**, *Obs.*)
well-earned, meritus.
well-trained, exercitatus.
well-wishers. (**175**.)
what. (**157** ; and see *who.*)
when (*interrogat.*), quando (**157**, ii.): *conj.*, cum (quum). (See Temporal Clauses, I.)
whence, unde; *interrogat.* (**157**, ii.); *correlat.* (**89**).
whenever. (**434**, and *Obs.*)
where, ubi ; *where . . . from* (= *whence*), unde ; = *whither*, quo ; *where in the world?* ubi gentium. (**294**, *Obs.*)
whether . . . or. (**168** ; see also **171**, *c, d,* and **467**.)
which (see *who*): *which of two*, uter (**157**, i.).
while (*conj.*), dum. (**180**.) See also Temporal Clauses, II.
while, for a, paulisper.
whither, quo. (**157**, ii.)
who, which (*that*), *what* (*relat.*), qui, quae, quod. (See Relative.)
who, which, what (*interrogat.*), quis, quae, quid (*subst.*) ; qui, quae, quod (*adj.*). (See **157**, i.)
whoever, quicunque : *often exp. by tense of verb.* (**434**, *Obs.*)
whole, totus, a, um ; *whole of.* (**60**.)
wholly (**61**): (*to despair*), de summā re, *i.e. of our most important interests.*
why, cur, quamobrem (**157**, ii.). (See also **174**, *a*, and *note.*)

---

[1] *Ultro*, before receiving, without waiting for, provocation, solicitation, etc : *sua, mea*, etc., *sponte*, of one's own impulse, without external pressure or advice.

wicked, the, improbi. (**50,** and *note.*)
wickedness, nequitia, *f.* (See note
  under *crime.*)
widow, vidua.
will, against my, me invito, *abl.
  abs.* (**420,** ii.)
willing, I am, volo, velle, volui.
win, I (*obtain*), consequor, i ; *win
  the day, I,* vinco, ĕre. (Intr. 40.)
wind, vent-us, -i, *m.*
wing (*of army*), cornu, *n.; on the,*
  332, I, *c.*)
winter (*adj.*), hibernus.
winter, I (*pass the winter*), hiemo.
  are.
wisdom, sapientia, *f.*
wise, sapien-s, -tior, -tissimus ; *all
  the wisest men.* (**375.**)
wish, I, volo, velle, volui : *could
  have wished* (**149**, i.): *I do not wish,*
  nolo, nolle nolui.
wish for this, I, hoc opto, are : volo,
  velle.
wishes (*against your*), = will. (**424.**)
with, (See S, and **332,** 2 ;) *weight
  with* (see *weight*).
withdraw-from, I, me recipio, ĕre,
  e, ex.
within, intra (**331,** 12); *of time,* **325;**
  within memory, post (**331,** 17, *b*):
  I am within a little of (**137,** I, *h*).
without (*prep.*), sine : *more often
  exp. by abl. abs.* (**332,** S, and **425**);
  ita ut (**111**) ; quin (**132,** *b*); *without any* (**360,** *note*).
withstand, I, ob-sto, are, -stiti
  (*dat.,* **244,** *b*).
woman, a, muli-er, -eris.
wonder, I, miror, ari.
wonderful, mirificus.
word, a, verbum, *n.* ; *words,* dicta.
  (**55.**)
word (*of honour*), fid-es, ei, *f.*
work, a, op-us, -eris, *n.*
work upon (*your feelings*), *I,* flecto,
  ĕre, flexi, flexum.
world (see **16,** *b*) ; *all the world,*
  nemo est quin (**80**); *in the, in the
  whole, world,* usquam : *the rest of*

the, ceteri homines ; ceterae gen-
  tes.
worse, pej-or, -us ; deteri-or, -us ;
  for the, in.
worst foe, enemy, superl. *of* inimicus. (**256.**)
worth seeking, gerundive of appeto,
  ĕre. (**393.**)
worthless, nequ-am, -ior, -issimus :
  see 224.
worthy of, dignus. (**285.**)
would that. (**152.**)
wound, vuln-us, -eris, *n.; national,*
  reipublicae. (**58.**)
wound, I, vulnero, are ; *wounded,*
  saucius (*adj.*) ; *I am wounded,*
  vulneror, ari ; saucior, ari (*se-
  verely*).
wrench from (*you*), *I,* (tibi) extor-
  queo, ĕre, -torsi, -tortum. (**257.**)
write, I, scri-bo, ĕre, -psi, -ptum ;
  write you word, ad te scribo.
wrong, a, injuria,[1] *f.; I do wrong,*
  pecco, are ; *wrong-doing,* peccare
  (**98,** *a*).

year, ann-us, -i, *m.; (space of) two,
  three, years.* (See *two, three.*)
yes (see **162**) ; *I say yes,* aio, *pres.
  part.,* aien-s, -tis.
yesterday, heri ; *of yesterday,* hesternus (*adj.*).
yet (*nevertheless*), tamen ; vero (*emphatic*).
yet, not, nondum.
yield (*to*), *I,* cedo, ĕre, cessi (*dat.*).
you, tu, *pl.* vos. (See **11,** *a*, *b ;*
  334, i.-iii.)
young, juvenis, junior. (**51,** *a,
  note.*)
your, your own (*sing.*), tuus : (*pl.*),
  vester (see **11,** *c*) ; *that of yours,*
  iste (**338**).
yourself (*emphatic*), ipse (**355**) ; (*reflexive*), te, vos (**356,** ii.).
youth (*time of*), adolescentia, *f.; in
  my* (**63.**) (See also **51** *a, note.*)

zeal, studium, *n.*

---

[1] *Injuria* is never used for "injury" in the sense of mere *harm* or *damage;* this
must be expressed by *damnum.*

INDEX OF SUBJECTS.

LATIN INDEX.[1]

---

[1] This Index is chiefly limited to words specially noticed. Many, therefore, which occur merely as examples, or in the Vocabulary will not be contained in it.

Printed by T. and A. CONSTABLE, Printers to His Majesty
at the Edinburgh University Press